Eyes Open
in
Shadowy Hall

Fate of Vaeldor
BOOK 3
written by

Ronald G. Bellar

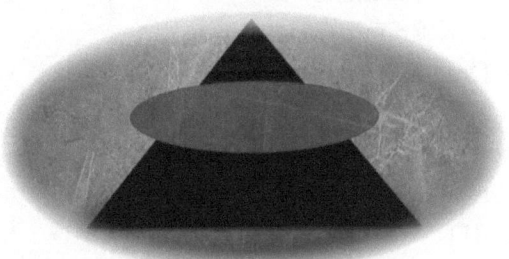

Vaeldor House LLC

Brighton, MI 48114

EYES OPEN
IN
SHADOWY HALL

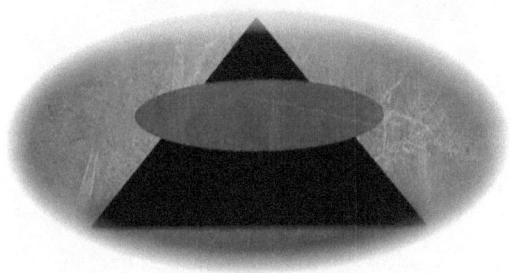

To my wife and son, Justiina and Ronnie.
They fill my life with love and adventure.

Dear Reader,

The Fate of Vaeldor is decided over several decades, and many characters are introduced throughout the series. For your convenience, a detailed glossary of names and pronunciations is provided at the back of Eyes Open in Shadowy Hall.

Some entries may act as small spoilers.

Fate of Vaeldor Series
(in reading order)

Alas! The One that Evil Brings
Might and Strength of Evil Bone
Eyes Open in Shadowy Hall

Visit Ronald G. Bellar's Facebook page at
https://www.facebook.com/vaeldorhouse

CONTENTS

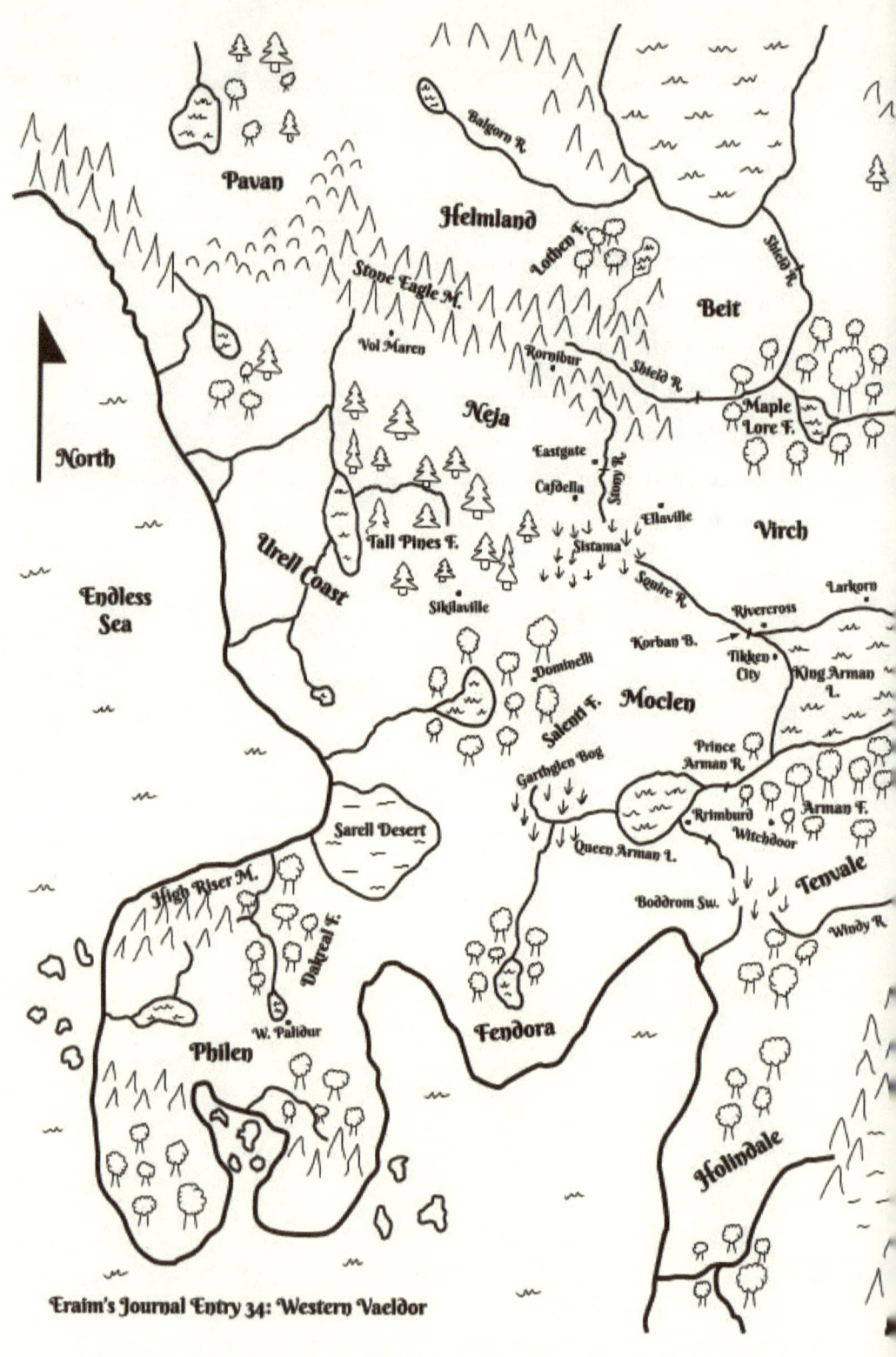

Pavan

Helmland

Balgorn R.

Beit

Lothen F.

Shield R.

Stone Eagle M.

Vol Maren

Rorylbur

Maple Lore F.

Shield R.

North

Neja

Eastgate

Stony R.

Ellaville

Virch

Cafdella

Sistama

Urell Coast

Tall Pines F.

Squire R.

Larkorn

Rivercross

Endless
Sea

Sikilaville

Dominelli

Korban B.

Tikken
City

King Arman
L.

Salem F.

Moclen

Prince
Arman R.

Arman F.

Garthglen Bog

Rrimburd

Witchdoor

Sarell Desert

Queen Arman L.

Tenvale

High Riser M.

Boddrom Sw.

Windy R.

Dakreal F.

W. Palidur

Fendora

Philen

Holindale

Andria
Wornduir
Coranthiar M.
Ekland
Bouldertown
Harbnum
Echo Valley Rapids
Selt
Maple R.
Lake Charal
Vermallon F.
Nira
Batorn Gulf
Steadshire
Berynye
House of Elgarroth
Peltagar
Orlenfel F.
Tribenor
Sendorum
Benasti F.
Batorn R.
Orlenfel R.
Compound
Great East R.
Candermane Tunnel
Palidur
Varlimor M.
Morimont R.
Lake Garaard
Kalmaar
Morimont
Sardina
Starlight L.
Darmhorog
Burmagaard
Serpent's Range
Southwood
Charabena
Ironside Keep
Barraday
Border Hills
Fire Hills
Denvale
Belsal R.
Marcove
Ladal M.
Mud Lake
Moon Lake
Kembald
W. Twin R.
Mentrial F.
Krimbror R.
Lumbrak
Endless Sea
Borkan M.
E. Twin R.
Stronghold
Desert of Fire
Dright Sw.
Trethel R.
Nomedd
Tarn Arum Jungle

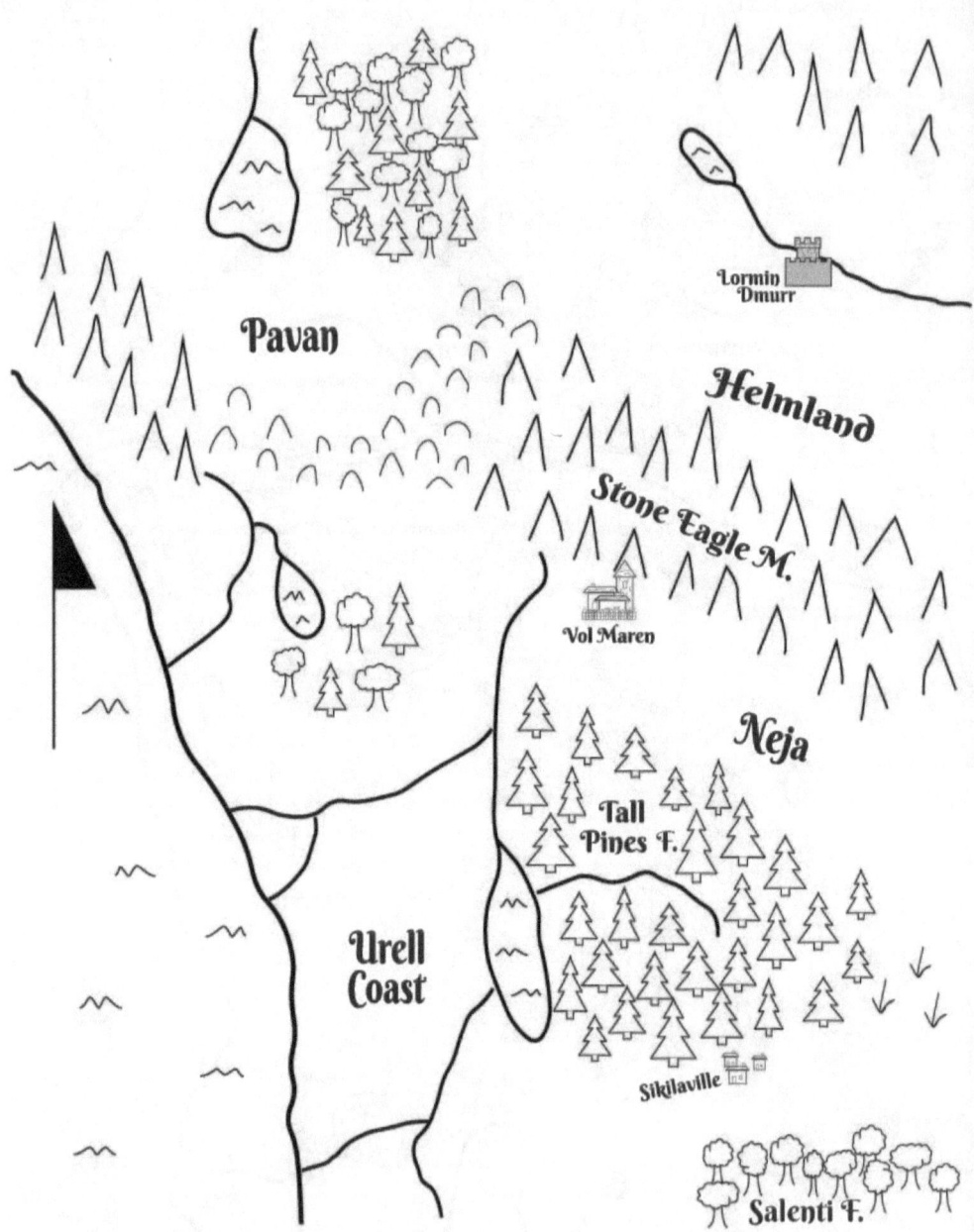

Pavan

Lormin
Dmurr

Helmland

Stone Eagle M.

Vol Maren

Neja

Tall
Pines F.

Urell
Coast

Sikilaville

Salenti F.

Eraim's Journal Entry 43

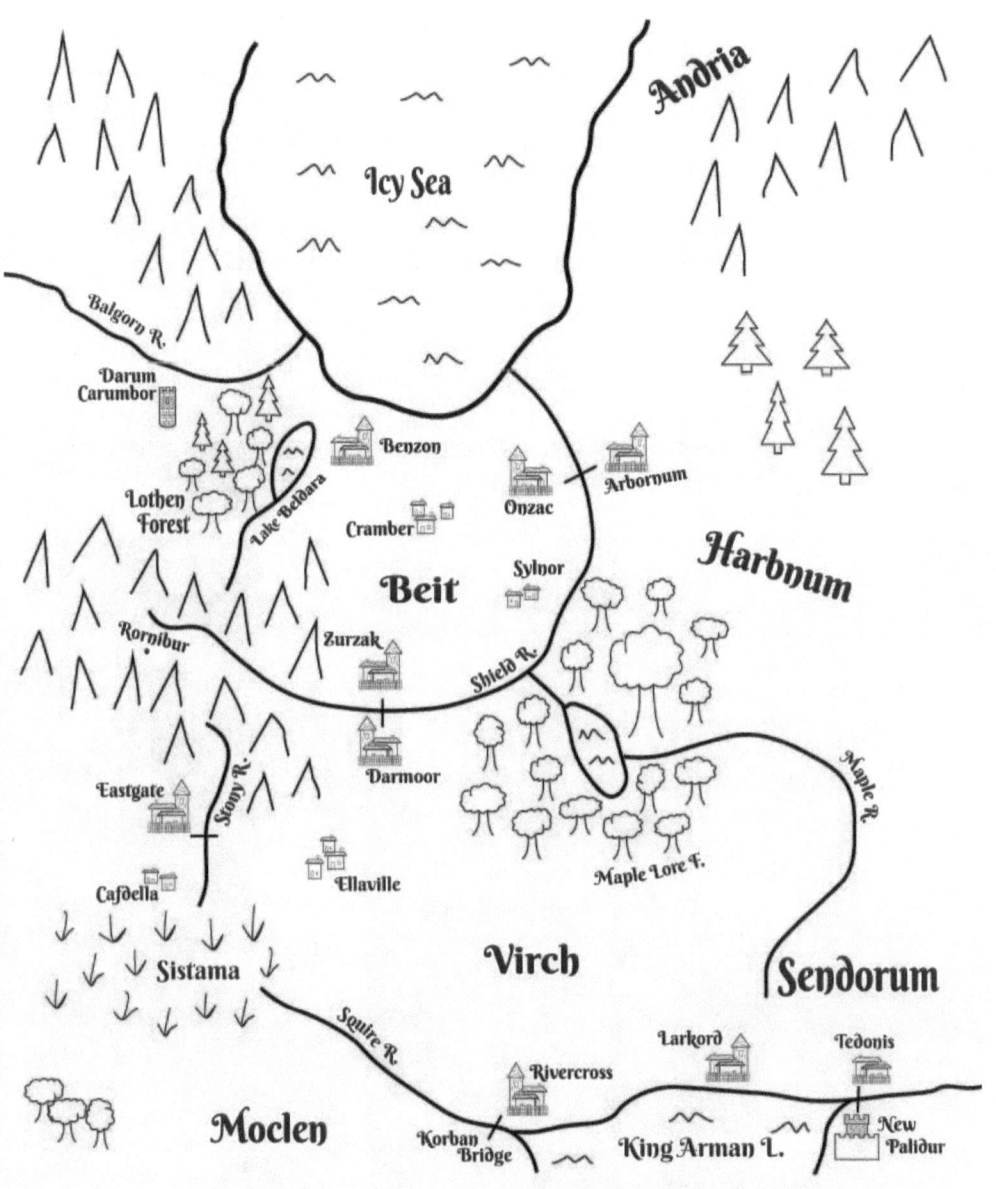

Eraim's Journal Entry 44

PROLOGUE

ПΘΜΕΘΘ

Vecnor wiped his brow as he gazed at the cloudless sky. The Nomedd sun beat hard upon the wasteland, but little did it bother the vultures circling overhead, nor the lizards and snakes eyeing Vecnor from the cover of rocks and dried brush. It was only spring, but already the land had suffered enough heat to match any summer within the northern realms.

Ahead stood the dark stronghold where the heroes of Vaeldor faced Trannum over twenty years ago. Though its master was long defeated, the small castle was as foreboding as ever. Not even goblins inhabited the hills to the north, nor the mountains just beyond them. Their continued absence was a reminder of the great evil that once occupied nearly all of eastern Vaeldor with its armies of undead. Many rumors existed about the fortress, stories of wicked spirits inhabiting its halls, but Vecnor doubted anyone had seen the necromancer's lair since the final battle, when Eraim's arrow shattered Trannum's skull.

Near the stronghold's shadowy entrance, Vecnor pulled Umbarc to a halt. The horse's feet shifted and its ears flicked as it inched away. Vecnor could not recall the last time he saw the animal this nervous, but the aura of malevolence radiating from the dark stones was unmistakable. He dismounted.

"Stay," he said, and he approached the opening, where the rotted remains of a door lay across the threshold.

He passed through the entryway, and at once the Nomedd heat surrendered to the chill permeating the structure. Vecnor's breath became heavy, obscuring his vision, but he found the cold comforting. The feeling did not last long, however, and shivers invaded. He walked briskly along a wide corridor, and at its termination he stepped over the very door Soren had kicked down, moments before Radaam killed the Soleran paladin.

The throne room smelled like an old tomb. Strewn about were several dunarchin corpses, appearing as armored skeletons, and a throne of bones presided over the grisly scene at the far end of the chamber. Vecnor had not been present for the confrontation, since he was fighting Trannum's horde in the Battle of the Dead Fields in Kalmaar, but he had heard the tale. He looked at the small piles of rubble decorating the flagstones, and he could envision the ghastly hands emerging to clutch at the feet of the living. To his right, Arrikan stood over her husband, Pallit, while Lorylla protected them from dunarchins. Against the wall to his left, Nilborg called upon the divine power of Soleran.

Vecnor turned to the throne, where Greyor and Rholmar battled Radaam while Trannum watched from before the large chair. A slab of stone lay near the morbid seat, four feet long and a couple feet thick, and a crack traveled down its middle. It had fallen from the ceiling two stories above to strike Greyor, but the dwarf miraculously survived.

Vecnor's gaze climbed the arcing stairwell to the right until reaching the partially destroyed balcony. Selanna and Eraim were there, wounded but refusing to yield, and Selanna cast spells while Eraim loosed an arrow from her bow. Vecnor followed the arrow's path into the eye socket of the necromancer and the orb resting therein. The skull exploded, and a few feet from the throne lay a crumpled black robe. It was all that remained of Trannum's body, as the bones had disintegrated with the destruction of the orb.

Vecnor stepped over and around the dunarchins' remains while crossing the room. Upon reaching the robe, he lifted it and gave it a few shakes, allowing the dust within to rain onto the floor. He then pulled a spoon-like shovel and collected the powder into a silver jar. As he closed the container, a voice spoke inside his mind.

It is time. Make haste.

Vecnor nodded and tucked the jar into his pouch.

He exited the castle to find Umbarc obediently awaiting his return. The horse snorted, hesitant to allow Vecnor to mount, but he climbed onto the saddle and they headed east.

CHAPTER 1

JUST A DREAM

The arrow flew swift and true, finding its way through the melee; and even as the skull shifted, the missile remained on target. The arrowhead pierced the orb within the eye socket, and a small explosion shattered the blue sphere and destroyed the skull. The rest of the skeleton turned to dust and the black robe collapsed into a heap. Then darkness...

A pair of eyes opened in the darkness. They shone blue, but illuminated nothing. And yet, a circular chamber was visible, as well as a black triangle, barely discernable upon the smooth stone floor. The shadows drew together above the triangle to form a figure cloaked in flowing robes, and as the eyes narrowed, the hint of a chuckle echoed from nowhere and everywhere.

The figure took to flight, racing through a series of underground tunnels and emerging among mountains. It ascended into the sky, blotting out the full moon for a moment, and plummeted into the valleys below. Gliding across the land with only its eyes giving away its location, a layer of frost was the only evidence of the shadow's passing. It traversed villages unnoticed—though many blankets were pulled tighter about the necks of sleeping folks—and flew over rivers and woodlands. At last, the figure came upon a walled city and slowed. It hovered above and just outside the walls, undetected while the glowing eyes scanned buildings of white stone until locating what they sought.

The shadow sped around the perimeter of the city, getting closer to its target before daring to proceed—its presence would surely be detected. It flew over the wall and into a large church, passing through the cracks of a window and entering a dark bedroom.

Lying on a bed of modest make was Nilborg, High Priest of Soleran. He was instrumental in the war against Trannum, and he aged well over the twenty-two years that had passed since. The chill that enveloped the room did not escape Nilborg's notice, and he awoke with a start.

Though his breath nearly blinded him, Nilborg was aware of the figure hovering next to the bed. He attempted to sit up, but its shadowy hand pressed against his chest and his body did not respond. The other dark hand rose, taking on a blue glow that turned white, and the palm lowered to Nilborg's forehead, afflicting him with a terrible chill that coursed through his veins.

His hand trembling uncontrollably, Nilborg reached for the door ten feet away. In his mind he screamed for help, but nothing escaped his lips. The shadowy figure smiled with its eyes, and it slipped back through the cracks of the window and disappeared into the night.

The door to Nilborg's room burst open and three priests entered in haste. They stopped and gasped...

Selanna sat up in her bed, panting. She had endured several bad dreams lately, but this was the worst one yet. None of the others had been so vivid, but they were all unsettling, nonetheless.

She rose and walked to the window, pulling her robe over her shoulders as she gazed at the trees of Salenti Forest. The darkness of night enshrouded the ground, but the large branches outside her treehouse glowed dimly in the light of the waning moon. She inhaled deeply as a warm breeze brushed her cheek in a vain attempt to chase away the chill of her latest nightmare. There would be no more sleep tonight.

She lit a candle with the touch of her finger and sat on her overstuffed chair, pulling a large tome from the nearby table. It was a book on ancient history she had "borrowed" from the Council Library in Tikken City a couple of weeks ago. *The Dragon Wars, and Who's to Blame* was the title. She would gladly have read it within the more-than-comfortable confines of the library, had she not grown tired of the many servants and Council wizards interrupting her with questions like *"Will you be here long?"* One wizard asked, *"Wouldn't you be much happier at home?"* She took the advice of the latter, even though it was common knowledge the Council did not allow books to leave the premises. It was awfully kind of him to grant her an exception.

Opening the tome to where she left off earlier that night, Selanna twirled a few strands of her golden hair and put her nose to the book. But she could not focus on the words. When she looked up again, the rising sun illuminated most of the room, but she still could not shake the images of her dream. She blew out the candle and closed the book.

Selanna stepped from her cottage and gazed upon Dominelli. It was the largest elfish settlement within Salenti Forest. Her home shared a wooden platform with a dozen other cottages forty feet above the ground, and several bridges led to other platforms. Selanna loved her home among the treetops, and she often wondered how elves of Vermallon and Orlenfel could stomach living on the ground like humans. It was so unnatural. Perhaps it was because they were much taller than the elves of Salenti, Dakreal, and Maple Lore.

Her thoughts were interrupted when Eraim silently climbed onto the platform. Ladders and stairs existed for such a task, but Eraim obviously chose to scale a nearby tree before jumping from branch to branch—again. It was amazing how one so small could accomplish such a feat so easily.

Though Salenti elves were the shortest of all elfish clans, Eraim was small even for a Salenti elf, standing just shy of five feet. She wore a black leather jacket that matched her sleek, raven hair, and her fancy sword, Mithkahr, hung at her side in a jewel-encrusted scabbard. Slung over her shoulder was her bow—the very weapon that released the arrow to end Trannum's reign—and strapped to her waist was a green pack.

Eraim smirked at Selanna as she pulled a small pouch from the pack. But then her smile faded. "Can you not sleep?"

Selanna sighed. "My dreams have darkened further, I fear. This last one was most disturbing." While Eraim counted rubies from the pouch, Selanna added, "I am off to New Palidur."

Eraim looked up with more than a hint of excitement.

Selanna knew her companion to be bored as of late. They had spent most of the last two decades within Salenti, since the end of the Necromancer War, and Selanna's excursions to Vermallon Forest to visit Elgarroth had been reduced to once every few years, as her mentor seemed unusually busy. Eraim loved Dominelli as much as Selanna, but lately Eraim acted as though the trees had become prison bars. That was likely the reason she had spent the night filching from a pompous elf visiting from Dakreal Forest.

Selanna and Eraim were sitting in Treetop Tavern the previous evening when the snob boasted of how Dakreal was better than Salenti, and that elves there lived like kings. Eraim took exception to those words, and the glint in her eye at the time did not escape Selanna's notice. Now, the Dakreal elf would learn what it was like to depend on others for food, drink, and shelter. Eraim loved to teach lessons.

"When do we go?" Eraim asked. "I have a horse to sell, and Tikken City would be the perfect place."

Apparently, the Dakreal elf would need to procure a way to get home as well. Selanna could not contain her chuckle.

"I am leaving shortly. But you do not have to —"

"I am packed already!" Eraim grinned.

The statement was no surprise. It seemed Eraim was always ready to go. Selanna gave in with a nod.

They collected their gear and descended to the ground level to fetch their horses. Dominelli did not possess stables, but there was a glade of thick, rich grass where the Salenti horses roamed and socialized until their elfish companions were in need of their services. A cool stream ran through the center of the clearing and a row of apple trees grew along its northern edge, and more than a thousand of the small horses were present — full-grown steeds at the perfect height for Salenti elves. The animals ranged from white to brown to black, although most of them combined the colors into beautiful patterns, and their manes and tails varied in length, as the horses had differing preferences.

Several gatherings of horses shared conversations with short whinnies, snorts, and stomps. To the western edge of the dell, a young elf wandered through a pack of enthusiastic colts and fillies, speaking to each of them in turn. Selanna remembered when her time came to choose her animal companion over two hundred years ago. She and Dandi bonded immediately. Presently, her mare was running toward her, happy to take her on her next journey, and beside Dandi was Lilli, equally excited to see Eraim. Selanna and Eraim greeted their animal friends with hugs and pats. Though neither spoke a language the other fully comprehended, a general understanding came easily enough, and the horses led the way to their saddles and gear.

Before leaving Dominelli, Eraim insisted they make a stop north of the city. Tethered there was a fine, full-sized horse, and Eraim pulled its reins from a branch. She then mounted Lilli, holding the extra animal in tow, and they departed on the path for Moclen.

Though an actual *path* did not exist, Salenti elves knew the way, and it was not long before the trees gave way to a wide-open plain. Selanna and Eraim then rode northeast with little rest for three days. It was unlike a Salenti elf to travel in such haste, but Selanna could not arrive in New Palidur soon enough. Thankfully, Eraim did not pry into Selanna's dreams. Instead, Eraim filled most of the time prattling on about the differences between Salenti and Dakreal, like how hobgoblins roamed Dakreal Forest's northern reaches, while Salenti was cleared of evil over a thousand years ago.

It was nearing dusk of the third day when Tikken City appeared on the horizon, butted against the King Arman Lake. The high walls concealed most of the buildings nestled within, but several taller structures were visible, as well as the dome of the Council Building at the eastern end. Laborers made their way from the fields and through the west gate, guided by the alluring smell of supper.

Though following the crowd and having a hot meal was tempting, Selanna turned Dandi up the northern road. Eraim's hesitation did not escape Selanna's notice, but she feared a night within the free city would stretch into two or three... or five. She needed to get to New Palidur.

Eraim frowned. "Do you wish to tell me of this dream?"

"Not yet." Selanna sighed. "Let us just ride. The market and taverns will still be here when we return."

"As you wish." Eraim aimed the extra horse toward the city and gave it a slap on the rear, apparently having lost interest in selling the animal. The mount headed for the open gate. "But I really think you should share some of your dream with me."

Selanna pursed her lips. "Why do you think elves of Dakreal are so wealthy?"

Eraim huffed. "They are a product of the dwarves in the High Riser Mountains!" She shook her head. "Everyone knows those mountains are loaded with precious minerals, and the whole kingdom benefits from it. If Dakreal elves lived in any other forest, they would be no better than the rest..."

Selanna held a brief smile, glad to have changed the subject.

The next couple of weeks sped by, as did Korban Bridge, Rivercross, and Larkorn. Water from the King Arman then collected into a channel, giving birth to the Great East River, and Palidur Bridge came into view. The bridge spanned a mile across the gorge, and beyond, New Palidur rested off the coast of the immense lake. Selanna's attention, however, fell upon Tedonis.

The small city occupied a field just north of the river. But Selanna remembered when the only feature the land provided was a simple road connecting Palidur Bridge to the many villages of Sendorum. That before Merssa, the greatest paladin since Vennimor, erected her first tent.

While most folks fled from the realms of undead occupation, Merssa remained as close as possible, beginning what had been referred to as *the compound*. A wall was constructed around the tents that were raised, and the tents became buildings. It was there that Merssa made plans for the impending Necromancer War, and the encampment served as the starting point to free the eastern kingdoms from Trannum's bony grasp.

After the war, the compound endured, and folks journeyed there to see where it all began. Several took up permanent residence, and Arbiss, the local lord, evolved the compound into the walled city it was today. Within, one could find taverns with names such as *The Front* and *The Compound*, but the most popular establishment was *The Golden Mace*. At the center of Tedonis stood a large building that served as a home for the current mayor. In Merssa's days, it was her headquarters, and it remained the only structure of stone within the walls.

Lord Arbiss had long been a friend to Palidur, even before it fell to the undead, and he gave full support to Merssa when the compound was young. As the area flourished with the war's conclusion, Arbiss renamed the settlement Tedonis. Most folks did not know it, but Tedonis had been the surname of Merssa's parents. Merssa Tedonis trained in Palidur as a child, and upon achieving paladinhood she changed her last name, as was customary, to something more befitting of her stature: Goldmace. It surprised Selanna that Arbiss had been aware of Merssa's true name, and it was a tribute she found to be just.

The small city never failed to give Selanna cause to reminisce, and Eraim did not interrupt—she was likely buried in thoughts of her own. Merssa had been the greatest leader and bravest person Selanna had ever met, and she missed the paladin dearly. With a sigh, she turned Dandi south and continued.

Palidur Bridge brought more delays as additional images flooded Selanna's mind. The magnificent construction of dwarfish craftsmanship passed over the raging water far below, but memories brought back the corpses of the South Army littering the road— brave warriors that sacrificed their lives to allow others to storm the undead-infested city of Palidur. Flying boulders crushed thousands of soldiers, and hundreds more were burned by flaming oil, and those making it across the bridge met a barrage of arrows from atop the Holy City's walls. Selanna had ridden behind the South Army in secret with the companies bound for Lornibur and the Fire Hills, and she passed over the devastation—it was a visage she would never forget. Presently, the bridge was in perfect order. There existed no evidence of chipping from flying rocks, nor scorching where the fires had burned.

At the midpoint of the bridge, Eraim gazed up at the enormous statues of Vennimor, founder of the original Palidur, and Bormungdaher, the dwarf king that saw the mighty bridge built. The boots of the monuments were continually bathed in the rapids below, while the heads provided housing for several birds overhead. Selanna shared her friend's view, admiring the work of the Varlimor dwarves. Just as with the rest of Palidur Bridge, the pillars no longer showed evidence of the bombardment they had endured.

Selanna turned her attention to the opposite end of the bridge, where New Palidur stood in all its glory. To her, the city looked exactly like Palidur of old, but she remembered Eraim's comments from years ago, when they first viewed it from this vantage point. Eraim insisted each tower possessed an additional window, and that the portcullis, visible through the open gates and in the raised position, owned two more bars than the previous one—Eraim had an eye for such details. Just as old Palidur, New Palidur was separated into three sectors, each dedicated to its own deity: Cafior of the land; Arronaus of the sky; and Soleran the Protector. And though one could not tell the districts apart from the outside, not with every building painted white, Selanna knew the streets and local garb of the sections to be brown, sky blue, and dark blue respectively.

It was still early when they entered the Cafior Sector. The brown cobblestones were exceptionally clean, very much reflecting the rest of the city, and a few people in brown cloaks milled about. Selanna and Eraim dismounted and allowed Dandi and Lilli to follow, and they headed west until reaching the monument of Merssa. There,

Selanna gazed at the statue. It was an incredible likeness of the paladin in her younger days, although it made her appear taller — Merssa had stood no higher than Selanna. And being made of rorbak, the mighty white stone from the Stone Eagle Mountains, the details were as sharp as the day the dwarves of Rornibur created it. Selanna and Eraim bowed their heads and shared a moment of silence.

They continued along the street until reaching the wall separating the Cafior and Soleran Sectors. The gate was closed. Selanna swallowed hard, trying to wash away the lump forming in her chest, and she approached the grim Cafior sentries standing before the wooden doors.

"I am Selanna. I request access to the Soleran Sector."

"Sorry, miss," one guard said. "There is to be no access until further notice."

Selanna felt ill. First her nightmare, and now this. The Soleran Sector rarely closed. Even in Palidur of old, when arrogance had ruled the Holy City, the Protectors of the Weak shut their doors only in times of war, and only once local commoners were safely gathered within the walls.

"We are personal friends of Rholmar and Nilborg," Eraim said. "As well as Montac."

Adding Rholmar's son, the current leader of New Palidur, could not hurt their chances of proceeding. But Eraim's words did not move the soldiers. Selanna doubted even the charming smiles she and her companion often employed to gain favor from humans could accomplish that feat.

"Sorry," the guard said. "This is by order of Grand Paladin Montac."

"What is going on?" demanded Selanna.

"Can't say."

Selanna's annoyance grew. "So be it!" She spun on her heels.

They headed to the center of the city, where the domed roof of the Grand Cathedral rose higher than all other buildings. A circular wall encompassed the structure, connecting it to the three sectors, and Selanna walked through the open gate and onto the silver cobblestones that filled the inner sanctum.

Shields of soldiers that fell while taking Palidur at the beginning of the Necromancer War lined the inside wall. Though faded, the tall works of iron were colored light blue across the top, brown on the right, and dark blue on the left, and they covered the stone barrier with almost no room to spare. Rholmar had placed them thusly, both as a reminder of those that perished, and as a way for the spirits of the departed to protect the Holy City they died for.

To the left, the Grand Cathedral occupied a bit more than half of the circle. The building's covered porch arced from the Cafior gate to the gate of the Arronaus Sector, and several statues of warrior angels held ready their weapons along the wide street, as well as high upon the cathedral around the dome. The sculptures were reconstructions of those destroyed by the undead, and added to their ranks were the likenesses of Merssa, Soren, and Hubrid. Soren, a well-respected High Paladin, perished in Trannum's stronghold during the final battle. Hubrid was not a part of the Necromancer War, but he sacrificed his life to allow a ship loaded with Palidurians to escape the downfall of the Holy City, making the war possible.

To the right was a magnificent fountain of whitewashed stone upon which burned the Eternal Flame. It was a feature added when New Palidur was nearly complete, as a tribute to the deity Silcor, for stories of Nidor's heroic contributions to the war effort abounded. Selanna sensed magic to be fueling the small fire, but it was a divine magic, and she often wondered how Rholmar had accomplished the feat. Beyond the fountain, the gate leading into the Soleran Sector was closed and manned by four soldiers wearing dark blue cloaks.

Selanna turned to the cathedral, where three flights of stairs rose to three sets of doors upon the porch. The doors and steps to the far left were painted brown, the ones in the middle dark blue, and to the right they were sky blue. Though Montac was the leader of the entire city, he was a paladin of Arronaus, so Selanna headed for the doors on the right.

A couple of guards in cloaks of light blue pulled the doors open before Selanna and Eraim—quite a change from Palidur of old, where outlanders were not allowed *near* the building. Within the hall beyond sat a third sentry at a small table. Dipping a quill into a bottle of ink and moving it to a piece of parchment, the soldier raised his brow and stared expectantly.

Selanna cleared her throat. "We are Selanna and Eraim, and we wish to see Grand Paladin Montac."

"I'm sorry," the guard said. "That's not possible."

"I am tired of this!" Selanna huffed. "I need to see him now, and I do not care if he is asleep or just begun breakfast!"

"Sorry, miss," the man said. "But he's not here. He left early this morning, and he's not expected back until this evening."

"And where *is* he?"

The soldier shook his head. "I cannot say."

Selanna muttered a few words in elfish the man obviously did not understand. Eraim nudged her nonetheless, for they lacked good manners.

"Aren't you friends of Lord Rholmar?" the guard asked.

Eraim jumped in before Selanna could offer the sarcastic reply darting across her tongue.

"Yes, we are."

"Well, *he's* here. He's eating breakfast. But I'd wager he wouldn't mind a visit."

Rholmar—Lord Rholmar, as he was called. Prior to the war, he was a paladin that proved just as arrogant as his city. Rholmar had traveled with Selanna into Tenvale to wrest one of Trannum's orbs from Solett, a wizard too weak to resist the orb's power, and he was present for Trannum's demise in Nomedd. Besides being a paladin of Arronaus, Rholmar had been the Duke of Philen, a title he left behind to rebuild the Holy City once Trannum was destroyed. Under Rholmar's guidance, New Palidur became greater than its predecessor, and though the free city appeared no different from the past, Rholmar forever changed the way it was governed. In days of old, the High Order made decisions concerning Palidur through debate and the casting of votes, and it was the Order's pride that failed to heed Merssa's warnings of the rising evil. While New Palidur still maintained the High Order, the group now served as advisors to the Grand Paladin, a position Rholmar held for years until retiring. His son, Montac, then accepted the title, having received the unanimous support of the High Order.

Selanna doubted the guard sitting at the table knew any of this about Rholmar. The knave probably saw him as just another aging, retired paladin, and offered the audience to get the *outlander* elves out of his hair. She stared at the man as several fitting comments raced through her head.

"We would be most appreciative," Eraim said.

Selanna gave a sniff.

The soldier made a quick entry onto his parchment and rose from his chair. "Please follow me."

He escorted Selanna and Eraim to a dining chamber, where Rholmar sat with his wife before a fine spread of boiled eggs, ham, apples, and bread. Though the couple were beyond days of adventuring, Rholmar and Ladonia had aged well. They looked up from their feast and smiled, but the expressions appeared forced.

"What a pleasant surprise!" Rholmar stood. "What brings you two here?"

"I was hoping you could tell me," Selanna said.

From the way Rholmar's eyes shifted to his wife and back, Selanna knew something dire was afoot. He sighed and took his seat. "It's Nilborg."

"No!" Selanna found it hard to breathe.

"What has happened?" asked Eraim.

Ladonia placed her hand on her husband's shoulder. "He has passed."

"Oh no!" Eraim paled. "Is that why the sector is closed?"

Rholmar shook his head.

"What has happened?" Selanna asked.

Rholmar took in a deep, shaky breath. "No one knows. He passed last night. And his skin... It was like ice."

"Trannum!" Selanna spat, not meaning to have said it aloud.

Rholmar's brows drew together. "Why do you mention that name? The necromancer was destroyed years ago. You were there."

"I am sorry." Selanna attempted to put the old paladin at ease. "It was just a bad dream I had. Please, continue."

Rholmar nodded, though his expression remained unchanged. "Soleran priests reported an evil presence, and they followed it to Nilborg's chamber. When they arrived, they found him shaking in his bed. He could not speak, so we received no account as to what had befallen him. He passed moments later. Montac has sealed off the sector to investigate. He does not want anyone entering or exiting until he's finished."

"I must see Nilborg," Selanna said.

Rholmar sighed. He nodded and pushed away his plate.

Selanna and Eraim followed the retired paladin into the Soleran Sector—there were no arguments before Lord Rholmar, and the gates opened without delay. The walk along the cobblestones of dark blue took longer than Selanna would have liked, as the aging warrior leaned upon a staff with every other step, but leaving him behind was not an option, for sentries roamed the streets, as if searching for something. Selanna considered herself a patient elf, but her anxiety grew with each passing second, and she had to bite her tongue until they arrived at last.

A handful of soldiers in dark blue cloaks guarded the entry to the large church where Nilborg resided. One soldier lifted his brow, but Rholmar raised his hand and the doors were opened. Beyond, several candles illuminated the main hall, as the rising sun scarcely touched the stained-glass windows, and a dozen guards moved about, carrying torches that cast shadows across the many pews. A white cloth covered an altar of blue stone at the far end, and farther back was a tall statue of a warrior with his chin held high and his sword pointing to the heavens.

Selanna and Eraim received a few glances as they followed Rholmar past the statue. A single door was set into the rear wall, and Rholmar went through it and into a corridor possessing several more doors. At the end of the hallway, a gathering of priests stood outside an open door to the right side. Most wore robes of dark blue, but one was dressed in brown and another in light blue. Selanna heard Montac's voice coming from within the room beyond.

"There's not much more we can do," Montac said. "We'll have to move the body and prepare it for burial as best we can. But let no one see him."

"Yes, Grand Paladin," voiced the priests, almost in unison. They then noticed Rholmar, and they parted before him.

"Father." Montac's expression was grim. "You came after all."

Montac had grown into a fine man. He surpassed Rholmar in size and inherited his mother's fair eyes and skin, and though he was only six-and-a-half feet in height, he reminded Selanna of Vecnor. The Grand Paladin was also well learned in politics and diplomacy, and it seemed all citizens of New Palidur held him in the highest regard.

"Selanna. Eraim." Montac acknowledged their presence. "I'm glad you're here."

Upon the bed, Nilborg lay with a rigid hand reaching out to no one. The priest's face was white and his lips and tongue blue, and terror-filled eyes stared without sight toward the door. Rholmar paled at seeing his longtime friend and averted his gaze. It was no wonder he had opted to remain at the Grand Cathedral.

Pity shone on Montac's face for his father, and the Grand Paladin turned to Selanna and Eraim. "The priests reported an evil presence within the church. It wasn't here long, but when they arrived..." He glanced at his father before continuing. "This presence was felt about the entire area, from what others have said, but no one saw anything. It was as if it was—"

"Made of shadow," Selanna said, just above a whisper.

"Perhaps." Montac frowned. "Do you know what it was?"

"No," Selanna answered hastily. Trannum was destroyed. And though her dream seemed more like a vision now, she did not know for certain what the shadow was. Still, her mind traveled back to Olinin, a marteese from Neja. The half-elf wizard had endured a terrible death just outside of Sistama, having experienced the freezing touch of the necromancer. Was it only coincidence that Nilborg suffered the same fate? Selanna needed more information. "But I shall look into it."

"That would be appreciated," Montac said. "For now, I suppose we should open the gates before the entire city is panicked." He eyed Selanna. "Will you be staying? Perhaps you should attend the next meeting of the High Order."

Selanna would never get used to hearing such a request. She recalled the first time Merssa sneaked her and Eraim into a meeting of the High Order, prior to Palidur's fall. The members exhibited such outrage that Selanna thought one of them might actually spit fire.

"Sorry." She shook her head. "I am on a pressing journey. But I shall return as soon as I can."

Montac nodded and began giving instructions to the priests.

Selanna and Eraim followed Rholmar back down the hallway. They exited the church and returned to the inner sanctum, where they exchanged hugs with the retired paladin and said their farewells.

Dandi and Lilli patiently awaited their return on the silver street, and Selanna and Eraim led the way back through the Cafior Sector.

"Is it not strange?" asked Eraim. "Nilborg's death reminds me of Olin —"

"Let us not speak of that now." Selanna sighed. "I do not wish to think about it. Not without more information. It will only lead us down a dark road."

Eraim nodded. "I understand."

Chapter 2

Tikken City

Selanna and Eraim rode at once for Vermallon Forest. Life in Sendorum and southern Harbnum seemed well and nothing slowed their pace, but after traveling several miles along Vermallon Road, they encountered a pair of merchants' wagons. One wagon faced east and the other west, unmoving before each other. Vermallon Road was a wide path of packed dirt, providing ample width for the traders to proceed, but there they were, each driver demanding the other move aside. Such a human thing to do.

In better days, Selanna might have stepped in to act as mediator—rather, she would have enjoyed the chaos she could have sown, easily doubling the time necessary to sort out the affair. But she was too occupied, and there was not a moment to spare. Turning to the trees, she urged Dandi south into the forest.

Selanna and Eraim hastened through the maples, birches, oaks, and cedars, encountering no Vermallon elves—at least, none willing to show themselves. The tall warriors had grown used to Selanna over the years, and it was possible they remained hidden while she and Eraim rode by. With no other obstacles, Selanna passed without effort through the halo of magic surrounding the House of Elgarroth—no trees mysteriously appeared and no strange, red-eyed wolves emerged from the underbrush to chase her off. In fact, she arrived quicker than she expected.

The cabin was dark and quiet, and no smoke issued from its chimney. Even the small firepit surrounded by logs was cold. Selanna could not recall a day when a fire did not burn there. Elgarroth was gone.

"Should we wait?" Eraim asked.

Selanna shook her head. "I feel time is too important. Let us make for Tikken City. Hopefully the Council will be of some help."

"And perhaps you will tell me about this dream," Eraim said.

Selanna gave a wry smile. "In due time."

Dandi and Lilli worked harder than any farm horse, bearing Selanna and Eraim back to Vermallon Road, through Harbnum and Sendorum, across Virch, and finally over Korban Bridge and into Moclen. Their animal friends did not complain, not even after completing the journey in under ten days with little rest. A befitting reward would be due once they returned to Salenti.

It was just after lunch when they reached Tikken City. From outside the walls, everything appeared normal, but Selanna sensed something to be amiss. Upon entering she found the streets crowded, as was usual for that time of day, but the many taverns were strangely silent and citizens bore expressions of concern and sorrow.

"What is happening?" Selanna asked a woman.

"The Seer..." the woman replied. "The Seer is no more."

Selanna's heart froze and Eraim gasped. Seac the Seer was better than one and a half centuries in age, but that was not surprising for a human mage — the flow of magical energy tended to stretch a wizard's lifespan. Seac had just begun training the next Seer, a process needing forty to fifty years to complete. He was too young to have died.

"How?" Selanna asked.

"No one knows." The woman shook her head. "And the Council has said nothing." Her eyes widened. "What does this mean?"

"I am sure all will be fine," Selanna said. But the same question echoed in her mind.

She and Eraim moved on until reaching the Council Building. The iron gates were closed.

"We are Selanna and Eraim of Salenti," Selanna called up to the single tower guard. "We request admittance."

"I know who you are," the man said. "And your request is denied.

The Council is not seeing anyone today."

Selanna released a sigh of frustration. First New Palidur, and now Tikken City. She raised her brow at Eraim and received a nod in response.

They rode to the nearest stables and quartered Dandi and Lilli, much to the animals' disliking. Normally, they left the horses untethered outside the buildings they visited, for the mounts would never stray, but there were too many people meandering about. They definitely owed Dandi and Lilli all the *orbo berries* they could eat when they returned to Dominelli.

"Do not feed them any of your dirty oats," Eraim said to the stableman. "Give them a few of these every hour." She held out a small bag of carrots.

"Yes, ma'am." The young man nodded vigorously. He looked about sixteen years in age and was clean for a groom, but the day had already saturated his clothes in perspiration.

"And there is no need to brush them," Eraim added. "And keep them in neighboring stalls, so they can speak to each other. Give them fresh water only—"

"Eraim?" Selanna crossed her arms.

Eraim sighed and handed the lad a few silver coins, bringing a smile to his face. "There will be more when we return." She batted her blue eyes, causing the young man to blush.

They walked to a nearby tavern and made themselves as comfortable as possible. But Selanna's desire to meet with the Council prevented her from relaxing. She bore no appetite, a feeling Eraim seemed to share, and they ordered a couple glasses of fine wine and sipped slowly.

"I cannot believe this." Selanna did not take her eyes from her goblet. "Nilborg was murdered. Seac is dead, and we know not how. We can neither find Elgarroth nor talk to the Council. It is almost like that prophecy...

"Eyes of old are kindled,
Master returns from below.
Frozen, righteous hand shall fall,
Sight is blinded in Shadow's wake..."

Selanna shook her head. "Or something like that. You probably remember it better."

Eraim frowned. "I know not of what you are saying. Where did you hear this?"

Selanna twisted her lips in thought. "Never mind." Her gaze passed through the window, where the setting sun had just touched the top of the city wall. "We best get going."

As she reached the tavern exit, Selanna noticed she was alone. An empty table in the corner held her friend's attention.

"What is it?" she asked.

Eraim glanced at Selanna before turning back to the table. Her eyes narrowed as she scrutinized the shadows of the corner, where the only light was cast by the slightly opened shutter of a nearby window.

"Eraim?"

"Did you not see it?" Eraim scanned the rest of the room. Several patrons were finishing their dinners and holding conversations. "There was a figure there. It wore a dark cloak. And I am almost positive I saw the same figure outside the Council Building."

Selanna looked again. There was no one there. "Are you sure?"

"I know what I saw," Eraim said. "It was fiddling with a small blade on the table. And I am sure it was looking our way."

A chill ran along Selanna's spine. "Come."

She headed out the door, and Eraim hastened to catch up.

They returned to the Council grounds on foot, where the dome of the audience chamber reflected orange above the wall. This time, however, they did not approach the gate. Eraim led the way into an alley out of view from the nearest tower, and she extracted a rope and hook from her pack. After a few twirls, she let the hook fly up and over the wall and pulled it taut, accomplishing the task on the first try.

Selanna enjoyed having a friend with so many talents.

Eraim scaled with ease, and Selanna followed. Upon reaching the top, Eraim gathered the rope and repositioned the hook while eyeing the barren courtyard. They descended after she lowered the rope, and she left it dangling as they made for the nearby servants' entrance.

The small door was unlocked and opened easily. Eraim moved silently as she walked along the empty corridor beyond, and Selanna did her best to keep up without making a sound. She learned long ago how annoyed Eraim can get with the slightest *scuff* of a boot or *swoosh* of a robe, and she did not wish to trigger the look she received on more than a few occasions in the past.

Eraim ignored several doors and halted outside an archway. From the pounding and clanging, it surely led to a kitchen. She took a peek before raising a single finger to reveal the number of occupants, and she slipped inside.

Selanna inched forward to have a look. Eraim squatted behind a table, hidden from a woman laboring over a cauldron, and she put a finger to her lips as she glared at Selanna. Selanna shook her head. She had not made even the tiniest of sounds! Besides, with the racket the cook was making, the woman would not notice a herd of sheep entering. Selanna released a silent sigh, earning another glare. She crouched low and entered.

Eraim continued around the room to an out-of-the-way corner, and there she opened a short, narrow panel. Beyond was a passageway. After receiving a nod, Selanna hurried into the passage, and Eraim followed, carefully pulling the panel shut.

The way was dark and dusty, but enough light shone through imperfections in the walls and ceiling to illuminate the corridor. Eraim squeezed by Selanna and led the way twenty feet before turning right, and they followed that passage thirty feet and turned left. After another thirty feet, the passageway ended and Eraim stopped to listen. There was no sound. She opened a second panel, and they stepped into the library.

The Council Library. Selanna's favorite place outside of Elgarroth's house and her own cottage. Shelves lined the room like tall pews and a few comfortable chairs faced a cold hearth, but no one was present. The large chamber contained more books than any library Selanna had ever seen, and it seemed there were tomes on just about any subject one could hope to find. Selanna would spend months within the room's walls, were it not for Council wizards insisting she leave after only a few hours. Over the past hundred years, she was sure she had visited more often than anyone not residing in the building, and still she had only read half of the shelves' contents. Her favorite books were on history, for Salenti records focused on events in which elves were involved, and the Council scribes did well to make anew all books and notes ever discovered. She took in a deep breath, delighting in the scent of candle wax, leather binding, ink, and parchment, and her gaze drifted to the library door, where Eraim tapped her foot and glared.

Selanna joined her companion.

Eraim listened at the door before cracking it open to have a look. Selanna peered over her friend's head, spying an empty hallway. Eraim opened the door and they headed right.

The corridors were very familiar now, and after a few turns Selanna and Eraim picked up the pace with no more attempts to remain hidden—they were far too deep into the Council Building to be deterred. A couple of servants saw them and gasped, too shocked to react, and the double doors to the audience chamber were reached without hindrance. Selanna moved past Eraim and pushed open both doors.

Eleven throne-like chairs were positioned in a semicircle atop a dais, and upon them sat the ten wizards of the Council, with the middle chair vacant. Seac the Seer's chair. Behind the wizards, a half-circle window revealed the shadows of Tikken City creeping across the King Arman Lake.

The elderly men were all speaking at once, so consumed by their conversation that they failed to notice Selanna's arrival. To the left of the doors was their chief steward, Mordan, appearing much too old to be carrying on with his duties. The steward had a full head of hair, though it was thinning and completely white, and his wrinkles were deeper than those of the wizards' upon the dais. Mordan's legs had a slight shaking to them as he stood at attention, and when he turned to see why the doors had opened, his shoulders slumped and he released a sigh.

"Selanna and Erimmuh—" A phlegm rattle accompanied Mordan's scratchy voice, bringing on a cough. He cleared his throat and finished his announcement. "Eraim."

The Council's chatter ended and their weathered gazes fell upon Selanna. Several members frowned while others glared, and it was then that she noticed Elgarroth standing among the shadows to the far side of the room. The timeless wizard smiled, and Selanna's stress melted away.

"I thought no one—" said the council member two seats to the left of Seac's throne. He shook his head. "Never mind. As long as you two are here, you might as well join us."

Selanna knew the wizards had never forgiven her and Eraim for stealing the orb they once possessed. But it was one of Trannum's orbs, and it needed to be destroyed. She and Eraim walked further into the room to stand next to Elgarroth.

"Nilborg is dead," Selanna whispered to her mentor.

"We know," Elgarroth said. "And Seac. In the same manner."

Fear crept down Selanna's spine again. But she had more to share with the wizard. "I had a dream, of a shadow—"

She sensed the eyes of the Council upon her. The vaulted chamber was silent, except for her whispers bouncing about the dome.

"Please," said the wizard that had addressed her already. "Tell us all about your *dream*." He did little to mask his sarcasm.

"Well..." Selanna hesitated. "It was of a shadow. And it attacked

Nilborg while he slept. It cast a spell of ice upon his body."

"A shadow?" asked the wizard three chairs to the right of the center.

"Yes." Selanna was unsure if the question bore the same sarcasm. "It was a great and terrible shadow. And it used a spell, much like the one Trannum cast upon Olinin more than fifty years ago in Sistama."

"Trannum?" The wizard on the right end raised his brow. "So now the necromancer has returned?"

"I did not say it *was* Trannum." Selanna sighed. "Only that this shadow used a power described to me before; one that Trannum performed upon Olinin. True, the shadow had blue eyes, just as Trannum's minions, but—"

"Here we go." The wizard to the right of Seac's chair waved his hand. "For years, you have been coming to us with nightmares. And that's all they are. Nightmares. Your mind has pieced together things you know, and fear has created illusions of Trannum."

"Did Seac not say that he found her dreams interesting?" Elgarroth asked.

"How would you know that?" The wizard one seat from the left end frowned. "Unless you have been spying on us. Is Selanna not the same elf that believed the rising of the dead to be a product of the Ancient Enemy of the North? And how did that theory turn out?" The wizard leered at Selanna with his final words.

Selanna was speechless. But it was not due to the wizard's query. Why would Seac be interested in *her* dreams? The thought occurred of mentioning she had had the dream several days before Nilborg was attacked, but a nudge from Eraim distracted her. Selanna turned to see her friend gazing into the far shadows of the room. She saw nothing. Eraim pursed her lips and shrugged.

Selanna returned her attention to the Council. "The fact remains that both Nilborg and Seac were killed by the same evil magic. And the only one known to have possessed that power was Trannum. I am not claiming it was the necromancer, but it could have been one that learned the magic from him. Perhaps Radaam."

"The missing Death Lords, Radaam and Anduiff," the member that first addressed Selanna muttered. "There has been no trace of the creatures since the necromancer's demise. As we explained many years ago, they were strongly linked to Trannum. And with the necromancer's destruction, they have likely secluded themselves from the world to fade away."

"Like the dunarchins?" Selanna asked. "Sightings of the undead firstborns have been reported over the past several years."

"Investigations by the Death Hunters have offered no proof to support such claims," said the wizard to the left of the middle chair.

Selanna huffed. "I, for one, find it intriguing that all sightings began around the same time, spread over hundreds of miles."

The wizard to the right of the center chair rolled his eyes. "Yes, yes. You have mentioned this on several occasions."

"And you have always dismissed it." Selanna cared not if they found her tone displeasing.

"What about the *Frozen, righteous hand?*" Eraim stole everyone's attention. "And *Sight is blinded in Shadow's wake?*"

The Council members glanced at one another.

"From what prophecy is that derived?" Eraim asked.

The member two seats to the left waved a dismissive hand. "We know of no prophecy bearing such words."

"But..." Eraim frowned at Selanna.

"Very well." Selanna had heard enough. "We shall not take up any more of your time. You obviously have this under control and need no assistance in finding the truth. Good evening to you all."

The Council stared in silence, unmoved by Selanna's comments, and waited for her to make good on her words as Mordan opened one of the large doors. She looked at Elgarroth, and the wizard nodded with a smile. Though she wished to speak with him, she could tell he was not finished with the Council.

She and Eraim departed.

Four servants awaited within the hallway, and three of them kept a careful watch over Selanna and Eraim while the fourth one escorted them to the exit. From there, the servant led the way to the gate, pausing when Eraim made a quick detour to the south wall to retrieve her rope. They were then ushered from the Council grounds.

It was dusk, and several lamps added life to the darkening street. Unsure of where to go next, Selanna began walking.

"Why did you not demand an answer to the prophecy?" Eraim asked after a couple of blocks were behind them.

Selanna raised a brow. "Why did you draw my attention to the shadows of the chamber?"

"Oh, um..." Eraim's face twisted into a frown. "I saw that figure again. But if ever I take my eyes from it, it disappears."

Selanna scanned the surrounding darkness, unable to shake the sudden feeling that someone was watching her. "How long has this been happening?"

Eraim pursed her lips. "Well, I first thought I saw it in New Palidur. And I am sure it was outside the gate to the Council Building earlier. It was in the tavern after we had our wine, and I saw it again within the audience chamber moments ago."

"A cloaked figure?"

Eraim nodded.

Selanna's chest tightened. Could it be the shadow from her dreams? "Let us return to the tavern." Perhaps she might find a clue as to what this cloaked figure was.

They arrived in little time, for the establishment was less than a hundred yards away. It was not as crowded as when they first visited, and Eraim went directly to the shadowy corner.

"Right here." She stood next to the vacant table. "I am sure it passed through the window."

Selanna checked the window. The shutters were latched from the inside. "In my dream, the shadow entered through the cracks of a window and into Nilborg's room."

Eraim scrutinized the tabletop. "Tux..."

"What?" Selanna looked to see what her companion had discovered.

Eraim wrinkled her nose. "Nothing."

Selanna saw three letters carved into the table: TUX. It had been done recently. "Who is Tux?"

"Well…" Eraim released a heavy sigh. "He is legendary in the ways of stealth. He is the one all thieves aspire to emulate. But it is quite an unattainable task."

"Really?" Selanna smirked. "I thought *you* were the best."

"I am no thief!" Eraim frowned. "Besides, I do not believe Tux actually exists. More likely, he is a creation of those who need such inspiration; those needing to believe all the things he has done."

"Then who carved his name?" Selanna teased.

"Legend says he leaves his name wherever he goes." Eraim stared at the letters. "But I have caught many wishing to *be* him doing just that. He is a myth. Nothing more."

"But that does not tell us who has been following us." Selanna abandoned her jovial tone. "So the next time you see this figure, do not let him from your sight. I should like to ask him, or whatever it is, a few questions."

CHAPTER 3

HUNTING TRIP

C ome on Fang!" called Daymyn. "Try to keep up!"

Baylun cringed. He had become accustomed to the nickname over the past dozen years, given to him due to the tooth protruding from his lower jaw on the right side, but Daymyn always said it with a certain meanness. Baylun had hoped his cousin would ease up on the subject, since they were on a hunting trip to celebrate him turning eighteen years of age, but neither of his cousins seemed to take that point into account. Not even his half-brother, Romik, showed him any favor.

"Yeah. Why can't you be more like your brother?" asked Desser, his blonde beard mixed with hints of red making him look more and more like Uncle Magneer every day.

"Come on, Fang!" Romik said, leading the way over the hills separating Urell Coast from the wild lands of Pavan.

Baylun looked at his older brother. No one would ever guess they were related. Baylun received his krukari heritage from his father, Gruelenor, who insisted he appeared more hobgoblin-like than Baylun. Baylun disagreed. Romik, on the other hand, had had a human father. Ballrik died in the war against Trannum, but it was said he had been quite comely, just as their mother, Lorin, and both of Romik's parents had added to his fair complexion. But their mother's beauty could not salvage Baylun's face, and he was reminded of this every time he caught people staring.

Baylun used to be jealous of Romik, a feeling that worsened when Romik was named Lord of Ironside Keep several years ago, receiving with it a noble status and vast wealth. Romik even carried a fancy broadsword, claiming it was a family heirloom to be wielded by the reigning Lord of the Keep. But Baylun's envy dwindled over the last year, when he spent nearly ten months learning to hunt with his father. While Romik was off training with Granduncle Arkor in the Varlimor Mountains, Baylun became an accomplished archer and tracker. Of his cousins and brother, only Desser might prove superior at tracking, for Uncle Magneer was an expert and often took Desser to distant places to train — Baylun rarely made it far from the walls of West Palidur. Baylun's talents would likely go unnoticed, however, for he rode to the rear of the group, and his opinions were never welcomed or called upon.

It was the tenth day of the trip, and Baylun followed as best he could atop the ass Daymyn procured for him while the others rode fine horses. Daymyn insisted the mule was necessary for transporting their prizes back to Philen, but Baylun knew his cousin to be making him the butt of yet another joke. Being so near to the Stone Eagle Mountains, they had seen black bears, large cats, and mountain goats thus far, but Romik continued north, seemingly uninterested in the animals. Baylun's brother had put the journey together, taking a month's holiday from the keep to execute it — Arkor made sure Romik enjoyed time outside the mountain pass. Romik did not divulge where they were headed exactly, but he assured them they would be well rewarded, unlike any hunting experience elsewhere.

"Much farther and we'll be leaving the hills," Baylun said, the usual saliva escaping through the gap his fang created.

"What?" Desser chuckled. "Tired already?"

"Must be the hobgoblin in you," said Daymyn.

"Enough." Romik glared at their cousin.

Although Romik enjoyed teasing Baylun, Daymyn went too far at times. Especially when reminding Baylun of his heritage. That was when Romik usually put a stop to things. And as they got older, Daymyn's tongue grew sharper. Perhaps it was his flowing black hair and piercing dark eyes, and the fact that he drew the attention of several maidens that Daymyn acted superior. But it was Baylun's birthday trip, and he was determined not to let his cousin ruin it.

"I can travel farther than any of you," Baylun said. "I'm just worried about you old folks passin' out."

The others laughed, though sarcastically.

"You get your sense of humor from your father," Daymyn said. "Meaning you don't have one!"

Daymyn received another glare from Romik.

Baylun did not care. He loved his father dearly, even if Gruelenor seemed apologetic, if not ashamed, for having passed on his krukari blood. Baylun saw his father as a great hunter and archer, and he heard a rumor that Gruelenor killed a Death Lord in the war against Trannum. His father denied such claims. People could say what they wanted about Gruelenor. No one would ever tarnish Baylun's opinion.

"At least tell us where we're headed," Baylun said to change the subject.

Romik grinned. "You shall learn that soon enough."

They continued until dusk and made camp. Romik insisted they guard through the night, for the rolling terrain carried a certain amount of danger, and Baylun took the first shift with his brother. They sat near the fire, watching the dark hills.

"Baylun," Romik said after the others were asleep. "Happy birthday."

"Thanks." Baylun offered half a smile. "And thanks for the hunting trip."

Romik shrugged. "This is as much for us as for you. But I did get you this."

He placed a leather-bound package onto the ground, one that had been strapped to his horse throughout the journey. It was obviously a double-edged axe by its shape. Baylun figured it was just another treasure Romik was waiting to show off when the time came. Baylun was partial to the battleaxe from his combat training, and he already possessed one, but Daymyn convinced him to leave it at home since there was little use for it on a hunting trip. But then he noticed the others had brought their swords. Why did he ever believe anything Daymyn told him?

He unwrapped the present and gasped. The weapon was exquisite. The blades looked to be of polished bronze, with small runes etched along each of the edges, and its three-foot haft was wrapped entirely in black leather, except for a bronze spike protruding from the bottom.

"It was made in Morimont," Romik said, "by the greatest dwarf weaponsmith ever to dwell there." He pointed to the runes on one of the blades, as if he could read them. "This one is named *Honor*, and the other is *Courage*. The smithy claims it to be constructed of rare metals found deep within the mountains. It is sharper than any blade crafted by human, elf, or dwarf, and he says it will learn your style over time so it can complement your skills."

Baylun gave his brother a wry smile. Was this another joke?

Romik held up his hand with a chuckle. "I'm just saying what the smithy told me! In any case, it's the sharpest thing I've ever encountered."

Baylun was in awe. "This must have cost you a fortune."

"Don't worry about that," Romik said. "Nothing's too good for my little brother."

Baylun enjoyed these moments, and not because of the extravagant gift. When it came down to it, he knew he could always count on Romik.

"Well?" Romik lifted his brow. "What are you waiting for? Give it a twirl."

Baylun stood and lifted the weapon. It was heavier than the one he left at home, but its balance was superior and it took almost no effort to swing to and fro.

Romik's grin stretched to one side.

Baylun played with the axe for a good portion of the night. But then came time to wake Desser and Daymyn, and after doing so he settled into his blankets, his hand firmly clutching the haft.

Come morning, they moved on, heading steadily north as the terrain allowed. More signs of animals were evident, but Romik paid them only a passing glance. After four days of traversing the rolling land, the hills came to an end.

"Pavan?" Baylun asked. "We're hunting in Pavan?"

"Too much for you?" teased Daymyn.

"Though I'd love to join you in this one," Desser said to Daymyn, "I must agree with Baylun. What do we know of this region?"

Romik grinned. "That it's abundant in wild boar the size of horses, albino elk, and bears with golden fur."

"The things you hear in that keep!" Desser shook his head. "You realize more than half of the stories aren't true."

Romik smirked. "But finding out which ones *are* is half the fun!"

Pavan. Baylun knew the name to be dwarfish, meaning *savage country*, and that many tribes of barbarians with no allegiance to any realm, or each other for that matter, inhabited the land. There existed no formal leadership or law, and the Pavish were rumored to be extremely territorial.

"Well, if we're to ride into Pavan," Desser said, "then I'm taking the lead. I don't want to wander into tribal hunting grounds. The barbarians must leave markers of some sort."

"Be my guest." Romik gave a regal wave.

Desser led the way across the grassy fields and scattered woodlands of ash trees, maples, oaks, and firs. The air was crisp and wild flowers abundant, and the Stone Eagles moved to the southeast, rising majestically above all else. They traveled another two days, taking care to remain within the southern portion of the realm, and over that time they found no signs of Pavish barbarians. Nor did they see any giant boars, albino elk, or golden bears. They did, however, begin to hunt at last, claiming a beaver, a wolverine, a couple of squirrels and rabbits, three foxes, and a deer. They also narrowly avoided a confrontation with a skunk. Through it all, Baylun exhibited his much-improved abilities from years past, and the others were openly impressed. His marksmanship with the bow left pelts unmarred, and his tracking skills were only slightly bested by Desser.

"Isn't it odd that we've seen no sign of barbarians?" Daymyn asked as they readied for the final day of the trip.

Romik gazed about the scattered trees surrounding their campsite. "It's strange, I agree. Perhaps they've moved on for the season."

"It's spring," Desser said. "And they're not birds."

Romik chuckled. "Let's just go. The sun's already risen, and we've only just finished breakfast."

"Yeah," Desser grinned to one side. "And we've yet to see giant boars and such."

"Ha ha." Romik smirked.

"Fang!" Daymyn snapped. "Stop playing with that axe and help us pack."

Baylun had been polishing the blades of his new weapon since he awoke. He grinned at his brother and cousins before wrapping the axe and securing it to his back.

They returned to the hunt, venturing a bit more north in hopes of discovering the fantastic game Romik mentioned. After a few hours, Desser brought them to a halt.

"These tracks are curious."

"Giant boars at last?" Daymyn held more sarcasm than conviction.

"Dwarves?" Baylun gazed at the wide footprints. They did not belong to animals, and they were too short for the barbarians.

"Not dwarves." Desser glanced at Baylun, as if to see if he was joking. "These are bare feet. Dwarves wear boots."

"Then what?" asked Romik.

"They're goblin-like," Desser stroked his short beard, "but a bit larger than the ones I've seen in the High Riser Mountains." He stood. "I'm sure they're goblins."

"Great." Daymyn sighed. "Now we have to be on watch for

barbarians *and* goblins?"

"Perhaps we should turn back," said Baylun.

"Easy, Fang!" Daymyn held up his hand. "You're not afraid of goblins, are you? Maybe they'll accept you as their king."

"How fresh is the trail?" Romik made no sign that he heard Daymyn.

"Less than a week," Desser replied. "But that's not what concerns me."

"There's at least three score," Baylun said.

Desser scanned the ground, his brow rising as he nodded. "I was going to say a dozen. But Baylun's correct. I didn't notice the three different groupings of tracks. I assumed they were all made by the same group. There's too much overlapping to know for sure, but I agree with Baylun's assessment." He turned to Baylun. "Good eye."

Baylun wanted to smile. Instead, he examined the surrounding woodland.

"What's that?" asked Daymyn.

Baylun followed his cousin's gaze to the north, where black smoke billowed into the sky.

"We've company!" Romik pulled his broadsword, watching the trees.

Daymyn and Desser unsheathed their blades and faced north while Baylun retreated several paces. He thought of pulling his battleaxe, but he had yet to use the weapon, so he opted for his bow. Even so, he had never been in actual combat, and his hands started trembling.

A dozen creatures rushed from the trees. They stood nearly four-and-a-half feet in height, and crude black helmets with narrow slits to allow for sight concealed their heads. Their shoulders were broad, making them appear almost like dwarves, but they lacked beards and ran barefoot upon wide, black feet. Dark leather armor covered their upper bodies and they wore ragged breeches, and they waved small axes, swords, and maces while emitting battle cries.

Romik was first to meet the attackers, swinging his broadsword with skill worthy of his title of Lord of the Keep. Arkor had trained Romik well, and he slew three before fending off a fourth.

Not far from Romik, Desser defeated one assailant while receiving a gash on his left arm. He favored the arm afterward and fended off three others, managing to strike down another.

Daymyn faced four attackers, and he withdrew a dagger with his free hand and smiled as he waved both weapons about. His father had been killed before he was born—rumor held that a Death Lord slew Solinin in Nira—so Uncle Magneer took charge of his battle training. But Daymyn also traveled throughout Philen, working with the realm's finest teachers when Magneer was away on extended hunting trips with Desser. Daymyn's hard work paid off as he parried and dodged an axe and mace, and he laughed while cleaving the head from one of his foes. He came up with his dagger, burying it into another opponent and releasing his grip, and followed with a low swing of his blade, crippling a third attacker.

Baylun's focus turned to a short warrior rushing toward him. He trained his bow and released the string, and the arrow pierced the creature's chest, dropping it to the ground. Baylun then pulled his axe and quickly shed its wrappings, but once he was ready, the battle was over.

"You want to use that thing next time?" Daymyn shook his head, pulling his dagger from a corpse.

"I..." Baylun looked around, feeling ashamed. "I'm sorry."

"Leave him be." Romik eyed Daymyn. "I've seen combat in the Varlimor Mountains, and Desser has fought goblins with Uncle Magneer. And you've bragged of many battles in your travels as well. Baylun has experienced nothing beyond shooting wild game." Romik turned to Baylun. "Don't fret, brother."

Baylun was not sure he deserved Romik's defense this time. What if one of them had been killed?

"I'm more interested in what these things are." Desser sheathed his sword and placed a piece of cloth over the cut on his arm.

"They look like dwarves," said Daymyn.

"They're not dwarves." Desser squatted above a corpse. "No beards. And they run barefoot, like goblins."

"But goblins don't travel beneath the sun," Romik said.

Desser nodded. "One way to find out."

He pulled the helmet from a fallen attacker. The creature's skin appeared as dried-out black leather, and two small teeth protruded from its lower jaw. The nose was flat and the eyes reddish in color, and stringy dark hair was thin upon its head.

"It definitely looks like a goblin." Desser frowned. "Except for the black skin. Goblins are more brownish."

"They're too tall," Romik added.

"Blackfoot goblins." Daymyn hovered above the two. "I learned about them in my studies. They're supposed to be extinct."

Desser gazed at the northern sky. The smoke was growing in mass and moving closer. "This was just a scout patrol. I think this puts an end to our little trip."

"I think you're right," said Romik.

Baylun rummaged through his pack, withdrawing herbs he had brought in case of an emergency. He purchased them from a merchant in New Palidur prior to leaving Philen. "Let me see to your arm," he said to Desser.

Baylun stripped the small leaves from the herb and discarded the stem. He then rubbed the leaves between his finger and thumb before mashing them in his fist with a bit of water from his flask. Too much water, and the healing properties would lose potency, so he fought to keep a steady hand.

Romik furrowed his brow. "Where did you learn to do that?"

"My father." Baylun turned to Desser. "Now let me see that wound."

Desser pulled up his sleeve. "And then we leave this place in all haste."

CHAPTER 4

TUX

It disappointed Selanna to learn Elgarroth had exited Tikken City without first seeking her out. She had left a message with a servant to be summoned once the Council's meeting with her mentor had ended, but after an hour passed with no word, she returned to the Council grounds to find he had gone. The wizards denied her audience to discuss their conversation with Elgarroth, but after she flashed a proper smile, a guard divulged that the *elf wizard* seemed troubled and departed in haste.

"This does not bode well," Selanna said while she and Eraim walked along the lamplit street. It was late, but Selanna had hoped to see her mentor before turning in for the night. "He is not easily shaken." She inhaled deeply and slowly released it. "He fears something. I know it. And we need to find out what."

"But I hardly believe *he* needs *our*—" Eraim froze, staring into the distance. "This way!" She bolted.

There was no time to ask questions, and Selanna hurried to catch up as Eraim raced into an alley. But when Selanna arrived, her friend was gone. She thought about calling out, but she feared she might anger Eraim. Allowing her eyes to adjust, Selanna spotted her companion in the darkness sixty feet ahead. Eraim was scrutinizing the dead end of the alley, and her focus climbed the wall to the right until reaching the rooftop two stories above.

Selanna approached, summoning her small light to have a better look. "Was it Tux?"

Eraim shot Selanna a sarcastic glance. "Hardly. But it *was* the cloaked figure." She scanned the building again. "Whoever it is, they are very skilled to have climbed this wall so quickly."

Selanna shook her head. "Why is it following us?"

"Perhaps it is keeping watch on us," said Eraim.

"But who is it?" Selanna frowned at the roof. "And why?"

Eraim sighed. "Should you not use your magic next time? So we can get some answers?"

Selanna nodded. "Yes. We need answers."

They stayed at an inn for the remainder of the night, but Eraim received no sleep. Instead, she kept an eye on the window, waiting for the cloaked figure to appear.

It did not.

Come morning, she and Selanna retrieved Lilli and Dandi from the stables to begin their journey back to the House of Elgarroth. Selanna admitted she was unsure if the wizard had returned home, but she had no idea where to go next. Eraim was too tired to think of anything else to do, not to mention distracted by the cloaked figure, so they left at once.

They rode north along the King Arman shore and crossed the Korban Bridge as dusk arrived. The lights of Rivercross were aglow to the northeast, and though the city was inviting, Eraim did not argue when Selanna suggested they ride through the night. The Rivercross Market would be closing anyway.

They continued beneath the moonlight along the eastern road, following the northern shoreline of King Arman Lake, and Eraim viewed every shadow with suspicion. It was not long before she felt eyes upon her and she halted. Gazing back, she sensed a shadowy figure atop a dark horse, just beyond her range of sight. But when she squinted to pierce the night, the road was barren.

"Is it there?" Selanna peered into the darkness.

Eraim twisted her lips. "It is out there." Perhaps it used magic to evade her.

"Let me know when it returns," said Selanna.

Eraim nodded, and they resumed their eastward trek.

An hour later, Eraim sensed the presence again. She cleared her throat, and she and Selanna spun their horses and bolted back down the road. The mounted stranger became visible, darting into the wilderness to the north, and despite the workload Lilli and Dandi had endured over the past several weeks, the gap closed. After nearly a mile, scattered trees grew more numerous and the shadows thicker, and as the cloaked figure neared to within thirty feet, it rounded a large tree. Eraim went left and Selanna right, but as they reunited on the other side, they saw the dark steed galloping without its rider.

"After the horse!" Eraim yelled to Selanna.

While Selanna continued the chase, Eraim pulled Lilli to a stop and scanned the branches above. The leaves were still, and nothing moved within the shadows. But she sensed something was there. She kept her focus on the darkness until Selanna returned with the black mount in tow.

Eraim recognized the animal to be a Batorn horse. When it came to speed and comfort, they were fine steeds, but there was something different about this particular beast Eraim could not place. She gave the branches overhead one last glance and huffed. "It has eluded us again!"

"Perhaps next time I will slow him with a wall of fire," Selanna said, sounding more than a bit annoyed. "Or knock him from his horse with a strong wind!"

"That would be unkind," said a voice to the south. It was elfish, and it belonged to a male.

Eraim and Selanna turned to see the cloaked figure ten yards away. It stood almost as tall as Selanna and was just as thin, and at least a chin existed beneath its hood.

"Who are you?" demanded Selanna. "And why have you been following us?"

"I am Eslimil Tuxendora," the figure replied, his voice deeper than Eraim would have thought. "And what I do is my business."

"Tuxendora?" spat Eraim. "Bah!"

Selanna lit up with realization. "Tux!" She eyed the stranger. "Show your face."

Eslimil reached for his hood, his hands appearing dark in the moonlight, and though they were slender, Eraim did not underestimate their skill. He pulled back the hood, revealing himself to be an elf. His skin was as dark as a gray elf's, but he lacked the height of the Orlenfel clan, seeming more in likeness to a Salenti elf. His hair was white, and his black eyes with white irises gave him an ominous appearance and further supported a gray elf heritage. But Eraim had never heard of the reclusive elves cross-breeding with others. Besides that, gray elves were warriors, and not masters of stealth. Eraim found him fascinating, but she did not lose sight of her annoyance with him and his ruse. He was just another thief.

"By whose authority have you trailed us?" Selanna asked again.

"Many would claim that title," Eslimil replied. "But in the end, I follow the path before me."

Selanna pursed her lips.

It puzzled Eraim that her friend was so irritated by the reply. She would have thought Selanna to be accustomed to such responses after years of conversing with Elgarroth. As for Eraim, she was losing interest.

"This is pointless," she snapped. "Be gone and bother us no more."

"I wish to speak with you," Eslimil said.

"Then why the games?" asked Selanna. "Why not just speak with us?"

"I do not converse in public," he replied. "And I had to be sure you were not followed."

"*Followed*?" Eraim raised a brow. "If anyone *else* was following us, I would know."

"Not the one *I* speak of," Eslimil said. "It travels through shadow more easily than even myself, for it *is* shadow."

Selanna's face paled. "The one that killed Nilborg?"

Eslimil nodded. "I saw it pass through the priest's window. I attempted to follow it afterwards, but it was too swift. Even for me." He paused when Eraim scoffed. "But I know it traveled into the north."

"Beit?" asked Selanna.

Eslimil nodded again.

"Do you lack the ability to traverse enemy terrain?" Eraim mocked him.

"I can slip through the slimmest crack without a sound, if I wish." He gazed at Eraim with his strange eyes. "I know you sleep on your left side most of the night. And though you hide a chest within the floor of your home with traps to stop the most accomplished thief, you carry items most valuable to you upon your body."

Eraim gasped. "You are a spy!"

"I am many things," Eslimil admitted. "But as to your question, I could not pass farther north because of something strange in the air. I first detected it several miles into Beit, but I knew not what it was. Then I encountered hundreds of corpses littering a small village, and I realized there to be a plague at work. It struck me ill for a week, but I did not remain long enough for it to take hold."

"A plague in Beit?" Eraim wrinkled her nose in disgust. "Good riddance."

"The land might be ruled by evil," Selanna said. "But do not wish evil upon its citizens. One cannot control where one is born." Her face lit up. "The Guardians!" She looked at Eslimil. "What of the Guardians?"

"My journey did not take me to Lothen, alas," Eslimil said. "I know not if the plague is there, nor the fate of the elves therein."

Selanna turned to Eraim. "We must see if they are all right."

Though Eraim had never been to visit the Guardians before, she was sure Selanna had. The band of Vermallon elves were charged with keeping a watch on Helmland in case Uustaag the Dark ever resurfaced. They accepted this responsibility, living lonely lives so that others might sleep without fear. Still, there were other matters to consider.

"What about the plague?" Eraim had no intentions of traipsing through a plague-infested land.

Selanna bit her lip in thought. "I have no magic to protect us from such a catastrophe." She spoke almost to herself. "We must continue to Vermallon."

"If it is Elgarroth you seek," Eslimil said, "he is not home."

Selanna frowned. "And how do you know that?"

"When he departed from Tikken City, he turned south."

Selanna shook her head. "You risk trouble beyond your means, Eslimil, if you follow too closely to one such as Elgarroth."

"I believe there to be a way to avoid the plague." Eslimil seemed undaunted by Selanna's warning. "Not all were affected. I saw soldiers during my departure that looked quite healthy, and they all possessed black canteens with a strange marking upon them. Perhaps the contents provide some resistance."

Selanna furrowed her brow. "Beitian soldiers?"

Eslimil nodded.

Selanna turned to Eraim. "I am going to Lothen."

"And you know I am going with you." Eraim released a heavy sigh. She then noticed Eslimil was gone, as was his horse, and she pursed her lips. "Now what?"

Selanna shook her head. "We will have to worry about him later. For now, we must seek the Guardians."

CHAPTER 5

DESERTERS

Selanna and Eraim returned to Rivercross late into the night. They knew no inns would be open, so they settled upon a peaceful hill outside the walls to gain what sleep they could.

It seemed only moments had passed when the sun peeked over the horizon, and Selanna doubted she had found any rest. Her mind was a torrent of thoughts and questions. What was the shadow? Why were Nilborg and Seac murdered? Why was there a plague in Beit? Was Eslimil really Tux? Hopefully, she would find answers to some of those queries.

She woke Eraim, and they entered the city to gather supplies. Merchants had just begun parking their wagons and a few taverns showed hints of life—Rivercross was not known for its early risers. They rewarded the peddlers willing to make ready their wares before breakfast, purchasing blankets, thick cloaks, and rations for the trip, with no attempts to haggle on price. They then visited a tavern that seemed pleasant enough, for Selanna preferred to eat as little on the road as possible—food was always better when it was fresh. After the meal, they mounted Dandi and Lilli and made for the city gate, riding through a meager gathering of shoppers making their way to the Rivercross Market.

It was a fine morning for a ride, and they set out on the northern road. As usual, Eraim paused to gaze back at the Korban Bridge—she never seemed to tire of the construction of white stone that defied time. Selanna found the perfectly chiseled faces of dwarfish lords fascinating as well, but the splendor of the rorbak used to create the structure held terrible memories for her. First there was Trannum's

49

cabin in Sistama, and then Trannum's tomb in the Stone Eagle Mountains. Both locations were horrible, and both had seen friends killed.

"Is that Romik?" Eraim asked.

Selanna spotted four men leading their horses along a trail south of the Squire River. It *was* Romik. And his brother and cousins. It seemed like ages since she last saw the young warriors, and emotions for their parents and grandparents nearly overwhelmed her.

"Romik!" Selanna called out, urging Dandi toward the Korban Bridge, and Eraim followed.

Of the four boys, Selanna knew Romik best. She rarely made it into Philen, having no business to tend to within the realm, but she visited Ironside Keep often enough over the past twenty years when passing into Marcove. The keep was a convenient stop, bearing memories both good and bad, and Arkor was one of the few living humans from the days when Trannum first surfaced. Selanna had known the one-armed warrior since long before the Necromancer War, as well as Romik's late father and grandfather, Ballrik and Vikur.

The boys met Selanna and Eraim on the bridge. They looked much older since Selanna last saw them. Baylun led a mule while the others held the reins of fine horses, and there were a few carcasses and pelts strapped to the krukari's mount. They had obviously been hunting.

"Selanna. Eraim." Romik smiled. "It has been too long. You remember my —"

"Of course!" Selanna dismounted and addressed Romik's companions. "Hello Baylun. Desser. Daymyn." She turned back to Romik. "How is Arkor?"

"He's well." Romik's smile faltered.

"What is it?" Selanna asked.

Romik looked at his cousins and brother. After receiving a nod from Desser, he turned to Selanna. "We encountered Blackfoot goblins."

"That is impossible," said Eraim. "The likes of them have not been seen since..." She bit her lip.

Daymyn pulled a sack from his mount and stepped forward. A dark liquid saturated the bottom, and from it he extracted a severed black foot and a scalp.

The trophies were disturbing, and while Selanna observed them her concerns deepened. The ancient tribe of goblins had been foot soldiers for Uustaag's army. But after the warlord's defeat, the fiends were never seen again. Her desire to seek the Guardians grew.

"We're taking these to Granduncle Arkor," Romik said. "We're not sure what to make of them."

"Where did you encounter these creatures?" Selanna asked.

"In Pavan." Daymyn admired his handiwork as he returned the bloody parts to the sack and tied it shut.

"And beneath the sun," added Desser. "I've never heard of goblins raiding during daylight. But take a look at this." He pulled a helmet from his horse and offered it.

Selanna gazed at the dark iron bucket. It was a bit crude in construction, possessing a narrow eye slit and small holes for air. Blood splattered one side.

"Try it on." Daymyn grinned.

Selanna eyed Solinin's son with disgust before taking the helmet and peering inside. It was filled with shadow, and she knew right away it was unnatural. The blackness swirled, and when she tilted it toward the sun, the shadows remained, keeping the interior buried in darkness.

Selanna looked at Eraim. "This is strong magic."

"Please," Romik said. "We do not speak elf. If this is more than a mere raiding party, we'd like to know."

Selanna considered the young warriors. They were the children of great heroes in the war against Trannum, now men themselves. "I know nothing for sure. But goblins are not capable of this kind of magic. How many were there?"

"We faced only a small number of their force, of that I'm certain,"

Romik said. "From the smoke we saw, there must have been hundreds."

Selanna twisted her lips, unsure of how much to share. "Blackfoot goblins disappeared after the Ancient Enemy of the North fell. They were foot soldiers, and wherever they marched, the dark legion followed." Horror gripped her heart as she revealed the information.

"What does this mean?" asked Romik.

"I am not sure," Selanna said. "But I aim to speak with the Guardians."

Desser frowned. "The elves of Lothen?"

Selanna nodded. It pleased her to know humans still possessed such knowledge. The Guardians had lived within Lothen Forest for well over a thousand years, watching Helmland for signs of the greatest evil ever to threaten Vaeldor—that is, the greatest evil since before Trannum. Often, Selanna found humans far too willing to forget history beyond a couple of centuries.

"How will you get there?" asked Desser. "Lothen lies north of the Shield River, between Beit and Helmland, does it not?"

"There is a way," Selanna said.

Outside the Council of Wizards and the elders of Vermallon Forest, few knew of the secret path. Selanna tricked Elgarroth into revealing it over fifty years ago—at least Elgarroth made it seem as though she did. She had used the path only a few times, before the Necromancer War began.

"If that's where you're headed," Romik stood up straight, "then we're going with you."

Baylun's head snapped toward his brother with unbelieving eyes.

Selanna studied the young Lord of the Keep; son of Ballrik; grandson of Vikur. She recalled the deaths of Romik's father and his father's father. Ballrik leaped through a gate, entering the world of demons to save thousands of lives—perhaps all of Vaeldor. Vikur died at the hands of Radaam while attempting to reclaim Ironside Keep. Did she have the right to involve Romik in her quest? Was it her decision to make? She released a heavy sigh before speaking.

"Very well. But know this: though Lothen Forest is home to the Guardians, it is not a safe place. And word has reached our ears of a plague that has invaded Beit. We are unaware as to how far it has spread."

Romik glanced at his company and turned back. "We're in."

After allowing the boys time to sell their pelts in Rivercross, they followed the northern road bound for Neja. They arrived in Ellaville a few days later, and Selanna was glad to see it had returned to a prosperous village filled with livestock and happy citizens. After the devastation brought upon it by ghouls over fifty years ago, it seemed no good folks would ever inhabit the place again.

They stopped at the Happy Ranch, the only tavern in town, and had a bite to eat—the last cooked meal they would enjoy before diverting into the wilderness. Selanna recalled when she entered the establishment after the undead attack of the past. It appeared differently then. It was called Larman's Brew, and the windows were smashed, the furniture broken, and blood stained the floors and walls. They found Larman, the proprietor, and his wife and two boys safely tucked away in the cellar; and they moved the family to Eastgate, where Larman opened Larman's Haven. To Selanna's knowledge, the innkeeper never returned to Ellaville before he died of old age, not even after the village was restored. Most likely he did not wish to relive the nightmare that killed hundreds, and Selanna did not blame him.

It was a couple hours past noon when they finished their meal, and Eraim drew Selanna's attention to the large windows facing the street. A covered wagon headed east, driven by two marteese. A female Selanna did not recognize held the reins, but there was no mistaking the identity of the male. Brem's hair was whiter than when Selanna last saw him and the thin mustache was new, but the dark spots scattered randomly about the priest's skin were undeniable. The blemishes served as a reminder of the undead critters Trannum released to infect the bodies of Selanna and her companions. Selanna and Eraim were spared the permanent markings only because of the healing sap Brem provided. Unfortunately, there had not been enough for everyone.

Eraim ran from the building, and Selanna and the boys followed.

"Brem!" Eraim hailed the priest.

Brem's face lit up when he spied Eraim. He placed a hand on the driver's arm, and the woman pulled the horse to a halt. Brem then dropped from the wagon.

"It has been too many years," he said.

Selanna thought it funny. She and Eraim had never cared much for half-elves, sharing the Salenti view that the dilution of their long-lived race was perverse. But after their time with Brem, surviving the mines of Lornibur and the battle against the necromancer, they shared a bond and no longer saw him as half-human. Neither did they see him as an elf, though. He was a priest of Frayorna, the Mother of Nature, as well as a good man.

Selanna smiled as Brem and Eraim embraced. But then the wagon driver stole her attention. The female marteese was a warrior, judging by the golden vambraces and form-fitted breastplate. Her red hair spiraled slightly below her shoulders, held back by a golden headband, and her sharp green eyes narrowed while they watched Eraim.

"You look well." Eraim glanced at the wagon driver as the woman climbed down behind the priest.

Brem rolled his eyes, scratching a dark spot on his cheek — Selanna wondered if they still itched, or if he scratched out of habit. "Allow me to introduce Kiryanna." He turned toward his companion.

Kiryanna nodded once, and her frown never wavered. Selanna thought it a pity, one so lovely hiding behind a seemingly permanent scowl.

"It has been much too long," Selanna said, accepting a hug from Brem. "And this is Romik son of Ballrik, Desser son of Magneer, Daymyn son of Solinin, and Baylun son of Gruelenor."

Each of the boys nodded with their introduction, and Brem

returned the gestures.

"Great men, your fathers," said the priest.

"Though I deeply wish there was time for a visit," Selanna added, "we are pressed."

"Actually," Brem glanced at the wagon, "I could use your help in a most important matter." He turned to Kiryanna, scratching a spot on his neck. "Perhaps we should move our cargo from the road."

Kiryanna climbed onto the wagon and drove it into an alley next to the tavern. A pen housed three dogs at the far end, and the animals expressed their excitement for the company's visit with many barks. Kiryanna dropped from the seat and moved around to the back, where a wooden door was chained and padlocked. After scanning the street, Brem turned to Selanna and Eraim.

"I came across something most strange." He pulled a key from his pouch and unlocked the padlock. "I am on my way to Tikken City to consult the Council of Wizards. Perhaps you have saved me the journey."

Brem removed the chain and opened the door. Within the shadowy compartment sat a pair of figures, one on either side. Sacks covered their heads and their hands were bound, and they wore the unmistakable garb of Beitian soldiers.

Eraim gasped. "Spies!"

"I'm not so sure." Brem scratched his arm. "If they're spies, they're using a new tactic. They sought me out to surrender."

Selanna furrowed her brow. "Surrender?"

"I think that is a matter best explained by them." The priest gazed into the wagon. He then nodded to Kiryanna, and she entered to remove the sacks before stepping out again.

The soldiers were human, with no remarkable features. Selanna could not even tell their rank. Their expressions were troubled and nervous, and she suspected it had nothing to do with being tied up in the wagon.

Brem climbed inside, and Selanna and Eraim followed. Romik and Daymyn stood to either side of the lovely marteese warrior outside the door, and Selanna almost giggled at their attempts to flirt.

"Are you from Neja?" Romik asked.

Kiryanna did not respond.

"Is that real gold?" Daymyn's eyes traced her golden breastplate to her mail skirt. He received an icy glare.

Within the wagon, Brem spoke gently to the captives. "I trust the ride hasn't been too uncomfortable."

"You have been most hospitable, under the circumstances," one soldier replied, his words slurring together—typical of Beitians.

"Good, good." Brem nodded. "Now, I would like you to tell your story to these friends of mine."

The soldiers looked at each other. The one that had spoken then turned to Selanna and Eraim and cleared his throat before beginning.

"There is a new leader in Beit. The Shadow."

Selanna held her breath, reliving the image of her nightmare. The wagon suddenly felt colder and darker than moments ago.

"Without a fight," the soldier continued, "it threw down our king and assumed power. Now all of Beit is under its control."

"Tux was right," Eraim whispered in Selanna's ear. But then Eraim amended her statement. "That is, the one claiming to be Eslimil."

Selanna nodded, wishing there was time to enjoy Eraim's angst about the strange elf.

"But that's not the worst of it," the soldier added. "It has brought with it some item of power. I know not what it is, but it has released an air of death that kills all living things."

"The plague," murmured Selanna.

"Not a plague." The man shook his head. "It is evil magic."

"I have been informed that Beitian soldiers are not affected," Selanna said.

"*All* living things are affected," he insisted. "But they provide us soldiers with an elixir. One swallow per day prevents the magic from entering the body."

"I have these tonics in my possession," Brem said. "But I'm no alchemist. I do not know what they're made of."

"What about the item of power?" Selanna asked the soldier. "Where is it?"

"I know not, alas," he replied. "The last I heard, it was taken north of Lake Beldara."

Selanna turned to Eraim. "That takes it close to Lothen!" She used the elfish language in hopes the soldiers did not understand.

"And along the road to Helmland," Eraim added in the same dialect.

"We must not delay any longer," Selanna said. "I fear the worst."

"Where are you headed?" Brem spoke in the common tongue.

Selanna glanced at the prisoners and back to Brem. "I do not wish to say in present company. But rest assured, we are looking into this shadow."

"Perhaps I should accompany you," the priest offered.

Selanna gazed into Brem's eyes. Though he appeared aged, she sensed his spirit was strong. He had done well over the past two decades, following in Olinin's footsteps.

"All right," she said. "And Kiryanna can continue to Tikken City with the prisoners."

"I'll do no such thing!" hissed Kiryanna from outside the wagon.

Apparently, Kiryanna possessed the acute hearing of her elfish heritage. Selanna was impressed. Even with Romik and Daymyn still attempting to penetrate the marteese's icy shield, Kiryanna had kept up with the conversation inside the wagon.

"She is sworn to my side," Brem said. "But we could hand over custody to Ellaville. They are good people here. I'm certain they'll see to things."

Selanna was not so sure, but they could waste no more time. She gave in with a nod.

CHAPTER 6

VAYLA

R holmar sat in the Grand Cathedral listening to his son, Grand Paladin Montac, give instructions to the Holy City's newest paladin. Vayla was a high-spirited warrior, and although she was not the first female paladin to walk the streets of New Palidur—nor the second, third, or tenth—Rholmar saw many special qualities about her. Vayla reminded him of Merssa, one of the greatest paladins the city had ever known. Though Merssa had been small in stature, she was larger than most in courage, faith, and dedication. She was the key figure in the war against Trannum, and she sacrificed much while ensuring the necromancer's defeat, including her own life. Now, Merssa was a celebrated hero in New Palidur, Sardina, Sendorum, Moclen, Philen, Kalmaar, and Marcove, the latter ruled by her son, Cavalor.

These thoughts flooded Rholmar, for Merssa had been a dear friend. And he could not shake the memories, because the young woman standing before Montac with a stone face of courage and determination was the spitting image of Merssa, right down to the knot of brown hair upon Vayla's head. Stranger still was the fact that Vayla was the daughter of Cavalor, the adopted son of Merssa and Borse, who bore not a drop of the late paladin's blood. How it was possible could only be explained as a miracle, and the young paladin's appearance never failed to fill Rholmar with awe.

Vayla listened to Grand Paladin Montac's latest report from across the lake. A few days after the murder of Nilborg, the Council of Wizards informed New Palidur that Seac the Seer had also been murdered. And now, less than a month later, the Council had acquired a couple Beitian prisoners. Though the wizards referred to them as defectors, Vayla was sure it was some devious plan to infiltrate the southern realms.

The captives reported there to be a plague upon Beit. This news was disconcerting to many, and especially to citizens of Virch and Harbnum, who were only separated from Beit by the Shield River. New Palidur decided to get to the bottom of this alleged plague, but finding willing souls was another matter—venturing into Beit was bad enough without adding an invisible cloud that killed all living things. Vayla's convictions were strong and her faith in Cafior's protective blessings unyielding, so naturally she volunteered.

Presently, Grand Paladin Montac was issuing Vayla's orders. And though her gaze was unwavering, she felt the eyes of Lord Rholmar upon her. It was a distraction, but only slightly. She had become as accustomed to it as she believed possible, under the circumstances.

Vayla grew up a princess in Castle Lambrak of Marcove. She had never known her mother, for the woman passed when Vayla was very young, but King Cavalor was the best father anyone could hope for. Vayla also benefited from her loving grandfather, Borse.

Borse was a mighty priest of Cafior, and from him Vayla learned to love the deity of the land. Borse shared stories of Vayla's grandmother, Merssa, commenting more than once that Vayla resembled the late paladin. It was not until her grandfather's passing that Vayla saw a statue of her grandmother on a hill in the wilds of northern Marcove. Her father took her there to bury Borse next to his greatest love.

Vayla was six years old at the time, and although she was sad, the sight of the monument left her in awe. The sculpture was well detailed, and Vayla could picture the woman completing all the tasks her grandfather told her about.

"There was a time when your grandfather and I could speak with your grandmother," Cavalor said as a tear made its way down his cheek. "We would lie on the grass and close our eyes, and she was there." He sighed. "Unfortunately, nothing lasts forever."

At Vayla's insistence, they lay head to head on the soft turf and attempted to resurrect the vision. Though Vayla failed to see her grandmother, a warm breeze swept over her and she breathed in deep. Something was there. She sensed it. But it was just out of reach. From that moment, Vayla knew what she wished to do with her life. She wanted to be a paladin.

After informing her father of her wishes, Cavalor smiled. But Vayla sensed sadness, as if he harbored some detail of which she was unaware. Her father later explained it was not enough to *want* to be a paladin, and that thousands of Palidurians led fulfilling lives as holy warriors—a point he would impress upon her many times throughout the coming years.

At age eight, Vayla began playing with wooden swords. Her father's personal guard, the zhokards, secretly encouraged this behavior, and they often sparred with her when her father was not around. When she turned ten, Cavalor became aware of these activities, but he was not outraged, as Vayla expected. She thought her father would lecture her on the appropriate behavior of a princess, but he was supportive, and even decided to train her personally.

At fourteen, Vayla had developed into a skilled warrior. She revisited her desire to become a paladin with her father and insisted she needed to go to New Palidur for proper training, but Cavalor was reluctant. He again spoke of the benefits of being a holy soldier, and though she listened to his words, she did not relent until he promised to let her go to the Holy City one day.

While awaiting that time to come, Vayla continued practicing and reading from her grandfather's books. It was in these books that she discovered her grandmother had defeated a Death Lord named Cadorn, as well as an entire force of evil creatures upon the hill where her statue stood. This only solidified Vayla's resolve.

Her sixteenth birthday was not a good day. Vayla realized she would never be beautiful, not like the princesses from every story ever written. To add to her angst, she had not grown very tall, standing only a few inches higher than five feet. Her father tried to comfort her, speaking of the heroic accomplishments her grandmother achieved at Vayla's height. He also added that one did not need to be a paladin to do great deeds.

"Why do you always say such things?" Vayla asked. "Why don't you like paladins?"

"You misunderstand," Cavalor said. "I have never shared this with you, but *I* wanted to become a paladin. It just wasn't meant to be. You see, it is not the choice of the warrior, but a bond between the warrior and Cafior."

"But grandmother was a paladin."

Cavalor gave her the same sad look he often did when discussing the matter. "Yes, she was. But she was not your grandmother by blood. She raised me as her own, and she was the greatest mother in all of Vaeldor. But we are not of her lineage."

Vayla was shocked. "Are we of grandfather's descent?"

"No." Cavalor placed a gentle hand on her shoulder. "But know this: I was a holy warrior. And now look at me. I'm a king!"

Vayla smiled. He could always make her smile.

Vayla thought hard on her father's words, and after a month she accepted them at last. Though she still wished to be a paladin, she was ready to accept any role the Holy City offered. She informed her father of her revelation, and it was then that he agreed to send her to New Palidur.

The Holy City fell short of Vayla's expectations. First, they placed her in classes with twelve-year-old boys. How had her father not known the age at which training began? Thankfully, this did not remain an issue for long. Vayla was already skilled with the sword and well learned in the ways of Cafior, thanks to her father and grandfather, and after only a year's time, they advanced her to join others of her age.

Vayla's next problem was with the statue of her in the middle of the Cafior Sector. Not a statue of *her*, exactly, but of her grandmother. And now Vayla's resemblance to the late paladin was uncanny. This led to many conversations with classmates — exchanges she grew tired of. Most were exploratory questions, to which Vayla had no answers — she had never met the woman! But some were of a teasing or jealous nature, and Vayla did her best not to react to those. The worst days, perhaps, were when her instructors held lessons concerning Merssa, and everyone expected Vayla to be an expert on the subject.

When it came to the city's older citizens, they gazed longer than Vayla was comfortable with, just as Lord Rholmar always did. Questions often accompanied these stares, like, "Do you know you're the spitting image of Lady Merssa?" It was more than Vayla could stomach. She became desperately tired of being compared to a woman she had never known. Tired of the staring. Tired of the willingness of others to please her for no other reason than her appearance. Some of her instructors claimed she was developing a bit of an attitude, but she did not care. She was not Merssa, and it was high time everyone got used to that fact.

A few months after Vayla turned nineteen, she received a summons from Grand Paladin Montac. Several of her classmates insisted she was in trouble, and a few thought she was being dismissed, but also there were those that believed she was getting special treatment because of her grandmother. Vayla ignored their assumptions and reported at once, ready for whatever awaited her. After all, she was not there to impress others. She was there to expand on her faith, her duty, and her love for Cafior.

As she stood before the Grand Paladin, a sensation that had plagued her stomach often as of late returned. It was not nerves, and she did not feel ill. It was a strange tingling. Perhaps it *was* nerves. She was then shocked when Montac informed her she was being promoted to Paladin.

"But..." She had a hard time finding her voice.

Montac raised his brow. "Yes? Do you take issue with this?"

"My lord. This isn't because of my grandmother... is it?"

The Grand Paladin's eyes bore into her. "First of all, it is no one's *choice* as to whether or not someone becomes a paladin. It is a bond formed between the individual and their deity."

Those words sounded familiar.

"And a paladin always knows when faced with another paladin." Montac paused, as if waiting for his point to register.

Vayla concentrated on the feeling in her stomach. The tingling persisted, and as she ceased to fight it, it grew pleasant and put her at ease. It had to be what Montac meant. She had experienced the sensation often over the past couple of weeks while walking the streets of New Palidur. She must have felt it every time a paladin passed by.

"Second," Montac continued, reminding her there was more than one point, "I am addressed as Grand Paladin Montac or Grand Paladin. I am not *my lord*."

"Yes." Vayla smirked. "My apologies, Grand Paladin."

As was customary when achieving paladinhood, Vayla changed her surname during a ceremony within the Grand Cathedral. She chose Starblade, combining her love of the mare her father had purchased for her and her preference for the sword. A celebration in the Cafior Sector followed.

After the festivities, Vayla journeyed home for a one-month leave. King Cavalor beamed with pride upon hearing the news, and the zhokards offered respectful nods. It was the closest Vayla had seen the elite soldiers come to showing affection.

The promotion had occurred seven months ago. Vayla was the youngest paladin New Palidur had ever known—a year younger than Merssa had been, according to Lord Rholmar—and here she was, receiving her first mission.

"Now gather your force," Montac said, returning her focus to the present. "You depart immediately."

Vayla bowed. "Yes, Grand Paladin."

Though she failed to hear most of his words, it was her third briefing on the mission, and she knew what she had to do. She bowed to Lord Rholmar, receiving a smile and a nod, and she left.

Outside the Grand Cathedral, Vayla's squadron awaited. Fourteen soldiers, holy warriors that had not achieved paladinhood, were mounted and ready to ride. They gazed at Vayla with stern expressions, knowing the mission ahead would likely claim several of their lives. The lead figure dismounted and approached as Vayla stepped onto the silver street surrounding the cathedral.

"Any news, my lady?" Captain Macurak asked, handing Vayla the reins to her mare.

Vayla patted Star's neck. The horse was chocolate brown with the blackest mane, and its eyes always brightened at the sight of Vayla, which had led her to name the animal Star. Star was from the region of the Batorn Gulf, where special horses were bred, and Vayla loved her mare deeply. Onlookers might have believed the mount to hold more value to Vayla than the dedicated warrior before her, but she was only lost in thought. The words of her captain then registered.

"The plans are unchanged," she said. "We ride for Arbornum."

Macurak bowed his head. "Very good, my lady."

Vayla sighed. "And Macurak..."

"Yes, my lady?"

"Quit with the title."

"As you wish." Macurak bowed again, his eyes darting left and right to spy others upon the road.

Vayla knew Macurak feared disrespecting her in front of other paladins. But she despised the distance her elevated position placed between her and those she trained with less than a year ago. Back then, they were equals. She climbed atop her mare, and after Macurak had mounted, she gave a nod.

"Move out!" Macurak shouted, and the contingent rode through the gate to the northeast and into the Cafior Sector.

The horses carried them across the brown flagstones and toward the outer wall. Many Cafior citizens nodded as they passed, and some said prayers, knowing the grim mission they had undertaken. There were also outlanders along the streets, either come to see the splendor of New Palidur or in town on some errand, and most of them moved aside with no greetings whatsoever.

Upon reaching the statue of Merssa, Vayla did not spare it a glance. The rest of her company, however, slowed to bow their heads and pray for the deceased paladin's guidance and strength.

The final gate sat open, and Vayla gazed one last time at the white buildings of the Holy City. She had only lived there a few years, but it was home. The tower guards held high their fists in salute, and she exited toward Palidur Bridge.

They rode across the Great East River and through Tedonis—another reminder of her grandmother. Beyond that, Vayla breathed a little easier as they headed northeast through Sendorum and into Harbnum.

Stops were at a minimum, and usually within taverns to refresh themselves, but they spent their nights on the road, for Vayla believed inn beds led to late starts. They veered west while in Harbnum and skirted Maple Lore Forest, and many of her contingent eyed the woodland with disdain or unease. Vayla ignored the ordinary-looking trees, holding no concern for the arrogant elves that dwelt therein. She had never met a Lorian personally, and she was convinced that rumors of the reclusive elves empowered fear of the unknown—a waste of energy in her opinion.

They pushed the horses for a time, and as they came to within a day of Arbornum, the city tasked with guarding the only bridge crossing the Shield River north of Maple Lore, Vayla slowed the pace. Many in the company would have preferred traveling through the night, she was sure, but to do so would bring them to Arbornum a few hours before dawn, and that was too soon. The city's gates would be shut tight, allowing no entry until the sun's light was felt.

They halted within a stone's throw of the forest come evening, and Vayla nodded for Macurak to issue the order.

"Camp!"

The holy warriors glanced at one another before dismounting. They erected tents and lit a couple of fires, and while they worked, Vayla spoke to Macurak.

"I don't like their attitudes."

"They were the finest soldiers willing to take part in this affair," Macurak said, not for the first time.

Vayla knew not all of them had been Macurak's first choices. But the fact that they volunteered spoke strongly to her captain of their faith and convictions, and he shared this wisdom with her more than once as well. Vayla also perceived that several of them held aspirations to one day attain paladinhood, and they hoped this quest would help achieve that goal. But she cared nothing about that. That was between them and Cafior.

"Willing to ride into Beit," she mumbled as she handed her reins to Macurak, "but afraid to camp outside a large gathering of trees. That hardly makes sense to me."

"Braving evil is one thing," Macurak said. "But the elves of this woodland are not necessarily evil. I believe it is a bit of a conflict. Are they truly your enemy if they are not evil?"

"Such the philosopher!" Vayla half-smirked.

"Yes, my lady." Macurak bowed, grinning at Vayla's scowl.

Camp was efficiently broken down come morning, and they arrived at Arbornum on time. But once within the walls of the city, delays were thrown at Vayla from every direction. The guards at the gate were obviously expecting her, for the doors opened without hesitation, but then problems arose.

Vayla was to be escorted immediately to the manor of Baron Weslin, but her escort was nowhere to be seen. When she insisted she could find the house on her own, the gatekeeper informed her that visiting soldiers were not permitted to walk the streets unaccompanied unless they left their weapons behind.

"That is ridiculous!" Vayla glared at the man. "I am a Paladin of New Palidur, and I am here on an urgent task."

"I'm sorry, my lady." The guard exhibited genuine empathy. "But that is the law." Before Vayla could explode with her next retort, the gatekeeper added, "There's The Guardian, just down the street. It is lunchtime, yes? Why don't you and your contingent head over there? It will be the baron's treat."

Vayla bit her tongue. The men were surely hungry.

Upon arrival at the tavern, she found no tables suitable for a party as large as hers. They had to stand outside while eating chicken legs and cornbread.

Vayla's escort showed up near the end of the meal with many apologies, claiming he had been informed she was to arrive tomorrow. From the sleep in the man's eyes and the alcohol on his breath, he probably did not know what the current day was.

The escort led them across the city, and after noticing the same buildings twice, Vayla wondered if he was actually from Arbornum. Upon reaching the baron's manor at last, a rotund butler did not improve matters.

"His lordship has stepped out for a moment," the man said with his nose in the air, "and shall be back within the hour."

It was enough to drive Vayla mad. Had it not been for Macurak's constant attempts to calm her, she might have punched the next person bearing unwanted news in the jaw.

Vayla and her men waited in the manor's library, staring at dusty books. The room was warm and stuffy, and some of her warriors began to nod off, so she ordered them to stand. After what seemed like three hours had passed—Macurak insisted it had only been slightly more than an hour—they were summoned to the baron's audience chamber.

The large hall was elegantly decorated with many tapestries and busts of unfamiliar men, and upon a fine maple throne big enough to seat a giant was Baron Weslin. The man was much older than Vayla, and he bore an expression that said *"I'm more important than you"* beneath his balding head. He gazed at Vayla and her contingent.

"Is this all that New Palidur has sent?" He raised his brow.

Vayla cleared her throat, and behind her a sigh escaped Macurak's lips.

"First of all," she said, "your guards leave much to be desired. They are unorganized and sloppy. Secondly, when a Palidurian Knight comes to call, and especially when you're aware of that call, you best have your *butt* planted in your seat on the day of her arrival. And now, to business."

The baron's mouth hung open for several seconds, and Vayla did not need to glance over her shoulder to know Macurak's head was downcast and shaking in disapproval.

Weslin's mouth shut as his face reddened. It was obvious he did not know how to respond. He could not send her away, because she was there for an undertaking so dire that none of his own soldiers possessed the courage to attempt it. He could not imprison her, not only for the same reason, but also because she was a Palidurian Knight, and no kingdom wished to fall from the Holy City's good graces. All he could do was release a slow, controlled breath and mutter. "Very well."

A servant entered bearing a large tray upon which rested a fancy crystal bottle containing red liquid, and a vine of grapes draped over one edge. Weslin waved the woman off, apparently no longer caring to provide refreshments to his visitors, and he sat back in his seat.

"As you may know," the baron said stiffly, "the plague attacking Beit is deadly to all things liv—"

"This we know." Vayla was still annoyed. "We have been informed of everything Tikken City has learned. We also know the Death Fog has not yet reached the eastern border, which is why we have been sent to cross the river here and not in Virch. So get on with what we do *not* know."

Baron Weslin took in another long breath, and Vayla again sensed his conflict. He assuredly wished for the plague to be stopped.

But at the same time, he would likely lose no sleep if she fell victim to its curse.

"My spies inform me that not all of Beit is bowing to its new king," Weslin said.

"The Shadow?" posed Vayla.

The baron paused, sighing at the interruption. "Yes, the Shadow King," he said curtly. "As I was saying, not all are willing to accept the fate the Shadow brings. Some have crossed the bridge under flags of surrender, and my prisons are full. Others, I am told, remain to fight for what is theirs. From the defectors, I have procured a so-called elixir the soldiers use to avoid contagion, and have enough stock for you and your contingent to last a week. From what I have learned, you will know when to drink it. The plague first appears as a common illness, with sneezing and coughing. It then attacks the body, making you waste away. Your limbs will ache. Your mind will cloud. Finally, you go to sleep and never wake."

Vayla detected the eagerness in the baron's voice at envisioning these symptoms overtaking her. "You need not concern yourself." She gave a sarcastic smile. "We will not succumb to such misery. We will put an end to it."

The baron nodded slightly. "I'm afraid that is all the information I can offer, since I'm sure you already know the Shadow possesses an item of power that has passed north of Lake Beldara."

"And the Council of Wizards believes the item to be responsible for the Death Fog," Vayla added, informing him she was, in fact, already aware.

Weslin nodded once. "And what of your plan to enter Beit. Do you intend to move forward with it?"

"We do."

"Frankly," the baron said, "I would have you proceed under a flag of parley, and perhaps slip—"

"Our plans are unchanged." Vayla was unconcerned with the politics between Harbnum and Beit. What did she care if Onzac became cross with Arbornum?

"Very well." Weslin sat back again. "If there's nothing else, I shall have rooms made available, and you may depart first thing tomorrow."

"I believe I have endured all of the city's hospitality that I care to," Vayla said. "So if you don't mind, we would appreciate an immediate escort to the bridge."

Baron Weslin visibly choked down his rage. "So be it."

CHAPTER 7

BEIT

Vayla set out with her contingent from Weslin's manor, led by one of the baron's officers along the streets and to the western edge of the city. After a mile, they passed through a gate and into the only part of Arbornum Vayla found acceptable. The area housed barracks, smithies, stables, practice areas, and hundreds of soldiers. The warriors marched from place to place, running drills or performing whatever duties they were given, and all appeared focused and disciplined. Perhaps Baron Weslin was not as useless as Vayla thought.

They approached the outer wall, this one taller than all others. Six catapults were situated to either side of the street, and piled next to each were boulders of various sizes. Dust and loose dirt covered the rocks, leading Vayla to wonder how accurate the operators of the weapons would prove if called upon. Atop the catwalks, soldiers kept watch over the west, and between forty-foot towers stood a massive portcullis, larger than any Vayla had ever seen. Beyond the iron bars was a pair of twenty-foot wooden doors, reinforced with steel bands and held by an enormous bar across their width.

With a wave from the officer to the northern tower, the portcullis slowly rose. Another winch then lifted the bar from the massive doors and the gates swung open to reveal the bridge over Shield River.

The arched stone stretched no less than fifty yards, and Vayla spotted a pair of thick chains secured beneath it twenty yards out and disappearing into the water. The chains resurfaced on the shore, where they were attached to multiple harnesses. Vayla learned in New Palidur that Andrian horses would pull these if an invasion was

73

imminent, breaking loose the bricks and making the structure unstable. Though she did not wish for war, she could not diminish her desire to see that plan go into action.

They passed through the gate, and to the left, Maple Lore Forest spread to either side of the Shield River. Vayla's gaze shifted to the water. The rapid current maintained its strength for miles and miles, all the way from its origination among the Stone Eagle Mountains — an impressive distance. It was the swiftest current outside the Great East River, creating the border between Virch and Beit until entering Maple Lore. It was then unseen until exiting the trees' northern reaches, and it separated Beit from Harbnum as it hurried to the Icy Sea. While traversing the forest, the river split, feeding a large lake in the middle of the woodland and giving life to the Maple River, and rumor held the Shield River to be fordable near this junction. But just as the Vircans and Harbanians, the Beitians would never seek this route for passage. Lorian elves permitted no outsiders within their realm, good or evil.

Vayla led her men to the bridge. A hundred yards beyond the stone construction stood Onzac, a walled city opposite Arbornum that served the same purpose. Vayla sensed the eyes of its soldiers upon her, daring her to cross without permission. They were probably blowing the dust off of their own rock piles at that very moment. Her next move was risky, but there existed no safe passage into the evil kingdom. She kicked Star into action.

The hoofbeats of her contingent pounded the stone behind her while they sped across the bridge. Ahead, activity was unmistakable atop the walls of Onzac. But Vayla had time, and before the city opened its gates or fired its catapults, she reached the opposite side of the river and turned south.

Vayla raced along the riverbank without making sure her men kept up, wanting to put distance between Onzac and herself before a detachment could hope to pursue. It was a bold plan, but decades of idleness, with no trespassers other than those under flags of parley, had surely left the city watch relaxed and unprepared. As well, the pressure of a new king and the threat of the Death Fog had to weigh upon the soldiers' minds.

Vayla continued two miles and the Beitians appeared—a cavalry over three times her troop's size gave chase. But they were a long way off, and her contingent rode the finest steeds in all of Vaeldor. Just as Star, the animals had come from the northern reaches of Kalmaar, near the Batorn Gulf, and they proved durable and swift as she pushed them harder and the distance increased. The Beitian force grew smaller until they disappeared altogether.

Maple Lore was now clear, its maple trees standing tall and proud. If need be, Vayla had every intention of entering the forest to elude the evil soldiers—damn what the elves might think! Her warriors knew this, and it was likely the chief reason they had been so uneasy while traveling along the forest's edge. But this decision would not come to pass, for hundreds of armed men arose from tall weeds and scattered bushes. Vayla was surrounded.

She pulled Star to a halt. How could the Beitians have been so prepared? How could they have known of her plans to breach their border? If Baron Weslin was involved in this...

Vayla viewed the enemy more closely. They did not wear Beitian uniforms or tabards, and their expressions ranged from determined to fearful. They were not soldiers, but hunters, farmers, and the like. Only half carried swords while others wielded pitchforks, scythes, hammers, and wooden poles shaved to points.

One man stepped forward, eyeing Vayla, and she knew right away he was a soldier of high rank. Or at least he used to be. He was tall and his shoulders broad, and several scars marked him as a seasoned warrior. Above his reddish, dapper mustache that curled into loops, his green eyes narrowed while he considered her and her company.

"You are of Palidur," he said in his slurry Beitian accent with a sneer.

With Beit having no ties to the realms beyond the Shield River, Vayla was surprised the man knew the common tongue. She nodded.

His gaze snapped northward, where the pursuing cavalry appeared. "Here they come!" he called out in his own language, of which all Palidurians were well versed. "Ready your weapons!"

The militia eyed the approaching horsemen, awaiting the next order. Some perspired heavily, their eyes anxious, and others held a steady hand with looks of ire—folks who had nothing to lose.

"Charge!" the man commanded, and three-quarters of the force ran screaming toward the Beitian pursuers.

The cavalry of trained warriors could certainly destroy the would-be-soldiers at least ten to one. But even at those odds, the riders would be slaughtered. The cavalry seemed to realize this, and they fled into the north.

The militiamen roared as they halted their charge, waving their weapons in victory. Vayla looked back at the man who had issued the order.

"What now?" she asked. Did he plan on taking her and her unit as prisoners? Unlike the Beitian cavalry, she would not run. She would kill as many as possible.

"Though I bear no love for you or your city," the soldier said with visible animosity, "I have no intentions of killing you... for now."

Vayla almost wished he would try after those words. If she struck him down, the rest of his men would likely scatter in fear.

"But you *will* accompany us," he added, sizing her up. "It's obvious to me why you're here. And we may be able to help one another."

Vayla considered him. She would rather make a dash into Maple Lore than consort with a Beitian. She took in a deep breath and released it. "Very well. I will go with you... for now."

The man gave a snort, almost smiling. His men appeared uneasy.

Vayla and her warriors rode alongside the militia to the southwest until they were just beyond bowshot of the forest. From there, they veered in a more southerly direction. The Beitians looked relieved to leave the trees behind—even more so than did the holy soldiers. It was obvious the people were not used to such labors and the pace was slow, and while they marched, the commander spoke to Vayla.

"I am General Burnod of Zurzak." His lips twisted into a scowl. "At least, I was."

Vayla held a level gaze. Zurzak hosted one of the most elite armies of Beit, positioned to guard the bridge against Virch. There was no way this man could be what he claimed. He surely played on her assumed ignorance. She glanced at the peasants surrounding her and scoffed. "My, what Beit calls soldiers these days."

Burnod looked at his men. "They are braver than any soldier hiding behind well-crafted arms and armor, allowing those they're supposed to be protecting to die." His tone held little patience. "This fog the Shadow releases..." Burnod shook his head. "I saw no choice but to desert my post."

Vayla did not respond right away. She realized the man to be telling the truth, but her dislike of Beitians made sympathy impossible. "And how will you take on the Shadow? Your men can scare off a small band of riders, but sooner or later a force will arrive that you cannot withstand. You are but a thorn in their side."

"Perhaps you should offer your encouraging words to my people!" Burnod came to a halt and eyed her with contempt. "The fact remains that we could have killed you and your men. But we allow you to live. And I think that should grant us a *bit* of courtesy."

"*Courtesy* is not freely given," Vayla countered. "For all I know, this is merely a trap, and you are delivering us to our cells."

"You'll see," Burnod said, and they continued without further words.

After a few minutes had passed, Macurak spoke quietly to Vayla.

"I don't think this is a trap. And I do not believe for a second that you do either."

"So?" Vayla kept her eyes forward.

"So what's the plan? There are no bowmen and they have no horses. We can just ride away."

"No." Vayla looked ahead at Burnod. "I want to see what they're up to."

As the sun dropped low in the sky, a town came into view. The collection of wooden buildings stood atop a rise, a half mile west of Maple Lore's border, and around it a ragtag fence was almost complete in its construction. To the north, cattle and sheep grazed beneath the watch of a few shepherds and a couple of hounds. Several men armed with bows were alert along the eastern perimeter of the village, barely protected by the fence, and they appeared relieved to see the militia's return.

"Report!" Burnod called out after he and his force had climbed the hill.

A man came running to stand in front of the ex-general, flanked by a pair of archers. "All's quiet, sir!"

"Very good." Burnod glanced over his shoulder at Vayla and her squad. "See to it these horses are stabled and well treated. And escort our guest and her warriors to the Silver Chalice and make sure they are fed."

"Yes, s—sir," the man stammered, glancing at Vayla. After a meaningful stare from Burnod, he composed himself and addressed the bowmen behind him. "See to the horses!" The soldier turned to Vayla. "Welcome to Sylnor, ma'am."

Vayla looked at Burnod, but the ex-general paid her no mind as he walked away. She returned her glare to the man before her, unsure of how to handle being called *ma'am* by one twice her age. With a sigh, she dismounted, and her contingent did the same.

They followed their escort along the main street of the small village. The road was in decent shape, obviously not knowing many horses or wagons over its existence, but the buildings were dirty and in need of repairs. Most of the roofs sagged, shutters hung, and chimneys were in various states, having lost a number of bricks. These details meant little to Vayla, however. The villagers held her attention.

Older men and several women performed chores and attempted to mend dilapidated structures. Other citizens tilled fields, butchered meats, and stitched leather into crude armor while smithies of limited skills fashioned weapons Vayla would never wield, not even if offered as a gift. Around the village, a dozen people worked on the wooden fence, a construction that would serve only to keep livestock in and never ward off advancing soldiers. Children ran about, but not for fun or games—they, too, prepared for an attack that would certainly come. The inhabitants were a miserable lot, and their dirty faces knew no smiles while they did their parts.

Vayla sighed. Burnod realized his village would eventually fall to the Beitian army, of that she held no doubt. But even with his limited resources, he would make sure they endured as long as possible, living on their own terms as best they could. It might have been commendable, were she not positive an underlying, self-serving reason surely drove the man.

The Silver Chalice came into view—an inn under reconstruction. Several older men were nailing boards around a newly framed second story, and others were placing slats onto the roof. Upon entering, Vayla found the building to be more of a command center and mess hall than a tavern or inn. The wooden walls were reinforced, the windows barred, and next to every door was a thick plank, so they could be secured should the need arise. It was obvious the structure would serve as a keep in the end, so the villagers might make a final stand before their demise. The scene was depressing.

"Vayla," murmured Macurak.

"I know." She was sure her captain shared her thoughts.

They were seated at a sturdy table, and after a whispered message from Vayla's escort to a man behind a bar, the servant disappeared into the kitchen. Moments later, he emerged with platters of bread, cheese, and smoked meat. He also provided a few pitchers of beer and mugs, all without mention of a price or a plea for a tip. The bartender then resumed wiping plates and cleaning mugs.

The food was fair, as was the brew, and Vayla's men proceeded to fill themselves. It was a much more accommodating meal than Vayla had planned for their first evening within the evil kingdom, and their expressions seemed better for it. Still, their eyes shifted as they awaited what was to happen next.

"What now?" Macurak whispered to Vayla.

"Now we wait." She took another bite of cheese.

"But for what?" asked Macurak. "To die with them?"

"I wish to see what their plan is," Vayla said. "If there's any way to use them to further our goal, we must."

"But Vayla—"

She elbowed her captain as Burnod entered.

"Now that I've seen to a few things," the ex-general took a seat at the end of the table, "we can get better acquainted."

Vayla nodded.

"You still have not told me your name." Burnod stared.

Vayla waited a few seconds before responding. "I am Vayla, Palidurian Knight of Cafior."

Burnod raised his brow, surprised or impressed—or both.

"And with me is Captain Macurak and my contingent of holy soldiers." She did not bother to inform him of which man was Macurak. He would figure it out if he had truly been a general.

"That wasn't too hard now, was it?" Burnod revealed not a hint of humor.

"Please," Macurak said. "It's obvious there is no love at this table. But it's also obvious we have a common foe, if only for today. Perhaps we can stop wasting time and focus on the problem."

Vayla and Burnod turned to Macurak. They then faced each other. Vayla gave a nod, and Burnod broke into a grin.

"The captain's right," he said. "I've watched Vircans and Palidurians from across the river for so long... Well, you may or may not understand my hesitation."

Vayla decided to get to the point. "Tell me all you know about this Death Fog. How do I stop it?"

Burnod's smile dropped and Macurak shook his head. The ex-general then spoke.

"As for your question, I do not know how to stop the plague. In fact, I know very little about it, other than it kills all things living. First you get the sniffles, and then your skin pales and dark circles form beneath your eyes. Then the sniffling disappears, replaced by vomiting, and you are fatigued. The vomiting ends, leaving you but a fraction of what you used to be... I've seen grown men weighing no more than a child. In the final stages, your body withers and blood seeps from your nose and ears. It takes less than a week, ending in death. Unless, of course, you possess the elixir provided by the Shadow."

"I'll drink nothing created by evil," Vayla said flatly. "There must be another way."

"No way *I* know of." Burnod shrugged. "Unless, maybe, you're made of shadow."

"Surely you do not expect me to believe you intend to sit here and await your death." Vayla narrowed her eyes. "Even if the Beitian army ignores your presence, the Death Fog will dispose of you. You cannot possibly have enough of the evil potion for an entire village."

"As comforting as your words are," Burnod said, "there are few choices available to us. We could die fighting the armies of Beit, or attempt to cross one of the bridges before either side kills us, only to become imprisoned if we survive."

His glare may have daunted the holy soldiers, but Vayla was unmoved.

He sat back and folded his arms. "No. We will hold our ground for as long as the gods allow, as free men. Who knows? Perhaps the plague will never arrive. Perhaps a miracle will save us. The people of this village deserve a chance to live or die however they choose. Better that than the alternative."

Vayla raised a brow. "Alternative?"

"Sacrificial pawns to the Shadow!" Burnod spat. "We were never told why so many must die, or what purpose it serves. But it is not an end I'll allow, not if I can help it."

Vayla considered the ex-general. He continued to speak the truth. As for the village he chose to serve out his exile, he surely bore an attachment. Perhaps his birthplace. A heroic story. A sad story. Vayla kept up her guard, exposing no emotions.

"Tell me about the Shadow," she said.

"No one knows when it first entered our land, nor where it came from." Burnod shook his head in frustration. "All I know is one day my orders were issued by King Vronik, and the next day he was dead. Killed at the hands of the Shadow." His face paled. "The Shadow summoned all generals to it, and I reported to Benzon to receive my new orders. It was then that its plan was revealed; a plan to sacrifice the citizens of Beit to the Dark One."

Vayla held her breath, knowing of which deity he spoke. Thard'Dun was the vilest, most evil deity from the deepest pits of Hell. Few uttered the name aloud, and even fewer openly worshipped him since the days of the Ancient Enemy of the North. Of course, for all Vayla knew, things were different on this side of the Shield River.

"And how is it the Shadow found enough willing subjects to carry out its plan?" she asked.

"Though there have always been those that followed the Dark One's ways," Burnod replied, "there are also those eager to do what they can to please the ruling power. And the strength of the Shadow is great, make no mistake."

Vayla furrowed her brow. "And just how are the citizens to be sacrificed?"

"The plague consumes their souls." Burnod's gaze fell to the table. "It creeps across the land, infecting all but the protected soldiers. Left behind are nothing but empty shells. And it's a fate worse than death, for those souls are sent to the Dark One.

"I have spent my entire life defending my people." Burnod eyed Vayla. "I could not play a part in this. Upon returning to Zurzak, I made my choice." He shook his head, gazing out a window showing the full darkness of night. "There were none under my command willing to join me. Too many were afraid. Others looked forward to the chance of throwing down their long-hated enemies to the south, no matter the cost."

"What?" Vayla could not conceal her shock. "The Shadow means to invade Virch?"

"That, I do not know for certain," Burnod said. "The Shadow's interests seem to be elsewhere. But for what purpose does it clear the land of all living souls? Why would it feed these souls to its deity, if not to fuel some power? These thoughts haunt my dreams."

"And you know of no way to end the Fog?" Vayla asked again.

Burnod shook his head. "You would have to go to its source. To do that, you must journey for days within the unseen cloud. And without the aid of the elixir, you will surely perish before reaching your destination."

Vayla bit her lip. "I shall need the evening to think. I'll make my decision by morning." She ignored the incredulous look Macurak issued.

Burnod nodded. "Very well. You shall have this night. But know this: you'll not be able to cross the bridge back into Harbnum. Onzac will be watching for you, and the plague has already reached the border near Virch. You are prisoners of Beit."

CHAPTER 8

MAPLE LORE

Macurak could not sleep. The cots provided were comfortable enough, placed within a single chamber to accommodate the entire company, but his mind was unsettled. Maybe it was their current predicament, trapped in an evil kingdom. Perhaps it was the dire mission that lay ahead, to battle an enemy you could not see; one you could not swing a sword at. Or maybe it was Vayla. He was used to her aloofness, as well as her poor manners when dealing with those outside of New Palidur, regardless of their station in life. But he did not understand her recent actions; her lack of empathy for a defeated people trying to hold on to what pride remained.

A hand touched his shoulder and gave him a shake. Looking up, Vayla was staring at him.

"Wake the men," she whispered. "We leave at once."

Now what was she up to? He had little time to consider the matter, for she had already moved away.

Macurak stirred the holy soldiers, and they dressed as quietly as possible in the darkness before following Vayla from the chamber. The tavern room was empty, and they unbarred the door and exited the Silver Chalice.

They marched down the street beneath the twilight of an early morning, encountering a handful of townsfolk. The civilians stared in shock, too afraid to speak, and a few ran off in haste. They reached the stables without delay, and once the horses were saddled and mounted, Burnod arrived in a long nightshirt. His face almost glowed red in the dim light.

"Where are you going?" he demanded.

Vayla looked down at the ex-general from her horse. "Our paths together end here. I fail to see where we can serve one another. You are here to die with your kin. Our fate lies to the northwest, as Cafior allows."

Burnod stared for what seemed like several minutes before speaking again. "At least take this." He tossed up a small jug.

Vayla seized the container. It was a black waterskin, and Macurak could make out two blue dots above three wavy purple lines painted on the side.

"It is the elixir provided by the Shadow," Burnod said. "There should be enough for a couple of weeks."

"I have no need—"

"I know your *pride* prevents you from using it," Burnod sneered, "but think of your men. Perhaps *they* might enjoy the chance to live a bit longer than you. Perhaps they might complete your mission in your absence, after your soul has been consumed."

Vayla looked at the holy soldiers. Their eyes were downcast, unwilling to put truth to the commander's words. Macurak held her gaze, hoping she would give Burnod's offer a second thought. She tossed the jug to the general. Macurak sighed.

"Cafior will guide us," she said, and she turned her horse to the west.

There were no attempts to stop them while they rode from Sylnor at a brisk pace, and the cool morning air swept across their faces as a couple of miles fell behind. Macurak then detected the sun's heat on his back as the way brightened, and Vayla came to a halt.

Ahead, a dark line stretched five-hundred feet in the distance. An army was marching on the village. Why so large a force, Macurak did not understand, but there was no mistaking the direction they aimed for. He studied them further, and he noticed some did not wear Beitian uniforms and no Beitian banners waved. Several were clad in black armor, and there were no flags at all. No horns sounded, and nothing showed them to be concerned with the horsemen in front of them.

Vayla looked left and right, as if considering riding around them. Macurak pulled his horse next to hers. "What now?"

Her expression was unreadable. "Back to the village."

Macurak hesitated. He did not know if he was glad she decided to offer the villagers help, or confused at risking the mission for an unattainable goal. He gave the order, and they left a cloud of dust in their wake as they sped into the east.

The low sun stung Macurak's eyes, and before long he spied Sylnor in the distance. One, then two, and finally three horns issued their warnings, and Burnod appeared at the shabby fence with a hundred unarmored men to see what the commotion was. The villagers seemed to breathe a collective sigh of relief upon seeing it was the Palidurians ascending the hill.

"Why have you returned?" demanded Burnod once they arrived.

"An army approaches." Vayla spoke loud enough for everyone to hear, using the Beitian language. "One you cannot hope to withstand. You must take your people and flee."

Burnod raised a brow. "And where would you have us go?"

"North. South. Wherever your path leads you." Vayla's tone remained cold. "We'll attempt to lead them away. We have bows and might gain their attention. Perhaps your departure will pass unnoticed."

Burnod held Vayla with a level stare. "No." Turning to the villagers, he shouted, "Now is the time! We shall let the Shadow know we will not go willingly to his dark deity! Today is the day to die in battle and enter the Halls of Brondor! Far from the clutches of the Dark One!"

Brondor worshippers? In Beit? Macurak did not think it was possible. As he viewed the citizens, however, he suspected Burnod might be the only one. A less-than-enthusiastic cheer resounded as the people left to prepare. Some looked scared, some confused, and others resigned to their fate.

"Blast it all!" Vayla dropped from her saddle, gaining Burnod's attention. "Gather your archers and place them on the western edge.

When we arrived yesterday, they were too scattered."

"Typical thinking." Burnod shook his head. "But with our lack of numbers and skill, they are better spread out, and less likely to fall in one return volley. I will disperse them along the fence and atop what buildings will bear their weight."

"And your unarmored men should be positioned to slow the enemy and do what damage they can," Vayla added as villagers took the horses and she and Burnod led the way toward the Silver Chalice.

"That is warfare for soldiers, not villagers," Burnod said. "They would lack morale, fall without causing *any* damage, and sadden those they left behind, killing their spirits without a fight."

"So *my* men are to lead the charge?" Vayla eyed the commander. "Or do we just ride around and cause confusion?"

"There will be no charge," Burnod answered. "We wait. Focus our strength together and use the village as cover. It provides only a slight chance for victory, but it's the best chance we have."

Vayla and Burnod stood on the front porch of the tavern, staring at each other. Macurak held his breath, awaiting Vayla's decision.

"Very well," Vayla said. "My archers will take point along the fence. The rest of us will settle near enough to guard their retreat when they fall back. You will place yourself deeper in the village with your men and flank those in our wake."

A grin captured Burnod's face. "Very good. They shall be so deployed."

Vayla turned to Macurak and the holy warriors. "No time to waste. Let's go."

A part of Macurak wanted to smile. Every once in a while, Vayla exposed her humanity. But they now faced impossible odds, and it was not like her to ignore orders—they entered Beit for a specific reason. Macurak wished to speak with her on this topic, but everything was moving too fast.

Vayla stood at a window in a small house near the fence along the western edge of the village. She gazed at the valley below, finally gaining a better view of the approaching force.

Hundreds of foot soldiers bearing pikes led the way, followed by swordsmen and then a cavalry. She estimated there to be more than a thousand. Behind the horses marched two hundred archers, and beyond them, yet another grouping, but Vayla could not see them clearly. They were more like monsters than soldiers, standing twice the height of the bowmen and three times their girth, and they walked on stout legs with immense arms dangling to the ground, appearing like black gorillas. As they moved closer, Vayla swore their eyes glowed with a violet light. She had never seen the likes of them before, and a chill ran down her spine as a tingling sensation invaded her scalp.

"Wait here," she said to Macurak.

She exited the house and raced along the street until reaching the Silver Chalice.

"Burnod!" she called out.

There was the muffled sound of the bar sliding from the door. The door then opened and Burnod exited, frowning while Vayla panted.

"We must flee," she said. "The slight chance of victory you hold does not exist. Not only do they outnumber us, but something else marches with them. Do you know anything about giant black gorillas?"

Burnod shook his head, his eyes narrowing. "I know nothing of gorillas. But we stand our ground."

"Blast the Brondor faithful!" Vayla's blood boiled. "You can't expect me to believe that everyone in this village will be welcomed into His Halls. These are farmers, not warriors. I fear a fate worse than death awaits all who fight beside you. Perhaps even yourself."

"We stay," Burnod said through clenched teeth. "So return to your post or flee with your men. The choice is yours."

Vayla shook her head.

She ran swiftly to the small house, where Macurak stood at the window.

"The archers have halted," he said, "and the foot soldiers have split. The cavalry now rides forth."

"And what of the gorillas?"

Macurak's brows drew together. "Gorillas?"

Vayla gazed out the window. The monsters were gone. The chill in her spine traveled down her legs, and she fell against the wall. What devilry was this?

"To the forest," she said, just above a whisper. She looked at Macurak, and the captain frowned. "To the forest!" Vayla repeated, more boldly this time as she regained her composure. "Sound the retreat in Beitian for everyone to hear."

"Yes, Vayla." Macurak turned to the others in the room. "Gather our men. We head for Maple Lore!"

"Yes, sir!" came an energetic response.

Apparently, they welcomed the rumors of the forest to the certain death that approached.

"Fall back!" the holy warriors shouted after exiting the house, all of them speaking in the Beitian tongue. "Fall back! To the east!"

The Palidurian archers were the first to heed the call, and the villagers were close behind, seemingly eager to comply. Vayla led the way, and the calls to retreat captured the streets. Burnod exited the Silver Chalice as Vayla drew near, and ire was plain on his red face, but there was no stopping the rout now—too many villagers had accepted the idea.

"I hope you're happy!" Burnod growled. "Had I known Palidurians were so easily shaken, I'd have led an assault upon your city years ago!"

"You'll thank me," Vayla said as she continued past the tavern and to the stables.

She and her men mounted and rode to the eastern edge of the hill, where half of the village was already gathered at the bottom. Several more were running, even rolling down the hillside to join them.

Vayla descended into their midst and shouted in the Beitian language. "To the trees!"

The villagers hesitated. Their lifelong fear of Maple Lore froze their legs, and they looked at each other in confusion. Burnod then arrived, rushing down the hill.

"Into the forest!" His voice held anger. "Quickly!"

The people moved across the field and toward the distant trees. When Burnod neared Vayla, he issued her a menacing glare, but he continued past without a word.

"Keep the rear!" Vayla ordered her men, and they rode slowly while watching the hill behind them.

The villagers made it halfway to the forest when Sylnor began issuing black smoke. Fiery arrows rained onto the eastern-most buildings, and moments later, swordsmen rounded the southern base of the hill. The mass of people making their way across the field did not escape the soldiers' notice, and many shouts ensued before a horn sounded.

"Faster!" Vayla commanded. "We've been spotted!"

The citizens of Sylnor ran, and not a moment too soon. Away to the north, the gorillas appeared. The enormous creatures lumbered toward the villagers, but not in the fashion Vayla would have thought. They did not pound their large fists onto the ground and run on all fours. They ran similarly to men, pumping their long arms with every step but covering more distance than any man could have hoped to.

The forest drew nearer, and Vayla knew it would be close. She rode to the northern side of the retreating people to offer protection, but at the speed the gorillas exhibited, they would surely smash through her and Star, as if passing through tall weeds. She pulled her sword and made ready her defense, nonetheless.

The monsters drew near enough for Vayla to see they were hairless, covered by perfectly jet-black skin, and the deep purple glow filled their eye sockets—no eyeballs were visible. The creatures snarled, revealing pointed black teeth, but they did not growl like animals, as Vayla expected. In fact, other than the pounding of their massive feet on the ground, they made no sound at all.

Macurak arrived at Vayla's side, as did the rest of her contingent, and the holy warriors loosed arrows. The missiles bounced from the monsters' smooth skin with no apparent effect. They released another volley with no better results.

"Ready your swords!" Vayla ordered.

She shook her head. She had entered Beit with a dire mission — her first mission. Why did she allow herself to be distracted? She put her men in harm's way to fight a battle that was not their own, and now they protected strangers, unknowing if the forest provided safety. She was charged with stopping a plague, and she would fail without barely having begun. People called her the reincarnation of Merssa Goldmace, the great High Paladin that led the war against the undead necromancer. But she was not Merssa. She could not even perform the one task given to her.

Hundreds of arrows exited the forest in haste — long-shafted missiles that pierced the creatures' black flesh. And though they failed to drop the gorillas, they gained the monsters' full attention.

Vayla looked back at the villagers. They were at the forest's edge.

"To the trees!" she commanded her men.

The Palidurians made a mad dash, catching up as the last of the crowd crossed the tree line. They slowed their horses to enter the woodland, and though the way was clear at first, low branches forced them to dismount.

"Farther in!" Vayla could not turn away visions of gorillas storming the forest. "We need more distance!"

"Halt where you stand!" a melodic voice sounded above the murmuring and rustling of Sylnor's people making their way around trees and through brush. It was elf-like, but sharp and menacing.

Everyone froze.

"Who speaks to us?" demanded Vayla. "Show yourself!"

An elf stepped from behind a tree. And then another. And another. Soon, an army surrounded the villagers and Palidurians.

The elves wore brown leather and stood taller than the average Salenti elf, but shorter than their Vermallon cousins. Most carried bows, all with arrows at the ready, while others held short, fancy swords. Their eyes revealed contempt.

"You will drop your arms and surrender," said an elf standing before them. It was the one who had spoken already, and his voice rang out loud and clear, as if amplified by the trees.

"We entered your realm only to escape the creatures you yourselves found it proper to attack." Vayla glanced over her shoulder. No gorillas pursued. "If you did not wish for us to seek refuge in your forest, you should have let us fall prey to them."

"What we choose to do is none of your concern," the elf sneered. "And our law states that no one outside our clan is permitted within Maple Lore. You have broken that law, and you must abide by its penalty."

Vayla saw no choice. With dire reluctance, she sheathed her blade. The law made little sense, but she would not lead the villagers from certain death at the hands of the evil army to an alternate death beneath the trees. Perhaps she would meet an authoritative figure to speak with on the matter.

The elves ushered them deeper into the woodland, walking for half the day, and the farther they pressed, the more majestic the trees became. Maples of normal growth gave way to towering pillars upon trunks several feet in girth, and the ceiling rose high overhead, providing ample room for even ogres to tread. Dusk then arrived and the forest darkened, and they entered a large area illuminated by dozens of torches and boasting many wooden buildings. Unlike Sylnor, these were in perfect order, some standing three stories to reach the boughs of the mighty maples. From the rooftops extended ramps to structures higher up, and higher still was another collection of houses atop wooden platforms.

Vayla gazed in wonder. It was a city layered within the forest like the towering dwarf home, Morimont. But instead of scaling the mountainside, this one climbed what must be Vaeldor's tallest trees.

Vayla spotted no less than four tiers, including the ground level where she stood, but she was sure the city continued upward. Perhaps a watchtower extended above the final branches and into the sky.

A vast cage of wood at the center of the ground floor caught Vayla's attention. It was as large as three inns, though there were no separate rooms, and at least fifty occupants were inside. The bulk of the prisoners were older, appearing to have known no other home for years. Most of them were Beitians, probably tasked with finding a path through the forest at one time, and a few Vircans and Harbanians shared the space.

"So the rumors of a giant prison are true," Macurak murmured to Vayla. "And from the looks of the prisoners, so are the rumors that no one ever leaves."

"Hey! Vayla!" Burnod walked at the front of the mass of villagers, wearing a sarcastic smile. "Thank you!"

The hilt of an elf's sword silenced the ex-general.

CHAPTER 9

LORIAN WIZARD

Vayla barely slept. It was a new day, and with the first sign of morning, Lorian elves began their daily routines while she sat and watched. The majority of the settlement's population were surely upon the platforms rising into the towering maples, but plenty of elves were coming or going, fishing in the nearby river, or milling about. Most walked past the cell without a glance, but every so often an elf sneered at the cage's occupants or a young Lorian made faces and taunted the prisoners.

Nearing lunchtime, warrior elves began arriving in various states of health, and the mangled remains of some were carried to places unknown. Vayla witnessed heated conversations now and again, but they were in elfish and she understood none of them. The battle with the gorillas must not have ended after the shower of arrows.

"Vayla." Macurak grabbed her attention with a harsh whisper.

The captain nodded to the opposite side of the cage, and she followed him there. Leaning against a tree twenty yards away was an elf who appeared to have a case of the sniffles. Vayla then spied another with the sniffles. And another. And another. There were no less than two dozen elves with pink noses, sniffling and wiping excess mucus.

"The Fog has reached Maple Lore," Macurak said, drawing close enough so no one else could hear.

"That's not necessarily true." Vayla scanned the treetops, as if she might see the cloud. "They may have encountered it outside the forest."

Macurak shook his head. "If it's not here now, it soon will be. We must get out of this cell."

Vayla bit her lip. Her captain was right. She turned to the nearest Lorian soldier. "You there!"

The elf did not look. None of them seemed to hear her.

"Excuse me."

Still nothing.

"Hey, you blasted pointy-eared knave!"

The forest quieted as every elf on the ground level glared at Vayla.

"They have the plague." She pointed at the sniffling elves. "Those, over there."

"A plague you brought with you, then!" spat a Lorian in the common tongue as he approached the bars. He was a soldier, and one of high rank. "Your entire race is a plague!"

The rest of the elves resumed ignoring the cage.

"Whatever you might think," Vayla said calmly, "the plague is invading your forest and will kill us all. I have come from New Palidur to find—"

"Palidur means nothing!" the elf hissed through clenched teeth. "And I will hear your tongue no longer. Keep it still or lose it!"

The soldier walked away to converse with others of his race.

"These elves are insufferable!" Vayla did not care who heard her. Just let them try to remove her tongue!

"Burnod!" Macurak called.

The ex-general looked at Macurak, rubbing the lump he received to his head the previous night.

"Tell them she speaks the truth," Macurak said.

Burnod snorted and turned away.

"You would let your people succumb to it now?" Macurak approached Burnod. "You'd allow them to become sacrifices to the Dark One?"

Vayla's captain held the attention of several elves. Their faces showed infuriation.

"You will pay for such insolence!" spat the elf that had addressed

Vayla. "You!" He pointed at Macurak. "You have ended your stay with us."

From the expressions of the cell's long-time occupants, Vayla knew these words bore no hope of freedom for her captain. She moved to Macurak's side, her hand reaching for the sword that was not at her waist.

"What is going on here?" came a calm voice, speaking in the common tongue.

Several Lorians parted as an elf wearing green robes approached the cell. Though he appeared no older than the others, the new arrival was obviously well respected, and he had possibly known a few of the larger trees when they were young. His white hair made his emerald eyes shine with the arrogance he carried, and his steps were confident while he gazed at the one that threatened Macurak.

"This *creature* has disrespected our city, making mention of things we speak not of." The soldier used the common speech in an obvious attempt to scare the prisoners. "I was about to—"

"Merssa?" The robed elf stared at Vayla with a furrowed brow.

Great. It was like she was back in New Palidur.

The elf shook his head. "Of course not. That would be impossible." He gazed into Vayla's eyes, making her more uncomfortable than even the elder citizens of New Palidur had. "But..."

"I am Vayla."

Several elves gasped, as if taken aback that she dared to speak. She did not care.

"I know," she added. "I look like my grandmother. I hear it *every* day."

The elf's eyes narrowed. "But your father... He was adopted. How could you—?"

"You seem to know a lot about my family." Vayla's interruption stirred a multitude of murmurs. "But I know not who you are."

"Forgive me." The elf revealed the tiniest smirk. "I am Wezlok. And I knew your grandmother, as well as your grandfather and father."

"Wezlok?" She knew that name. Not only did the teachings of New Palidur mention Wezlok's part in the war against Trannum, but her father had spoken in depth about the Lorian wizard with the highest of praises. She could not recall all the details, but that much she remembered. "I've read about you. Somehow, I thought you'd have been older, or taller, or... something."

Wezlok stared for several seconds without speaking. Vayla bit her tongue. Her instructors described the elf wizard as aloof and unpredictable, and she did not want to bring unnecessary punishment to her contingent. Wezlok's smirk then stretched to one side of his face and he turned to the elf soldier.

"Set her free."

"But Master—"

"Dresnian!" Wezlok's tone chased the gathered elves back a step or two. "You dare to question my authority?"

Dresnian's shoulders slumped, and he gave a short response in the elfish tongue. His ire then returned as he approached the cage door.

"No." Vayla halted Dresnian and caused Wezlok's brow to rise. "I stay with my people. Free us all, or leave me to share their fate. The Death Fog is invading your forest as we speak, and I have come to put an end to it. So either allow us to carry out our quest, or leave us to die with the rest of you."

Wezlok frowned. "What makes you believe the plague has invaded Maple Lore? There is magic in place to prevent such an occurrence."

"Look at the sick." Vayla nodded at the group of elves displaying what Burnod had explained to be the first signs.

Healthy Lorians moved away from the ailing bunch, and those exhibiting symptoms were suddenly alarmed.

"Your magical wards are obviously ineffective," Vayla said. "Either the Fog has entered the forest, or the elves have brought it with them. Either way—"

"Enough." Wezlok waved a hand.

He approached one of the sick, seemingly unconcerned with contracting the virus. His eyes narrowed as he studied the elf, and after a minute, he returned to the cage.

"What you say may be true," Wezlok said, and Vayla could almost feel the entire city stop breathing. "But what hope do *you* bring? How will *you* end it?"

Vayla looked into the piercing green eyes, knowing she could offer no hope. She also realized she could not lie to this being. "I make no promises. All I can offer is for me and my men to ride north, as we originally intended. We shall find the source of this plague and put an end to it, or we will die trying."

Wezlok's expression was suddenly sad. His face then straightened, and he spoke to Dresnian, still using the common tongue. "Let the Palidurians go." He turned to Vayla. "You shall proceed with your quest. As for the Beitians, they are safer here than elsewhere." Beneath her questioning gaze, he added, "They will be fed and watered. Do not worry."

Vayla did not like the way the wizard spoke, as if he were caring for cattle. But she let it go. "I also require one of them to accompany me. Burnod, ex-general of Zurzak. He knows the realm better than any here."

Wezlok nodded. "So be it." He turned to Dresnian. "Free the one called Burnod."

"And our horses," Vayla continued with her demands.

"Of course." Wezlok bore a sly grin now. "Will there be anything else?"

Though the question was surely rhetorical, Vayla stood in thought while Dresnian opened the cage and her men exited. "Yes." She eyed the wizard. "I would like your assistance as well."

The village gasped.

"That goes without saying," Wezlok said. "How could you hope for success without *me*?"

Vayla gave a wry smile. But he was probably correct.

Vayla sat upon Star, and her contingent was ready to ride. The Lorians supplied Burnod a horse from their own stock, and he waited on its fancy green saddle with a permanent scowl.

Vayla was unsure which made the ex-general more uncomfortable: having to use an animal provided by the forest folk, accompanying her and her men, or marching into the Death Fog. In the end, she did not care. He had protested when the elves pulled him from the cell, claiming he wished to remain, but after speaking with an elderly couple—probably his parents—he gave in. Though Burnod refused to believe it, Wezlok's words were likely true. The Beitians would be safer in the cage than roaming Beit, and they had no immediate need of their leader. Besides that, time was short, and Vayla had been honest in her reason for including the ex-general. He knew the land better than any book she had read or scouting report she had received.

Wezlok emerged from the trees upon a fine gray horse. The wizard stopped next to Vayla and gave her a nod, his lip still twisted ever so slightly in the form of a grin.

"We ride northwest," Vayla announced, mostly to Burnod and Wezlok, as her men were aware of the plan. "From what we have learned, the source of the Death Fog lies there. And we must make haste. According to Burnod, the plague takes less than a week to complete its cycle. Our immediate task is to exit the forest unseen, so we will first head southeast."

"Perhaps exiting *seen* would be more expedient," said Wezlok.

Vayla shot the wizard a glare. Now that he was one of her company, all feelings of intimidation were fading. "Your words remind me why I don't travel with wizards. They never say what they mean."

"On the contrary," Wezlok shrugged, "I say exactly what I mean. Let them see us. It is easier, and will take less time."

"But—"

"There is a magic I have performed before," Wezlok said. "With your father and grandparents, in fact. And... several times since."

Vayla eyed the wizard. "Very well." She turned to the others. "We'll exit the forest with Wezlok's assistance and make for Benzon." Not wanting to waste time with questions, Vayla ignored Burnod's opening mouth and Macurak's rising brow. "Move out!"

Wezlok guided them through Maple Lore, taking a route unimpeded by dense undergrowth. They made it to the forest's border without hindrance, and it became obvious their march with the Lorian soldiers the previous day had followed a purposeful path, as Wezlok's course took only a couple of hours. Vayla dismounted and moved to the woodland's edge to scan the surrounding territory, and Macurak and Wezlok joined her. She spied nothing but open fields.

"The invading army has secured themselves within what remains of the human village," Wezlok said, gazing in Sylnor's direction. He then looked from north to south. "There are a couple of roaming patrols, and one heads this way. Not more than a score of humans."

Another memory came to Vayla, of her father speaking about Wezlok's extraordinary vision. Though all elves could see well over long distances, her father insisted Wezlok's sight traveled farther than even elves at times. According to Cavalor, Wezlok once imparted this vision to him to fire a crossbow over two miles with short range accuracy.

"Any sign of gorillas?" Vayla asked.

Wezlok frowned. "Gorillas?"

"Dark, hairless beasts," Vayla said. "They were with the invading army. Your archers fired upon them. I don't believe they were actually gorillas, but for lack of a better name..."

Wezlok scanned from left to right. "No gorillas."

"Good." Vayla turned to the holy soldiers, who had dismounted. "We'll overpower the patrol after luring them into the woods." She singled out five of her men. "Ready your bows and take out anyone attempting to retreat."

"Yes, my lady," the soldiers responded.

Vayla eyed Wezlok. "And what about you?"

"I shall make sure your men do not fail," the elf said.

Vayla held a level gaze. "Do what you must." She then mumbled to herself. "This is why I never enlist the aid of wizards."

Wezlok's tiny smirk returned.

Vayla and her contingent awaited the arrival of the patrol. Nineteen soldiers in Beitian uniforms arrived on armored mounts, trotting along the edge of the woodland and peering into the trees. Eight possessed bows, and their body language held them ready for the slightest twitch of a branch. Their formation was tight, with those closest to the forest holding shields toward the trees, and each bounce of the horses rattled their chain barding in perfect rhythm. The music grew louder as they neared.

Vayla lifted her gauntlet, and the holy warriors waited with grim faces. After balling her hand into a fist, one of her men went into action, standing just inside the tree line and stumbling among the brush like an incompetent lookout.

The Beitians spotted the movement and turned, breaking their rhythm as their archers slowed to spread out. The others dismounted and drew swords to approach on foot. At that moment, Vayla noticed one of the bowmen was dressed in black armor. He held a black bow with a dark arrow to the bowstring, and while the other soldiers' eyes moved hastily about the forest, his were eerily calm. Emotionless.

Vayla's men dodged behind trees as arrows arrived—all but the black arrow—and the missiles stuck into maples, bounced off boulders, or pierced the forest floor. The evil soldiers then entered the woodland, spreading out to search the brush, and the holy warriors advanced. Being superior in skill, the Palidurians dispatched over half of the enemy without receiving a wound. Vayla's archers dropped five bowmen as well. The Beitian swordsmen attempted to retreat, but none of them escaped Maple Lore.

A couple of arrows found their way into Vayla's men, and the return fire reduced the enemy to four. The Beitians scattered—all but the soldier in black—but did not make it far before well-placed arrows dropped them from their saddles. One missile pierced the dark archer's thigh, but he was seemingly impervious to the pain while he aimed his bow. He let loose the string, and the black dart streaked into the woods, striking a holy warrior in the shoulder. The dark bowman turned his mount and rode away, and Vayla was sure he held a satisfied grin.

"Drop him!" she commanded.

The archers fired, but their arrows were suddenly off the mark, landing around the retreating figure—it was as if they feared gaining his attention. The tall grass to either side of the horseman then bent toward him, like opposing winds colliding, and there was a *clap* as the dark archer abruptly ceased to move. It was as if he and his horse had been crushed between invisible walls. A second later, both rider and beast collapsed into a gruesome heap and the grass settled.

Vayla turned to see Wezlok's hands planted firmly together. It was a disgusting but effective spell, and she could not help feeling a trace of nausea for what the archer must have experienced at the very end.

"Vayla!" Macurak's voice stole her attention. "You're needed!"

Macurak stood over the holy warrior that received the black arrow. The wound should not have been fatal, but the soldier was deathly pale.

"Poison!" She rushed to him.

Macurak's face was grave. "His heart pounds heavily."

Vayla lifted the chain shirt, and through the soldier's tunic she detected the rapid heartbeat. Ripping the fabric to gain a better view, she gasped. A black web extended from the wound, creeping toward the middle of his chest. Each extension sprouted others, and it continued to grow.

"Cafior!" Vayla had never seen anything like it. She recited a prayer, unsure of what else to do.

The soldier convulsed as the web encircled his heart. Vayla grabbed a handful of soil and held it up while she spoke her words of healing, but before she could rub it onto the soldier's skin, he ceased to move. His heart stilled, and his final breath escaped as black ichor issued from his mouth.

Vayla stared in horror. "What evil is this?" Never had she heard or read of such a thing.

"That is exactly what it is," said Wezlok. "It is evil, true and deep. An ancient weapon long forgotten."

Vayla rose to face the wizard. "Then it's good I am here." She hoped she exhibited more confidence than she felt.

Wezlok lowered his brow. "It *is* uncanny, the similarities."

"Get one thing straight, elf," Vayla snapped. "I am not Merssa."

Wezlok responded with half a grin.

Vayla shook her head. She closed the fallen soldier's eyes and recited another prayer, hoping to usher him into the Halls of Cafior.

The other injuries received by her men were not serious. Vayla treated them with healing herbs, soil, and prayer, and while she worked, the rest of her contingent pulled the dead Beitians into the trees to conceal them. As for the wandering horses, Lorians collected the beasts and led them into the woodland. Vayla did not realize the elves were nearby, and she wondered why they did not help with the battle. Then again, why would Lorians help anyone outside of their clan?

Once Vayla finished caring for the wounded, she walked to the edge of the trees. The only evidence of the skirmish was the mangled mess that was the dark archer and his mount. But there was nothing to be done about that. Hopefully, it would go unnoticed a while longer.

"How does this magic of yours work?" she asked Wezlok.

The elf closed his eyes and took in a deep breath. He opened them as he exhaled, and he viewed the Beitian corpses. Next, he gazed at the company, and Vayla noticed a brief shimmering in his irises.

"It is done," he said.

Vayla looked around. Nothing had changed.

"All will appear normal to us," Wezlok said. "To be otherwise would risk your men hurting each other. It will not be so for the enemy, however."

"Which of us is the man in black?" she posed.

Wezlok smiled. "Does it matter?"

Vayla shook her head in annoyance. "Mount up!"

They rode from the cover of the trees, and Vayla's hand never strayed far from the hilt of her sword. She did not know how much trust to place in the elf wizard, but as they traveled across the fields nearer to Sylnor, the occasional soldiers they encountered never paid them a second glance. It continued this way, even as they rounded the hill and veered north. By the time dusk arrived, the village was beyond sight. The spell had worked.

CHAPTER 10

DEATH FOG

The morning sun shone across the open fields of Beit. Vayla squinted into the light, but it was too bright. There was likely nothing to view anyway. Onzac was surely beyond sight for even Wezlok to detect.

Though they had ridden most of the night, the Batorn horses remained strong. New Palidur spent an enormous amount of gold to acquire the beasts, knowing there to be no animal better suited for the quest. It surprised Vayla that Wezlok and Burnod had kept up on their ordinary steeds. Either the elf used magic to enhance the animals' abilities, or they *were* creatures of magic.

After a quick break to chew on dried meat, the company mounted and headed northwest. It was the direction Vayla had desired to go throughout the night, but Burnod insisted they travel due north to avoid roads and populated areas. There had been no encounters with Beitian squadrons or travelers thus far, so Vayla allowed the ex-general to continue leading the way.

The morning was still young when Burnod brought them to a halt. Bodies decorated the ground ahead. There were no prying eyes that Vayla could detect and Wezlok remained silent, so she focused on the corpses while she approached.

A dozen humans lay dead about a campsite. The remains of a fire sat cold in the middle and everything seemed to be in order—there did not appear to have been a conflict of any sort. Vayla dismounted.

The first corpse she inspected caused her to balk. It was a shell of a man. His pale skin sagged, as if he had lost weight quickly and recently, and dried blood marked its escape from his ears and nostrils.

The nose was chafed, as if there had been excessive rubbing, and the eyes were sunken and underlined by dark half-circles. Though the skin was wrinkled and the hair gray, Vayla sensed the man had not been elderly when he died.

"It's the plague," Burnod said.

The ex-general raised his elixir and took a drink. He then offered the canteen to Vayla. After receiving her glare in response, he held it out to the rest of the squadron.

Vayla looked at her men. Several gazed longingly at Burnod while the others searched the grass for answers. Macurak appeared unsure. Wezlok bore his usual calm demeanor, staring at Vayla as if curious to see her next action.

"Do *you* wish to drink from the evil general's potion?" Vayla asked the elf.

"Now just a moment!" Burnod's cheeks turned red.

"While you were guests in my forest," Wezlok used an interesting term to describe their imprisonment, "I examined that tonic. Would it interest you to learn that it is concocted from the waters of Balgorn River?"

"It would not," Vayla replied.

Though Wezlok referred to it as the Balgorn River, it was known by another name as well. Blood River was what most civilized folks called it. The water was forever tainted red upon Uustaag the Dark's defeat, after his body was cast into its current. Vayla's convictions to refuse the elixir had been strong, and now they were unbreakable. Then a thought occurred to her.

"Just a moment." She looked at the wizard. "How could you possibly know it was made from the Blood River? You would have to have been to Helmland to ascertain such a deduction."

"It is possible my travels have taken me thusly," Wezlok said. "It is also possible I had another undertake the journey for me. How I have come by that knowledge is inconsequential."

Vayla glared at the elf. What purpose did it serve to be so unrevealing? Do wizards learn early in life how to avoid giving direct answers? Is there a school of magic that trains them to do so? All it did was confuse people and cause unnecessary anger, sometimes leading to additional questions and wasting more time. She wanted to throw Wezlok into the Blood River!

"Excuse me," said Burnod. "Evil is a matter of—"

Vayla had no interest in hearing the rest of the statement, and she addressed her contingent.

"Now you know what is in that container. I will not allow its poison to rot *me* from the inside. Cafior protects me. I leave it to each of you to determine the strength of your faith; that He will do the same for you."

The soldiers glanced at one another. Some then gazed into the distance, some eyed the canteen, and the others returned their focus to the grass. None of them accepted the drink.

Vayla searched the remainder of the campsite, finding women and children among the dead. There appeared to be two or three families from the looks of the corpses, and within packs and trunks were clothing, food, water, and a small amount of gold. Several yards away was a dead horse.

Macurak shook his head. "They were fleeing the plague."

"But they didn't make it." Burnod pointed out the obvious while taking the gold from the trunks.

Vayla sneered at the ex-general.

"What?" Burnod shrugged. "*They* won't be needing it. It might come in handy."

"From what direction did they come?" Vayla asked her captain, knowing his tracking skills to rival that of any ranger.

Macurak answered while glaring at Burnod. "Northwest."

Vayla nodded. "Well then, there's nothing left to learn here. Mount up."

They rode another hour before a village came into view. It was one of several villages they had encountered thus far, and Vayla began to veer around it as they always did. But Wezlok brought her to a halt.

"That place is dead." The elf stared at the distant buildings. "I see only corpses. And I hear nothing."

"That would be Cramber," Burnod said. "We're another day or two from Benzon, depending on stops and rerouting. We're sure to encounter soldiers soon."

Vayla gazed at the village from atop Star. Such merciless killing. And for what purpose?

Macurak sneezed. His nose was pink, and he brushed the back of his hand across it to wipe away escaping mucus. He sniffed.

Vayla sniffed—most likely a reaction to Macurak's sniffle. But then she felt her nose running. She observed the others of her contingent. Their noses were pink, and they looked at one another with darting eyes as the sniffles invaded. It was the plague. Only Burnod and Wezlok appeared unaffected.

"What do we do?" Macurak's tone held a touch of panic.

"Why are *you* free of symptoms?" Vayla demanded of the wizard.

Wezlok shrugged. "I assure you I did not imbibe the Balgorn antidote. Perhaps it is that I am an elf."

"Other elves showed signs." Vayla grew increasingly suspicious. What was Wezlok not telling her? "You are *not* immune."

"I make no pretense of being immune," Wezlok said calmly. "Only that all of you are human and I am an elf. There is no reason to believe we will be affected equally. Whether by length of incubation or arrival of symptoms."

Vayla shook her head and turned to Macurak and her men. "If you wish to partake of the evil elixir, that is your decision. I will not judge you for this choice. That is between you and Cafior."

Half of the holy soldiers dismounted and hastened to Burnod, and the ex-general appeared to take pleasure in distributing his Blood River concoction.

Vayla was disappointed. Even with the scratchy sensation in the back of her throat and her eyes growing warm, she knew deep down that Cafior would provide. He would not allow her to perish at the hands of the evil plague. But she could not be the others' keeper.

They needed to choose their own paths.

She looked at Macurak, who appeared conflicted. He gazed at her for several seconds before nodding. He would not be drinking from the flask. Good. She could always count on her captain.

Once everyone was ready, they rode around the village and returned to their northwesterly trek. The late-morning sun chased away the final traces of the cool night air, and moisture saturated Vayla's underclothes. She coughed a few times, sniffling more often as they pressed farther, and she heard several others doing the same. She glanced at Wezlok. The wizard still showed no signs of having contracted the plague. Vayla thought of demanding answers, insisting the elf explain why he remained healthy without the elixir, but it would do no good.

The day saw the frequency of trees increase, and they halted among a copse of evergreens for lunch. Vayla had not planned to stop, but the burning in her eyes was annoying and she decided it was best to close them, even if only for a short time. She sat on a bed of pine needles and propped herself against a knotty tree to do just that.

"There is no evil in saving yourself from the plague."

She opened one eye to see the ex-general hovering. To her surprise, there was no humor or arrogance in his tone, and he bore not the slightest hint of a grin. Her other eye opened, and she glared without answering.

"I must admit," he added while brushing his mustache with his index finger, "it surprised me to learn you were a paladin. You're quite young for such a title. Perhaps your inexperience clouds your mind on this matter."

"My mind bears no clouds," she said flatly. "It is my faith in Cafior that stays my hand. It is He that I will put my trust into, not your evil drink, and not in you. If there were more faith in this realm of yours, it might never have come to its current predicament."

"As young as my daughter would have been," Burnod mused. "But a tongue as sharp as my wife's." He walked away.

Vayla was about to close her eyes again when she noticed Wezlok standing nearby.

"What if the plague kills you and your men before you reach Benzon?" the elf asked. "You do your cause no good."

"Did you come along just to see if I die?" She closed her eyes to stop the burning. "Why don't you make yourself useful and conjure me some cold water?"

There was silence. Vayla opened an eye to find the wizard still staring. Surprisingly, his expression showed no anger at her words. Instead, they revealed curiosity, if not pity. Why did he pity her? Because he still believed her to be Merssa?

"I don't know what relationship you shared with my grandmother," she said. "But I have never met the woman, I never shall, and I have no regret on that matter."

"Of course." His sarcasm brought back his smug smile. "All you need is Cafior and a few good swords."

"What do you want?" Vayla emphasized each word.

"It is not cold water that I offer," he held a small flask, "but healing sap from Maple Lore. I do not know if it can counter the plague, but it might be worth a try."

"I have herbs from New Palidur." She closed her eyes. She then opened them as curiosity got the better of her. "Is this sap why you still show no signs of contagion?"

Wezlok frowned. "I admit, I was awaiting the first sign before trying it. And though you do not see any evidence, I experienced the slightest tickling in my nose and throat, not very long ago. But it has subsided. So I offer it to you."

"Do I look that bad?" Vayla posed.

"Well," his brow lifted, "the dark circles under your eyes are not very becoming. It reminds me of a time when Merssa—"

"All right!" Vayla stood. She had not tried her own herbs, knowing she might need them after she rooted out the Shadow. But if there was a chance the Maple Lore sap could counter the plague, it was worth a try. "How much do you have?"

"Enough for four applications."

That was insufficient to treat her men, but she accepted the flask and opened it to smell the contents. It was like honey. She went to Macurak, who had also found a tree to rest against. The dark circles beneath his eyes made it appear he had not slept in days, and his face was ashen, except for his pink nose.

"I have some sap the mage gave me." Her voice led Macurak to open his eyes. They were bloodshot. "It might counter the plague."

"What about you?" he asked. "You should treat yourself first."

"She has *Cafior*," Burnod sneered, suddenly standing too close.

Vayla glared at the ex-general.

"It won't work," Burnod said. "Only the elixir from the Shadow has that power."

Vayla turned to Macurak. "I'm not sure if you're supposed to drink it or rub it somewhere."

She bit her lip and looked at Wezlok, who was sitting no less than twenty yards away. The elf had obviously heard her words with those pointed ears of his, and he made a motion to rub it under the eyes, across the forehead, and beneath the nose.

"I guess we rub it in."

"You first," Macurak said.

"Oh, isn't this precious!" Burnod received glares from both of them.

"Why don't you check the perimeter?" Vayla said through clenched teeth.

The ex-general left with a shrug.

Vayla turned to Macurak. "I have Cafior. But you—"

"No." Macurak was firm. "Take care of the men first. The ones who still suffer."

Vayla eyed the holy warriors that had accepted the elixir. Though they sniffled and wiped their noses, the plague had not progressed for them. Not like the other six soldiers—or her and Macurak, for that matter. She called four of the six ailing warriors to her and applied the sap as Wezlok demonstrated. They were grateful and offered many thanks.

"I'm not sure it will work," she said.

They appeared relieved all the same.

After a bit more thought, Vayla went to her pack and extracted several herbs. They were a special plant known as Vermallon Dusk. Rholmar had given them to Vayla as a gift for her journey. With a sigh, she pulled her mixing bowl and began tearing the leaves. She grabbed loose dirt and held it high, saying a prayer, and added it to the bowl. After sprinkling in a trace of water, she mashed the mixture until it was blended.

She called to her the other two soldiers that still suffered, and she smeared the concoction on their faces in the same manner as the sap, rubbing it into the skin as best she could. What did they have to lose? Once finished, she looked at Macurak. The captain's gaze told her he would accept no help until she treated herself. Reluctantly, she gave in, and she cared for Macurak afterward.

"My, that looks nice." Burnod grinned.

Vayla lacked the energy to deal with the ex-general, so she returned to her tree and closed her eyes. Her stomach roiled as her breakfast attempted to make its way back into the world, and she released a slow breath.

Vayla must have fallen asleep, and she awoke to Macurak shaking her. By the sun's position, it could not have been a long sleep, but time was lost. Blast the plague! At least her stomach had calmed and her eyes did not burn.

"I think the herbs are working." Macurak offered a hand and pulled her to her feet. "I feel much better, and the sniffles seem to have abated."

Vayla realized her own sniffles had ceased as well. In fact, all the soldiers appeared to have improved. She looked at Wezlok, who still watched her with curiosity.

"Mount up!" she called out.

It was just past noon, and they resumed their trek to the northwest. Villages cropped up more often, but the settlements were no different than Cramber and no one opposed their progress. The ill effects of the plague continued to lighten for Vayla, but when they set up camp among another grove of pines that evening, the soldiers she had not treated started vomiting and she grew concerned.

"I know what you're thinking," Burnod said. "But it's not the plague. The elixir takes some getting used to. When I first drank—"

"Macurak!" Vayla summoned her captain. "Gather those I did not tend to this morning." She rummaged through her pack to extract more herbs.

"I do not think that will be necessary." Wezlok stood just behind Vayla. "I have applied no healing agents, and the plague has failed to progress."

"But I thought you said…" Vayla was confused. Did he not use the sap?

Wezlok shook his head. "I wished to see how the plague worked. But now I am free of symptoms."

Vayla furrowed her brow. "Is that because *elves* are superior to *humans*?"

"While I agree with your assessment," Wezlok said, "you miss my meaning. I do not believe there *is* a plague anymore. At least, not in this region. Perhaps it would be better to save what is left of your herbs."

Vayla considered the elf's words. "Very well." She glanced at the ailing soldiers. "They probably deserve upset stomachs for imbibing the Blood River."

Burnod's head shook while Macurak's shoulders slumped.

Vayla ignored their reactions and addressed her captain. "Have the healthy men guard in shifts tonight."

Macurak nodded and carried out the order.

The night grew cool and they had a fire. Though the vomiting ceased and the holy warriors appeared to have overcome the negative effects of the potion, Vayla ordered them to turn in for some solid rest. Only the flames then made a sound, and she stared at Burnod from across the fire. The man seemed occupied.

"What can we expect from Benzon?" Vayla asked.

The ex-general gazed at her a moment, issuing a sigh before giving his response. "Outside Zurzak, it's the most militant city in Beit. It was reinforced to guard the border against Helmland. Even after Uustaag's defeat, it remained so."

Vayla found it odd to hear someone not from New Palidur speak the Ancient Enemy's name so freely, without the slightest hint of hesitation or fear. She did not know if she should be impressed or disgusted.

Macurak frowned. "Why would you guard against Helmland? Were they not Beit's only ally?"

"That is the ignorance of the southern realms." Burnod appeared to have tasted something foul. "To use words you might understand, Helmland was like an older brother. A *cruel* older brother. Beit seldom had a choice in its cooperation with Uustaag's plans."

"Your king seemed willing enough." Macurak gave a sarcastic chuckle. "Within the *southern realms*, only Benasti Forest takes krukari as kings."

Vayla found Macurak's point to be well placed. She enjoyed hearing someone other than herself show some intelligence.

"It was Helmland that began the line of krukari kings!" Burnod was hot now. "And what help did we ever receive from the south to resist?"

"It's not the job of other realms to establish your monarchy." Macurak's passion showed he was feeling better. "You could have staged a revolution. Instead, you mounted invasions upon the *southern realms*."

The conversation was getting interesting.

"That was before my time!" Burnod insisted.

"And today you vigorously guard your borders against us," Macurak added, "instead of trying to improve your situation."

"We do what we must to survive!"

"It's no wonder the Shadow was able to usurp your throne." Macurak was relentless. "And now your soldiers willingly follow that creature, allowing their own people to die." He turned to the fire. "Beitians have no spine."

Vayla held a smile of satisfaction. She could not have put it better. Well, she probably could have. Burnod fell silent.

"The Beitian in our company has forfeited his life to fight this Shadow's reign." Wezlok gained their attention. "Though I believe all humans to be weak in their own ways, this particular human has given up everything to perform the very actions you suggest."

"A bit too late," Macurak said flatly.

Burnod glared at the captain. "Why is it you brought me along?"

"It was not my decision." Macurak glanced at Vayla.

No one spoke for several moments. The ire in Macurak's eyes paled only slightly compared to that of Burnod's.

"I assume the city is walled." Vayla returned to the original conversation.

"What?" Burnod appeared confused.

"Benzon!" Vayla snapped her fingers twice. "Please, keep pace."

Burnod bore an incredulous look, his mouth agape.

"So we'll need to find access," Vayla continued. "I'll not play the part of a prisoner or Beitian soldier, so we need another way."

"Well..." Burnod gathered himself. "The major watchtowers are on the northwestern side of the city, to spy the approach of Helmland forces along the road. The southern edge isn't as heavily guarded, but they won't allow the likes of you to enter."

"What about you?" Vayla posed. "Will they allow *you* to enter? Are they aware of your treason?"

Burnod scowled. "I doubt it. They may have heard rumors, but there's been no time to verify them just yet. The armies are gathering at Zurzak, and things are a bit chaotic. Perhaps I can get us in."

"Not us," Vayla said. "You. You will gain access and get us in another way."

"No." Burnod shook his head. "It would be better for me to enter with your contingent. It will be much easier to sneak *you* in, and not twenty people."

"No." Vayla grew annoyed. "We lack the proper garb to disguise my men as Beitian soldiers."

"That doesn't matter." Burnod shifted his position. "Around these parts, uniforms are more of an option. Only high-ranking officials wear them."

"But *you're* out of uniform," Vayla pointed out.

"I can explain that," Burnod said. "I'm easily recognized."

Vayla raised a brow. "What if you're a wanted man?"

"I doubt that will be the case." Burnod's frustration crept back into his voice. "But if that's a concern of yours, perhaps the wizard should disguise us again."

"No." Vayla held a level stare. "Wezlok remains with me and Macurak. This Shadow is obviously a creature of magic, so I distrust the use of magic while our presence is unknown."

Wezlok appeared impressed. Vayla disregarded the notion. She was not there for his approval.

"Macurak should be with me," Burnod said. "Someone needs to lead your men."

"Were you not a general?" Vayla put her hands out in mock question. "*You* can lead them."

"Will they obey my orders?" Burnod returned her sarcasm. "The hated enemy?"

"They'll do what I say," Vayla said. "They'll follow you."

"I'm amazed you'll allow *me* to lead," Burnod muttered.

"It's settled then." Vayla nodded. "When we arrive, you and the holy soldiers will ride into Benzon and gain access for me, Macurak, and Wezlok."

"No." Burnod shook his head. "We will not ride. If things go awry and we need a hasty departure, we'll not want the horses confined within the city."

Vayla gave him a sidelong stare. She did not trust the man.

"Besides that," Burnod said, "one look at your animals will see them seized by officials." He observed the horses. "They are more beautiful than any steed in the realm." Turning to Vayla, he added, "It's a practice that has become all too common, leading men such as myself to leave our horses elsewhere and enter on foot."

Macurak snorted a laugh, causing the ex-general to frown.

Vayla conceded with a nod. "The plan is set. Now tell me everything you know about the Shadow."

CHAPTER 11

BENZON

Vayla's contingent rode through the following day, stopping briefly for lunch. From the looks of their supplies, they had a week's rations left—plenty for the remainder of the journey, if all went well. Several hours before dusk, Vayla spied a large force moving in their direction—a Beitian army.

"South!" she commanded. "Quickly!"

They pushed the horses hard for half a mile and came to a halt. The army was beyond sight.

"There's no way they didn't see us." Burnod looked at Vayla. "But they'll believe us to be bandits. Hardly worth their efforts."

"Then we'll ride west and skirt around them," Vayla said.

Burnod shook his head. "No good. We'll be discovered."

Vayla scowled at the ex-general. "You just said we aren't worth their efforts."

"That doesn't mean their commander won't be interested in any loot we might have pillaged." Burnod's tone insisted that should have been common knowledge. "He'll have scouts moving east and west to see if we try to ride past. He'll not be concerned if we get away, but he'll not turn down the possibility of adding a few coins to his purse."

Vayla thought of how Burnod took the gold from the dead campers. "This realm disgusts me."

"We should continue south at least another mile," Burnod said. "After that, they'll believe we have ridden off and call off the scouts."

"Won't they wonder how we have survived the plague?" Macurak asked.

Burnod shook his head. "Not at all. We could have come across the elixir and discovered its benefits." After these words, he took a drink from his flask.

Vayla sighed. Though it would take longer to reach Benzon, it needed to be done. "Very well."

They proceeded south at a steady pace. Half an hour passed. Then an hour. Vayla eyed Burnod, and he shook his head. They continued another hour and Vayla brought them to a stop.

"Surely we can change paths now," she said in frustration, gazing at the lowering sun in the west.

Burnod glanced at the sky before looking north. There was no sign of the army. He grinned. "I believe this will suffice." He gave a nod. "We should reach Benzon well after dusk."

"Wait." Vayla furrowed her brow. "You led us this far on purpose? Just to arrange our time of arrival?"

"Well," Burnod shrugged, "you're a hard lass to reason with. It was an opportunity, and I took it. Arriving during the light of day would have been disastrous. The plan needs the cover of night to work."

"I am no lass!" Vayla glared at him. "I am Vayla. Paladin of Cafior. Knight of New Palidur. You will not perform such an action a second time."

"My apologies." He made a mocking bow. "We shall return north immediately."

Wezlok moved very near to Vayla and spoke so no one else could hear. "At least he does not see you as someone you are not, I suppose."

The comment confused Vayla at first. But then she grasped the elf's meaning. Did Wezlok treat her as if she were Merssa on purpose? Was it a game? But the mage had a point. Outside of Macurak, it was a rare find to meet one that did not compare her to the dead paladin. Burnod had probably never heard of Merssa. Vayla sighed. None of that mattered. They needed to get to Benzon.

They veered west for a mile before heading north, and when dusk arrived, they continued beneath the young moon. Vayla spied the many fires of the Beitian force, the army having settled within a large field, and it seemed she held her breath until the encampment faded into the south. A few miles later, with the full darkness of night upon them, the lights of Benzon appeared in the distance. Vayla picked up the pace.

The walls of the city rose greater than thirty feet, concealing most of its buildings. The lights Vayla detected belonged to the turrets and windows of many towers.

"This is where we part," said Burnod.

Vayla nodded, noting the concerned expressions her men held, the soldiers now lacking their Palidurian markings. She asked a lot from them, but Cafior would see them through if their faith proved strong enough. And if any of them did not survive, He would accept them into His Halls.

Vayla led Macurak and Wezlok to the eastern edge of Benzon, staying beyond sight of any krukari that might be manning the towers and well outside the detection of humans. Wezlok took the lead before long, and as they neared a small woodland Burnod had described, they ushered the horses into hiding. Though the trees were dense, a clearing existed within, just as Burnod promised.

After securing the animals, Vayla made her way back through the woods until Benzon came into view. Again, Burnod had spoken the truth, as the spacing between the towers along the eastern wall left a blind spot for the city watch. Not even a krukari would see her if she stepped from the trees and walked straight up to the wall.

Macurak and Wezlok arrived, and they stood on either side of Vayla. To her right, Macurak fidgeted.

"What is it?" Vayla looked to make sure her captain was okay.

"I still wonder if this is the best course of action," he said. "We could have had our men find out if we *need* to enter Benzon and then get out. The source of the plague might not even be here."

Macurak made this argument the previous night, and Vayla understood his hesitation. It was not fear of the city for her captain, but fear of failure.

"This is where the Shadow resides," Vayla said. "Whether or not the source of the plague is here, the Shadow is behind it." She gave a nod. "We go after the snake's head."

"It is time." Wezlok grabbed her attention.

Vayla was grateful for the lack of moonlight while they followed the wizard across the dark field. As they neared Benzon, the small hairs on her arms stood and a chill ran along her spine—a powerful evil was near. An aura of ice then surrounded her as she reached the wall, and the air was suddenly befouled, like discarded bandages that had covered festering wounds. Her eyes darted about, as if every shadow was a possible enemy ready to strike, but she saw nothing to be afraid of. She noticed Wezlok's face had paled, seeming to glow, and his expression was not confident for the first time since she met him.

"This is not good," the mage said quietly, turning to Vayla. "It is a Death Lord."

Macurak trembled, appearing anxious to return to the trees. Vayla's mind raced, and she fought the chill with a silent prayer before addressing the elf.

"Death Lord? The creations of Trannum? Destroyed for more than twenty years?"

Wezlok shook his head while searching the sky. "Not all were destroyed. Radaam and Anduiff disappeared."

"I was told that without Trannum, they should have faded away," Vayla said. "The Council of Wizards assured us this was true."

"Information attained by fools!" Wezlok revealed annoyance. "You cannot simply *wish* them out of existence."

"How do we get our men?" Macurak asked.

His words were spoken louder than Vayla was comfortable with, and she looked at her captain's ashen face. It was not his fault—the fear was unnatural. But he needed to control it.

Vayla forced her thoughts to the Death Lord. Or was it Death Lords? They were the greatest creations of Trannum. Vayla's father had fought in the Necromancer War, battling legions of zombies, ghouls, wraiths, and creatures called dunarchins. Cavalor had seen two Death Lords, Gulthar and Jurak, during the war, and he described them as terror incarnated. The very presence of the undead kings was said to animate the dead. Vayla was prepared to deal with the Shadow. But the Shadow *and* Death Lords?

"This complicates things," she muttered.

"Yes." Macurak nodded vigorously. "We should extract our men immediately. For all we know, Burnod is part of a complex trap to draw us into the city."

"No!" Vayla's focus had been on combating the Shadow, and now Macurak's words struck her. A trap? Did matters just get worse? She bit her lip.

"That is how you know she is thinking," Wezlok said to Macurak. "Her grandmother used to bite her lip."

Vayla's teeth retreated. Blast that wizard! She gazed along the wall and across the surrounding territory. No soldiers were mobilizing against them. It could not be a trap. Burnod's feelings for Sylnor had been genuine, and Cafior would not allow her to walk so easily into an ambush. Still, the situation was changed.

"I cannot fight the Shadow *and* the Death Lord," she said, hoping only one of the undead kings was present.

"Other than Merssa," Wezlok lifted his brow, "no one ever faced a Death Lord alone. Lest you credit the tales about Vecnor."

"Never met him," Vayla muttered.

Vecnor was another name mentioned more times than she cared to hear. All these figures from the past with unbelievable stories attached to them... Vayla did not believe them. At least, not most of them. She had endured Selanna and Eraim several times while growing up at Castle Lambrak; it appeared they were friends of her father. The elves were reputed to be powerful as well as resourceful, but Vayla knew them as tricksters that loved to laugh at other people's misfortunes. As Vayla got older, she avoided the two, for their eyes became just like all the others—pitiful orbs gazing upon their long-lost companion.

"We have *you*." Vayla looked at Wezlok. "And you survived. Surely you know how to handle a Death Lord."

"Death Lords do not get *handled*," Wezlok said. "As for my part, I was with your father when he faced Gulthar. I did what I could to aid those fighting, but I did not directly combat the undead king."

Vayla stared at the elf. "Then you shall have to assist Macurak and the others while I take care of the Shadow."

"This is not a good plan." Macurak seemed unable to shake the fear. "I say we get our men out as soon as the door opens."

As Macurak finished his statement, Vayla's hand went to her sword. Seams had appeared on the wall, outlining the secret entrance Burnod had divulged—a portal known only to a few within the city, according to the ex-general. Burnod claimed he needed to activate it from the inside, and it was how Vayla was to gain access. As the hidden panel opened, a shadowy figure stood before Vayla and she held her breath.

"Come in! Quickly!"

It was Burnod's voice.

Burnod possessed no light, but Vayla could see he was alone. Where were her men? Was it a trap? With her hand on her hilt, she entered the city, and Macurak and Wezlok followed.

Vayla scanned the immediate area. They were at the dead end of an alley, and to either side, buildings blocked the view of the surrounding towers.

"I have ill news," Burnod said in a hushed voice. "The Death Lord has returned."

"*Returned?*" Macurak exhibited outrage. "He was here before? And you didn't tell us?"

"He has not been here for twenty years!" Burnod glowered. "I thought they were all destroyed."

"Where are my men?" demanded Vayla.

The ex-general calmed himself. "Not far. They're safe, and they await our arrival."

"If this is a trap," Macurak grabbed Burnod's arm, "I will cut you down."

Burnod yanked his arm free. "Follow me!" He scowled as he moved along the alley.

Vayla looked at Macurak. Though his suspicions were warranted, there was no turning back now. They crossed that line at the Shield River. She followed Burnod.

The alleyway stretched twenty yards and turned right. Around the bend, it split right and left. Burnod headed left, and at the next intersection he veered right. They were in a maze, but the ex-general proceeded without hesitation along the dank cobbled paths. All doors remained closed and the windows were dark—it seemed there was no one to notice their presence.

The fear in Vayla's stomach increased, as did the chill, and everyone's breath grew thick when they exited the alley onto a wide street. A few illuminated windows suggested life, but silence ruled the evening and there was still no one to be seen. Burnod headed right, following the edge of the street and passing several doors. Shingles revealed many of the buildings to be shops, but everything was closed for the night. The castle drew nearer with every step, rising above the structures ahead and to the left, and after the next turn the stronghold came into view. The road stretched a hundred yards before spanning a moat and ending at the castle. A dozen openings showing torchlight dotted the first level, but the upper levels were dark.

The chill rose from Vayla's stomach and into her chest.

They walked a bit farther, and Burnod picked up the pace as he turned down another alley. Vayla wondered if the ex-general felt the chilling fear, or if he was accustomed to such things. But it was not the time to ask. After traversing a couple more turns, they entered an open area teeming with soldiers. Vayla pulled her blade halfway while Macurak drew his entirely, but she relaxed her grip when she recognized the voices of her holy warriors.

"Thank Cafior!" one soldier said.

"Did Burnod tell you a Death Lord is here?" another warrior

asked urgently.

"Be quiet!" Burnod hissed.

"I know," Vayla said to calm her men before turning to Burnod. "What is going on here? Why does the city seem abandoned?"

"When I was younger," Burnod replied, "the Death Lord, Jurak, came twice that I'm aware of. And while he was a guest of King Vronik, Benzon appeared much as it does this night, though there were more soldiers present. This time, according to the gate captain, they sent the soldiers to the south and east. There's a skeleton crew manning the towers."

Vayla gasped. "They're preparing to invade!"

Burnod inspected the rooftops, avoiding Vayla's gaze. His eyes then met hers and he sighed. "I had no idea this was coming, I swear!" He grimaced. "I removed myself from duty two months ago."

"The Shadow divulged its plans to slay your people," Macurak said, "but it did not tell you of its intentions to mount an attack upon the other realms? You take us for fools!"

Vayla bit her lip. "Why would the Shadow kill its inhabitants and *then* wage war?"

"It is obvious." Wezlok spoke from the shadows behind Vayla. "The Death Lord makes it so."

"Please! Elf!" Vayla's shout caused all but Wezlok to cringe and scan the alley. "Pretend we are not wizards and speak more words!"

"The very aura of the Death Lord animates the dead," Wezlok said. "Did you not learn that?"

Vayla knew that fact well. But having never faced a Death Lord, and believing they did not exist anymore, she failed to make the connection until now. "It's going to raise those killed by the plague," she murmured.

Wezlok gave a nod. "Correct. And by doing so, it will increase the size of its army one-hundred fold.

The alley fell silent.

"Well." Vayla pulled her blade. "At least the guard over the castle will be light. We'll be able to confront the Shadow and Death Lord without too much distraction." She ignored the wide-eyed faces around her. "My focus will be on the Death Lord. I must destroy it before its plan bears fruit."

"Those are easy words to say." Burnod shook his head. "But to follow through on them is another matter. Half your men will flee when faced with the Death Lord."

Vayla looked at her warriors. There was no mistaking their fear.

"Cafior is with us, make no mistake." She held her chin high. "How else do you explain the plague failing in its attempts to stop us? Do you think it a coincidence that we are here at this very moment? Let Cafior's Will enter your hearts and fuel your spirits. Let evil lie at our feet and know that it is no match for His Might!" While she spoke, the eyes of her men narrowed and several nods ensued. She turned back to Burnod. "Cafior is with us. Now let's go."

They moved from the alley and approached the castle. Strangely, the portcullis was raised and the large entry doors were open, as if they welcomed Vayla's arrival. She said a prayer to Cafior for strength.

They passed beneath the iron bars and through the doors. Torches burned in sconces, illuminating corridors to the left and right as well as a carpeted hallway straight ahead, and there were no guards. The cold now stung Vayla's nose and fingers, and she gripped her weapon tighter and proceeded along the carpeted passage.

A set of double doors at the end of the hall opened into the throne room. A dozen torches left the corners of the chamber in shadow, and as Vayla entered, those shadows came to life with points of blue light. She froze, holding her sword ready, and the lights advanced, revealing themselves to be the eyes of horrific undead. They looked like zombies, but Vayla sensed them to be something much worse. While zombies exhibited rotting flesh, these creatures appeared to have had their lives sucked from their bodies, leaving yellowish skin wrapped tightly about their bones, and their eyes burned with hatred and skill.

"Dunarchins!" said Wezlok. "Decapitation is the swiftest death!"

"Circle Wezlok behind me!" Vayla ordered. "Burnod on my left. Macurak to my right. Do not let them touch the wizard!"

The fear in Vayla's chest crept into her throat, but a quick prayer reduced it to a mere annoyance and she charged. She reached the closest dunarchin and allowed it to attack first, easily fending off the blade before bringing her sword around in an arc. She sliced through the neck of the undead warrior, and the dunarchin fell as its head rolled several feet away.

The next dunarchin protected its neck, and Vayla struck its chest, stomach, and leg, the latter wound hampering its movement. But the fiend showed no pain as it attacked. Though skilled, the dunarchin paled compared to Vayla, and she severed its sword arm before cleaving its head.

Macurak and Burnod had taken down a dunarchin each, and three others were motionless outside the soldiers' circle. Two holy warriors had fallen as well. To the rear, Vayla's men fought human guards attempting to flank them, and five Beitians lay dead. Wezlok stood in the middle of the protective circle, releasing small globes of flame that reduced four dunarchins to ashes.

After defeating another undead warrior, Vayla spied a pair of dunarchins converging on Macurak. The captain took a defensive stance to keep from being flanked, and Vayla cleaved one from behind, removing its head. Macurak then went on the offensive, issuing a lethal blow to the other.

The room fell silent, and Vayla assessed her squadron. Macurak had taken a minor wound to his left arm, four holy soldiers were motionless on the floor, and five others showed injuries, three of which would need tending to.

"Do not touch the bodies!" Wezlok said as a couple of the men checked on their fallen companions.

The warriors pulled back just as the dead soldiers and Beitians began to stir, and though surprised, the holy warriors were well trained and reacted accordingly. The zombies presented little resistance, but the looks on the soldiers' faces, having to destroy the corpses of friends, were disturbing.

"Do not forget the effects of the Death Lord upon the dead," Wezlok said.

Vayla withdrew herbs and patched all wounds as quickly as possible. It was not her best work, but they needed to keep moving. She then closed her eyes and concentrated. A vile, slimy feeling seeped from the ceiling.

She turned to Burnod. "Where are the stairs?"

"This way." The ex-general headed for the far end of the chamber.

They came to three doors spaced evenly apart, and Burnod passed through the middle door. Beyond, a wide staircase covered by a blue carpet rose to the second floor, and a cold white mist drifted down the steps. Burnod hesitated, his confidence suddenly replaced by indecision. Vayla began to climb.

Upon reaching the top, a corridor stretched left and right. Macurak and Wezlok were close behind while Burnod lagged, and the holy soldiers followed the ex-general with darting eyes. Vayla concentrated again, and the hairs on the back of her neck rose. Her scalp tingled, and a sweeping feeling of woe emanated from the passage to the right. The Death Lord or Shadow was there, if not both.

Vayla moved along the hall, following the evil aura. She passed several doors until reaching a set of fancy double doors at the corridor's termination, and when she reached for the latch on the left, she noticed her hand was shaking. Swallowing the fear, she pushed open the door.

Beyond was a large room. The left side possessed a canopied bed, hearth, wardrobe, three chests, and a wash basin. To the right were living quarters, including a second fireplace, plush chairs, a table holding a crystal decanter and goblets, and a set of doors, currently open and revealing a balcony outside. A body rested upon the bed, and a tall figure stood amid the chairs, armored in black plates and masked by a dark helm. In the evil warrior's left hand was a black sword, and the right held an axe of the same color. Blue eyes similar to a dunarchin's burned beneath its helmet, and Vayla's knees shook as those lights pierced deep into her soul.

"It is Anduiff!" Wezlok said. "Ancient Lord of Benasti."

Vayla pointed her blade at Anduiff. "Where's the Shadow?"

The Death Lord tilted its head. "I thought you were dead." Its voice was strangely hollow.

Vayla was not sure why, but her legs froze. Was it because the creature had spoken? Or had it cast a spell on her? Then its words registered, and anger broke her limbs free.

"Confusing me for Merssa will be your last mistake!" She readied her sword.

Anduiff waved a hand at the bed, and Vayla took a sideways stance as the body swung its hairy feet over the edge and slowly rose. The figure resembled a krukari. It was attired in torn and bloody remnants of royal garb, and blue points of light shone from its empty eye sockets. Sharp teeth were visible through missing lips and the skin of its fingers were peeled back, forming bony claws.

"King Vronik?" Burnod's tone held both shock and disbelief.

Vronik hissed as he leaped into the air and glided toward Vayla's company with surprising speed. While two holy soldiers fled from its path, one stood firm and struck the horrific creature with his blade. The weapon sliced through Vronik's ribs, and the king dug its claws into the soldier and bit into his neck. A brief scream was all that escaped before the holy warrior's head fell to the floor.

Burnod moved to confront Vronik, and Vayla faced Anduiff. The Death Lord was upon her, swinging his axe, and she sidestepped the attack. She countered as the weapon struck the flagstones, but Anduiff's sword knocked her blade aside.

"Dunarchins!" cried a holy soldier.

They were surrounded again.

Vayla focused on the Death Lord, and she could hear the battle behind her. The creature that Vronik had become continued to hiss and snarl while Burnod yelled obscenities, and explosions sounded as Wezlok surely released magic against the dunarchins. Macurak then arrived at Vayla's side.

"Zhokard Standard!" Vayla said, having shared with her captain the battle styles taught to her by her father's ageless personal guards.

Macurak moved to Anduiff's left, forcing the Death Lord to turn. Vayla then slashed her sword several times, drawing Anduiff's attention, while Macurak darted to the rear of the enemy and issued a thrust. The captain's blade pierced the black plate, but Anduiff spun, yanking the weapon from Macurak's grasp and across the chamber. The Death Lord's axe followed, and Macurak dropped to the floor, narrowly evading the sharpened edge.

Vayla came in low and thrust her weapon upward. Her sword managed only a minor wound as the dark armor turned her blade, but no blood issued forth. With barely a glance at Vayla, Anduiff kicked her in the chest and knocked her prone. A chilling sensation crept across her breastplate, invading her body, and she suddenly felt as if she were naked in a winter storm.

Anduiff pressed Macurak, who stood with only a knife in his hand. Vayla called upon Cafior's Strength while she regained her feet, and she cried out as she charged. But Anduiff paid her no heed. The dark king swung both weapons, driving the captain against the fireplace. Macurak thrust his knife, failing to penetrate the Death Lord's armor, and Anduiff's sword struck. Macurak collapsed.

"No!" Vayla shrieked in both anger and distress.

She launched a flurry of attacks, but Anduiff fended off her strikes. He countered, and Vayla parried the blade and dodged the axe. Their dance continued around the furniture until one of the chairs exploded, showering the Death Lord with debris, and Vayla used the momentary distraction to lunge. Her attack cut deep into the black plates, and before Anduiff reacted, she yanked her weapon free and set her feet.

Anduiff held Vayla with his gaze. She had penetrated the armor near the neck, where a bluish steam now issued. Then came a horrible sound: a screeching roar from the balcony that ended in a hollow hiss.

The noise captured Anduiff's attention, but his eyes returned to Vayla and he stepped toward her. The screech sounded again, and again Anduiff froze.

"We will finish this once my army is complete," Anduiff said in his hollow voice, and he fled through the open doors.

Vayla gave chase, but the Death Lord was too fast. It was as if the heavy armor bore him no hindrance. Upon reaching the doors, she halted, paralyzed by another visage of terror. Anduiff sat astride a skeletal beast perched on the balcony, and the back half of its elongated body extended beyond the edge while its hind legs gripped the railing. The monster possessed the same glowing eyes as the Death Lord, and its skull rose atop its long neck. It lunged, issuing a sickly yellow cloud filled with specks of black ash, but before the fog washed over Vayla, she was yanked backward and the doors slammed shut.

Vayla hit the stone floor hard and looked to see who had seized her. Ten feet away, Wezlok stood with his fists to one side, as if he had just pulled on a rope. She returned her attention to the balcony. The screech sounded again, but it faded into the distance and the chilling fear diminished.

"No!" Vayla climbed to her feet.

The Death Lord was surely wounded, and now he was getting away. She raced to the doors, but they were held fast. She spun and scanned the room.

The chamber was quiet. The battle was over. More than a score of dunarchins were splayed across the floor, and Vronik's corpse did not move. Besides Wezlok, Burnod and six holy soldiers stood, and from the wounds upon the dead warriors, Vayla knew they had become zombies, and that her contingent had been forced to kill their friends—again.

Her eyes snapped to Macurak. The captain sat on a chair with a blood-soaked cloth held against his side.

"The Shadow is not here," Wezlok said. "Now that Anduiff has departed, I am sure you know this to be so."

Vayla concentrated, searching beyond the freezing pain in her chest from Anduiff's kick. The evil was indeed gone. Without a word, she ran to Macurak.

"How are you?" She knelt next to the chair.

"I can walk," Macurak said through clenched teeth.

Vayla pulled the cloth from Macurak's side to expose a nasty gash. "You'll not move!"

Macurak coughed, and more blood seeped from the wound.

Vayla fished through her pack, withdrawing all of her herbs, as well as a small pouch of blessed Palidurian soil and a vial of holy water. She mixed the ingredients together, muttering while she worked. "*I can walk...* Such a fool!" After creating a good paste, her eyes moved to the hearth. It was dark. Then, as if she had willed it, the logs took to flame. Looking over her shoulder, she saw Wezlok with a single finger extended toward the fireplace.

"This will hurt," Vayla said to Macurak.

"Oh?" He laughed briefly before coughing. "I don't think I can feel more pain than I do now."

Vayla brought a flaming log to the gash and cauterized the wound. Macurak screamed. After tossing the log into the fire, she applied the healing paste. She used a bit more than half of the mixture, and Macurak passed out as she finished.

"There are a few others in need," Wezlok said.

Vayla looked back. Burnod stood over Vronik, still staring in disbelief. The ex-general possessed several wounds, most of them appearing as long scratches and bite marks. The soldiers bore injuries of their own, but none of them appeared to be life threatening.

"What was that creature on the bed?" Vayla whispered.

"Trannum took pleasure in his creations," Wezlok said. "Perhaps it was one of those, unseen during the war twenty years ago."

Vayla nodded and sighed. She needed to tend to the others. After that, she was at a loss as to what came next. She set out to end a plague, and regardless of Wezlok's suspicions that it had run its course, she was not so sure. And now, Anduiff was raising an army of undead. She could not face both problems by herself. The only thing she could think to do was report to Grand Paladin Montac. But how would she get to New Palidur? Armies were gathered at the bridges and zombies would be roaming the kingdom. Cafior was testing her. She looked at Wezlok.

"We cannot stay here," he said. "Anduiff may yet return, and he will not be alone. What is left of your men are in no shape to fight, and I cannot take on an entire army." His eyes narrowed. "But I believe I know of a way out."

CHAPTER 12

LOTHEN FOREST

Selanna and Dandi led the way with Eraim and Lilli beside them. Brem and Kiryanna were next, sitting atop horses Eraim purchased in Ellaville, and then came Romik with Desser and Daymyn to his sides. Baylun brought up the rear.

Selanna again thought it odd that the young krukari sat on a mule while the other boys rode fine steeds, but she suspected she knew why. The lads often teased Baylun when they were younger, and Selanna assumed that pastime had survived the years. Even though Baylun's father, Gruelenor, resembled a hobgoblin more so than a human, Selanna hoped Lorin's fair looks might temper Gruelenor's rough appearance in their offspring. Unfortunately for Baylun, it was not so, and he had it worse than his father. At times, Selanna preferred not to look at him.

"A secret path through the Stone Eagles..." Eraim said, stirring Selanna from her thoughts.

They followed the road west from Ellaville, and Eraim gazed at the mountains growing larger with each passing minute.

"I do *love* secret paths," she continued. "Of course, I am not too keen on the destination in which it leads. And I will need to squeeze it onto my map. I simply detest mountain travel. Why could it not be a secret forest trail?"

Selanna smiled. Eraim's nervous babble was always calming.

The Stony River was not yet in view when Selanna turned north. There existed no path, but she moved at a brisk pace, knowing the way, and they used every last trace of sunlight before setting up camp. After a hasty meal, Eraim disappeared into the shadows to keep watch for unwanted visitors while the rest of the company sat around a fire.

Conversation was light. Brem spoke of life in Neja over the past decade, centering on the worship of Frayorna and of his teachings to people of mixed-race families. Romik added a few stories about Ironside Keep, mentioning more than once that he was Lord of the Keep—for Kiryanna's benefit, no doubt. Not to be outdone, Daymyn brought up the encounter with the Blackfoot goblins, boasting of how he killed half of the enemy himself. Desser rolled his eyes and Baylun remained silent.

"But I let my cousins handle the other half." Daymyn shot Kiryanna a wink. "I only wish Selanna hadn't disposed of my trophies." He tossed another branch onto the fire with a sour face.

Selanna had, indeed, made sure they burned the foot and scalp before leaving on their current journey—besides being disgusting, the goblin parts bore a pungent odor.

Daymyn's statement brought back Selanna's concern for the thought-to-be-extinct race, but she pushed it away, preferring to enjoy the boys' attempts to impress Kiryanna. Selanna wondered if they noticed the marteese's seeming lack of interest in things they said. Kiryanna sat next to Brem with her focus pinned to the growing darkness—that is, unless Brem spoke. During those times, the marteese listened, but always with one eye fixed on their surroundings. Selanna also wondered if Brem was aware his bodyguard had feelings for him.

"I wish to hear what Selanna knows of the Shadow." Desser stared at Selanna, having brought silence to the camp.

Selanna sighed. So much for happier thoughts. But she supposed they needed to know more about what they faced, little as that information was.

She began with Nilborg's death, but she did not mention that she had seen it in a dream. She pointed out that Seac's death had been accomplished in a similar manner, and that she believed the Shadow to be responsible for both. Her report concluded with the Shadow passing into Beit and the plague that followed, but she omitted her encounter with Tux.

"And the plague kills all living things lacking the antidote we obtained from the Beitian soldiers," she said.

Everyone remained quiet, their faces pale. Having lost interest in conversing, they settled in for some rest.

The night was peaceful, and with the dawn they continued their trek. The eastern reaches of the Stone Eagle Mountains were then due north, and Selanna aimed straight for them. By nighttime, they were camping within the mountains.

The next day revealed the Path of the Guardians at last, though it was overgrown and hard to discern at times. It weaved through the rough terrain for several hours before depositing them onto a ridge overlooking a long valley. Below were many firs, oaks, and maples, almost appearing as bushes from the company's vantage point, and a wide river cut through them, rushing off to the east and becoming the Shield River. The view was in contrast to the mountains they had seen thus far, which exhibited scant vegetation at best.

The ridge bore them westward until the light failed, and they set up camp within a small clearing existing just for that purpose. Selanna did not know who had made the campsite, but she used it when journeying to Lothen Forest. Not a blanket went to waste as the night grew frigid, and they ate from their packs and gazed at the starry sky while the wind danced with the campfire. For an hour, the battle between the crackling flames and the breeze was the only sound. But then Desser spoke.

"If my calculations are correct, we are north of Rornibur."

"You are correct." Selanna was impressed. "The dwarves helped to make this pass long ago, when the Guardians were first placed. I doubt any in Rornibur are aware of its existence anymore."

"Who are the Guardians?" Desser seemed genuinely intrigued. "I mean, I know they're elves, but who *are* they? Salenti? Vermallon? Do they live in Lothen? Raise families?"

Selanna considered her response. Desser had always been an

adventurous soul, in search of knowledge of faraway places, so she obliged.

"Long ago, the Ancient Enemy of the North was defeated and cast into the Balgorn River. This we all know. The river, as I am sure you have learned, was tainted red afterwards and called the Blood River. After the battle, Vermallon elves remained behind to search for the body of Uust —"

"Please." Brem raised a hand. "I have a hard enough time speaking the necromancer's name. Don't mention the Enemy's name."

Selanna offered a smile of pity. Elgarroth had used Uustaag's name so often in her presence that it lost its power. But she acquiesced.

"The Vermallon elves searched the river for weeks, but the warlord, as they referred to the Enemy then, could not be found. Because of the unfathomable power the Enemy exhibited, the elves were not convinced he had been killed. In fact," she glanced at Brem, "this *power* is also the reason many feared to speak the Enemy's name. They believed that doing so would awaken him."

"But what about the Guardians?" Desser asked.

"Without a body to serve as proof of the warlord's demise," Selanna returned to the young ranger's question, "the Vermallon elves insisted a watch be placed upon Helmland. And being the only forest north of the Stone Eagles, Lothen was selected to host the sentinels, or Guardians, as they are called. The Guardians reside in the forest, and they keep watch over Lormin Dmurr, the Enemy's citadel, for signs of the warlord's return. Each elf pledges their service for not less than one hundred years, about a fifth of their lifespans, but most have spent their entire lives there. They do not have children, as caring for families would complicate matters. They have, in essence, sacrificed their freedom so that all others of Vaeldor may live normal lives. Vermallon elves remain the sole muster of the Guardians, for they consider themselves the greatest warriors of all elves."

"Of all *races*," muttered Eraim, but Selanna doubted any of the boys heard the comment.

"So, you think there's activity in the citadel?" asked Romik.

Selanna sensed a touch of fear in the young lord's voice. "If some shadow has taken the throne in Beit, possessing an item to release a plague, then I believe the Guardians will have useful information on the subject."

Her response did not answer the question, but only Eraim seemed to notice. Selanna did not know what to think. But she would see if the Guardians had any news of life in Helmland, as she always did when visiting Lothen.

"The battle against the Ancient Enemy of the North was more than a thousand years ago," Romik said. "If the Enemy survived, surely he'd have made his presence known. Besides, he would have passed long ago from old age."

"Though mortal bodies are fragile," Selanna pointed out, "evil often finds a way to endure. The war against Trannum was proof enough of that."

"Could the Shadow be the Ancient Enemy?" Daymyn ceased in his quiet, one-sided conversation with Kiryanna. "Maybe that's why the Blackfoot goblins have returned."

Selanna's heart almost skipped a beat at the thought. But she shook her head. "The Enemy was never known to be sneaky, as the Shadow has proven to be. And I am sure it murdered Seac to hide something."

"I'm more concerned with the plague." Daymyn eyed one of the flasks containing the elixir. "First off, how can we be certain these tonics will protect us? And how will we know when it's time to use them? After one of us drops dead? And is there enough for all of us?"

Selanna raised her hand. "I am sure you could go on and on with such questions. But if you are not comfortable proceeding, you are welcome to remain behind."

Daymyn gave a wry smile and fell silent.

"We should get some rest now." Selanna stood and stretched.

"We have an early start tomorrow, if we are to cross the valley before nightfall."

They returned to the ridge as soon as the sun illuminated the way. The path allowed for a single-file march for most of the day, but a few hours before dusk it widened. The trail then turned north, and after another mile, they happened upon a large cave and Selanna halted.

"We'll have to leave the horses here," she said.

She received looks of confusion from all but Eraim. Eraim dismounted and led Lilli into the cave, where she began filling her pack with supplies from her saddlebags. As Selanna did the same, everyone followed their lead.

A pair of troughs were carved into the rock on either side of the spacious cavern, one large and one small. A steady stream of cool mountain water kept the larger one filled, and the excess flowed into a natural basin with a narrow hole leading to an unknown location. Straw covered the floor, and a few empty shelves were fastened to a wall—a perfect makeshift stable.

Selanna unsaddled Dandi, and Eraim did the same with Lilli, acting as if she had been here before. But Selanna knew her friend to be resourceful, and Eraim observed and understood everything in front of her—she even filled the smaller trough with meal from a barrel near the entrance. The others unloaded their horses and placed all items to be left behind on the shelves, except for Daymyn, who looked troubled.

"These are expensive animals," he said.

Selanna could not help but glance at Baylun's mule.

"I purchased them because they're trained for rough travel," Daymyn added. "They should have no problem crossing a valley."

"You misunderstand me." Selanna smirked. "But soon you will see."

She knew the lad to be thoroughly confused. But he gave in and unsaddled his horse.

Eraim placed a gentle hand upon Lilli's chin and spoke in the elfish tongue. "Guard. And let none wander."

Lilli whinnied and nodded.

Kiryanna seemed impressed. Selanna doubted the marteese had ever encountered a Salenti horse before.

They returned to the ridge, which arced steadily to the east, and after walking a mile, everyone understood Selanna's meaning about crossing the valley. She fought the urge to giggle at the looks of shock and horror that overtook the boys.

In front of them was a narrow bridge of rock suspended five hundred feet above the woodland. The gap was no less than thirty yards across, and there existed no railing or rope to steady oneself—the chief reason Selanna wanted to complete the task before shadows engulfed the mountainside.

Selanna was the first to step onto the two-foot-wide path, and she crossed its length swiftly and without mishap. Eraim followed, and then Brem and Kiryanna.

The boys hesitated. After a couple of deep breaths, Romik proceeded, though at a much slower pace, and his group of young warriors filed behind him. At one point Romik stopped, and Eraim offered some helpful advice.

"Do not look down!"

Selanna practically saw Romik's heart pounding in his eyes. She knew the bridge would stir anxiety within the humans—it had been constructed with elves in mind—and that was why she went first. She held ready her magic in case it became necessary.

Romik resumed his pace, and Daymyn and Baylun showed just as much apprehension behind him. To the rear, Desser appeared less concerned—the young ranger had surely spent half his life in the mountains with his father, Magneer. At last, the boys were safely across.

"Well that was interesting." A glare for Selanna accompanied Daymyn's sarcasm.

Selanna noticed the boys searching among the surrounding boulders for places to get comfortable.

"No time to rest," she said, much to their obvious dismay. Crossing had taken longer than expected, and they needed to cover more ground by nightfall.

They continued along the ridge for another couple hundred yards before a trail materialized on the left, leading north into the mountains. As they made the turn, the sun dipped beyond the western peaks and shadows moved in on a cool breeze.

The path slanted downward and loose rocks played with their footing, but Selanna did not slow the pace. At one point Brem stumbled and Romik reached out to help, but Kiryanna was quick to intervene and steady the priest—all the while glaring at the young lord. They continued, even after night was upon them, until reaching another resting station. There, they set up camp, and exhaustion allowed for sleep to come easily.

The next day passed swiftly, and by dusk the southwestern reaches of Beit appeared in the distance. A river vanished over a cliff ahead, and beyond that, the current continued through the mountains and across the fields to the north.

The company made camp once more within tall rock formations to the side of the path, and they moved on early the following morning. It was not long before they reached the cliff, where they stood atop a beautiful waterfall. The water cascaded several hundreds of feet into a pool that fed the river, and somewhere beyond sight, the waterway emptied into Lake Beldara. It was an amazing view, but Selanna's desire to reach the Guardians grew stronger with each passing moment, and she pressed on with barely a glance.

They descended step-like stones along the fall's western side. The way was slick and an icy mist sprayed often, but the steps were wide and there were no mishaps. Soon they were level with the collecting water, where the roar was almost deafening.

They followed the current north down the mountainside, and after a mile the land leveled and the river broke free of the rough terrain. To the northwest, a dark line formed upon the horizon—Lothen Forest was two days away.

Selanna picked up the pace, but after a few hundred yards, a rancid odor assailed her senses and Eraim's gasp halted the group.

"Look at the water!" Eraim wrinkled her nose.

Dead fish lined the riverbank as far as Selanna could see.

"I think it's time to use the potion." Daymyn appeared more than a bit nervous.

Selanna nodded, and everyone took a drink from the canteens. The elixir carried a musty odor and tasted almost like blood, causing most of them to gag, but they kept it down. They then continued, but at a slower pace, as Selanna's stomach was unsettled.

The next few hours saw everyone's nerves on edge, waiting to see if the antidote worked. They encountered no living creatures, but the rotting corpses of birds, squirrels, raccoons, and many other small animals added to the foul stench of the fish. There were also no Beitian citizens, for the secret path lay beyond civilized lands, but it seemed insects were unhindered by the plague and feasted upon the carcasses—a few sampled the company as well.

With the coming of night, Selanna did not wish to stop, and she received no arguments, not even after Eraim, Desser, and Brem vomited—likely due to the elixir. Though the desire to speak to the Guardians remained Selanna's driving force, she heard whispered words from some of the others, providing additional reasons to continue. Daymyn feared he might not wake again if he slept; Desser's concern lay with being discovered by Beitian soldiers; Kiryanna was tired of the constant stink; and Brem wished to find an alternate water source before his supply ran dry. Romik presented no differing opinions, and Baylun said nothing.

They marched under the young moon for a couple more miles, and Selanna continued north when the waterway bent to the northeast, taking with it the odor of decay. At that point, they stopped for much needed rest. The break did not last long, however, and they moved on after less than two hours.

They veered northwest, placing the line of trees directly ahead, but the forest remained half a day away. With the rising of the sun, Selanna realized they had made good time, and she eased the pace as each of them took another drink from the Beit canteens. Still, nothing impeded their progress and not a living creature was seen, and Lothen Forest was before them at last. Selanna stepped beneath the trees without hesitation.

Evergreens populated the woodland, mingled with maples, cedars, and birches. On the few occasions Selanna had been there, she saw many breeds of birds and small game, but now the remains of those animals were scattered about the forest floor.

"We should see a Guardian soon," she whispered to Eraim, refusing to believe the plague could defeat the elves.

Eraim scanned the trees and underbrush and shook her head. "There is no sign of anyone having been here recently."

"That is not unusual," Selanna said. "Most of the Guardians roam the western edge of the woodland. And the few that patrol this area remain hidden until they can discern the motives of visitors."

Eraim eyed the treetops. "No one hides from me."

"Hello!" Selanna called out. "I am Selanna of Salenti. I am here to speak with the Guardians. Please show yourselves."

Only the buzz of happy insects answered.

They moved farther into Lothen, walking out the day with no obvious path. As the forest darkened with the evening, Selanna came to a stop. She was exhausted, and the fatigue in the company's movements did not escape her notice.

"We best get some rest," she said.

They lit a small fire and sat on the ground. Though the air was not as chilly as within the mountains, it was cooler than what they were used to and they pulled their blankets over their shoulders.

"Where are the Guardians?" asked Romik.

"They probably do not wish to show themselves." Selanna attempted to sound positive, but concern gnawed at her stomach. It was not like the Guardians to allow strangers to wander freely for so long.

"Shouldn't we have seen something by now?" Daymyn looked at Selanna. "Perhaps the body of an elf?"

Selanna glared at Daymyn, displeased with the question. "That we have *not* seen one gives me hope they are all right."

The camp fell silent, and everyone but Eraim settled in for some sleep. But before anyone found rest, a frozen gust swept through the leaves and the fire was snuffed out.

Selanna sat up in alarm, as did the others, and she gazed about the dark trees. There was nothing. Another icy wind crossed the campsite, and upon it were screams of pain and anguish. The cries grew louder as the gust rose in strength, and also Selanna detected whispers and chants. The wind swirled, lifting pine needles, leaves, and dirt, and fear suddenly gripped her—she needed to get away from the screaming.

She ran, making her way through the trees as fast as she dared, but the shrieking wind followed. She darted left and right, and still it found her. This continued for what must have been half a mile and the gust diminished, taking with it the screams and whispers.

Selanna regained control and looked around, thankful Eraim was with her. The rest of the group then rambled through the forest and joined them—Kiryanna and Brem led the way, with Baylun bringing up the rear.

"Where are you going?" Eraim panted.

Selanna scanned the trees. "Did you not hear the screams?"

Eraim shook her head slowly. "I felt a chill wind. But I heard nothing."

Selanna turned to Brem.

"I sensed something upon the wind," the priest said. "Some kind of presence. But it's gone now."

Selanna sighed. She had no idea where she was, and they had left their blankets and some of their gear behind. Thankfully, Eraim still wore her backpack and the boys and Kiryanna had been quick enough to grab theirs. Eraim could probably lead them back, but would that be wise?

Selanna shook her head. "We will settle here."

"Maybe we should walk until morning," said Daymyn.

"I doubt you can see past the next tree," Eraim muttered.

Eraim was correct. Human vision at night was inefficient, lest they be in an open field beneath a full moon. Brem and Kiryanna surely possessed the vision Selanna and Eraim enjoyed, and krukari sight was just as strong, so Baylun would be fine. But the other boys were lucky they did not stumble into thorns and other undesirable vegetation during their run through the woodland.

"We will have to wait until the light returns." Selanna lowered onto the ground to seal her decision.

With reluctance, they all sat.

No fire was lit, and no one bothered to lie down; they leaned against trees in the darkness, facing each other. Minutes later, the wind returned, swirling and carrying screams louder than before, and everyone rose.

"Are those screams?" Eraim searched the forest with wide eyes.

"Nobody move!" Selanna shouted.

She closed her eyes, concentrating on the sounds while her hair flew about her face. The cries were almost deafening, but it was the whispers that Selanna focused on. Then she heard words spoken.

"Mees! Mees!"

It was the elfish call for alarm.

The gust headed north through the woodland, and Selanna opened her eyes to see the uneasy faces of her companions. But there was no time for explanations.

"Follow me!" she said.

Branches swayed in front of Selanna as she tried desperately to keep up with the wind. She knew the boys would face difficulties, but the others would just have to lend them aid again. The trees thinned, allowing her to pick up speed, but after a mile the gust vanished.

Selanna stood in a small clearing dully illuminated by moonlight. Eraim was with her with questioning eyes, but Selanna had no answers. Kiryanna and Brem then arrived with the boys close behind.

Romik frowned at Selanna. "What—?"

The wind returned, moving from east to west. Selanna trailed after it another few hundred yards and it vanished yet again. Her heart then climbed into her throat and she found it hard to breathe.

She stood at the edge of Lothen Forest, overlooking the eastern reaches of Helmland. Half a mile away, a long road lay beneath the dim light, passing from north to south before disappearing into the west, and upon the other side rose a dark tower. The tall, menacing structure wore a gathering of storm clouds like a crown, and firelight shone from several openings while an eerie violet glow issued from the highest two windows.

Eraim gasped. "It cannot be..." she said, just above a whisper as the rest of the party joined them.

Selanna's skin crawled and goose bumps invaded. "Darum Carumbor has life."

"What is Darum Carumbor?" Brem whispered, as if the tower might hear him.

Selanna nearly choked on her reply. "The watchtower of Helmland."

CHAPTER 13

THE CRYSTAL

The situation continued to worsen for Baylun. It all started with a simple birthday. *"Don't let anything happen to your brother,"* were the last words his mother said; directions given to Romik. Then came the hunting trip that led to fighting Blackfoot goblins in Pavan. That should have been a sufficient reason to go home, but Romik decided they would speak with Granduncle Arkor. Why not speak to Baylun's father? Gruelenor was just as knowledgeable and had also fought in the Necromancer War.

Next, they ran into Selanna and Eraim. Romik *knew* Baylun was uneasy in the presence of beauty. And not only were the elves the most beautiful creatures Baylun had ever known, they were accomplished in their abilities—it was said they issued the killing blow to Trannum! Beauty *and* power? Baylun's uneasiness turned to complete anxiety. If that were not enough, Romik decided they would accompany the elves into Beit; a realm of evil. Baylun's parents would not approve, but what could he do? Brand himself a coward in front of his brother, his cousins, and the lovely elves?

So Baylun followed, unwilling to utter a word. The last thing he needed was to douse the elves with the saliva that sprayed every time he talked. Silence, however, became difficult when the priest joined the group. Brem, the spotted marteese, often spoke quietly to Baylun about the hardships of being a half-breed, and how those hardships could become strengths. Baylun offered only shrugs and nods to communicate, but Brem would not take the hint.

Then there was the priest's lovely companion. Romik and Daymyn showered the poor marteese with attention, a habit of theirs

151

whenever they encountered an attractive female, and they teased Baylun, insisting Kiryanna made eyes at him when he was not looking. All Baylun noticed were expressions of pity. At least Desser never played those games. Desser's only contributions were to smile.

They journeyed into Beit, only to find everything dead. Why would they go any farther? What would Mother think if she knew? Or Father? After reaching Lothen Forest, they never found the Guardians Selanna spoke about. Instead, they were greeted by a screaming wind—a wind that apparently whispered to Selanna and led them to Helmland.

And now they marched into Helmland!

"Get up Baylun!" were Romik's words well over a month ago. *"I gotta surprise for you, birthday boy!"* This was definitely a surprise, and one Baylun could do without. Did Romik not need to return to Ironside Keep? Was his leave not ending soon?

What were they doing here?

Baylun sighed.

They made their way across the dead land and toward Darum Carumbor beneath the shadows of the dying night. The broken soil crumbled under Baylun's boots and occasional rocks were kicked, but it seemed there was nothing to detect their approach. As they drew to within a couple hundred yards, however, Baylun spied figures exiting the structure, and he knew Eraim had seen them as well.

"Get down!" the small elf hissed.

They crouched low. But what good would that do without trees or boulders to conceal them? If hobgoblins, krukari, or elves were among the tower group, Baylun and his companions were sure to be discovered.

Over a hundred figures issued from Darum Carumbor, marching with torches toward the road and the company, and Eraim ushered everyone several yards to the south and had them lie flat. As the contingent drew near, Baylun saw they wore Beitian tabards. They passed by, seemingly unaware of anyone hiding in the darkness, so they had to be humans. They turned north on the road skirting Lothen Forest, and once their lights had grown small, Eraim stood and brushed herself off. The others did the same.

"It seems it is Beit that brought the tower back to life," said Brem.

"More likely the Shadow," muttered Selanna. "But why has it come here?" The elf mage pursed her lips as she gazed at the company. "I am going inside."

"We're with you," said Romik, obviously forgetting his promise to Mother to keep Baylun safe.

"Yes, of course." Brem viewed the sky. "But the sun will rise within the hour."

Baylun glanced overhead, where the few stars defying the haze were fading.

"Then let us make haste." Selanna nodded at Eraim.

They hurried toward Darum Carumbor, and soon Baylun saw it clearly. From a distance, he believed the circular structure had lain in shadow, but now he realized dark bricks made up its walls. Surrounding the flat roof were eight smokestacks, issuing fumes that seemed to fuel the storm clouds hovering above. The battlements showed no signs of watchmen and there existed no moat or drawbridge. An iron portcullis was the only visible guard to deny entry, but the gate was in its raised position.

Eraim hesitated twenty yards from the opening. "Do you think it is a trap?" she asked Selanna.

Selanna shook her head. "Highly doubtful. The Shadow likely does not believe anyone could survive the plague long enough to trespass."

Highly doubtful? Should they not be sure?

"With that in mind," Eraim said, "perhaps we should have another sip of the elixir. No telling what might happen once we enter."

Selanna nodded, and everyone drank from the canteens. It was a horrible concoction, but better than the alternative.

Eraim sighed. "From what remains, we have enough for two

more days."

The small elf used her native tongue this time, a language Gruelenor had insisted Baylun learn. So Baylun understood every word. He knew his brother and cousins never bothered to study elfish, and he suspected the elves assumed none of them were fluent. He decided it best not to react to anything they said.

"That is not enough to see us safely back to the Stone Eagles," Eraim added.

"We are beyond turning back." Selanna also spoke in elfish. "No sense worrying the boys."

Brem and Kiryanna exchange looks. Romik and Baylun's cousins remained clueless.

Eraim pulled her fancy little sword from its jewel-encrusted scabbard, and the blade radiated a soft red glow. Kiryanna drew her sword as well, revealing it to match the rest of her golden equipment. Romik unsheathed the Sword of Ironside, and Daymyn and Desser readied their weapons. Baylun took in a deep breath and grabbed the axe from his back.

"Be prepared to use it this time." Daymyn winked at Baylun.

Baylun ignored his cousin. But he made a silent vow to never again freeze in battle.

They climbed a stone ramp and passed beneath the iron gate and into the tower. Torches burned in sconces along a curving corridor stretching left and right, and ahead were stables. Baylun scanned the walls and ceiling, searching for some form of resistance. He saw nothing.

Eraim entered the stables with her blade ready. She turned to Selanna and shook her head.

"Empty," Selanna whispered to the company.

They headed down the left passage with Eraim at the lead. The corridor arced around the perimeter of the tower, and after sixty feet, a wooden door was on the inside wall. Eraim listened before slowly opening the door, and beyond, another hallway stretched twenty feet to a second door. The little elf crept in with the company several paces behind, but then she halted.

"Do you hear that?" Eraim whispered to Selanna.

"Sounds like metal pounding on metal," Selanna whispered back. Baylun heard nothing.

Eraim nodded and pointed upward.

The noise came from above?

The small elf opened the door to a round chamber, and Baylun detected the sound at last. It was a rhythmic beat, like a smithy going about his work in a distant room. A staircase ascended the wall to a trapdoor in the ceiling, and four racks held lances, bows, axes, and swords. The weapons were black in color. Another trapdoor was in the center of the floor, and Eraim and Selanna approached it while Romik and Daymyn examined the weapons.

Baylun joined the elves as Eraim pulled a ring, lifting the door to reveal a damp chamber below. Skeletal remains filled the room — prisoners, judging by the shackles fastened to their wrists — and Eraim closed the hatch, wrinkling her tiny nose.

"These are made of black steel." Romik grabbed a sword. He then dropped the weapon as if it had bitten him, and it clattered to the floor.

Everyone froze. The pounding continued its rhythmic beat. After a few seconds, Selanna checked on Romik.

"What happened?" she asked.

"I don't know." Romik held his hand close, wincing as he stared at the dark blade. "It felt as if my hand was on fire."

Baylun saw no evidence of burns on his brother's gauntlet, but it was definitely shaking.

Brem scrutinized a lance without handling it. "These weapons are touched by evil." He turned to Romik. "But you did not hold the sword for long. You should recover shortly."

"Let us move up the stairs," Selanna said.

Eraim scaled the steps, and the company ascended in single file to a landing where iron rungs led to the trapdoor. The small elf climbed to the top and cocked her head to one side, and she made a motion to Selanna that Baylun did not understand.

"Ready your weapons," Selanna said quietly.

It was an unnecessary command. Their weapons had been ready since reaching the tower.

Selanna moved against the wall, allowing everyone to pass. Brem stood aside as well, and Kiryanna climbed the ladder with her golden sword in hand, followed by Romik and Desser. Lacking any more space on the rungs, Daymyn and Baylun remained on the landing.

Once Eraim saw all were ready, she tightened her grip on her fancy blade and pushed the door open. She then passed through the opening with such speed that Baylun nearly missed it when he blinked.

"Who are you?" a voice demanded with slurred words.

Kiryanna scrambled into the room, and Romik and Desser hastened up the rungs. Daymyn and Baylun followed as the sliding of chairs and the clash of steel ensued.

Within the chamber were four guards dressed in black chain armor. Two lay at Eraim's feet and the others were motionless beneath Romik and Kiryanna. Desser held his sword ready, but everything was still. Even the pounding had ceased. A table was in the center of the room, and Baylun was sure the soldiers had been sitting. The chairs were toppled and drinks were spilled, as the men had obviously rushed to defend their tower against the invaders.

"I sense a great evil," Brem said once he entered. "It is above us."

Baylun looked at the ceiling and around the room. There existed no means of ascending, but there were four doors evenly spaced about the round chamber.

Eraim went to the door nearest to her and listened. After a couple of seconds, she approached the next door on her left.

The door opposite from Eraim opened, and in rushed a dozen men. A few of the warriors wore black chain shirts, and they raised bows and pulled dark arrows from their quivers. The remaining soldiers were dressed in black plate armor, and they charged, brandishing swords of the same color. All at once, the enemy chanted senseless words in unison.

Romik and Desser converged on a warrior to the right side of the table, and they struck him down without difficulty. Kiryanna and Daymyn fought next to each other on the left, dropping two more.

Baylun hurried to join his brother, but as the droning chant sped up, the enemy moved faster—that, or Baylun moved slower. He realized it was the latter when he noticed his companions' sluggish movements, and they worked desperately to defend themselves. His eyes then grew wide as the archers took aim, but a green light flashed and the bowstrings snapped. Selanna must have beaten the restricting magic! A red glow swung to Baylun's left, and he saw Eraim's fancy sword growing in brightness. Eraim went on the offensive, darting about with great speed and striking down a soldier.

Baylun readied his axe as a warrior rushed him. The man held no snarl, smile, or show of any emotion while he voiced the chant of the enemy, now deafening in Baylun's ears, and he brought his black sword in a vicious arc. Baylun's arms did not want to move, not very quickly, but somehow he knocked the blade aside. He continued the axe's momentum, twirling it overhead and down onto his attacker, but he did not think he could complete the maneuver before his opponent struck again. The guard must have shared this belief, for he made no effort to defend himself, and Baylun cut the soldier down when the axe picked up speed and easily sliced through the dark breastplate. The warrior's steel body crashed to the floor, the clatter swallowed by the inane chant.

Baylun's heart lifted. Selanna had surely restored everyone to normal. But then he noticed his companions still struggled—except for Eraim. The small elf worked hard to assist Daymyn and Kiryanna while preventing the enemy from reaching Brem and Selanna. Kiryanna had taken a wound, and Daymyn was on his knee with his sword held high—the archers had pulled black axes, and one was bearing down on him. On Baylun's right, two soldiers pressed Romik while another had Desser backed against the wall.

Baylun arrived at his brother's side, and he severed the leg from one attacker with ease; the man fell, but continued to chant from the floor without a whimper of pain. Romik's second opponent turned, bringing his sword up in time to parry Baylun's next attack, and the axe shattered the blade. Baylun followed with the bronze spike, thrusting it into the man's eye and landing a gruesome blow. He then spun, swinging his weapon and decapitating an enemy soldier approaching him from behind — it was the one that had been pressing Desser. Baylun did not realize the man was there, but he sensed that danger was nearby.

Only five chanting warriors remained, and the drone weakened, allowing Romik and Desser to move quicker. After Romik finished the wounded guard at his feet, he and Desser met the advance of two archers swinging axes.

Baylun saw the rest of his companions were back to normal as well. Kiryanna struck down the enemy before her while Eraim dropped another, and Daymyn skewered the one towering above him. Daymyn then joined Romik and Desser, and they defeated the final soldiers.

The chamber fell silent, except for Kiryanna. Baylun knew the marteese had received a gash on her forearm, and she gritted her teeth while panting.

"It burns!" she hissed.

Brem ran to her, pulling a jar from his pouch and immediately inspecting the injury. The wound was not enough to cause the pain Kiryanna exhibited, but from the cut a black web grew, extending toward her shoulder. Brem closed his eyes and recited a prayer, and while he spoke, the web receded. The priest continued until it vanished altogether and the gash closed, and Kiryanna breathed easier.

Brem turned to Selanna and frowned. "The evil weapons deal evil wounds. My spiritual healing is not nearly as strong as Nilborg's had been. I'm not sure how many more times I can treat such an injury." He looked around. "Is anyone else hurt?"

Everyone shook their heads.

"Well then," the priest nodded, "luck is with us."

"Why couldn't I move?" Romik asked Selanna.

Baylun's brother appeared both angry and frightened. Had Baylun not arrived when he did, Romik and Desser would certainly have suffered wounds much worse than what Kiryanna received.

"I have never experienced such a chant before." Selanna viewed the bodies. "I will be better prepared next time."

"The malevolence in their words was powerful," Brem said. "Much too powerful for mere soldiers to possess. There is a greater evil, yet unrevealed."

"How was it you were able to move so quickly?" Daymyn asked from behind Baylun.

Baylun turned to see his cousin was speaking to Eraim.

"It was Mithkahr." The elf smiled at her sword, the blade having returned to a dull, red glow. "Mithkahr is too powerful for their little chant."

"What about you, Baylun?" Desser posed quietly. "Is your axe a *Mithkahr* too?"

"There is only one Mithkahr!" Eraim had obviously heard the comment. "But I did notice you moving freely." The elf gazed curiously at Baylun, as did Kiryanna next to her.

"Lucky for us all," Selanna said. "But there is no time for explanations. We need to move on."

Romik shared a smile and nod with Baylun while Desser placed an appreciative hand on Baylun's shoulder. Daymyn's eyes narrowed upon the axe.

Eraim approached the door the guards had used to enter. "We might as well go this way."

She passed through, and everyone followed.

A corridor extended to a hallway arcing to the left and right. Eraim looked both ways before closing her eyes.

"I hear faint whispers," she said. "But I cannot tell from where they are coming." She turned to Selanna.

The mage shook her head.

Baylun detected nothing.

Eraim pursed her lips and headed down the corridor to the left.

They came to a door, and after pressing her ear to the wood, the small elf opened it to reveal barracks. A score of bunks filled the room, but it was devoid of occupants.

Eraim continued along the passage, and they encountered a short hallway on the left leading to a door. The elf ignored it and moved forward. Baylun figured it returned to the chamber where they had just battled the soldiers.

Not much farther ahead, the curving tunnel presented another door on the inner wall. Again, Eraim listened, and seconds later, she opened the door and cautiously stepped through.

A burning hearth and metal basin containing hot coals dominated the room. Nearby were bellows, an anvil, a few hammers, and a barrel of water, and scattered around the chamber were pieces of black armor.

Eraim pointed to a stack of black iron bars, looking at Selanna with a raised brow. After the mage nodded, Eraim used Mithkahr's edge to roll a couple of them into a bag. The small elf then scanned the room once more and moved back to the door, and everyone stepped aside to allow her by.

They continued around the tower, passing another hallway that likely returned to the central chamber. Upon encountering a third inner-wall door, Eraim gave a listen before swinging it open. A guardroom possessed a table, four chairs, four crossbows, and a crate of arrows. Beyond that, the room was empty, save for a small staircase extending above the ceiling and to a landing with a single door.

They ascended, and Baylun finally detected the whispers Eraim mentioned earlier. He did his best to ignore the sound, still haunted by the chanting soldiers. Eraim pushed the door open and they entered.

They were at the edge of a circular chamber. The room surely occupied the entire third level of the tower, and suspended from the ceiling about its center were four braziers, burning with an odd smelling incense and spewing a purple haze that covered the floor. Within the middle of the braziers was an enormous crystal, perfectly diamond shaped and set upon an iron base, and though it appeared black, it pulsed with a violet light. A figure dressed in a black robe with purple trim stood at a podium beyond the large gem. He showed no interest in the intruders as he read from a tome, whispering an eerie chant and moving his hands in some strange ceremony.

"Stop him!" shouted Brem.

With amazing speed, Eraim sheathed Mithkahr and pulled her bow, and the robed man continued ignoring them as she drew back an arrow. She released the string, and the missile buried deep into the man's throat. He held a look of shock as he choked on the blood flowing freely from the wound, and he somehow possessed the strength to lift the book and cast it into a nearby brazier before collapsing.

"Get the book!" Selanna said as it caught fire.

They advanced, but Eraim was first to cross the room. She again wielded Mithkahr, and she struck one of the chains supporting the brazier, spilling the tome and several violet coals onto the mist-covered floor. The book still burned, and Eraim quickly stomped it out.

"The crystal." Brem moved closer to the large jewel, which now emitted a steady glow. "It is the source of the evil. It must be destroyed."

A breeze swept across Baylun's lower body, and the haze swirled as it rose like purple tendrils up his legs. His knees stiffened, and walking was nearly impossible as he attempted to approach the gemstone.

The fog had climbed everyone's legs, and their steps were rigid. Romik and Desser were next to the crystal and they swung their swords, but their blades clanged off the finely chiseled gem without leaving a mark. They dropped their weapons, clutching their wrists and wincing.

The mist now reached Baylun's waist, bringing him pangs of nausea, and Eraim appeared ready to vomit as it wrapped around her chest. Selanna waved her hands, releasing a spell of lightning, but the energy rebounded from the jewel and threw her across the room until the wall halted her. The elf collapsed into the haze.

Baylun needed to do something. He raised his axe and forced his way past Kiryanna—the marteese gaped with wide eyes, apparently rooted to where she stood. His heart rate increased as the mist neared his chest, and after a couple more steps he brought down his weapon, slicing into the crystal and cutting loose a shard.

The enormous gem vibrated, filling the room with a drone that rattled Baylun's head. The vibration ended seconds later when the jewel disintegrated into a cloud of violet powder, and the evil fog receded to the floor, releasing its hold on Baylun and his companions. Sunlight then dimly illuminated the chamber through windows Baylun had not noticed, brightening the purple haze that still issued from three of the braziers.

Eraim wiped her mouth, having vomited, and Kiryanna checked on Brem. Selanna rose, her robes a bit charred and her skin burned in several places, but she moved without difficulty. Romik, Daymyn, and Desser gazed at Baylun in wonder.

"Very good," Daymyn said, looking at the axe more closely.

"Yes," agreed Desser, still shaking the pain from his wrist. "Well done."

"I'm proud, little brother." Romik placed a hand on Baylun's shoulder.

"It wasn't me," Baylun whispered to Romik. "It was the axe."

"Maybe." Romik eyed the weapon and then Baylun. "Maybe not. A mighty thing it is, but I wasn't lying. The dwarf claimed it would derive its strength from its wielder."

Baylun gave a wry smile, unwilling to accept any credit.

"Brem," Eraim said, now at Selanna's side. "We need your assistance."

The mage had evidently suffered more than Baylun realized.

"Let us first leave this chamber." The priest glanced at the braziers. "It makes me ill."

Baylun's nausea had subsided with the destruction of the crystal. Perhaps Brem was affected differently.

"What about the stairs?" Desser stood at the base of a narrow stairway climbing the wall to yet another trapdoor. "It surely leads to the roof."

How had Baylun missed the stairs and windows when he first entered?

"Can you make it up the steps?" Brem asked Selanna.

The mage nodded, and Brem offered her a shoulder to lean on.

Kiryanna's eyes narrowed while the priest escorted Selanna to the stairs. Romik then stepped in to relieve Brem of his burden, and the marteese warrior relaxed.

Desser led the way up, pushing open the door to reveal the sky, and the company began filing onto the roof. Eraim hesitated within the chamber, and she carefully lifted the remains of the burnt tome from the floor. Baylun then saw her eyes lock onto something else. She pulled a piece of cloth from her pouch, circling an area of the haze, and grabbed the shard Baylun had cut from the crystal and placed it into her pack.

Eraim looked at Baylun. "Up the stairs with you. Move on, now." She motioned with both hands, appearing much like Baylun's mother urging him to go outside and play.

Baylun complied.

The remains of three ancient ballistae littered the eastern side of the battlements, but there were no soldiers atop the tower. And though the smokestacks continued to feed the dark clouds, allowing no view of the sky above Darum Carumbor, the air tasted fresher than before and the land did not seem so dim beneath the easterly sun—though the haze remained.

Baylun breathed deep to expel the evil fumes that had invaded his body while scaling the stronghold. To his right, Brem finished placing a salve onto Selanna's cuts and burns. The priest then moved from person to person, tending to their wounds. Baylun had none.

Eraim gazed across the rooftop. Why was Darum Carumbor alive? It had lain dark since long before her days. And what evil spell had the enemy employed? How could soldiers recite chants, creating magic while they battled? Eraim knew of no one outside of the gray elves capable of battle magic. And watching Selanna struggle... Eraim had not seen that since they faced Trannum and his Death Lords. Selanna was much more powerful now.

Eraim's attention fell to a burnt page in her hand. It had fallen free from the damaged tome she carried. The parchment was mostly destroyed, but a legible portion at the bottom grabbed her notice. The letters appeared to have originally been written in blood, now brown and weathered.

... THROUGH MIGHT OF THE SHADOW, HE WILL SEND THE DUKE TO ONCE AGAIN EMPOWER WE OVER ALL ELSE; AND THROUGH THE PORTALS OF ULTIMATE MALEVOLENCE, THE LAND SHALL FLOOD WITH THE MINIONS OF DARKNESS; AND ALL WILL BE UNDER THE MIGHTY FIST OF POWER, WITH THE GREAT ONE CLOSE BEHIND...

Lower on the page, beneath an unreadable section, were symbols she did not recognize. Anxiety crept into her throat.

"Selanna!" she called out. "You must see this."

Selanna moved closer to look over Eraim's shoulder, and Eraim felt her friend's body stiffen.

"Selanna! Eraim!" Desser gained Eraim's attention.

The young ranger stood on the western edge of the tower, gazing into the distance. She and Selanna hurried to see what had caught his eye.

The landscape was more desolate than even Neja and Nomedd as far as Eraim could tell. Under the struggling morning sun, nothing grew upon the cracked and broken soil. Patches of it were black and others brown, and though there were no signs of water, moisture stained the dirt in several areas. The road from Beit continued across the plain and into the west, almost indiscernible from the surrounding terrain, and over a mile away, a large force marched deeper into Helmland.

"What *are* they?" asked Romik.

Everyone now gazed into the west.

Desser shook his head. "They're too far away. Perhaps they're Blackfoot goblins."

"No." Eraim saw them clearly enough. "They are humans. About a thousand in all. Some are Beitian soldiers, but others are dressed as those that opposed us today."

Brem sighed. "What is happening?"

"I am not sure." Selanna's eyes were troubled, but then they narrowed with conviction. "But I am going to find out."

"We do not have enough elixir for such a journey," Eraim said in elfish.

"We will not need it." Selanna gazed at the company, using the common speech. "The crystal was the source of the plague, of that I am certain. But if any of you wish to return to safer lands, you may go back the way we came. I am following that army."

The young men looked at Romik. Desser seemed nervous while Daymyn appeared eager. Baylun was hard to read, as usual—he very much reminded Eraim of Gruelenor.

"We're with you." Romik never glanced at his cousins or brother before committing them.

"As are we," said Brem.

Kiryanna nodded.

"Let us get from this tower, then." Selanna headed for the trapdoor.

CHAPTER 14

THE SHADOW

Selanna felt sick while they trailed after the army. She had not contracted the plague—she was sure the destruction of the crystal ended that threat. But never had she been west of Lothen Forest.

It was Helmland; a wasteland unlike any other. There were no cities, no villages, and almost no trees. The trees that existed failed to rise to any real height and bore no leaves or needles. In patches where grass and weeds grew, they were straw-like and climbed no higher than a couple of inches. The sun provided warmth, but it remained distorted through a haze covering the entire dominion, and the air was as dry as a desert. There were no ponds or lakes, and though the soil often appeared moist at a distance, those areas turned out to be ash-like and small clouds arose when trod upon. South of the Stone Eagle Mountains, Neja was a hard country lacking in fertility, but thousands of people made lives there. Even outside Trannum's abandoned stronghold in Nomedd, where no settlements existed, birds and reptiles populated the area. Here, there were no animals. The only life Selanna witnessed consisted of insects, all of the carrion variety; and other than the pests' minute noises, a distant buzzing rose in pitch before falling and ending, only to start again from another direction. Selanna wondered how Uustaag could have housed armies within a realm bearing no food, and the only water source was that of the Balgorn River along the northern border.

Trailing the large force was not difficult, for the soldiers marched a slow pace. They posted no scouts, nor guards when they camped, and they seemed uninterested in all things around them. Eraim made sure the company kept enough distance to avoid notice, nonetheless.

On the morning of the fourth day, twelve dead soldiers were left behind where the army had halted the previous night. The corpses lay face down, arranged with heads pointing toward central locations to form two circles—or perhaps six-pointed stars—and pooled beneath their throats was blood.

"These men are from the rear ranks," Eraim said. "They wear cloaks and helmets, while those toward the front are armored in chain."

"They fight one another like hobgoblins." Daymyn looked at Baylun. "No offense."

Baylun sighed.

Selanna often wondered if Gruelenor was aware of the teasing his son put up with. But Baylun was a man now, and the world was not kind to krukari. He would have to figure it out for himself. Then Selanna noticed Brem speaking softly to Baylun.

"Move not to anger. Remember, it is impossible for others to see through the eyes of a half-breed. Take pity on their ignorance and resist urges to impress them, for it only empowers their feelings of superiority. Live your life for you." He patted Baylun on the back and gave an encouraging smile.

"He's my cousin," said Baylun without interest.

Brem frowned.

"Perhaps they battle each other for favor." Romik stared at the corpses. "Or maybe it's just the will of evil."

"Possibly sacrificial," Eraim suggested. "Their weapons are sheathed."

"Perhaps." Selanna gazed at the army marching away. "I only wish I knew where they are headed."

"Judging by the mountains," Desser eyed the peaks of the Stone Eagles fading to the south, "we are bearing northwest, and have been since we left the tower."

Selanna looked to the north, and at the edge of her sight was a dark line. Balgorn River. She first noticed it late last night, and she hoped the army would veer a bit more south. But it was becoming clear they would not.

"I see the river as well." Eraim spoke in elfish.

"I dislike this." Selanna used the common speech as her chest tightened. "We head for the dark citadel. Lormin Dmurr."

Though Selanna was sure no one in the company had ever been to the ancient fortress of Uustaag, she saw shivers, as if chills had coursed down their spines.

"Is it wise to continue?" asked Desser. "Perhaps it's enough to know where they're going. Maybe we should return home and gain reinforcements. Our rations are depleting, and I've not seen any sign of game in this wasteland."

"There are many reasons to turn back." Selanna looked at her companions. "But I must discover what the Shadow is up to."

"We might make use of these uniforms," said Eraim. "Just in case."

They distributed the cloaks and helmets showing the least amount of blood. The boys had no problems fitting into the gear, but they were a bit long and wide for Selanna and the others and the helmets were ill-fitted, especially in Eraim's case. Selanna hoped they would not get close enough for these facts to matter. They opted to carry their helmets for now, and they continued trailing the marching force.

Over the next day, the haze grew thicker, making the soldiers appear as wavering shadows in the distance. A few more bodies were left behind, but they revealed nothing more. Soon, the Balgorn River drew close enough for everyone to see.

Selanna gazed at the water. Something was amiss. Legends held the river to be tinted red, but it appeared black, and the haze seemed to rise from it. Adding to her concerns were the ruins just south of the Balgorn and less than half a mile to the northwest. Crumbling dark walls corralled equally dark buildings against the river, and the marching force headed straight for them. Then Selanna noticed an even greater army approaching from the west.

Eraim gasped. "Blackfoots! At least five thousand."

Selanna brought the company to a halt as the humans ceased their progress just outside the ruins. The goblins continued into the wreckage, and the humans followed.

Selanna drew in a deep breath, her heart beating in her throat. "Let's go."

They reached the entrance shortly after and passed over the remains of a gate. The once-thick doors of stone lay shattered in thousands of fragments, and at the end of a wide aisle was a twisted portcullis, rusted and discarded. Watch towers once stood to either side, but all that remained were piles of rubble. From history books, Selanna knew a massive gatehouse once served as guardian to the dark citadel, but an explosion destroyed it when the Alliance for Good attacked. A part of her wished she had seen that.

Within the ruins, a wide road led through crumbled buildings that had surely housed Uustaag's soldiers. The decay was not wholly due to time, however, as the invading army of centuries ago made sure nothing survived and no chamber went unchecked. Dark trees were scattered, still unclothed but not so fragile as the ones seen thus far. Their girth was mighty but twisted, and it appeared as though grim faces of torment had settled upon their trunks.

Selanna picked up the pace, gaining ground on the army until it halted near the river. There, Lormin Dmurr stood atop an enormous pillar of rock extending from the riverbed, and a bridge of stone joined it to the land. It was said that no catapult or spell existed to scratch the dark citadel's surface, leading Selanna to believe it to be made of rorbak, just like Korban Bridge and Trannum's cabin within Sistama. Looking at the jet-black bricks, she now knew that was not the case. It was surely constructed of something completely foreign.

The Blackfoot goblins congregated to the left side of the bridge, and other armies were present as well. To the right were at least two thousand minotaurs, massive man-like creatures with bull-like heads, and next to them stood an army of hobgoblins and krukari. Beyond the goblins was a force of trolls. The swamp monsters' arms dangled just above the ground, and saliva drooled from their long fangs as they gazed down at the Blackfoots.

The humans did not move to either side of the bridge. They marched onto the arched stone and toward the dark fortress.

"Hurry!" Selanna put on her ill-fitted helmet.

She ran to catch up with the army. She did not know if everyone followed, and she had no time to check, but Eraim was beside her as she reached the tail end of the humans, just before passing the other battalions and as the last soldiers set foot on the bridge. Selanna fell into rank, feeling thousands of eyes upon her and her costume, but nothing was said and no alarms sounded.

The bridge arched fifty yards to the open gates of Lormin Dmurr, and the dark flagstones invaded Selanna's boots with a dull chill. The onlooking armies then roared, and Selanna nearly jumped from her skin. But the cheer was not meant for her. They directed it at the top of the citadel, sixty feet overhead. There, storm clouds gathered while an icy wind stirred, and upon the roof was the Shadow—the very image that passed through Nilborg's bedroom window.

The ghostly form hovered above the battlements as its blue eyes scanned the horde below. It raised its hand, and within was an object Selanna could not see clearly, for darkness obscured it. The roar grew louder and a grunting chant began, but Selanna lost sight of the Shadow when she passed through the gates and into the citadel.

The entire company was with her, and their eyes darted about. Selanna also noticed that Brem's spots had grown darker, and he was scratching vigorously. Kiryanna slowed to check on the priest, and Eraim grabbed the warrior's arm to keep her moving.

A high ceiling gazed upon the enormous entryway illuminated by several torches, and corridors led left and right. Ahead, a short hall ended in a pair of doors fifteen feet tall. The soldiers wearing the dark armor disappeared through the doors while the rest split down the side hallways.

The entry was nearly empty when Eraim's sharp whisper alerted Selanna to the fact that she had stopped moving.

"Which way do we go?" Eraim looked each direction, including back across the bridge.

Selanna shook her head. She did not know. "We need to get to the roof."

"What about Brem?" asked Romik.

Brem's skin was turning blue and his spots oozed pus and blood, reminding Selanna of a time over twenty years ago.

"I don't understand what is happening," Brem said through chattering teeth. "It's just as it had been in Trannum's stronghold!"

Selanna looked around. They were alone in the entry hall. Down the passage to the right, not far away, was a normal-sized door, and she nodded at it. Eraim raced over to give it a listen, and Selanna joined her as she opened it to reveal a small room devoid of occupants and furnishings.

"Wait in here." Selanna stepped aside.

Brem made his way with Kiryanna's assistance. Kiryanna glared briefly at Selanna before flashing a concerned gaze at the boys, and she closed the door behind her.

Romik's brow furrowed. "Is it wise to leave them?"

"It will have to do." Selanna sighed. "Brem will draw too much attention. And I do not know if we will be able to protect him."

"Now what?" asked Daymyn.

"We are garbed as those that headed right and left." Eraim eyed the corridors and then ceiling. "But my guess would be that the big doors get us to the roof fastest."

"Lead the way," Selanna said.

Eraim gave a nod before moving swiftly and pressing her ear to one of the large doors. She opened it with some effort, and after a glance she passed through. Romik went next, followed by Daymyn, Selanna, Desser, and Baylun.

Beyond was a hall bearing a long table broken into several pieces and surrounded by smashed chairs. At the far end, torchlight illuminated an immense throne of granite, and farther on, a wide staircase climbed to a balcony encompassing the entire chamber. A dozen doors were present on either side, and more were visible around the balcony as well. The room was unoccupied.

Eraim led the way across the hall, and as they neared the throne, Selanna noticed hundreds of scratches showing failed attempts to topple the massive chair. They then scaled the steps, and Mithkahr's red glow intensified when Eraim reached the top. The railing of the balcony was in poor shape, rotted and cracked, and portraits that once lined the walls between the doors lay in shambles on the floor.

"There are many footprints in the dust." Eraim's words bounced around the chamber. "They go to absolutely every door!" She studied the tracks and lifted her head. "There is a single set of boots passing through the first door."

The door Eraim indicated was larger than the others, just as the ones leading into the room where they now stood. Selanna nodded to proceed.

Eraim cautiously pushed opened the door and led the way through. It was another high-ceilinged room, well lit and possessing three more large doors. Eraim continued scrutinizing the floor and approached the door on the right. After completing her routine, she pulled it open with both hands.

A tall corridor curved away to the right with torches every ten feet, and Eraim led the company along its length. They passed through a broken door and into yet another empty chamber, this one consumed by darkness. Mithkahr's light revealed a stairway to the left, ascending through a hole in the ceiling.

Nothing opposed them while they climbed the steps, but upon entering the room above, everyone halted. They stood at one end of a dark temple, and the air was deathly cold—a feeling Selanna had not experienced since she last faced a Death Lord. Though the furnishings were destroyed, six pillars that did not reach the ceiling encircled the center of the chamber, and from each, a faded black triangle stretched across the floor to point at a crumbled altar in the middle.

A muffled roar sounded, and Selanna raised her hands with a

spell on her lips, looking for the Death Lord. But it had come from the armies outside.

"Why is it so cold?" whispered Romik as he shivered.

Eraim held up her hand to silence the Lord of the Keep, and she crept to the pillars. Selanna followed while the boys spread out, and as she neared the circle, she noticed the triangles were not black, but dark violet, and old blood stained fragments of the stone altar.

Mithkahr's glow illuminated three free-standing arches beyond the columns. Two faced each other while the third one faced the altar. Their purpose was not clear, for they supported nothing and led nowhere. They were made of white stone and covered by strange runes written in blood, and most of the symbols held trails slinking their way to the floor—the writings were fresh!

Selanna moved around the pillars to gain a better view, and she noticed a stairway leading to the ceiling. Flashes of lightning highlighted an opening at the top of the steps as thunder shook the foundations, and a sensation came over her, one she had never experienced before. It was as if an ocean of malevolence descended, and shivers worked their way from her head to her toes—an evil presence approached.

"Hide!" she warned the company, placing a pillar between her and the stairs.

Romik, Daymyn, and Desser did the same, and Eraim hurried to join Baylun as he disappeared down the steps. Mithkahr's light winked out.

Just when Selanna thought the air could get no colder, she was proven wrong. It was like an icicle piercing her lungs every time she inhaled. Then came a whispering chant that seemed to exist in her head, for it had no origination, and a grayish light spread across the room from the direction of the arches.

Selanna chanced a peek, and she saw the arch to the right emitting the glow. The opposite archway then lit up, this one reddish, and the two combined to create sickly swirls dancing upon the far wall.

"Ahhhh! Selanna..."

The whisper was everywhere, and the eyes of Selanna's companions snapped in her direction, so they had heard it as well. Even Eraim poked her head from the stairwell to give Selanna a questioning look.

"How nice it is to see you again," the whisper added.

Selanna could not believe her ears. It had to be a trick.

"Trannum!" She stepped from behind the pillar.

The Shadow materialized, hovering amid the three arches. Its eyes were the same shade of blue Selanna grew to despise all those years ago, and they narrowed upon her.

"But you..." She could not find the words to continue.

"*Please!*" the whisper hissed sarcastically. "Did you think defeating me was so easily accomplished? You mortal fools have yet to witness my true power!"

Selanna felt the blood rush from her face.

"Eraim is here too." Trannum sounded amused.

Eraim stood at the top of the stairs with Mithkahr in hand, and she paled as she viewed the wraith-like being.

"You did a naughty thing, little elf, destroying my bones." The eyes narrowed further. "How many more rats are hiding, I wonder?"

"I know not what you are up to." Selanna regained Trannum's attention. "But you will pay for what you did to Nilborg and Seac!"

"*Pay?*" The whisper seemed to chuckle. "I have paid with centuries. But at last I possess what I have sought for so long." Trannum raised a shadowy hand, and clutched within was the strange item he displayed before the horde earlier. It remained cloaked in billowing darkness, making its true form impossible to discern. "And now you shall witness my reward!"

Trannum turned his back to Selanna to face the final arch. He chanted while raising the item overhead, and the archway lit up with a swirling violet mist.

"No!" shouted Selanna.

She conjured a blast of fire, pooling as much power as she could gather in haste while targeting the dark object. The spell struck, creating an explosion, and Trannum shrieked as the item was launched from his hand and through the opening in the ceiling, as if fired from a mighty crossbow.

Trannum spun to face Selanna, his eyes taking on a reddish tint. "How dare you! You are nothing! You have already failed. Your lives are meaningless and your souls are forfeit! Step forward and receive your doom!"

Selanna felt the urge to surrender, an emotion Trannum had placed upon her long ago. She saw her companions lower their weapons—even Baylun entered the room with his head bowed. But she was stronger this time. This time, she would not allow it.

"Heed not his call!" she said aloud. "For the voice you hear is false! Raise up your weapons and fight the poison of his evil words!"

The company lifted their weapons, appearing to have regained control, but their eyes still showed fear.

"Well done, Selanna." Trannum chuckled. "I see you have grown since last we met. But you are nothing in the face of what is coming. Can you not *feel* the very foundations shake? You are too late!"

With his final hissing words, his shadowy presence hovered to the ceiling, and the tower shook, as if something a thousand feet tall approached. The pounding grew heavier until it seemed the giant stood just outside the citadel. Within the central arch, a silhouette disturbed the violet mist. The figure ducked beneath the ten-foot archway to gain access into the chamber and rose to its full twelve-foot height. It wore black armor with spikes protruding from the shoulders, and upon its massive head was a diabolical helmet. It reminded Selanna of the demon Hezeb, with its elongated snout containing many sharp teeth, and from the top protruded ram-like horns, reminiscent of the demon Ragab. Strapped to the figure's back was an enormous hammer, while a sword, no less impressive, was sheathed at its side.

The warrior removed its helmet, and Selanna stared in horror. It was a monstrous krukari, the most hideous of its kind. Its eyes were of different colors, one violet and the other red, and within them burned a true evil that drove into the pit of Selanna's stomach. The warrior took in a deep breath and roared at the ceiling, causing the stone to crack and rain dust onto the room. It seemed the howl would never end.

Selanna needed to put the monster back from where he came. She thrust her hands forward, sending an invisible force to topple a small building, and the magic washed over the krukari like nothing more than a breeze. The figure ceased its roar and turned its eyes on her.

"These mortals wish to do battle with you, Master," Trannum hissed from the ceiling.

Master? Who would Trannum consider his *master*?

The krukari took in a breath and slowly released it, as if enjoying the fresh scent of a bouquet. "No mortal can battle me." Its gravelly voice mustered more fear than any Death Lord could have summoned. "But it has been too long since I bathed in the cries of terror. They are mine!"

Eraim could not believe her eyes. She desperately wished to find a place to hide. With the roar of the enormous krukari, Baylun bolted down the steps and Daymyn was close behind. Romik and Desser were too terrified to move.

Eraim took in a deep breath, calling upon Mithkahr's strength, and she hurried to the boys to urge them along. She watched Selanna's spell fail, and the krukari announced his intention to destroy them all.

Romik and Desser broke free of the paralyzing fear and raced down the stairs. Eraim followed, slowing to look at Selanna.

"Go!" Selanna ordered.

Eraim descended to find the boys in no need of direction as they sped through the open doorway. She then heard an explosion above. Selanna was buying time for their escape.

"Get Brem and get out!" Eraim shouted after the retreating warriors.

She looked up the stairs. There was little she could offer in the way of help, but she had to do what she could. As she placed her boot on the first step, however, she was forced to dodge aside when Selanna came crashing to the floor beside her. Selanna released a gasp, and Eraim returned to the stairs with Mithkahr ready.

"You must flee!" Blood sprayed from Selanna's mouth with her words.

Eraim helped Selanna to her feet while thunderous footsteps approached, and the krukari's presence canceled the eerie light from the temple. The monster held its sword, and the blade danced with wisps of violet smoke. Eraim did not know what the fumes meant, and she did not wish to find out.

"I have you!" Eraim lifted her companion over her shoulder, inciting a small squeak, and she ran from the room as fast as she could.

"I can run," Selanna said once they entered the arcing hallway.

Selanna was in great pain, evidenced by the tattered robes and burns about her face and hands. But there was no hope of escape if Eraim had to bear the weight of two for the entire duration. She set Selanna on the floor.

"Sometimes I forget how strong you are." Selanna's voice sounded more annoyed than impressed.

They ran along the corridor and through the guardroom. Upon reaching the balcony of the next chamber, they found it teeming with black-armored warriors that chanted in unison. But it was not the same chant as in Darum Carumbor. Eraim readied Mithkahr, but none of the soldiers moved to impede, and she and Selanna descended the stairs.

Additional guards stood in open doorways within the lower room, continuing the chant with hateful glares. Still no one made a move to obstruct Eraim and Selanna, and they raced over the broken chairs and to the other side. As they reached the large doors, the chanting grew in strength, and the heavy boots of the krukari crashed onto the steps behind them.

They passed through into the entry hall to find the boys leading Kiryanna and Brem from the citadel. The priest's skin was a deeper blue now and his movements stiff, and Baylun scooped him up without losing a step.

"He's coming!" shouted Eraim, and the pace of those before her quickened.

They ran onto the bridge, stepping beneath a dark sky. It should have been early evening, but it appeared as though night had captured the land. The stones shook as the krukari exited the citadel, his long strides equaling five of Eraim's running steps, and he gained as she neared the bridge's far end. The armies roared with excitement while they watched, moving to either side of the road as if to get a better view.

There was no hope of escape, and Eraim could not imagine what terror awaited them once they were caught. The pursuing monster was at her heels as she stepped from the bridge...

The heavy footfalls ceased.

Eraim risked a glance to see what new devilry was at hand. The enormous warrior stood at the end of the bridge, as if he could move no farther. The krukari released a roar into the sky to cause the entire compound to tremble, and he sheathed his blade and pulled the hammer from his back.

With another bellow, the warrior swung the mighty weapon onto the ground. The land shook, causing the company to stumble as they continued across the ruined outpost, and fissures opened, stretching like fingers from Lormin Dmurr to collapse already crumbled buildings and swallow trees.

Eraim and her companions were hard pressed as the growing cracks sprouted crevices of their own. Several were narrow and easily jumped, but others widened enough to consume a wagon and the horses that pulled it. Worse still, some became aglow and produced heat to surpass that of the hottest bonfire. The smoldering gaps illuminated the dark realm, and the company avoided them as they exited the ruins.

Everything exploded.

CHAPTER 15

ALL ALONE

Desser had been running beside Romik across the ruins of Lormin Dmurr. But after a loud crash and shaking of the ground, several fissures opened before them, slowing their progress. They hurried around the larger ones and jumped the smaller ones as they exited the compound.

Then everything erupted.

How much time had passed since the explosion, Desser did not know, but it could not have been long. His beard was singed and his ears were ringing, and everywhere the crevasses hissed while issuing steam.

He detected a pounding to his left. Turning, his knees almost buckled. Beneath dark clouds that pierced the ground with lightning, an army of Blackfoot goblins approached, and minotaurs were in their wake.

Another noise drew Desser's attention. He whipped around to see Romik shouting from across a glowing chasm. The words then registered.

"Desser! You must hurry!"

Desser hastened to the fissure. Within, magma bubbled twenty feet below the surface. He looked at Romik, and he saw Daymyn and Baylun as well, but there was no sign of the others.

"Where's Selanna?" he shouted above the hissing steam.

Romik shook his head. "The elves are gone! And Brem and Kiryanna!" He peered left and right along the chasm. "You need to find a place to jump!"

Jumping was risky. The heat was too great and the distance

questionable. Meanwhile, the army drew nearer with every passing moment. Desser then spotted a narrowing of the gap, but it would take him toward the advancing force. It was impossible to reach without being seen, and he would lead the enemy to his cousins.

Desser sighed, his mind racing. How did they get here? It was supposed to be a vacation; a hunting trip in the north. He was not supposed to die. But what choice did he have? He could not risk the lives of his kin.

"Go on!" he shouted.

Romik stared, either in disbelief or feeling he did not hear Desser's words correctly.

"Go!" Desser repeated, gesturing for his cousins to move away.

Again, Romik balked, and this time he shook his head. A conversation took place next; perhaps an argument between Romik and Daymyn. Daymyn waved his arms while speaking, and Romik appeared to grow angry as he threw his Beitian helmet into the glowing crevasse. Baylun provided a comment, and Romik's expression was suddenly forlorn.

Daymyn walked away.

Baylun shared one last word with his brother, his hand on Romik's shoulder. Desser's krukari cousin then sent a look of compassion across the gap—as compassionate a look as Baylun's face could muster. After depositing his Beitian helmet into the crack to join Romik's, Baylun trailed after Daymyn.

Romik stood alone. His eyes were glossy above the fumes and smoke, and his shoulders slumped as he shook his head. He gave a half-hearted wave, and he turned to follow his brother.

Desser watched his cousins fade into the haze, wishing things were different.

The creatures were almost upon him, and he bolted along the fissure, running in what seemed like a westerly direction. After a hundred yards, he stopped and pulled his backpack. There were several supplies within, some having been loaded for the unsuccessful hunting trip and others picked up in Rivercross. He grabbed what food he possessed, perhaps a day's worth, and crammed it into his pouch. He then extracted his blanket and tossed it on the ground.

"There," he said to no one, and he ran.

The blanket was the first piece of the trail Desser hoped would lead the army of monsters away from his cousins. He threw down his rope as the large fissure to his left ended, and he turned south, discarding his spikes and a small hammer.

Desser maintained a quick pace, taking short rests and placing several more objects onto the path. He dropped three leather straps, his block of salt, skinning knives, and his extra clothing—a few articles at a time, starting with the Beitian uniform. He soon ran out of items and left the pack itself. All he possessed were the clothes on his back, the leather armor he wore, his sword, waterskin, and the pouch containing his rations.

The night had assuredly grown late, and the sky remained dark even after Desser passed beyond sight of the storm clouds. Fewer fissures blocked his progress, and most were easily jumped; and though several still glowed with magma, providing more heat than was comfortable, they illuminated the way and he avoided falling into the darker openings. He attempted to remain on a southerly route, but there had been no hint of the Stone Eagle Mountains to guide him, and the larger cracks forced him to change course often enough that he lost his bearings.

After another mile, Helmland quieted. The steam hissing from the crevices had calmed. Large rocks now dotted the landscape and there was no sign of the enemy, so Desser hid among a collection of boulders to find a moment's rest.

Desser awoke. It was morning, but the haze made it difficult to know the exact time. The sun seemed to be high, so it must be nearing noon. He had slept longer than he planned.

His shaky limbs lifted him from the hard ground to begin another day, and he scanned the surrounding terrain. The fissures were dark, many of them releasing wisps of smoke, and in the distance stood the Stone Eagle Mountains, now visible within the daylight. Nothing stirred.

Desser sat, feeling lost and alone. Thoughts of Romik, Daymyn, and Baylun then crossed his mind, and he took in a deep breath. Giving up was not an option. He ate what food remained in his pouch to gain some energy, and as he finished the meal, he heard marching feet back the way he had come. He stood and squinted into the northeast, where a line of dark soldiers headed his direction. Blackfoot goblins, by the size of them.

Desser ran, and a blaring horn chased after him. He was spotted. Blast! He had hoped to lead them farther before that inevitable event.

Picking up speed, Desser stumbled when his foot caught the edge of a narrow crack. He staggered a few steps and regained his balance, but then he came to a stop, his spirit sinking further. In front of him marched another force — the enemy had encircled him while he slept! Though their forms were hazy, he knew them to be taller than the goblins. Minotaurs.

There was nothing left to do, and Desser pulled his sword. He was out of food, nearly out of water, and his body was fatigued far worse than any moment he could recall, even when trekking for days through the High Riser Mountains with his father. Desser thought of his parents. He recalled the last time he saw them, when they wished him luck on his hunting expedition. They did not know where he was headed, nor where circumstances would take him afterward. He was going to die alone in an evil land, and his parents would never learn how his end had come; how he had spent his final breath killing as many vile creatures as he could. Though he would fail to overcome enough to make a difference, Desser did not care. If only there was a way to inform his parents of his demise; a way to be sure they did not sit up late, waiting for their only son to return.

Desser charged the goblins.

The enemy line was erratic, the fissures making it impossible to keep an even front, and the haze caused their bodies to waver, as if they were dancing. As Desser came upon the first goblin, its form stabilized and he brought his sword across. The small warrior failed to lift its axe in defense, and his blade cleaved its head.

Strangely, the enemy did not converge on Desser. They underestimated him, and they would pay for that mistake. He moved on to another goblin.

A pair of the dwarf-sized monsters charged, and Desser took a wound to his left leg from one while he cut down the other. He knew there to be pain, but he refused to acknowledge it, and he felled the second goblin.

A roar resonated behind Desser as he advanced on his next foe — the minotaurs were closing. He dropped three more goblins, desperate to kill as many as he could, and took wounds to his arm and ribs. He then braced himself as the flanking army arrived, but they did not strike him. In fact, they were not minotaurs, but men, and they carved into the Blackfoots' ranks.

With renewed strength, Desser slew at least a dozen goblins while the surrounding warriors savagely attacked. He knew they must be Pavish barbarians by their painted faces and the strategies they employed. They emitted war cries, swinging large axes and hammers and thrusting long spears, and showed little interest in protecting their own bodies. Several of them fell, but they held no fear and battled until the enemy was utterly destroyed.

Desser panted, exhausted beyond what he thought possible. The wounds he had taken were now in full force, and he dropped to his knees.

A large barbarian approached with angry eyes. Blood spattered most of his muscular body, and a wide, diagonal stripe of white paint ran from his right temple to his lower-left jaw. He shouted something Desser could not comprehend, and Desser shook his head. The warrior repeated the words.

"I don't understand," Desser said. "But I welcome your timely arrival. Never have I been so glad to encounter — "

A blow to the back of his head knocked him unconscious.

CHAPTER 16

DEATH FROM ABOVE

R omik stared across the wide fissure at his cousin. The explosion had isolated Desser, and an army was fast approaching.

Desser was two weeks younger than Romik, and though they were cousins, they had spent enough time together to be brothers. The hardest part of becoming Lord of Ironside Keep had been leaving Desser in Philen. Romik tried several times to convince his cousin to move into the stronghold—Desser loved the mountains, and it seemed a perfect fit. But the ranger was reluctant to live so far from his parents, Uncle Magneer and Aunt Kalette.

Romik understood, and though he missed his mother and half-brother dearly after moving away, Lorin and Baylun were in good hands with Romik's stepfather, Gruelenor. Romik never knew his own father, but many winters of training at the keep led him to love his Granduncle Arkor in Ballrik's stead, which made the transition to Lord of Ironside a bit easier.

The bond between Romik and Daymyn was different. The three-month gap separating Romik and his youngest cousin posed no issue, but throughout their youth, Daymyn spent half of every year traipsing around Philen with his mother, Aunt Della. Daymyn often told wild stories about his adventures, including thieves in dark alleys, bandits across the plains, and pirates off the coast; and though Romik and Desser doubted the plausibility of most of them, it was these stories that encouraged Romik to finance the hunting trip where this entire ordeal began.

Presently, Daymyn insisted they honor Desser's plea and leave him alone in Helmland. Why was Daymyn so willing to abandon his cousin? What if it was Daymyn on the other side? Would he want his cousins to leave *him*? Would Desser remain to help? Then Baylun placed a hand on Romik's shoulder.

"Brother," Baylun said in his raspy, spittle-filled voice. "We must go. You know Desser is only thinking of our safety. And you would do the same."

Baylun was a lot like his father, in that he did not often offer advice. And he was correct. Romik would have insisted on being left behind. After a teary-eyed wave at Desser, Romik and Baylun hastened to catch up with Daymyn, who was already thirty yards ahead.

They traversed the broken land by the light of the glowing chasms at a quickened pace, and after a mile Daymyn halted. There, they placed their hands on their knees. They had been on the move with barely any restful sleep since entering Beit, and Romik's legs quivered. But the lava had risen to the top of several fissures, and though there was no sign of pursuit, the heat was getting unbearable. They needed to keep going. Baylun and Daymyn looked at Romik, their expressions plagued by fear and worry. Romik nodded, and he led the way as they took off at a jog.

After another hundred yards, a screech echoed from the sky. It was a sound Romik had never heard before: a hollow roar ending in a hiss. He gazed back, and gliding through the air was a beast he could only assume was the animated skeleton of a dragon. He learned from his uncles about undead dragons—horrible creatures serving as mounts to Trannum's Death Lords. But never had he seen one, and none of the descriptions prepared him for what he now faced.

The monster was at least thirty feet long, and though its wings were but skeletal remains of its living days, they carried the dragon across the night sky. Fine points of blue light lit up its eye sockets, striking fear into Romik's stomach, and what appeared to be brown gas seeped from its jaws. Romik remembered horrible stories about the creatures' breath, a cloud reducing all it touched to withered corpses. His heart raced.

He shoved Baylun to the left and Daymyn to the right—his cousin landed just shy of a smoking crack. Having no time to save himself, Romik pulled his sword and braced for the attack. But the deadly vapors did not come.

The dragon passed a few feet above Romik's head, and one of its bony talons grabbed hold of his torso. The four-fingered claw yanked the breath from his body and snapped a couple of his ribs, but he retained his sword while the monster climbed.

Romik lost sight of Baylun and Daymyn as the ground retreated, and the fissures grew finer, appearing as if someone had drawn random lines on dark parchment with glowing orange ink. Though the elevation would surely kill Romik if he fell, he swung his blade, and his steel clanged off the massive leg bone. But the monster maintained its grip.

The creature descended as it circled, and Romik feared it to be returning for his brother and cousin. Pain coursed through his chest as he hacked harder at its leg, but the dragon did not seem to notice. The ground then smashed into his body and he bounced a couple of times—he was free.

Romik was beyond hurting. His limbs refused to move. He tried to speak, but he could barely draw a breath. The world then exploded, and he was weightless for several seconds until the ground met him again, just as unforgiving as the first time.

His eyes closed.

Chapter 17

Into Enemy Hands

Baylun's ears rang after the explosion at Lormin Dmurr, but he heard his cousin clearly.

"There's no saving him!" Daymyn said to Romik above the hissing fissures while Desser stood beyond a wide chasm, beckoning them to leave. "He knows it. And so do you. We must go before we're all killed."

It pained Baylun to admit it, but Daymyn was correct. And so was Desser.

Daymyn led the way, and they ran single file around the larger cracks. Baylun possessed no energy, but fear and anger kept his legs moving, as well as guilt for leaving one of his cousins behind. After what seemed like a mile, they halted to catch their breath. But the break did not last long before Romik gave a nod and they took off again.

Then came a horrible screech from the sky.

Baylun could not believe his eyes. He heard stories about Death Lords riding undead dragons, and from out of his nightmares, one of those monsters descended upon them. Romik shoved Baylun aside as the beast arrived, and when he regained his feet, Romik was gone.

Baylun gasped. "No!"

He spotted his brother clutched within a talon of the horrific monster as it sped away to the south, and his mind raced. Though his quiver held several arrows, he lost his bow in the explosion at Lormin Dmurr. Even if he had retained it, what good were arrows against a dragon of bone? He pulled his axe.

To Baylun's left, Daymyn was yelling.

"Let's go! Before it returns!"

Baylun ignored his cousin. They had already abandoned Desser. He was not leaving Romik too.

The dragon descended as it turned. Good. Let it come. But then it veered to the west and Baylun panicked. Before he knew it, his axe was spinning through the air. He did not remember throwing it, but his arms were extended and his body lurched from the momentum of heaving the weapon. His mind must have gone numb, and he had done the only thing left, as impossible as the distance was. But the runes etched across the blades took on a glow, and the axe spun faster, flying as swiftly as any arrow and disappearing into the darkness.

A flash lit up the sky, as if lightning had struck, and the massive skeleton crashed a mile away. Shortly after, an explosion followed.

"No!" Baylun gaped. What had he done? There was no way his brother survived the crash *and* the explosion. And he lost the weapon Romik gave him.

"They're coming!" Daymyn's voice snapped Baylun from his shock.

An army of minotaurs approached, and among them were a few gorillas with glowing purple eyes.

"Romik..." Baylun turned back to the west.

"Even if he lives," Daymyn shouted, "there's no way we can get to him. I'm leaving. Are you with me?"

Baylun looked at his cousin, and he saw terror, somehow mixed with growing annoyance. Meanwhile, minotaurs tramped around fissures while gorillas effortlessly jumped over the cracks. Though large themselves, the bull-men were humbled by the size of the giant apes, and a gorilla snatched a minotaur moving too slowly and ripped it in half. The sight was enough to power Baylun's legs—he did not wish to find out what it was like to be torn apart, no matter how short the experience might last. He trailed after Daymyn, who was already ten paces ahead.

Hours passed before they stopped again. Morning was upon

them, though the sun struggled to penetrate the haze, and the enemy had disappeared some time ago. Baylun wondered if he and Daymyn were the prey the monsters pursued.

"We must hide." Daymyn looked around. "I need rest. Just an hour or two."

Baylun searched the surroundings. The fissures had grown narrower, no longer showing signs of magma, and the steam rising from them was a lazy emission. The cracked, dusty land stretched far to the south and west while the chasms ended in the east, and the only trees visible were pitiful and scattered. Short of jumping into a crevasse, there was no place to conceal him and his cousin.

Daymyn shrugged. "I guess here's as good as anywhere."

They sat against a pathetic tree Baylun guessed to be a birch. White bark was peeling about its bole, and it rose no higher than seven feet, with a few leafless branches extending from its contorted trunk. Baylun faced north and Daymyn west, and they remained alert for any evidence of pursuit.

A half hour passed, and the distant buzzing they heard upon first entering Helmland returned. Other than that, Baylun detected nothing.

"I can't believe you threw your axe away." Daymyn shook his head. "That weapon was amazing. And now all you have is a knife."

Baylun stared at the hard ground.

"I know you don't like to speak," Daymyn said. "But you're going to drive me mad with your usual silence."

"Until we find Romik," Baylun muttered, "I have nothing to say."

Daymyn sighed. "We can't go back, Fang. If Romik survived, he'll seek safety. But there's no way to help him."

Rarely did Baylun react to the nickname his cousins enjoyed throwing at him anymore. On this occasion, however, anger stirred within. "My name is Baylun!"

"Okay! Okay!" Daymyn raised a hand, as if defending himself from a strike. "But you know I'm right. All we can do is keep moving. There's no turning back."

Daymyn was correct. There was nothing to be done. If the gorillas caught them... The thought brought pain to Baylun's midsection.

"Let's just get going." Baylun forced himself to his feet. He did not wish to talk about it anymore.

Daymyn stood, and he removed his Beitian helmet and tossed it at the nearest fissure large enough to claim it. It missed the mark, bouncing a few yards farther to lie upended on the dusty soil. He then dug some dried meats from his pack and sighed. "You have any food left?"

Baylun checked his stock. He possessed little more than the handful Daymyn held. He shook his head.

"Well," Daymyn said in a jovial tone, his dirty face failing to detract from his charm, "we'll have to see what gets us first. The minotaurs or starvation."

Evidently, he had not seen the gorillas.

They walked southward to conserve energy while eating the last of their food. Baylun had some water left, but no more than a day's worth, and the nearest water source was in Beit. He did not trust the lake near Lothen, however, nor the river that fed it—he was sure the plague still existed, regardless of Selanna's beliefs. Perhaps if they returned to the waterfall...

As evening arrived, the land quieted, and all that remained of the fissures were mere cracks. Mountains appeared ahead, and Baylun realized just how far they had traveled. It was an impressive feat, had he the care to give it more thought. As it was, his interest lay in the concealment the rugged terrain might provide.

They continued through the night, resting often, but the breaks never lasted more than half an hour. By midday of the following day, the mountains provided rising land and stones of various sizes. Baylun located a grouping of enormous boulders atop a hill capable of hiding them, and amid the rocks they discovered a pair of skeletons, one large and one small. Both were dressed in tattered animal skins.

"What do you make of this?" asked Daymyn.

The larger skeleton was of a man at least six feet tall, and the smaller was a female, a foot shorter. The male sat against a boulder, cradling the woman on his lap.

"Come on, Baylun." Daymyn lowered his brow. "Do what you and Desser do. Look at the dirt."

Baylun sighed. It was pointless, but he acquiesced. "It's a man and a woman." He inspected the ground. "The tracks are almost entirely faded, but there's only one set. From the man."

"Maybe the woman's prints are too old," suggested Daymyn.

Baylun shook his head. That was not the case. From the impressions, the man carried the woman, and from faded stains on the clothing, he had been bleeding. Perhaps both of them were injured.

"They came here to hide," Baylun said. "They were wounded, and they died here."

Daymyn shrugged. "Their secret's safe with me." He sat across from the corpses. "As long as they don't mind the company."

Baylun felt sorry for the two. Who were they? Where were they from? Most of all, how did they get here?

"Have a look." Daymyn eyed the tattered packs lying next to the skeletons. "Maybe they have something useful."

It was wrong to rob the dead, but Baylun and his cousin were desperately low on supplies. He rummaged through the belongings. There was no food to speak of and the waterskin was dry. The female possessed an empty quiver, but no bow. Then Baylun noticed a long wooden handle. It ran beside the male skeleton's leg and beneath a part of the boulder. He pulled on the haft and saw a hammerhead at its other end. It was a maul. Not an exceptional weapon by any means, but it was better than the knife strapped to Baylun's waist.

"What have you there?" Daymyn craned his neck to see what Baylun held. "*There's* a spark of hope. Now I won't have to protect you."

Baylun gave a wry smile. A *spark of hope*? It was just a hammer.

But Daymyn was correct, and Baylun felt more secure with the haft in his hands.

"You take first watch." Daymyn sat back and close his eyes. "Wake me in a couple of hours."

Baylun stood, staring at the maul. It was a heavy weapon, but he could handle it. He looked at the skeleton and wished he could thank the warrior.

With a deep breath, he moved about the rocks to keep guard.

Baylun was not sure how long he slept. The sun was still hard to read, but it must have been at least a few hours. Daymyn, who was on guard, dozed nearby. Baylun sighed and pulled the hammer.

His limbs hurt and his legs shook, but he forced them into action and scanned the northern terrain. There was no sign of minotaurs or gorillas.

He reflected on the latter. Had they truly been gorillas? He had seen the animals a few times at a distance while passing through Fendora, but never did they appear so large. The purple eyes proved them to be something different, and in the glow of the fissures, their bodies had appeared hairless and their skin glossy.

There was a noise, not far to the east. Baylun crouched, and he crept around the boulders until he spied four humans relieving themselves on nearby rocks. They wore Beitian uniforms, appearing much like the soldiers he and Daymyn followed from Darum Carumbor.

Baylun returned to rouse his cousin, putting his finger to his lips. Daymyn nodded in understanding. Baylun then led the way around the boulders, and Daymyn smiled upon spotting the soldiers. The men were engaged in a competition while they completed their task.

"Think you can handle two of them?" Daymyn whispered without taking his eyes from the Beitians.

What was Daymyn thinking? What if killing these men brought the attention of an army? Baylun wished to voice his concern, but

Daymyn had already drawn his blade and crept forward. Baylun shook his head and followed—once Daymyn set his mind on a course of action, there was no stopping him. They would just have to deal with the consequences, whatever that entailed.

The nearest soldier detected their presence as they approached to within twenty feet, and he shouted a warning. Daymyn struck swiftly, gashing the man's chest before the Beitians pulled their weapons.

Baylun charged, swinging the maul overhead and onto the next opponent. The man made the mistake of trying to parry, and the thick haft bore down, barely losing any momentum. The hammerhead crashed into the Beitian with enough force to crush his skull twice over.

Baylun turned in time to sidestep a thrusting blade, and he swung his maul low, snapping the attacker's leg. The soldier fell with a cry of pain, but Baylun felt no pity as thoughts of Romik fueled his mounting rage. He twirled his weapon, smashing the man's face in a brutal manner, and the sound almost made him gag.

To Baylun's right, his cousin defeated the final Beitian with a thrust into the stomach.

"Good." Daymyn nodded. "You didn't bloody the uniforms much." He began undressing the corpse with the smashed-in face.

Baylun was confused. "What are you doing?"

"Same thing the elves had us do," Daymyn replied. "We'll use their uniforms to pass through." He noted Baylun's hesitation and ceased in his actions. "Do you really think we'll get by Darum Carumbor without being spotted? Look at what the explosion did to the uniforms we're wearing. They'll never do."

Baylun scanned the open land. To the northeast, a large group of soldiers were setting up camp, far enough away to have missed the screams of their comrades. He estimated there to be two hundred in all. And just as the force that marched to Lormin Dmurr, they posted no watch.

How had an army approached without alerting Baylun or

Daymyn? How long did Baylun and his cousin sleep? They were lucky to have gone undiscovered.

"Fang!"

Baylun turned with a finger to his lips, pointing at the gathering.

Daymyn moved closer to have a look, now half dressed in the dead soldier's uniform. He smiled. "Just as I hoped. This is going to be easy."

Easy? Nothing had been easy since Baylun left his house for the hunting trip. He sighed and began undressing the man with the crushed skull.

The gear was a tight fit, but it would work. The helmet, however, was covered in blood, cartilage, and bone fragments, and it bore a large dent. Baylun held it up. He doubted he could squeeze it onto his head. He noticed Daymyn was wearing a helmet from one of his own victims, both of whom possessed wounds to their torsos. Baylun retrieved the helmet from Daymyn's other slain opponent, feeling a little foolish.

"They'll know we don't belong," Baylun said as he buckled the last belt into place. "Especially me." He looked at Daymyn. "At Lormin Dmurr, the krukari were with the hobgoblins. Not the humans."

Daymyn gave a wry smile. "Did you learn nothing from Eraim and Selanna? We'll follow at a distance. Then, when we get the chance, we head for the secret path. They probably won't notice a couple of soldiers wandering into the south. They haven't even realized these four are missing!"

Probably? Not a great plan. But Baylun could think of nothing better.

The Beitians' waterskins were half full, and Baylun and Daymyn combined the contents to fill their own canteens. They also found pouches of dried meats and breads and removed them as well. Baylun balked at the containers of anti-plague elixir, but he thought better of it and they each grabbed one.

"By the way," Daymyn said. "You used that weapon like you've owned it for years. Quite impressive, really."

Baylun pondered his cousin's words. The battle had happened so fast that he failed to realize how easily he swung the hammer about. The maul was heavy and awkward, yet he wielded it without difficulty. Still, it was not his axe.

The next task was hiding the bodies. Baylun did not search long before finding a place to the southwest where enough rocks existed to bury them. The chore took a while, and the sky grew dark, and in all that time no one came looking for the dead soldiers.

Baylun breathed a little easier.

After dusting themselves off, they returned to the site where they fought the Beitians. Several fires burned within the enemy encampment below, but nothing moved in the darkness that Baylun could detect. He took the first shift while Daymyn rested, keeping watch on the army as well as the surrounding territory. Halfway through the night, he woke Daymyn and settled in for some sleep.

Baylun was awakened by Daymyn. The sky was brightening beneath the haze and the Beitians were breaking camp.

They made one last check of their gear to make sure everything was in place. Then, just as they had followed the force into Helmland, Baylun and Daymyn trailed after the group, hanging back far enough to avoid detection. Baylun saw no other enemies throughout the march, and he and Daymyn halted when the squadron camped again, each of them taking a shift to guard the night.

With the morning they continued. They walked another day, and as dusk arrived, Baylun spotted the glowing windows of Darum Carumbor within the encroaching darkness. The soldiers appeared to head for the tower, but Baylun wondered if they would continue along the road and back into Beit. Then came the sound of pounding hooves.

Three mounted warriors approached from the north. The riders wore black armor, and pointing skyward were short, dark lances.

Baylun thought of making a break for the distant mountains, but they would never outrun the horses. Daymyn stared at the soldiers with calm eyes.

"What are you two doing?" one rider demanded as they pulled their mounts to a stop. The man spoke the common tongue without the hint of an accent, and his light hair and fair skin suggested he hailed from Moclen, or perhaps Urell Coast. "Get your hides into the tower! Or you shall taste my Dun lance!"

Baylun did not know what a Dun lance was, and fighting three mounted soldiers would not be easy. But now that he and Daymyn had rested, he felt they stood a decent chance of victory. He reached for the maul, but Daymyn's words froze his hand.

"Very sorry, sir! We were, shall we say, relieving ourselves, and the contingent left us behind. I guess we weren't missed."

"Shut your mouth and get in the tower!" the rider hissed.

"Right away, sir!" Daymyn shot Baylun a glance, and he ran toward Darum Carumbor.

Baylun took one last look at the riders before catching up with his cousin.

What were they doing?

CHAPTER 18

RETURN TO LOTHEN

Eraim removed the misfitted helmet and shook her head clear. The explosion had sent her tumbling and her body hurt, but she was more concerned for her companions. Lormin Dmurr was a silhouette on the horizon, and hundreds of fissures had taken up permanent residence, several of which emitted orange light. To the south, the cracks extended into the dark, desolate land, and many were taking on glows of their own while others issued hissing steam, adding to the already growing heat.

There was movement to the left. It was Selanna.

Eraim rushed over. "Are you all right?"

Selanna sat up. Her singed hair dangled across her face and her robes were even more tattered and scorched than before. She gave a forced smile, the blood covering her chin now mixed with dirt.

"I have taken part in more explosions than I care to today." Selanna's chuckle became a cough. "But I am well enough." She cleared her throat and looked around. "Where are the others?"

Eraim shook her head. "I did not know which way was up, let alone where the others were thrown. We best begin looking for them."

She helped Selanna to stand.

They did not travel far before discovering Kiryanna. The marteese was unconscious and blood coated the front and right side of her scalp. Just as with Selanna, her Beitian helmet was missing. Eraim tapped on the warrior's cheek while Selanna continued the search.

"Eraim!" Selanna shouted. "We cannot stay!"

Eraim looked to see what Selanna had found. A horde of dark shapes were moving south from the compound. Her heart sank.

Kiryanna awoke, and she was suddenly overcome with panic. She glanced at Eraim and searched the landscape. "Where's B—Brem?"

Eraim pulled the marteese to her feet. "We have not seen him. But we must be on our way. The armies of Lormin Dmurr approach."

Kiryanna shook her head, almost hysterical. "No! I cannot!"

"There is no time to look," Selanna said firmly, having returned to Eraim's side. "To stay is to die."

"Perhaps he is all right." Eraim did her best to sound positive. "He may be seeking safety at this moment."

Kiryanna stared at Eraim with angry eyes before scanning the area. The marteese shook her head, exhaling her frustrations.

"The army is coming," Selanna said. "We are leaving now. I hope you will join us."

"Fine!" Kiryanna growled. "And his blood shall be on your heads!"

Eraim shared a glance with Selanna, understanding her companion's urgency. They did not need to leave for the sake of their own lives. They needed to inform others of their discovery. If they died, evil would be allowed to grow into... Eraim feared to finish the thought.

They moved southeast, slowing often to allow Selanna brief periods of rest—Eraim's friend was in an awful state. The lava-filled crevasses lasted another half a mile, and a mile farther the chasms ended. After that, the air cooled and there existed few obstacles. The glow of the fissures then diminished until Eraim could see them no more, and she and her small group continued in the dark, relying on their elfish sight.

Several hours passed with no sign of pursuit, so Eraim halted to tend to her companions' injuries, and Selanna summoned a small light to assist her. Kiryanna exhibited a dozen cuts, though the bleeding had stopped. Selanna was scratched, burned, and bruised in so many locations… It was amazing she had kept the pace. Fishing through her pack, Eraim pulled what healing herbs and medicines she had, all the while keeping an eye and ear on the surroundings. Other than Selanna and Kiryanna, nothing moved or made a sound. She went to work, mixing the ingredients, and she could not help observing the conversation between Selanna and the marteese warrior, the latter's gaze fixed upon the northwest.

"I know Brem means a lot to you." Selanna placed a sympathetic hand on Kiryanna's arm. "But the enemy will not relent. We cannot go back. Not yet."

"Do not speak to me as if I am naïve!" Kiryanna ripped the tattered Beitian cloak loose and cast it aside.

Eraim sighed at the thought of leaving a trail behind, but she said nothing.

Kiryanna eyed them both. "I realize we have witnessed something terrible. And word must reach those that might fight it." Her attention returned to the northwest. "The only reason I remain is to make sure you two get out alive and do just that. Then I shall return, come what may."

"You are in love," Eraim said.

A tear rolled down Kiryanna's cheek. "My life was empty. But now, I have purpose and understanding, and…" She bowed her head. "I do not think I would call it love. But with time… Every moment I spend in thought beckons me to leave you and find him."

Eraim was a bit confused. Perhaps the marteese had not known Brem as long as she assumed.

She returned to her task and treated their wounds. Selanna offered a grateful smile; Kiryanna refused to make eye contact. Eraim and Selanna then discarded their Beitian attire—there was no point in keeping the ragged garments—and Eraim scattered them, hoping to confuse anyone tracking her and her companions.

"We best get moving," Selanna said once Eraim finished, and the magical light faded.

They walked through the remainder of the night and into the

morning with no sign of the enemy, nor anything else outside the pitiful trees. Eraim estimated there to be a bit more than a day before they reached Lothen Forest, and she suggested they rest their legs, so they stopped and consumed what little food and water they possessed. Exhaustion beckoned Eraim to lie down, a weariness reflected in Selanna's and Kiryanna's eyes, but after an hour they pushed on.

That night, Eraim's attention snapped to the starless sky. "I hear wings! To the west."

She searched, but saw only darkness. Then two points of blue light appeared, followed by an enormous beast. A dragon of bone! Eraim's heart raced. She had thought—or rather hoped—they had all been destroyed.

The monster eyed them as it flew overhead. It then took a wide arc to return from the south, and it released its sickly yellow breath. Eraim scrambled from its path while Kiryanna stood defiantly with her sword, and Selanna waved her hands to the side, summoning a wind to disperse the evil cloud before it arrived.

Selanna turned as the monster sped by, her eyes narrowing while she tracked its flight. Eraim knew her friend to be exhausted, but Selanna found the energy to launch three balls of fire. The flaming spheres raced across the sky, striking the dragon in the head, ribs, and tail; and after the explosions subsided, there was a crash in the distance.

Eraim released her breath. "Well done!"

Selanna pursed her lips. "I am not so sure. Who knows what I have just alerted to our location?"

The relief Eraim felt vanished.

They resumed their trek, turning due east, and after several miles they stopped to rest. Though the healing herbs had nearly finished mending their injuries, no one found sleep, so they passed the time taking inventory of their gear. Selanna had very little. Nothing disturbed them, and they moved on once the sky brightened.

By midday, Darum Carumbor was in sight, sitting within the

permanent haze. Eraim saw no activity, and she led the way toward Lothen Forest, remaining south of the faded road. With a couple hundred yards yet to go, a dozen mounted soldiers exited the structure. The riders wore the same black armor as those that occupied the tower days earlier, and they carried short, dark lances. The horses broke into a run, heading right for Eraim and her companions.

Eraim turned to the forest. It would be close, but they could win the race to the trees. Her heart then sank when another rider emerged from the woodland. It was a trap!

"We are cut off!" she shouted as she pulled Mithkahr. "But I shall clear a path."

She charged the single horseman as fast as her exhausted legs could carry her, and the closer she drew, the larger the warrior and horse became. With only sixty feet between them, she noticed two large swords strapped to the rider's back, and he and his mount were suddenly as big as...

Eraim gasped. "Vecnor!"

Though Vecnor's face lay hidden by his full helm, Eraim knew it was him. He extended his giant gauntlet as he rode past and scooped her onto his saddle.

"Your arrival is most timely!" Eraim's feelings of hope soared as they raced toward Selanna and Kiryanna.

Six of the enemy mounts were without riders, and the animals fled to the tower while the unhorsed warriors encircled Selanna. Kiryanna had managed to climb atop a horse still bearing an evil soldier, and her golden blade viciously entered the man's back. Dumping the corpse and taking control of the animal, the marteese turned to oppose the other mounted warriors.

Umbarc sped toward the horsemen, and Vecnor released the reins while drawing both swords — Eraim had to duck to avoid the scabbards. With unwavering balance, he steered away a lance with one sword and thrust the other deep into the soldier's chest. The warrior fell from the horse with a muffled cry.

Two more riders approached, and while Vecnor focused on one, Eraim climbed to her feet and faced the other. Leaping from Umbarc, she struck down the soldier with Mithkahr, and she rolled to soften the blow as she landed on the hard soil. She then rose to her knee to check on her companions.

Selanna had taken care of the unhorsed warriors, evidenced by the smoking suits of armor lying around her, and Vecnor defeated the rider he faced. Kiryanna timed a swing perfectly to knock the point of a lance into the ground, and the dark weapon lifted the soldier from his saddle. He teetered only a moment, and the marteese decapitated him.

Vecnor moved on to defeat the final horseman, but another score of riders issued from Darum Carumbor.

"More are coming!" Eraim shouted.

Sheathing Mithkahr, she grabbed her bow. She hesitated to use the weapon against heavy armor, for the plates were hard to penetrate, and to make matters worse, only a dozen of her arrows had survived the explosion at Lormin Dmurr. But she needed to reduce the number of foes before the melee started. She dropped two soldiers as they began their charge, each requiring a couple of arrows, and trained her next shot... The target fell before she released the bowstring, pierced by a single arrow. Then another fell. The missiles had come from Lothen Forest!

Eraim's heart rose. The Guardians were alive. She saw no elves, but it must be them, and she dropped two more riders while the Guardians impaled four others. The remaining soldiers retreated to Darum Carumbor.

"To the trees!" shouted Vecnor.

Selanna sat upon Umbarc in front of Vecnor, and he ran the massive steed past Eraim, scooping her up a second time and placing her behind him. Kiryanna followed on the tower horse. While they rode swiftly toward Lothen, the low droning of a horn shook the ground for several seconds.

"They prepare another attack," Selanna said.

206

"That may not matter." Eraim could not contain her excitement. "The Guardians are here! Did you not see their...?"

A single figure holding a long bow stepped from behind a tree. It was no taller than Selanna and wore a black cloak, and the hood disallowed any view of its face.

"Eslimil," Eraim muttered as they came to a stop before the archer.

Tux lowered his hood. "Sorry to disappoint you." His horse exited the trees and he mounted.

Vecnor removed his helmet and hooked it to his saddle. He then ran his hand through his sweaty, dark hair and turned to Kiryanna. "Leave that horse and ride with Tux. That animal has been trained, and we cannot trust it."

"You know Tux?" Eraim asked Vecnor, casting a sidelong glance at the gray elf.

"Words are better saved for later," Vecnor said. "Let's move."

Kiryanna dismounted, but she did not join Tux. She gazed back into Helmland, where a squadron of archers and another score of lancers were exiting Darum Carumbor.

"What are you waiting for?" Tux held little compassion.

"I did what I said I would do." Kiryanna looked at Eraim and Selanna. "Now I will return. Dead or alive, I must find him."

"Just as you worry for him," Selanna said, "my heart aches for the young warriors that traveled with us. They are children of friends of mine, and I must explain to their parents what has transpired. The only way to help them, if they still live, is to return with a proper force. And the only way to avenge them if things are otherwise remains the same. In the short while that we have known you, you have proven yourself an excellent warrior. I do not believe Brem would wish you to throw your skills away, nor your life. So please, come with us. If not for yourself, then for him."

Kiryanna gazed west, taking in a slow, deep breath. The dark force was crossing the road. She grabbed Tux's outstretched hand and climbed onto the saddle.

Eraim was relieved. But she could not help noticing the glare meant for Selanna. It was one of hatred. Did Kiryanna blame Selanna?

There was no time to dwell on such matters as Vecnor urged Umbarc beneath the trees.

They ventured deep into the woodland, unceasing until dusk arrived. There was no sign of pursuit. Fear then crept into Eraim's heart as the air became deathly cold, and for a moment the tree trunks appeared wicked, as if haunting faces had developed within the creases of their bark.

Selanna looked at the darkening sky through a window in the canopy of leaves. "I was wondering when they would arrive."

The terrible screech of an undead dragon echoed through Lothen, and the branches stirred as the beast passed only inches above the trees, traveling from east to west. Eraim glimpsed the monster, as well as the armored figure atop its back. The Death Lord continued west, taking the chill with it, and the forest returned to normal.

"I do not think it saw us." Eraim was more hopeful than certain.

"We best move a bit farther," said Vecnor. "If the Death Lords are arriving, it's only a matter of time before dunarchins follow."

"Dunarchins?" Eraim found it hard to breathe. Other than Selanna speaking of the undead firstborns to the Council of Wizards, Eraim had not thought about them for years. But now, memories flooded her: zombies, ghouls, wraiths, and dunarchins. All those decades of battling the necromancer, the undead, the Death Lords... It was supposed to be over.

Vecnor gave her a sympathetic eye, followed by a wink and a smile. Normally that would have warmed her heart, but on this occasion she found no comfort.

The night grew darker with every step, and after a couple of miles, Vecnor came to a halt.

"A short rest should not prove ill," he said.

Eraim noticed the slightest shake of the head from Eslimil aimed at Vecnor. The imposter did not agree. But the gray elf dismounted, and the others did the same.

Vecnor worked well in the darkness for a human. He set down his pack after withdrawing fresh blankets for everyone, and he placed his near a tree, avoiding any underbrush that might have otherwise made him stumble. Eraim always wondered about the tall warrior's adeptness, and this time she decided to pry.

"Are you human?"

He ceased in his actions to stare at her.

"Or an elf?"

Vecnor frowned. "What is that supposed to mean?"

"Nothing," Eraim said coyly. "But I am never sure if I address Vecnor the human, or the wood chopping—"

The return of the screaming wind interrupted the forest. Eraim could not believe she had forgotten about it. Vecnor and Tux grew alarmed, but Selanna halted them with a shout.

"Hold!" Selanna put her hands up as Vecnor and Tux headed for their horses. "Everyone be still."

Vecnor held a questioning gaze, but he complied. Tux grabbed his reins with a look of doubt.

Selanna closed her eyes while the gust played with her tattered robes and tossed her singed hair about. Then came the whispers. She heard words forming again, but this time they did not call for alarm.

"Come..." the whisper beckoned. "Come with us."

"Come..." many voices echoed. "Come..."

Selanna opened her eyes. "They want us to follow them."

"Who?" Vecnor's hand went to one of the swords on his back.

"I am not sure," Selanna said. "But they did not lead us astray the first time. We must go before they vanish."

The wind moved to the north, and though it was not the direction she and her companions needed to travel, Selanna followed without hesitation. After several hundred yards, the gust ceased its northward movement and swirled upward and downward. The trees swayed and groaned while their leaves thrashed about.

"Here," the voice whispered. "Here you are safe. Here you must sleep."

"Here you must sleep," voices echoed.

The wind subsided and everything stilled.

"We are safe here." Selanna scanned the ground. "We must sleep."

"I know not of whom you were speaking to," said Tux, "but talking trees in an evil land..."

"It is not the trees." Selanna turned to the gray elf. "The voices spoke elfish."

"Still," Vecnor frowned, "I'm not so sure we should sleep."

"They said we *must* sleep." Selanna looked at Vecnor. "Not that we *can* or *should*." She considered the large man. One such as he would never comply with the request, especially not when issued by a ghostly wind. Besides that, the ghosts said *you* must sleep. Did they mean her? "*I* will sleep. Perhaps then I might learn more."

Selanna could see that Eraim held doubts. Kiryanna showed no emotion beyond the daggers shooting from her eyes. Vecnor sighed, and he dropped the few blankets he had evidently gathered before joining the pursuit of the wind.

"Very well," he said. "Get as comfortable as you can. I'll take first watch. Then Tux. From the looks of you three, you should *all* sleep."

Eraim was insulted. Why would Vecnor issue orders for the Tux imposter to guard? She was the perfect guard, and Vecnor knew it. At least *she* did not pretend to be some legendary figure. And why did Vecnor appear so comfortable in the trickster's company? Were they friends?

Vecnor offered food and water from his pack while Tux disappeared into the branches of a tall maple tree. Eraim accepted the bread and berries, and it did not escape her notice that they tasted like home. But she made no inquiries on the subject—she knew she would get an Elgarroth-like answer. After the meal was finished, Selanna and Kiryanna laid down while Vecnor walked the perimeter.

Eraim crept after the large warrior.

"Vecnor?" she said as she neared, so as not to alarm him.

He glanced her way before returning his attention to the forest, where the darkness should have been beyond his ability to penetrate. "It's good to see you."

A brief smile crossed her lips. "It has been too long... as usual. But I must ask you about Tux. Do you *know* him?"

The warrior nodded. "I've known him for some time. Don't worry. You can trust him."

"But is it really *him*?"

Vecnor's grin stretched to one side. "The legend himself."

Eraim frowned. "But the tales are old. And he appears as young as I."

Vecnor shrugged.

"Then again," Eraim added, "age probably holds little meaning for you."

Vecnor scrunched his brow, as if considering the comment. "I've never put much thought to it. All elves appear young to me."

Eraim held a wry smile. "Of course." Another Elgarroth-like response. She then returned to her query. "What *is* he? He appears as one from Orlenfel, but he is shorter, like my kin."

"He's both."

Eraim stared in disbelief. Gray elves never mingled with elves of other clans, unless it was to share information.

"Take my word for it." Vecnor's expression left no room for jest. "Tux is trustworthy." He smiled. "Now, you really should get some sleep."

"All right." She turned toward the campsite. "But if you hear *anything*, you are to wake me. I do not want you getting in over your head." She gazed back at him. "And we are not finished with this conversation."

Vecnor looked as if he wished to say something. Instead, he gave a single nod.

CHAPTER 19

THE BLACK STICK

Selanna awoke with a start. She thought she heard a distant scream. It was still nighttime, and Eraim and Kiryanna were sleeping. Vecnor sat against a tree with his eyes shut, and one of his swords rested on his lap.

It must have been a dream.

Leaves rustled, as if something approached, and Selanna stood. She was about to voice a warning when she spotted several tall elves. They were transparent, like white lights in the dark forest, and passed through trees without a misstep. One stopped in front of Selanna, gazing at her with bright, noncorporeal eyes.

"Are you...?" Selanna stammered.

The elf's jaw dropped, as if surprised. "We are the Guardians." His voice was hollow—the same voice that whispered earlier. "I do not know how it is that you can hear me, but I am greatly relieved that it is so."

"What has happened?" Selanna asked.

"I cannot stay long," the ghost looked over his shoulder, "for evil approaches, and it will take all of our strength to keep them away."

Selanna had so many questions. Why were they ghosts? How was it she could see them? What evil approached? She nodded, leaving her queries unasked.

"As to our demise," he said, "it was an army of dunarchins. They invaded Lothen over thirty years ago, in numbers too great to withstand."

Selanna gasped. Thirty *years* ago?

"The dunarchins scoured the forest," the image continued,

"searching for an item given to our keeping long before my time. They could not find it, and they departed for Helmland. But they returned with reinforcements... Blackfoot goblins. They resumed their search, still without success, but they would not give up. They returned again and again—"

The ghost flickered as he looked to the south with wide eyes. Selanna wished to inquire as to what the item was, but his head snapped back and he spoke in haste.

"Time grows short, so let me say that they found the item at last. I know not what its properties are, only that we were to protect it at all costs. It was taken only recently, but somehow has retur—"

The image faded, as did the other Guardians.

"Wait!" Selanna searched the trees. They were gone.

The ground shuddered, as if enormous animals thundered through the forest. Suddenly, Selanna's vision pierced the woodland, and she saw six gorilla-like creatures rambling toward her company without a care for the forest's well-being. Their skin was a deep black color, lacking body hair, and their eyes were made of hideous purple vapors. They bore no weapons, but their arms appeared capable of rending an ogre.

"Mees! Mees!"

Selanna's warning went unnoticed. Not even Eraim stirred.

"Vecnor!"

He did not wake.

Selanna rushed over to shake the large warrior, but her hand passed through his shoulder. She was a ghost, just like the Guardians. She turned to her blanket. Her body rested peacefully on the forest floor.

Gazing back, Selanna saw the gorillas surrounded by swirling winds—rather, by the Guardians. The ghostly forms swarmed the creatures with transparent swords, and the apes swung enormous fists. To Selanna's surprise, the attacks did not pass harmlessly through the combatants—the phantom weapons tore through the dark flesh and the fists brought visible pain. The Guardians did not yield, and a gorilla disappeared in a black-and-violet cloud that shriveled leaves and caused branches to rot. Then another monster vanished. And another. Soon, the gorillas were gone. But so were the Guardians.

The forest fell silent.

Selanna sat up with a gasp.

Vecnor opened his eyes, his grip tightening on the hilt of his sword. "What is it?"

His voice stirred Eraim, and she pulled Mithkahr as she stood. The blade did not emit its red glow, so no evil was near. Kiryanna awoke, and Tux dropped from the branches.

Selanna shook her head and looked around, wondering if it had been a dream. Then she noticed a black stick lying beside her blanket. It was two feet long and perfectly smooth. Had it been there all along? Though shadows obscured it before, she knew it to be the item Trannum displayed atop Lormin Dmurr, and again before the gates. How had it gotten here? She realized she held her breath, and she released it.

"We are not safe here any longer." She kept her focus on the stick. "Do not ask me how I know, for I do not think you would believe me. But our protection has diminished."

Selanna used her blanket to wrap the stick, careful to avoid contact. Vecnor's eyes never left her while she secured it in one of Umbarc's saddlebags, but he posed no questions.

"Let's go," he said once she finished her task.

Selanna and Eraim rejoined Vecnor on Umbarc while Kiryanna rode with Tux, and they headed southeast in silence. They maintained a steady pace, and after refreshing the horses at a creek while the sun illuminated the canopy, Vecnor turned due east.

Selanna kept watch on the ground, trees, and sky, but there were no signs of dunarchins, gorillas, nor any other collection of enemy forces she had witnessed over the past week. Had she seen the gorilla creatures correctly? What were they? Did they come through one of Trannum's portals? She had more questions than answers, and her desperation to speak with Elgarroth deepened.

They soon left the cover of Lothen Forest and began the journey to the river. Upon reaching the slow-flowing water, the odor of the animal corpses and dead fish was a hundred times worse than before. Selanna's heart then sank when she detected the approach of pounding hooves.

"Mees!" Eraim voiced as Selanna opened her mouth to do the same.

Tux and Vecnor turned their mounts to the north, where a group of horsemen appeared.

"A score of horses," Tux said. "But only half bear riders."

A second later, Selanna saw he was correct. How did his vision travel farther than her own?

Vecnor unsheathed a sword, and Eraim and Tux lifted arrows to their bowstrings. Selanna observed Tux's weapon for the first time, and she marveled briefly at the smooth gray wood. It was unlike any bow she had ever seen. She also noticed his arrows were nearly twice the length of Eraim's.

"Wezlok?" Eraim drew Selanna's attention back to the horsemen.

The distant mounts came to a halt, and the riders stared at Selanna's party. Wezlok was in the lead. Selanna had not seen the Lorian wizard since he left Castle Lambrak over twenty years ago, following Trannum's supposed demise.

"Vayla?" Eraim lowered her bow.

Selanna spotted the paladin. Vayla... Daughter of Cavalor. Granddaughter of Merssa. The last time Selanna had spoken to Vayla was in New Palidur, when the young lady first reported to the Holy City for training. Since then, it seemed Vayla was too busy for guests. What was she doing here? Did Cavalor know?

Both groups rode toward each other. As they neared, Selanna noticed all but Vayla and Wezlok bore injuries.

"Vayla!" Eraim hailed the paladin. "Why are you here? It is not safe."

"I am on New Palidur business." Vayla's grim expression revealed not a hint of a smile, nor relief at seeing friendly faces. "And of course it isn't safe. Why are *you* here? And what *happened* to you?"

Selanna ignored the last question—she must be a sight. New Palidur business? She should have known. But why would Montac send one so newly promoted? One so much younger than other paladins? Why would Vayla willingly enter a plague-infested land? Perhaps Palidur did not know about the plague. As Selanna observed Vayla, her heart saddened. It was as if she was staring at Merssa. Of course Montac was aware of the plague, and of course Vayla had been willing to walk into danger. She was more like her grandmother every day.

"We all agree it's not safe," Vecnor said. "So let's leave this place in haste."

Vayla gave a single nod.

Wezlok showed no emotion.

"At last!" Kiryanna dropped from Tux's horse and headed toward the riderless mounts. "Mind if I take one of these?"

A soldier holding the reins of a spare animal looked at Vayla. After receiving a nod from the young paladin, he relinquished the horse.

Selanna followed the marteese's lead, and she picked a Batorn steed for herself. Though not as nice as Dandi, the breed had never disappointed her before.

Eraim climbed to Vecnor's front and remained on Umbarc.

Vayla had hoped Wezlok was mistaken, but it was not so. It *was* Selanna and Eraim. How was it the two just happened to be in Beit?

Vayla went to great lengths to avoid the elves. They visited Castle Lambrak every year throughout her youth, back when they could make a child laugh. But things changed once Vayla turned fourteen, and she busied herself training extra hard with the zhokards whenever the mage and little thief were present. And it was strange how often they could be found in the Holy City. Even now, Selanna and Eraim envisioned Vayla's grandmother, and the large man sitting behind Eraim on the giant horse mirrored their gazes. Vayla detested their pity-filled expressions. At least the half-elf in the golden armor appeared disinterested, and the gray elf with the bizarre eyes seemed more concerned with their surroundings than Vayla's appearance.

"We are headed to a secret pass," Vayla informed Selanna. "It connects —"

"We follow the same route." Eraim interrupted. "But how do *you* know of it?"

Vayla turned to Wezlok. He stared back, offering no help. In Benzon he mentioned, *"...a path known only to the Guardians,"* or some such nonsense. But now he had nothing to say.

"In any case," Selanna said, "we shall ride together. It will be safer."

To this, Vayla agreed.

They followed the river toward the Stone Eagle Mountains at a decent pace. The odor was horrible, but Vayla ignored it, and either no one else smelled the rotting carcasses, or everyone was too weary to make mention of it. It did not escape Vayla's notice that the white-eyed elf sat atop a Batorn horse, or that the large warrior's steed was surely from the Andria region. She found the image of the big man and Eraim odd; like a father giving his child a ride across the country.

Well before evening, the mountains loomed ahead, as did a tall waterfall. Eraim and the huge warrior led the way through the foothills in what seemed to be random directions, but then a trail suddenly appeared. As they neared a pond fed by the falls, Eraim murmured to the man and he halted the group.

"We will have to turn the horses loose," Eraim said. "The way ahead is not for them."

Vayla glared at the elf. Star was a gift from her father, and she had no intentions of losing the mare.

"If I may." Macurak rode forward, still favoring his side. "Is there no other path? We are wounded and weary. To ask our men to walk through the mountains would be impossible under the circumstances."

"We only need to walk for a couple of days," Eraim said. "There are horses waiting to carry us beyond that."

"And I have healing herbs that should help." The white-eyed elf drew a frown from Eraim.

Macurak glanced at Vayla, an apology etched on his face. She appreciated his attempt, but she would take care of it.

"I'll not leave Star behind."

"I know how special animal friends can be." Eraim exhibited pity. "But —"

"I shall look after Vayla's horse." Wezlok finally spoke. "Do what you must with the others."

"Your mare will be fine," the large warrior behind Eraim said in his handsomely deep voice. "Do not think for one moment that I plan to abandon my steed. You can trust Umbarc to deliver Star to you." He patted the horse's enormous neck.

Trust? What trust should Vayla have for this stranger and his mount?

Wezlok moved next to Vayla. "Worry not," he said quietly before addressing Selanna. "Star shall accompany us."

Selanna's eyes narrowed on Wezlok. "Very well."

"At the very least, you will want to dismount." Eraim climbed down from the giant horse, and everyone followed her lead.

Now that the tall warrior stood, Vayla realized he was the largest man she had ever seen. He was much bigger than Grand Paladin Montac. She could only imagine the terror one might feel when faced with his wrath — that is, one lacking Cafior's Favor. After grabbing several packs from his saddle, he muttered something to Umbarc, and the mount whinnied and nodded. Vayla then stared in wonder as the horse appeared to speak to the others, and they trotted off to the north like a pack of wild animals — Star attempted to follow, but

Vayla held the reins tight.

Eraim led the way, and they ascended rocky steps to the right of the waterfall. It was not a particularly arduous climb, but Vayla's men struggled at times, especially Macurak, and she assisted them as best she could while leading her mare. Dinnertime came and went as they reached the top, but they moved on, veering south and leaving the falls behind.

The trail disappeared after fifty yards, but Eraim remained firm in her directions. The sound of rushing water then diminished to a distant roar as shadows stretched across the mountainside, and a dark, narrow path appeared between towering walls of stone. Selanna held aloft her fist, and when she opened it, four small lights rose to hover overhead and illuminate the way.

Debris plagued the trail, presenting difficulties for Star, but the mare was a smart animal and did not slow their progress. After another half hour, Eraim entered a clearing surrounded by tall rocks and dropped her gear. It was obvious the area had been used many times for camping, but it was surely not intended to house horses and Star gave it a cramped feeling. Vayla did not care. She led her mount to the far edge and pulled Star's brush from a saddlebag.

Vayla had just begun grooming her mare when Eraim appeared next to her, holding several unfamiliar herbs. The roots were still attached, the nodes were swollen, and little white flowers budded at the end of slender shoots while long pink blossoms were crushed at the top of each stem.

"Here they are." Eraim held a sly grin as she glanced at the gray elf, who was starting a fire.

Did she steal them?

Eraim turned to Vayla. "Humans call them Unicorn's Blood, but do not let the name bother you." She lifted the plants and gazed at them. "You must grind the roots. And cut into the nodes, not between them." She looked at Vayla. "The flowers have been crushed to keep the pollen from escaping, and the more pollen you extract, the better. But do not include the petals. The rest... I am sure you know what to do."

Eraim's face was smeared with dirt and shrouded by disheveled, dark hair, but it exuded happiness and hope. Vayla found the corners of her mouth twitching, wanting to smile in return. Instead, she retrieved her mixing bowl and holy water.

She followed Eraim's directions, and it was a little disturbing when she cut into the nodes and red fluid oozed out. That explained the "blood" part. Once the ingredients were combined, she held a fistful of soil and recited her healing prayer. Cafior's Touch warmed the dirt, and she added it to the bowl. After sprinkling a bit of holy water, she gave it another good mixing.

Visiting each of her men, Vayla changed their dressings and used the healing concoction. She treated Macurak last, and it pleased her to see the captain's progress. Had she not run out of her own supplies, a couple more applications would have done the trick. She hoped the Unicorn's Blood was as potent as Eraim suggested.

Once finished, Vayla helped Macurak to his blanket and made sure he ate some of the bread, meat, and nuts provided by the giant warrior. Her captain chewed slowly, and after he had his fill, she took her portion of food and wandered to the northern edge of the campsite.

A window in the tall rocks allowed a view of the waterfall, as well as the river extending into Beit. The night hid most of the visage, but the growing moon sparkled off the water, making it easy to forget the dead animals Vayla knew to be there.

"Please," Selanna said, joining Vayla, "tell me why you are here."

"To fail," Vayla murmured.

"To fail?" Selanna frowned. "At what?"

Vayla sighed. "I was tasked with putting an end to the Death Fog."

"The plague?" Selanna's brows drew tighter together. "But you have *not* failed. The plague is ended."

Vayla looked at the elf. Was the mage trying to make her feel better?

"We discovered its source in Darum Carumbor." Selanna's tone became grave. "The tower was occupied."

Vayla knew that name. Darum Carumbor was a small fortress that guarded the entrance to Helmland. Palidur invaded the tower centuries ago when marching against the Ancient Enemy, and wiped out the dark soldiers within. The structure proved impervious to all attempts to topple it, so Palidurian priests invoked wards to keep evil from ever inhabiting it again. "Impossible."

"I swear," Selanna said. "We encountered warriors bearing vile weapons. And they serve... No. I will not speak of that yet. But know this: a magical crystal generated the plague, and that crystal has been destroyed. Your quest has been fulfilled."

Unless Selanna was mistaken, Vayla's mission was truly over. Did it matter that she was not the one to complete it? She supposed that would be up to Grand Paladin Montac.

"What have I missed?" Eraim's squeaky voice entered the conversation.

Why was it Vayla never detected the small elf's approach?

"I have just informed Vayla that the plague has been stopped." Selanna never took her eyes from Vayla.

Eraim's face paled. "Oh, that. Did you mention — ?"

"No." Selanna was quick to interrupt her companion.

Vayla sneered at Eraim. "Shouldn't you be playing with your giant?" If she had to deal with the elves, one at a time was preferable.

"Who? Vecnor?" Eraim looked at the tall warrior.

"*Vecnor?*" Vayla gazed at the man. Was it the same Vecnor from the stories? The Vecnor Wezlok spoke of? The one who single-handedly defeated a Death Lord?

Strangely, the large man appeared to have overheard them and he glanced their way.

"You have not met him?" asked Selanna. "He was a dear friend of Mers — "

"All right!" Vayla had heard enough. "I told you why I'm here. Why are *you* here?"

The elves looked at each other. Selanna then spoke.

"You have heard of the Shadow?"

Vayla nodded.

"Well, the trail of the Shadow led us here," the mage said. "We sought the Guardians to see what they might have heard or seen…" Her eyes moistened. "Sadly, the Guardians are no more. We were then drawn to Darum Carumbor, where we shattered the crystal emitting the plague, and from there we entered Helmland. Nothing more needs to be said about that at this time, other than it appears Trannum was not destroyed. He *is* the Shadow."

Vayla felt sick. Probably lingering effects of the plague. At the opposite end of the campsite, Wezlok blanched. He had surely been listening.

"That explains why Anduiff was in Benzon." Vayla bit her lip.

"You faced a Death Lord?" Eraim looked as if she had seen a ghost. "You could have been killed."

"Please!" Vayla was not about to be mothered by the small elf. "Cafior is with me."

Selanna stared at Vayla as if she wished to say something. She then spoke to Eraim.

"Anduiff must be the Death Lord that flew above Lothen." She sighed. "Unless Radaam has arrived as well."

Vecnor and the gray elf did not move to join the conversation, but it seemed their necks were craning to listen.

"Who is the elf?" Vayla nodded at the one with the gray skin.

"Nobody," muttered Eraim.

"He is Eslimil Tuxendora." Selanna flashed Eraim a smirk before returning her attention to Vayla. "You may call him Tux. And the marteese is Kiryanna. She was… She *is* the protector of Brem, priest of Frayorna."

"The man there is Burnod." Vayla looked at the Beitian, who was the only one still eating. "He was general of Zurzak."

Selanna gasped. "Then he is —"

"With me," Vayla said. "And the rest of them are my men."

223

Eraim held a mischievous grin. "Who is the handsome warrior you assisted onto the blanket?"

What the elf *thought* she knew, Vayla did not care. She looked at Macurak. He was sleeping, and she realized he must be handsome to most women. She noticed the same of Vecnor and Tux, as well as Burnod. Kiryanna was beautiful too. Add Selanna and Eraim to the picture and Vayla was surrounded by beauty. Even the holy soldiers were above average, making Vayla feel quite ordinary and out of place. But appearances did not matter. She had no time for such nonsense.

"He is Captain Macurak," Vayla replied. "A competent soldier."

Eraim's smile shifted to Selanna, who smirked. What in Cafior's name were those two implying? Vayla focused on the valley below.

"Selanna!" Vecnor said. "When will you share with us the item you took from Lothen?"

Selanna opened her mouth, appearing as if she had been caught stealing from a merchant's wagon. Good. It served her right. And what item was Vecnor speaking of? Vayla and Eraim followed the mage back to the fire, and Eraim seemed just as intrigued as everyone else.

Selanna pulled a rolled blanket from Vecnor's gear and carefully opened it, revealing what appeared to be a black stick. But it was not an ordinary stick. It was perfect. Perfectly smooth and unmarred by scratches or pocks. Other than that, it was unimpressive.

"What is it?" Kiryanna broke her silence, though her angry expression remained.

"I do not know." Selanna frowned. "I suspect it is a key. Trannum used it in Lormin Dmurr."

"One key for multiple gates?" asked Vecnor. "Is that possible?"

"I did not believe it to be so." Selanna sighed. "But—" Her eyes snapped to Vecnor. "How did you know about the gates?"

Vecnor shrugged. "Someone must have mentioned them."

Selanna looked at Eraim, who shook her head. The mage turned to Kiryanna. The marteese shrugged.

"Lormin Dmurr?" Vayla knew that name well. All Palidurians learned about the citadel of the Ancient Enemy. What were the elves doing in that dark place?

Selanna considered Vayla, as if deciding whether to share. "We shall speak of that later. As for the stick, it is a key Trannum used to open three portals. I did not think it was possible that a single key could create multiple gates, but I also have doubts as to where this item has come from. I hesitate to touch it."

"Who was the krukari?" Kiryanna demanded. "The one who chased us across the bridge? The one that stood twenty feet tall?"

"It was only twelve feet," murmured Eraim.

"Krukari?" Vayla glared at Selanna. The mage was hiding things. Why?

"And how is it that Trannum is still alive?" Kiryanna added. "I thought you two destroyed him."

Selanna nodded. "Indeed. But then there is the final verse of Seac's prophecy."

"*Power shatters, dust does fall; Eyes open in shadowy hall.*" Eraim recited the lines Vayla had learned from her studies.

"They were Trannum's eyes," Selanna said. "I know not how, but he has survived." She turned to Eraim. "I am not even sure it was Trannum you destroyed."

"Did you know?" Eraim barked at Vecnor, fists on her hips.

Vecnor put up a hand. "I wasn't there."

"That is no answer!" Eraim appeared angry. "You are not Elgarroth!"

Vayla recognized that name as well. Elgarroth was an elf wizard often mentioned in Palidur, and many of the stories were contradictory. The only thing Vayla knew to be fact was that he had assisted in planning the Necromancer War.

"We need more minds on this." Selanna looked as if she was speaking to herself. "We must seek the Council of Wizards."

"What about Elgarroth?" Eraim posed.

"Apparently we can't get answers from *him*," mumbled Vecnor.

"He has been hard to track down as of late." Selanna ignored the large warrior. "I doubt he is home." She glanced at Tux, who gave the slightest shaking of his head.

"We best get some rest," Vecnor said. "There is still a distance to travel."

Vayla realized Selanna neglected to answer Kiryanna's question about the krukari. She let it go... for now.

Come morning, Vayla awoke to find Vecnor keeping watch. She would have insisted on guarding a portion of the night herself, but riding for days with little rest, not to mention overcoming the plague, had left her drained. The only other person awake was Kiryanna, who was sharpening an impressive golden sword. Tux was missing, but Vecnor did not seem concerned, so Vayla checked on her captain.

Macurak awoke while she removed the bandages, but he remained still. It impressed Vayla to see his wound had nearly recovered. Where did Eraim acquire those herbs? Or rather, Tux? Macurak stood without assistance once Vayla applied fresh wrappings, flexing his arm and testing his side.

"Don't do too much," she said quietly, not wanting to wake the holy soldiers just yet.

Macurak smiled and nodded, and she realized he was definitely a handsome man. But it changed nothing.

She approached Vecnor. The warrior held one of his blades, and it was as long as Vayla was tall. Why did he wear black? He would look like Anduiff if he wore the full helmet lying with his gear.

"I have been told you destroyed a Death Lord single-handedly," she said. "Is that true?"

"Do you always say what comes to mind?" Vecnor raised a single brow. "I suppose you would. That's the way—"

"Yes, I know!" Vayla scowled. "You obviously knew my grandmother!"

"I was *going* to say that's the way of paladins." Vecnor smirked.

"But now that you mention it—"

Vayla stomped off. "When do we depart?" she voiced aloud, stirring everyone within the campsite.

Once their gear was packed, the company resumed their trek. Vayla walked to the rear with Wezlok so she could lead Star, and Macurak and her soldiers marched before her. They stopped briefly for lunch and again for dinner, and with the holy warriors returned to full strength, they continued through the night.

Shortly after sunrise, they came upon a valley plunging deep below. It was breathtaking, and Vayla stared in disbelief when she spotted the narrow bridge spanning its breadth.

"How are we to cross that?" she demanded.

Vecnor chuckled. "Very carefully."

Did he think he was funny?

"It is sturdy," Eraim said. "No winds blow here. You just need to maintain a steady pace."

"But Star..." Vayla looked at her mare.

Wezlok measured the bridge. "Leave Star to me."

The humans paled upon seeing the narrow bridge, but Selanna took no pleasure in their expressions of fear and shock. The young men she left in Helmland still haunted her.

She allowed Eraim to cross the gorge first, and she was close behind. Tux went next, followed by Kiryanna and Vecnor—the large human moved almost with the grace of an elf. Vayla's soldiers and Burnod then ambled across with wide eyes, and Selanna held her hands forward, adding support as necessary until they reached the other side. That left Vayla, Wezlok, and Star.

Wezlok worked his magic, lifting Star off the ground before pulling the weightless mare along the bridge. The horse trembled, but Wezlok offered comforting words and kept it calm.

It touched Selanna to see Wezlok behave so. He was a Lorian, and Lorians did not do favors for anyone other than Lorians. She could not imagine what had affected Wezlok so strongly that he was willing to do this for Vayla, but she suspected it had something to do with Merssa. Wezlok had accompanied Merssa into Andria to track down one of Trannum's orbs from the barbarian chief, Dimarr, and again with the South Army that marched from Sendorum to Kembald. Merssa never arrived at Castle Lambrak, and over the years, Selanna could get none of the participants to speak of the manner in which her death had occurred. Normally, Selanna experienced a small void when gazing at Vayla. It was a sadness for the late paladin; the hero Vayla would never meet. But now Selanna fought back a tear for Wezlok. It pleased her to know that he could feel.

Everyone was across at last, and Eraim led them to the cave containing Dandi and Lilli, as well as the other horses their original company had ridden. Selanna thought of the animals they left behind, and she hoped Umbarc had taken them to safety.

Eraim beamed at Lilli. "It is grand to see you," she said in elfish.

Lilli nuzzled Eraim, and Dandi nudged Selanna toward the cave exit. Her animal companion was ready to leave.

Macurak accompanied Vayla on Star, and her men doubled up on the mounts belonging to Romik, Desser, and Daymyn. After convincing Dandi to bear Tux, Selanna joined Eraim atop Lilli. Kiryanna rode the horse she brought from Ellaville, and Burnod maintained a scowl while sitting on Baylun's mule — Vayla seemed pleased that there had been no other choices for the general. Vecnor appeared comical, seated on the steed Brem had used, but Selanna made no comments. There was too much on her mind.

They exited the cave and headed south.

CHAPTER 20

COUNCIL OF WIZARDS

Eraim rode atop Lilli with Selanna seated behind her, and they led the way to the next campsite. There, they settled in for another night, eating dinner around a fire.

The holy soldiers remained together, speaking quietly while Vayla and Macurak discussed their report for Montac. Selanna sat with her eyes shut, Kiryanna brooded, and Vecnor continued eating well after the meal had ended—a body that large surely needed more fuel than most. Burnod kept to himself, pouting near the entrance of the campsite. Eraim did not worry about the Beitian running away— several opportunities to do so had come and gone, and Vayla seemed unconcerned. At the opposite edge of the clearing, Tux scrutinized his long arrows one at a time. Eraim decided to speak with the gray elf before he disappeared, as he did every night.

"From where have you procured such arrows?" She eyed the dark shafts. "I thought them to be of Vermallon make, but now I am not so sure. They pierced the armor of those riders more efficiently than my own."

"They are from Orlenfel." Tux said, his ominous eyes never straying from his task.

His deep voice continued to contradict his appearance. It reminded Eraim of Xorlunder, the gray elf commander that fought in the Battle of the Dead Fields and perished at Gruzim's hand.

"Do you check them every night?" she asked.

"Do you not?" Tux stared along the shaft of an arrow. He furrowed his brow and placed it aside and away from the others. "The constantly changing climates and elevations can influence them. I must make sure I use only those that remain perfect."

Eraim had never considered that. It might account for her occasional misses, an incident plaguing her maybe once out of every hundred shots. It was not a pattern she wished to endure if she could avoid it. Her eyes moved to Tux's bow. "What of your bow? Is it from Orlenfel?"

Tux looked up, pausing in his efforts. "It was a gift." He lifted the weapon and offered it.

Eraim grabbed hold of the gray wood. It bore almost no weight and it was warm to the touch. Though it seemed fragile, she doubted it was easily broken. Her own bow held a special place in her heart and she would never think of parting with it, but if she did, she wanted one just like this. It did not feel like a tool, but an extension of her arm. Her fingers tingled.

Tux retrieved the weapon, a smirk leaning to the right side of his face. "There is not much I am able to tell you about it. I am sorry."

Eraim was getting used to that. When your best friends were Selanna and Vecnor, you seldom received any information.

"Do you possess magic?" she asked. "When I journeyed with the likes of Xorlunder and Lorylla, they exhibited certain abilities. Magical talents. Is that how you disappear?"

His smirk spread across both cheeks. "I do what comes naturally to me, just as you do what comes naturally to you. I have been watching for some time, and I understand the legend that follows you."

Eraim was taken aback. "What legend? I am no thief!"

"No." Tux chuckled. "You are definitely no thief. You are much more than that. Now if you will excuse me, I must keep watch on the night."

Eraim returned to the fire, confused and frustrated. She was no legend. She was just Eraim. And there was nothing wrong with that.

Everyone slept except for Vecnor. He sat, watching the flames dance. Eraim joined him.

"Am I a legend?" she asked.

He smiled. "You are to me."

Her frustrations melted away.

Eraim continued sharing Lilli's saddle with Selanna, and they exited the mountains as the sun illuminated the countryside. The path disappeared after a few miles, an event Eraim had expected, but she remembered the way and they did not slow. She gazed at the terrain, wondering what magic was at work to hide the trail. Surely horses passing back and forth would have left signs. But the ground remained unmarred.

Upon entering Virch, they aimed for Ellaville, and Eraim's thoughts wandered to the subjects plaguing her most. Why did Selanna avoid answering Kiryanna's question about the krukari at Lormin Dmurr? Who was he? Only one answer seemed feasible, but Eraim hesitated to bring it to mind, afraid to put any truth to it. She shuddered. It could not be so. The half-hobgoblin was just another monster brought about by Trannum. It had to be. Then there were the Guardians, visible only to Selanna. Eraim possessed senses every bit as good as her friend's, so why had she not seen or heard them? She wondered about Tux. Where did he go at night? Was it truly to guard? Vecnor trusted him, but that only showed how gullible humans could be. Though Vecnor was no mere human, he was still human. Was he not? And since when did he not give direct answers to Eraim's questions? Well, perhaps he did not always give direct answers to *every* question. Vecnor had been unreachable for the most part over the past decade, and the times that Eraim tracked him down, he proved more aloof than usual. The only practical reason was that she continued to uncover truths about his seemingly ageless life. But that topic would have to wait.

They reached Ellaville, and the company cleaned themselves and restocked their supplies. Eraim, Selanna, and Kiryanna purchased new clothing with gold from Eraim's emergency stash, and Selanna used her magic to regrow all hair lost or singed from the explosions they endured. Kiryanna almost smiled. They remained in town for the night and left early the following morning.

The pace was hard while they traveled south. Eraim failed to track the days, and she was relieved when they reached Tikken City at last—she needed some familiarity in her life. They passed through the gates, and she noticed Tux was gone. She did not know when he parted company and it was useless to bring it up, so she said nothing.

It was just after noon, and everyone was tired from the road, but they continued across the free city to its eastern edge. The Council Building gates were open, and it surprised Eraim when guards claimed the wizards were awaiting their arrival. Grooms immediately tended to the horses, and as usual, Eraim and Selanna issued instructions to Lilli and Dandi so the humans could lead them to the stables.

Servants ushered the company inside. Upon reaching the audience chamber, they found ten Council Wizards seated on the thrones with the middle chair vacant. Elgarroth was also present.

"We have been briefed as to where you have been," one wizard said with a glance at Elgarroth. He then turned to Selanna. "So what news is it you bring from the Guardians?"

Selanna sighed and shook her head. "If only it were that simple. I am afraid the Guardians are no more."

The information barely stirred the room, but Eraim detected a slight widening of the Council members' eyes. None of them spoke for several seconds, so they were probably doing that trick where they communicated without words. It was an annoying talent.

"Perhaps you can enlighten us," said a wizard. He sat two chairs to the right of the empty throne.

Selanna released a frustrated breath. Eraim's friend had suggested a possible connection between Helmland and Trannum on more than one occasion over the past five decades, but the Council always scoffed. And now, when it was too late to do the Guardians any good, the wizards wished to hear what Selanna had to say. It reminded Eraim of when the High Order of Palidur did not listen to

Merssa, leading to the city's downfall. Hopefully, this time would be different.

Selanna spoke with a controlled voice, beginning her tale with her and Eraim encountering the boys outside Rivercross. After mentioning the Blackfoot goblins, she nodded at Eraim.

Eraim lifted the sack she removed from Lilli before entering the building, and she extracted the helmet Desser presented to them on Korban Bridge. Mordan entered to take the item for later inspection by the Council, appearing nervous while he handled it—or perhaps he shook from old age.

Next, Selanna spoke about Ellaville and their meeting with Brem and Kiryanna. Upon mentioning the Beitian deserters, the wizards nodded, obviously having questioned the prisoners already.

Selanna advanced the story to Lothen Forest and the whispering wind that led to the discovery of Darum Carumbor's occupation. The plague-crystal brought the Council intrigue, which increased when Eraim produced the small fragment Baylun cut loose. She carefully removed it from her pack with a cloth, avoiding direct contact.

"Perhaps we may study the shard?" the wizard on the far right asked, to which Selanna nodded.

Eraim was surprised with her friend's assent. But also she was grateful to be rid of the crystal. She worried it still contained a trace amount of the plague. Mordan accepted the item, having Eraim set it within a small coffer. He appeared to shake even more than before as he carried the box from the chamber.

Selanna continued, speaking of the tome from Darum Carumbor, and Eraim recited the incomplete passage they discovered.

"...through might of the Shadow, He will send the Duke to once again empower We over all else; and through the Portals of Ultimate Malevolence, the land shall flood with minions of darkness; and all will be under the mighty fist of power, with the Great One close behind..."

Eraim pulled the remains of the charred tome from her pack, and again Mordan entered. He carefully removed the book, the steward now covered in sweat and out of breath—and still shaking.

The worst part of the journey was then shared: the trek across Helmland and into Lormin Dmurr. Several Council members leaned forward, and Selanna's voice was suddenly dry and cracked. She revealed the Shadow to be Trannum, and nearly choked on a lump in her throat when she spoke of the gates and the emergence of the krukari warrior. Selanna still did not give the monster a name, allowing Eraim to hold on to hope that it was someone other than the obvious.

Elgarroth then shattered that hope.

"It seems Uustaag has returned."

A chill traveled the length of Eraim's spine, and she desperately wished to return to Dominelli and hide in her bedroom. Even Vecnor's face paled.

The wizard to the left of the empty chair stood in outrage. "We do not speak that name here!"

"That hardly matters anymore," Elgarroth said. "The Ancient Enemy of the North has returned. Now, perhaps, is the time to become familiar with his name."

The wizards murmured among themselves.

Selanna cleared her throat, recapturing the Council's attention. She then resumed her report, speaking of the flight from Lormin Dmurr and the names of those left behind. She concluded with the return to Lothen Forest and the meeting with the ghosts.

Eraim thought it odd. Though Selanna informed the Council of the Guardians' demise at the hands of dunarchins, she failed to mention that she had spoken to their spirits in a dream. She also omitted the black stick, and she never uttered Tux's name.

The small door leading to the wizards' quarters opened, and a man dressed in Council robes entered. It was Fenreil, the new Seer. He was much younger than the other wizards, probably in his early fifties, and he was the only one of their order not bearing white hair— his was dark. His beard was not quite an inch long and his eyes were kind, and he smiled at his guests, making him seem out of place with his colleagues.

"Sorry I'm late." Fenreil took his seat on the center throne.

The wizard to the Seer's left raised his brow. "Have you completed your studies?"

Fenreil stared at the Council member. "I need a break."

"Do you think that wise?" asked a wizard farther to the left. "Vaeldor is without a proper Seer."

Eraim understood the wizard's point. Selanna explained the situation to her after Seac's murder. A seer was born once every century, but they seldom realized they carried the Sight until around age fifty. Upon discovery of their talent, they reported to Tikken City. There, they trained for at least forty years, headed the Council for the next sixty, continued their services while tutoring their successor, and retired with what remained of their two-hundred-twenty-year lifespan. Or something like that. With Seac's assassination, Fenreil had only received a few years of training, and the Council was now tasked with the matter—a skill none of them possessed. The wizards worked together to interpret visions of the Seer, but they did not know what it was like to actually *see* those visions well enough to explain them so that they *could* be interpreted. Or something like that. Presently, the Council was a bunch of old mages trying to make decisions, since there existed no experienced seer to guide them.

"I am not a child." Fenreil held a sidelong gaze at the one who had spoken. "I will continue with my exercises shortly." He turned to the visitors in the chamber and smiled. "Now, what seems to be the problem?"

Eraim thought him handsome for a human, a trait far beyond any other member of the Council. She could see Fenreil charming guests in ways Seac had never been able to. But Vayla appeared unimpressed. She had been scowling with her arms folded across her chest since arriving, and she chose that moment to unload her frustrations.

"The problem is that Uustaag has returned, Trannum is not dead,

Helmland and Beit are massing their forces, and Vaeldor lacks a proper seer!"

Vayla sounded so much like Merssa. It tugged at Eraim's heart.

"This is a waste of my time." Vayla looked at her warriors. "We are leaving for New Palidur."

She exited the chamber with her company in tow, including Wezlok—the Lorian held a slight grin. The room was silent until the doors shut.

"Palidurians..." muttered Fenreil.

Now it was Selanna's turn to scold the Seer.

"I thought she phrased it quite nicely. I shall return once you are ready to discuss what is to come next."

Selanna turned on her heels and exited the chamber, and Eraim, Vecnor, and Kiryanna followed. Elgarroth remained behind.

"The Council cannot help us," Selanna said while they walked to the rear exit of the building where the stables were located. "Vayla is likely headed to the docks to obtain a ship to New Palidur." She sighed. "That young lady is more like Merssa than she knows or wishes to be. But I have faith that Montac will have a proper reaction." She spun as they reached the final door, staring at Vecnor. "Can we count on you for counsel? Or do you plan to disappear for another ten years?"

Vecnor stood without speaking for several seconds. "I am at your disposal." He bowed his head.

"Good." Selanna looked around. "Where is Tux?"

Eraim shrugged.

Selanna pursed her lips before addressing everyone in the corridor. "Meet me at The Jeweled Scabbard near the southern gate. It is a fine establishment with private rooms. If there are any errands in need of your attention, please attend to them quickly, and be there in one hour's time."

She opened the door and headed for the stables.

CHAPTER 21

THE NEW SEER

After purchasing fresh green robes from the Tikken City Market, Selanna proceeded to The Jeweled Scabbard to clean up and don her new clothing. Once finished, she secured a private dining chamber, and there she waited.

She had called for the meeting to begin one hour after they exited the Council Building, but an hour and a half had passed, and the only other person present was Kiryanna. The marteese arrived on time, still wearing her scowl, and she had not said a word.

Selanna sat with a glass of wine untouched before her, as was the wine she ordered for Eraim and beer for Vecnor—Kiryanna refused any beverage. But it was not the tardiness of Selanna's companions that held her in a trance. Trannum was alive. Uustaag had returned. She could not remember how many years it had been since the Wind of the Dead interrupted a warm summer afternoon in Rivercross, raising the departed. It was barely a day later when she presented the possibility of Uustaag's involvement to the Council, a theory that Seac disavowed. And now she wondered if the brave people of Vaeldor could unite yet again. The war versus Trannum had been hard enough. How could they hope to succeed a second time?

The door opened and Eraim entered.

"It's about time!" snapped Kiryanna.

"Sorry." Eraim glanced at Selanna.

"It is fine," Selanna said. "We can get started. I doubt Vecnor is coming."

"He is here." Eraim smiled deviously. "That is why I am late. I was making sure he attended."

The door opened again, and Vecnor ducked to enter. The room suddenly seemed smaller.

"You're late!" Kiryanna spat.

"My apologies." Vecnor bowed and took a seat.

A knock sounded, and Selanna's head snapped to the door. Had Tux returned? She was even more pleased to see Elgarroth enter.

"You're late!" Kiryanna scowled.

Elgarroth lifted a brow as he sat. He then nodded at Selanna. "Please, proceed."

Selanna suddenly felt lighter with her mentor's presence. Taking in a deep breath, she placed her hands on the table to steady them. "I do not expect to make decisions tonight. We first need to determine what the questions are, and where to find the answers."

"I have a question." Kiryanna's glare was almost frightening. "When do we go to Helmland?"

"There are several friends missing," Selanna said, "and rescuing them is part of the plan. But that will take some time. For now, let us speak of what we know.

"Trannum is alive, and Anduiff has returned." Selanna looked at the room's occupants. "Somehow, Trannum has summoned Uustaag back into Vaeldor, which explains why the warlord's body was never found. Trannum also released a plague onto Beit to enlist its citizens into his undead army, and from what Vayla said, that army now marches to the bridges to await the coming war. The Guardians are dead. And some of our friends were left behind."

Kiryanna's squirming did not escape Selanna's notice.

"We have not seen Radaam yet," Selanna added, "but I am sure he will surface."

"So what?" Kiryanna's eyes dug into Selanna. "You defeated Trannum before, and he had twenty Death Lords at his disposal."

"There were not twenty Death Lords," Eraim muttered.

Selanna had heard many variations of the war against Trannum. Twenty Death Lords; fifty Death Lords; she and Eraim destroyed Trannum; Xorlunder destroyed Trannum; Greyor destroyed

Trannum. The version depended on where one was. In the end, it had been a group effort.

"Apparently, we did *not* defeat Trannum." Selanna eyed Elgarroth, hoping for insight into the matter.

"If I were to venture a guess," Elgarroth spoke slowly, "I would say Trannum abandoned his body before animating it. He must have placed one of his orbs within the skull, granting him the ability to use the skeleton; to speak through it as if it were him. He turned all attention on Nomedd while his true plans were executed far away, in Helmland."

The room fell silent for several seconds.

"*Eyes open in shadowy hall,*" murmured Selanna. "The final verse."

Everyone stared at her.

"I do not know how it is possible, but I have seen this *hall*. At least, I believe I did. In a dream." Selanna shifted in her chair. She had never wholly admitted her dreams to anyone—not even Eraim. "It was a round chamber, and upon the floor was a black triangle. The Shadow... Trannum... He emerged from that triangle and flew through a series of tunnels before rising above mountains."

Eraim frowned. "Rorbak?"

"Of course!" Why had Selanna not thought of that? She felt foolish. She should have revealed her dreams to Eraim long ago. "We did not fully search the tomb, not after Trannum placed his spell on us. And we never returned. Palidur sent soldiers to investigate, but there is no reason to assume they found Trannum's hall. If it *is* there."

"And what about the other prophecy?" Eraim asked.

Selanna knew her friend to be referring to the gibberish from weeks ago. She was not even sure where she had heard it, or if it was real. Had that been a dream as well?

Elgarroth furrowed his brow. "Something about the *Eyes of old*?"

Selanna's jaw dropped. She did not remember sharing any of it with Elgarroth. Beneath her mentor's gaze, she nodded.

"And the *Righteous hand,*" added Eraim.

Selanna thought hard. It was coming back to her, although

slowly.

Elgarroth tilted his head. "The *Crystal of Doom*?"

Selanna sat up straight as she recalled the verses. "Let me try." She closed her eyes, allowing the words to come to her.

"Eyes of old are kindled;
Master returns from below;
Frozen righteous hand shall fall;
Sight is blinded in Shadow's wake.

Crystal of Doom, Air of Death;
Shadow's prize arrives at last;
Portals three, the Duke returns;
Savage land is broken.

The key! The key!
The Duke is leashed;
Release the minions,
March the hordes.

Shadowy hall, undisturbed;
Underlings hold the power;
Trap is sprung, treachery arises;
Scorching death avails.

Lords take flight;
March begins;
Borders crossed;
War is waged.

Within, without, the final stand;
Golden sun, Flame of Life.
Tools enriched with bones of dust;
Immortal to mortal, shadows fade;

Evil storm, fire cracks;
Gates are, the key;
Star affixed in holy hand;
Flame, not flame."

She opened her eyes. Everyone was staring again. She turned to Eraim. "Surely you remember it better."

Eraim shook her head. "As I said, I have never heard this before."

"You relayed it perfectly." Elgarroth smiled.

"But..." Selanna attempted again to determine where she had heard it.

"We will speak on that later." Elgarroth seemed to read her thoughts. "For now, what can we ascertain from this prophecy?"

Eraim had already removed a quill, a jar of ink, and a piece of parchment from her pack, and she scribbled at a hectic pace.

Selanna reflected on what she had recited, the words clear in her mind. "The *Eyes* were Trannum's, opening after Eraim destroyed his remains. And he is the *master* that returns." She looked at Elgarroth for confirmation.

He gave a nod.

"The *Righteous hand* must refer to Nilborg," Selanna added.

"And the *Sight is blinded* was the murder of Seac," said Vecnor.

The large man surprised Selanna. But he often found ways to do such things.

"The crystal and the plague are the next verse." Eraim scrutinized her completed work.

"I saw the gates that make up the *Portals*," Selanna said. "And we all witnessed the land being broken. The *Duke* is surely Uustaag."

"So what of the *Shadow's prize* and *the key*?" posed Eraim.

"*The key*..." mumbled Selanna. "The black stick!" She pulled the item from her pack, still wrapped in the blanket, and unrolled it for all to see. "Trannum used this to open the three gates." She turned to Elgarroth. "But does not every gate need a key unique unto itself?"

Elgarroth stared at the stick. Selanna wondered if he heard her question.

"What is it, Master?"

"This is not of our world," he replied slowly. "I have never seen it before, though I know of it. Welmirth, the wizard that cast down Uustaag, hid it, that it might never again be used."

Selanna recalled her conversation with the ghost. "The Guardian spoke of dunarchins scouring Lothen Forest. They searched for over thirty years and found it at last."

"Lothen Forest..." Elgarroth appeared lost in thought. "He kept it close, knowing Uustaag's minions would search far and wide." He eyed Selanna. "I doubt it has only been thirty years that they sought this item. I am sure it was more than a thousand years when they realized it lay at the edge of their border."

"But what *is* it?" Selanna asked.

"It is power." Elgarroth's expression was one Selanna had never seen before: deep concern; almost fearful. "You speak of gates and keys," he said, "but I do not believe what you saw in Lormin Dmurr are mere gates. They are openings, created by Uustaag over a thousand years ago."

"Openings?" Selanna frowned. "I do not understand."

"This is indeed a key," Elgarroth said. "But it is a creation of Thard'Dun, and it is more powerful than any key that has ever existed. It does not merely open gates between worlds. It attempts to adjoin them. Uustaag gained his power from Thard'Dun by surrendering his soul. In essence, Uustaag became an extension of Thard'Dun through that key. Welmirth believed the dark god rescued Uustaag at the last moment, before his imminent death in the Battle of Balgorn, and that the power was granted through the key. Now, I know his beliefs to have been correct."

"But if this is the key," Selanna said, "then we need only pass it through the portal." She stared at nothing, realizing the flaw in her statement. "But which portal?" After a moment, she decided. "The center arch."

"But what of the other gates?" asked Vecnor. "Do we allow

whatever lies on the other side free rein into Vaeldor?"

Eraim raised her brow. "Surely they will be easier to deal with than the Ancient Enemy."

Elgarroth gave Eraim a fatherly look. "I am sure you realize that to be unacceptable."

Selanna did not understand. "How can three gates be closed by a single key?"

"Let us come back to that question," Elgarroth said. "What about the next line of the prophecy, after *the key*?"

"*The Duke is leashed.*" Eraim twisted her lips in thought. "Uustaag did not pursue us. From what I remember, he did not step from the bridge of the citadel."

"Exactly." Elgarroth held a weak smile. "From what I know, from what I believe, and from what I feel, a part of Uustaag exists within this stick. When he surrendered to Thard'Dun, a piece of his soul was placed inside it. That is why he is leashed. Without the key in his possession, he is tethered to Thard'Dun's world."

"But the gates were closed when I first saw them," Selanna said. "How did Welmirth close them without sending the key through?"

"Welmirth was a powerful mind," Elgarroth mused. "He did not trust returning this item to Thard'Dun, so he took it. And he had not the power to destroy it, so he hid it. The openings were then canceled, leaving Uustaag trapped within the dark god's realm until the key could be recovered."

"That brings us back to my question," said Selanna. "How did Welmirth close the portals without using the key?"

Elgarroth held a crooked grin. "It was once said that Welmirth was the right hand of Vou." He sighed. "But as for your question," he shook his head, "I do not know."

Selanna's shoulders were suddenly heavy. Elgarroth did not know? How was that possible?

"But Welmirth wrote many journals," Elgarroth added. "And I shall look into it."

"At least Uustaag cannot leave his citadel," said Eraim. "He is scarier than a Death Lord by a hundredfold."

"No, he cannot." Elgarroth eyed Eraim. "But do not fool yourself. He will send his minions to retrieve the stick. Whomever holds the key will be in constant danger."

Eraim stared at the black stick, as if it were a snake about to strike.

"So now we go back to Helmland?" Kiryanna's fingers drummed a dangerous beat on the pommel of her golden sword.

"No, my dear." Elgarroth offered a sympathetic smile.

Selanna's mind went to Romik and the boys, and her stomach was suddenly queasy. "We must send word to the parents of those we left behind." Saying the words stirred anger within, pushing her focus back to the task at hand. "And we need to return to Trannum's tomb in the Stone Eagle Mountains."

"We must also spread word," said Vecnor. "The kingdoms of Vaeldor need to know what is coming. Especially the realms of Virch and Harbnum."

Selanna pursed her lips. "But it will not be like last time. Merssa is not here to lead us." She sighed. "As much as my heart wishes it to be so, Vayla is not her. I only pray Montac can unite the kingdoms." She looked from Vecnor to Elgarroth. "And we cannot assume the enemy will sit idle for years while we launch a coordinated attack. They may very well strike first. So the realms must rally soon."

"I'll spread the word," said Vecnor. "Most kings will listen to me."

Selanna realized they might not see Vecnor for a while—again. But there was nothing to be done.

"After we speak with the parents of those left behind," she said, "I plan to enter Trannum's tomb in the Stone Eagles. That is as far as I can plan until we learn more."

Eraim and Vecnor nodded. Kiryanna shook her head, glaring at the table.

Selanna found Elgarroth readying his horse outside The Jeweled

Scabbard. The streets were quiet, and the few people wandering about appeared intoxicated. Eraim had gone with Vecnor and Kiryanna to retrieve the horses, leaving Selanna alone with the wizard.

"Master?" She approached. "You said you would speak of the prophecy. Where have I heard it?"

"You have not." He smiled, but said no more.

"Please, Master." Her chest tightened. "Do not be evasive. Why do I know it?"

"Because you are a seer."

"A seer?" She frowned. "But I am not human."

His brow lifted. "Who said only humans birth seers?" He chuckled. "Elves do so as well. We just do not share that knowledge with the world. In fact, only the elf seers know that elf seers exist."

Selanna was not sure she followed his meaning. Besides that, she had a hard time accepting his words. She then realized what he had not said. "*You* are a seer?"

He nodded. "It is a burden. And just as the humans, it is my job to train my successor. That is what I have been doing these many years."

"But that cannot be!" Selanna's head spun. "I do not have visions. I do not have the Sight. And it was I that sought *you* in the beginning."

"You *do* have the Sight," Elgarroth said. "You have been using it for some time. Trannum standing on a bridge, sending forth his minions to recover his orbs; Nilborg's murder; the prophecy you recited... Just to mention a few. As far as you seeking me out for mentoring, you would be surprised how easy it was to make you see it that way."

"No." Selanna shook her head. It was impossible.

"Then there is Lothen Forest, and your dream encounter with the Guardians' ghosts."

Selanna thought back. She had mentioned speaking with the Guardians, but not that it had been within a dream. She left that part out, knowing the Council would not believe her. "I did not even tell you about that!"

"I am the Seer." Elgarroth spread his hands. "I saw it. And no other elf or wizard could have experienced what you did. Only a seer. I have known this about you since the day you were born."

"But they were just ghosts."

"Not just ghosts." Elgarroth looked at the stars dotting the night sky. "They were memories. That was why Eraim could neither hear nor see them." He eyed Selanna. "But *you* interacted with them." He paused. "Now, the wind... That was another matter. It was their spirits roaming the forest, and that is why the others felt them. Some may have even detected the screaming of their demise. But they could not hear the whispers."

Selanna pondered this. Eraim mentioned hearing only screams. Another thought then occurred. If Trannum killed Seac because he was the Seer...

"Did Trannum try to kill you?"

Elgarroth shook his head. "He does not know elfish seers exist. As you have probably guessed, he killed Seac to keep things hidden. The final verse of Seac's last prophecy came close to revealing too much. And had we been without the prophecy before the Necromancer War, the outcome might have been much graver."

"But my prophecy does not even rhyme," Selanna pointed out.

"That is a human thing." Elgarroth frowned. "I believe they force it to rhyme. Very odd. Mine have never been so."

"Why do you tell me this now?"

"It is time," he said. "Time to focus your skills. It is time for you to prepare."

Horror grabbed hold of Selanna. "Are you passing on? I am not ready—"

"I am not leaving any time soon." He offered a comforting smile. "But remember this: it is the Seer's job to help. To guide. It is not for us to be the hero."

"But what about Trannum and Uustaag?" She understood his statement, but she could not desert her friends. Not now.

"What if you perish in this affair?" Elgarroth posed. "Where would Vaeldor be with Fenreil as the only Seer? He will require many more years before he is ready to advise anyone."

Selanna wanted to laugh at the comment. But she could not. Anger mounted within. "I cannot abandon them! Being the Seer will just have to wait."

"Very good." Elgarroth nodded. "Very good."

CHAPTER 22

GRAND CATHEDRAL

Vayla left the Council Building feeling utterly disgusted. The wizards were of no use. Losing Seac made them obsolete, and she would waste no more time listening to their babble. She needed to return to New Palidur.

She led her men to the docks, and Macurak retrieved Star while she sought a ship to carry them across the King Arman. There were few to choose from, as most were out on fishing expeditions or docked for maintenance, but under her stern gaze, she located a captain willing to acquiesce.

To her surprise, Wezlok remained with her. The elf said nothing of his intentions, but he appeared glad to be finished with the Council. Vayla figured he must be eager to return home, and sailing to New Palidur would get him more than halfway there.

The weather was fair and the winds steady, but the voyage took longer than Vayla expected. She did not converse with anyone during the day-and-a-half journey. Instead, she spent most of her time with Star, who had sailed enough to tolerate the trip, or watching fishermen on other boats cast their nets and pull in their hauls. Macurak's injuries had fully recovered, and he confiscated Burnod's weapons and kept watch on the ex-general. Vayla was unsure what to do with the Beitian. Perhaps Grand Paladin Montac would provide guidance on the matter.

The sun passed overhead until it was low in the west on the second evening, and the Holy City came into view. There existed no better sight than New Palidur at sunset, as seen from the lake— sunsets at Castle Lambrak were boring. A score of ships were anchored alongside the many piers stretching hundreds of feet from the shore of silver stones, and three white towers stood tall, watching the Tikken City ship that arrived unlooked for.

Once the vessel docked, Vayla was first to disembark amid soldiers donning dark blue cloaks — holy warriors of Soleran tasked with keeping the harbor safe. She was immediately recognized, and she instructed the Soleran lieutenant to reimburse the ship captain for his troubles and make sure Star arrived at the Cafior stables. The officer appeared displeased with the orders, but that was not Vayla's concern.

She led her contingent along the silver street and toward the gate, and she could not help noticing Burnod's eyes darting about — he had likely seen nothing so glorious. His face then paled upon entering New Palidur proper, where the streets were dark blue and torch runners ignited suspended lanterns in preparation of the encroaching night.

Vayla continued until reaching the divider wall separating the Soleran and Cafior Sectors. There, she addressed the six holy soldiers; the only survivors of those that accompanied her and Macurak into Beit.

"You may return to your quarters." She noticed Macurak's disappointment — yet again — and she added, "I thank you for your skills and sacrifices. Those that we lost will be honored."

She glanced at Macurak while the warriors departed. He appeared satisfied. She turned to Wezlok.

"Thank you, Wezlok. Your companionship has been both interesting and beneficial. You do your kinsmen proud."

Wezlok stared for several seconds. "Do not pretend to be what you are not. It insults us both."

"Very well." Vayla took in a breath. "You are a most uncomfortable and infuriating presence. But your magic is impressive at times. I wish you speed returning home."

Wezlok smiled. "Much better. But I think I shall see what your Grand Paladin plans to do about the mess outside my forest."

Vayla was not surprised.

She headed for the Grand Cathedral at the center of the city, followed by Macurak, Burnod, and Wezlok. The gates to the inner sanctum were open, and the dark blue street gave way to silver cobblestones as Vayla passed through. Though night had not yet captured the sky, the Eternal Flame atop the fountain illuminated the shadows with the help of several lanterns, and a handful of holy soldiers walked about, some of them offering nods. Vayla returned a few of the greetings while she approached the Cafior entrance on the left side of the cathedral.

"I never got a statue made in *my* likeness." Burnod's slurred voice brought Vayla to a halt.

She turned to see the ex-general viewing one of the many statues along the silver street. Merssa. This particular sculpture depicted the woman in a combat stance and holding a simple mace. A mace? Afraid to spill evil blood on the soil? Vayla disagreed. Cafior accepted the blood of his enemies, drawing it deep into the land so that its stain was lost and forgotten.

Vayla noticed the grin Macurak attempted to cover up. "Yes, I'm very important," she said to the ex-general, and she proceeded toward the cathedral. "You should see the larger statue of me in the Cafior Sector. You're lucky to have made my acquaintance."

She climbed the steps to the covered porch, where a pair of guards wearing brown surcoats were alert before double doors of the same color. The sentries eyed her companions, and they each opened one of the doors to reveal a third soldier—also dressed in brown. The man sat at a desk, and he looked up as he dipped a quill into a bottle of ink.

"Vayla, reporting to the Grand Paladin," she said. "You may have received word from the docks of my arrival."

"Yes, my lady." The soldier scribbled onto a piece of parchment. "And who should I enter as your guests?"

"Captain Macurak, the Lorian wizard, Wezlok, and the evil General Burnod."

Burnod released a cough. Vayla paid him no mind.

The guard made the entries and then stood to open the next door, and Vayla followed him through.

They walked a long hall bearing a brown carpet, passing several doors and statues of departed Cafior heroes. Vayla tried to ignore the final statue to the right of the large doors leading to the High Temple, but again Burnod stopped. It was another Merssa, this one displaying the woman in flowing robes.

"I don't think this is you." The ex-general narrowed his eyes. "She looks older."

Vayla sighed and motioned for their escort to open the doors.

Within the High Temple, Grand Paladin Montac sat on a throne of granite built by the dwarves of Varlimor nearly two decades ago. The base was brown, the arms dark blue, and the seat light blue, and three jewels were set across the white back, including a brown tourmaline, an aquamarine, and a sapphire. The gems sparkled beneath a divine glow hovering in the center of the dome; a light that never failed to shine. Seats meant for the High Order were on either side of the throne. The chairs to the right were dark blue, light blue, and brown for the High Priests, and the High Paladins' seats of the same colors were to the left. None of the High Order were present. Instead, Lord Rholmar and Lady Ladonia occupied two of the paladins' chairs, Rholmar the one dedicated to Arronaus and Ladonia the one for Cafior.

Lord Rholmar gazed at Vayla, as he always did, and his eyes were moist while he smiled. Why was he in attendance? Should retirement not occupy one's time with fishing or travel?

"Welcome back, Paladin Vayla." Montac tilted his head. "And Captain Macurak."

Macurak bowed low. "Thank you, Grand Paladin."

Montac's focus shifted to Vayla. "What news do you bring of the plague?"

"The plague is no more," Vayla replied. "Or so I'm led to believe."

The Grand Paladin raised a brow. "Is there some doubt in the matter?"

"I was not a witness to its demise," she said. "But Selanna and Eraim destroyed an evil crystal, and afterwards the effects of the plague seemed to fade."

At the mention of the elves, Montac and Rholmar lifted their chins a bit higher.

"In the end," Vayla added, "I was unsuccessful in the mission I was charged with."

"I see." Montac's brows drew together. "I heard you arrived with only seven of the soldiers under your command."

Vayla shook her head. "Beit is an awful place."

Burnod cleared his throat. Vayla ignored the ex-general and continued.

"We faced an army, rebels, creatures I have never seen, undead, and the Death Lord, Anduiff."

The eyes of those sitting before Vayla grew wide, and she hesitated, unsure if she wished to say more. But what choice did she have?

"It appears Trannum was not defeated, as everyone believes."

Montac's fingers curled into fists. Ladonia paled. Rholmar pounded the arm of his chair as he stood.

"What proof have you to support such a claim?" the retired paladin demanded.

It was the first time Rholmar exhibited an expression other than pity for Vayla. It was outrage, with a hint of fear. She almost preferred it.

"Please, Father." Montac held up his hand until Rholmar sat, and he returned his attention to Vayla. "What makes you believe the necromancer still lives?"

"Selanna," she said.

Rholmar squirmed, but he remained quiet.

"According to the mage," Vayla continued, "Trannum now uses the form of a shadow, and he resides in Helmland."

Montac's frown deepened, and he raised his hand to silence

Vayla while he absorbed the information. "Selanna believes this?" he asked at last.

Vayla nodded. "She does. And she reported Darum Carumbor to be occupied."

"How can this be?" Montac spoke quietly, as if to himself. He looked at Vayla. "We have received no such warning from the Guardians."

Vayla shook her head. "Selanna claims the Guardians are no more."

Montac stared at her for several seconds. "What was Selanna doing in Beit?"

"From her account," Vayla replied, "she followed the path of the Shadow. She traveled with Eraim, Vecnor, Tux, Kiryanna, Brem, and a group she referred to as *the boys*. Brem and the boys were no longer with her when we met."

"Is there anything else we should know about Selanna's travels?" Montac asked.

"She has an item," Vayla said. "It is a smooth black stick, pure and unmarred, but otherwise unremarkable. She seems very interested in it, perhaps even fearful. She claims it to be a key that Trannum used to open multiple gates in Lormin Dmurr. And the one called Kiryanna spoke of a large krukari within the citadel. Elgarroth claims it to be Uustaag, but I do not know if the Council agrees."

"It cannot be him!" Rholmar was as white as a ghost.

Montac looked at his father. "We will discuss this with the Order." He returned to Vayla. "Is there anything else to report as to *your* journey?"

"Beit is massing armies at both bridges," Vayla replied. "It is my belief they plan to march with forces both living and undead, since Anduiff animated those killed by the plague, but I don't know when. Also, I should mention that we departed from the evil land by way of a secret trail through the Stone Eagle Mountains. Apparently, it is the Path of the Guardians."

Montac clapped his hands twice, and a servant entered.

"I want a search sent out for Selanna or Eraim," the Grand Paladin said. "Issue a *strong* invitation for an immediate visit. I also want contingents dispatched to Sendorum, Virch, and Harbnum. And send word to the king of Sardina that I request an audience."

"Right away, Grand Paladin." The servant bowed and exited.

Montac turned to Vayla. "Who are your guests?"

"I have with me Captain Macurak, whom you already know. Just as the soldiers that returned with me, I ask that he be honored for skill and bravery. And for those that did not return, I request a memorial of honor."

Montac gave a nod. "It will be so."

"Also with me is the Lorian wizard, Wezlok." Vayla looked at the elf.

"I knew I recognized you." Rholmar turned to his son. "He was instrumental in the war against Trannum."

Montac nodded. "So I have been told."

"And he was instrumental in our survival in Beit," Vayla said. "I request that a horse be issued, or at least an escort, so he may return to his forest."

"That will not be necessary." Wezlok showed no emotion. "I shall find my own way, in my own time."

"Very good," Montac said after a moment. "Until then, you are an honored guest of New Palidur."

Wezlok held a wry smile.

"Finally," Vayla glanced at Burnod, "I have with me the ex-general of Zurzak. Burnod."

"Indeed." Montac gazed at the Beitian with interest, as well as a touch of hostility. "He will be placed in our dungeon."

Vayla gave a nod while Burnod gasped. She then saw one of the many expressions of disappointment Macurak kept at the ready for her. Did he understand he was not her father? She sighed.

"If you please, Grand Paladin?" She gained Montac's attention as he leaned over to speak to Lord Rholmar.

"Yes?"

"Burnod deserted his position in the Beitian army, and he worked as our guide. With his help, we traversed the realm with little resistance, as well as received insight as to what we were to face. He could be a great source of information against Beit."

Montac looked from Vayla to Burnod and then back. "I agree. And that is a service he can provide from within the dungeon."

"If it pleases you, Grand Paladin," Vayla added quickly, "I would take him into my keeping. For services and loyalty he has shown..." She failed to find the proper words, and her own words took over. "It's just not right, my lord. Although his company is unpleasant and he's misguided, his assistance was invaluable. And he's no coward. He shouldn't have to spend his days—"

"Enough!" Montac raised his hand. "He will be your responsibility while he is a guest in New Palidur. And he's not to leave, nor to be left alone." Montac sighed and stared at Vayla. "Regarding your earlier statement, do not find failure where it does not exist. Though you were not the one to destroy the crystal, you accomplished so much more. You represented your city well." He continued to stare. "And it's Grand Paladin Montac, or just Grand Paladin. Not *my lord*."

"Yes, m… Grand Paladin." Vayla bowed.

"You are dismissed." Montac waved her off.

Vayla led the way from the High Temple and back onto the silver street. Full night was now upon New Palidur.

"I see this city is as boring as ever," said Wezlok.

"Why are you still here?" snapped Vayla. "Don't you have Beitian prisoners to take care of?"

The elf smirked. "In due time." He then frowned. "Why did you not speak of the gorillas?"

Vayla pursed her lips. "I was to report on the mission and its particulars. The gorillas are another matter and will be discussed at the proper time. Did I not mention '*creatures I have never seen before*'?"

"Why are you keeping me with you?" Burnod demanded. "I'm not under the impression you care for my company."

"I do not." Vayla eyed the ex-general. "But you might be useful. And if that status changes, I shall escort you to the dungeons myself. So you're with me... for now."

"Very good." Burnod held a devious grin. "I'm at your service... for now."

"What next?" asked Macurak.

"I have some reading to do." Vayla thought of all the information she had gathered, and how many questions she now possessed. "But first I must get out of this armor." She looked at her captain. "I'll meet you at the library."

Macurak nodded, and they exited the inner sanctum, passing through the gate and onto the brown streets of the Cafior Sector.

After walking half a mile, Macurak left for his quarters while Vayla continued toward her apartment with Burnod. Wezlok followed. Vayla did not know why the elf remained, and asking was pointless — she would receive no straight answers. But it was getting late, and she could waste no time on the subject at present. More important matters needed her attention.

CHAPTER 23

NEW RECRUITS

Baylun stood on the rooftop of Darum Carumbor, gazing across the surrounding fields. To the north was the Balgorn River, and to the northeast the motionless black water mirrored the road, disappearing between a small mountain chain and Lothen Forest.

Lothen Forest... Baylun's eyes often rested on the trees longer than they should. He remembered when he and his brother and cousins followed the elves into that woodland. Selanna and Eraim were supposed to be heroes, but Baylun had his doubts. Romik and Desser were likely dead, and he and Daymyn were now property of Darum Carumbor.

Baylun and his cousin were mistaken for foot soldiers when they tried to escape Helmland over three weeks ago, and they played the part to stay alive. As it turned out, the contingent they had followed was on their way to the tower for training. Several of the new arrivals realized Baylun and Daymyn had not marched with them, but they appeared hesitant to say anything. They seemed both fearful and respectful of Baylun, solely because he was krukari. It was strange.

Daymyn was asked a few times where he and Baylun had come from while eating meals or bunking at night, and his quick mind contrived a story. He explained they were pirates off the coast of Philen, and that they enjoyed wreaking havoc on the king's port towns. He further claimed the Shadow was so impressed with their combative prowess that he recruited them immediately and sent them to the tower.

It was a believable lie, since the trainees were a collection of soldiers and outlaws from various realms—although most of their stories were much simpler. Some felt mistreated by their lords; some enjoyed spreading chaos; and others simply desired power. Most were misguided souls, and several worshipped the evil deities, Shadia and Demoligius, while a handful paid homage to the Dark One, Thard'Dun. Baylun could not begin to understand how they were all brought together. Did the Shadow seek them out one by one?

Since entering the tower, Baylun and Daymyn proved their skills in combat to be superior to the other recruits. Though Baylun missed the axe his brother gave him, he found the maul did not feel so awkward. He twirled the weapon with ease, incorporating the haft into the melee almost as much as the head, and impressed all onlookers. It reminded him of how easy his battleaxe had been to use. Romik claimed the axe would learn from him, but he believed it to be the other way around.

Presently, Baylun was surrounded by the enemy. Most of the soldiers seemed normal people, and they accepted him, never commenting on his jutting tooth or overall appearance. It was odd, and so much different from his life in Philen.

His shift was nearly over, and he looked forward to getting some rest. He felt as if he had not slept in days, as worry of discovery made sleep a difficult task to sustain. He and Daymyn could not stay hidden forever.

"Baylun!" his troop leader called from the stairs leading into the tower's top floor. "Captain Rozall demands your presence. Immediately!"

Baylun held his breath. Had his deepest fear come to light? Just by thinking about it for too long? Dark priests scrutinized him and Daymyn after they arrived, checking their ears, eyes, and noses; testing their muscles, elbows, and knees. The priests then stood back, staring for what seemed like hours. Baylun believed they had been probing his mind, and now he provided them with the proof they needed—they were surely reading his thoughts.

He headed down the stairs, noting the concerned expressions of his comrades atop the tower. Seeing the captain was rarely a desirable occasion.

Baylun entered the chamber that once possessed the large crystal. The Dun Crystal. The four braziers hung from the ceiling, issuing the purple haze that covered the floor—the one Eraim cut had been mended—but the iron frame that displayed the gem was gone, and an ornate throne of brass rested in its place. Normally, the room contained soldiers learning the Chant in preparation of becoming Dun Soldiers or Dun Lancers. It was the same chant that nearly rendered Baylun and his friends immobile the first time they ascended the tower. Priests used the chamber as well, either teaching the Chant or praying in front of the chair. Baylun had yet to see anyone sitting on the throne, but he often suspected an invisible being was there, watching him.

He walked through the purple mist and to the far door. When he followed Eraim and Selanna, the door sealed this level from the one below. At present, it remained open, and he passed through and onto the arcing stairs. The fog descended only a few steps before dissipating, leaving Baylun to wonder what happened to it after that.

"On your way to the captain, Baylun?" posed a soldier playing cards with three other guards in the next room.

"You best keep your eyes on Forban." Baylun's words led the one who had spoken to turn as another guard attempted to cheat.

"I'll gut you, Forban!" the man growled.

Baylun chuckled as he exited the guardroom, but the looks of pity did not avoid his notice. It was strange, getting to know the soldiers as friends. The first time he entered the tower, he and his companions slew several guards. Now, Baylun wondered if any of *them* had been funny. Did they cheat at cards? Did they have families? It was easy to view the enemy from afar, never thinking about such things. Baylun sighed. Would he remember these questions once he and Daymyn made good their escape?

Escape… An event drifting further and further away every day. On more than one occasion, Baylun thought a window of opportunity presented itself, but his cousin always disagreed. Daymyn did not trust the wide-open field they needed to cross. They would surely be spotted, and Dun Lancers would run them down with ease. Baylun's cousin was probably correct.

He stepped into the curving hallway, and he heard the rhythmic pounding—the noise he and his companions detected while scaling Darum Carumbor. It came from the smithy, where a large krukari worked day and night. The strange black metal was transformed into the Dun weapons and armor, a skill apparently few possessed, and tower authorities coveted this particular smith. No one spoke to the krukari or disturbed him, and if he owned a name, Baylun was yet to hear it spoken. The blacksmith had been the one manning the anvil when Baylun's company invaded the tower, but the krukari was ordered to vacate the room before they reached this level. This confused Baylun. If the enemy was aware of his company's presence, why did they allow the crystal to be destroyed? It made no sense. He headed the opposite direction.

Baylun paused upon reaching the captain's quarters. He stared at the latch, hesitant to open the door. Was Daymyn on the other side, awaiting Baylun to join him for the penalty of being spies? There was no choice. Baylun entered.

Daymyn was not there. Captain Rozall was alone, sitting behind his desk and reading from a parchment. He was a cruel master that preferred to train soldiers with a barbed whip. Fortunately, Baylun had never received such reinforcement, and to his knowledge, neither had Daymyn. Would this be the first time? Baylun supposed it was better than the alternative. Some of those reporting to Rozall's office were never seen again.

"You wanted to see me, sir?" Baylun stirred the captain from his reading.

"Baylun." Rozall's voice was low and steady. He set the parchment aside and sat back.

Sweat beaded on Baylun's forehead. Rozall's eyes were level; unemotional. They were always unemotional. That was the way of most soldiers once they learned the Chant; once the priests declared them *worthy* to learn the Chant. It was as if their compassion had been removed. They still exhibited occasional laughter and anger, but never while on duty.

"Baylun?" Rozall's brow lowered. "Is your mind wandering again?"

"Sorry, sir." Baylun needed to get control over his thoughts.

"Wandering minds distract from the Message," Rozall said. "How can you hope to receive the Message if your focus is elsewhere?"

The Message... Baylun was tired of hearing about the Message. He did not even know what it was. Nowhere in his training had the Message been explained, though the priests brought it up often enough in conversations. Only a handful of the top recruits had received the Message, and they left the tower shortly after completing the Chant ritual.

Baylun's mind was wandering again, and he forced himself to focus on Rozall. "Yes, sir. Of course."

"I have news that is not particularly to my liking," Rozall said evenly.

This was it. Rozall knew. Or he suspected something.

"You are being elevated to lieutenant, beginning immediately."

Baylun's jaw dropped. Lieutenant? Him? Why would anyone make *him* a lieutenant? It must be a trick.

"It is against my better judgement." Rozall seemed more interested in the back of his fingers than Baylun's presence. "You have yet to receive the Message. But others have been convinced. Your skills in battle are extraordinary and the men seem to have the utmost respect for you." A disturbing grin stretched across his face. "Why, one recruit even cried out your name, as if you might arrive to save him."

Rozall chuckled. An evil chuckle. It was the first emotion Baylun ever saw the captain express, and it was unnerving. And why would a recruit be calling Baylun's name? What had Rozall been doing to make the soldier need saving?

Once Rozall finished reminiscing, he said, "You will gather your personal belongings and move to the officer's barracks." He frowned. "And there's another issue. Why do you hold on to possessions?" He shook his head. "Well, once you receive the Message, all will change."

Baylun definitely did not want this Message.

"The master arrives soon," Rozall added, "so the men *must* be better. They'll not like the consequences if they are otherwise. *You* will see to their training personally." He eyed the hammer on Baylun's back. "You may want to try your hand at something with an edge. Perhaps an axe. Dun weapons cannot be made into hammers. They need to enter the blood to be effective."

Baylun was afraid to move or speak. He was in a nightmare. He then noticed Rozall had resumed reading his parchment.

Without another glance, the captain said, "That is all, Lieutenant Baylun."

Baylun exited, and he walked numbly to the central chamber. It was the main training room, and several soldiers were present. They ceased in their exercises when Baylun closed the door, and the tower fell silent—except for the blacksmith's pounding. Baylun lifted his head and saw the trainees standing at attention. While half of them bore grins, the others showed a mixture of respect and pain—those having failed in their sparring matches.

"Lieutenant Baylun!"

Baylun did not know who had spoken, or how the news had already gotten out, but everyone responded.

"Lieutenant Baylun!"

Baylun nodded, and he headed for the trapdoor.

He climbed down the iron rungs to the descending staircase and made his way to the ground level. The circular room still contained the weapon racks, but most of the black weapons were gone, having been distributed to worthy soldiers that received the Message and learned the Chant. Though the smithy worked night and day, the racks rarely held more than half a dozen weapons.

Baylun exited the chamber and turned right. He passed the first door on the inner wall, the entry to the Dun Lancers' quarters, and continued to the next door. The barracks.

Before he opened the latch, Daymyn and a guard named Ruson appeared down the corridor, laughing while they headed his way.

Daymyn stopped and smiled. "Well. Lieutenant, is it?"

Baylun did not want to be reminded. But another soldier was present, so he had to play the part. "That's me." He tried to sound light.

"Couldn't have happened to a better man!" Ruson beamed. He then changed the subject. "You'll never guess what we've been up to."

Baylun lifted his brow.

Daymyn chuckled at Ruson. "Do you jest? A lieutenant has no time for such things."

"Seriously, though," the soldier said. "We just constructed a trap at the entrance."

"A trap?" Baylun had not heard of any plans for a trap.

"Yeah." Ruson glanced at Daymyn. "With the pull of a lever around the bend, you can shower acid on anyone breaching the tower." His smile broadened. "Let's see someone break in here again!"

"Acid?" Baylun frowned.

Daymyn flashed his usual sarcastic grin as he spoke to Ruson. "I think that's beneath him now." He turned to Baylun, his expression sincere. "But you are to be congratulated, Lieutenant Baylun."

"Agreed," Ruson said. "I'm honored to follow you, sir."

Would Ruson be so willing if he knew the truth? Baylun was not so sure.

A week passed, and Baylun spent most of his time training soldiers in the art of heavy weapon combat. But also he was made commander of a squadron to patrol the surrounding terrain. It would have been a perfect opportunity to escape, except for the fact that Daymyn was not with him. All the same, he enjoyed breathing fresher air.

Another week later, Baylun was sitting in the lieutenants' quarters when an intense cold descended onto the tower—a strange occurrence, since the days had been surprisingly warm. The chill grabbed hold of Baylun's bones and a creeping fear stirred within his soul. Next came a horrible sound; a familiar sound. It was the cry the undead dragon made before grabbing Romik and flying away, and it echoed across the sky.

The door to the chamber opened, and Lieutenant Slythe stuck his head inside.

"The new master is here," Slythe said. "Everyone to the top floor."

Baylun joined the other officers as they filed up Darum Carumbor, and the higher he climbed, the colder it became. Upon reaching the throne room, Baylun's knees shook and his heart raced. It relieved him slightly to see he was not the only one suffering, as a couple others shared in his ailments. Captain Rozall was perfectly calm.

A warrior covered in black armor sat on the brass chair, and from the eye slit of the helmet shone two blue dots. Baylun knew right away it must be a Death Lord.

"All hail Lord Radaam!" Captain Rozall shouted.

Everyone raised a fist. "All hail Lord Radaam!" they echoed in unison.

Baylun only mouthed the words, and it seemed the blue eyes shifted his way. His lip quivered, and he bit it to keep it still while attempting to hide behind another lieutenant.

"Get in line to welcome the new master!" Rozall ordered.

Baylun fell as far back as he dared, and one by one, the officers greeted Radaam and kissed the dark gauntlet before stepping aside.

Baylun's heart pounded as the line inched forward.

Two lieutenants were ahead of him.

The pounding filled his ears.

One more.

The glowing eyes burned into Baylun as he reached the throne. To either side of the brass chair, priests glared down their long noses. Radaam extended the black gauntlet.

Bowing, Baylun spoke as clearly as his chattering teeth allowed. "Welcome, Master."

He kissed the metal glove, and a stinging chill shocked his lips. It was more than a sting. It was a stabbing sensation that pierced the back of his skull and traveled deep into his lungs. He pulled away, hoping he did not do so too quickly, and followed the lieutenant that preceded him.

Baylun sensed the Death Lord's eyes on him, and he swallowed the urge to cry out for the pain. He realized two others were doing the same while the rest displayed excited grins.

"We have not received the Message," Slythe whispered to Baylun, his voice shaking. "That is why he affects us so. But don't worry. We shall be worthy soon enough."

The Message. Again. Baylun needed to escape before it was too late.

CHAPTER 24

BOMAHNI

Desser awoke. It was dark, but the sunrise was not far off. He stepped from his tent and breathed in the crisp air. Every morning in Pavan was crisp.

He gazed at the village — at least, that's what the Pavish called it. It was more like a traveling campsite. When Desser first arrived, he thought it to be temporary lodgings for the army, but he realized it was just how the Pavish lived. They dwelt in tents all year long, even through the winter months, moving from place to place like migrating animals. Presently, it was summer, and only the mornings and nights were chilly. The encampment sat among the hills north of the Stone Eagle Mountains, less than a mile from the Helmland border. It seemed the barbarians believed the hunting there to be best.

Desser remembered when he first viewed the campsite over a month ago, after being caught in the middle of a battle between the Pavish and Blackfoot goblins. The savages rendered him unconscious once the conflict ended, and he awoke within their camp-village, dressed in a tunic and clean-shaven. And with the manacles attached to his feet, escape was impossible. There were no other prisoners that Desser could see. So why did they keep him?

They put him to work a couple of days after he arrived, but with the wounds he received from the goblins, he was only capable of menial tasks. So his days were filled with cleaning tools and threshing and winnowing the wheat. The injuries did not stop the men from treating him harshly, however, and they enjoyed pushing him around when he did not comprehend their orders. As a result, he spent hours in dire pain.

At night, a woman tended to his lacerations, but she was not very good at her job. Though Desser was no expert with healing herb preparation, he knew her process to be flawed, and it would take him longer to recover than was necessary. When he attempted to correct her, she met him with a slap and more harsh words he did not understand. After several days, he made the woman see that he only wished to help, and when she reluctantly allowed his assistance, he impressed even himself. Before long, Desser was teaching all the women the proper ways to prepare herbs and dress wounds, his limited knowledge notwithstanding.

His nurse also brought him scraps to eat twice a day, as well as a sour-tasting draft to wash it down. The food was tepid and bore teeth marks from the one that failed to finish it, but it was better than starving.

Once Desser was physically able, they changed his occupation to chopping wood. A few days later, he seized the opportunity to show a hunter a more efficient way to skin an elk. He received a smile, the first one meant for him in some time, and they promoted him to skinning and cleaning animals after the daily hunts concluded.

The next week was easier. The tribe seemed appreciative of Desser's contributions and allowed him a bit more freedom, although they kept him clean-shaven and the shackles remained. They showed him slightly more patience when he failed to understand their words, and instead of being struck or pushed around, he received raps on the top of his head.

They soon permitted him to eat with the villagers, and he was grateful to no longer receive leftovers. But his meals were still served to him by his nurse, whose name was Barrelda. When Desser noticed all the men having their food brought to them, he felt a little more comfortable with the custom—only his mother had ever catered to him in such a fashion. Even the draft tasted better.

After another week, Desser held an understanding of certain words and phrases. It was not enough to hold meaningful conversations, but he could promptly respond to most of the commands issued to him. He also picked up on the fact that the women were not mere servants, for they trained with weapons every afternoon. He later discovered it was their duty to be ready for combat if a dispute broke out with a rival tribe. Besides that, the constant threat of Blackfoot goblins forced the women to stay sharp.

One day, while Desser was tanning a bear hide, he watched a practice session. The women placed too much of their weight forward, trying to put every bit of strength into their attacks, and it left them vulnerable. As Desser thought back to when he first encountered the barbarians, he realized the men fought the same way against the Blackfoot goblins.

Over the next few days, Desser convinced Barrelda to bring her spear to his tent after dinner, and he demonstrated to her a proper stance. She resisted, of course, but seemingly only to remind Desser he was not in charge. She caught on quickly, and it surprised Desser to see her teaching other women the same lesson the following day.

Life continued to improve, and the men allowed Desser to join the hunt. Although he did not take part in any actual hunting—they used him as a lackey—he appreciated not having to wear the heavy shackles during those times. He found the Bomahni, as the tribe was called, to be excellent hunters, but he still had a few tricks he was able to teach them about tracking and trapping. They occasionally ran into Blackfoot goblins when exploring in the east, and the Bomahni enjoyed those skirmishes almost as much as encountering large game. The barbarians were savage in combat and fought well, and Desser noticed some of the techniques he had shown Barrelda being utilized—apparently there were no secrets within the tribe.

More than once, Desser stared longingly at the Stone Eagle Mountains during the hunts, contemplating escape. He would give anything to know his cousins were all right; to see that Vaeldor was safe from the evil he witnessed—the goblins were proof enough of the enemy's continued existence. But escape was impossible. Too many barbarians surrounded him at all times, and if they caught him, he would lose the rapport he had worked so hard to achieve. Still, the temptation grew.

Presently, Desser shook his head clear. The feeling that someone was outside his tent had stirred him from his slumber, but he saw no one other than the Bomahni that patrolled the night. He returned inside, where a transparent image of Selanna stared at him.

Was he dreaming?

"Hello, Desser." She held a sympathetic smile. "I am glad to see you are healthy."

"How...?" he stammered. "Where...?"

"That is not important." Her expression became serious. "I need you to stay with these people. You must convince them that Helmland is as much an enemy to them as they are to the rest of Vaeldor. We need them to fight."

"But..." His mind raced. "What about Romik? And Daymyn and Baylun?"

"I am sorry, but I have not yet located Romik," she replied. "I *am* looking. Daymyn and Baylun are hiding, but I cannot contact them. It would not be safe for them."

Desser nodded. He appreciated her honesty about Romik, but part of him wished she had lied. To put his cousin from his mind, he focused on what she was asking.

"How do I convince the Pavish of anything? I can barely communicate with them."

"You communicate better than you believe," she said. "And there are those among them that understand you more than you know. You must find a way."

The weight of her request descended onto his shoulders. How could he incite an entire tribe of savages? A village of warriors that lived to hunt and fought to survive? They were not marauders that initiated combat. They protected what was theirs. "I'll... try."

"You *will* find a way." It was as if Selanna had read his thoughts. "And once you do, you must wait for the right moment. Marching too early would bring devastation."

He frowned. "When will that be?"

"I will send word, somehow." She seemed unsure. "You will know."

"I'll do my best." It was the most he could offer.

The tent flap opened, and Desser turned in alarm. It was only the wind. When he looked back, Selanna was gone.

Was she a dream? Was he still asleep? No. It had been real. But how could he accomplish what she asked? There was no choice. He had to try.

Desser banged his fist on his chin and paced. He had seen enough barbarians killed by Blackfoot goblins to realize the hatred Bomahni held for the little monsters. It was his best option.

The flap opened again. It was Barrelda. Relief washed over her face and she uttered something in her language Desser did not comprehend.

"I'm afraid our time will soon come to an end." Desser sighed. "Pity. Funny as it sounds, I have enjoyed your company."

Her eyes grew wide, all signs of relief vanishing, and she shook her head.

Desser stared, his brows drawing together. "You understand me?"

She suddenly resembled a scared rabbit, and she sought the tent flap for escape.

Desser seized her arm. "You understand."

She relaxed her muscles and sighed. "Many speak common tongue." She spoke slowly, enunciating each word. "It only way to make trade with non-tribes."

"All this time?" Desser grew annoyed. "All this time, you could have told me exactly what you wanted? Exactly what I was supposed to do?"

"It forbidden to use!" Her expression was wild, but her tone was apologetic. "Only for trade."

Desser understood. The Bomahni were proud and valued their way of life. They were not so savage as the southern realms believed, but they were barbarians nonetheless. Then another thought occurred to him.

"Why are you here?" he asked. "It is not yet sunrise. The hunt doesn't begin for a couple of hours at least."

"Dream."

"What?"

"Dream," she added more emphasis. "I had dream you were gone." She shook her head. "Just dream."

Was it a dream? On the same night Selanna shows up for a visit, Barrelda dreams of him escaping? In any case, Selanna's words rang true. The Bomahni understood him.

"Please," she begged, "no more speak. Do not tell."

"No one will know." He gave a reassuring smile to calm her. He did not wish to bring her undue stress.

Desser did not return to his blanket after Barrelda left. For the next hour, he pondered the task before him. Come sunrise, he stood outside his tent, watching the men gather for the day's hunt. A hunter headed his way, bearing the key to unshackle his feet.

Today, Desser would begin communicating by speaking freely, all the while pretending he did not realize they understood. He would reveal things, and they would have no choice but to think on his words.

CHAPTER 25

THE CAVE

Silence rang in Romik's ears. A stabbing sensation in his chest prohibited any deep breathing, and his eyes did not want to open. He recalled the hissing steam and the rush of air from his flight with the undead dragon. Then the explosion and pain. So much pain. He hurt all over.

Something rustled nearby, and Romik held his breath to listen.

It was quiet. Very quiet.

He opened a painful eyelid.

Impenetrable darkness surrounded him.

He resumed breathing.

The rustling started again—a presence hovered over him. Romik reached for it, but his arms would not move. He was tied down! He struggled to break the restraints, but his pain doubled for the effort and he cried out.

"Hush," came a soft voice. A man's voice. "We know not what's out there."

The voice sounded familiar, but Romik was unsure. He tried again to penetrate the darkness, but it was too deep.

"It's me, Brem," the man said. "I apologize. You must be blind in this cave. Many of your bones are broken, and I have secured you to begin the healing process."

"Brem?" Romik did not recognize his own voice. It was dry and cracked, like an old man's.

"I'm sorry," Brem whispered. "We can't risk any light just yet. So try to sleep. You need lots of rest."

"How long have I...?" Romik could not think straight.

"Where...?"

"Hush, young warrior. Sleep."

Romik opened his eyes. Things were different. He was in a cave illuminated by a small fire. He turned his head as far as his injuries allowed, and he saw a narrow tunnel exiting the chamber. Nothing moved or made a sound outside the occasional crackling of the flames. He was alone.

He tried to sit up, but he could not. No restraints prevented it, but splints fastened to his arms and legs were like stone weights, and all attempts to move brought surges of pain. On the floor nearby sat a mixing bowl, stained by a brown liquid, and several torn pieces of cloth that might have once been a shirt. Romik surrendered all hope that the journey into Helmland had been a bad dream.

A noise came from the tunnel. Romik tilted his head to see Brem entering the chamber. The marteese appeared thinner than Romik remembered and his cheeks were covered by stubble, and although the dark spots covering his body no longer oozed, they were definitely more noticeable.

"Ah, you're awake." Brem spoke louder than before. "Good. I was getting worried. The last time you woke was four days ago."

Four days? It seemed like four minutes!

"Where are we?" Romik managed. His voice had not improved.

"Helmland." Brem frowned. "At least I think we're still in Helmland. I was separated from everyone when the ground erupted. I know not how far I was thrown or how long I had been there, and I found no one else when I awoke." His ashen face paled further, making the dark spots shine all the more. "I abandoned my search when I spied the strangest creature I had ever laid eyes on. I'm not even sure I can accurately describe it. It was an odd shape. There was no distinguishable head, but it possessed a single eye and a large mouth. Instead of arms or legs, it had four tentacles, and it hovered above the ground. I hid until the thing passed, and then moved away as fast as I dared." He sighed. "I must have walked for two days.

"Once I arrived in the mountains, I found this cave." Brem scanned the room. "As far as I can tell, I have been here a couple of weeks. I'm not completely sure." His eyes drifted to his pouch on the floor. It bulged with whatever contents it held. "I ran out of food and water some time ago, but there's a small pond and wild berries nearby. I'm afraid berries are all we have to eat, since I'm no good as a hunter or fisherman."

"It's been two weeks?" Romik barely finished the last word when a fit of coughing assailed him.

Once the spell passed, Brem answered. "*I* have been here that long. Which is three days longer than yourself. I only found you because of an explosion a few miles to the east. I investigated, hoping to find a friendly face, and there you were, lying among a bunch of dragon bones. And let me tell you, you're not an easy lad to haul. I had to remove your armor. Even then, it took me a few hours."

"What about Baylun?" Romik feared the answer.

"I have seen no sign of the others." The priest's shoulders slumped. "But I dare not search too far. I have never been good at sneaking, and I have no intentions of being discovered by that floating creature."

"What about my sword?" Strength returned to Romik's voice.

"I retrieved your gear," Brem replied. "I knew once you were back to health that you would need them. Your armor, sword, and axe are right over here."

The priest moved to the side of the chamber, where Romik saw his chain shirt and the Sword of Ironside. Baylun's axe was there as well. Why was Baylun's axe there? Had Romik's brother arrived to rescue him? Was Brem hiding the fact that Baylun was dead?

"Where did you find the axe?" Romik's heart paused while he awaited the answer.

"Strangely enough," Brem said, "I found it in the dragon's crumbled skull. I only noticed it because of the glowing runes, although they darkened shortly after I removed it. Did this not belong to your brother?"

So that was why the dragon crashed. Baylun must have thrown the axe. But how was it the runes were aglow? The dwarf who sold it to Romik prattled on about the axe's special qualities, but Romik took it as nothing more than a push to make a sale. It was a marvelous weapon, but glowing runes?

Brem moved to Romik's side and began pouring the contents of a vial into the mixing bowl. The liquid oozed out, and while it did so, Brem recited a prayer.

Once the priest finished, Romik asked, "What's that?"

"Maple sap." Brem added a couple more ingredients to the mix. "Lucky for us, there's a maple tree growing just south of this cave, up the slope a bit. Mother Nature has blessed us with this fortune, and it's the only reason you still live."

What was the marteese talking about? How could tree sap keep Romik alive?

Brem dipped two fingers into the bowl and spread the sticky concoction across Romik's wounds. A pleasant, tingling sensation chased away most of the pain, and Romik exhaled as his muscles relaxed.

"I think you should be able to sit up for a short while now," Brem said upon completion of his task.

Romik tensed while the marteese lifted his upper body into a seated position, but the discomfort was not as bad as he expected. He looked around the chamber, and he detected a hint of sunlight shining from the tunnel. It seemed brighter than the sun that shone over Helmland the last time he viewed it.

Brem fed Romik berries from the pouch and helped him to drink water — his arms were not yet ready to feed himself. The berries were tart and hardly filling, leaving Romik wanting for meat. The priest then enjoyed some berries, and Romik was surprised he maintained his balance once the marteese's helping hand withdrew.

"What's your plan?" Romik ventured to ask while Brem chewed.

Brem sighed. "I'm still thinking about that. I came here to hide from the tentacle creature. But then I found the cave to be surrounded by everything I need to survive, although I wouldn't mind a nice rabbit stew once in a while. I'm convinced Frayorna led me here, and finding you confirms that. I was *meant* to find you. And once you're healthy enough, we'll figure out what it is we are here to do, and where it is we're supposed to go." He eyed the tunnel. "I just wish I knew that Kiryanna and the others were okay."

Romik nodded in agreement. As to what he and Brem were supposed to do, he was at a loss. He had seen the enormous krukari that trailed after them from Lormin Dmurr. What could a wounded warrior and a spotted marteese possibly accomplish?

CHAPTER 26

THE CRYPT

Selanna was out of breath. The incantation Elgarroth taught to her had worked—one of several spells she learned in haste while preparing to be the next Seer. She communicated with Desser, relaying to him Elgarroth's message, and she was sure he would do his best to make the situation work. Projecting her image had been easier within Elgarroth's home in Vermallon Forest, where she practiced at shorter ranges. This time, she extended the spell many miles to cover the distance between Pavan and the inn room in Vol Maren, where she now sat. And that had taken a fair amount of power. She did not know for certain Desser would succeed, but she had to leave that to hope.

Her stay at the House of Elgarroth lasted a month, and she spent nearly every waking hour learning and practicing magic. *Projecting* was one of the more impressive lessons, but another was a spell her mentor called *linking*. This incantation provided the ability to see through the eyes of those she was well acquainted with, so long as she was aware of their general location.

"That is how you know what transpires around you!" Selanna said to Elgarroth. "How you kept track of the war versus Trannum."

"It is." His expression became serious. "But I caution you: You did not grant this ability for personal gain, or to assist you in protecting only the futures of those you care about. To abuse His Gifts... I cannot tell you what the consequences might be. It has never been done."

"I understand."

"And," he added, "the more you use the Sight, the more the Sight comes to you. But keep in mind that you may have several visions of the same occurrence, all bearing different outcomes. You see, the future is yet to be determined, because we can never truly know the actions others will take until they take them. There are multiple paths of possibility, and determining the proper route to achieve the desired outcome is not often clear."

"I believe I understand." Selanna hoped her words rang true.

As the days passed, Selanna's fear that the war was fast approaching grew; and though her mentor insisted her companions in Helmland were in no immediate danger, he admitted things could change quickly. At her insistence, he granted her request to depart, regardless of the lessons she had yet to learn. The last piece of advice he imparted was to search for Desser in Pavan and for Romik and Brem in Helmland. He gave no clues as to the whereabouts of Baylun and Daymyn, and he warned her not to seek them, for her presence would likely be detected and endanger the two.

After exiting Vermallon Forest, Selanna responded to a summons from Grand Paladin Montac, and she informed him of everything she saw and heard during her time within the enemy realms. Montac's expression was grim when she confirmed Uustaag's return, and he sat silently for a couple of minutes, staring at nothing.

The following day, New Palidur issued heralds to all kingdoms, as if taking charge of Vaeldor's defenses; just as Palidur did the last time Uustaag threatened the world. Before Selanna's arrival, Montac had focused only on Beit, and he sent a thousand Palidurians to both Harbnum and Virch to help secure the bridges. Now, the entire city was on alert, and every paladin, priest, and holy soldier prepared for war.

Over the next few weeks, messengers from Sardina, Sendorum, Marcove, Kalmaar, and Nira reported to New Palidur, all bearing promises of armies within the month. The Urell Coast offered no soldiers, instead shoring up their border to the north. Moclen, Philen, and Neja contributed, but their battalions marched directly to the Virch-Beit bridge.

From the Varlimor Mountains, Morimont issued not only an army of dwarves, but a dozen enormous ballistae with blunted missiles—weapons they employed against the undead dragons in the Necromancer War. Selanna heard great things about the giant crossbows, and she was glad to have them. Morimont also sent word that Rornibur would provide additional dwarves when the time came.

From Salenti, Vermallon, and Orlenfel Forests, thousands of elves swore an oath to see the Ancient Enemy vanquished. Of the three tribes, the Orlenfel muster was the smallest, but the gray elves' ability to combine magic with archery and swordplay would make them seem four times their size.

Selanna spent a month in the Holy City, and though the time passed swiftly, she did not lose track of the days. She needed to depart for Neja. When she arrived to the Grand Cathedral to relate this to Montac, she was delighted to find King Cavalor of Marcove holding council with the Grand Paladin. Cavalor, son of Borse and Merssa, had been present during the planning phase of the Necromancer War, and his keen mind would prove an asset in the weeks to come.

With Cavalor were his thirteen zhokards—warriors that did not age and could not be killed by normal means. The zhokards were an unintentional creation of Trannum's that turned against him, and as long as their black hearts remained within their chests, they overcame grim fates that mortals could not. They kept their identity secret from Trannum, afraid of what he might do to them if discovered. That changed after Cavalor's arrival at Castle Lambrak. It pleased Selanna to see the zhokards willing to face their creator once again.

Selanna regretted having no time to spend with Cavalor. In years past, the king enjoyed speaking of his late mother as much as Selanna did, and she remembered several nights in Castle Lambrak doing just that. But there was work to be done. She offered a brief farewell and headed north.

She rode into Harbnum and then Virch to check on the bridges.

Soldiers were arriving every few days to either location, and everything seemed secure. If the massing of armies affected the enemy's plans, Onzac and Zurzak did a good job of hiding it. If only there had been time for a closer look.

Selanna proceeded to Vol Maren in Neja, where she now readied herself for mountain travel. She needed to revisit the tomb Trannum occupied many years ago, when he began his first assault upon Vaeldor. She needed to see what she had missed.

Her last journey into the Stone Eagle Mountains had been a taxing affair. With that in mind, she decided to begin as soon as the city gates opened — Merssa would have been proud! She awoke well before the rising of the sun to pass her message on to Desser, and after donning her gear, she headed downstairs to the Ogre's Breath tavern. Within, Eraim was already sitting at a table. Selanna's friend had risen early to entice the innkeeper into making sure breakfast was ready. It would not be a tasty meal, but something was better than nothing.

Selanna missed Eraim dearly over the past couple of months — it had been decades since she last spent as much time without her friend's company. They parted in Tikken City before Selanna reported to Vermallon Forest to train with Elgarroth. She did not explain why she needed to go alone, for her mentor forbade even Eraim from knowing she was a seer. As luck had it, Vecnor was still in the city, and he happily accepted Eraim's companionship while he spread word of the impending war. As well, Eraim assumed the responsibility of speaking to the families of those left in Helmland, and she used the opportunity to recruit former companions for the mission into Trannum's crypt. Selanna would have loved to hear about her friend's excursion with Vecnor when she arrived in Vol Maren the previous night, but the hour had been late and they needed rest.

Magneer entered the tavern next, his face eager. He had a bit more girth than in his younger days, and he wore a thick beard that was a mixture of gray, brown, and blonde. Unlike his father, Pallit,

Magneer had never been a King's Ranger in Vol Maren, but Eraim sketched a detailed map from what she remembered of their first trip to the rorbak, and he was more than capable of guiding them.

Rorbak... The precious stone that defied time. The dwarves of Rornibur kept its location secret, and only they possessed the knowledge to work it. Over ten centuries ago, Trannum placed his crypt among the mighty white stones and the region became plagued by the undead. Rornibur abandoned their treasured rock afterward, deciding it to be cursed, and dubbed it the Forbidden Area. Following the supposed downfall of Trannum, the evil faded and Rornibur resumed mining the rorbak. The dwarves then produced several monuments and buildings, always for a hefty price, but they constructed the statue of Merssa in New Palidur at no cost. The notion of returning to the rorbak haunted Selanna. It held many terrible memories for her.

Nidor and Gruelenor arrived, bringing Selanna's focus back to the tavern. The barbarian paladin was as tall as ever, with a physical presence only bested by Vecnor. Gruelenor's face was stern, but his eyes lacked the bitterness they constantly displayed in the past.

Though he was only half-hobgoblin, Gruelenor's countenance suggested otherwise. It was a trait Selanna found revolting. After discovering his deepest secret, however, it no longer surprised her. Selanna first learned of Gruelenor's heritage after the Necromancer War ended; that the krukari had been the eldest son of Gruzim, one of Trannum's foulest Death Lords. From what she understood, Gruelenor kept that knowledge from his closest friends. In the end, he assisted in his father's destruction, marking the turning point of the Battle of the Dead Fields. Gruelenor's past was known to very few, and Selanna thought it best to keep it that way.

Nidor seemed in good spirits, all things considered, and it was likely due to Holindale's allotment of warriors to the impending war. It disappointed the dark-skinned paladin when his kin were slow to join the conflict against Trannum twenty-two years ago, but the territory's chiefs quickly banded together for the cause this time, and the army of Dales in Virch did not escape Selanna's notice when she passed through. Nidor was surely proud.

Though Selanna had never witnessed it herself, she heard about Nidor's ability to draw upon Silcor's Healing Flame, enveloping his hands with fire. He used this divine gift to mend wounds, just as a powerful priest might use prayer, or so she had been told. It was also rumored that Nidor's eyes and sword lit up while battling the undead in Kalmaar, and that the holy fire slew the enemy faster than any weapon.

Selanna had seen little of Nidor over the past decade, since the paladin became a mentor to Dales wanting to fight in the name of Silcor, the fire god. But when Nidor found time to venture from Holindale, Gruelenor was usually at his side. The two shared a bond that pleased Selanna, and though she did not comprehend its depth right away, she realized it to almost rival that of hers with Eraim.

Greyor stifled a yawn while stepping through the tavern door, and Selanna was grateful to see Clanghorr hanging on the dwarf's belt. The ancient battleaxe was the only weapon to challenge the strength of Mithkahr—although Baylun's axe presented a mystery Selanna hoped to investigate further. In Greyor's hands, Clanghorr destroyed the Death Lord, Velgaad, as well as many dunarchins, and over the past two decades, the dwarf slew hundreds of goblins while protecting Morimont from raiding parties in the Varlimor Mountains.

Everyone was now present, except for Vecnor.

Selanna turned to Eraim. "Will Vecnor be joining us?"

Eraim gave a curt shake of her head. "He has been a bit edgy as of late. Said he has affairs to tend to. And he declined my assistance, if you can believe that. Probably working with Tux!"

Blast! Selanna had counted on Vecnor's help. And now that he was out of Eraim's sight, there was no telling when they might see him again. Once they finished with the tomb, Selanna would use the linking incantation to locate him if necessary.

All but Selanna and Eraim slurped the gruel provided by the

Ogre's Breath, and various frowns resulted. Magneer sneered at his spoon; Gruelenor swallowed hard to force down a mouthful; and Greyor held back his long beard to sniff his bowl more than once, as if to make sure it was actual food. Nidor seemed the least disgusted by the meal, as his only reaction was to raise one of his eyebrows. The Dale's shaved head displayed tattoos of fire traveling up his dark scalp, starting just above the ears and at the nape of his neck, and Selanna wondered if it ever lit up with flame. She shook the thought and addressed the company.

"Thank you for joining us. As a reminder, we are entering the crypt where Trannum dwelt for more than a thousand years. The last time Eraim and I delved into its tunnels, we fought ghouls, an army of skeletons, and a demon called Ragab."

At the mention of the demon's name, Nidor's jaw tightened and the color drained from Magneer's face. Selanna was certain Gruelenor shifted in his chair as well. It was rumored the three had battled Ragab when they were younger.

"I know not whether any of those things are there anymore," Selanna admitted, "but I am sure it will be guarded in some way."

"We do not know the room you seek is actually there, correct?" Magneer asked.

Selanna sighed. "That is correct." Though she firmly believed the tomb to contain the necromancer's hall, she had no proof.

"Then why waste time on such an expedition?" Magneer looked around the table, as if he pointed out the obvious. "We could just as easily sneak into Helmland to find those you left behind."

Selanna expected the ranger to make that argument. Eraim warned her of Magneer's outrage back in Philen, when he was first approached. It was not until Eraim informed him the search for his son could not begin until they investigated the tomb that he agreed to take part in the mission. Selanna might have assured him Desser was all right, but it would have done no good. Had she told Magneer his son was in Pavan, he would already have left.

"Though it is distant," Nidor said in his deep voice, "I sense strong evil to the north."

"From what Eraim told us," Magneer turned to the paladin, "it may be Uustaag you feel."

It surprised Selanna how easily people grew comfortable uttering the krukari's name.

Nidor held a regretful expression for the ranger. "The warlord is in Lormin Dmurr. I doubt I can detect him at this distance."

"What are we looking for once we arrive?" Gruelenor asked Selanna.

It never failed to surprise her when Gruelenor spoke. The krukari still said little, but in his younger days he was practically mute. Selanna credited Nidor with Gruelenor's new outlook on life. Of course, the destruction of his father also aided in his growth, perhaps leaving nothing more for him to hide from his friends.

"Unfortunately, I do not know," Selanna replied. "But I am certain I will recognize it when I see it."

"That sounds encouraging," Magneer mumbled.

The door opened, and Kiryanna entered. The warrior's tardiness had Selanna believing she decided not to accompany them. Kiryanna was the only one outside of Eraim that Selanna spoke to about her conversation with Elgarroth; that Brem and the boys were safe. She hoped it would keep the marteese from making any rash decisions. She nodded at Kiryanna, who remained next to the exit, as if eager to depart.

"Let us be on our way," Selanna said to the others.

They headed south on foot along the paved streets, and the city gates were opening when they arrived. A path then took them north around Vol Maren's towering walls and to the foothills where they met up with a King's Ranger—a soldier tasked with keeping creatures of the mountains from harming Vol Maren and its citizens. Eraim had recruited the man's assistance at the Ogre's Breath the previous evening.

The ranger offered only a nod in greeting, and he led them up narrow paths into the Stone Eagle Mountains and onto the Barren

Trails. It was an arduous trek, constantly leading them along the rising terrain, and few words were spoken, even when they camped within ranger resting sites through the dark hours. By midday of the third day, the guide wished them luck and bid them farewell. Magneer then took the lead.

Following Eraim's map, Magneer left the trails behind. They spent the rest of the day hiking and climbing, and occasionally loose gravel threatened to send at least one of them back down the mountainside. But Magneer's skills prevailed and there were no mishaps. With an hour of sunlight remaining, the air cooled and the ground leveled. They had arrived.

The area was not as Selanna remembered. She recalled the rorbak to have held strange formations, like misshapen logs and freestanding pillars scattered about, and parts of the mountains were made of the stuff. Now, the white pillars and logs were missing and most of the mountains showed signs of having some of their stock removed. One wall bore not even a scratch, however. It was pure rorbak, perfectly flat, and it contained the hidden entrance to the crypt. As Selanna neared, a chill penetrated her cloak and she struggled to draw her next breath. She understood why the dwarves had avoided it.

Eraim ran her hands along the white stone. Upon locating what she sought, she pushed in a square section no bigger than a couple of inches per side. A hollow *click* sounded, followed by the rattling of a chain, and a large block of rorbak pivoted slowly into the mountain. Once the door had fully opened, the rattling stopped and a dark chamber was revealed.

Selanna summoned three floating lights and willed them to enter, chasing the shadows to the edges of the room. It was just as she and her companions had left it. The enormous octagonal chamber was deathly quiet, and each of its walls bore a single door. One was open, five were shut, and a couple had fallen from their hinges. On the far side, before the open door, the skeletal remains of fifty ghouls littered the floor.

Selanna recalled the battle against the ghouls from decades ago. She envisioned Pallit on the left side, receiving a savage bite to his leg while defending Bayn. In the middle, Vikur and Vecnor destroyed ghouls at an impressive rate, and Gruzim, not known to be Lord of Benasti at the time, slew a dozen of the creatures with his spear. Arkor was to the right, using his false arm as bait, and he hewed all the undead foolish enough to sink their teeth into the wood.

Arkor... Selanna missed having the one-armed warrior's companionship. He never replaced his wooden arm after shattering it on a Death Lord during the Necromancer War, but he proved an apt commander of Ironside Keep without it. Besides that, he was human, and too advanced in years to have taken part in this quest. Even Merssa would have been too old... had she survived the war.

Selanna walked to the center of the room, her steps echoing from wall to wall. Painted on the floor there was a faded black triangle with a blue oval breaching two of its sides—Trannum's symbol. A large circular section of stone in the middle of the oval once covered the secret entrance to the crypt, but it rested to the side, where Vecnor had placed it long ago. Evidently, no one bothered to return it. Selanna issued a mental command, and her lights swooped near. One then dropped into the shaft to illuminate iron rungs while the others hovered overhead.

"I believe Clanghorr knows this place." Greyor's voice rumbled across the hall.

The dwarf was correct. Dozens of severed ghoul limbs decorated the far end of the chamber as evidence. But Clanghorr knew a different hand back then. Poluran had wielded it. And though it proved a lethal weapon, it became much more than that in Greyor's possession. Selanna had no explanation as to why. Perhaps if they succeeded in the war against Uustaag...

Greyor descended the ladder, followed by Nidor, Gruelenor, Magneer, and Eraim. Selanna went next, and Kiryanna brought up the rear. The frozen rungs deposited them onto a landing, and they walked a short distance along a tunnel before the wall to the left ended, leaving them on a ledge within an enormous cavern. The ceiling rose high above, undetectable in the shadows, and the drop-off had Selanna wondering if a bottom existed.

Shifting currents played with their loose clothing, and the company hugged the wall while they made their way a couple hundred feet to the path's termination. The chasm then stretched ahead of them as well as to the left, and on the right was an archway adorned by leering demonic skulls. Greyor passed beneath the arch and to an identical one not far away, where he stopped and looked at Selanna.

"This was the hall of endless skeletons," she said, remembering the horde of undead.

She sent her lights forward, revealing a hundred smaller versions of the first two archways evenly spaced around a rectangular room and filled with cobwebs. A twenty-foot path extended across the chamber, free of the dust that coated the rest of the floor, and ended at a third larger arch. The remains of the skeletal warriors Selanna and her companions destroyed the last time were gone.

"When I say so," she said, "run through the other arch. Everyone." She took in a deep breath. "Go!"

Selanna eyed the smaller archways while they hastened across the room, but the cobwebs remained still. No undead emerged. They exited the chamber and slowed to a walk within the adjoining corridor. Selanna glanced over her shoulder, and she was grateful to see no skeletons pursuing.

Greyor led the way along the tunnel and around a bend. The hallway possessed several doors to the left and right, but Selanna motioned for the dwarf to continue.

After the next turn, they were met by a set of oversized doors with brass pull rings. One door stood open, revealing half of the pentagram occupying the floor of the circular chamber beyond, the blood used to sketch it now faded and brown. Greyor opened the second door, providing a full view, and the battle versus Ragab came to Selanna's mind. The summoning circle contained the lanky demon as a type of sentry. It killed Bayn, grievously injured Vikur, and battered Merssa before the company defeated it. Selanna eyed the scorching of Ragab's fire on the wall in a couple of places, and she could almost hear the gurgling that rolled in the back of the monster's throat whenever it grinned.

Greyor proceeded across the pentagram, crushing the fragments of the ram skull that Merssa shattered long ago. Selanna held her breath, wishing she had instructed him to go around, but the pentagram offered no resistance.

She returned her attention to the way ahead, where a ring of bone extended from a fanged skull to one side of a door. Greyor pulled the ring, and the wide door swung open.

They entered the final hallway. Halfway down the corridor's length was a door to the left, and another was at its termination.

"The evil grows strong," Nidor said, just above a whisper. "We are on the right path."

Selanna's stomach churned. Though grateful for Nidor's confirmation, she was reluctant to discover what awaited them once they arrived. Greyor looked at her, and she nodded at the far door. The dwarf marched forward.

Within the next room, Selanna held her breath. The laboratory had changed little. Many candles rested in holders, their wicks cold and dark, but their illumination was unnecessary as Selanna's lights rushed inside. To the right, a packed bookshelf covered the wall, and to the left, a couple of tables displayed stains and broken bottles, as well as fragments of the components the bottles once contained. On the opposite wall, runes formed an arch where a portal of darkness once allowed dunarchins access. Now, the gate was gone, and there existed only the wall to fill the space. Before the archway stood a podium of black rock where Trannum once read from a tome. The book was missing.

Though there were no occupants, Selanna's muscles tensed. "Search the room." Her throat was suddenly dry. "There must be another door."

While the company spread out, Selanna wandered to the bookshelf, hoping there might be something useful—or at least interesting. But the titles suggested books one typically found in every wizard's library. Nothing concerning the undead or gates. Were they the same volumes as the last time?

The bookshelf moved, nearly causing Selanna to jump from her skin, and it swung open to reveal a dark passageway. Turning, she saw Eraim staring from the podium, having just worked a mechanism on its base.

"This way," Selanna said to her companions.

Her lights raced to her, and one of them entered the passage. The width of the corridor was enough for two to walk abreast, and to either side stood four-foot statues of squatting demonic creatures that faced each other. Their mouths made up more than half of their bodies, wide open and showing forked tongues and hundreds of pointed teeth. Selanna wrinkled her nose.

Greyor moved forward with Clanghorr in hand, but when he stepped between the statues, their eyes came to life with a red light. The runes upon the axe's blades lit up, and Greyor cried out as he stumbled back into the laboratory.

Nidor rushed to the dwarf. Greyor panted, but otherwise appeared unharmed, and he did not take his focus from the sculptures.

"It was like my bones were being ripped from my body!" he said.

Selanna studied the demonic forms. The light of their eyes had dimmed. She concentrated, and their magical auras became obvious. She felt foolish for not checking earlier—what kind of Seer would she be if she failed to notice things under her nose? Reaching with her mind, she probed the magic, tracing its lines to find their origins. The power was strong. She had no doubt it was death magic, and she delved deeper, penetrating the essence to determine its exact function. She gasped, turning to Greyor.

"You are lucky to be alive." She shook her head. "Only the undead can proceed. It will rip the life from anything else attempting to pass."

Greyor searched his body, as if making sure it was all there.

"I believe Clanghorr saved you," Selanna said.

"Wouldn't be the first time." Greyor narrowed his eyes on the statues. "So how do we get past them?"

Selanna studied the demons. She did not know.

"Can we just destroy them?" asked Magneer.

Selanna had not thought of that. She concentrated again, revealing to herself the magical auras. She sensed no protective magic. Trannum likely could fathom no one daring to attempt entry after witnessing the trap.

"Yes," she said, hoping she did not miss anything. She checked again. Nothing changed. "Yes. I believe we can."

Greyor stepped forward. "Say no more!"

Selanna cringed as the dwarf brought down Clanghorr. The runes lit up when the weapon struck, and the blade sliced through the stone, severing the leering head of the demon on the left and crumbling it to pieces. There were no explosions or ill effects that Selanna noticed, and before she knew it, the other head was destroyed as well. Greyor then took in a deep breath and bolted into the tunnel.

"Wait!" Selanna shouted too late.

The dwarf gave her no time to make sure the magic was gone. He looked back with a raised brow, unharmed, and she breathed a sigh of relief and motioned for him to continue. Greyor shrugged and proceeded, and the others followed.

The corridor was natural, having never known a pick or chisel, and the height and width varied while the company progressed. The air was musty and dank and the floor moist, and the only sound outside Greyor's armored steps was the constant dripping of water. A downward slope was obvious, and after twenty yards the cavern twisted left and right until Selanna lost track of the direction they traveled. The only thing she was certain of was that they continued deeper into the mountain. After a mile, the tunnel widened and the ceiling rose to forty feet, displaying many stalactites. A bit farther and the passage opened up completely.

Everyone froze. Selanna's lights spread out to reveal a monstrous cavern, and contained within was a small village. If not for the ceiling of darkness, Selanna was certain the ledge outside Trannum's crypt would be visible a thousand yards overhead. She turned to the dark buildings, and her dream of the Shadow racing from its hall came to her in a flash.

She gasped. "This is the place."

CHAPTER 27

THE FORGOTTEN

Selanna gathered her lights to better illuminate the immediate area. Flat-roofed constructions made of dark bricks stood on either side of an equally dark cobblestone street, and stalagmites rose like deformed conical trees, having developed from centuries of dripping water. Though the buildings were in various states of ruin, the architecture was surprisingly creative for an underground village tucked away from the world. Exquisite pillars supported eaves of stone over the face of each building, and wooden doors exhibiting rot and swelling, as well as chewed edges along their bottoms, were set within decorative arches. Upon the corners of each rooftop sat gargoyles of skeletal fiends wearing hoods; some had tongues extended, some bared claws, and all possessed multiple fangs. The street passed between the buildings, disappearing as it curved to the right, and it was obvious stalactites were responsible for the damaged portions of the cobblestones and the structures. Selanna gazed upward, appreciating the distance the stones had fallen to wreak their havoc.

"Why would the undead have a village?" Greyor mumbled. "Don't they just need a grave to crawl into?"

"It is hard to know for sure." Selanna watched the shadows. "Perhaps it is for the more intelligent undead. There may be a part of them that craves some semblance of the life they once lived. The wizard, Melac, claimed dunarchins held quarters in Ironside Keep."

The dwarf sniffed.

"There is definitely evil here," Eraim said, her sword glowing with a red light.

"I am certain it is the presence I sensed in Vol Maren." Nidor eyed the gargoyles. "And it is strong."

"Ragab?" asked Magneer, his knuckles white upon the hilt of his sword.

The paladin shook his head. "I do not believe so. It is something very different."

Selanna gathered her courage with a deep breath. "Let us get started. Be prepared for anything."

The first building on the left was partially crumbled toward the rear, but the rubble allowed no view of what lay inside. Greyor forced open the reluctant door, breaking it free from its hinges to gain entry. It was hard to tell what the space beyond had been used for, as most of the roof covered the floor and the furnishings were buried. Among the debris were fragments of wood, feces, dead rodents, and bones of various sizes. A few of the bones appeared humanoid, but most had surely belonged to small animals.

They moved to the next structure, finding it much the same. Not all of it was in shambles, however, and a couple of chairs faced a hearth. The fireplace showed no signs of recent use and the chairs were in a poor state, their faded material ripped and the stuffing removed—likely used to make a nest somewhere.

"This place is deserted," Greyor said. "We should spread out."

"No!" Selanna spoke louder than she intended. She cleared her throat and calmed her voice. "No. We have yet to discover the evil that resides here. We stay together."

Nidor nodded.

Greyor led the way across the street and they entered two more buildings. The first was the remains of a workshop, apparently used to cut stone, and the other was a library. Selanna might have found the latter interesting, had the books not been completely destroyed.

A puddle surrounded the steps of the next entrance, forcing the party to soak their boots in three inches of cold water. Greyor then opened the door to reveal another library. This one maintained all four of its walls, three of which were covered by stone shelves bearing hundreds of books. A candle burned on one of two tables, and seated with its back to the company was a hooded figure in a black cloak. A pair of tomes lay open before it.

Greyor pointed his weapon at the room's occupant. "Who are you?"

The figure rose and slowly turned. It was a skeleton with glowing blue eyes. Bony hands pulled back its hood, revealing a thin black crown with a bright blue jewel resting between two points.

"I am Gortran." It sounded like a whispering serpent. "It is very nice to make your acquaintances."

"*Nice?*" Greyor gripped Clanghorr with both hands.

"*Very* nice." The skeleton's hiss stretched the last word. "I have been down here for so long, with no one to talk to." It glanced at the bookshelves. "Books have been my only friends."

Selanna stepped forward. "Who are you? And why are you here?" She did not believe the creature's seeming innocence. It was undead, bearing eyes reminiscent of a Death Lord's.

"I am Gortran." It spread its hands to either side. "I am the keeper of the books. I have been here for so long... I cannot remember anything else."

Selanna looked at Nidor. The barbarian paladin shook his head with a furrowed brow.

"Why do you not leave, since you are so lonely?" Selanna asked.

"Leave?" Gortran mused. "I can never leave. I am cursed to remain for all days."

"Cursed by whom?" Selanna pressed.

"Cursed..." Gortran gazed upward, as if searching his memory. "The name is old. Very old. One of great power... Power greater than any of his time. And the books are precious to him..."

"Selanna!" Kiryanna called harshly from beyond the door.

The marteese had remained outside of each building while the company completed their searches, keeping an eye on the street. Gortran continued to prattle on about the books as Selanna exited the library.

Kiryanna stood on the porch, gazing at the rooftops across the road. "The gargoyles."

Selanna looked up at the sculptures. Their eyes had taken on a blue glow. Her jaw muscles tightened and she released a frustrated breath. "It is stalling us!"

She scanned the surrounding shadows. Nothing else had changed. But then two robed skeletons with glowing blue eyes appeared from around the bend, hovering rather than walking. The trap was sprung.

"To arms!" Selanna cried out.

Eraim and Magneer charged from the building in response, but before any others followed, the library door slammed shut.

The approaching skeletons made gestures, summoning power Selanna recognized as attack magic. One discharged a bolt of lightning while the other launched a ball of fire. Selanna raised her hands, tearing the flooded portion of the street and lifting the cobblestones as a wall to intercept the spells. After the ensuing explosions, she allowed the bricks to collapse into a pile of debris. One skeletal figure remained, and it darted into the building on its right.

Selanna fired a green sphere into the library door, splintering the wood. The room was empty. Bookshelves still lined the sides of the chamber, but most of the back wall had collapsed.

"Where did they go?" Magneer's voice was desperate.

Kiryanna rolled her eyes. "Through the rubble!"

"Look out!" shouted Eraim.

Selanna turned to see the robed figure hovering atop the building it had entered. It cast a bolt of lightning, and everyone scattered. The attack struck the library, forming cracks across the structure's surface, but it remained intact. Selanna returned lightning of her own, and the creature dropped from sight, leaving her spell to strike the cavern wall and rain stones onto the empty roof.

"I will deal with this thing," she said. "You three find the others."

Magneer and Kiryanna rushed into the library.

Eraim did not move. "I am with you."

Selanna shook her head while eying the skeleton's hiding place. "No. Stay with them. I will be fine."

She issued a silent order to one of her lights, and it obediently hovered above Eraim. Eraim reluctantly entered the library with the light close behind.

Selanna approached the building across the ruined street, emitting an invisible field of magic. Her spell penetrated the walls of the structure, and she detected the skeleton inside, moving along the left wall toward the back. The undead wizard rose, and this time Selanna was ready when it appeared above the roof.

The skeleton's hands moved in preparation of a spell while its eyes scanned the library. It did not notice Selanna. She launched four green spheres, and the balls darted over the roof and exploded. The skeleton hissed as it retreated into the building.

Selanna ran to the door. It was locked. She stood back and splintered the wood, just as she had the library door. Within was a tidy room containing a hearth, a divan, and two comfortable looking chairs, and a pair of doors were to the rear.

Moving to the left door, Selanna pulled it open. The skeletal wizard hovered beside an elaborate bed, and it cast a dart of shadow from its finger. Selanna steered the attack aside with a wave of her hand, and the bolt tore through the stone wall, creating a three-foot hole. She responded with a spell of force, crashing the skeleton into the wall next to the bed.

The figure's hood fell, revealing a black crown holding a bright blue jewel. Unlike Gortran's crown, this one possessed a single point instead of two. Selanna released another spell of force, then lightning, then force again, and finished with a ball of fire. The skeletal wizard went on the defense, but it only managed to deflect one of the force spells and the lightning attack. Once the explosion of fire subsided, nothing remained but a pile of bones and a burning robe. The iron crown rattled to the floor.

Nidor watched while Gortran continued to babble about the lonely library. Then came Selanna's shout from outside.

"To arms!"

Gortran waved a bony hand after Magneer and Eraim exited, and the door slammed shut. Gruelenor tried unsuccessfully to force it open as Greyor charged the undead wizard.

The skeleton launched a bolt of lightning, and Greyor raised Clanghorr. The axe canceled the spell as its runes illuminated with a white light. Greyor then swung the mighty weapon, slicing Gortran's left hand from its body.

Nidor moved to support the dwarf, but the evil mage exploded the back wall with a wave of its remaining hand. A passage of worked stone was revealed, and Gortran fled with great speed, gliding several inches above the floor. Nidor followed Greyor over the rubble with Gruelenor close behind, but as soon as they entered the tunnel, the ceiling above the breach collapsed, plunging them into darkness.

Flames engulfed Nidor's sword to illuminate the corridor. The passage traveled ten yards and turned left, and Greyor disappeared around the bend. Nidor and Gruelenor hastened to catch up, and when they arrived at the corner, they saw the dwarf rambling down a long tunnel. In the distance, Gortran fired another bolt of lightning, and again Clanghorr devoured the spell. The skeleton then waved its hand downward, and chunks of the ceiling drove Greyor to the floor.

Nidor stopped to help Greyor from beneath the rocks. The dwarf shook his head and immediately picked up the chase, regardless of the blood running down his scalp—he held more determination than anyone Nidor had ever met.

Another thirty yards and the tunnel ended. Gortran was gone, and there was nowhere else to go.

"Must be a door." Gruelenor stepped forward. "I'll find it."

Greyor swung Clanghorr into the corridor's end. The weapon cut through the stone like a mighty pickaxe through soil, collapsing a portion of the wall into a pile of bricks and revealing a dark chamber beyond. Greyor crashed through the breach, and Nidor and Gruelenor ducked as they followed.

They entered a large dining hall. Dust and cobwebs decorated four stone tables, each of them set with enough fine silver to serve a dozen people. Gortran was not present.

"The dog runs and hides!" Greyor snarled. "It has tasted Clanghorr!"

Nidor sensed the skeleton to be near. "Stay alert."

"Such rude guests!" Gortran's voice hissed from everywhere.

Nidor spied movement across the room, but when he squinted, he saw nothing. His eyes flared, giving his vision an orange tint, and the wizard was revealed to him, hovering a couple of feet above the floor while blending into the darkness. It seemed to draw nearby shadows to it, making the air about it murkier than it should have been. It waved its hand, and a table upended onto Greyor, pinning the dwarf. Clanghorr fell to the floor.

"Where in Silcor's flaming name is that thing?" Gruelenor scanned the chamber with an arrow to his bowstring.

Nidor never tired of hearing his friend's passion for the fire god. Not even when Gruelenor was abusing the deity's name.

"Help Greyor," Nidor said without looking away from the undead wizard. "I will stop this evil."

Gortran's eyes followed Nidor while he circled the end of the tables, and its skeletal hand gestured as it whispered a chant. Nidor charged with a roar, ready to face whatever magic assailed him, but Gortran turned, and from its finger issued a bolt at Nidor's companions. It was a dark essence, deeper than black—the opposite of light. The spell passed through Gruelenor and into the wall, knocking the krukari to the floor and collapsing the secret passage.

Nidor wished to go to his friend, but he needed to destroy the evil mage before it brought further harm. The orange tint of his vision deepened as the enemy flew away from him in haste, and though his body temperature soared while he pursued, he felt no pain. Gortran's gaze fixed upon him, and its hand rose slowly as he neared—much too slowly to intervene. Nidor swung his sword, the weapon appearing like pure flame, and it seared through robes and bone, detaching the skeleton's right arm. Nidor attacked again and again, cutting the wizard in half and then decapitating it. Gortran's eyes darkened and the bones collapsed.

A sense of weightlessness held Nidor for a moment. His vision then returned to normal and he fell to the floor, covered in perspiration and panting. He pushed himself to his feet and rushed to his companions.

Greyor knelt beside Gruelenor, staring at Nidor with mouth agape but saying nothing. Gruelenor's eyes were closed. The black bolt had grazed the krukari's left shoulder, exposing much of the bone, which was in several pieces.

Nidor controlled his breathing while whispering a prayer, and Silcor's Healing Flame engulfed his hand. He placed the fire on Gruelenor's arm below the injury, uncertain if he possessed the ability to heal such a wound, and he was grateful when the bones fused together and new flesh rapidly formed.

Gruelenor was soon whole again, but he remained pale. His heart pounded at an alarming rate, as if trying to escape—the evil spell was not through with him yet.

Nidor closed his eyes and placed his hand over his companion's chest. He penetrated deep, wrapping the Flames about Gruelenor's heart and mouthing another prayer. The beating slowed.

"Thank Silcor," Nidor whispered.

Gruelenor awoke, and his eyes darted about the room as he sat up.

"You are safe," Nidor said. He turned to Greyor, who still gaped at him. "How is your head?"

Greyor's brow furrowed. "How did you do that?"

"I have been able to summon Silcor's Healing Flame for many years now. I thought you knew this."

The dwarf shook his head. "Not the healing. The fire thing?

Against the skeleton?"

Nidor helped Gruelenor to his feet. The krukari nodded in thanks, his color returning.

"What fire thing?" Nidor frowned. "I struck it down."

Greyor turned to Gruelenor for help.

Gruelenor shrugged. "I was unconscious."

"You became fire!" Greyor blurted. "One moment you were running across the room with burning eyes, and the next you're a burst of flame. You surrounded the wizard and burned through it until it fell to pieces! Then you dropped to the floor as you again."

Nidor looked at Gruelenor.

Gruelenor shrugged again and shook his head.

"Silcor provides His Gifts as He sees fit." It was all Nidor could think of to say.

Eraim joined Kiryanna and Magneer in the library, where the back wall lay in ruin. Magneer inspected the left edge of the rubble while Kiryanna stood in the middle of the room, watching Eraim with a steely gaze. The marteese remained angry with Selanna for not seeking Brem before this affair. And while the knowledge that the priest and the boys were alive was enough for Eraim to stay focused, Kiryanna evidently did not feel the same. It was unfortunate that there were more pressing matters than rescuing people Eraim cared about. But that was the situation she found herself in, and there was nothing to be done but see the mission through.

Atop the rubble pile, Eraim located a tunnel just beyond a small opening.

"There is a passage," she said. "Kiryanna and I should be able to make it." She looked at Magneer. Even if time had not added a few extra pounds to the ranger, he would not fit. "I doubt you can squeeze through." She observed what remained of the ceiling. Several cracks stretched from the tunnel and into the library, sifting dust onto the floor. "It is not stable enough for digging."

An explosion outside the building stole their attention. Eraim thought of checking on Selanna, but her friend could take care of herself.

"Why would they go into some tunnel?" Magneer stared at Eraim, as if she had the answer.

Another explosion sounded from the street, and Eraim glanced at the open doorway as her frustrations mounted. With a sigh, her thoughts returned to her missing companions. She blew on Selanna's light, wishing for it to move away, and it surprised her to see the glowing ball fly to the center of the room. Peering into the darkness beyond the rubble, she allowed her eyes to adjust.

"The tunnel turns left." She looked left, as if her vision might pierce the library wall. "It must connect to another building."

"We should return to the street," said Magneer. "If they moved deeper into the village, I'm sure we'll hear Greyor sooner or later."

The ranger had a point. Greyor was rather loud most of the time. Eraim nodded, and she slid down the debris.

They exited the library and froze. Selanna was gone, but that was not what held Eraim's attention. The village was different. An ambient light pulsated, causing the shadows to move, and the buildings seemed to bulge and retract as if they were breathing. Selanna's ball returned overhead, but its glow changed to gray and it illuminated nothing. The scene sickened Eraim, and she noticed her companions were pale—their stomachs had surely soured as well.

"What's happening?" a distorted voice asked—one much too deep to belong to any real person.

Eraim turned to see it was Kiryanna that had spoken, and the marteese appeared just as disturbed as Eraim by the sound.

"Dark magic!" Magneer said, his voice exactly like Kiryanna's.

Eraim shook her head, unsure of what to do and not wanting to speak. Where had Selanna gotten off to? She waved for the others to follow and headed toward the next building. At the very least, they would check each door until they found their companions.

They passed over the cobblestones Selanna destroyed while

shielding them from the undead wizards' attack. It was tricky with the rubble shifting about, and Eraim believed it was Magneer that cursed a couple of times as they progressed. Following the street did not prove as problematic, but the warping steps of the neighboring structure were an interesting task, though not too difficult as long as Eraim did not focus on her feet.

"Let me go first," said one of Eraim's companions—she did not know which.

Magneer stepped past her and opened the door.

They entered a tidy drawing room. To the left, a stool was neatly tucked beneath a table bearing a burning candle. On the right side, a comfortable-looking chair sat before a cold hearth, and beside it was a small table holding an exquisite ewer and goblet. Unlike the fireplace, the furniture did not expand and contract, though it moved with the shifting floor. On the back wall was an open door, through which Eraim spied a bed. There were no occupants.

"They're not here," someone pointed out the obvious—likely Magneer.

Eraim inspected the ewer and goblet. They were of fine silver and had obviously been dusted, but they were dry. The chair was clean, and it appeared to have been used often. She shook her head. She still could not fathom the undead requiring such accommodations. Perhaps Selanna was correct in thinking the intelligent undead enjoyed comforts they had once known.

Her attention went to an open book beneath the candle on the table, and she crossed the room to have a peek. Its runes seemed familiar, but she did not understand them. Probably the Ancient Moclen Script Selanna loved to read. Eraim placed it into her pack.

Magneer exited the bedroom, having finished his search, and shook his head.

They returned to the street. The village was unchanged. Eraim led the way past the next building, as it was more than half crumbled, and proceeded to the neighboring structure. The constant breathing of the stone continued to play with her mind as she climbed the steps, and the wall lashed out, inflicting searing pain to her right arm and causing her to lose hold of Mithkahr. She turned to see that a gargoyle had struck her. She dodged its other claw, and as she did so, the expanding building met her and knocked her to the cobblestones.

Eraim scrambled away on hands and feet to retrieve her weapon, but the warping street made it difficult to pinpoint Mithkahr's location and she missed. The ground then shook when the gargoyle landed next to her. She lunged, reclaiming her sword, and rolled onto her back as the monster descended with its fangs bared. Driving Mithkahr upward, Eraim pierced the monster's throat. The living statue exploded into small bits of stone, forcing her to cover her face in defense.

Regaining her feet, Eraim saw her companions battling a pair of gargoyles. Kiryanna's golden blade rang off the body of her foe, inflicting minor damage, and she possessed a scratch across her cheek and an injury to her stomach. Blood soaked Magneer's left leg while he swung his sword, and he evidently had a hard time judging his opponent's position, for his weapon whistled through the air twice without making contact.

Eraim detected a rhythm with the expanding and contracting of the village, and she moved with the motions toward Kiryanna. The gargoyle either did not see Eraim's approach or did not care, and Mithkahr cut easily through its midsection. Eraim turned away, avoiding the shower of stones that ensued.

The final gargoyle bore down on Magneer as he tripped on the steps. Eraim raced to the ranger's aid, reducing the creature to pebbles with a single blow, but the fiend had already buried its teeth into Magneer's shoulder, leaving a nasty wound.

The village fell silent, except for Magneer's grunts of pain. No other gargoyles moved, but at least a dozen of the statues gazed downward from nearby rooftops.

Kiryanna assisted Eraim in lifting Magneer to his feet, and they helped him onto the porch. The marteese then held the ranger steady while Eraim forced the door open and made a quick survey of the room beyond. Dust-covered shovels and picks were scattered, and a few tables possessed hammers and chisels. Along the rear wall existed a couple of doors, but the chamber was otherwise empty.

They ushered Magneer inside and seated him on the floor next to a table. The ranger clutched his shoulder, gritting his teeth and scanning the area.

"Watch the door," Eraim instructed Kiryanna, hating her voice.

With her left hand held over her stomach wound, the marteese reported to the entryway with golden sword at the ready.

Eraim eyed the interior doors. Mithkahr's glow had been constant since entering the village, so she could not depend on her weapon to let her know they were safe. She just had to chance it.

She pulled a healing herb from her pack, a small plant from her homeland called Salenti Magic, and crushed it in a bowl while adding water from her flask. She worked quickly, dipping bandages into the herb mixture and wrapping them about Magneer's shoulder and leg while he winced.

"I need Nidor," the ranger's voice that was not his said.

Eraim knew her herbs to be no match for the paladin's miraculous healing powers. But they were the finest of their kind, and Merssa had shown her the best way to prepare them over fifty years ago. It was the most they could hope for until Nidor was found—if he was found.

Kiryanna flew across the room, crashing into the wall between the inner doors, and Eraim grabbed Mithkahr and jumped to her feet to face the doorway. Nothing entered. She peered over her shoulder to see Kiryanna on hands and knees, spitting blood onto the floor.

An eerie presence crept into the shop, and Eraim turned to find a hooded skeleton filling the entrance. Its glowing blue eyes bore into her, paralyzing her legs, and she raised Mithkahr as if it were a shield.

"More rats…" the undead figure hissed, its dry voice unaffected by the distortion haunting Eraim and her companions.

It sounded like Gortran, but it was not Gortran. The black crown atop its head possessed three points instead of two.

"You should not have infested this place," the abomination said. "This is where rats come to die."

A deep blackness formed upon the skeleton's bony fingers as it raised its hand. It reminded Eraim of a spell Trannum cast at Selanna long ago, and her eyes widened as her mind raced, but still her legs would not move. Someone then called out from beyond the door. Eraim did not understand what was shouted, and the voice was not distorted nor a raspy hiss. It was gravelly, like that of an old hag. The skeleton turned its back on her to fire the darkness as a single bolt onto the street, and an explosion followed shortly after.

Eraim broke free of the fear and charged, thrusting Mithkahr into the undead wizard. There was another explosion, and the figure dissipated into a billowing mass of shadows and vanished. Eraim swung again to make sure it was not invisible. Nothing. And there was no one outside.

Kiryanna suddenly stood next to Eraim. It surprised her the marteese could move.

"Where did it go?" Kiryanna's horrible voice asked.

Eraim shook her head. Where was Selanna?

Nidor kept watch while Greyor inspected the caved-in tunnel. The dwarf looked up and down the pile of debris and knocked on a couple of larger-sized rocks before turning to Nidor with a furrowed brow. Though the blood no longer flowed from Greyor's scalp, the paths of its seepage traced several of his wrinkles to his thick mustache and long beard. Nidor had tried to tend to the wound, but the dwarf insisted there was "no time to play with scratches."

"We don't have the tools to return by this path." Greyor sniffed. "If we had a couple more dwarves... Maybe. Fire and arrows are no help."

Nidor glanced from his flaming sword to Gruelenor's bow. Gruelenor relaxed the tension on his bowstring.

"We are still in the village," Nidor said. "We should find the others. I am sure they are looking for us."

They headed for the room's only door, but as Greyor reached for the latch, the air about them changed. Everything darkened, and the room came to life, as if the stone began to breathe.

"What in the name of—?" Gruelenor frowned. His voice had come out shrill, like the high-pitched squeal small children made.

"What's with you?" Greyor's voice was identical. The dwarf issued Gruelenor an accusatory glare. "What did you do?"

"He did nothing." Nidor sounded no different than the other two. "It is dark magic." He nodded at the exit.

Greyor opened the door and proceeded, but after a few steps he halted. "Meldar's hammer!" His words would have made the exclamation comical if not for the evil lurking around every corner.

Nidor exited to see the warping effect was not exclusive to the dining hall. The entire village expanded and contracted, and an eerie glow pulsated like a heartbeat.

"Above you!" a shrill cry came from behind.

Nidor jumped from the porch and onto the street, staggering as he landed on the shifting cobblestones. A gargoyle with glowing blue eyes then crashed heavily onto the stairs, breaking loose a chunk of the top step and cracking most of what remained. It lunged at Nidor, but Clanghorr cut through its midsection and it exploded into a shower of stones.

Another thud sounded beside Nidor and he spun, reflexively stepping aside and avoiding the lashing claw of a second gargoyle. He struck it with his sword, chipping its stone hide, and Gruelenor's arrow bounced from its head with no apparent effect. Greyor charged, but the dwarf must have misjudged the steps, and he dropped his weapon as he tumbled down the fractured stairs.

The gargoyle pounced, driving Nidor to the street and scratching his chest as he held its shoulders at arm's length. The creature then moved in slowly with its fangs, and Nidor squirmed free, grabbing his sword as he rolled to his feet. He struck the monster again, snapping his blade in two.

Another pair of gargoyles landed, and Nidor maneuvered to keep all three in front of him as he cast his broken weapon aside. Greyor emitted a high-pitched roar, advancing with Clanghorr back in his hands, but when the dwarf swung he hit nothing — the warping likely threw him off the mark.

Nidor's internal temperature rose, and the village changed as the orange tint to his vision returned. The buildings and cobblestones still breathed, but the area about him stabilized, and he saw the enemy clearly. A gargoyle lunged, and he caught hold of its wrists, but its strength was great and it forced him back. His hands then erupted with fire, and though similar to the Healing Flame in appearance, it burned hotter and liquified the stone in Nidor's grasp. The gargoyle's claws fell to the street. The fiend showed no pain and bit into Nidor's shoulder, and he grabbed its jaws to pry open its mouth. His hands melted its fangs and half of its head, and its body shattered.

Greyor had dispatched one of the other gargoyles, and the dwarf pursued the final creature up the steps where Gruelenor fended it off as best he could with his sword. Clanghorr destroyed the monster with a single blow.

No more gargoyles moved.

Nidor's hands returned to normal and the pain of the bite set in. But that would have to wait. Bringing forth Silcor's Healing Flame, he went to check on his companions.

Greyor bore fresh injuries to his chest and arm, and his side had been gouged twice. Gruelenor suffered only scratches. The dwarf submitted this time, and he winced briefly at Nidor's touch, following the gesture with a grateful nod. Nidor then breathed easier upon applying the scorching relief to his own shoulder.

"You know your flamin' eyes are still burning?" Greyor asked in his high-pitched voice. He then laughed, sounding like a child giggling. "Too bad there's no one else here! I'd love to hear King Kolermane speak in this place!"

Nidor scanned the village, and his vision continued to penetrate the veil of warping. An old woman shouted in the distance — a croaky, hag-like voice — but he could not understand the words. It came from around the bend in the road.

"This way!" he called out in his squeaky voice.

An explosion sounded as Nidor hurried toward the shouting. Around the turn, Selanna stood in the middle of the street, launching four green spheres at an open door. The target of her attack was another robed skeleton, this one wearing a black crown with three points. The spheres struck, and the creature vanished into a cloud of shadow.

Eraim, Kiryanna, and Magneer ran from the building with weapons ready. Magneer and Kiryanna appeared to have taken injuries, and they moved gingerly down the stairs. Eraim then said something Nidor did not understand, but instead of a high-pitched squeal, the small elf's voice was strangely low and distorted. Stranger still, all three of them passed Selanna without acknowledging the mage. Selanna raced up the steps and entered the building.

Nidor looked at Gruelenor and Greyor. "What devilry is this?" He then turned to Magneer. "Magneer! Over here!"

His shrill voice failed to gain the ranger's attention.

"Magneer?" Gruelenor's head swung from side to side. "Where?"

Nidor realized only he could see the others. He chose not to explain. There was no time, and he was not sure his companions would understand. "Follow me!"

Eraim led the way onto the street, moving slow enough for Magneer and Kiryanna to keep up. She scanned the buildings for the old hag that had stolen the undead mage's attention, but the breathing village was empty. There was no sign of Selanna or her missing companions, and no robed skeletons.

"Come," she said, irritated with herself for forgetting not to speak.

They moved deeper into the village, and Eraim detected the

distant squeal of a child. She listened, but she could not discern what it was saying or where it came from. A sudden surge of heat nearly overwhelmed her, but it burned for only a moment and her aches faded. Checking her arm, the wound from the gargoyle had vanished. She looked back, and Magneer appeared confused while he worked his newly mended shoulder in circles. Kiryanna gasped as her wounds closed before their eyes.

"I don't know what just happened," the marteese said in her warped voice. "But did anyone else hear children?"

Magneer gazed suspiciously up and down the street, but he said nothing.

Eraim was not sure what to think. The village had an odd sense of humor, attacking and healing them. She did not like it, but Magneer and Kiryanna were in better shape for it. She nodded for them to follow and continued briskly down the road.

Around the bend to the right, piles of rocks lay about the entrance of a large building. The steps were damaged in several places and the door sat open. Eraim was certain the rock piles had once been gargoyles, and she moved carefully up the broken stairs that shifted beneath her feet.

Beyond the entry was a dining hall. Three stone tables were arranged as if a grand feast had been planned centuries ago, and a fourth table was upended, its settings strewn across the floor. To the right, a mound of rubble blocked what appeared to be a passage, and against the opposite wall was a pile of ashes and bones. An iron crown sat near the burned remains, bearing two points and a blue gem.

"Gortran," Eraim muttered. She hated her voice!

"They were definitely here." Magneer's face brightened. "They're probably nearby."

Movement at the entrance caught Eraim's attention, and she saw the robed figure with the three-pointed crown hovering in the doorway. She had no choice. She yelled an alarm.

"Mees!" Ugh!

Eraim dropped to the floor when the undead wizard issued a

black light from its skeletal hand. The darkness raced past, narrowly missing her, and searing pain encompassed her body, as if the bolt had pulled at her very life force. She cringed as she fought the urge to cry out, and a table behind her exploded when the spell struck. She prayed she never experienced a direct hit from the evil magic.

Kiryanna charged with her golden sword, but the mage waved its hand and the marteese crashed into the wall. The undead wizard then launched lightning at Magneer, forcing the ranger to dive behind the overturned table — Eraim hoped he had escaped the attack.

Though her joints ached and resisted all movement, Eraim pulled herself from the floor and raised Mithkahr. Her heart climbed into her throat as she waited for the glowing eyes to return to her, but they did not. The creature floated into the room and spun, issuing a jet of flame through the doorway. Lightning then launched from its fingers at a random wall.

The strange burning sensation Eraim experienced on the street returned, and her pain subsided. She knew not what magic was at work, opposing the evil that surrounded her, but she needed to make the most of it. She charged.

The skeleton whirled to face her, and she saw the darkness reforming in its hand. But one of its legs fell from its body and it launched the spell to the side at no one. A high-pitched shriek followed, like a child's scream, but Eraim ignored it and swung Mithkahr, severing the mage's remaining leg. It hissed, again dissolving into billowing shadows, but the old hag's voice called out and the robed skeleton reappeared exactly where it had been. Eraim slashed her sword before the creature could summon more evil magic, and Mithkahr sliced into the black robe and through the ribs and spine. The undead wizard collapsed.

The warping effect ended and the world returned to normal. Selanna stood in the doorway, and to the left, where the deadly bolt had removed a sizeable chunk of the wall, Nidor tended to Greyor. Gruelenor was nearby, scanning the room with an arrow to his bowstring.

"Thank Galenfial!" Eraim's voice was restored as well.

She then noticed Greyor was unconscious. Dirt and blood covered the dwarf's face, and the runes on his axe were aglow. Her heart raced.

"Is he all right?" she asked Nidor.

"He will be soon," the paladin replied, applying his flaming hand to Greyor's head.

Healing flames! It was Nidor that mended her wounds earlier. But how had the paladin accomplished the task? Did the others see through the magic?

Gruelenor lowered his bow as his brows drew together. "I don't understand where you all came from?"

Perhaps only Nidor had seen through the ruse.

Magneer rushed to Gruelenor, and the two shared a brief hug. Since when did the men show affection for one another?

"What just happened?" Eraim asked Selanna.

"It was a spell." Selanna entered the room. "And a powerful one. One I could not counter." She looked at Nidor. "But somehow *you* saw through it."

Nidor stood. The glow of Clanghorr's runes had faded, and Greyor was alert. Nidor helped the dwarf to stand.

"Silcor guides me," the paladin said as he moved to Kiryanna to inspect her injuries.

Selanna gave a wry smile, apparently unsatisfied with the Dale's explanation. She then turned back to Eraim. "I believe the skeletons created distinct spaces of existence; of distorted reality. They used them to separate us." She looked again at Nidor with a puzzled expression.

"*Brakkeet*!" Greyor's face twisted in disappointment. "Our voices are normal." He glanced at the undead wizard's remains. "At least Clanghorr got to shave a leg off that thing!"

"In the end, it tried to escape into shadow," Selanna said. "But I was ready for such a maneuver this time."

"What were those black missiles?" Eraim asked, the memory sending a shiver down her spine.

"I know not for sure," Selanna replied. "I suspect it is a form of necromancy, and a spell more powerful than I would have thought possible from these undead mages."

"The evil is not gone." Nidor looked around the room, having finished tending to Kiryanna. "But it has faded."

Selanna nodded. "We must find what we came for. Before something else awakens."

"It would help if we knew *what* we're looking for," grumbled Magneer.

Selanna sighed. "I agree."

They exited the dining hall and began searching the surrounding buildings, discovering a tavern, a woodwork shop, a wizard's laboratory, and another library. The tavern and shop looked to have been forgotten, and the laboratory items were dried up or smashed. The library was intact, and upon entering, Eraim remembered the book she picked up.

"I found this in what I assume was one of the mages' quarters." She pulled the tome from her pack and handed it to Selanna.

Selanna glanced at the book and set it on one of three tables. She then scanned a nearby shelf and chose a couple more books before taking a seat.

"Keep searching," she said to the group. "I shall see what I can learn here. Come back if you find anything you do not understand."

Eraim hated to leave her friend alone again. It did not work so well the first time. But she left with the others, and two of Selanna's lights followed.

They checked four more buildings, finding nothing beyond rubble and ancient remains. With only half a dozen more to go, Eraim spotted a lone structure off the road and tucked away from the village. It seemed to be hiding in the shadows, and she almost missed it. While the company headed toward the next building, she moved closer with one of Selanna's lights, but the illumination failed to penetrate the darkness.

"Over here!" she called out.

Eraim's companions arrived shortly with Selanna's other light. Even with both glowing spheres, the shadows remained undisturbed.

"What have we here?" Greyor did his best to speak in a child-like voice. He looked at Eraim with a grin that quickly faded. "Just practicing for when I explain my journey to those back home."

Eraim shook her head.

Three steps led to the octagonal building's only visible door. The air grew bitterly cold as Eraim ascended onto its small porch, and the shadows swallowed her, as if she had stepped from a lit room and into a dim one. It reminded her of the cloud hanging over Sistama. Though the structure appeared dark from a distance, its bricks were gray, and unlike the other doors, this one was of black stone.

Someone grabbed Eraim's arm, and she jumped. It was Greyor.

"Perhaps Clanghorr and I should go first," he said.

Eraim realized she had been reaching for the door, and she pulled her hand away. "The house in Sistama..." She looked from Greyor to the others. "It was trapped. Simply opening it alerted Trannum to your presence. We need Selanna."

Greyor shrugged. Nidor and Magneer nodded. Gruelenor and Kiryanna gave no response.

They exited the shadows, and it was as if they stepped from winter and into summer. But the village was surely just as cool as when they arrived. The library was not far, and they hastened inside to find Selanna reading. A dozen tomes lay open on the table.

"They were his apprentices." Selanna looked up. "The skeleton mages. They have been here for more than a thousand years."

Eraim wondered if the apprentices were alive when they first called this horrible village home. "We found something. But we need your help to enter. I believe it possesses the same ward as the cabin door in Sistama."

"Yes, of course." Selanna rose from the chair.

They returned to the shadows and icy aura of the octagonal

building, and Selanna scrutinized the door.

"It is definitely the same as the one in Sistama."

"What are we to do?" asked Eraim. "There is no chimney for me to crawl through this time." She detested the memory of entering the swamp cabin alone.

Selanna revealed a small grin. "That will not be necessary. I was not strong enough back then. But much has changed over the years."

She stared at the door, pursing her lips in concentration. She did not make any movements or gestures, and after a few deep breaths she turned to Greyor.

"You may open it," Selanna said.

The dwarf pushed. Nothing happened. He used his whole body, and the veins on his forehead bulged while the door swung slowly inward with the sound of stone grinding on stone. Once fully open, he breathed a little heavier and stepped forward, and the others followed.

Beyond was a single chamber. Bricks made up the outer edges of the floor, and a circle encompassing most of the room exhibited a smooth surface with no visible seams. There were no furnishings, but in the center of the circle was an image Eraim knew all too well: a black triangle. Unlike the triangles where Trannum was concerned, the blue oval breaching two of its sides was missing and it possessed a golden border filled with violet sigils.

Selanna paused at the circle's border before proceeding to the triangle, and though it went against Eraim's better judgement, she followed. The triangle was perfectly black; not a scratch interrupted its darkness. But then Eraim noticed it was not so at the triangle's points. Selanna evidently made the same observation.

"Holes." Selanna's whisper echoed around the chamber, as if multiple people uttered the word in succession.

Eraim looked closer. One point of the triangle bore a single hole. The next point had two holes, and the final one had three.

"The crowns." Eraim's whisper bounced about in the same fashion, and the words did not overlap one another.

Selanna's eyes brightened. "Nidor, Gruelenor, Magneer." The reverberation continued. "Retrieve the crowns, please."

Retrieve the crowns, please...Retrieve the crowns, please...

"You will find one in the sixth building on the left from the beginning of the village."

You will find one in the sixth building on the left...from the beginning of the village...from the beginning of the village...sixth building on the left...from the beginning of the village...

She spoke faster. "Bedroom door to the left side. Be on your guard."

...Be on your guard... Bedroom door to the left side... Be on your guard...

The three nodded and departed.

Greyor stepped to the edge of the triangle. "Very interesting!" He did his shrill voice imitation, and he grinned as it resonated around the room.

Kiryanna almost smiled.

Eraim shook her head. "What exactly have we found?" She ignored the echoes that followed.

"I have my suspicions," Selanna said, and she did not wait for the bouncing words to finish before speaking again. "But I am not sure. I believe I know why he uses a triangle as his symbol."

Eraim raised her brow. "His apprentices?"

"No. I do not believe so." Selanna continued staring at the symbol. "I think it has to do with the crowns. That was not a wizard's book you found, but a pupil's. I doubt the skeletons we faced had the power to defend the village the way they did. I believe the crowns enhanced their abilities. And I believe the crowns are the key to discovering what we came for." She looked at Eraim, still ignoring the echoes. "If I am correct, they are made of a material similar to the black bars you took from Darum Carumbor. I do not think they are of our world."

The men returned, their mission a success. Eraim noticed right away that the points of the crowns matched the holes exactly.

"Set them outside the triangle," Selanna said. Once they did so, she added, "Everyone stand beyond the circle. Just in case."

Again, Eraim hated to leave her friend's side. But she complied.

Selanna took the crown with a single point. She turned it upside down and pressed it into the single hole in the floor. She did the same with the other two crowns, setting them into their respective places around the triangle. Upon placing the final crown, the triangle shimmered, like rippling black water. A small blue light appeared in the middle, veiled in shadow, and Selanna stepped back. The light grew larger and brighter, as if something deep below moved toward the surface, and the circle elongated. A two-foot-long oval crystal then emerged, rising to a height of three feet, and there it hovered, emitting the same blue glow as the apprentices' eyes; the Death Lords' eyes; the dunarchins' eyes. Trannum's eyes. Eraim did not need Selanna to mention the power it contained. She could feel it.

"Your bag." Selanna reached out to Eraim, her focus remaining on the crystal.

Eraim balked. Did anyone else notice the echoes had stopped? Her skin crawled and she no longer wished to enter the circle, but she could not reach Selanna's awaiting hand from the perimeter. With a sigh, she stepped forward, pulling one of her fine sacks. Selanna accepted the bag and scooped it over the crystal from underneath. The shape of the item settled at the bottom of the sack once it closed.

"Let us leave this place in haste," Selanna said. After a moment, she added, "Grab the crowns. And there are a few books I need to retrieve from the library."

CHAPTER 28

SEARCH PARTY

Nothing opposed Selanna and her companions while they exited the tomb and returned to Vol Maren. After an evening's stay at the Ogre's Breath, they mounted and began their journey across Neja with the morning. Selanna spent several hours every night reading from the books she had taken while the others slept, hoping to learn more about the enemy. But most of what she discovered was trivial at best.

The days raced by, and upon arrival in Eastgate, they stopped at Larman's Haven. Selanna's mind drifted back five decades as she scanned the tavern room, envisioning the plump innkeeper, Larman, scuttling about with eight tankards in his hands and a sincere smile from ear to ear. Her fondest memory of the bald man was the joy he radiated when Merssa entered, as well as the hug that ensued. Larman and his wife, Fellna, grew to be respected citizens of Eastgate and lived productive lives, but those lives ended years ago from old age. Now, one of Larman's boys continued the tradition his father set before him, including the rotund belly but lacking the shiny head, and the establishment was as popular as ever. The innkeeper beamed when he spied Selanna and Eraim.

"Welcome! Welcome!" He hurried over. "We're full up. But I always keep a private chamber ready, just in case the most beautiful elves happen upon our fair city!"

"Thank you, Malen." Selanna smiled. "I see your children are still helping out."

Malen's two adult daughters and his youngest son moved around the room, serving customers. His daughters were old enough to begin lives of their own, but evidently chose to remain with the family business.

"All but the eldest." Malen's grin failed. "Larman has marched with the army for Virch. He and his Uncle Lindow."

Though the lad went by the same name, Malen's oldest son was nothing like the original Larman. Muscles replaced the extra mid-section, and a passion for the blade led Larman Junior down a different path, one reminiscent of Malen's brother, Lindow. A seed was planted in Lindow for adventure when he was young. Selanna believed it began with the horse ride he shared with Merssa after the family was rescued from the devastation of Ellaville, and the many visits from Merssa and Vecnor to Larman's Haven afterward nurtured that seed. Lindow became an impressive swordsman over the years, and he rose through the ranks in the Nejan army. Now, apparently, he was among thousands of soldiers holding the southern bridge against Beit, and young Larman was with him. Selanna understood Malen's apprehension. Unfortunately, there was no comfort she could offer.

"We will not be staying long," she told the innkeeper. "I would appreciate an early lunch."

Malen nodded. "To be sure."

He led them to the private dining room. Though a bit cramped, the chamber possessed enough chairs for everyone and they took their seats. Malen's daughters entered shortly after, bearing two pitchers of beer and a bottle of wine, and Malen brought in a couple of trays, one holding a pile of steaming vegetables and the other covered by chunks of beef. As always, the innkeeper refused any recompense. And as usual, Eraim placed a few gemstones within his daughters' hands after he left, more than covering the fee.

They had nearly finished the meal when the door opened and Malen rushed in. He was out of breath and his face lacked color.

"Some folks came looking for you just now!" he said to Selanna with wide eyes.

"Oh?" Selanna held the slightest hope that Elgarroth was among them. "Where are they?"

"Gone!" Malen shook his head. "I know not who they were, but I didn't like the looks of them. They didn't even speak. Only gave me a note." With trembling fingers, he handed Selanna a piece of parchment. "I denied having seen you for some time..." He looked unsure of what else to say.

Selanna read the note.

SELANNA?

It was the only word written.

She was suddenly concerned. "What did they look like?"

"They were hooded and wore masks." Malen was sweating more than usual. "There were three of them."

Selanna frowned. "Masks..." Only in Eastgate could people walk around in masks without turning heads. She looked at Eraim, who nodded and headed out the door.

"Did I do right?" Malen's lower lip quivered.

"You did." Selanna gave a smile to ease his stress. "I thank you, and we shall be leaving soon."

"Very good." Malen bowed twice. "To be sure."

Elgarroth had warned Selanna about this back in Tikken City. Everyone stared at her, but she waited for the innkeeper to leave before explaining.

"It seems one of the search parties has arrived. They seek an item I possess, and it appears they are aware that I have it."

Magneer sat up straight. "What item?"

"There is no time to discuss it," Selanna replied.

"What do we do?" asked Gruelenor.

He would not like her answer. None of them would. But Selanna had no choice.

"Eraim and I must proceed alone. It will be safer that way."

"Is that wise?" Nidor's brow furrowed. "What if you need our help?"

Greyor snorted. "Clanghorr does not fear men in masks."

"Let me just say that we can move much swifter if we are alone."

Selanna also hoped those seeking the black stick would ignore her companions once it was gone.

Kiryanna pursed her lips. Now that they found Trannum's hall, the search for those left behind was supposed to begin.

"You should all head for Tikken City," Selanna said. "I promise we will meet you there."

The marteese's shoulders lowered slightly.

The door opened and Eraim entered.

"They are ready," she said.

Selanna looked at the others. "I suggest you wait no less than half an hour and then depart."

Eraim went to the room's only window and cracked open the shutter, brightening the chamber. After spying the alley outside, she opened it further and climbed onto the ledge before dropping from sight. Selanna moved to follow, and Nidor was suddenly beside her.

"I will see to the others." He offered his hand.

Selanna accepted the Dale's assistance, and he effortlessly lifted her onto the window ledge. A sweet warmth came from his touch, and she was sorry for its absence when his hands pulled away. She sensed him to be a special paladin, and it reminded her of Merssa's connection with Cafior.

"Thank you," she said, and she dropped into the alley.

Eraim held Mithkahr ready, and it shone a dim red light, only visible due to the shadow the neighboring structure provided. Evil was near. But not too near.

They crept to the edge of the alleyway and had a peek onto the sunlit street. Nothing seemed out of the ordinary. Skirting the front of the building on their left, they passed a couple of closed doors and reached an alley where Dandi and Lilli obediently awaited. Selanna was glad to see no thieves had attempted to hassle their animal friends—an obvious conclusion, since there were no bodies nearby. She and Eraim mounted.

"I shall take the lead," Selanna said, and she proceeded onto the street.

The city gate was not far from Larman's Haven, and they rode at an easy pace, scanning every being on the wide street. Most of the citizens went about their day, and there were a few men that ogled Selanna and her companion—a typical and annoying occurrence within the Nejan community. Selanna then spied a figure with a low hood, and the shadows did not completely conceal the bronze mask beneath. The figure's robe was black and out of place for the heat, and its head tilted back, revealing dark eyeholes aimed her direction.

"I see it," said Eraim. "And now that it has seen us, can we please leave?"

Selanna stared a moment longer, wishing there was time to learn more about the masked figure. "Yes. Let us depart."

They picked up the pace, and nothing opposed them while they exited Eastgate. But three more figures wearing dark cloaks and bronze masks stood near the only bridge crossing the Stony River. They were perfectly still while gazing Selanna's way.

"Dunarchins?" asked Eraim.

"I do not believe so." Selanna's focus remained on the strangers. "And though I would like to know who they are, we cannot afford a confrontation. Not with the items we bear."

"How are we to cross the Stony?" Eraim posed.

Selanna looked up and down the river. The bridge marked the only fordable area the waterway knew. She and Eraim could ride across without using the patched-up stonework the Nejans had constructed, but she did not wish to be caught in the middle of the Stony if the masked figures attacked. To the south, the current picked up speed and was too deep to traverse, and beyond that was Sistama. Though Selanna had not ventured into the swamp since the expedition to Trannum's cabin, the memory of the odors, slimes, freezing temperatures, and ghouls were uninviting. Tall Pines Forest presented the least risk, even with the large population of wolves roaming about, but the excursion would take too long.

"They are coming," Eraim said.

Two of the figures approached while one remained on the bridge, and a couple more emerged from the city. It was time to move.

Selanna turned Dandi to the south, and she and Eraim ran their horses two hundred yards before stopping near the riverbank. Selanna then concentrated, pulling forces from the surrounding energies and fusing them together. It was not a simple spell, but it was easy enough for her, especially since it only needed to accommodate her and Eraim.

"Follow me," she said once she finished. "*Exactly* behind me."

Selanna urged Dandi forward, patting the horse's neck and whispering in a comforting tone. "I am with you. You are safe."

Dandi trembled while stepping over the river, but the mare's hooves never touched the water. After a few steps, the animal's muscles relaxed. Behind Selanna, Eraim offered words of encouragement to Lilli and they followed. Selanna kept Dandi on a straight line, and the farther they moved, the easier the pace became. The Stony River rushed below like a pack of excited mongrels competing for a dangling treat, but the horses soon reached the far bank and stepped onto firm ground.

Selanna released her hold on the magic, allowing the forces to disperse to their unseen places among the water, mountains, fields, and sky.

The hooded figures arrived at the riverbank. Their eyeholes gazed briefly at the rushing water and then at Selanna, but they made no attempts to cross.

Selanna nodded with satisfaction. "Let us make haste."

"Gladly," said Eraim.

Selanna did not wish to lead the hunters into civilized areas if she could avoid it, so she and Eraim rode southward along the river. The way became overgrown, but living in a forest prepared Dandi and Lilli for such conditions, and they covered more ground than would have been possible had ordinary mounts accompanied them. Besides that, only Batorn steeds could rival a Salenti horse's ability to travel with little rest, and the pace was almost constant.

They stopped at last as the sun dropped low in the west. Ahead, the darkest storm cloud engulfed the Stony River, fallen from the sky centuries ago to conceal Sistama. The humans called it Silent Marsh, and Selanna learned how fitting the name was, for no sound emitted from within. But it did not come close to describing the horrors the swamp contained, and Selanna understood the shiver invading Dandi's back. At one point, Selanna thought she and Eraim would die in that awful place.

They veered east to put the cloud behind them, and Selanna's nerves eased as the distance grew. But as the bog faded from sight, there was movement at its edge. Selanna squinted. She saw nothing. She turned to Eraim, who's expression was somewhere between doubt and fear.

"A gorilla?" Eraim asked.

"Gorilla?" Selanna frowned. "From the swamp?" She had only known the animals to dwell in Holindale and Fendora.

"It was not normal." Eraim wrinkled her nose. "It was very large. And its eyes glowed."

"Blue?" Selanna assumed.

Eraim shook her head. "Violet."

Violet. The color of the fog upon the floor of Darum Carumbor; the triangles in Lormin Dmurr; the swirling mist within the gate; Uustaag's right eye. This gorilla was not Trannum's minion. It belonged to Uustaag. A shiver raced down Selanna's spine — she would rather face the undead.

"Where did it go?" she asked.

Eraim narrowed her eyes while scanning the darkening countryside. After a few seconds, she pointed to the north. "There!"

Selanna spotted the creature bounding toward them. Its skin was the purest black and completely hairless, and its eye sockets exhibited wispy violet lights, but no eyes. Its legs were longer than a gorilla's, allowing it to run more like a human, and its arms were long and extremely muscular. The monster snarled, showing off its pointed black teeth as it closed, but no roar or any other sound escaped its thin lips.

"What do we do?" Eraim's voice held a slight tremble.

"We have no choice." Selanna slid from her saddle, not wanting to risk any harm to Dandi.

Eraim dismounted as well, and she sent Lilli to safety as she pulled her bow.

The gorilla was forty yards away when Eraim loosed her bowstring. The missile bounced harmlessly off the creature's smooth chest. At thirty yards, she released another arrow. The missile caromed from the ape's head, leaving no mark. Eraim held her next arrow steady, staring intently with her right eye. Twenty yards away… Fifteen yards… Ten yards… She fired, and the shaft pierced the beast's left eye socket until only the fletching was visible. The creature slowed to shake its head as the violet light faded, and its mouth looked to cry out, but no sound emitted. The gorilla then resumed its charge, bearing down on Eraim.

Eraim dropped her bow and rolled aside, returning to her feet with Mithkahr ready. The monster, meanwhile, pounded its fists where she had stood, and the displacement of dirt sprayed in every direction. A pair of depressions resulted, a foot deep, and the vegetation issued traces of smoke.

Selanna launched a spell of fire, but the gorilla did not appear to notice as it sprung at Eraim. Eraim jumped to the side, barely avoiding a slamming fist, and the creature placed its other hand on the ground and kicked with both feet. Selanna reached out, pushing her companion with a magical force as gently as she dared, and Eraim tumbled safely away, tucking her sword and flattening into a roll.

The gorilla turned its good eye on Selanna.

She released four green spheres, but the spell fizzled on the dark skin, leaving the monster unmarred. She then raised a field of magic when the ape leaped twenty feet overhead. The shield served only to alter the beast's trajectory as its massive frame crashed through, and it missed Selanna by mere inches. Its thunderous landing challenged her balance, but she retained her footing; and in their nearness, an aura of ice invaded her body. Unlike the pleasant warmth Nidor radiated, the cold exuded evil and fear, like the air surrounding a Death Lord but with much less reach. Selanna scrambled away as it swung its fist, and the breeze in the attack's wake caused her to stumble and fall into a seated position.

The gorilla's mouth opened into a snarl, as if in pain, but it still had no voice. It spun, and Selanna saw Eraim holding Mithkahr. The blade dripped a thick purple blood, and a fine line was visible on the creature's back, oozing the same substance.

Selanna launched her green spheres again, aiming for the gash left by Eraim's attack. Three of the four orbs found the mark, and the beast lifted its head to the sky to emit another silent roar.

The gorilla lunged at Eraim, and Selanna cringed when her companion leaped onto the beast's shoulders and dangerously close to its black teeth. Eraim plunged Mithkahr into the remaining eye socket, burying the sword to the hilt, and the monster collapsed without so much as a whimper. Tumbling with the ape, Eraim freed her blade from the enormous skull and rolled away. The gorilla ceased to move.

"Yuck!" Eraim pulled a cloth from her pouch to clean the goop coating her weapon. She then discarded the rag, her lips twisted into a sneer at the substance serving as blood to the strange fiend.

Selanna memorized the monster as best she could. It twitched, and she and Eraim jumped. But it moved no more.

"That thing is like ice," said Eraim. "I could feel it through my boots." She retrieved her bow. "Let us get away before another one finds us."

They mounted and headed southeast into the night. Upon finding the Squire River, they followed the waterway east for a day and a half. Korban Bridge then appeared in the distance.

"They are there." Eraim nodded at the cloaked figures meandering about the grand white stones arching over the waterway.

They wore masks, just like the ones in Neja.

Selanna formed another path of magic, and they crossed the water without notice. They continued south until the bridge fell from sight and then veered southeast. Once the King Arman Lake was in view, they turned due south, following the shoreline and remaining well off the road.

It was late when they arrived at Tikken City, and the gates were closed. But the tower captain recognized Selanna and Eraim, and a smaller door opened to allow them access.

"The Council said to watch for you." The soldier shut the door behind them. "They expect you'll pay a visit first thing in the morning."

It did not surprise Selanna that the wizards were aware of her arrival. She expected Elgarroth was in the city as well, but somewhere other than the Council Building, and she headed for The Jeweled Scabbard. Eraim followed without question. Upon reaching the establishment, they dismounted, and Selanna grabbed the sacks containing all they had collected from the crypt.

A barmaid greeted them at the door. "You must be Selanna. Someone is waiting for you."

The woman led them to a private dining chamber, where Elgarroth sat at a table. Two plates covered by splendid looking fish and vegetables awaited them, as did goblets of wine.

"Welcome." Elgarroth stood briefly while they seated themselves and the door shut. He smiled, but his eyes were troubled. "We have much to discuss. But first you should eat."

Selanna's mind was too occupied to feel hunger, but she took a bite to satisfy her mentor. The fish was delectable, and eating was suddenly all she could think about. She and Eraim enjoyed the meal, and while they ate, Elgarroth helped himself to the books they had brought, opening each and scanning pages at random. Once the food was gone, his smile vanished.

"The situation grows more dire with every passing day," he said.

"Indeed!" Selanna nodded vigorously. "I have so much to tell."

Elgarroth smiled. "Now that you know that which I have shared, we can move on to things I have learned while you were away."

Her shoulders slumped. Of course Elgarroth had been watching her. It was his responsibility. She glanced at Eraim, who appeared confused. Selanna wished she could explain.

"From these books," Elgarroth lifted a tome, "it is obvious the undead wizards you faced were Trannum's apprentices at one time, and his caretakers afterward. To that extent, they were able to draw from Trannum's power; from the crystal you found."

Selanna had not mentioned the crystal. She hoped that fact escaped Eraim's notice.

"The crowns also possess crystals," Selanna said. "Do they contain Trannum's power as well?"

Elgarroth shook his head. "The smaller crystals are but tools used by the apprentices to draw upon the master crystal. Alone, they have no power. But the crowns... They are another matter." He pulled the two-pointed crown from one of the sacks and placed it on the table. "They are foreign to our world, but they are not the same as the black bars you brought from Darum Carumbor. While the bars are an unholy iron, the crowns are more of a magical element. They enabled you to open a small portal to where Trannum kept safe his most guarded treasure. My belief is that the crowns are also tools, but unlike the crystals, they are a path to foreign magic. And I am convinced they made it possible for Trannum to achieve all he has over the centuries; the ability to channel this magic into Vaeldor and bend it to his will."

"Will he know we found it?" asked Eraim. "The crystal?"

"I do not think so." Elgarroth turned to Eraim. "Just as the orbs from years ago, he cannot sense its location. Only that it is."

Selanna sighed. "Then we cannot yet destroy it."

Elgarroth shook his head.

"But with the orbs, you both claimed destroying them weakened Trannum," Eraim pointed out. "If we truly possess the last of his power, should we not be done with it?"

Elgarroth gazed at Eraim with fatherly kindness. "It is not easy to understand. Magic rarely is. Let me just say that if we were to destroy it, right here and now, Trannum will feel its loss. That would leave him with only the energy he retains in his current form. And while that would seem preferable, it provides him with time to prepare. He will acquire power to replace that which he lost. He would, in effect, become more dangerous. Less arrogant."

"But if we wait until the right moment..." Selanna understood Elgarroth's point.

Eraim picked up the line of thought. "We can catch him off guard. Fight him when he is at his weakest."

Elgarroth sat back with a nod. "Precisely."

Eraim's eyes grew wide. "We must carry that thing to Lormin Dmurr?"

"That is not all." Elgarroth turned to Selanna. "You must also bear that which Uustaag desires."

"The black stick." Selanna felt the blood drain from her face. She leaned forward, closing the gap between her mentor and herself. "What have you found?"

Elgarroth drew in a deep breath, either calling upon memories or preparing to share horrible news—or both. "The black stick, as we know, is not from Vaeldor. Uustaag received it as a gift, after he opened his first portal into Thard'Dun's world. According to Welmirth's journals, it grants Uustaag a sense of immortality. It contains his mortal soul. For that reason, the Dark One was able to retrieve him when he was defeated at the Battle of Balgorn. While the stick remains, death for Uustaag is not permanent."

A shiver traveled along Selanna's scalp and down her arms. She had been carrying the item for weeks now.

"This arrangement made Uustaag part of the Dark One's world, as well as part of our own," Elgarroth continued. "Thard'Dun wanted it this way, for until his plans are fully realized, his minions can only endure Vaeldor for so long. There is an element of Thard'Dun's world they need to survive. It would be like one of us trying to live underwater, except the Dark One's minions are capable of holding their breath for weeks instead of minutes."

"Is that why the creature we faced made no sound?" asked

Selanna.

Elgarroth nodded. "But Uustaag is different. The part of him belonging to our world allows him to survive here, while the part of his being that is foreign is anchored to Lormin Dmurr. If Uustaag recovers the stick, he will be free to roam."

Eraim shook her head. "Then why do we not destroy it?"

Elgarroth held an empathetic smile. "It is more than just a vessel for Uustaag's soul. It is a powerful artifact. As I suspected, it does not merely open gates. It creates holes between worlds; pathways that cannot simply be closed. Welmirth knew this. And though he realized Uustaag to be contained within the item, he dared not destroy it without knowing the consequences of such actions."

"How did Welmirth close the holes?" Selanna asked.

"With the stick," Elgarroth replied. "Not only does it possess the power to open pathways, but it can also *stitch* them shut." He paused. "Think about torn fabric. Once the tear exists, it is always there. You can sew it, but the scar remains. After Trannum acquired the item, he used it to remove the *stitches*."

"And now the gates are open," Selanna said slowly.

Elgarroth nodded. "And while they remain so, Thard'Dun's minions have access to Vaeldor, such as the krahluk you faced outside Sistama. But also there are zreekans, a more cerebral minion. They are oddly shaped creatures bearing a single eye, and in place of their legs are four tentacles they use more like hands." He looked at Selanna, his expression leaving no doubt as to his sincerity. "They are capable of magic unlike any used in our world. Trannum has evidently known these beings for some time, for the dark power you witnessed in the forgotten village was zreekan magic, and they must have taught it to him. The masked individuals you encountered were zreekans. They can change their bodies to appear human-like, but they cannot form a second eye. So they wear masks."

"Let me see if I understand," Eraim said. "We must return the one item Uustaag needs to Lormin Dmurr to close the holes? While strange gorillas and floating octopuses hunt for it? And we will face

Trannum, whom we failed to defeat even with Vaeldor's greatest heroes, all the while possessing that which he holds most dear?"

Elgarroth gave a weak smile.

"And they know I have the stick," Selanna said. "I do not see how we can complete such a task. Uustaag and his underlings surely sense its presence."

"You are correct." Elgarroth's confirmation made Selanna's skin crawl. "As we speak, there are minions headed for Tikken City. So our time is growing short."

Eraim gasped.

"Do not worry." Elgarroth raised a hand. "We will be gone before they arrive, and Tikken City is prepared for the possible attack."

Selanna did not feel relief. Fear and confusion seemed to be the only emotions that existed. "How did Welmirth hide the stick from them?"

"It was not always a stick," Elgarroth said. "It was once a pendant, ripped from Uustaag's neck during the Battle of Balgorn. Welmirth reshaped it to what you see now, and he hid it within Lothen Forest. But the enemy has seen and held it in its new form, and they are now attuned to it. It must be reshaped again."

Selanna possessed no reshaping magic. Even if she did, how could she tamper with a powerful item from another world? Thard'Dun's world? The Dark One was the strongest of the evil entities, banished by all other gods to dwell alone. According to legend, the evil deities required assistance from the deities of good to accomplish the feat.

She looked at Elgarroth. "How?"

"Arman Forest," he replied.

Arman Forest! The reputed resting place of Vou's mortal remains. A forest laden with magic. A woodland where no paths exist. It was the reason Tenvale became a realm of wizards; a society of mages desiring to be near the Forest of Vou, as they referred to it. Criminals were often sentenced to cross its border, never to be seen again. It was said that simply stepping around a tree at the edge left the victim hopelessly lost, for time and space were unpredictable and leaving a trail was impossible. It was also rumored that magic ran wild among the trees, and a mere apprentice could unleash power greater than the most accomplished mage, or a master wizard might be reduced to a lowly prestidigitator.

"How did Welmirth accomplish such a task?" Selanna had trouble believing her mentor's statement. "He would never have found his way out again."

"There is... a way." Elgarroth said. "For those that know it, and are willing to risk it."

Selanna's stomach roiled. She was both fascinated and terrified by the prospect of entering Arman Forest. It then occurred to her they could throw the stick into the trees and let it be lost forever. Then Uustaag would never achieve his prize. But that was not an option. The holes would remain open in Lormin Dmurr. Why had Welmirth not left the stick in Arman Forest after closing the gates? Selanna thought of asking, but she was sure Welmirth had his reasons. Another issue then came to mind.

"What about those that journeyed with us into Trannum's crypt?" She had almost forgotten. "They are to meet us here."

"Do not concern yourself." Elgarroth patted her hand. "I have someone awaiting them in Rivercross. They will be informed of where they are to go next." He grinned. "And I am sure they would not want to follow us into Arman."

"I would rather journey back into Helmland than enter that forest!" said Eraim.

"Actually," Elgarroth raised a brow, "you shall not be accompanying us."

Selanna was as shocked as Eraim looked.

"I have a boat ready to carry you and Lilli to Larkorn," the wizard told Eraim. "From there, I need you to go to my house. You will know why when you arrive."

"This is the life I chose," Eraim muttered. "I travel with wizards, so I get wizard explanations. Even at a time like this." She lifted her brow and stood. "I will be off and let you two have your fun in Arman Forest." She turned to Selanna, failing to conceal her anxiety. "I hope to see you again."

"I shall see you soon," Selanna assured her friend.

Eraim headed for the door, hesitating to reveal the slightest of smiles. But her eyes betrayed her concern. She left.

For several minutes, Elgarroth seemed far away. Selanna did not disturb him. She realized her mentor must be using the Sight. When his focus returned to the room, he spoke.

"Time grows short. We leave at once."

Elgarroth retrieved his horse from a nearby stable. Selanna thought it odd, but his steed was of the Salenti breed, and she could not recall him ever riding it before. Had he hidden it all these years? Of course, she knew he possessed the power to alter its appearance — an illusion he taught her over three decades ago.

They exited the city's southern gate and rode at a hard pace through the night and two days more. Nearing dusk on the third evening, they halted off the shore of King Arman. Elgarroth treated the horses to a couple of apples each, and he allowed the animals to wander along the water's edge and gather their strength.

Arman Forest was in sight, where the King Arman emptied into its western region to give life to the Prince Arman River. The water then flowed swiftly to the Queen Arman Lake and beyond. The river held no magical properties that Selanna was aware of, but she wondered if it was the same within the woodland.

"We do not have long," Elgarroth said while they ate sweetbread he pulled from one of his packs.

"How close are they?" Selanna looked over her shoulder at the deepening shadows. Nothing moved.

"They are far enough." Elgarroth gazed to the north. "There was no attack on Tikken City, since the stick was not there." He turned to Selanna. "The hunters require rest, though not much. But it is enough to maintain several miles between us. We are safe."

Selanna breathed a bit easier.

"There is something else that concerns me, farther north," Elgarroth said. "It is the chanting you witnessed in Darum Carumbor."

Selanna remembered the dark soldiers all too well. She had been powerless to prevent the slowing effect their chanting placed on her and her companions. The enemy fought almost like the undead, without pain even after receiving a debilitating strike. The memory sent a chill to her extremities.

"Thard'Dun worshippers call it the Chant," Elgarroth said. "It is learned only when one is ready to surrender themself to the Dark One, and their soul becomes tainted forever. They no longer care whether they live or die, so long as they die for Thard'Dun. Even death from old age is not acceptable." He looked at the star-filled sky. "Darum Carumbor was constructed solely for this Chant. And just like the orbs that produced the Wind of the Dead years ago, the tower is capable of projecting the Chant for miles. This happened when allied forces fought Uustaag the first time, lending its effects to the warriors of Beit." His gaze returned to the distant north. "Darum Carumbor is almost ready to perform that task again. And this will make the impending war much more difficult."

Selanna frowned. "But not all Beitians are Thard'Dun worshippers. How can it assist them as it does those speaking the Chant?"

"The Beitian soldiers have been drinking the taint of the Balgorn River for some time now."

Selanna gasped. "The elixir?"

Elgarroth smiled. "You and your friends did not consume nearly enough to be affected, I assure you."

She released her breath. "That is good." Then something else occurred to her. "But how is it you see Darum Carumbor? Is it through Daymyn or Baylun?"

"No. As I mentioned, doing so would risk their lives."

Did that mean one or both of the boys were at the tower? Elgarroth's stare suggested he would offer no more information on the subject.

"Darum Carumbor will need to be resolved if casualties in Beit are to be minimized," he said. "But that is a future conversation. For now, it is time to enter the forest."

"Should we not first cross into Tenvale?" Selanna asked. The ferry was not too far away.

"Why would we do that?" Elgarroth shrugged. "We require but a single tree." He looked at the woodland to the south. "From there, crossing the Prince Arman is irrelevant."

Selanna had not thought of that. Stepping around any of its trees could place them deep into the forest. There was no need to enter Tenvale.

"I believe I will take the stick now," Elgarroth said.

He pulled a pack from his horse, and from within he produced the three crowns. He then extracted the black iron bars and the crystal shard from Darum Carumbor that Eraim had relinquished to the Council of Wizards. Selanna's heart raced as he did so without care to avoid touching the latter items with his bare hands.

"Do not worry," he said. "They are quite safe. At least, they are at the moment."

Though Selanna's interest piqued, she remained silent and handed him the black stick. He repacked the bag with the stick at the bottom and strapped it to his horse. They then mounted, and Selanna followed the wizard to the south.

CHAPTER 29

GIFT OF FLIGHT

Eraim traveled through the night aboard a decent sized craft. She and Lilli were the ship's only guests, and though the crew appeared inconvenienced by the voyage, they made no ill comments. In fact, they spoke no words to Eraim at all. She remained with Lilli for the entire trip, feeling no need for a cabin, and conversed with her mare to pass the time.

"Do you think Selanna will be all right?" she asked.

Lilli snorted—a normal response given by any horse. But when uttered by a Salenti horse, it meant so much more to the elf it was paired with. Eraim and Lilli had grown together and played together. And they understood one another.

"Yes, Lilli. Of course Dandi will be fine." Eraim patted the mare, trying to reassure herself as well.

Though nervous about Selanna entering Arman Forest, Eraim was grateful her friend would not be alone. Elgarroth would be there. And with Elgarroth, anything was possible. It was the only thought granting Eraim comfort on the matter.

A few hours before sunset the following day, the small ship docked along a pier in Larkorn. Eraim and Lilli disembarked with no salutations forthcoming from the sailors, and they followed a stone path until the city surrounded them. Eraim figured she should find an inn and gain some rest, but her brain was alive with thoughts and she doubted she would sleep. Puzzles plagued her mind. And she was tired of puzzles. Elgarroth, Selanna, and even Vecnor rarely said what they meant, and they always left Eraim to figure everything out. She mounted, deciding it best to begin the journey to Elgarroth's house and unravel the mystery the wizard presented to her.

She rode across Sendorum, sleeping beneath the stars over the next couple of nights. Though Selanna preferred being nearer to civilization and eating fresh food, Eraim found comfort in the wilderness. And she did not fear unwanted company, for Sendorum had few roaming bandits to speak of, and Lilli would help to guard through the dark hours.

On the third evening, she arrived in Tribenor, the largest city of the realm. It was rife with activity, and the streets teemed with people entering or leaving the many taverns. Also present were soldiers from various kingdoms, either on their way to one of the bridges crossing the Shield River or stationed in Tribenor to await further orders — perhaps enjoying their final days. It was a sad thought, and it moved Eraim's mind to Romik, Desser, Daymyn, Baylun, and Brem. How long could they avoid enemy detection? What horrors were they enduring? Would they ever know freedom again? Will they be the same people if that chance came to pass? The questions were depressing.

With no vacant inn rooms to be found, Eraim headed east and slept outside the city. She became eager, however, and well before the dawn she mounted and continued.

Eraim spent long hours in the saddle, and by nightfall of the next day she entered Vermallon Forest. She followed Vermallon Road a few miles and then camped among the trees. The forest was not so tame as the fields of Sendorum, so the break was kept short, and she and Lilli each took a turn to guard.

They returned to the road with the brightening of the sky, and nothing impeded their progress except for a pushy merchant shortly after lunch. The peddler led five wagons, and he attempted to convince Eraim of her need for several items she had no interest to buy. She pretended not to understand the common speech, but when the merchant began speaking in the elfish tongue, she nocked an arrow to make her point. Guards reached for their swords, but the merchant calmed the situation and urged his wagons onward.

In the end, Eraim arrived at the House of Elgarroth two days early. The clearing was empty, but smoke issued from the cabin's chimney, so someone must be home. She had visited Elgarroth nearly every year for greater than a century now, but she had never set foot inside the dwelling—she doubted even Selanna had been permitted to enter. She approached the door, but a deep voice from the side of the house brought her to a halt.

"Over here."

Eraim turned, expecting to see the muscular elf servant.

It was Tux.

She wrinkled her nose. "What are you doing here?"

"I am here as a favor." His white pupils scanned the trees, as if searching for unwanted visitors.

"A favor to whom?"

Tux shrugged. "Does it matter?"

Eraim sneered. Another puzzle. "Was it Elgarroth? Or perhaps the strong *elf* lad?"

"Please." Tux's expression was stern. "It is obvious you have figured out much, but you are far from knowing everything."

What did he mean by that? Eraim was unsure of how much she knew, but she held several suspicions. She assumed Elgarroth used magic to disguise Vecnor as the elf servant. She believed the two worked together, though she was yet to figure out why. For the past twenty years, she played their game and did not expose their secret while delving deeper to learn more. She had hoped to gain some insight when traveling with Vecnor before the expedition into Trannum's crypt, and though they shared laughs and pleasant conversations, the large man became guarded any time she even thought about probing for knowledge. Why did no one speak of the fact that Elgarroth and Vecnor should have passed away decades ago from old age? Eraim did not share these thoughts with Selanna. She loved Selanna dearly, but she suspected her friend was keeping secrets as well. Of course, Eraim knew Selanna wished to be just like Elgarroth, so secrets were inevitable.

And now there was Tux. What part did he play in this game? He stared at Eraim, still unsmiling. Elgarroth was always warm and welcoming; Vecnor was strong and imposing. Tux was... mysterious. And what was he referring to? What did Eraim not know? It surely had something to do with the strange Salenti-Orlenfel elf standing in front of her.

"Time grows short." Tux interrupted her thoughts. "You will learn everything you need to know soon enough."

He walked to his horse and pulled a quiver holding a score of his special arrows from the saddle. He tossed it to Eraim.

"What...?" She was unsure what to ask.

"It is a gift," Tux said. "To fulfill a request."

She lifted a brow. "What do you owe Elgarroth to honor such a request?"

"We all have done things. We all have things to do. And we all owe somebody something, whether or not we wish to. In the end, what does it matter who I owe or who you owe? Or the reasons why? I have something to do, and so do you. Hopefully, this gift makes *your* something easier."

Elgarroth could not have said it better! Eraim did not know whether to be grateful or suspicious.

"Thank you." It was the best response she could conjure.

She looked at the arrows, remembering how well they pierced the plate armor outside Lothen Forest. It was a grand gift. She pulled a single arrow and admired its length. The longer the shaft, the greater the opportunity for flaws. But these were flawless. She also noticed they were dark gray—she originally believed them to be black. A nice red shaft would have been much more to her liking. She decided she was grateful.

"May they serve you well." Tux climbed onto his horse. "Wherever your path leads."

"Thank you," Eraim repeated. She then frowned. "Wait. Where is it I am supposed to go next? Elgarroth told me to come here, and I assumed I would get direction once I arrived. In truth, I expected to find Vecnor."

"I see." Tux showed no emotion. He stared for several seconds, as if in thought. "I suppose you can accompany me... for a while."

Accompany Tux? That could be interesting. A part of her wished to say no—she still doubted he was the legendary figure from the past. But still...

She strapped the arrows to Lilli and climbed onto her saddle. "Where are we off to?"

"Here and there." Tux's eyes drifted to the quiver. "Do not forget to check your flights regularly."

CHAPTER 30

HARBNUM BRIDGE

Vayla sat in a field north of Arbornum among the many Palidurian tents. Ten thousand holy soldiers were present, half of the army that departed from the city two months ago. The other half marched to Darmoor, the military outpost guarding the bridge over the Shield River in Virch.

It pleased Vayla that her father and the zhokard warriors accompanied the Holy Army. As well, many soldiers she had grown up with were among the thousands of Marcs that joined the cause, ready to defend the realms. King Cavalor was usually with Grand Paladin Montac in the war tent, discussing battle plans. Vayla did not receive invitations to these meetings. She understood she was not a High Paladin, but she took slight offense, nonetheless. It further annoyed her that Burnod was often summoned to the war councils, and the ex-general never shared any information.

Vayla spent most of her time with Macurak, drilling holy soldiers and keeping them ready. Burnod and Wezlok were never far behind, the former because he remained her charge, and the latter because... Vayla did not know why Wezlok still followed her. Maple Lore Forest lay to the south, and the elf could easily return home. But he lingered, offering no explanations.

Currently, Vayla enjoyed the warmth of a fire, as the Harbnum nights had been growing cold. Macurak, Burnod, and Wezlok were with her, of course, but also present was a gray elf.

Lorylla was taller than most, making Vayla feel even shorter than usual, and the elf warrior held a presence that could not be ignored. Vayla thought Lorylla to be a larger version of Tux, for she bore the same gray skin and white pupils on black eyes, and though the female elf did not appear overly strong, Vayla did not doubt the warrior's skills in battle. Lorylla wore dark gray chainmail and a fancy sword hung from her belt. She also possessed an exquisite bow, five feet in length, and it currently rested beside her.

Since Vayla's encounter with Tux, she did some reading on the gray elves of Orlenfel. But there was little knowledge to obtain in New Palidur libraries on the subject, and she still lacked a firm grasp of the secretive race. She discovered Lorylla to be the daughter of Xorlunder, a gray elf hero at the Battle of the Dead Fields in Kalmaar, and it reminded Vayla that Lorylla had been there to face Trannum in Nomedd. Vayla held instant respect for the elf. But Lorylla's presence did nothing to lighten Vayla's mood.

"All this waiting is maddening," she spat, staring at the fire. She was a bit cranky, as weeks of preparing the holy soldiers had grown tedious. It did not help that Burnod spent yet another day within the war tent, and he again refused to divulge what they had discussed.

"A day without combat is a day of peace," muttered Burnod.

"Is that what they say in Beit?" Vayla sneered. She was tired of his voice.

The ex-general scowled. "I only mean that I do not look forward to marching into Beit. You have no idea how hard it will be. There is a reason your realms never attempted to invade."

"Yes," Vayla said. "Because there's no desire to occupy your silly land. It offers nothing to the prosperity of the other realms."

Burnod gave her a level stare. "No. Your realms know they cannot possibly win."

"No." Vayla eyed the man. "Our realms do not want the task of housing and feeding your people."

Burnod sighed, turning to the fire. "What people?"

Vayla experienced a twinge of guilt. But the ex-general thought he was always right, and it was annoying.

"Do you two always argue?" asked Lorylla, her deep voice never failing to catch Vayla off guard.

Macurak nodded. "They do."

"It is almost entertaining," said Wezlok.

"We're not arguing!" Vayla and Burnod voiced at the same time. They then looked at each other.

Burnod returned his gaze to the fire.

"Across the bridge is Onzac." Vayla spoke as if giving a report. "It is stocked with no less than ten thousand zombies; victims of the plague. Beyond the city are five thousand living Beitian soldiers, ready to enter combat once the zombies have wrought sufficient damage. We expect Anduiff will join the battle on an undead dragon when he can raise enough fallen allies and enemies alike to cause maximum devastation. If things go poorly for him, and they will, he'll return to Benzon to regroup and protect the entrance to Helmland."

"We know all of this," Macurak said. "We are reminded every day."

"What we don't know is what we're waiting for." Vayla glared at her captain. "We have our targets. We have our goal. And we are aware of what we're up against. Why do we wait?"

"You think it will be *so* easy," Burnod scoffed. "Every contingency must be considered. It's the only way to avoid disastrous surprises." He looked at Vayla. "What if there are *two* Death Lords? What if there are dunarchins instead of zombies? What if the Beitian soldiers are all armed with crossbows? They'll not hesitate to use them while we battle the undead. What care is there if they strike walking corpses? Would you allow your impatience to bring unnecessary casualties to your men?" He smirked, turning back to the fire. "You'd make a fine Beitian general."

Macurak stood. "Watch your tongue, sir!"

And so, another conversation with Burnod ended the same way it always did. Macurak's fuse for the ex-general grew shorter with each passing day. In fact, Macurak was quicker to anger than Vayla lately, and his outbursts kept her own temper in check.

None of Burnod's points caught Vayla off guard. Thanks to her father, she knew the very concerns Burnod brought up were discussed in the war tent. She was even aware of the Chant after a visit by Tux and Eraim a few nights back. Besides that, they could not march until all fronts were ready. But sitting around was infuriating. With every passing day, they risked their soldiers losing the spark that drew them there. And too much time to consider the totality of what lies before them could lead to poor morale.

"If you will excuse me." Burnod rose. "Nature calls."

The ex-general sighed when Macurak stood to join him. Had Macurak remained seated, the responsibility would have fallen upon Vayla. She appreciated her captain sparing her that duty.

Vayla returned her attention to the fire. But then she noticed Lorylla's stare.

"Don't tell me." Vayla eyed the elf. "You knew my grandmother."

"I met her once," Lorylla said.

"Well, I'm not her," Vayla sneered.

"No. You are not." Lorylla sat up straight. "She was the very best humans had to offer in leadership and courage."

Vayla was unsure if she should be insulted or angered. Or both. The elf's calm demeanor made it hard to tell if the words were meant to be harsh. Even if Lorylla had voiced an insult, it pleased Vayla to find someone that agreed with her. Wezlok, however, stared at the gray elf, and though the Lorian wizard's face remained stone, the slightest hint of discord shone in his eyes.

"Why have you blessed our fire with your presence this evening?" Wezlok asked once Lorylla returned his gaze. "Are your folk not stationed farther to the north?"

"They are." Lorylla looked at Vayla. "But I had to see for myself."

Vayla sighed.

Burnod returned to the campfire and stood before Vayla.

"I apologize." The ex-general bowed. "I didn't mean to insinuate that you are no better than a Beitian general."

Vayla spied the steady eyes of Macurak behind Burnod. She would have loved to witness the conversation leading to that apology!

"Think no more of it." She turned back to the fire. "For one to be insulted, one must first hold respect for the insulter."

Macurak shook his head. He disapproved again.

Burnod stared at Vayla. The corner of his mouth twitched, as if he held back a smile. He burst into raucous laughter, and Lorylla let go a smirk—the first expression the gray elf exhibited that night. Vayla did not understand why, but she laughed as well. Macurak sighed and chuckled. Wezlok opened a book and began reading.

Vayla made a check of the perimeter, as she did every evening. Numerous bonfires created halos of light, and soldiers that should have been sleeping drank and shared laughter. But her focus lay mainly across the Shield River at the undisturbed darkness. It was not her duty to patrol, but the time alone helped her to sleep.

The final two hundred yards of her path took her around the command tent. The neighboring tents housed Grand Paladin Montac, the High Order, and other generals and people of import, and she saw her father as she neared his quarters. Cavalor was speaking with one of the zhokards, and the soldier nodded and ran off. Her father then noticed her presence and waved her over.

"My darling daughter!" He spread his arms wide.

Vayla allowed the hug. Her father *always* insisted on a hug. This particular embrace, however, lasted longer than usual. It made her feel like a young girl again.

"What is it?" she asked once he released her, noticing the concern in his eyes.

"It is time," he said. "Tomorrow."

The words lit up Vayla's nerves, but her father did not seem to share in her excitement. He appeared as though he wished to say more.

Vayla frowned. "What is it?"

"Nothing." He forced a smile. "Just... Keep Wezlok close. He's a fine wizard. And... Be safe."

He embraced her again and placed a kiss on her forehead. After another forced smile, he entered his tent.

Vayla returned to her quarters, both excited and scared. The day was arriving at last, and this time she would not fail Cafior. During her first visit to Beit, she had to make decisions for the betterment of her small force, pushing her from the path Cafior set before her. This time, she would march with an army. This time would be different.

Vayla found Macurak pacing outside her tent. The others had retired for the night, and no one sat around the dying fire except for Wezlok, still absorbed in his reading. Her captain's expression exhibited either concern or anxiety. Maybe both.

"What is it?" She became alarmed. "Did Burnod escape?"

"No." Macurak sighed. "Burnod does not *wish* to escape."

"No?" she posed. "Do not let him catch you off your guard. He is a Beitian."

"Please, Vayla," Macurak said. "Don't ignore what is right in front of you. Burnod has no desire to return to his life. His family is safely tucked away in a Lorian prison, and he is likely branded a traitor. He is not part of some elaborate ruse to betray us at some point. Surely you realize this to be true. And Wezlok only remains because of something from the past. Something to do with Merssa. It's all so obvious."

"I take nothing for granted." She released the grip on her sword.

"Do you not?" He raised a brow. "It seems you have a talent for ignoring that which is under your nose." Macurak shook his head. "I know we will soon march into the clutches of evil once again. And this time will be much more dangerous." He hesitated, as if unsure of what to say. "You are always focused on your path with Cafior, and I love that about you..." He fell silent, his cheeks flushed.

What did she do wrong? What was Macurak angry about now?

"I know I often disappoint you," Vayla said. "And I know I tend to go too far when speaking to Burnod... as well as a few other whelps we have crossed. But that is who I am. I am a Paladin of Cafior. I cannot always waste time acting *properly* to avoid hurting the feelings of others. Not when pressing matters are at hand. My service to

Cafior is all that matters."

"It's not *all* that matters," Macurak muttered.

Why would he say such a thing? She was a paladin! Her duty was to Cafior above all others. Did he not understand that? Perhaps that was why he never attained paladinhood.

"Look." She touched his arm, attempting to mend whatever it was she did or said to make him behave so. "We march tomorrow. It has not been announced yet, so don't —"

"Tomorrow?" Macurak spoke too loudly.

Vayla was sure Wezlok had heard. But the elf likely did not care. "Yes!" She whispered, trying to bring down his voice. "I know you have been on edge. It is to be expected. I, too, have been losing my patience. All this sitting around —"

Macurak pulled her close and kissed her. She tensed, her hand moving to her sword. But then she relaxed enough to allow the blood to flow to her fingertips. Macurak released her and stood back, staring.

Vayla was confused. What caused him to behave so? If Wezlok were capable of humor, she would suspect the elf of having cast a spell on Macurak. It had been too long since she last healed her captain and she had not saved his life recently, so neither of those could be the reason. Was he homesick? Vayla missed her home and her church. She tired of the worship tent used by every priest of every religion. It was not right. She was at a complete loss, and now she had stood silently for at least a minute.

"Never mind!" Macurak turned away. "I'll see you in the morning." He entered his tent.

Vayla did not move. Did Macurak fear for his life? She understood how people fell prey to such feelings. But to die in the service of Cafior was glorious! There *was* no better reason. And tomorrow would present Macurak the opportunity to show Cafior his resolve. Was the kiss for luck? Vayla needed no luck, and Macurak knew that. So it must have been for *his* benefit. Perhaps the battle against Anduiff was on Macurak's mind. But why kiss *her*? She shook her head and entered her tent. She would have to leave it be for now.

"He loves me?" Vayla said aloud, sitting upright in her bunk. The realization had shocked her into waking.

It was still dark, but it had to be morning. The noises outside suggested breakfast was being prepared. Vayla dressed in her brown tunic before donning her Cafior tabard, and she strapped on her weapon belt to hold everything together.

Stepping from her tent, the morning was not as dark as Vayla had thought. But it was still early. Cooks and servants toiled over fires and readied plates and mugs, and Wezlok sat alone near an exhausted firepit, reading from his book. Did he ever sleep?

"No armor today?" the elf asked without a glance.

Vayla looked down. She had worn her armor every moment while outside her tent. It was not that she expected battle, but it comforted her. Most paladins preferred to be armored at all times; prepared for anything.

"I'll... don it after breakfast," she said.

"Must be your late night." The elf remained immersed in the book.

Vayla was not sure what he meant by that. She stomped off, deciding she did not want to know.

She walked the perimeter under the brightening sky, still unsure of what to think about Macurak's actions. Eraim called him a handsome man back in the Stone Eagle Mountains, and the elf made insinuations after Vayla took the time to be sure he recovered from the wounds he endured in Benzon. The thought caused her to halt. Why *had* she taken such care of Macurak? Sure, he needed treatment. But when did she ever provide more than herbs and bandages? *Did* she have feelings for her captain?

"Lady Vayla!"

Vayla turned to see a zhokard soldier. It was Grimmen. "Yes?"

Grimmen frowned. "What's the matter? I called you four times."

"What is it?" She wished he would just say what he came to say.

"The king sent me." Grimmen spoke of her father. "You are to report to the command tent at once."

This was it! She nodded and headed back to don her armor.

Upon arrival at her tent, Vayla saw Macurak and Burnod eating breakfast while Wezlok sipped from a mug—the usual meal for the elf. Macurak glanced at her and continued to eat. Vayla entered her quarters.

While strapping on her breastplate, she pondered the situation with her captain further. But there could not *be* a situation. Grimmen had to call her name four times to get her attention. She could not afford distractions. Not now. War was upon them, and the outcome was all that mattered. Perhaps it was the thought of dying that made Macurak behave the way he did. It did not matter. Vayla needed to remain focused. Besides that, he *was* a handsome man, and he deserved a woman of less complication; a woman possessing a more agreeable visage. Once the war ended, he would see that for himself.

Vayla exited the tent and looked at the others. "It's time," she said, and she marched toward the command tent.

CHAPTER 31

ONZAC

No horns sounded. There were no mobilizations that anyone could see outside Arbornum. They needed to catch Onzac off guard.

A few hours of sunlight remained, and Vayla readied Star near the eastern gates of Arbornum. Macurak, Burnod, and Wezlok did the same with their mounts. There were attempts to remove Wezlok by a few officers, but the elf would not yield in his resolve to stay. Montac threatened to expel the wizard personally, but Cavalor eased the Grand Paladin's temper with words Vayla could not hear. Vayla also noticed her father speaking with Wezlok for several minutes. It was a reminder that they had traveled together in the Necromancer War. Cavalor concluded the meeting by placing his hand on Wezlok's shoulder and issuing a firm nod—the former obviously to the wizard's disliking.

Vayla's nerves were alive with anticipation. She entered the city, where the Palidurian cavalry of over five thousand crowded open squares, wide streets, and alleyways, and they fell in line as she rode to the west. The hooves on the cobblestones and the jingle of the horses' mail were music to Vayla's ears, and she led the mounted warriors at a brisk pace.

Upon reaching the western edge of Arbornum, the doors opened and Vayla entered the final courtyard. A dozen soldiers manned each of the catapults, and the practice equipment had been cleared to make room for her squadron. At the far end, the thick portcullis sat in an upraised position, but the wooden doors remained shut, blocking any view of the bridge over the Shield River. Vayla halted to take in a deep breath before slowly releasing it, and behind her the cavalry fell silent. She nodded to her captain.

Macurak raised his left hand, and the doors swung inward with the cranking of the winch. Vayla urged Star forward, steadily increasing her speed, and by the time the gates were open, she charged through and onto the arched bridge.

Star's hooves pounded the stone, reaching the apex in haste, and she sped up as she continued down the other side. No immediate attacks came from Onzac, as the city was surely unprepared, and once across, Vayla steered her horse south along the river, just like the first time she entered the evil realm. She glanced over her shoulder at the five hundred riders following, and an equal number broke off to the north in pursuit of High Paladin Zeratar. The rest of the cavalry halted on the bridge.

Vayla raced two hundred yards before pulling her men to a stop. Just as Burnod had reported, the catapults of Onzac failed to reach the bridge, and those tracking Vayla and the horses riding north only covered areas thirty degrees to either side—according to the ex-general, fear of a Harbnum invasion was not taken as seriously as one from Virch. The attacks brought no harm, and once the boulders crashed down, another thousand riders split to the south and north while the catapults were reloaded.

Vayla smirked at the enemy's incompetence.

A thousand horsemen were now under her command, and she rode Star to the west until Onzac was due north. There, she again halted.

"Wezlok!" she shouted, and the elf arrived at her side. "What do you see?"

Wezlok shot her an odd look. "Your grandmother asked me that very question to begin the Necromancer War at Palidur Bridge."

Vayla sighed.

He squinted at Onzac. "No archers. The gate is opening. Zombies approach."

The mass of figures heading Vayla's way staggered like a

drunken army, and she estimated five thousand to have exited the city. Another five hundred horsemen joined her force, and again boulders crashed away to the northeast. Vayla nodded to Macurak.

"Lancers!" the captain called out, raising his right hand.

Eight hundred cavalrymen moved forward, holding lances like flagpoles. Macurak pointed northward, and they kicked their horses into action, speeding across the field and toward the oncoming army.

Vayla nodded again.

"Fall in!" Macurak shouted, and the remaining riders formed rows behind Vayla with swords ready.

Vayla charged, trailing the lancers by fifty yards with Macurak and Burnod at her sides. The long weapons ahead of her lowered, and the vanguard crashed into the enemy, skewering hundreds of undead while the battle-trained horses trampled hundreds more. The lancers drove a wedge into the middle of the zombie horde, and Vayla veered to combat those on the left—half of the swordsman followed while the others broke right. Though armed, the walking corpses barely penetrated the horses' armor, and the unorganized force was quickly defeated.

Vayla estimated her losses to be sixty lancers and two hundred swordsmen—a more than acceptable outcome. To the south, a thousand reinforcements headed her way. She continued toward Onzac.

On her order, Macurak issued the next command, and the lancers dropped their long weapons and closed ranks as they pulled shields. Behind them, two hundred riders readied bows. Just as Vayla expected, zombies holding crossbows appeared atop the city wall and fired, but the shields proved effective and only a score of soldiers and a handful of horses fell. The Palidurian archers countered, releasing a volley that had been dipped in holy water and dropping more than half of the enemy with steaming wounds. What remained of the undead bowmen made one last feeble attack, and the return fire cleared the ramparts.

While the archers worked, the newly arrived Palidurians readied ladders and rushed forward on foot. The shield wall advanced, leading the way, and the ladders soon rose up to the parapets.

Vayla signaled Macurak, and he dismounted to lead the soldiers up the wall. Opposition arose once he reached the top, and the new arrivals showed skills beyond mere zombies.

"Dunarchins!" Wezlok sounded more disgusted than fearful.

It was just as Vayla had anticipated. But five hundred Palidurians now stood upon the wall and hundreds more were climbing. The dunarchins were not enough to stop the invasion. She then spied Macurak leading a squadron along the battlements to the east, while the rest of the holy warriors entered the gate tower.

Vayla lifted her hand as her attention shifted to the city gate. Her men succeeded in their task and the large doors opened, and she lowered her hand to signal the charge.

Just beyond the gate, Palidurians spilled from the ramparts to combat a group of dunarchins. Vayla rode into the enemy with a thousand cavalrymen in her wake, and they carved into the evil force, clearing the wide street in less than ten minutes. The southern entrance was secured—Vayla hoped the northern assault succeeded as well.

She scanned the immediate area. Buildings of dark stone filled the city. Several of the structures were more like small towers than businesses or houses, and they possessed many windows from which dunarchin archers attacked.

"Storm the buildings!" Vayla ordered as an arrow narrowly missed her.

Soldiers bounced off reinforced doors while attempting to gain access, and help came when a hundred men bearing fifty battering rams passed through the gate. Thudding of the rams ensued, followed by crashes of success, and Vayla led the charge into a newly arrived company of zombies and dunarchins to the north.

The differences between the undead combatants were vast. Dunarchins lacked the rotting flesh, looking more like dried-out corpses with tightly wrapped yellow skin, and they fought with the skill of living warriors. The zombies were a nuisance for the most part, counting on their massive presence, and though they outnumbered the dunarchins ten to one, the undead firstborns killed three soldiers for every victory the zombies claimed. Even so, the enemy force was no match for the Palidurians opposing them, and the holy warriors cleared the area in less than an hour. Vayla estimated another three hundred soldiers had fallen for the effort.

She ordered a squadron to maintain control of the gate, and she led the rest of the cavalry east. Just as the roads through Arbornum, the streets were wide enough to accommodate military movements, and though resistance met Vayla at every turn, she and her men could not be deterred. After a mile, they reached the city's eastern side.

They entered an area similar to the western edge of Arbornum. A walled field harbored eight catapults, but the large weapons were unmanned, as Macurak and his squad had already defeated the enemy within. Macurak continued issuing orders, and holy soldiers lined the walls and raised the united flag of New Palidur: a sun setting beyond a single mountain beneath a dark blue sky. A massive roar followed as the host from across the river charged into Beit.

The assault upon Onzac had been an easy one, but that came as no surprise. Zombies were not soldiers. Vayla did not allow the ease of the battle to fool her, however, and she wondered why they encountered no living resistance. And where was Anduiff? She twirled her hand overhead and pointed to the west, and the cavalry took to the streets while those on foot stormed the buildings, flushing out the undead.

Nearly a week had passed since the taking of Onzac. Grand Paladin Montac set up a command center within the largest manor available, and Vayla reported to the building, responding to a summons. The messenger had tracked her down outside the city wall to the south, where she was supervising the gathering of the dead. There, Palidurian priests performed last rites. History held the ceremony to prevent those slain from rising in the presence of a Death Lord. Palidur had administered the same blessing to living soldiers as a defense in the Necromancer War twenty years ago, a practice Vayla found abhorring. There were not enough priests to administer such a service for this war, however, and only the Palidurians received it before the march. Vayla declined.

The manor was lavish. Vayla had seen many buildings while sweeping for enemies, finding cold and drafty structures lacking anything she considered one of life's comforts—it appeared low-ranking Beitians led very harsh lives. Once she entered the large house, she realized where the city's gold had been spent. Expertly crafted sculptures adorned the halls and exquisite tapestries decorated every room. Most of the statues reflected war, depicting Beitian soldiers holding decapitated heads or dancing on corpses. There were also statues of krukari warriors glaring hatefully onto the chambers they overlooked.

Vayla found her father and the Grand Paladin standing in a dining hall. Maps covered a large table, and the two were engaged in a conversation that halted upon her approach.

"My darling." Cavalor embraced Vayla again.

"Please, Father." She glanced at Montac.

The Grand Paladin smirked. "Let us get right to business."

"Yes, my lor—" Vayla cleared her throat. "Grand Paladin."

"First, let me commend you on your suggestion of using Burnod," Montac said. "He has been most helpful with his information."

Though Burnod was of the enemy, Vayla was not wholly comfortable with the Grand Paladin's comment. Was she *using* Burnod?

"We march on Benzon next," Montac continued. "We'll split our forces to approach from the east and south, as we discussed, but we'll also send a contingent to make sure all has gone well in Zurzak. As of now, we have had no word."

Vayla had not expected to hear from Zurzak so soon. Besides Burnod's claim that the southern city was much more fortified than

Onzac, she understood Darmoor would not begin until two days after the forces at Arbornum marched. The primary reason had been to draw some of Zurzak's soldiers into the north. Vayla supposed Montac grew anxious to know that reinforcements would arrive on schedule.

"What would you have me do, Grand Paladin?" Vayla asked with a bow of her head.

"You are young yet for one of your rank," Montac replied, "but you have shown great leadership and instinct. Your idea of dipping arrows into holy water worked better than anyone expected." His grin stretched to one side. "You will lead the force to approach Benzon from the south."

Vayla's heart rate increased. "I thank you for your trust." She bowed again, working hard to contain her excitement. "I will not let you down."

The Grand Paladin nodded. "You shall take five thousand Palidurians and an army of twenty thousand from various realms. Lorylla of Orlenfel will be at your disposal, as well as Eimell of Vermallon. They are both leaders among the elves, and should serve you well as captains."

Vayla gave a nod. She then frowned. "What about Macurak? He has been my captain since my rising to Paladin."

"Macurak has proven himself a competent leader, deserving of high marks once this is over," Montac said. "For that reason, he shall march with the force aimed for Zurzak."

Vayla's heart stopped. Macurak had always been with her. He knew her. He knew what she was thinking most of the time. His kiss still troubled her, but he was focused now. She wanted him with her.

Cavalor placed a hand on her shoulder. "It is for tactical purposes. From what I've heard, he's a very competent scout."

Her father read her like no other person could. Vayla composed herself—she did not want to cause her father worry—and she refocused on the days ahead.

"Who shall lead the force east of Benzon?" she asked.

Cavalor cleared his throat. "That will be me."

His reply almost caused her to choke. Originally, her father was to remain in Onzac until Benzon's defeat. Vayla had assumed Grand Paladin Montac would lead the eastern assault.

Cavalor read Vayla's expression again, and he grinned. "Let me just say that I have unfinished business with Trannum."

"But should a king march into this battle?" Vayla asked.

"I have argued this topic in every way," Montac said. "Your father is set on his path, and we could not ask for a better general." He looked at Cavalor. "He was, after all, trained by the very best."

Great. Merssa again.

"I shall remain here," Montac continued, "and finish the preparations for the march into Helmland."

Cavalor nodded, as if in thanks.

"Dwarves of Varlimor have arrived from across the bridge." Montac turned to Vayla. "You will have a thousand under your command, answering to Greyor, and they will bear the mighty ballistae capable of dropping undead dragons from the sky."

Greyor. Everyone in New Palidur was aware of that name. Not only had the dwarf fought against Trannum in the Necromancer War, but he was highly regarded for his part in the Holy City's reconstruction after the war's conclusion. It was also said he wielded an axe of the gods. Vayla was very interested in seeing such a weapon.

"Orders are being issued as we speak," Montac added. "Your captains await you at your quarters to prepare for tomorrow."

Tomorrow? That was not much time.

"Thank you, Grand Paladin." Vayla bowed. "And King Cavalor." She bowed again, receiving the expected wry smile from her father. It always filled her with a small amount of satisfaction.

Vayla departed from the chamber, her mind racing. She disliked the thought of Macurak not supporting her. She depended on him for both military assistance and to keep her in line.

The door opened behind her, interrupting her thoughts. Her

father entered the corridor.

"Wait!" Cavalor approached. "I want you to take Grimmen."

Grimmen. One of the zhokards. In truth, he was the zhokard Vayla knew best. The others were aloof, preferring to speak among themselves or with her father. To Vayla's surprise, they also appeared comfortable in Wezlok's presence, though the wizard did not seem too pleased with *their* company. Outside Vayla's father, Grimmen had provided her the most training in swordplay. Other zhokards taught her as well, but none of them showed as much interest in the matter as did Grimmen.

"But he is of your personal guard," Vayla said. "He should be protecting you."

"To be honest," Cavalor scratched his head, "he requested this assignment. I believe he is worried about you."

Worried? Because she did not hear him call her name last night? "But—"

"Please." Cavalor placed a tender hand on her shoulder. "He will make a fine replacement for Macurak. And I hesitate to mention it, but he has a personal reason as well, though I doubt you'll like it. Long ago, he was a soldier under your grandmother's command—"

"Fine!" she said, harsher than she had intended. That was all she needed: another set of eyes seeing her dead grandmother!

Cavalor embraced Vayla again. "Take care, my daughter."

Vayla exited the manor and walked along the dark streets. Night was in full swing, and torchlight sprung from several tower windows while soldiers patrolled the city on high alert. All remained quiet.

She reached the inn where she was stationed, and upon entering the tavern she found her captains seated at a table. Lorylla fiddled with a dagger on the tabletop, and a second elf, one Vayla assumed to be from Vermallon, stood in recognition of her arrival. He had pale skin and dark hair, and he wore a black cloak over green leather. He was tall, but a few inches shy of Lorylla, and leaning against the wall next to him was an impressive bow with etching from tip to tip. Although remarkable, Vayla doubted any bow could compare to the one Tux wielded. She never had the opportunity to see Tux use the weapon, but she suspected its efficiency was unmatched.

Also at the table was a dwarf. He ate from a tray of meat and drank from a pitcher of beer, and he did not seem to notice Vayla's arrival. When the male elf rose, the dwarf stopped chewing to offer Vayla a nod and returned to his meal. The Vermallon elf was as far from the dwarf as possible while remaining part of the group, but Lorylla appeared unconcerned while she sat next to the stout warrior.

"I am Eimell," the standing elf said. "I served as a scout to Tikken City many years ago. Two thousand Vermallon warriors are ready to march."

"Thank you." Vayla claimed the chair at the end of the table.

Eimell took his seat. "I must add that I met your grandmother once."

Vayla sighed.

"Though our meeting was brief," he added, "I understand her to have been a great hero among humans."

"Yes." Vayla offered no enthusiasm.

"And let me say that you are the spitting image—"

"Let us get to business," Vayla said.

The elf frowned.

Wezlok and Burnod entered. It surprised Vayla to see the two carrying a conversation, but it ended when they reached the table. Burnod took a seat next to Eimell while Wezlok grabbed a nearby chair and sat several feet away. Eimell scowled in the Lorian's direction.

"Our orders are to march on Benzon from the south," Vayla said. "We will then make a concerted assault upon the realm's most militant city with an allied force out of the east."

"Second most," Burnod muttered.

"What?" Vayla stared at the ex-general.

"Second most militant," Burnod replied. "Zurzak is the *most* militant city."

Vayla held her level gaze for a moment and then turned to the others to continue. "We will likely encounter Death Lords and undead dragons."

"No problem." The dwarf licked his fingers now that the meat was gone, and grease made the upper portion of his long, dark beard gleam.

"This is Greyor," Lorylla said. "He is a great warrior and a dear friend."

It was an odd friendship. But Vayla knew little about gray elves. Perhaps they did not hold the same disdain for dwarves as did other elves.

"Leave the dragons to us dwarves." Greyor exuded confidence.

"Very good." Vayla gave a nod. "I have seen your weapons for the bone dragons, and I'm impressed with your ingenuity." She turned to Eimell. "I will also depend on your folks' legendary archery skills."

The Vermallon elf revealed a sly grin and nodded.

"And Lorylla." Vayla eyed the gray elf. "Isn't your kind the ones full of magic?"

Eimell's smile dropped and Lorylla's brow raised.

"I have not the time for secrets," Vayla said, and she was sure Wezlok smirked. "We are preparing to march, and I need to know everyone's capabilities." She directed the last statement to all at the table.

The meeting lasted a couple of hours. Vayla learned enough to realize Orlenfel elves were much better suited as archers and Vermallon elves as warriors. Though both were excellent with the bow by reputation, the gray elves possessed the ability to add elements of magic to their arrows. In the end, Vayla would need all of their bows, as well as their blades. Greyor placed onto the table his *god axe*, and Vayla was not disappointed. The double blade was of polished silver with runes etched along its edges, and black leather wrapped its brass handle that ended with a spike. The dwarf referred to the weapon as Clanghorr, and he spoke as if it were a person. Vayla was eager to see it in action.

The hour was late when the meeting concluded, and the tavern emptied until Vayla sat alone. She thought of seeking Macurak to wish him luck, but then Grimmen entered.

"I'm surprised to find you awake," the zhokard said. "We have long days ahead."

"Yes." She sighed. He was right. "I shall get some rest."

The morning buzzed with activity. Vayla's forces were gathering outside the eastern edge of Onzac, and she sat on Star, watching the collection of humans, elves, and dwarves assemble. But her mind was elsewhere. On the northern side of Onzac, her father readied his army for the march, and she feared for him. To the south, Macurak prepared for Zurzak. Vayla wondered what awaited her captain in the days to come.

Grimmen arrived at Vayla's side. "All are assembled."

"Just a moment," she said. "I shall return shortly."

She urged Star to the field south of Onzac, searching through hundreds of soldiers and avoiding marching ranks. She then spotted Macurak issuing orders from the ground. He would become a favorite of his new commander before the day was spent, of that Vayla was sure. She moved closer and dismounted.

"Lady Vayla." Macurak used her proper title with his superior standing nearby. "It is good to see you."

Vayla looked at the paladin general: High Paladin Nyer of the Soleran Sector. He was more than twice Vayla's age and well known for his skills with the sword. Macurak was in excellent hands.

"I don't know why they are sending you south," Vayla said to Macurak, perhaps with more annoyance than she intended.

"It is for the good of Vaeldor," he responded in soldier-like fashion. "I'm honored the Grand Paladin is even aware of me."

He was right. It was momentous for a holy warrior to gain recognition within his sector. But for a captain to be acknowledged by the Grand Paladin... That was truly special. Still, Vayla did not like the situation.

"I wish you a safe journey, my lady." Macurak bowed. "May Cafior guide you."

Vayla grabbed Macurak by the breastplate and pulled him down, placing a kiss on his lips. "You better stay alive," she ordered him. "And Cafior guide you," she added, letting him go and returning to her horse.

She could sense Nyer's stare while she rose to her saddle, but she ignored it. She cast one last glance Macurak's way. Her captain appeared speechless, reminding Vayla of how she felt when he did the same to her. Served him right.

Urging Star northward, Vayla noticed Wezlok watching from atop his horse. She did not know what the mage thought, and she did not care. He followed her as she rode past.

Her army was ready when she returned, and Vayla nodded to Grimmen as she joined her captains at the lead. The zhokard raised his hand, and a horn sounded to begin the journey; and the cavalry started slowly forward while the soldiers marched in their wake.

They passed across the fields west of Onzac, trampling vegetation while aiming for the village of Cramber. To the northeast, the army of Vayla's father was a dark line. The south revealed nothing of Macurak's force. Behind Vayla, Onzac grew smaller with every step.

There came a distant crash—an explosion of stone. Vayla turned as another explosion sounded, and one of Onzac's towers collapsed. Then another. And another.

"What devilry is this?" she demanded.

"There is an attack upon Onzac!" said Lorylla.

"It must have come from within," added Eimell.

"This is not good." Wezlok gazed at the city with narrowed eyes. "A wall has just crumbled, and I see black gorillas—krahluks, Eraim called them. There are also zreekans. Odd looking creatures." The wizard looked at Vayla. "It was a trap. We are sealed within Beit."

Vayla gasped. "Montac!"

Not only had the Grand Paladin remained behind, but half of the High Paladins and High Priests were with him, as well as thousands of Palidurians. One by one, towers continued to crumble, and additional sections of the city wall collapsed.

"We must move forward!" said Lorylla.

The gray elf was right. Vayla needed to continue with the mission. Onzac was not without an army, and she would have to trust they were up to the task. Even her father's soldiers had resumed their northward march. She nodded to Grimmen, and the horn sounded to proceed.

CHAPTER 32

ZURZAK

Macurak traveled with a much smaller army than those meant for Benzon. But the entire force was mounted, allowing them to make the journey to Zurzak in three days if everything went well. A thousand of the riders were Palidurians, and the other four thousand hailed from Harbnum, Sendorum, and Kalmaar. The Palidurians led the way behind Nyer, followed by the Kalmirans that comprised half of the overall regiment, and the Sendors and Harbanians brought up the rear.

Macurak rode at Nyer's side, ready to perform the same duties he had for Vayla. He was honored that Grand Paladin Montac had taken notice of him, and to say it had caught him by surprise was an understatement. But he could not help regretting his removal from Vayla's command.

Vayla's kiss was ever on his mind. His interest in her began during their Cafior studies, a year before she rose to Paladin, when they were often paired together for various exercises. He remembered being uncomfortable in her presence, partly due to her likeness of the heralded Merssa Goldmace—not to mention her relationship to the hero of old—and also because of her intense focus. But then he came to know her. Other students did not understand Vayla, and Macurak was quick to put them in their places when they spoke ill of her. That was when he realized he had feelings for her.

After Vayla's ascension to Holy Knight, Macurak hoped to follow in her footsteps. But he was still unworthy. At first he was disappointed, but he grew to accept his status, and he was more than happy to serve beneath Vayla when the chance arrived. His affections

371

continued to grow, and he dreamed she might one day feel the same. But as time passed, he wondered if she was capable of love. Several women attempted to distract Macurak from Vayla, women of substantial physical beauty, but they never compared—Vayla possessed a beautiful soul.

The battle against Anduiff almost cost Macurak his life, and the way Vayla cared for him afterward was endearing. He thought he had finally broken through her shield. But then everything went back to normal.

After learning they were to reenter Beit, the fear that one of them might perish forced Macurak to take stronger measures. He kissed her. And though it took her a while, she kissed him in return. And now they would likely never see each other again. Life had a funny way of twisting a knife into one's heart.

"That was an interesting farewell," Nyer said.

Macurak turned to his commander, hoping his expression had not given away his thoughts. "Yes, High Paladin."

"Big plans lay before that young paladin." Nyer raised his brow. "Plans that may keep her life quite busy." He eyed Macurak. "But I suppose all will be moot if we fail to achieve victory."

"My lord," Macurak said, "we *will* achieve victory. Cafior will see to it."

"Very good." Nyer turned his eyes forward. "May Soleran smile upon us."

The High Paladin fell silent.

What did Nyer mean by *quite busy*? Was the paladin general suggesting Vayla would not have time for love? Macurak took in a deep breath. He needed to focus on the war. Nyer was correct in that nothing mattered if they failed.

They rode throughout the day, encountering only abandoned villages. Unlike Cramber the first time Macurak entered Beit, these towns were not littered with corpses. They were barren. The cavalry spent a couple of nights within inns and vacant homes, and though the ghost villages gave most soldiers an eerie feeling, including

Macurak, the security of sleeping indoors provided for solid rest.

On the morning of the third day, Macurak became anxious. According to Nyer, they should have met up with Darmoor forces the previous evening, but not even a scout came from the south. After a few hours of riding, the paladin commander halted, and he frowned while scanning the countryside.

"What do you think, High Paladin?" Macurak asked. "Shall we send forward the scouts?"

Nyer remained silent for several seconds. "You lead them," he said at last. "Search and return."

Macurak gave the signal, and he joined the scouts as they advanced.

They rode at a good pace, spreading out until Macurak saw only the immediate soldiers to his left and right, and the host fell from sight. Macurak was not out of place. He had spent many years working with the trackers of New Palidur, and he excelled in the craft. The Holy City pushed its students in every occupational direction to find their strengths, and Macurak would have made an excellent scout. But then Vayla requested that he be her captain, and that was that.

Trees dotted the landscape, sometimes clumping together in small groups. Macurak rode through a few of these groves to check for spies, but he found nothing. In fact, there was no evidence of any traffic over the past month. After taking Onzac, Grand Paladin Montac surmised that the living enemies had reported to Zurzak. So why was the land so barren? With mouths to feed, there would be frequent hunts reaching far and wide. But Macurak saw nothing to suggest such actions. Of course, the plague had likely wiped out all the game. So what did the Beitians eat? Macurak did not want to know.

They pressed deeper, and Macurak knew Zurzak to be fast approaching. But no enemy soldiers existed to spy his presence. Looking to his sides, he waved his hand back and forth and made a fist, and the distant riders repeated the gesture. He waited several minutes until the scouts signaled again, a motion starting high and sweeping low. There was nothing to report.

Macurak took in a deep breath. There was no sense going back yet. The command had been to search and report, and if the High Paladin was anything like Vayla, he would not appreciate Macurak returning empty-handed. Besides, he was certain something lay just ahead. He motioned the scouts forward.

With a wary eye on the surroundings, Macurak picked up the pace until he detected a distant sound. The clamor of combat lay ahead. He pressed harder, and Zurzak came into view, settled at the bottom of the next hill. The battle for the bridge was at hand; a contest that should have ended two days ago. From Macurak's vantage point, at least half of Zurzak and Darmoor were burning, and hundreds of corpses littered the riverbank while hundreds more rode the current into the east. Flaming arrows and boulders flew back and forth almost constantly, proving Zurzak to have greater range and capabilities than Onzac, and explosions sounded on both sides of the bridge, as mages surely worked for either army.

Macurak gasped. Once Vayla reached her destination, she would be in need of reinforcements from Darmoor. Benzon was believed to host a battalion of no less than forty thousand, and if Helmland chose that moment to enter the fray...

Macurak signaled the scouts to return, and he spun his horse. They traveled as swiftly as the mounts could carry them, covering several miles, and reached the cavalry a few hours past noon. Nyer advance to meet Macurak while the scouts gathered to him in haste.

"Zurzak still holds the river!" Macurak said. "The enemy is well prepared. Much better than Burnod supposed."

Nyer nodded, his expression grim as he stared blankly ahead. But his silence did not last long.

"Double time," he ordered Macurak.

Macurak pumped his fist up and down and pointed south. The message spread quickly through the ranks, and the horses proceeded at a canter.

Though the scouts' animals had been worked hard already, there was no time for concern while they pushed across the southern region of Beit. The hill rising above Zurzak then arrived faster than Macurak thought possible, and the cavalry halted while he and Nyer rode forward. Other than the darkening sky, the scene was unchanged.

Nyer scanned the city. "See the breach to the east?"

Macurak eyed the crumbled wall on the near side. "Yes, High Paladin."

"Take the Kalmirans there. But hold back until my signal." Nyer's gaze moved to the far side of Zurzak. "I'll lead the others through the western breach. When the enemy responds, you enter and make for the southern edge to disable the catapults."

"What about the archers?" Macurak watched another volley of flaming arrows exit the evil city. There were hundreds, if not thousands.

"They will be a problem," the paladin admitted. "But we must get our allies across the bridge." He turned to Macurak. "No matter the cost."

Macurak nodded as a lump formed in his throat. He would never see Vayla again.

He issued the lieutenants their orders, and the men departed in haste, carrying word to the ranks. Before long, the Kalmirans gathered to the east. A pang of jealousy struck Macurak while the Palidurians rode away, but it was proper for the High Paladin to lead them. The Kalmirans were renowned for their combative skills, and they had fought well in Onzac, but the Holy City cavalry was superior to all others. The Palidurians, Sendors, and Harbanians descended the right side of the hill behind Nyer, disappearing from view. They reappeared in the valley as a shadow stretching beneath the moonlight, circling toward the far end of the city where the western opening lay.

Macurak and the Kalmirans proceeded at a steady pace. They neared the eastern breach in little time, but remained a hundred yards back and waited. Macurak's heart pounded while he listened, and he soon detected a change in the battle's tone. A horn then blasted from the far side of Zurzak.

He raised his sword, and the horses bolted forward. As they reached the bottom of the hill, the Kalmiran cavalry roared, risking discovery while charging the breach. It was not the method in which Palidurians operated, but the Brondor worshippers knew no other way—they were not ones for stealth. As Macurak feared, their advance did not escape attention, and several Beitians moved to block access through the rubble that once formed part of the wall. Macurak steered his horse into the human and krukari soldiers, allowing his mount to crush a couple while he dispatched a few with his blade, and the Kalmirans stormed recklessly into Zurzak with an overwhelming show of force. Though Palidurians would have done things differently, the Kalmirans' tactics were effective and they quickly secured the area.

A wide street led to the south, and Macurak and his contingent followed the road at a brisk pace. Resistance was light at first and overcome with relative ease, but the farther they pressed, the stronger the defenses grew—it seemed they had grossly underestimated the number of troops inhabiting the city. Fires and crumbled buildings forced Macurak to seek alternate routes, but he maintained a southward trek, even when ambushes from surrounding alleys and towers killed hundreds of his men. The Kalmirans defeated the ground forces quickly and rode past the archers with as much speed as was possible, and after an hour they reached the southern edge of Zurzak at last.

They charged through the open gates and into a walled-off courtyard resembling Arbornum's western end. A score of catapults dotted the field, but only seven were functional, as the others were destroyed or burning. Thirty soldiers operated each working catapult, but Macurak was more concerned with the city walls. Archers crowded the ramparts, using fire-filled barrels to light their arrows, and additional bowman attacked from towers that had survived the onslaught thus far—five out of ten by Macurak's estimation. Worse still were the two dozen dark mages upon the wall, launching spells of destruction across the river.

Macurak shouted above the din, dividing the Kalmirans into their squads, and he led twenty riders into the soldiers operating the nearest catapult. Five Beitians fell either beneath his horse or by his sword, but an explosion showered him with debris and almost knocked him from the saddle. It had been a flaming boulder. He steadied his mount, and he saw the catapult burning, as were eleven Beitians. Eight Kalmirans and their horses were also splayed upon the field, slain by the friendly fire.

An arrow struck Macurak's horse, launched from the ramparts. More than a hundred enemy archers now faced inward, and Macurak dropped from the saddle to use his steed as best he could to shield his body. A volley descended, and forty mounted Kalmirans and just as many horses fell, including Macurak's. One arrow pierced Macurak's shoulder. Spells then issued from the wall, and Macurak sought cover behind the burning catapult, narrowly avoiding a small explosion. Another blast erupted ahead of him—the mages had him pinned.

The Kalmirans did not hide, and their bravery astounded Macurak. Even as spells and missiles reduced their numbers, those remaining in the courtyard continued the assault upon the catapults while others battled their way into towers and onto the ramparts. They defeated nearly a third of the soldiers atop the walls, and the Beitian archers and wizards shifted their attention to the more immediate threat.

Macurak ran to the stairs the Kalmirans used to ascend the wall, but after climbing the first few steps, the friendly fire ceased and he paused. At that moment, the stairs above him exploded, launching him back onto the field below. Had he continued on his path, the attack would have been a direct hit. As it was, every part of his body screamed out in pain. He struggled to his feet, and a roar sounded to the south—the allies were storming across the bridge!

The cranking of a winch resounded, but the south gate did not move. Instead, a section of the field lifted like an enormous trapdoor. It was twenty feet square, and from the hole issued krahluks—the same creatures Macurak saw outside Maple Lore Forest. The gorillas were as large as four men with fists the size of children, and one pulverized a Kalmiran horse and its rider with a single downward swing. Another ape-like beast looked at Macurak, and it began bounding toward him, closing the gap in haste.

Macurak turned to the stairs. There were no steps left to climb. He checked the gate to the north, but a strange creature hovered there. It possessed only one eye, and four tentacles writhed about its base—a nightmare Eraim had called a zreekan. If that were not enough, another arrow struck the ground near Macurak's foot.

He calmed his mind and took in a deep breath. He had completed the task given to him and provided an opening for the allies to cross the Shield River. But he would never again see the outside of the evil city. His only hope lay in Cafior granting him a quick death— hopefully not at the hands of the advancing krahluk.

What looked like rain streaked horizontally overhead, and scores of Beitians fell from the wall. It was a shower of arrows. The one-eyed monster blocking the north gate then rotated to face the dark street behind it, and additional arrows pierced its body—enough to kill three men. The creature dissolved into a mess of goop.

Nyer had surely arrived, but would the Palidurian cavalry be able to combat the mutant creatures advancing from below? Macurak then noticed it was not the Palidurians storming into the courtyard, but an army of elves. Lorians swarmed the field, and half of them advanced with swords while the rest utilized bows with deadly accuracy.

Macurak turned in time to evade the pounding fist of the charging krahluk, and its attack shook the ground. He lunged, thrusting his sword, but the blade snapped upon the creature's hide. Scores of arrows then struck the beast, making it appear almost as a porcupine, and the monster danced back with its mouth wide open.

But it made no sound. Another fifty missiles impaled the krahluk's body and it collapsed.

Shutting out the pain, Macurak lifted a sword from the field. The main gate was now open and the Darmoor allies surrounded the handful of krahluks that remained. The enormous apes crushed two and three soldiers with every swing of their deadly fists, but once the Lorians joined the fray, the monsters were overwhelmed. Atop the walls, the Kalmirans cleared the ramparts of all enemies, and through the north gate charged Nyer and the Palidurian cavalry. The battle for Zurzak was won.

The relief Macurak experienced was great, but the pain his body endured returned and he fell to his knees. A soldier appeared at his side and pulled him up by the arm.

"I've got you." The man held him steady. "Here. Bite this."

The soldier ushered something into Macurak's mouth, and he bit down by reflex. Juices coated his tongue, and his muscles relaxed as the aching eased.

"Are you a paladin?" Macurak asked through clenched teeth, staring at the ordinary-looking warrior.

"No," he said. "I'm Captain Larman of Neja."

Macurak was not sure what to think of a Nejan coming to his aid. Though New Palidur no longer scorned the kingdom of cutthroats openly, neither did they extend amiability toward the realm's citizens. But this was a time of war, and they were on the same side.

"Thank you, Captain. I'm Captain Macurak. If I may ask, what did you give me?"

"An herb from my homeland," Larman replied. "I have plenty." He pulled a handful from his pouch to reinforce his claim. "I prepare them myself. My uncle showed me how. They will ease the pain, but they are no cure."

Macurak looked about the field. The battle was over, and Nyer rode forward to meet with the general out of Darmoor. Though the man sat on a horse, he was obviously tall, and he held a strong resemblance to the captain tending to Macurak.

"Is that your uncle?" Macurak asked.

"It is." Larman grinned. "General Lindow of Neja."

CHAPTER 33

THE STORM

Vayla knew Benzon to be drawing near. She had ridden for more than a week across Beit, or rather fought her way across, as several small armies opposed her. The first couple of days they battled zombies and skeletons, overcoming the enemy with minimal casualties. The next few days brought battalions of living soldiers and dunarchins, and fatalities were higher, but still within the acceptable range. In the end, she made good time, all things considered.

Presently, they rode due north, and Vayla's head swam with apprehension. She was concerned about the battle ahead; concerned for her father; concerned for Macurak. She could not remember a time when so much worry plagued her, and it pained her stomach. Why had she allowed Macurak to affect her so? It was a matter she needed to do without, and she pushed him from her thoughts.

Wezlok cleared his throat, and Vayla turned to see the mage nod at a gathering of dark clouds ahead. She squinted. They were the same storm clouds she had been riding toward for the past hour. Nothing more. Nothing less.

Another quarter mile passed, and Lorylla spoke.

"Benzon is ahead."

Vayla still saw only dark clouds. She then realized Wezlok had spied the city well before the gray elf. Why did he not just say so? Clearing his throat and nodding was not a warning. The world would do fine without mages!

"Deploy the troops," Vayla ordered her captains.

She stared at Wezlok while Lorylla, Eimell, Greyor, and

Grimmen issued their commands. She loathed to speak to the wizard, but what choice did she have?

"What do you see?"

Wezlok's eyes narrowed. "There is a storm," he pointed out the obvious, "but it is not natural. If I were to guess, I would say Anduiff is not the only presence in Benzon."

"The Shadow?" Vayla preferred that name to the alternative. Uttering Trannum always seemed to bring Merssa up in conversation.

"I think not," Wezlok said slowly. "Though one might believe that to be the case, past experience offers doubt. It is not his way."

Vayla glared at the elf, and he sighed.

"It is unlikely Trannum dwells within the city." Wezlok spoke with obvious annoyance. "My guess is that Radaam is there as well as Anduiff. Radaam was and remains a battle wizard, and he is capable of brewing the storm before us. He is formidable and will complicate things. But I believe your leaders considered the probability of his attendance."

Vayla lifted a brow. "Was that so hard?"

And yes, they had taken the possibility of Radaam's presence into account, though it was an event they hoped to do without. So be it.

The gray elves gathered to Vayla's right while Vermallon elves assembled to her left. Behind her stood the Palidurians, Sards, Harbanians, and Nirans. The Holy City muster was smaller than Vayla had wished for, so she stationed them at the head where they might apply the most influence. Beyond the humans were the Varlimor dwarves, though Vayla could not see most of them from where she sat upon Star. The dwarves she did see toted the giant ballistae meant for undead dragons, in case any of the beasts entered the battle. She fully expected they would.

Vayla faced the distant clouds and waited—an uncomfortable wait. Day became night, but they erected no tents, and soldiers ate where they stood and took turns resting on the ground while staying in rank. Vayla was not hungry, and she remained upon Star, watching the sky.

"You should rest," Grimmen said as the darkness deepened. "I will remain alert for the signal."

Vayla considered the zhokard. He could go longer than most without sleep, but she feared being unprepared when the signal arrived. Then Wezlok spoke.

"Rest."

The wizard addressed Vayla more gently than she thought possible. She looked at the elf and was suddenly relaxed. Coming from him, the words sounded appealing. She dismounted, grabbing a pack from Star to use as a pillow, and laid on the ground.

Vayla awoke. It was morning. She rose to find Grimmen on watch, as well as thousands of soldiers. The city was certainly aware of their presence, but nothing had come through the night. Wezlok and Burnod were awake, and though Vayla knew the ex-general to have received rest, he appeared paler than the day before.

"No signal?" Vayla asked Grimmen, already knowing the answer. He would have wakened her otherwise.

"Not yet, Princess," Grimmen said.

Vayla stared at the zhokard, his formal address catching her off guard. She had not been called by her royal title for years. Most times, she forgot she ever *was* a princess. Burnod furrowed his brow, his expression one of confusion, but he said nothing.

"And the city is unchanged," added Wezlok.

Had the wizard remained awake throughout the night? Vayla did not ask.

The day wore on, and the sun traveled overhead.

"I hate to bring this up," Grimmen said, "but we are nearing the deadline."

"I know!" Vayla's anxiety drove her to speak more harshly than she intended. She sighed. The attack was to occur with or without her father's army or reinforcements from Darmoor. Their absence was likely the result of ill tidings, and she needed to begin the assault before aid could come to the city. But two hours remained before they needed to march. She calmed her voice. "It's not time just yet."

Another hour passed, and the second hour was nearly spent. Still nothing. Fear filled Vayla's heart—fear for her father and the war.

"Ready the men." She spoke almost too softly, but Grimmen heard her words and shouted orders at the nearby captains.

Twenty minutes passed. The time to march had come and gone, and still Vayla balked.

"Vayla," Burnod said.

"Hush!" She searched the sky. King Cavalor did not make it, and no scouts arrived with news from Darmoor. Or of Macurak. Her spirit sank, and she whispered a prayer to Cafior.

"I only wish to say this is as far as I go." Burnod spoke quietly, having ridden to her side. "I do not dare accompany you any farther. In case the Chant begins."

Vayla looked at the ex-general. He was a good tactician and an abled swordsman. She hated to leave him behind. They had been warned about the Chant and the effect it imposed on those having depended on the Blood River concoction to counter the plague. Burnod had consumed the elixir regularly for weeks. Vayla suggested the absence of the potion for more than a couple of months might suppress the power over the ex-general, but Grand Paladin Montac did not wish to take any chances. Vayla disagreed. Besides Burnod's skills as a warrior, his knowledge of the city was too great to do without.

"You ride with me." Her words brought looks of shock to Burnod and Grimmen.

Wezlok appeared uncaring.

Burnod shook his head. "But—"

"Signal the men!" Vayla ignored the ex-general. For good or evil, she would have his help.

Grimmen hesitated. He then waved his arms, and the northward march began.

The storm grew closer, and Vayla saw Benzon at last. The dark walls stood tall and light shone from the towers, but the city rested like a sleeping dragon. Her battalion drew to within half a mile. A thousand yards. Five hundred yards. Benzon showed no reaction, but a constant breeze came out of the north. Eight hundred feet. Six hundred feet. The wind rose in strength, and large birds now circled the city. Vayla counted half a dozen of the winged shapes, and she suspected they were undead dragons. Hopefully she was mistaken. She dared not ask Wezlok, for hearing the truth would serve only to fill the men's hearts with fear.

At two hundred yards, boulders raced across the sky. A dozen of the projectiles launched from beyond the wall, and the majority of them sailed over the army and toward the ranks farther back — the dwarves. Vayla heard shouts through the wind, as well as cries of pain. The city was attacking the ballistae.

One hundred feet. Another volley of rocks crashed into the main body, and the ensuing screams were much closer than before. A boulder streaked for Vayla, and she maneuvered Star as best she could, but a ball of fire struck the projectile, reducing it to a harmless shower of pebbles. Vayla did not need to look to realize it was Wezlok's doing.

The time for one of Vayla's contributions to the campaign was at hand. She motioned for Grimmen to give the order, and after he did so, the dwarves went to work. The Varlimor warriors had reported to Arbornum with their giant ballistae to drop undead dragons from the sky. But Vayla had additional plans for the weapons. Several trees were felled along the edge of Maple Lore Forest days before the march began, and though Wezlok was none too pleased, no Lorians arrived to turn them away and the dwarves tripled the number of projectiles they had brought. Those extra logs now flew overhead. The tree-sized missiles did not need many direct hits to destroy the gatehouse, and sections of the wall either crumbled or received cracks from ground to parapet.

Vayla signaled for the host to charge.

Crossbowmen arose atop the undamaged portions of the walls, but the Orlenfel and Vermallon archers dropped them before most of them released a bolt. The elves then blindly launched arrows over the wall to cause as much chaos as they might, and several explosions ensued—arrows loosed by the gray elves.

Vayla's plan was executed better than she had imagined, and she thanked Cafior for his guidance. She was further encouraged when a hawk flew overhead, and a leather thong streamed from its talon. Her father had arrived!

Thousands of Beitian soldiers poured from the city. Humans, krukari, and dunarchins made up their ranks, and they charged like barbarians, without any order. Vayla met them head on, swinging her sword left and right from atop Star. She struck down at least a dozen evil combatants, but the enemy fought savagely and her mare stumbled after receiving a wound.

"To me!" she called.

Palidurians led by Grimmen responded, as well as Burnod, and Vayla fell back to dismount. She slapped Star upon the rear, sending the horse to safety, and returned to the melee.

Screams of the undead dragons filled the sky, and several non-Palidurians gave ground with wide eyes. A pair of the skeletal beasts descended, and one of them collapsed when a tree-missile snapped its spine in two. The other dragon swooped low, issuing a yellow cloud from its maw and wiping out over fifty allies and enemies alike. The resulting corpses were hideous, dried-out husks, and Vayla was further disturbed when a chill captured the battle and the dead began to stir. A Death Lord drew near.

"Trust nothing dead!" Burnod shouted.

Arrows continued to enter the melee from the elves, each missile true and finding only enemy warriors. But even as they were slain, they returned shortly to the fray as zombies. Grimmen fought with reckless abandon and fell several times, but his zhokard heart denied death, and surprise took the Beitians when he rose again—he did not become a zombie, as the evil soldiers had expected. Being neither wholly alive nor undead, the presence of the Death Lord had no effect on Grimmen, and he made his way to Vayla's side while she battled the horde.

Horns sounded to the west—another force approached. This came as no surprise, and the Vermallon elves drew their weapons as they joined a squadron of dwarves charging to meet the newcomers. Half of the gray elves also pulled their swords, and Vayla could not suppress the awe she experienced from seeing them fight. Their tall forms leaped over twenty feet in the air, slashing with glowing blades that emitted steam in the growing chill.

Two more undead dragons fell, crushing friend and foe. It was an unavoidable consequence, and allies decapitated many a former companion's head before the resulting zombies crawled from the wreckage. Another skeletal dragon remained high above, and atop its back was a figure with cold blue eyes shining beneath the darkened sky. It was a Death Lord, and it raised a hand, summoning a score of lightning bolts from the clouds and into the rear ranks. Though Vayla could not see the outcome of the attack, she was sure scores of soldiers had fallen and would soon turn to the side of evil. The dark rider proceeded south toward the dwarves and their monstrous bows.

A horn sounded to the northeast. Cavalor had intercepted another enemy force there. This allowed Vayla to concentrate her efforts on the gate and the west, and she prayed her father found success in gaining access to the secret entrance, where he was to insert paladins into the heart of the evil city after destroying the door.

The battle raged on, and Vayla's arms grew tired. She had slain more enemies than she cared to count, not to mention those that needed to be put down a second time, friends and foes alike. But she pressed on, drawing nearer to the gate. The Death Lord returned, and the most recently deceased rose up to surround her, but fire from Wezlok protected her flank and she destroyed those before her. The undead king unleashed more horrible spells, and explosions sounded behind Vayla as the Death Lord continued to grow the zombie army and trap her between opposing forces. But she could do nothing about that now.

Another tone reached Vayla's ears from the south—one she had been anxious to hear. The Darmoor reinforcements had arrived! Her thoughts went to Macurak, but she pushed them away. Even if her captain had survived, there was no guarantee they would see each other again. All that mattered was her relationship with Cafior, and her energy rose with that realization.

She battled her way into Benzon at last. Unlike Onzac, the entrance was not an open field bearing war machines, but a collection of towers upon gray streets of brick creating a myriad of paths in every direction. Catapults rested atop the wider turrets, now unmanned, and shaved trees launched by the ballistae were settled among collapsed buildings, where dozens of corpses struggled beneath the rubble to join the fight.

The streets were empty, but arrows rained from hundreds of slits within the tower walls. The gray elves took to their bows, and though only a few of their shots found paths through the narrow openings, the explosions of those striking the walls proved just as effective. Flying debris showered the street, and very few missiles were forthcoming in defense of the city afterward.

The only sounds then came from outside the wall to the south and west. The Darmoor reinforcements fought those in Vayla's wake while the Vermallon elves and half of the dwarves from her army battled... Vayla had no idea what they faced.

"I should leave!" Burnod stood twenty feet behind Vayla. "We have been lucky so far, but—"

"With me!" Vayla glared at the ex-general. "We need you!"

"I cannot..." He was as white as a ghost. "I refuse to bring you harm! I'm sorry."

He ran through the broken gate.

"Blast!" Vayla had no time to chase him down. The sun was descending, and she needed to reach the castle before nightfall—darkness would hamper her human troops against the krukari and the undead.

She returned to the task at hand and eyed the brick streets. The towers and buildings were strategically placed to narrow the approach of invading forces.

"Palidurians and dwarves to me!" she commanded. "Kalmirans, left! All others, right! Orlenfel, support!"

While the troops carried out her orders, she hurried along a central street. The chill of an undead king then returned, and she cursed the fiend—whenever the tide turned in her favor, a Death Lord intervened. Many explosions echoed to Vayla's right, and she prayed for her soldiers there.

She reached an open square a half mile inside the gate. Nothing moved, but she slowed her advance, untrusting the stillness. Every alley to the north then teemed with warriors in dark armor, and strange words suddenly rode upon the wind, droning in Vayla's mind. Selanna and Eraim were supposed to neutralize the Chant, but evidently they had been unable to do so. The Beitian soldiers charged.

"Run!" Grimmen shouted, stepping between Vayla and the enemy.

Vayla did not move. She refused to retreat. But then Wezlok's hand fell upon her arm and her head spun. Once the rotating stopped, she was back at the entrance of Benzon, just inside the broken gate. Wezlok was not with her, and neither was her battalion. Scattered soldiers from Darmoor battled zombies and dunarchins in her army's wake.

Burnod entered the city, and he struck down a Nejan and a Philander before turning to face Vayla. He charged.

CHAPTER 34

DARUM CARUMBOR

Eraim traveled far with Tux after departing from the House of Elgarroth. During that time he was a bit more talkative, though still tight-lipped, and she found she tolerated his presence. He even shared in Eraim's enjoyment of teaching rich braggarts lessons. After witnessing some of his talents, she had to admit he really was the master of stealth. But he was part gray elf, and he enjoyed natural abilities she could never know. She would never compete with him, for she *could* not compete with him. He did not even play the same game. And as she became comfortable with this knowledge, she appreciated his company all the more.

They spent a couple of weeks riding through Arbornum and Darmoor, sharing news and information—Tux knew much of what transpired between Eraim, Selanna, and Elgarroth, and Eraim wondered if he had been spying. They also sneaked across the Darmoor bridge into Beit during the darkest part of the night, a feat both terrifying and exhilarating, and entered Maple Lore Forest unnoticed until reaching a village rising into the trees. There, Tux spoke with a Lorian elder. A large cage containing hundreds of humans dominated the ground at the bottom of the town, and it disgusted Eraim. Tux paid it no mind. The temptation to free the people was strong, but where would they go if not into Beit and its impending war? Besides that, they did not appear malnourished. Eraim made a mental note to return after the war and set things to right.

From there, she and Tux passed through the forest, fording the Shield River where it was surprisingly tame. So why did they risk crossing the Darmoor bridge in the first place? Eraim figured Tux enjoyed showing off to a certain extent. They encountered four more Lorian villages comprising high bridges and buildings stacked within the trees, but it seemed Tux was well known, and no one hindered their progress.

They entered Virch and journeyed to Ellaville, where Tux claimed they were to meet up with Selanna. Eraim's friend was there indeed, as were Kiryanna, Magneer, Nidor, and Gruelenor.

Eraim's eyes moistened as she embraced Selanna. Her friend was in one piece. When the hug ended, Tux was gone. Eraim shrugged — it was an inevitability she knew to be coming.

"What was it like?" Eraim asked Selanna. But after the words escaped her lips, she was not sure she wanted to know anything about Arman Forest.

Selanna smirked, seeming to read Eraim's thoughts, and changed the subject.

"I have a gift for you." Selanna held a dagger with a black metal handle. She unsheathed it to reveal the blade to match, as if the weapon was forged from a single piece of ore. "This may prove more effective against foes not of our world." She slid the dagger back into its scabbard.

Eraim balked. Was it a product of something they acquired from Darum Carumbor or Trannum's crypt? The thought of possessing an object of the enemy was frightening. It was bad enough Selanna toted such items. Eraim noticed the others carrying similar daggers, and she accepted the gift.

After a night at the local inn, they departed early the next morning. Eraim and Lilli led the company west, with Selanna and Dandi at their side. Behind them rode Nidor and Magneer, and Kiryanna and Gruelenor brought up the rear.

Eraim and Selanna shared small talk, but Selanna still said nothing about her journey into Arman Forest. Eraim's feelings on the subject varied from grateful to irritated, as she remained unsure if she wanted to know. But she detected something different about Selanna.

Something troubling. She would have to keep an eye on her friend when she could afford to do so.

Before reaching the Stony River, they turned north and journeyed into the Stone Eagle Mountains. By evening of the second day since leaving Ellaville, they reached the first campsite along the Path of the Guardians and settled in for some rest.

The night was cool, and Eraim sat next to a boulder and out of the wind while inspecting her arrows. They were perfect. As she checked the final arrow, she noticed Selanna's grin. Eraim shrugged. Tux was wise to make sure each and every arrow was up to the challenge. Upon completion of the task, she joined Selanna beside the fire.

"Will you not tell me what troubles you?" Eraim asked, just above a whisper.

"It is nothing." Selanna sighed. "It is everything." She looked at Eraim. "It is taking the item the enemy desperately wishes to obtain to their very doorstep. It is possessing Trannum's source of power. It is life about to change forever, and not knowing if it is for good or ill." She placed a hand on Eraim's shoulder. "You are the best friend I have ever known, and the craftiest companion anyone could hope for. I fear for you. I fear for all of us." Her shoulders slumped. "I wish Vecnor was here. And... I wish Merssa was here."

"Do not concern yourself for me." Eraim offered a confident smile. "I have Mithkahr. And I will protect you with all my being."

"No!" Selanna said urgently. She then calmed. "No. You must watch out for yourself. Who knows what friends we will lose to this war? I cannot have you die saving me. I *will* not have it." Sincerity shone in Selanna's moistened eyes.

"Fine." Eraim gave a wry smile. "You have not needed my protection for some time anyway." She stood. "Now get some rest. We can ill afford for you to be weary."

Selanna laid down, and Eraim took her position to guard the night.

Eraim awakened to Nidor's touch. The paladin had finished the final watch. The morning was cool and dark, and the company ate breakfast while continuing along the path. As the sun rose high, they followed the ridge overlooking the scenic valley where the Shield River began, and they arrived at the stable-cave a few hours before evening.

After quartering the horses, Eraim made sure plenty of food and water were available while her companions gathered gear from their mounts.

"This could be the last time you see me," Eraim said quietly to Lilli in the elfish language. "If you run out of water or food, lead the others to safety."

Lilli whinnied and nodded, and Eraim detected sadness in her animal companion's body language.

The company left the cave and continued in single file. After another mile they reached the valley bridge, and doubt filled the eyes of Magneer and Gruelenor.

"I know you explained this to be a narrow crossing," said Magneer, "but no warning prepares you for this. It's breathtaking, to say the least."

"It really is wider than it looks," insisted Eraim. "I will show you."

"No!" Kiryanna stuck out her arm to stop Eraim. Though the marteese's expression had softened with each passing day since departing from Ellaville, she appeared eager now that Helmland and Beit were drawing near. "I will go first."

Eraim shrugged. "If you insist."

Kiryanna walked gracefully along the bridge with complete confidence. Once the marteese neared the midpoint, Eraim stepped onto the narrow path to follow. Movement among the boulders on the other side then caught her eye, and she halted. Pulling her bow, she nocked an arrow.

"What do you see?" Selanna asked with alarm.

"We are not alone." Eraim scanned the far rocks.

"Perhaps it is Tux," said Selanna.

Eraim shook her head. If it was Tux, she would not have seen him. "Kiryanna! Watch yourself!"

Kiryanna drew her blade, and at that moment several dunarchins emerged from their hiding places across the gorge.

"How can this be?" Selanna lowered her brow. "This path is unknown!"

Eraim released one of the gray arrows, and it pierced the eye socket of a dunarchin, passing through its skull. A hole resulted, and the undead firstborn fell into the valley below. The remaining dunarchins raised bows with the exception of one, whose fingers crackled with energy.

Before the evil warriors could release a volley, Eraim dropped another from their ranks. She then dodged a few arrows, and it impressed her to see Kiryanna deflect a couple of missiles with the golden blade while keeping perfect balance. But the marteese would be hard pressed to continue with such actions.

Eraim launched three more arrows while the dunarchins reloaded, and each missile reduced the enemy's number—she loved Tux's craftsmanship! Gruelenor used his bow to fell another, dropping the enemy to a dozen.

The dunarchin mage released lightning at Kiryanna, and Selanna redirected the spell into the cliff with a wave of her hand. With her other hand, she pulled back, and the dunarchin was jerked over the gap. The undead firstborn disappeared into the valley without a scream.

An arrow sank into Selanna's leg, and one bypassed Kiryanna's defenses and pierced her stomach. The marteese nearly fell from the bridge. Eraim continued picking off the enemy one by one, dropping two more while Gruelenor claimed another.

A ball of fire streaked across the chasm—it amazed Eraim that Selanna retained the ability to unleash such power with the pain she surely endured. But upon reaching the other side, the flame became

Nidor! The paladin stood among the undead firstborns with his burning sword, and he struck down four of the enemy before they pulled their blades. Kiryanna ran to join Nidor, and Eraim and Gruelenor continued supporting them with their bows. The dunarchins soon collapsed and the battle ended.

Eraim hurried to Selanna. The arrow was deep into her thigh, most likely stuck in the bone. Eraim was afraid to touch it.

"Sit." She helped Selanna to the ground.

On the other side of the gap, Nidor used his fiery hand while removing the arrow from Kiryanna's stomach. Once he completed his task, Eraim waved him over, and he hastened across the bridge with confidence unusual for a human.

"Move ahead and make sure the way is clear," Nidor said to Eraim.

Eraim stared with her mouth agape. Who put the paladin in charge? Of course, he had become quite an accomplished leader over the past couple of decades. It was impressive how he remained in the background thus far, following the lead of Eraim and Selanna while offering no judgements or complaints. Eraim complied.

Upon the other side of the bridge, Kiryanna searched the rocks for more undead. Eraim looked at Mithkahr as she arrived. There was no glow.

"You may relax," she told the marteese.

Kiryanna nodded, surprisingly without a scowl. The marteese then handed Eraim half a dozen Orlenfel arrows, having removed them from the dunarchin corpses.

"Thank you," Eraim said, wiping the arrows clean and returning them to her quiver, all the while scanning the mountainside for more. She had to make them last.

Magneer crossed the bridge, and Gruelenor followed, both moving with extreme caution. Selanna went next, showing no sign of a leg injury, and Nidor brought up the rear. The company then followed the path north with weapons drawn until reaching the next campsite, and after making sure the area was clear, they dropped their packs and prepared to rest.

"They should not have been able to discover this path," Selanna said to Eraim while they sat by the fire. "It has magical wards in place to prevent detection. One would have to know exactly where to look. Even then, they could easily lose their way."

Eraim remembered how often the trail disappeared before her eyes. Had she not memorized the way the first time, she might have gotten lost amid the mountains. "Do you have any thoughts?"

"They had to be shown the path," Selanna said. "There is no other explanation."

This did not sit well with Eraim. She could think of no one capable of such a deed.

The night saw little sleep, as everyone was on high alert, and all but Selanna shared in the watch. Lacking the ability to see in the dark, Magneer guarded with Nidor. Eraim would have thought the paladin to suffer the same deficiency, but his eyes lit up with fire, and he appeared to pierce the shadows as good as any dwarf or krukari.

With the first sign of morning, they gathered their gear and returned to the path. They continued to hold their weapons ready while they walked, but nothing revealed itself and Mithkahr detected no evil. The pace was hard until dusk, when the waterfall appeared to the north, and they stopped for the evening.

Again, the night passed peacefully, and by the time the sun illuminated the land, the company stood at the top of the waterfall. Eraim did not hesitate to descend, and the roaring water filled her ears, even after the stairs deposited them next to the pond. From there, the current held a moderate flow toward Lake Beldara miles away.

They headed north, guided by the river until it exited the mountains, and Lothen Forest came into view to the distant northwest. Small skeletons were scattered—a reminder of the dead animals decorating the landscape the last time Eraim traveled this route. She pushed the memory from her thoughts, taking care not to step on any of the remains.

The company continued without a break, bringing Eraim slight fatigue. But she said nothing. The others surely suffered as well. A couple hours after dusk, they drew to within a hundred yards of the forest.

"We will camp under the trees," Selanna said.

No one argued, and they moved on beneath the growing stars.

They entered Lothen, and the shadows made it seem like a moonless night. Selanna summoned two of her small lights to illuminate the way, and they walked another half mile before stopping.

Everyone made themselves as comfortable as possible. Eraim took the time to inspect her arrows, finding them perfectly straight — even those used against the dunarchins. They were impressive, indeed. She then gazed about the trees, remembering the wind that led them on an all-night run. Selanna claimed it to have been the Guardians' spirits. The thought still brought Eraim chills.

The hour grew late, and Magneer and Gruelenor turned in while Nidor stood guard. Eraim did not feel sleepy. Darum Carumbor plagued her mind, and she looked into the east, as if the tower would be revealed to her — it worked for wizards. She saw only trees.

"The war goes as well as can be expected." Selanna sat against a tree with her eyes closed.

"But how do you know?" Eraim asked.

Had Elgarroth taught Selanna how to see without looking?

Selanna sighed. "I just know. Vayla has reached Benzon, and she awaits her father's arrival. But ambushes have delayed Cavalor."

Eraim shook her head. She appreciated the news, but it was just more confusing wizard stuff.

Selanna opened her eyes. Eraim expected the usual smirk her friend held when being vague and causing confusion, but Selanna's expression was serious. In fact, she appeared tired.

"You should get some rest," said Eraim.

Selanna nodded and closed her eyes.

Morning arrived much too quickly. Having taken the final leg of the watch, Eraim awoke the others. It was yet dark, and the northern air chilled her lungs, but the sun's warmth would soon reign. This became a reality a half hour into their trek.

As evening arrived, they reached Lothen's western edge, as near to the tower as was possible while remaining beneath the trees. Darum Carumbor was silent while smog issued from its multiple chimneys, and the portcullis was up. A drone then filled the air, and within it Eraim detected strange words. She listened, and her nerves tingled as a cloud slowly spread across her mind and her muscles stiffened. But the sensations retreated when she grabbed hold of Mithkahr.

Selanna gasped. "The Chant!" She fished items from her pack and handed them to each of the company. They were pendants. "Wear these. Quickly!"

Eraim inspected the necklace. It was made of gold and bore what appeared to be a small black crystal. But when the light hit it, she realized the jewel to be dark violet. It reminded her of the shard she had procured from the enormous gem Baylun destroyed; the shard that had been turned over to the Council of Wizards. Eraim thought about questioning her friend on the matter, but Selanna was slipping one of the chains around her neck, and the others did the same. Eraim put it on.

"They are charms," Selanna said. "They should counter the Chant."

"*Should*?" Magneer frowned.

"Unfortunately, there is no time for stealth." Selanna ignored the ranger. "We must go now."

They left the cover of the forest, dashing across the two hundred yards separating them from the tower. Nidor challenged Eraim's speed, as the paladin's strides seemed to be fueled by the heat exuding from his body, and Kiryanna kept a good pace for one dressed in armor, trailing them only slightly. A gong sounded as they approached to within twenty yards, and the portcullis began to lower. Eraim halted and readied her bow.

Nidor raced forward, sheathing his sword and grabbing hold of the bottom crossbar. His muscles strained beneath the weight as he ceased the gate's descent, and he was defenseless when tower guards appeared in response to the alarm. Eraim fired two arrows, one after the other, and a pair of soldiers fell. Kiryanna then stood beside Nidor, blocking Eraim's path, and the marteese skewered a defender through the bars. The final soldier gashed Nidor's stomach, and Kiryanna issued a blow to make the man run down the corridor to the right.

It amazed Eraim that Nidor did not lose his grip. He lifted the gate overhead by the time the company arrived, and Eraim was further surprised to see he bore no stomach wound. Had he healed himself without his flaming hand?

Eraim slung her bow over her shoulder and unsheathed Mithkahr while entering the tower. Once everyone was inside, Nidor let the gate crash down behind him. The corridor arced to the left and right, and Magneer headed right with Kiryanna at his side. Eraim went next with Nidor, and Selanna and Gruelenor followed, the krukari holding an arrow to his bow and watching their flank.

"Here!" a voice hailed from around the bend.

Eraim gasped. She knew the voice to be Daymyn's. Magneer must have recognized it as well, for he ran along the tunnel.

They rounded the tower, and Daymyn came into view. The lad wore enemy garb and held a sword, and an urgent expression was on his face.

"You must hurry!" he called out. "The Chant has begun! The upper floor projects it to the Faithful!"

They rushed toward their lost companion, and Baylun appeared, charging from the opposite direction. He was larger than Eraim remembered, and taller as well. Had she not known him, she would have thought him scary to behold, an impression likely driven by the rage in his eyes. As he neared Daymyn, he shouted in a commanding tone.

"No!"

Eraim stared in horror as Baylun's large hammer fell. Daymyn raised his sword in defense, but the blade failed to alter the weapon's path and the hammerhead crashed onto his skull.

Daymyn collapsed.

"No!" cried Magneer, rushing down the hall faster than Eraim thought possible.

Magneer drove Baylun into the wall, lifting his blade to the young krukari's throat. Gruelenor pushed past Eraim and the others, and he shouldered Magneer, breaking Baylun free and knocking the ranger's blade to the floor.

The Chant continued.

CHAPTER 35

CHANGE OF ALLEGIANCE

Baylun lost track of how long he had lived in Darum Carumbor. Constant training made the weeks slip by, as did the sound of the Chant being practiced every night. He still had not been invited to learn the Chant, and he prayed that event never came to pass.

He gave up hope of escaping and returning to the life he once enjoyed in Philen. Daymyn was the only reminder of those days, although his cousin no longer called him Fang, and Baylun found he missed the nickname. Of course, referring to him in such a manner within earshot of another soldier would see Daymyn suffer grave consequences. Baylun understood his cousin's restraint. Lately, Baylun faced the reality that his only likelihood of escape would come as a rescue. But who would be saved if it took much longer for that rescue to arrive? His mind was slipping away.

Baylun's rank of lieutenant made life a bit easier. But it also kept him beneath Captain Rozall's critical eye.

"Still not worthy of the Chant?" the captain often asked. "Is there something wrong with you? Don't worry. You'll receive the Message soon enough."

Baylun did not *want* to receive the Message.

Evidently, the captain's concerns did not prevent Baylun from rising to First Lieutenant, his third promotion since coming to live in the tower. He was now second in command beneath the captain, although Rozall answered to Radaam and sometimes the Dun Priests.

Several of Baylun's underlings were elevated from tower guards to Dun Soldiers, and some became Dun Lancers if their riding skills were adequate. These men had all learned the Chant, and afterward their attitudes showed significant changes. They laughed less. They angered less. Only traces of their original personalities remained. And though they had been loyal to Baylun, he had no doubt they would strike him down without remorse if ordered to do so.

The chill Radaam exuded took some getting used to—most of the tower's occupants wore heavy cloaks—and Baylun eventually learned to shut out the unnatural fear. At one point, Baylun was made to display his skills in combat before the Death Lord, and during the bout he perspired heavily, even within the room of ice.

"You performed well," Radaam said after the exhibition, his hollow voice sending chills down Baylun's already frozen spine. "I can see you ruling this tower one day." The glowing eyes turned to the Dun Priests, allowing Baylun to release the breath he held while they rested upon him. "See to it he receives the Message."

"We live to serve," the three priests said in unison as they bowed.

The cold walls were closing in. Baylun's new life gnawed at him, and he wondered how much longer he could hold out before his true self was discovered. The fact that he saw Daymyn less did not help, as his cousin now served under another lieutenant's command, and their meetings were reduced to occasional corridor pleasantries. The anxiety in Daymyn's eyes was a cause for concern, but the presence of others did not allow for any genuine conversations. One day, Baylun caught Daymyn alone in the mess hall.

"You fought in front of Radaam?" Daymyn asked, his expression revealing both awe and fear.

"Yeah." Baylun shuddered. "How are *you* holding out?"

"*My* job's easy!" Daymyn chuckled. "*You're* the one climbing the tower!"

"I don't know how much longer this ruse can last." Baylun kept watch on the closed door. "I'm afraid of losing myself. I'd rather lose my life."

"Don't speak that way!" Daymyn grabbed Baylun by the arm—

an event punishable by a hundred lashes. "You *must* play the part. That is how I have survived. Become what they believe you to be, and they'll be none the wiser."

"But the Chant..."

"Your will is strong," Daymyn said. "They cannot prevent you from being you, no matter what. I believe that. If you have to learn the Chant, then learn the blasted Chant. If you need help remembering who you are, then lean on me. I'm here for you."

The conversation ended when a servant entered to clean the tables. And that was the last time Baylun had spoken to his cousin without prying ears.

Learn the Chant? But what if it changed him? What if Daymyn could do nothing to stop it? And why would Radaam want Baylun to rule the tower? Were his battle skills really that impressive? His cousins had never thought so. Besides, there were plenty of cruel candidates to govern once Radaam moved on—a widely known inevitability.

Presently, Darum Carumbor was much warmer, as Radaam had left over a week prior, and Baylun walked along the rounding corridor on his way to see Captain Rozall. The meetings with the captain happened so often as of late that Baylun had grown numb to the man's intimidating presence. In fact, he was numb to many things that once put him on edge. Even the priests were more annoying than scary.

Rozall smiled when Baylun entered—a surprising expression.

"Welcome, Baylun."

"Thank you, sir." Baylun took a seat at the captain's gesture to do so, and he set his hammerhead on the floor. "I'm confused as to my summons. There's nowhere else for me to go, unless I'm to take *your* chair."

Yes, Baylun's nerves had certainly grown numb.

Rozall's smile dropped. It then returned, becoming more of a sly grin. "We have decided it is time."

Baylun frowned. "Time?"

"Lord Radaam's orders were clear," the captain said. "You need to progress. Although you've not yet received the Message, it is time to become part of the Chant."

Baylun's face drained of all blood. He did his best not to show the worry those words provoked, turning his thoughts to the conversation with his cousin. Daymyn insisted Baylun could resist any change the Chant brought upon him; assured him he would have help if he needed it.

Rozall's smile vanished, and he sat back in his chair. "You don't look pleased." His face moved to anger. "You continue to disappoint me, Lieutenant. I have been patient, as have the priests. But it's time to move forward, whether you're ready or not. The Chant begins today! Forces are mobilizing, and we can wait no longer."

"Forces?"

"Do not play the fool!" Rozall stood as his face turned another shade of red. Anger was an emotion the captain rarely displayed, and it took Baylun by surprise. "Do you think we are so blind as to not realize who you are?"

These words struck Baylun, and he looked around the office... For what? An escape? The room's only door was behind him. And then what? There was nowhere to go. Did they know he came from Philen? Fresh from his birthday hunt with his brother, who was now lost to Helmland? Did they know who Daymyn was?

"Yes, Baylun." The captain retook his seat, his demeanor suddenly calm. "Since the day you arrived, you have reeked of treason. I have requested time and time again to be done with you, but Lord Radaam would not hear it. Not after the Dun Priests found Lord Gruzim's blood running through your veins."

Gruzim? The Death Lord that fell in the Battle of the Dead Fields? The priests were mistaken.

"Your skills in combat are impeccable," Rozall muttered. "I'll give you that. But your talents are no good if they are not on *our* side. So the decision has been made. We are to project our efforts into Beit this evening, so you *will* become a part of it without further delay."

The captain smiled, like a greedy merchant finding a gullible rich man. "The enemy nears, and the Chant will reign once again... It has been too long." Pleasure captured Rozall's expression, and a moan escaped his throat.

At that moment, the Chant began. It vibrated the stone walls, and Rozall's eyes brightened as they returned to Baylun. Baylun had heard it practiced every day, but this time it held a perfect rhythm, like when he first entered Darum Carumbor with his brother, only stronger. He did not have his axe, and he wondered how long before his body stiffened; before Rozall moved too fast for him to counter. But nothing changed.

"Feel it enter you," Rozall said adoringly. "It is power. Daymyn swore you would come around. Perhaps this was the path we needed to travel all along, descendant of Gruzim."

"Daymyn?" Baylun's head spun.

"Ah, yes. Daymyn." Rozall grinned. "How eager he has been to take part in all things. He received the Message weeks ago, after revealing a secret entrance into Helmland; a path used by the Guardians to spy on us." Rozall leaned forward. "But he is not permitted to learn the Chant. Not until he convinces you to do so first. *You* are the one Radaam wants. But don't worry. Once your head is right, you may keep Daymyn at your side. Everyone needs lieutenants, after all."

Baylun did not remember reaching, but his fingers were wrapped around the haft of his hammer. Captain Rozall continued to grin — an evil smirk ripping at Baylun's core — and the Chant was disorienting Baylun's mind. He refused to give in, and he brought the weapon up, clearing the desk and striking Rozall across the head. The force crushed the captain's skull. As Rozall collapsed, Baylun was already opening the door.

The Chant soured his stomach, and he ran, afraid that stopping meant being slowed for good. Within the central chamber, only two guards were present — those having learned the Chant were gathered to the upper level. The men saluted Baylun and spoke, but their words did not register. Baylun heard only the deep droning, and his mind was bent on Daymyn while he descended through the trapdoor. He barely noticed the gong warning of an attack upon the tower.

Could Daymyn have really told them about the secret entrance through the Stone Eagles? The path Baylun knew to be his only hope for escape? No. The captain had been trying to trick him.

Baylun continued along the outer corridor of the first floor when he heard Daymyn call out.

"Here!"

The shout came from around the bend.

How did Daymyn know Baylun was coming to... What? Warn him? Speak to him? What would Baylun do once he faced his cousin?

He ran faster.

Daymyn came into view, and farther up the passage was Uncle Magneer! Baylun's heart leaped, as if he might soon awaken from his nightmare. He then spied Kiryanna, Eraim, and Selanna. And was his father behind them?

"You must hurry!" Daymyn yelled. "The Chant has begun! The upper floor projects it to the Faithful!"

Baylun held his breath. The Faithful? Why did Daymyn refer to them as the Faithful? Then he saw his cousin reaching for the handle. Daymyn was waiting for the right moment to spring the acid trap!

Anger fueled Baylun, and his insides burned as he sprinted. How could Daymyn betray him? Betray their friends? Uncle Magneer had practically raised the man. As Daymyn grabbed hold of the dark lever, Baylun gained his attention with a shout.

"No!"

It was all the distraction he needed, and he swung his weapon with both hands. Daymyn tried to fend off the blow, but the hammer was too heavy and Baylun too strong. He drove his cousin's blade down, and the hammerhead crashed into Daymyn's skull, crushing it even harder than it had Captain Rozall's.

Baylun was unable to move. Had the Chant finally grabbed hold? The next thing he knew, Uncle Magneer forced him against the tower wall and put a sword to his throat. Magneer hissed something, but Baylun's shock and the Chant made the words sound like gibberish. Then Baylun's father arrived, shouldering Uncle Magneer away.

Baylun watched his uncle's weapon clatter to the floor. He stooped to pick it up, but a powerful hand impeded him, pressing its warmth against his chest.

"Hold, young warrior." Nidor's deep voice roused Baylun's senses.

"What have you done?" Eraim could not take her eyes from Daymyn's body.

"Traitor!" said Magneer, still held by Baylun's father. "Strike him down!"

"Leave him be!" Gruelenor carried a lethal tone.

"Stop!" shouted Selanna.

Everything went silent. No one spoke, though Baylun saw lips moving. Even the Chant had ceased. Baylun realized he viewed his saviors through tear-filled eyes, and he was sure he emitted a sob. But he heard nothing. He had waited forever for his rescuers, enduring the temptations of the surrounding evil. His cousin had not been strong enough, and Baylun killed him. Baylun wanted to die.

"Baylun," came Selanna's voice, calm and soothing.

He looked up and saw only her. The others were gone.

"Why, Baylun?" the elf asked. "Why did you strike Daymyn?"

Baylun was not sure he could break the silence. But it did not matter. He could not say the words. He turned to the lever on the wall, where Daymyn's hand had been, and pulled it.

Acid showered the corridor back the way Baylun's rescuers had come. His friends and family were present again, and he could see their gaping mouths as the hallway smoked and eroded. His father released Magneer with a shove before lifting Baylun's hammer and returning it to him.

The Chant resumed.

Selanna addressed the company. "No more needs to be said at this time. We must bring the Chant to an end, before irreparable damage is done."

"What about my nephew?" Magneer glanced at Daymyn and shot a glare Baylun's way.

Baylun looked at his cousin's body, his heart breaking further. He averted his gaze—the mess was unbearable.

"Nothing can be done about that right now." Selanna held no sympathy in her voice. "The Chant is everything." She turned to Baylun. "What should we expect?"

Baylun hesitated beneath Magneer's continuing scowl. He wondered if his uncle remembered he was a nephew too.

"Minimal guards," he managed at last. "Most of them are on the upper floor, performing the Chant. Over forty Dun warriors have arrived over the past week. The Chant has never been this strong before."

"Radaam is obviously not here," Selanna said to the others. "But I am sure there will be Dun Priests."

"Three priests," Baylun confirmed.

Selanna nodded. "Lead the way."

Baylun gripped his hammer. Eraim looked from him to Daymyn and back again, disbelief holding her mouth agape. Kiryanna bore a look of pity. Nidor's face was kind, as it had been throughout Baylun's life. Selanna gazed intently, urging him to proceed.

He stepped around Magneer without making eye contact. As Baylun moved past his father, a friendly hand touched his shoulder. At least someone was glad he still lived. Baylun was not sure he agreed.

He led the way into the central chamber, ascended the stairs, and climbed the iron rungs to the trapdoor. Upon entering the second-floor training room, Baylun saw the two soldiers that had been there earlier. They were young, still unable to receive the Message or learn the Chant. When Baylun had asked what guided them to join the tower in the first place, their stories about growing up in Beit revealed they had known no better life. He wished he could convince them to leave Helmland and never return. But it was too late for that.

The guards perked up as Baylun stepped forward, but when Nidor and Kiryanna rose from below, their jaws dropped.

"Lieutenant! Behind you!" shouted one soldier as they pulled their swords.

Baylun moved aside, unable to do what needed to be done. These men were yet innocent. But they were eager as well, and would don the black armor when the time came. Kiryanna and Nidor made an easy time of the two, and the room quieted—except for the Chant.

Magneer sneered at Baylun. "Friends of yours?"

"You leave him be," Gruelenor growled.

Magneer faced Baylun's father. "What use is he if he is unwilling to fight his comrades?"

"Leave him be." Gruelenor emphasized each word.

"He doesn't even wear a charm." Magneer looked at Selanna. "I thought this chant was supposed to freeze people or something."

"I sense no evil from Baylun." Nidor placed an unwanted hand on Magneer's shoulder. "But there is much evil higher up. I suggest we concentrate on that."

Uncle Magneer appeared displeased with the paladin's words, but after one last scowl, he ceased glaring at Baylun. Gruelenor's eyes were thankful, and Nidor gave him a nod.

"Proceed," Selanna said to Baylun.

Baylun led the way from the room and into the outer corridor. The pounding of metal now rang above the Chant, and he turned toward the smithy.

"You have a brave soul." Kiryanna spoke just loud enough for Baylun to hear. She walked next to him, revealing the slightest of smiles. "Others cannot understand the bravery and strength it takes to do what you did. But I do. Some cannot see past the krukari."

She sounded like Brem. This time, however, Baylun did not mind so much.

They reached the forge. Even with the Chant going on, the smith was hard at work—production of the Dun items stopped for nothing.

"We might want to..." Baylun stared at the door. He turned to

Nidor. "He is the only smith in Helmland with the ability to shape the black metal. The things he makes are pure evil."

Nidor's chest puffed out, and he entered the room. No scuffle ensued. No screams. No yells. The constant pounding ceased, and Nidor reentered the hallway and gave Baylun a nod. Baylun never cared for the smith anyway. The krukari spoke to no one; ate meals with no one. He simply created dark weapons and armor, day and night. Good riddance.

Baylun entered the final guardroom, and the Chant grew louder than ever. On the far side, stairs rose to the chamber where the Chant was being performed, and purple smoke drifted down the topmost steps before dissipating into nothing. There were no guards.

The others followed as Baylun ascended, but when he neared the top, Nidor halted him with a hand on his shoulder. The barbarian paladin strode by, his eyes flaring with fire to match the flame surrounding his blade. Baylun proceeded.

The purple mist covered the floor of the upper room, and in place of Radaam's throne was a construction Baylun had helped to build over the past week. They removed a circular portion of the ceiling to reveal the sky, and suspended from that hole was an enormous brass cone. The cone's wider end protruded through the roof, and the narrow end descended into the chamber and split into several smaller channels angling in multiple directions. A score of soldiers recited the Chant, and their words passed through the apparatus and projected across the countryside. Baylun had not known what he was creating at the time, and now he had another reason to hate himself.

The warriors speaking the Chant were unarmored, and they took no notice of Baylun's companions while they entered the room. Baylun thought it strange, but he had expected many more Dun Soldiers.

Nidor stepped forward. "Cease this noise! Or face Silcor's Wrath!"

Without alarm, anger, or any other emotion, the chanters pulled their weapons and faced the company. They continued their drone while marching at the intruders, their eyes barely seeming to focus.

Nidor advanced, striking down two of the soldiers with relative ease. Baylun moved to the paladin's side, and he slew another. Kiryanna arrived to skewer one, and arrows Baylun knew to be from his father's bow pierced two more.

And so the melee went. The defenders of the room, normally enjoying the disadvantage the Chant placed upon their foes, marched to their deaths. The Chant then ended, and a single Dun Priest was all that remained. He stood on the far side of the chamber, next to the stairs ascending to the roof.

"So predictable!" The priest sneered.

"Your evil spell has failed." Nidor pointed his flaming blade at the robed man. "You are defeated!"

"Ignorant fool!" spat the priest. "It is you that are defeated. Daymyn said you would come. He said you would never suspect the trap!"

"You lie!" Magneer stepped past Nidor.

"And you must be the father-uncle he mentioned." The priest chuckled.

Baylun was dumbstruck. How could the priest have known Daymyn had an uncle? One that had taken the place of the father he never met? Solinin died fighting the Death Lord Gruzim before Daymyn was born. Solinin, who turned out to be the son of Tarm, evil duke-turned-king of Kalmaar, and Mayry, the queen mad with power and slain by Cavalor in Marcove. Some said that Cavalor had been Solinin's brother, and that Daymyn was cousin to Vayla, a young paladin in New Palidur Romik had mentioned. It was a confusing tree to map out. Baylun shook his head free of the distracting thoughts. Daymyn had evidently revealed much to the enemy, and Magneer surely realized this, for he was speechless.

"Yes," the priest hissed. "The Dark One's Message was received by your young warrior, of whom I assume is now dead. But no matter. We will find some use for him yet. Just as soon as all of you have joined him!"

Heavily armored Dun Soldiers marched down the steps from the roof. Worse still, Baylun heard the jingling of armor below, as Dun Soldiers ascended to trap him and his companions. There were more than forty. Where had *they* been hiding?

Eraim placed herself between the warriors climbing from below and Selanna. Next to the small elf, Gruelenor dropped his bow and pulled his sword, and Magneer joined them. Baylun stood with Nidor and Kiryanna before those descending from the roof, and he could sense the heat from the Dale rising. It was as if he were too close to a bonfire, but the warmth brought no discomfort. On the contrary, it was soothing.

The Dun Soldiers began the Chant anew, and this time it pounded harder on Baylun's nerves. Somehow, he continued to suppress it, and his companions remained unaffected as well. Baylun charged, and Nidor and Kiryanna were beside him.

He swung his hammer, crushing the shoulder of the first soldier he faced. Though the Chant failed to affect Baylun and his friends, it empowered the Dun warrior to fight almost like the undead, and the man did not wince as he countered with his sword. Baylun brought up the butt of his weapon, smashing the man's nose, and followed with the hammerhead for a fatal blow.

A blade sliced Baylun's cheek, issued from the right. He ducked, narrowly evading a second strike. He came up with his hammer beneath the jaw of the attacker, and the soldier's head snapped back in a most unnatural manner as the man flew into his comrades.

The recipients of the flying corpse were two of four guards opposing Kiryanna, and they were knocked prone. A Dun Soldier lay dead at the marteese's feet, but she had taken a wound to her leg and limped heavily. Kiryanna seemed grateful for Baylun's unintentional assistance, and she skewered one of the foes in front of her. In her efforts, she overextended to the point of danger, but Baylun crashed into the other attacker before the man could expose her mistake. He bounced the Dun Soldier off the wall and brought the hammer around, crushing the man's breastplate into his ribcage.

The warrior fell, never to rise again—unless Radaam returned.

The room seemed to shrink as more evil soldiers entered from both staircases. Baylun's father appeared to have taken a couple of wounds, as did Uncle Magneer, and Eraim danced about with her fancy sword, slicing through the enemy's armor as easily as if it were made of leather. Several charred remains of Dun warriors littered the floor—surely the work of Selanna—and Nidor and Kiryanna were back to back. The barbarian paladin stood above the enemy, seemingly fueled by the heat he exuded, while the marteese slowed and looked to fail at any moment.

At the far side of the chamber, the Dun Priest conducted the Chant, and a dozen soldiers stood guard before him. The dark cleric needed to be stopped.

Baylun charged into the bodyguards, many of whom he had trained personally. But since receiving the Message they had changed a great deal. He bore no friendship for them, and he brought his hammer around in a wide arc. The weapon smashed one guard into another, knocking both to the floor, and he followed the maneuver with a punch, staggering a third soldier. A blade then sliced the back of Baylun's leg, cutting deep. But it was not enough to slow him, and he spun, crashing his hammer into the attacker. Without looking to see the results, he continued the spin, catching a warrior approaching his flank on the side of the head. The Dun Soldier fell.

The priest's words grew louder than all others in the room, but it was not one priest. It was all three, and they spoke as one. Where had the other two come from? Baylun glanced at his father, who stood over a dozen defeated foes. A dark crystal around Gruelenor's neck shattered and his movements became rigid.

Baylun's muscles tightened as the intensified words attempted to grab hold. He fought with all his soul, dropping his shoulder and ramming forward, and received several sharp pains as he plowed through the final three soldiers protecting the clerics. He collapsed onto a priest, pinning the man to the floor, and the evil zealot failed to maintain the Chant.

Baylun moved freely again, but his injuries prevented him from rising. He rolled from the priest and discovered a dagger in his stomach. He cast it aside, satisfied he had given his companions a chance, but horror struck him to see they still moved slowly—only Nidor and Eraim were unaffected by the evil magic.

Baylun would not be rescued in the way he had hoped. His wish had been to return to Philen; to his parents; to his life. Across the room, his father fell to one knee. Uncle Magneer was nowhere to be seen. Baylun's wounds burned, and he was sure black tendrils worked their way beneath his skin to attack his heart. Even the priest he had tackled was standing, and the man lifted the dagger from the floor.

A bright light caught Baylun's left eye—his right eye was blinded. Flames engulfed Nidor's body from head to toe, and Baylun felt the heat from across the twenty-foot gap separating them. Though the warmth had been welcoming before, it now radiated life, and Baylun's wounds vanished and his right eye cleared. All at once, his strength returned. Nidor became a silhouette within the fire, and the Chant failed as the soldiers revealed fear and withdrew, holding up their arms to keep the heat away.

Nidor exploded.

CHAPTER 36

CHANGE OF PLANS

The Chant did not affect Vayla the way she had been told it would. She was supposed to move slower or the enemy was supposed to move faster. The only noticeable result was the blank faces of the Beitians, including Burnod's, and their lips moving to form words they did not utter. That, and the fact that Burnod was trying to kill her.

Burnod swung his sword, and Vayla easily knocked it aside. She countered with her gauntlet to his face, breaking his nose, but he showed no sign that he felt the pain.

"Fight the Chant!" Vayla yelled.

As she parried his next strike, a score of Beitian warriors joined the ex-general, all of them sharing the same emotionless stare. Vayla did not wish to kill Burnod, but she would if necessary, and battling him plus another twenty soldiers presented her with very few options. Allies in Nejan and Moc uniforms then arrived, evening the odds.

"I have the lead figure!" Vayla said. "Take the others!"

The warriors did as ordered, and she fended off three more attacks from Burnod. She spun low, sticking out her foot and dropping the ex-general to the street. He attempted to regain his feet, and she stepped on his sword hand while moving the tip of her blade to his throat.

"Do not move!" she said.

The droning Chant abruptly ended. Other than the wind, the only sound was the clamor of battle within and outside the city.

Burnod blinked rapidly and glared at Vayla. "What in the name

417

of Brondor are you doing? Where did you even come from?"

"You were possessed by the Chant." Vayla pulled her weapon away and helped the ex-general to his feet. Around her, the allied soldiers overwhelmed the enemy, clearing the area without delay.

"Blast!" Burnod placed his hand over his broken nose. "I told you to leave me behind!"

"You brought me no harm," Vayla said. "Your skills are as outdated as your rank among Beitians."

Burnod sheathed his sword. "Then I guess I'm lucky to have a *Paladin of Palidur* around to help me."

The Chant began anew. It was much stronger this time, and Vayla's muscles tightened. Burnod pulled his weapon as the far-off look returned, and from the alleys issued another five hundred Beitians.

Within the square, the enemy butchered the allied soldiers at an alarming rate. Vayla could not match Burnod—he moved too quickly—and she barely knocked his sword aside. A flash of light then struck the ex-general in the back, knocking him to the street where he ceased to move.

Thirty feet away stood Wezlok. His actions were sluggish, and he disappeared as a group of Beitians converged on him. Vayla wished to give aid, but she could scarcely protect herself from the evil soldiers closing in on her. A dwarf then arrived, moving every bit as fast as the Beitians, if not faster. It was Greyor, and the runes on his axe were alive with the white-hot fire of a dwarfish forge.

Greyor dropped the four Beitians around Vayla in little time, slicing through their armor as if it were made of soft cheese. He then left body parts in his wake as he raced to Wezlok and cleared the attackers there. Greyor lifted the mage and zipped across the square to place the elf at Vayla's feet.

Wezlok's injuries were many. He was alive, of that Vayla was sure, but dark veins were spreading beneath all exposed skin and he was bleeding out fast. And she was powerless to help him.

The dark clouds vanished, revealing the aging sun, and the Chant stopped—again. Allied forces moved normally as they stormed the area, clearing it of Beitians—again. The sounds of battle dwindled.

Vayla quickly withdrew a silver vial from her pouch. She carried only three doses of the special Palidurian elixir, as it was rare, and she pulled the stopper and poured the contents into Wezlok's mouth. The elf's wounds closed immediately and his breathing eased as the dark tendrils vanished. His eyes fluttered, and they focused on hers for a moment.

"Thank Galenfial." He sat up, appearing more relieved with Vayla's safety than his own.

Vayla helped the elf to his feet. He brushed the dirt from his robes, his aloof expression returning. She then checked on Burnod.

"He should be fine," Wezlok said. "But he will be in no condition to fight for several hours."

Vayla checked anyway. Burnod was unconscious. She scanned the sky, listening for evidence of the Chant. Nothing. Thinking it better to leave him sleeping, she turned to a Nejan warrior.

"You!" she called. "Get this man indoors. I care not where, as long as no enemies are present."

"Cafior's Hammer!" The soldier stared at Vayla in wonder. "Lady Mer—?"

"I swear if you call me Merssa, I shall have your tongue!" She had no more patience to offer.

"I'm sorry," the man stammered. "It's just... I met her when I was a lad."

"I doubt that." Vayla sniffed. "Her dislike of Nejans was well known."

"No. It's just that..." The soldier seemed desperate to explain.

Vayla noticed he was no mere soldier, but a general. She sighed and faced him, allowing him his say.

"I was born in Virch. She gave me a ride to Eastgate; me and my family. She rescued us from the ghouls that devastated Ellaville."

"That's a delightful story." Vayla was still uninterested. "But this man needs immediate attention. And... bind him. But he's no prisoner."

"Captain Larman!" the general shouted over his shoulder.

A younger soldier responded, a few years Vayla's elder. He shared an obvious resemblance to the general.

"Get this man indoors," the general ordered. "And be sure to clear the building first. Bind his hands, but treat him well."

"Yes, general!" the captain said. He then barked instructions to other soldiers, who carried Burnod away.

"I'm General Lindow." The tall man bowed. "And the captain is my nephew, Larman, named after my father."

"Thank you for caring for my companion." Vayla nodded. "Continue to hold the entrance."

"Lindow!" Greyor smiled as he joined Vayla. The runes on the dwarf's axe no longer glowed, but the weapon was no less impressive. "Is Larman with you?"

"He is," the general said. "I was just saying to—" He glanced at Vayla.

"Don't say it!" Greyor put up his hand with a chuckle. "Lady Vayla doesn't like to hear it."

"I understand." Lindow's eyes showed he did not. "But I must admit, that horse ride with... the paladin... It changed my life. Her passion... I began worshipping Cafior and became a soldier because of her. Now I'm a general of Neja, and my soldiers show Cafior proper respect."

Vayla regarded the tall man. "Very good." She was genuinely impressed. A simple horse ride? Perhaps some of Merssa's stories were worthwhile... were there more time for such things. "I must be off."

"I apologize." Lindow bowed. "I shall secure the area at once." He called his captains to him and issued the orders.

Vayla looked at Greyor. "Your arrival was timely. I thank you."

"The approach to Benzon is secure to the south, and the bone dragons fly no more," the dwarf said. "The Death Lords avoided our attacks and fled to the west."

"Blast!" Vayla turned back to the general. "General Lindow!"

He immediately returned. "Yes, Lady Vayla."

"The enemy has retreated. Find High Paladin Nyer. He should have marched north with you. Tell him Paladin Vayla is heading to the castle to ready the march for Helmland."

Mentioning the High Paladin's name steered Vayla's thoughts to Macurak for the first time since entering Benzon. She wished to know that he was all right, but she pushed him from her mind. The war had to matter more.

"Yes, my lady." Lindow showed more respect than was usual for an outlander general. Most of them were arrogant.

"And find me my horse!" she added before turning to Greyor. "Relocate your folk to the north gate and guard the skies."

Greyor nodded and scuttled off through the destroyed gate.

Vayla looked to issue her next command. Soldiers scurried about, searching towers and dragging bodies beyond the city wall. Wezlok was the only one left.

"Come with me," she said.

They marched north along the streets. Vayla did not know exactly how to get to the castle, but the fortress rose high and she needed no guide. The battles were far from over, and the clash of steel and shouting were heard now and again, so she kept her sword ready. As thoughts of krahluks and zreekans came to mind, she made sure Wezlok still followed. Not only did the elf keep up, but he walked closer than usual, scrutinizing every shadow.

"What did you do to me?" Vayla scanned nearby alleys and windows. "How did I return to the gate?"

"A simple spell," Wezlok replied. "Well, not simple for most wizards. But easy enough for one such as myself."

"Sorry I asked," Vayla grumbled. But there was something she needed to know. "Why? Why are you protecting me?"

She could tell Wezlok halted. She stopped and turned. He was staring at her.

"You will not like the answer," he said plainly.

"Like it or not," she placed a hand on her hip, "why? You nearly got yourself killed."

"Better me than yourself." He continued to speak in a level voice.

"Out with it, mage!"

"Merssa."

Merssa? That was it? What kind of explanation was that?

Wezlok sighed. "Your grandmother was the bravest person I ever had the privilege of knowing."

Vayla detected sincerity from the elf. And he referred to Merssa as a person and not a *human*—or any of the other colorful, descriptive words he normally employed. Vayla was unsure if she should delve any further, but it did not matter. Wezlok continued.

"And it was I that led her to her death."

"*What?*" Vayla frowned. She had not only studied her grandmother in New Palidur, as was required, but she learned firsthand from her father and grandfather. Merssa died in combat, but not before killing Cadorn, one of the strongest of the Death Lords.

There was the slightest shimmering in Wezlok's eyes. "I made it possible for her demise."

Vayla hoped to Cafior the elf did not weep.

"She sacrificed herself so that Trannum could be stopped," he added. "So that her husband and her son might live. So that *I* might live. I could never repay this debt to her... until now." Wezlok spread his hands with the last two words.

Vayla was speechless. Lorians did favors for Lorians and no one else. She realized her mouth hung open, and she snapped it shut as she lifted her chin. "Cafior watches over me. I need no guardian."

"And neither did Merssa." The elf's stare did not waver.

"Just... Don't get in my way." She continued toward the castle.

After weaving through another mile of streets filled with allied soldiers, Vayla and Wezlok came to an open square. Just as the other clearings, corpses from either side of the war were strewn, some exhibiting gruesome wounds. But what caught Vayla's attention was the sound of her father's voice.

She rushed through a short alley and into another clearing to find him directing soldiers. Upon spotting her, his smile stretched from ear to ear and he released a powerful sigh.

"My *king*!" Vayla said in the humorous way she always had while growing up.

"My *princess*!" he responded to get even, and he gave her a grand embrace. "Wezlok." He looked past Vayla, adding a respectful bow of the head.

"Cavalor." Wezlok ignored all formalities.

"Vayla! There you are!" Grimmen arrived with the rest of the zhokards. None had been lost in the battle and all were present. "We have been searching for you. One second you were there, and the next..."

"We have the wizard to thank for that," Vayla muttered, though not as sarcastically as she wanted to.

"We are still rooting out the enemy," Cavalor said. "They are a slimy bunch and hide beneath every rock. All things considered, Benzon fell much too easily."

"Just as Onzac." Vayla searched the sky. The sun was nearly set. "I believe they fell back to form a solid front. It's as if we were *supposed* to take Benzon."

"For what purpose would they abandon the city to us?" posed Nyer, stepping next to Vayla.

Vayla glanced over her shoulder to spy Macurak. The captain released a small, almost hidden smile. Though her spirit rose, she forced her attention back to the conversation.

"Did you see the krahluks in Onzac after our departure?" she asked her father.

"Yes." Cavalor's expression was grim. "It was most disturbing. But there was nothing to be done. Grand Paladin Montac held the city with a sizeable army, and we had our orders."

Nyer frowned. "Has there been any word from the Grand Paladin?"

"None," Cavalor replied. "But there has been no time."

"The creatures appeared from within Onzac after we departed," said Vayla. "It could very well happen here too. We must be on our guard."

Cavalor looked back at Grimmen. "Let it be so."

The zhokard nodded, and he led his contingent away.

"We fought some of those krahluk gorillas in Zurzak." Nyer shook his head. "If not for the Lorians, we might not have arrived here as soon as we did."

Wezlok's eyes showed the slightest hint of interest. But it quickly dissolved.

Cavalor furrowed his brow. "Lorians?"

"Yes, King Cavalor," Nyer replied. "But they refused to accompany us afterward."

"If they joined the battle, there was sufficient reason," Wezlok said to Cavalor, seemingly oblivious to the sneer the High Paladin issued for the interruption. He turned to Nyer. "We are not the barbarians you take us for."

Vayla remembered the giant cage, and the way she and the Beitian villagers were treated like animals. She did not agree.

Nyer ignored the wizard's comment and returned his attention to Vayla and Cavalor. "So we return to the question. Why allow the city to fall?"

"A trap," said Vayla. It was the only explanation. "They wanted us to enter Beit. I know not about the battle for Zurzak, but they practically welcomed us in Onzac. And now the Death Lords have fled. They didn't even raise all the dead they could have."

Cavalor's expression darkened. "They are luring us deeper."

"Surely they are flanking us," Nyer said. "Herding us like cattle."

"Even if that is so," Cavalor rubbed his chin, "we must continue with the plan. I see no other option."

"Yes." Nyer drummed his metal fingers on the pommel of his sword. "But we cannot proceed as the plan dictates. If they are driving us into Helmland, they might already be approaching

Benzon. Who knows if Grand Paladin Montac will arrive before they do? That is, if the Grand Paladin is able to do so. We need to fortify the city." He looked at Cavalor, as if for confirmation.

"Agreed." Cavalor nodded. "We must hold Benzon for as long as possible."

"It is an assignment of death." Nyer took in a deep breath and slowly released it. "I'll stay."

"What?" Vayla could not believe her ears. "But you—"

"The city will be in need of me," Nyer said. "And perhaps I can delay the enemy long enough for the rest of the plan to execute properly, Soleran willing."

"But without the Grand Paladin to lead the army, the responsibility falls to you," insisted Vayla.

"This is my decision." Nyer gave her a hard stare. "*You* will carry on in my stead. It almost seems fated to be so." He mumbled the last part. "I'll do what I can to slow the enemy, if not defeat them. There's no hope if we are pinned between two forces upon reaching Lormin Dmurr. And I can trust no one else with Benzon's defenses. Who knows? Grand Paladin Montac may yet arrive."

Nyer was right. Benzon needed a paladin to command such a mission. And he was the best one for the job.

"I'll need soldiers to replace those from Onzac that were meant to hold the city," Nyer said. "And it would do well to have Vermallon archers and a squadron of dwarves with at least two of their ballistae, in case dragons return."

Cavalor nodded. "It will be so ordered."

Vayla glanced at Macurak, and her heart skipped a beat. Was her captain to remain in Benzon too? She searched desperately for something to say to address the question, but her mind was blank. From the look in Macurak's eyes, he searched for the same words.

"If I may." Wezlok addressed Nyer. "It seems we are shorted a captain, as Burnod is in no shape for the march ahead. He does, however, have an extensive knowledge of this city's defenses and would be most beneficial in your efforts."

"A good point." Nyer raised a brow, appearing suspicious.

"Perhaps Macurak should retake his position beneath Vayla," Wezlok said. "The assault upon the citadel can hardly suffer the loss of another commanding voice, and he is more than capable. And I have noticed that *humans* seem to hold him in high regard."

Vayla held her breath. It was as if Wezlok had read her mind. If she found he was doing so, he would answer for those crimes! But his point was a solid one.

"Let it be so." Nyer nodded, allowing Vayla to breathe.

CHAPTER 37

THE NEW PLAN

Eraim looked around the chamber. The evil soldiers and priests were dead; burnt into poses of terrible agony. There was no chanting, no hammering, no whispering. The room was deathly silent. Even the violet haze that once hid the floor had disappeared, and the large horn emitting the Chant to the surrounding territories was cracked and crumbling. Selanna appeared confused. Gruelenor helped Magneer to his feet, and Kiryanna did the same for Baylun. Nidor was gone.

"Nidor?" Gruelenor scanned the room.

The krukari raced to where the paladin had last stood; where the barbarian had shed a flame so bright and hot, yet soothing and filled with security. It did not escape Eraim's notice that every injury she received during the battle was mended, or that Magneer had suffered a crippling blow, and he now walked without assistance.

"He is gone," Selanna said softly.

"Where?" Anger and pain shone on Gruelenor's face.

Selanna shook her head with visible heartache.

Eraim knew Nidor to be the best friend Gruelenor ever had. The two had bonded during the Necromancer War. She sheathed Mithkahr and approached the krukari.

Gruelenor's eyes welled to the brim, and tears Eraim did not think possible flowed. She stopped short of the warrior when she spotted a twinkle upon the floor, barely noticeable next to a charred corpse. Stooping, Eraim found a perfectly chiseled fire opal the size of her palm, and trapped within was a wavering flame. She touched the gem, and the soothing warmth of Nidor's aura traveled up her arm and filled her soul. She lifted the jewel and noticed everyone was watching.

"Nidor…" she murmured.

Gruelenor wiped his tears, mesmerized by the opal, and Eraim placed it into his large hand. He closed his fingers and shut his eyes, inhaling deeply.

"I'm sorry." Magneer put his hand on Gruelenor's back.

Gruelenor nodded.

Magneer turned to Baylun. "And I am sorry to you." He embraced his nephew. "You were always the strongest of the bunch. I never should have doubted you."

Baylun was the strongest? Eraim supposed the ranger had a point. They were all good boys, but in every test of greed, romance, and bravery, Baylun remained true to himself. In the end, poor Daymyn did not possess the strength to resist what the enemy offered. Or perhaps his desire for power was misunderstood by those that loved him. In either case, what was done was done.

Selanna went to Gruelenor, and the krukari allowed her to handle the fire opal.

"It is him," she said. "Nidor's spirit lies within this stone." She handed it back to Gruelenor. "Keep it with you."

Gruelenor nodded. After staring at it a few seconds longer, he placed it into his pouch.

The shriek of an undead dragon reached Darum Carumbor, followed by another. The calls surely came from different beasts, for they resounded from two directions. A deathly chill then invaded the tower and Eraim pulled Mithkahr. But the cold retreated, and the next screech faded into the west. Eraim eyed the charred corpses littering the floor. None of them moved. She relaxed, but she did not sheathe her blade.

"What does this mean?" Magneer peered through the hole in the ceiling.

"I am not sure," Selanna said. "But the allies will join us soon. We need to leave."

They descended the levels of the tower, finding scores of fallen enemies. Every one of them was completely charred, and none had animated with the passing of the Death Lord. On the bottom floor, they reached Daymyn's body. It had been spared Nidor's fire and his head was mended. Daymyn remained dead, but he appeared as he had in life.

"Thank you, Nidor," whispered Magneer.

"Let's take him from this place," Gruelenor said in his gravelly voice.

Magneer lifted Daymyn, and he led the way over the pock-ridden corridor—the acid had run its course and the floor was dry. The portcullis looked to have been blown out of its track and lay several feet outside, and the air about Darum Carumbor was clear beneath the aging sun.

Another two thousand burned corpses littered the field surrounding the tower—where had they all come from? Eraim noticed the haze was not gone, but it had retreated and blurred everything beyond half a mile. Surely that had been the reach of Nidor's fire.

Without a word, the company headed east for Lothen Forest. Eraim searched the sky and distant landscape, but nothing stirred. Upon reaching the trees, they entered the woodland, hiking thirty yards before Magneer came to a stop. They stood within a small clearing, a serene spot where the orange sun trickled through a break in the canopy, and he set Daymyn on the soft ground.

Magneer and Gruelenor pulled spades from their packs.

Baylun watched his father and uncle dig the grave. He waited nearby, ready to assist, but neither yielded in their labors, not even when the sun fell beyond the trees and Selanna's glowing spheres illuminated the clearing. While the two dug, Kiryanna stepped next to Baylun without making eye contact.

"You were brave back there," she said quietly. "You saved my life, and you almost died trying to stop the priests. You carry yourself like a hero."

Baylun did not respond. He did not want another Brem-like lesson at the moment, but neither could he bring himself to feel annoyed. A hero? He was a defeated krukari that wanted to go home; wanted to find his brother; wanted his cousins back. He wanted to forget about Darum Carumbor.

"As I told you," Kiryanna continued, "I have personal knowledge of what it means to know betrayal by those you love. For me, my appearance is my curse. Seldom do others see beyond it, and I have learned what they will do to obtain it. Evil things. Until I met Brem."

Baylun glanced at Kiryanna. Her appearance was a curse? She was beautiful. He supposed, to a certain extent, she received stares as much as he did, but stares meant for her were of a different sort. Did that make it any better than his situation? It gave him something to consider.

"Mourn your cousin's death," Kiryanna added. "But bury your guilt with him. You are important in all of this, of that I am sure."

She placed a friendly hand on his forearm and offered a smile that lasted but a second. It was the first real smile he had seen penetrate the marteese's stone façade. It made her seem less lethal, even if only for a moment. But it vanished, and she walked away, pulling her sword and eyeing the trees.

Gruelenor and Magneer placed Daymyn's body into the hole.

"She is right."

Baylun jumped. Eraim stood on his other side. Had she been there all along?

"If not for you," Eraim said, "this war might already be lost."

Baylun appreciated the words, but he was not ready to accept what he did. Had he been stronger, had he spent less time pitying himself, he might have been there to steer his cousin down a better road. Or maybe he would have lost himself as well. He sighed. His rescue was supposed to be a happy occasion. But the only joy he experienced since entering Helmland, besides seeing his father, was the hug he received from Uncle Magneer. His uncle raised Daymyn as best he could, and perhaps the man felt responsible. Baylun was just glad Magneer learned the truth, as dire as it was.

"We shall remain here until the others arrive," Selanna said after Magneer and Gruelenor finished placing dirt over Daymyn's body.

Baylun looked around. Eraim was gone. Had he imagined her standing next to him a second ago?

Selanna seemed unconcerned about her friend's sudden absence. "It will be a day or two, so get as comfortable as you can."

Few words were spoken within the clearing. Eraim and Kiryanna kept watch, returning occasionally to check in; Selanna meditated; and Magneer and Gruelenor cleaned and sharpened their blades. Baylun received several nods and smiles from his father, but they did not speak to one another. Gruelenor did not enjoy conversing, and Baylun had inherited that trait. He desperately wished to ask his father a question, however, and once Gruelenor and Uncle Magneer finished their task, Baylun found his father stretching his back at the edge of the clearing.

"I'm proud of you," Gruelenor said at Baylun's approach. "I could not have survived what you went through."

"Of course you would have," insisted Baylun. "You're a much greater warrior than me. You would have escaped weeks ago, without having to wait for a rescue."

"No." His father shook his head. "You're wrong. And you are a fine warrior."

"Thanks to you." Baylun offered half a grin. But it vanished as he found the courage to ask that which needed answering. "Are we descendants of Gruzim?"

Gruelenor's eyes fell to the forest floor, and he seemed to hold his breath for several seconds. His gaze remained downcast when he responded at last.

"Why do you ask such a question?"

That was not the outright denial Baylun had hoped for. But it was his answer. How could they be related to a monster? Did this mean evil flowed through Baylun's veins?

"Never mind." Baylun released a sigh of defeat. "It's nothing."

Silence followed. Baylun thought he received a look of pity from Selanna on the other side of the campsite, but the mage turned away to speak to Uncle Magneer while the man started a fire. Baylun's father pulled the glowing fire opal from his pouch.

"I once wondered what you are wondering right now," Gruelenor said. "But this man, the greatest man ever to live... He showed me I was wrong. No. He taught me *why* I was wrong." Gruelenor looked Baylun in the eyes. "We are who we make of ourselves. Your stay here proves that. Let no one tell you who you are. *You* choose your destiny. As Silcor's Fire burns within our souls, we forge the steel our spirits need to combat evil." He recited the words Nidor had uttered often enough when visiting their home in Philen. "And this jewel will be a constant reminder of who you are."

To Baylun's shock, his father handed him the fire opal. Gruelenor and Nidor shared a friendship greater than any Baylun had ever witnessed, except for that between Baylun's mother and his aunts, and maybe Selanna and Eraim. The opal belonged to his father. But the look in Gruelenor's eyes said he would not take it back.

The warmth of the gem entered Baylun's body and spread to his fingertips, toes, and the top of his head. He felt no fatigue and his aches and pains vanished, not that many existed since Nidor exploded in the wave of fire. Now that Baylun thought about it, his father had dug Daymyn's grave with twice the energy of Uncle Magneer. The opal must have been the fuel.

Gruelenor placed his arm around Baylun's shoulder and they walked to the campfire.

The night progressed, and though no one showed an appetite, Selanna insisted everyone have a bite to eat. After placing the first morsel into his mouth, Baylun remembered how food was supposed to taste, and he found he was famished. He had eaten Darum Carumbor's gruel for so long, he forgot what flavor was. Once the meal ended, they settled in for some sleep.

Selanna received little rest. When morning arrived, she was wide awake. She replayed the events of the prior days throughout the night, trying to put things together with the prophecy. Daymyn's betrayal explained the dunarchins on the Path of the Guardians — *treachery arises*. But if Trannum placed them there, then he underestimated his enemy. She could not help thinking the necromancer was up to his old tricks, and she desperately wished to know what plan he had set in motion.

Then there was Darum Carumbor. The threat had been real — *trap is sprung*. It would have led to the deaths of her and her companions had Nidor not... She did not know exactly what Nidor had done. But Trannum could not have possibly anticipated the paladin's action — *flaming death avails*. And why did the Death Lords pass over the tower without stopping? Perhaps Nidor's wave of energy warded off the undead kings, and they realized Darum Carumbor had fallen. If that was the case, Radaam and Anduiff had already carried that message back to their master — *the final stand*. Troubled times were ahead.

Eraim entered the clearing. "They approach. Cavalor and Vayla lead the way."

Grand Paladin Montac was not leading the army? Selanna recalled a glimpse from one of her dreams, where Vayla charged at the head of an enormous force into a cloud of war. She sighed. Would any part of the plan remain intact? Elgarroth once referred to the final conflict as "Vayla's battle" when they were in Arman Forest. Perhaps he had seen the vision as well.

Everyone lifted their gear and readied to travel. Eraim led the way from the trees, and to the north, a mass of elves, humans, and dwarves marched south along the road connecting Beit to Helmland. Riding before the force were King Cavalor and his zhokards, Vayla and her captain, Wezlok, General Lindow, and Melac. Selanna had not seen Melac for years, since his employment with Queen Elloria in Kalmaar. He appeared just as muscular as ever, though much older, and small gray hairs sprouted around the perimeter of his scalp, which used to be shaved. It was good to see him.

Once the army arrived, Vayla barked an order, and a hundred soldiers entered Darum Carumbor. Cavalor then approached with Vayla and his entourage, dismounting as he neared.

"It seems all of Beit was a trap," Cavalor said, with no form of a greeting. The king's face was grim. "We will have an army on our heels, unless High Paladin Nyer has anything to say about it. I assume it will be a sizeable force, and one not completely of our world."

None of this surprised Selanna. Trannum was cunning, but she believed this to be Uustaag's doing. The evil krukari was a master tactician in his efforts to conquer Vaeldor the first time, according to Elgarroth.

"The tower was a trap as well," Selanna said. "But not one we were meant to survive, I am sure."

"It was the same in Zurzak." Vayla slid from her saddle, and Macurak took her reins. "But we were meant to survive Onzac and Benzon." She looked at Selanna. "My guess was that we were to battle Radaam and Anduiff here at Darum Carumbor."

"Another battle we would likely win at some cost," added Cavalor. "But the Death Lords would have pulled out before the battle's end to pool their resources at Lormin Dmurr."

Vayla shook her head. "And with that much strength before us and a force behind us, we would be slaughtered."

"Then what are we to do?" posed Eraim.

"We honor the plan." Vayla radiated confidence. "We finish this."

"But you said it is a trap," Eraim pointed out.

Vayla stared at Eraim. "I refuse to believe Uustaag knows every element of our plan." She turned to the others. "He has lost before, and I doubt he is the sort to believe he can be defeated again. We have—"

"Please don't say we have Cafior!" Melac rolled his eyes, as if he

434

had heard the statement more than a few times already. "The Battle of Balgorn had the likes of Vennimor, founder of Palidur and one of the greatest paladins ever known. And I'm sure they possessed many more paladins than we currently hold, since most of ours were lost in the city battles or left in Benzon."

"Yes, Kalmaar wizard." Vayla glared at Melac. "And they also had the likes of Welmirth, the greatest *wizard* ever known." She returned her attention to her father and Selanna. "We have knowledge the allies of the past did not possess. We know about Uustaag's minions, thanks to Elgarroth." Vayla looked at Selanna. "And I know you have something on Trannum, for you have mentioned very little of your plan for dealing with the necromancer. You also have knowledge of the magical gates Uustaag employs, though I admit I'm ignorant of your explanations. But I know *you*, and you're competent enough in that arena." She turned to Gruelenor, Magneer, and Greyor. "In the not-so-distant past, many of you dealt successfully with Death Lords. And there are only two this time. As far as goblins and minotaurs, I have no fear." She eyed Melac. "And yes, Cafior is with us. As well as Arronaus and Soleran."

"And Silcor," said Gruelenor.

"And Meldar!" Greyor nodded.

"Galenfial," added Eraim in a voice less boisterous.

"Frayorna!" Kiryanna shouted from thirty yards away.

"And Brondor!" hollered a man Selanna recognized as Deeyon, a Brondor priest sent by Queen Elloria of Kalmaar, and his following responded "Brondor!" from where they stood among the rest of the army.

Though Vayla made no mention of the krahluks and zreekans, Selanna was sure the young paladin did not underestimate those foul creatures.

"Vayla is right," said Cavalor. "We must follow through, for there's no turning back. But we'll need to adjust the plan for it to work. Our advantage lies in that we're aware of the trap. And we must trust that the part of our plan very few know about has remained secret."

Cavalor and Vayla were correct. And the others needed to hear those words, but not from Selanna. She was grateful for their wisdom.

Cavalor turned to Vayla. "Ready the troops while Selanna and I have a word."

Vayla looked at Selanna. Selanna had not thought it possible for the young lady to appear even more like Merssa, but she was wrong. It was like having the old paladin back, and she could not stop the chills from cascading down her body. Vayla nodded before climbing onto her saddle. With a gesture for Macurak to follow, the paladin rode toward the army still amassing between the forest and tower — an awesome sight to behold!

Selanna and Cavalor walked away from all ears, and Eraim paced them at a distance of thirty yards with one of the long arrows nocked. Selanna realized her friend would hear every word, but at this point, she did not care.

She spoke to Cavalor about Darum Carumbor. It pained the king to learn of Nidor's fall — Selanna knew he held the utmost respect for the Silcor paladin and his kin. The Dales arrived to the first war versus Trannum at the most opportune time, saving Cavalor and his companions from certain death. As well, Nidor visited Marcove nearly every year, and everywhere he went, people were put at ease. Cavalor was also saddened to hear about Daymyn's betrayal.

"I met Daymyn once," Cavalor said. "When I learned Solinin had been my brother, I wished to say something... But I could not. Daymyn lived on the other side of the world with his mother and cousins. He had a good life. He did not need that type of confusion. I sent gold, anonymously of course, to provide him the easy life he should have enjoyed..." He shook his head. "Perhaps I was part of the problem."

Selanna was torn. But for Cavalor's sake, she needed to share her observations of the past. "It is only to ease your soul that I say this, but there was always something in his eyes. Worry yourself not. In the end, his path headed toward evil. For years I said nothing, for his fate was not yet decided, but I knew of the possibilities. I had hoped the love of his mother, uncles, and cousins would..."

"I understand." Cavalor nodded. "And I thank you for your insight. But, please —"

"No one else needs to know." Selanna gave a sympathetic smile.

"And now to business." Cavalor thankfully changed the subject. "One part of the plan remains unchanged: the army will march on Lormin Dmurr."

Selanna looked at the dark tower to the northwest. "I only wish we did not need to leave a detachment in Darum Carumbor. Knowing what we know."

Cavalor raised a hand. "Worry not. With the forces we left in Benzon, we realized we could spare no others. But Wezlok has presented us with another option."

"Wezlok?" Selanna was taken aback. The Lorian wizard had never played a part in any plan as far as she was aware.

"Yes." Cavalor's eyes became downcast. "It is something he performed in the past... when..."

"I understand." Selanna did not know what magic Wezlok employed when Merssa made her stand against Cadorn, and she did not wish for Cavalor to relive the painful memory.

"Well," Cavalor continued, "let's suffice it to say the tower will be manned, and we'll not lose a life in the process."

"For that, I am grateful." Selanna tried to show more relief than she felt.

"But... Vayla..." Cavalor's expression was troubled.

Selanna shook her head. She took in a deep breath to explain the issue again. "Vayla cannot come with us. She is a paladin, and a forceful presence. The enemy will detect her approach. Even Nidor was to join the army at this time. Besides, without Montac or Nyer, who else can command the troops?" She did not mention her vision of Vayla at the lead, nor Elgarroth's comment about *Vayla's battle*. Neither would do the Marcove king any good.

"I know." Cavalor sighed. "But I fear for her. She is smart; much smarter than I was at her age."

"You are humble," Selanna said. "I remember a young warrior ready to march to Trannum's door. But I know of what you speak."

"I cannot bear to lose her." Cavalor paled. "That would be a fate worse than death."

"I understand." Selanna placed her hand on his arm. "For me, it would be like losing Merssa twice in one lifetime. If I could change things, I would. But this war needs her. Your faith in Cafior is strong. Have faith that He will see her through."

Cavalor shifted his feet. "Thank you. But if she must march with the army into a known trap, I'm sending my zhokards with her."

The plan called for the zhokards to join those traveling in secret. They were an exceptional fighting force. But there was no changing the king's mind, and Selanna nodded.

"Now let us discuss the part of the plan that needs adjusting," she said.

Chapter 38

Mountain Trek

The company headed southward toward the Stone Eagle Mountains in silence. Eraim kept watch on their surroundings once they entered the haze beyond Darum Carumbor, and it felt as though they had left all life behind. Magneer led the way, followed by Cavalor, Baylun, Kiryanna, Gruelenor, and Selanna. Eraim brought up the rear.

The hard soil wore upon Eraim's feet. They walked out the rest of the day and into the night, and as the terrain rose with the foothills, Selanna conjured one of her lights to hover overhead. Seconds later, Eraim detected a spark in the darkness. It was the signal, and shortly after, dwarves issued from their hiding places among the boulders.

The stout warriors were from Rornibur, the only dwarfish city within the Stone Eagles. Their appearance made Varlimor dwarves seem clean and their beards grew only half as long, but they were the strongest and tallest of their race, standing as high as Eraim, if not higher. Though they lacked the ingenuity of their Varlimor cousins, they made up for it with brute strength. Still, they carried a reputation for a delicate touch when creating works of art from stone. The statue of Merssa in New Palidur and the Korban Bridge were a testament to that belief. As repugnant as Eraim found their mannerisms, she was glad to have them on her side.

"Selanna?" the lead dwarf said in a deep voice. He stood just over five feet in height and his beard was longer than those of his kin, nearly touching his waist. His nose was as big as Eraim's fist—probably bigger—and he wore a suit of plate armor with a large pick fastened to his back. By the look of the tool, it had been designed for combat and not mining, and from the gouges on the haft, it had seen many battles.

Selanna dismissed her light and allowed the hazy moon to take over. "I am Selanna."

"I'm Keelord," said the dwarf. "Cousin of Poluran. Cousin of Millord."

Those were names Eraim had not heard in a long time. Poluran had been the first to wield Clanghorr. She encountered him on Korban Bridge while he battled skeletons fifty years ago, and he proved to be a skilled warrior, if not a careless one. Millord possessed the great axe next, and he accompanied Eraim into Lornibur in the Varlimor Mountains when they attempted to sneak up on Trannum's stronghold. Greyor, the current owner of Clanghorr, was part of that journey as well.

Keelord was not as large as Millord had been, but slightly bigger than Poluran. His nose was bent in a few different directions — probably broken more than once.

"Were you able to get the horses?" asked Selanna.

Keelord whistled, and the dwarves brought forward a score of mounts — more than was necessary, since the zhokards were not present. It disappointed Eraim to see none of the animals were of the Batorn variety. They stood taller, and she would have to actually *climb* onto the saddle. But it was better than walking.

"Twenty horses, as requested," said Keelord. "They are warhorses from Neja, so they should not spook easily." The dwarf scanned the countryside. "But from what I've been told, there are things out there that could still do the job."

"Very good." Selanna nodded. "About your orders..."

"We are to begin our march come morning," Keelord grumbled. "It will be done."

Selanna gave a wry smile. "There has been a change of plan."

"An army marches in the wake of the host," Cavalor said. "We need a strong force to follow them and strike from behind once they reach Lormin Dmurr."

"But that force must remain unseen until the time comes," Selanna added.

Keelord nodded while he absorbed the information. Several seconds after Selanna and Cavalor stopped speaking, his head ceased to bob, and he looked at Selanna as if a thought had occurred. "*We could do that.*"

Selanna and Cavalor appeared to release the same sigh.

"Excellent!" Cavalor said. "Vaeldor is eternally grateful!"

Everyone mounted while Keelord spoke to his warriors. Kiryanna refused Magneer's assistance in climbing onto her saddle, but she expressed appreciation for Gruelenor's help with the same task. It seemed to Eraim the marteese only enjoyed the company of other half-breeds. Kiryanna had spent more time talking with Gruelenor than any other during the journey to Trannum's crypt. Surely that was not the message Brem had been trying to convey. Eraim shrugged. Grabbing hold of the saddle strap with both hands, she pulled herself to the stirrup and jumped atop her horse.

After wishing the dwarves well, the company left the unmounted horses behind and rode west along the edge of the mountains. Gruelenor now led the way, possessing superior night vision to Magneer, and time passed slowly while they traveled beneath the struggling moonlight. The air was cool, though not as chilly as Eraim expected for a northern realm, and when morning arrived, the sun's warmth was immediately felt.

"We have at least four days ahead," Cavalor said after they halted for a short break. "And there's no drinkable water to be found, so ration what you have."

"Some of us have been here before." Kiryanna's tone offered little respect.

Eraim thought it odd to speak to a king in such a manner. Magneer's mouth opened, but Cavalor raised a hand to silence the ranger. Of course, Cavalor knew what it was like to march into almost certain death. And he was no ordinary king—privilege had never been a part of his upbringing.

After a cold breakfast, they returned to the trek. Magneer took the lead, and he continually scanned the ground ahead, but there were no signs of recent tracks. They rode until dusk with only a brief stop, and after the sun was set they rested for a couple of hours before moving on.

Another night passed without mishap, and the following day trudged along. As evening neared, Magneer dismounted to search the dusty soil. Eraim urged her horse forward to join the ranger, and Gruelenor and Baylun followed.

"A force has been here," Magneer said. "At least a couple hundred. And the footprints are too big to have been made by humans."

"There are hoof prints as well." Eraim gazed at the tracks nearer to the outer edge.

"Yes." Magneer seemed surprised she had noticed. "But they are not horses. They walk on two legs, with no shoes."

"Minotaurs," grumbled Gruelenor.

"Powerful beasts," said Baylun. "Once a group of them stopped by the tower. They're more intelligent than I would've thought, but still not too bright."

"All the same, we must avoid them." Eraim scanned the mountains to the south and looked west and north. There was nothing. She peered back the way they had come. Nothing. "Whatever was here is gone. Let us hope they stay gone."

Eraim returned to the rear, glancing at Selanna and knowing her friend had heard every word. No report was necessary.

That evening, they discovered a grouping of boulders large enough to hide them from prying eyes and stopped for some rest. They camped without a fire and without unloading the horses, and come morning, they picked up and readied to move on. Eraim noticed Selanna was missing, and she searched until locating her friend.

Selanna sat with her back against one of the large rocks, staring into the distance. Eraim had seen her companion like this more often lately, and she knew better than to interrupt. She figured it had something to do with Elgarroth, but she never pried, for Selanna would give no explanations.

Cavalor approached, probably to let them know it was time to go. Eraim put up a hand to halt him.

Selanna's eyes fluttered. "Are we ready?"

Eraim gave a wry smile and pulled Selanna to her feet. They returned to the others and mounted.

By lunchtime, the day saw the arrival of fissures Uustaag's hammer had created. Most of the cracks were narrow and no fire or lava seeped from them, but smoke rose steadily and the air grew hot and sticky. Eraim wondered how comfortable a Death Lord felt farther to the north, where the heat was surely more prominent.

"I did not realize they reached all the way to the mountains," said Selanna. "This could slow us if they grow too wide."

Eraim held on to hope the path would remain clear.

Hours passed, and Selanna's fear went unrealized. Though the fissures forced them closer to the Stone Eagles at times, making them travel on rougher ground for short distances, the journey remained on schedule as far as Eraim could tell. Evening was then upon them, and they settled among another collection of boulders within the foothills.

Eraim sat atop an enormous rock during her shift to guard. It was a dry, boring night, much warmer than previous ones, and all was quiet. Nearing the time to wake Gruelenor, she spotted something moving in the darkness back the way they had come. It was a group of somethings. Narrowing her eyes to focus, the silhouettes became minotaurs. They stood eight feet tall with horns upon their bullish heads, and dark, matted hair covered their muscular bodies. They appeared to be tracking her company.

"Mees! Mees!" she hissed before fitting one of Tux's arrows to her bowstring. "Minotaurs!"

Eighteen minotaurs wielding large axes approached to within a hundred yards. Eraim heard her companions readying their weapons, and she raised her bow, but she did not draw back the arrow. She did not want to start the beasts running — few things were deadlier than a stampeding minotaur.

Her friends were ready, concealed among the rocks, and they watched her expectantly. The minotaurs were fifty yards away... Forty... Thirty... Twenty. Eraim pulled back. Ten yards... Five. She released the string, piercing the chest of the lead figure, and it fell with a bull-like scream. Her companions came out of hiding as Selanna's lights illuminated the area, and Eraim nocked another arrow, ready to assist at the first sign of trouble.

Baylun led the charge with his massive hammer, and he struck the head of a minotaur. Its skull was so thick that the weapon only staggered the beast, but Kiryanna followed with a thrust, and her sword penetrated deep into its chest. The minotaur stumbled, and the marteese pressed, slashing several more times until the monster collapsed.

Magneer made quick work of another minotaur with the assistance of a couple arrows launched by Gruelenor, and Cavalor dropped one by himself, showing his skills had not diminished over the years.

The element of surprise ended, and the minotaurs released angry snorts as they attacked. Baylun knocked aside the axe of one and smashed the knee of another, dropping it to the ground. He ducked, evading a second swing, and planted his hammer into the chest of the downed beast, never shifting his focus from his attacker.

Kiryanna darted about a minotaur, issuing several cuts while dodging an axe that made her appear small. She did not detect the enemy to her left flank, and Eraim slew the creature with a single arrow into its tiny brain — it amazed her the missile had penetrated its skull.

Magneer and Cavalor stood side by side against four minotaurs. They dropped one while Eraim shot another through the throat, but an axe sliced into Magneer's leg, forcing the ranger to the ground.

Cavalor was then occupied with protecting Magneer, nearly receiving a wound for his efforts. Gruelenor's arrows staggered one of the remaining minotaurs, and Cavalor returned to the offensive.

Eraim heard stomping from thirty feet away, where a small group of the bull-men readied to charge. She shot two, killing both, but four others gained speed and lowered their horns.

One ran at Gruelenor, and the krukari jumped behind a nearby boulder as it arrived. The minotaur smashed into the large rock, creating a wide crack from top to bottom.

Another minotaur crashed into Cavalor. The king dodged most of the blow, but he was knocked several feet through the air and landed hard on the ground.

The third beast aimed for Magneer, who still reeled from his injury. But as it drew to within five feet, it slammed into an invisible wall—Selanna's work, no doubt.

The final advancing enemy had Kiryanna in its sights, but before it could trample the marteese, Baylun hurtled into its side. It surprised Eraim to see the krukari throw his entire body into the monster, and she was further amazed that he pushed it from its path and into a boulder. Kiryanna leaped onto the creature's back and thrust her golden blade to the hilt, killing the beast.

The minotaurs were down to ten.

Gruelenor switched to his sword and faced the one that had split the boulder. Staggered, the minotaur shook its head, and the krukari slashed its throat. He then ran to Magneer and lifted the ranger over his shoulder. The bull-creature that hit Selanna's invisible wall worked its way around to threaten them both, but Eraim pierced it through the heart. Another stood between Gruelenor and the rock where Eraim was perched, and lightning streaked from Selanna's fingers, enveloping its body and causing it to tremble and collapse.

Somehow, Cavalor found the strength to return to the battle, and two more minotaurs lay dead at his feet. He then dropped to a knee, favoring a nasty gash on his side. Another hulking monster approached, and he struggled to lift his sword, but Eraim placed an arrow between the beast's eyes and it fell.

Baylun continued twirling his hammer with surprising power, striking a minotaur three times and killing it. Eraim swore he had taken a wound to his arm, but he fought without hindrance.

Kiryanna took down one of the enemy, still showing no injuries while dancing out of the minotaur's reach. Her focus was again narrow, and she failed to notice another beast charging from her right. Eraim sent an arrow completely through its eye and out the back of its head—a gruesome but efficient shot.

Ten minotaurs became one, and the beast charged into Baylun. Baylun dropped his hammer and caught the horns, but his strength paled to that of the minotaur's and it drove him into a boulder. Selanna released a spell, knocking the monster aside, and Eraim place an arrow through its heart. Baylun collapsed.

Kiryanna rushed to the young krukari, but Baylun stood on his own and lifted his weapon from the ground. He appeared unharmed.

Eraim dropped from her rock, staring at Baylun in awe.

"How are you able to move?" asked Kiryanna as Selanna arrived.

Baylun looked ashamed. "I think it's this." He pulled the fire opal from his pouch. "It's Nidor."

Selanna reached for the gem, and Baylun did not stop her. She held it high, gazing into its orange flame. She then approached Magneer.

"Hold this." She extended the jewel.

Magneer's leg was a mess. The axe had cut through the bone. He clenched his fist about the opal, still cringing, and his face eased as his wound vanished.

"Amazing!" He stared in wonder. "Nidor's healing... It's in this gem!"

"It is more than that," said Selanna.

She took the opal—Magneer appeared sad to let it go—and moved to where Gruelenor checked on Cavalor. She handed it to the king, and the gash on his side closed immediately. His other cuts and bruises disappeared as well.

He gazed at Selanna. "Thank you."

"All thanks belong to Nidor." Selanna retrieved the opal.

She passed the jewel around until everyone had a turn, handing it to Eraim last. Though Eraim had received no wounds, she enjoyed the blessed warmth nonetheless.

"Nidor's gift." Gruelenor's expression was solemn. "Or perhaps Silcor's. I'm not sure."

"A special gift indeed." Eraim peered into its flame. "But what shall we do with it?"

"Baylun should keep it safe," Selanna said.

No one argued.

Eraim returned the jewel to Baylun, and he placed it in his pouch. She could not help noticing Kiryanna's gaze, still settled on Baylun and filled with shock and gratitude. The charging minotaur would have crushed the marteese had he not intervened. Was it bravery? Or foolishness? It reminded Eraim of Dellen back in the cabin in Sistama. Dellen had leaped before the demon Hezeb when it attacked Merssa, and he did not survive. Would Baylun throw himself into the same fate?

"There are no other enemies." Selanna surveyed the countryside. "Since we are awake, we may as well depart."

It was strange that Selanna had not used more magic during the battle. Eraim considered asking why, but they had always shared a mutual respect. She did not tell Selanna how to be a wizard, and Selanna did not tell her how to do... everything else. Perhaps her friend was saving her power for Lormin Dmurr.

They grabbed their gear while Eraim retrieved her arrows. She reclaimed all but the two stuck within minotaur heads—their dense skulls snapped the shafts when she attempted to remove them. She was sorry for the loss, but grateful for those she still possessed.

Selanna allowed the magical lights to diminish, and they moved on in the darkness of the early morning. Fissures appeared ahead and to the north, glowing among the shadows, and the heat increased. The horses perspired more heavily then, as did Eraim, and she

447

wondered how her companions could stand it in their much heavier armor.

Once the sun arrived, the company headed into the mountains for a brief rest, due more to the temperature than fatigue. Eraim was then grateful for the extra waterskins their mounts were stocked with—she requested two for each before the war began, but the dwarves saw fit to equip four.

After an hour, they returned to the trek, finally turning north. The smoking cracks grew more numerous and several erupted with steam or bursts of flame. Worse still, the air was hazier as the rising smoke added to the atmosphere, and the heat became distressing. Eraim then spied a large force to the northwest, and her shoulders slumped. It was hard to be sure, but they appeared to be Blackfoot goblins, and there were more than a thousand of them.

CHAPTER 39

FORWARD MARCH

Vayla rode at the lead of the massive army—over eighty thousand soldiers headed to Lormin Dmurr. A part of her mind was in Onzac with Grand Paladin Montac, and another was in Benzon with High Paladin Nyer. She prayed for their safety. She also wondered how far behind her the enemy followed. Other questions arose, like why she was put in charge of the allied forces and not one of the other holy knights—older paladins with more experience. She supposed no one had experience for what lay ahead.

As the miles passed, she grew to value General Lindow. The Nejan was an efficient leader, and he would have made a fine holy soldier—perhaps a captain, had he trained in New Palidur. She appreciated that Lindow stopped mentioning Merssa's name, although she sometimes caught him staring.

Lorylla and Greyor rode at the front, ready to issue orders to their soldiers when the time came. And though the Vermallon elves remained in Benzon, Nyer granted Eimell leave to march with the army, and he traveled beside Lorylla.

From Kalmaar was the wizard Melac, who Vayla's father had mentioned a couple of times in the past, and he was next to Wezlok. Vayla thought it odd the mages said no words to one another, but the muscular wizard seldom had anything interesting to say. Also from Kalmaar was a Brondor priest allocated by the Kalmaar queen. Vayla did not know what to think of a holy man of the battle deity. She preferred priests of New Palidur, and while many of them marched with the Palidurian footmen, Deeyon rode alongside Melac.

Then there was Macurak. Her captain was returned to her, and he gave her reports, as was his duty. But always he lingered, as if wanting to speak further. Vayla knew it must be about the kiss, but there was no time for that. She could not afford the distraction.

They marched throughout the day, spilling far beyond the edges of the only road the realm possessed. Vayla had never seen such a wasteland, and she guessed a desert would have been more accommodating. The haze was annoying, making the handful of trees seem to move, and a few carrion birds circled... What? Vayla had yet to see any signs that animals roamed Helmland.

At dusk, the army halted and erected tents. The night was cool and bearable, but fires were lit nonetheless, for they comforted the soldiers, and captains deployed guards around the perimeter. Vayla detected evil, as she had since entering the realm, but it remained far off to the northwest. The dead kingdom would likely present nothing unless a Death Lord were to fly overhead. She doubted that would occur.

Vayla sat by a campfire with the other leaders, and Macurak handed her a bowl of stew and took his place next to her. Lindow was opposite Vayla, and to her left, Lorylla and Eimell were immersed in a conversation, speaking in the elfish tongue. Greyor was on the other side of the gray elf, polishing his axe, and Wezlok read from his book, sitting just outside the firelight. Melac and Deeyon joined the group, carrying bowls and discussing Death Lords.

"Of course your magic does not work so well," Deeyon said. "You draw energy from Vou. I, on the other hand, use *divine* power. Better still, it is divine strength granted by Brondor."

"As I mentioned," countered Melac, "even divine power has had difficulties dealing with these monsters."

"But I'm a priest of Brondor." Deeyon held up a finger. "He is the god of battle."

"I assume you have never *seen* a Death Lord?" Macurak raised a brow.

"Of course not." Deeyon looked down his nose at the captain. "If

I had, we would not be having this debate."

"They're reanimated corpses of the most terrible kings ever to rule," Macurak said. "Each of them masters of combat. An aura surrounds them to bring seasoned warriors to their knees. You speak of magic versus divine power? Many priests have faced them. I suggest you talk to them before reaching any conclusions."

Well put, though Vayla would have added more emphasis behind the words.

Deeyon sniffed. "You refer to Palidurian clerics."

Vayla stopped chewing to glare at the braggart.

"They're all well and good," the priest continued, "but they worship deities of the land, the sky, and the protection of others. They are not *Brondor* priests."

Vayla did not like Deeyon. She especially hated the way in which he spoke. His words were uttered as if they were matter of fact and not opinion; as if he was bringing to light the obvious. It almost made her wish to see the priest faced with a Death Lord. Her own experience with Anduiff was not a memory she liked to dwell on, however, and she could not wish that fate on anyone.

"Death Lords *are* formidable." Vayla's tone brought the conversation to a halt. Her eyes bore into the fire. "Mortal weapons cause them little harm. To touch them brings a freezing ache that stiffens your soul. They possess fighting styles unknown in our time, but they are aware of *our* techniques, giving them the edge." She looked at the illuminated faces surrounding her. Lorylla and Eimell had ceased their discussion while Greyor continued polishing his axe. "After my encounter with Anduiff, I researched past battles. The only warriors to have beaten a Death Lord single handedly are Vecnor and... Merssa." She had the slightest difficulty getting her grandmother's name out. "I met Vecnor. And though I did not have the chance to see him fight, I have no doubt he is an unstoppable force."

Several heads around the fire nodded.

"I found no descriptions of his stand against Dunuthar, however, as no one was present," Vayla said. "Merssa was also alone when she defeated Cadorn, a battle that claimed her life, so there's no record there either." She eyed Greyor. "Greyor destroyed Velgaad by decapitating it with Clanghorr."

The dwarf paused to issue a nod, though there was more hate than pride in his expression.

"My father, King Cavalor, destroyed Gulthar by separating his head from his shoulders as well," Vayla continued. "Vecnor defeated Gruzim at the Battle of the Dead Fields the same way."

"So we need to sever their heads." Deeyon nodded, as if he had known it all along. "That is good information for the others to have. This is why we discuss such things."

"But it will not be as easy as that." Vayla stared at the Brondor priest. "As I said, they're masters with their weapons. Some even cast spells. It's true a few have been made to limp or suffer limited use of an arm, but in every case, it came at great cost to the attacker. The Death Lords surely realize how their kind have been defeated in the past, and they'll likely be ready to defend against such attacks, unless arrogance claims them."

"A Brondor priestess *did* face a Death Lord." Greyor spoke without looking up from his task. He then gazed at Deeyon. "I believe you call her Queen Elloria." He returned his attention to Clanghorr. "The *best* way to combat a Death Lord is to impose a group effort." He looked up and grinned. "And then get out of Clanghorr's way."

Vayla smiled. She liked Greyor.

Conversations continued, but in softer tones, and Vayla allowed her mind to wander to the days ahead. She was leading a battalion to Lormin Dmurr; to occupy the enemy so her father and his companions could gain access into the citadel. The army would suffer heavy casualties, pinned between evil forces, and there was no guarantee of survival or victory. As well, there was no assurance her father's group would achieve their goal. The troops had no knowledge of this. If they had, they might never have made the journey. Most of Vayla's captains were aware. It pained her not to inform the others — Nyer forbade her to do so.

A part of Vayla wanted to join her father's company; to combat the evil within Lormin Dmurr. But Selanna warned that if she drew too near, the citadel defenses would become impenetrable before they reached its gate. Vayla needed to fight with the army so that others could do what was necessary. She wondered if her grandmother had ever faced such a dilemma.

"Vayla." Macurak's whisper snapped her from her thoughts. "A word, please."

Vayla fought the inclination to sigh. "Now is not the time," she said coolly, and she saw disappointment on his face. "The mission must be more important than all other things."

"It *is* more important," Macurak insisted. "But that doesn't mean —"

"Yes!" She stared into his eyes. "It means *all* other things. I'm sorry, but I must remain focused. There can be no distractions."

"Yes, Lady Vayla," Macurak mumbled as he rose and collected their dirty bowls.

She hated when he called her that. She stood to go to her tent and noticed Wezlok's quizzical expression aimed her way. Shaking her head, she continued.

Come morning, the tents were broken down and everything made ready to depart. It pleased Vayla that Macurak did not pout about their conversation the previous night — he seemed absorbed in his duties. Good. Perhaps he understood better than Vayla had hoped.

They marched along the road a few hours before Wezlok grabbed Vayla's attention. The wizard was staring into the distance.

"They have reached Darum Carumbor."

Vayla waved her hand, and Macurak signaled the commanders to bring the army to a halt. She had not expected the enemy to reach the tower so soon, and it was cause for alarm. Had the fight in Benzon not gone well? Did Montac ever arrive?

"What is happening?" Vayla asked.

"There are no Beitians," the elf said. "Only Dun Soldiers and krahluks. Wait. I see zreekans as well. Not many. They have taken the bait. They are shooting arrows. Now they storm the tower."

The narration was fascinating. Vayla envisioned the evil warriors invading Darum Carumbor to fight a phantom enemy, wishing she could see it for herself.

"Wait!" Wezlok raised a hand, as if issuing an order. "The zreekans have realized the deception. The army is pulling out."

Wezlok curled his fingers into a fist and then opened his hand. Shortly after, a distant rumble of thunder rushed across the sky. The elf's lips stretched into a rare grin and he turned to Vayla.

"What happened?" she asked.

"Just a little fun for myself." His grinned remained. "A reward befitting the enemy's plague upon my forest."

Vayla could only imagine what the wizard had done. He mentioned nothing but a ruse to slow down the evil army, but he had clearly executed something more dire. Vayla wished she had seen that as well.

"Why do *you* not possess such power?" Deeyon asked Melac.

The Kalmiran mage ignored the priest.

"Will they not know we are aware of their presence now?" Eimell's expression was one of concern.

"It does not matter at this point," General Lindow replied. "Their trap has been set, and nothing will deter them from it. They'll follow us to Lormin Dmurr, as they had planned to do already."

Lindow was correct. He impressed Vayla again.

They resumed the march. Though the cavalry could make the journey in three days, the army needed at least five. More than six and the plan would be in jeopardy. Vayla did not want to arrive too early, but she pushed through lunch without a proper break and continued until evening. She would rather slow the pace later than try to make up time if necessary, and she did not wish for the army following them to gain any ground.

As the sun sank into the west, Macurak gave the signal and the commanders shouted their orders. Camp was then made ready and a watch put in place. The foot soldiers appeared relieved for the break, as well as the chance to eat a decent meal, and the cooks went to work.

Macurak carried on with his duties, pleasing Vayla that he continued to understand her point. But he spoke little throughout the day other than to issue reports from scouts. Of course, there had been nothing to report — Helmland seemed content to offer no resistance.

The night sky was a dark, blank canvas, and the air remained warm. Vayla was nearly finished grooming Star when Macurak came running.

"My lady!" He was panting

"Please, Macurak!" she snapped. "You know my name!"

"You must see this!"

Macurak led her to the southern side of camp. In the distance were fires — thousands of flickering lights covering a wide area from east to west.

"It is in response to Darum Carumbor," Macurak said. "They realize their presence is no longer secret, so they try to intimidate the ranks; to shake our courage before Lormin Dmurr."

Macurak was right. Vayla had not wanted to throw away a couple hundred soldiers defending a tower that could not be defended, so she let Wezlok handle the situation. Had the explosion gone too far? She supposed it did not matter now. Hopefully, that decision had not been her first failure.

"Have the commanders inform the troops that multiple bands of Blackfoot goblins have been spotted," she said. "Tell them the goblins were cowardly and avoided confrontations. That should put their minds at rest."

"It will be done, my lady."

Macurak ran off before Vayla could respond to the way he addressed her. Perhaps he did not understand the situation after all.

She shook her head. The enemy was playing with them. Anger

threatened to get the better of her, but then an idea took form. She headed back to her tent to have a moment alone. Upon spying Wezlok, she gave a curt nod for him to join her.

"Are you regretting my little show at the tower?" asked the wizard after entering her tent.

"No." Her voice was harsher than intended, but it was her growing annoyance. "I rather wish I could have seen it, to tell you the truth."

"I see." Wezlok raised a suspicious brow. "Then to what do I owe this rare invitation?"

"The magic you used," Vayla said, "within the tower, and back in Maple Lore when we rode past the enemy..."

"If you wish for me to disguise an entire army," he spread his hands, "that would be impossible. And if you want me to make us disappear, it would fail, because they are aware of our position."

"No." She eyed the elf. "That's not what I'm thinking at all. It's quite the opposite. I just need to know if it's possible."

Wezlok furrowed his brow. "Opposite..." A smile then stretched to one side.

"You best not be reading my mind!" Vayla's words did not contain enough anger to express her meaning.

"Mind reading is not within my power," he assured her.

"My idea. Can it be done?"

"Of course." Wezlok spoke just above a whisper, and Vayla saw his thoughts churning. "I have performed it before, more or less."

"Excellent!" Vayla smiled.

Wezlok nodded and exited.

Finally, Vayla felt she could sleep.

CHAPTER 40

BETWEEN TWO ARMIES

The morning sun had yet to illuminate the mountainside, and Romik had just finished working out with his sword, determined to keep his skills sharp. Brem entered the firelight wearing a frown, and Romik readied his weapon.

"What is it?" He looked over Brem's shoulder, as if the enemy were close behind.

"The tree." Brem shook his head. "It yielded no sap this day."

No sap? Romik had grown tired of sap. For uncounted days he ate berries in sap, berries cooked in sap, mashed berries with sap. The mountains presented no game, big or small, so berries and sap were the only sources of food. Romik tired of the berries as well, but the taste of the sap made their meals more of a chore than a pleasure. Brem insisted the juices of the tree provided all the nutrients the berries did not, thanks to the blessings of Frayorna. But why did the goddess not provide better flavor?

"I guess it's just berries, then." Romik shrugged. "So be it. We should still have plenty of water."

There was no way the pond had run dry.

"It is a sign." Brem's face was grave. "It's time for us to go."

As much as Romik desired to leave their hiding spot and find a path to friendlier realms, fear of discovery kept him within a hundred yards of its entrance, and he never went out at night. The cave sheltered them, and not even the one-eyed monsters had learned of their presence.

"Perhaps we can find another tree." Romik suddenly wished for a plate of berries and sap.

Brem shook his head. "It is a sign from Frayorna. If we are to survive, this is our opportunity. We must leave. Immediately."

Romik found it hard to breathe. The enemy was out there. The cave was not exactly comfortable, but it was their sanctuary. He then thought of Baylun, his mother, his cousins, and Granduncle Arkor. Had he grown too content with hiding? He sighed. It was time to find his family. He sheathed his sword and nodded.

They gathered their gear, comprising little more than a single blanket, two full waterskins, and the clothes on their backs. Brem had no weapon to speak of, but while Romik donned his chain shirt and strapped Baylun's axe to his back, the marteese left the cave for several minutes, returning with a long branch.

Romik frowned. "A stick?"

"A staff." Brem smiled. "From the blessed tree. It yielded this to me without tools, and it will carry the Strength of Frayorna."

Romik nodded. With the help the goddess provided already, he was not about to doubt the priest's word.

They exited the cave. To the north lay the fissures, most of them dark and issuing wisps of smoke. The west held Pavan and its savages, and the east led to Darum Carumbor and Beit. Baylun had gone east. Romik headed east.

Though not as accomplished as Baylun or Desser at tracking, Romik was not without skill, and he determined there had been no traffic through the area recently. Still, the first mile put his nerves on edge. It seemed nothing existed to notice them while they rounded smoking fissures beneath the rising sun, and their eastward trek was often interrupted when the wider cracks pushed them northward.

They halted upon reaching a collection of large bones scattered over a thirty-yard stretch.

"This is where I found you," said Brem.

Anger swelled while Romik viewed the skeletal remains of the monster that had borne him away. He noticed the broken skull, and his mind shifted to thoughts of his little brother. How often had he and his cousins teased Baylun about his heritage? Romik had nothing against krukari. In fact, he had always liked Gruelenor. Romik counted on his step-father above all others when he was younger. As well, Gruelenor had no shortage of stories about Ballrik, and Romik *loved* stories about his father.

Romik pulled Baylun's weapon from his back and stared at it. He wanted to return it to his brother, as if that would make Baylun's birthday right again. If only they had not taken that blasted hunting trip...

"Here's your pack!" Brem called out.

Romik's backpack hung from a talon that had separated from the dragon's body, and most of the contents were strewn across the ground. His food was there, although covered in dirt and obviously stale. He reached out, tempted to eat some, but Brem placed a hand on his arm.

"I would not," the marteese said.

Romik abandoned the thought.

The only useable items consisted of a few torches, a couple of tinder boxes, flint and steel, a spade, and a small hammer. All useless. The heat was steadily growing, so they needed no fire, and Romik did not want to reveal their location to prying eyes with torches at night—Brem saw well enough in the dark, thanks to his elfish heritage. Romik grabbed the hammer and shovel, though he could think of no immediate need for them. If he died, he did not wish to be buried in this forsaken realm. If the time came, perhaps he would simply dive into a crevasse.

They moved on, and as evening neared, the cracks emitted more heat than they had in the southeast. As well, the growing darkness showed many of them to be glowing from fires or lava contained below. Though this kept the night from getting too dark, it also led Romik and Brem to drink more water than they had planned.

They continued beneath the black sky, with Brem leading the way. The priest steered Romik clear of fissures hiding in the shadows, and they walked until Romik's legs felt to give out. Brem then located an area far enough away from the heated fractures to gain some rest.

They sat back to back until morning, but Romik found no sleep.

As soon as the sky brightened, they picked up again. Romik's sword remained sheathed so his arm would not tire, but he constantly scanned the countryside for enemies. The land presented nothing beyond the fissures, and though his vision did not penetrate the haze and smoke, he was sure no monsters were hiding nearby.

They continued eating berries throughout the day. The fruit was not filling, but it was better than starving. Romik could not recall the last time he had had a nice piece of meat to chew on, and he wondered if his teeth were fit to accomplish the task if he ever found the chance again.

Noontime must have come and gone, but Romik did not notice. The sun was beginning its descent into the west when Brem issued a warning.

"To the right!"

Romik gazed into the blurry east, attempting to pierce the haze. He saw nothing. But then a dark line appeared on the horizon. Brem then directed Romik's attention to the west, and he spotted another line. He and Brem were trapped.

Why did the enemy care about two insignificant beings? A human and a marteese posed no threat to the giant krukari's plans, whatever they might be.

Romik pulled his sword, and Brem readied the staff. They would not give up. Romik was Lord of Ironside Keep, and Lords of the Keep did not surrender.

"Are you sure you read your signs correctly?" Romik attempted to slide humor into his tone.

"I am sorry, my young friend," Brem said.

"I'll take the army to the left." Romik chuckled. "You handle those on the right." A brief thought crossed his mind that he was going mad.

The forces closed in. The lines were long, and there was no hope of running north or south to avoid them. Besides that, Romik was sure he and Brem had been spotted. Why else would the enemy choose now to bring the walls together? The approaching soldiers veered left and right, surely stepping around steaming cracks, but the pace remained constant.

"Blackfoot goblins!" said Brem.

Romik looked over his shoulder. The warriors to the east were not large, but he could not see that they were goblins — how badly he wished to view things the way elves did! He turned back and saw those to the west were closer and stood taller. Hobgoblins? The two breeds often worked together, but only when a powerful master organized them. And one did not get mightier than the Shadow and the giant krukari.

Romik faced the hobgoblins, holding his sword in both hands. "Thank you, Brem. Thank you for extending my life these past months."

"Today we make our deities proud." Brem held the staff near the middle and gave it a twirl.

The hobgoblins approached to within fifty yards. They stood as tall as men and were well muscled, and blue and white paint covered their faces...

They were not hobgoblins. Hobgoblins did not paint their faces, and Romik had never heard of them wearing animal skins as armor. They were Pavish. Romik was unsure if that improved the situation — Pavish were not known to hold any regard for folks of the southern realms.

"Barbarians!" Romik shouted.

A horn sounded from the Pavish, and the warriors pounded their weapons either upon their chests or on crude wooden shields. They were forty yards away when a single barbarian charged — a strange way to begin the battle. The lone figure yelled and waved his sword overhead, his voice drowning in the grunts of his comrades, and he was smaller than the others. And instead of an animal skin, he wore... leather armor?

"Desser!" Romik could not believe his eyes. Beneath the paint was his cousin!

Desser continued running around and jumping fissures to remain ahead of the mass of savage warriors, and Romik bolted forward, yelling his cousin's name. He was not sure if Brem had heard him, and he did not look back. He worried his madness was taking over.

Why would Desser be marching with Pavish? Wearing war paint? At that moment, Romik did not care. He then realized Desser called his name as well, and they reached each other thirty yards ahead of the Pavish.

"What—?" Words failed Romik. Not only was Desser's face painted, but he lacked facial hair. Was it really him?

"Hold still!" Desser said.

Desser fumbled a jar from his pack, nearly dropping it, and pulled off the lid to reveal a white paste. He dipped his fingers into the container and smeared the substance first onto Romik's face and then Brem's—the priest was suddenly beside Romik with a look of hope. After a glance over his shoulder—the Pavish were fifteen yards away—Desser extracted a smaller jar containing a blue powder. He placed his white-covered fingers in the powder and began patting it over parts of Romik's cheeks. Upon doing the same to Brem, Romik noticed Desser turned some of the paste blue.

"We can't pass as Pavish!" Romik said. "I don't know how you have fooled them."

"We're not fooling anyone!" Desser returned the jars to his pack and pulled his sword. "Now fight with us. You'll see."

"*Us?*" Romik stared at the barbarians ten yards away. The savages' furrowed brows revealed pure hatred, but their eyes glared right through him. Yes, his madness was taking over.

Desser made hand gestures at the Pavish. Romik had no idea what the signals meant, or how his cousin knew them, and he turned to face the Blackfoots. The goblins were thirty feet away, their faces hidden beneath the full helms that allowed them to walk in the daylight. They did not look like much in the way of size and strength, but they outnumbered the Pavish at least two to one.

A blaring horn sounded behind Romik, followed by a thunderous charge. He advanced with the barbarians, slashing one and then two goblins. The Sword of Ironside was light in his hands, as it surely thirsted for battle, and he hacked a couple more without taking a wound.

The Pavish drove into the enemy, seemingly unconcerned with Romik and Brem, and Romik laughed as he felled another Blackfoot. A short sword struck his chest, but his armor turned away the blade. He would sport a nasty bruise tomorrow, and the thought fueled his laughter as he carved down a few more goblins.

The number of evil warriors grew, and they mobbed the Pavish, attacking three to one. Four goblins charged Romik. He swung his sword in an arc to slow their advance, and when he brought it back, he scored a gash across the lead goblin's chest. The second goblin ducked beneath Romik's weapon and thrust a dagger into his side. Despite the sting, he shoved the fiend away. Desser joined Romik, slashing one of his foes, and Brem's staff cracked the helmet of another. Romik skewered the fourth.

"You're wounded!" Desser shouted at Romik.

Blood flowed, but there was no pain, and Romik laughed harder. He charged into five goblins, hacking down two, and Desser and Brem were beside him again, dropping one each. A female barbarian joined them and killed the fifth goblin.

An explosion behind the Blackfoots launched dozens of the creatures into the air, all of them on fire. A fissure must have erupted. Another explosion sounded, closer and to the left, and to the right, a few goblins fell with arrows in their backs. And was that a cavalry charging into the enemy's flank?

Mounted warriors entered the battle from behind the goblins, trampling a score of the evil soldiers and striking several more. One rider was a small female dressed in golden armor—Kiryanna? And next to her was a large krukari, swinging a hammer from side to side and crushing the enemy. It looked a lot like Baylun, only much bigger.

It *was* Baylun!

Romik stopped laughing. This was not a dream. His brother had returned; Desser had returned. And now Selanna and Eraim appeared. The pain of the injuries the goblins inflicted became unbearable, and Romik fell to his knees.

A morningstar crashed into his face.

CHAPTER 41

REUNION

Baylun did not know why his brother's face was painted like the Pavish. But there was Romik, fighting against the Blackfoot goblins. And then Romik fell.

Baylun dropped from the saddle, feeling stronger with the ground beneath his feet. He twirled his hammer, crushing goblin after goblin, and roared as he raced to Romik, causing the enemy to balk. Several barbarians were there, seemingly unconcerned with his approach, and while they held off the goblins, Baylun pulled the Nidor-jewel from his pouch and placed it in his brother's hand. Romik's wounds closed, but he remained unconscious.

Baylun spotted his birthday present strapped to Romik's back. How was that possible? Certain his brother would be all right, Baylun grabbed the axe. The haft was perfect in his grasp, like an extension of his arm, and he charged, swinging it with one hand. The blades cut through his foes with ease, and their blood splattered his body as he hacked into their ranks. It then seemed the world had silenced, and his roar was the only sound as he dropped the last two Blackfoots with a single swing.

Baylun realized he had indeed been the battle's final voice. The goblins were no more, and thousands of painted warriors stared — several grinned and nodded their approval. Even Baylun's father stood with mouth agape. The only one not staring was a barbarian in leather armor with his back to Baylun, and the warrior held his hands up to the Pavish.

Romik was sitting, and Brem was there, also with a blue-and-white face. Tears filled Romik's eyes as Brem helped him to his feet,

465

and he rushed to Baylun.

Baylun accepted his brother's embrace, noticing Romik was shorter than he remembered.

"You're alive!" Romik stepped back. "And you've grown! Where have you been? Where's Daymyn?"

Baylun did not know how to answer the latter.

"Darum Carumbor claimed Daymyn," Magneer said. "I'm sorry."

Romik's joy became disbelief. He then stared at the fire opal still clutched in his hand. "What's this?" He held up the gem.

"It's Nidor," Baylun replied, taking the jewel and placing it into his pouch. "What's left of him."

As the Pavish drew closer, it was obvious the barbarian wearing the leather armor was Desser, and his face was painted too. Relief nearly overwhelmed Baylun. Desser had survived!

Selanna approached, and Desser greeted her with half a smile.

"I received your message," he said. "Unless it was a dream."

Message? What was Desser talking about? From the looks of Baylun's companions, they were just as confused.

"It is good to see you well." Selanna did not bother to address Desser's comment.

A barbarian taller than Baylun approached. The warrior was wrought in muscle, and an animal hide strained to cover his body. Under the face paint was an angry expression.

"This is Pargahnu," Desser said.

The large man offered no greeting or reaction. Baylun wondered if he understood.

"He's chief of the Bomahni, and..." Desser glanced at the warrior. "He's my father-in-law."

No words came to Baylun. Upon seeing Romik's gaping jaw, he realized his mouth hung open as well.

"And that is my wife, Barrelda." Desser gestured at a woman a few paces behind Pargahnu.

"It is a great pleasure to meet you." Selanna bowed to the chief.

"I know it is not your custom, but time is short, and I do not speak your language. For that reason, I implore you to break tradition for the good of your tribe, as well as all of Vaeldor."

Pargahnu maintained his glare. He sniffed. "Fine," he grumbled.

"If you would please follow me," Selanna said, and she led the barbarian to the west, followed by King Cavalor and Eraim.

"You're married!" Romik slapped Desser on the back.

Desser smirked. "It just sort of happened."

Barrelda stood to the side, showing no emotion and appearing not to understand. But after hearing the chief speak, Baylun wondered if that was the case. Her dark hair was tied into a knot, and her bare arms and legs revealed strength. Her gaze wandered Baylun's way, holding a curious expression.

Baylun turned to glimpse Kiryanna hugging Brem, and the priest appeared as if the world was lifted from his shoulders. The two conversed, both of them smiling all the while.

"I guess we never had a chance with that one," Romik said to Desser, gazing at Kiryanna. "Too bad."

Baylun observed the marteese warrior. It was nice to see her happy. A part of him then grew angry with Brem, and he knew not why. Though the advice the priest offered made Baylun uncomfortable, Brem had always been kind and there was no reason to harbor animosity.

"Whoa, brother!" Romik stole Baylun's attention. "I believe she's spoken for."

Baylun sneered as he turned away from Kiryanna. *This* form of teasing he did not miss.

Magneer pulled Desser aside to have a private word, and Barrelda remained quiet, pretending not to listen. Baylun could tell she pretended, for her jaw clenched and relaxed in obvious reactions to what was said.

"Romik!" Gruelenor approached, wearing a grin.

"Uncle Gruelenor!" Romik gave Gruelenor a short embrace. "It's grand to see you! I never thought I'd see anyone again." Romik looked at Baylun, his smile fading. "I think I almost lost myself. Everything seemed so unreal."

"Nidor put you to right," Baylun said.

"Yeah... Nidor." Romik's brow furrowed. "You'll have to tell me all about that."

"Another time." Baylun glanced at Kiryanna. She was still smiling. Her eyes caught his, and she nodded. Baylun returned his attention to Romik and his father.

"Your mother is not happy with the birthday trip," Gruelenor said to Romik.

Romik let out a raucous laugh.

They proceeded to exchange stories. Romik spoke about how Brem had found him, and their time in the cave. Baylun mentioned only that he and Daymyn were trapped in Darum Carumbor, and that Gruelenor and the others rescued him. Gruelenor described the journey into Trannum's crypt. Baylun shuddered.

"So Trannum was never destroyed?" Romik shook his head. "And the giant krukari is... the Enemy?"

"Uustaag," Gruelenor said. "You can say it."

"Even if I don't wish to?" Dread filled Romik's eyes. "So what happens next?"

"We have an army marching on Lormin Dmurr." Gruelenor gave a wry smile. "As for us, we're heading for the dark citadel."

"What about Pavan?" asked Romik. "We can escape through the barbarian region."

"I will not." Desser returned with his wife and Uncle Magneer. "The Bomahni were convinced to join this war. They are Barrelda's people, and I will not leave them to finish what we started."

"But we didn't start it." Romik appeared angry.

"We cannot leave evil to its own devices," Brem said as he and Kiryanna joined the group.

"Yes, of course." Romik gazed at the dirt. "I'm sorry. I think living in the cave and eating berries and sap has blurred my thoughts."

Brem chuckled.

"Worry not," Magneer said. "No one in their right mind would go willingly into Lormin Dmurr. So it's a good thing we're not of sound mind." He winked.

King Cavalor approached, and Selanna and Eraim were close behind. The elves carried a hushed conversation in their own tongue, their expressions solemn.

"We're moving to the west," Cavalor said, "where Chief Pargahnu claims the land is less plagued by these blasted cracks. There, we will make our final camp before Lormin Dmurr. So say what needs to be said, because everyone must rest this night." He nodded and joined Selanna and Eraim.

Baylun shared a look of concern with his father and Romik, and he took in a deep breath as he fiddled with the fire opal.

At Selanna's insistence, the corpses littering the area were dropped into fissures—the mage feared a Death Lord might discover them and create another army. The Bomahni made quick work of the chore, and upon completion there was yet an hour of sunlight remaining.

Gruelenor retrieved their horses and offered to share his saddle with Romik, and Magneer did the same with Desser. Desser declined, preferring to walk with his wife and the rest of the Bomahni. Magneer joined his son, allowing Romik to ride alone, and Brem joined Kiryanna atop her mount. They then left the bloody field behind.

Though the hike was surely taxing after clearing the bodies, Uncle Magneer and Desser showed no fatigue, and their laughs rose above the marching feet and hissing steam. Baylun enjoyed seeing his uncle's sense of humor returned. His father watched Magneer and Desser as well, but then Gruelenor turned to Baylun and Romik.

"I wish your mother could see you two." His eyes glistened in the light of the glowing fissures. "She misses you both dearly."

"I'm sorry, Uncle Gruelenor," Romik said. "And I'm sorry to you, Baylun. I'm sorry my life has been so easy while both of you—"

"I've had a great life." Gruelenor looked at Romik. "For me, my life began when I met your father. And since that day, I have learned what it means to truly live."

Romik smiled. "You have been a father to me. I am grateful for everything you've done for Mother, and for what you have given me." He turned to Baylun. "And I am truly proud of you, brother. You have grown into a great man, and a formidable warrior."

"You have always been there for me," Baylun said to Romik. He looked at his father. "Both of you. There were times I wished... Well, that doesn't matter. I have come to realize I'm proud of who I am. And you have both helped me to *become* what I am."

Baylun quieted, afraid he might sob. It seemed his brother and father did the same.

Chief Pargahnu had been correct about the diminishing fissures. Smaller cracks still existed, but they did not radiate much heat and the world became more comfortable. The Bomahni spread out with no obvious organization, and they settled in for the evening.

Several fires were lit, and Baylun's company gathered around one while Selanna, Eraim, and King Cavalor resumed their meeting with Chief Pargahnu. The barbarians kept busy with their own affairs, including removing their face paint—Desser produced a liquid to do the same for Romik, Brem, and himself. The Pavish continued speaking in their own tongue, a language making them seem angry all the time, and Baylun occasionally peered over his shoulder to make sure the shouting was not meant for them. It seemed the Bomahni had forgotten he and his companions existed.

There were no cooks, and the Pavish produced rations for themselves, leaving Baylun's company on their own for dinner. Romik practically drooled at the sight of Baylun's food when he pulled it from his pack. He remembered his first meal after escaping Darum Carumbor, and he handed all he possessed to his brother. He then stifled his laugh when Romik gobbled every crumb.

Barrelda joined their gathering after dinner ended. Her war paint was now removed, and Baylun could see she was quite fetching. She carried several mugs in her hands, one per finger, and began distributing them, starting with Desser. Desser smiled and said something in her language, and she returned a curt nod.

Once everyone was served, Desser stood and raised his mug. "Here's to Daymyn; to those who have fallen; and to those that fall in the days to come."

"Here! Here!" they resounded, and everyone drank.

The draft was hot in Baylun's throat, and he nearly gagged. It was horrible! Several others could not hold it in, and they spit the liquid into the fire, making the flames roar with glee. Desser laughed, and Baylun detected the slightest smirk from Barrelda—the two had no problem draining their mugs.

"It takes about a month to get used to." Desser wiped a tear from his eye.

Baylun looked around the campfire. Here they were, only miles from the doorstep of Uustaag the Dark, and everyone was smiling and talking. Many of them would likely die tomorrow or the day after, fighting for the freedom of those who could not do so. But the faces before him were full of life, reminding him why they headed to their doom. None of them knew the ordeal he had survived, nor the struggles he had faced. A Death Lord's blood ran through his veins— one of the cruelest Death Lords in history. And the enemy had had plans for him. They were grooming him to be a leader of the forces that aimed to destroy the lands of his family and friends. The thought made the night seem darker.

He reached into his pouch and wrapped his hand around the fire opal, and the warmth spread throughout his body. Nidor had been a man of pure good; the noblest soul ever to exist. Baylun looked at his father. Gruelenor was a good man as well. Baylun took in a deep breath and let it slowly exit his lungs. Evil had tempted him, and he had been willing to die to deny it. In the end, he would have taken on the entire tower of Darum Carumbor if it had come to it. Gruzim meant nothing to him.

"Ah, my young krukari warrior." Brem squeezed in between

Baylun and Romik, patting Baylun on the knee. "My, how you have grown strong!"

Baylun looked at the priest. The dark spots were clearly visible without the war paint. Baylun was in no mood for encouraging words, and he took a gulp of the disgusting drink. Thankfully, Brem spoke to Romik; and strangely enough, Romik appeared happy for the conversation. Perhaps their time in the cave had formed a bond.

Another body squirmed between Baylun's father and himself, and he turned to see Kiryanna. She smiled at him, and he was suddenly self-conscious.

"There is no end to the wonders of your battle skills," Kiryanna said. "With or without your axe. You are quite impressive."

Baylun could not prevent the smirk from invading the right side of his face. He remembered being hesitant to fight when he first encountered Blackfoot goblins in Pavan. How long ago that day seemed. It felt like years.

"My father taught me." Baylun glanced at Gruelenor, who was occupied with watching the starless sky.

"After tonight," Kiryanna lifted her chin, "I would be honored to fight by your side, if you will fight by mine."

"Of course." Baylun's eyes met hers, and he suddenly felt foolish. He had been fighting beside her since they rescued him from Darum Carumbor. Had he understood her correctly? She probably meant fighting on the *same* side. But why would he fight otherwise? Did she know he had Gruzim's blood in his veins? No. That was silly. And now he was staring with Silcor knows what type of expression on his face. He had not intended to make it awkward. "I mean, it has been a pleasure having you as a companion. You're a remarkable warrior. I'm honored to be on your side."

She squinted, as if reading his turmoil. "I have told you about my past, at least in part. But from the beginning, *you* have never gazed upon me the way others do. *You* have never used lies to impress me. And you have proven yourself noble at every turn."

Baylun did not agree. He had *always* noticed how attractive she was. But he was ugly. He knew of nothing uglier. His mother was beautiful, and he held much respect for her. He respected all things beautiful, for he learned they inhabited the world not for him, but as inspiration; as reasons to do good.

"I mean to fight *by* your side," she said. "For too long, I was unknowing whether or not you lived. Until we found you in that horrible tower. I will not be left unknowing if you survive Lormin Dmurr. And you shall know of my fate as well. And if Frayorna smiles upon me... and Silcor upon yourself... then we will walk away from this war together."

"Me?" Baylun was sure he misunderstood. "What about Brem?"

Kiryanna's brows furrowed. She smiled again and placed a kiss on Baylun's cheek. "I give him all the love a father deserves, even if he is not my own."

Baylun found no words. Love was not meant for him... if that was what she offered. Kiryanna seemed to understand his hesitation, and she smirked as she patted his hand. He decided he should say something, in case she waited for reciprocation. He opened his mouth.

"Sorry to break this up." King Cavalor stood just outside their circle. "It's time to discuss tomorrow."

Selanna and Eraim arrived, and Cavalor explained the plan moving forward, which was altered from what Baylun originally understood. It appeared the enemy had been trying to recruit the Pavish for several months. The barbarians would now *accept* that offer, and Baylun's company would arrive within the Bomahni force and make their way into the citadel unseen. Cavalor reminded them they needed to deal with Trannum as well as Uustaag, and that Selanna had a plan for the necromancer. But that plan would not be revealed until necessary.

"The power of the enemy is strong," Selanna said. "I dare not share the information for fear of Trannum probing your minds. So trust in everything I tell you when the time comes. This is the only way."

Baylun saw several things wrong with Selanna's plan. What if something happened to her before she could relay her instructions? But then, she was Selanna. What could possibly happen to *her*?

"Now get some rest, everyone." Cavalor brought the meeting to an end, his tone leaving no room for argument. "We leave before dawn."

"Come, dear." Brem helped Kiryanna to her feet.

Baylun's anger for Brem returned, even though it was silly. Kiryanna placed her hand on Baylun's shoulder, giving him a stern nod, and she left with the priest.

"What was that all about?" Romik frowned as he watched Kiryanna walk away.

"Let's get some sleep," Gruelenor said to Baylun and Romik, failing to conceal his grin.

After Kiryanna and Brem took their places upon blankets, Baylun followed his father to their resting spot.

CHAPTER 42

THE WALL

Eraim felt tiny marching amid the Pavish. Even the barbarian women were tall and muscular. She would have loved nothing more than to remain atop the mount she had ridden across Helmland, but the Bomahni rode no horses, and it would have rendered her and her companions readily visible. So she trudged along with the company, traversing the hardened soil and weaving around the scars Uustaag inflicted upon the land.

Part of the meeting with Pargahnu the previous night had frustrated Eraim. Like Desser, the chief mentioned receiving a message from Selanna, but Selanna continued with the conversation, as if the words had gone unsaid. Was it another secret Elgarroth and Selanna shared? In some ways, Eraim felt alone. Selanna had always wished to be more like Elgarroth, a goal that was realized more and more every year. But Eraim never imagined her friend treating her the way Elgarroth treated others. What would she do if Selanna found herself a house to live in, hidden away from the world? Eraim supposed she had a couple hundred years to figure that one out. But none of that mattered if they failed to defeat Uustaag. That needed to be her focus.

She marched alongside Selanna and Cavalor in the middle of the barbarian force, and their companions were grouped with Desser and his wife, Barrelda. Eraim considered Barrelda. The woman spoke only in her native tongue, but she did not fool Eraim. Just as with Chief Pargahnu, Barrelda certainly understood all that was said around her. Eraim was truly happy for Desser, but curious as to how a marriage happened so quickly between people so different from one another.

Though the heat was unpleasant, no one complained, not even when the discomfort increased with the rising of the sun. The distant buzzing of insects returned with the daylight, as if whatever made the noise was accepting of the current lay of the land. A couple of miles farther, the fissures were wider and closer together, forcing the Bomahni to close ranks, but then new constructions came into view: stone bridges spanning several of the chasms.

The bridges were surprisingly sturdy, allowing for a northerly route, and the evil citadel soon appeared. The protective wall had been rebuilt, making the compound seem impenetrable, and surrounding it were multiple armies, including minotaurs, trolls, hobgoblins, Blackfoot goblins, krukari, and Dun Soldiers. Each group was segregated within large encampments, and it seemed they were enjoying merriment in their own ways. Beyond the wall, Eraim spied additional minotaurs, as well as Dun Lancers. Farther back, Lormin Dmurr stood over the Balgorn River. The stone was darker than Eraim remembered. Circling beneath storm clouds above the citadel's roof was a pair of undead dragons bearing the Death Lords.

Eraim forced herself to breathe.

As instructed the previous night by Selanna, Pargahnu led his people to join the evil horde without speaking to anyone. Eraim thought it odd, but it appeared there was no one to speak *to*. Everyone was just *there*, with no obvious leadership or direction. Upon reaching a vacant spot along the twenty-foot-high wall, the chief brought his army to a halt and they settled in.

An essence of evil filled the air, and Eraim was grateful no paladins had accompanied them. Even among the barbarians, Nidor would have been a beacon beneath the Death Lords' watch. Having Brem's presence made Eraim nervous enough, but Selanna assured her she need not worry. Still, she did. Eraim also noticed Brem's spots had become darker again, and he absently scratched at them. She tried not to stare.

Selanna sighed, gazing at Lormin Dmurr. "Now we wait for

Vayla."

Eraim detected concern in her friend's voice.

Night was upon them, and Eraim made her way along the wall surrounding Lormin Dmurr. Surprisingly, the fissures ended fifty yards outside of the compound, and their glow provided a menacing light, as well as more heat than anyone could hope for. Still, several fires were visible among the armies. Eraim figured the campfires that existed were likely for cooking purposes. She gazed at the nearby minotaurs, wondering if they cooked their food or preferred it raw. She decided she did not wish to know the answer. That might lead to images of what it was they were eating.

She continued past the minotaurs, remaining out of sight. Though most of the evil troops had excellent vision, she was not worried about being spotted while she carried out her task. The glow of the fissures beyond the armies cast sufficient shadows to hide her from even the most alert guards, but there were no guards to avoid. Eraim had covered over half of the wall so far, searching for a point of access other than the only visible gate, but she had had no luck. The stone was solid. And since a gap of thirty yards existed between the hordes and the wall — the distance kept the citadel within view of the monsters' encampments — Eraim had been able to search every inch.

She moved nearer to the krukari force, and she realized it was a collection of krukari, hobgoblins, and humans. Humans... They differed greatly from elves, and Eraim had given up trying to figure them out.

She continued with her inspection, and she found it at last. A secret door! The dark stone hid it well, especially within the shadows of the night, but nothing could remain hidden from Eraim. It was the entrance she and Selanna were hoping for.

A familiar voice caught Eraim's attention, and she stood up straight. Vecnor was among the krukari, hobgoblins, and humans, laughing with the lot of them. His black armor made it appear he had been separated from the nearby group of Dun Soldiers, and he was twice the size of the largest warrior around him. He gave a haughty laugh as he grabbed a half-hobgoblin by the breastplate and issued a headbutt to drop the krukari with a very bloody nose. There was a roar of laughter from the onlookers, as well as several slaps on Vecnor's back.

"Funny or not," Vecnor said, "there will be no more jokes about my mother being an ogre!"

The crowd burst into more raucous laughter.

Eraim froze. Vecnor's gaze then turned her way, and she sank deeper into the shadows.

"I must relieve myself," he bellowed in barbaric fashion, and he headed for the wall.

Eraim's heart pounded. Why was Vecnor with these *things*? How long had he been there? Was this the reason he had gone missing? She was used to him showing up when they needed him most, but never had she seen him among the enemy! Had she misread him all these years? Did Selanna misread Elgarroth as well? Had the two been minions of Trannum all this time? Trannum was old and cunning, and he had had centuries to devise his plans. How else was the necromancer able to stay one step ahead of Eraim and her companions? Was Tux a part of it?

Eraim attempted to move back the way she had come, but Vecnor veered toward her. There was no avoiding him, and she pulled Mithkahr. Her blade's red glow reflected in Vecnor's eyes, making them appear ominous.

"Put that away!" he hissed.

Eraim slowly complied. But her hand remained on the hilt. Vecnor stood facing the wall, and she turned away in disgust.

"I'm not relieving myself," he said quietly. "But I must play the part."

"Then... you are not...?"

"You think me capable of evil?" He stifled a chuckle and raised a brow as he pretended to water the wall.

Eraim felt foolish. But lately, her world was changing in so many ways. She was glad Vecnor was not one of those changes. Or was he?

"Of course I'm not evil," he said. "The door you just located was discovered weeks ago by Tux. That's why I led this contingent to this very spot. To keep it clear."

"Tux?" Eraim tried to understand what was happening. "Does Selanna know you are here?"

"I don't think so." He furrowed his brow. "I'm not entirely sure how much she knows... yet."

"What are you doing here?" Eraim glared at him. "*How* are you here?"

"I'm here to help," Vecnor said, as if it had been obvious. It probably should have been. "And I have been here for a month." He gazed over his shoulder. "It hasn't been easy."

"Is that why the servant was not chopping wood at Elgarroth's house when I met Tux there?"

Vecnor grinned in response to her contemptuous tone.

"It seems Elgarroth's servant has been absent a lot over the past decade," Eraim added. "How *has* the old wizard gotten along without all that firewood?"

"I have been sneaking soldiers into Helmland for weeks now." Vecnor left her questions unanswered. "Even so, we are greatly outnumbered, and we have to blend in."

"Have you not been *relieving yourself* for some time?" Eraim looked at Vecnor's men. They appeared drunk.

"No one will be surprised by my long absence for such a task." He winked, appearing the Vecnor Eraim knew.

For the moment, she did not feel alone.

"But time is short." He dropped something on the ground. "Get that to Selanna. She'll know what to do with it." He turned. "Don't open it," he said as he walked away.

"Wait!" Eraim held no fear of being overheard by the boisterous soldiers.

Vecnor looked back and lifted a brow.

"I…" The words were lost to her. There was too much to say and no time to say it. "Be safe."

He winked again and continued on his way.

Eraim sighed, watching until Vecnor joined the evil army. He seamlessly entered a conversation, and no one seemed to mind.

She stooped to lift a small bag, thankful Vecnor had not actually relieved himself. The sack felt empty, and a leather strap secured it. After one last glance to memorize the door's location, Eraim returned to the Bomahni.

Selanna was near the middle of the barbarian camp, staring blankly at a fire. Cavalor was with her, but his concentration was bent upon sharpening his sword. Eraim took a seat next to Selanna and remained quiet. Cavalor looked up from his task to nod in recognition of her return, but he said nothing, and Selanna continued watching the flames.

Eraim's companion was far off again. Of course. This might have upset Eraim earlier, but Vecnor's unexpected presence gave her hope, even if only for the time being. Still, nothing erased the fact that the battle within Lormin Dmurr would soon begin.

"Were you successful?" Selanna stirred Eraim from her thoughts.

"Of course!" She was slightly offended. "Would I have returned otherwise?"

"Excellent!" Selanna smiled, though it seemed more from relief than happiness.

"And…" Eraim hesitated, unsure of what to say. She placed the bag on the ground next to Selanna. "I received this."

Selanna gazed at the small sack for a few seconds before nodding. "Very good." She tested its near weightlessness and tucked it beneath her robes without explanation. "It all begins tomorrow, shortly after the sun rises." She turned to Eraim. "It has been a pleasure having you as a friend."

Chapter 43

The Battle Begins

Lormin Dmurr lay ahead. Others had described the fortress, but nothing prepared Vayla for the visage before her. The citadel rose above the Blood River, a waterway appearing black and not red at all, and the many dark buildings around the stronghold were not so crumbled as Vayla had been informed. Even the wall and gatehouse were intact.

Most of the fissures that hampered Vayla's progress over the past couple of days could be traced back to the fortress, where they drew closer together. It was a deadly maze that would constrict the battle and make mounted combat risky, even with the many bridges crossing the gaps. Vayla was ready for this obstacle and had planned accordingly. Still, she wished she could remain on Star.

She studied the bridges. Though the pathways would allow the enemy to approach from multiple directions, the restrictive alley prevented them from surrounding her army. She chose this particular field for just that reason.

Her attention shifted back to the compound. Beyond the wall, creatures moved about. Vayla could not tell what they were, but her main concern lay with the multitude of evil gathered outside to serve their most horrible master. Her father was among that horde, as well as Selanna and Eraim and the company they led from Darum Carumbor days ago. But Vayla knew not where they were. The only information Selanna shared the previous night, when the elf mysteriously appeared in Vayla's tent, was to avoid bringing harm to warriors possessing blue and white paint on their faces.

Vayla took in a deep breath. She then turned to Macurak and

nodded. Her captain pulled a strip of white cloth from his pack and rose up in his saddle, waving it in the air. All at once, soldiers extracted their own cloths and tied them to their non-weapon arms. Half an hour had been wasted that morning while the entire army rummaged through belongings to procure enough white clothing to go around, but Selanna insisted on it. The marking was necessary to avoid attacks from the barbarian allies, since Vayla's force did not possess war paint. She would have declined to color her face anyway.

As much as Vayla hated to part with Star, she dismounted. Wezlok could not rescue her mount this time. She patted her horse on the neck, and the cavalry followed her lead as she sent the mare on its way into the east. Hopefully Star found friendlier grounds.

Macurak waited for Vayla's next command, but she hesitated. She offered him a smile, a gesture he seemed unable to return, and then nodded. Macurak circled his hand and thrust it forward, and the commanders joined their troops as the march began.

A horn emitted from the citadel—a low tone seeming to widen the chasms. Vayla thought it would blow forever, but it ceased at last, and the enemy marched against her. She could not see them clearly at first, but as the gap between them closed, the lead warriors' size made them obvious.

"Blackfoot goblins," Wezlok said. "Behind them are hobgoblins and trolls. Then minotaurs and Dun Soldiers. The Pavish follow, along with a group of humans and krukari."

Good. The barbarians were toward the rear. That would be advantageous.

Vayla looked above Lormin Dmurr. The Death Lords circled the fortress upon their steeds. The undead kings would eventually enter the melee, but she knew not when. She would have to wait and see.

The Blackfoots remained on a direct path while the trolls and hobgoblins split. As the goblins approached to within fifty yards, Vayla looked back at Wezlok. The elf nodded, and she lifted her sword and charged. The roar of the Palidurians and Sards followed, and the goblins advanced against them.

Wezlok's magic took effect, and four replicas of Vayla emerged from her body and rushed in different directions. The same happened for the Palidurians around her. Flawless illusions swarmed the enemy, and the Blackfoots attacked, but their swords, hammers, and axes passed through the images. The goblins were then hesitant, and Vayla and her soldiers made easy work of the front ranks.

Once the goblins realized who the true attackers were, the spell ended. But Vayla's force held the advantage. From her right flank, a cloud of arrows descended onto the Blackfoots' rear ranks, and the left flank mirrored that assault. Both volleys looked to have been effective, but the left side was launched by the gray elves, and several explosions ensued.

Hobgoblins approached from the right while trolls charged from the left. A horn sounded, issued by the gray elves—the Orlenfel warriors switched from bows to swords to combat the trolls. The human archers fired a volley into the hobgoblins, and the Nejans and Philanders advanced in opposition to the foe, led by Lindow and Larman.

Macurak was beside Vayla, and fifty Blackfoots lay in their wake. The goblins were scattered and failing fast. But they were only pawns, and their goal had been to slow Vayla's men and bring them fatigue while the minotaurs approached. Vayla nodded at Macurak, and at his next opportunity he blew his horn. The Palidurians and Sards then pulled back as the Marcs and Harbanians followed the Kalmirans to challenge the bull-creatures.

Deeyon utilized two swords at the lead of the Kalmirans. Vayla shook her head. He was to remain with the other priests to aid injured soldiers, fighting only when necessary. Deeyon exhibited skills to support his words from nights ago, however, dropping a minotaur, and Vayla could not help being impressed. Melac was present as well, outside the enemy's reach, and he cast spells of fire to assist the troops.

The minotaurs were formidable, and the rear ranks lowered their heads and charged. They rammed their large horns into Kalmirans, launching the soldiers across the battlefield, and trampled several others in their stampede. Though the Kalmirans fought with exceptional skill, the minotaurs were capturing the field.

Vayla and Macurak still panted. She had wished to rest a bit longer, but she nodded to her captain, and he gave the signal. The Palidurians and Sards advanced.

Just like the last time, Wezlok's magic made Vayla's force appear four times their number. The minotaurs fell for the ruse, charging through illusions and becoming unbalanced when there came no resistance. A few even rammed into each other. Several of the bull-creatures were slain, but it did not take them as long to figure out which images were false, and Wezlok ended the spell again.

Trolls entered from the left with gray elves on their tail, and hobgoblins spilled in from the right. The Dun Soldiers were yet to arrive—Vayla glimpsed the dark warriors combating the Pavish. Mocs and Dales stormed the trolls, outnumbering them four to one, but with the reach of the monsters' claws and the power of their massive jaws, they did not seem so few.

A horn sounded to the rear. The trailing force approached. Vayla did not know what the new army consisted of, but another tone followed and she breathed easier. The Stone Eagle dwarves had arrived as well.

The undead dragons then grew in size as they sped toward the battlefield. Vayla retreated from the melee to issue commands, but the minotaurs drove back the Palidurians and a few broke through. She side-stepped a minotaur's charge and slashed with her blade, placing a gash upon its leg. The beast was hobbled, but it spun with a snort and brought down its axe. Vayla nearly raised her sword to parry the blow, but she was glad she jumped away instead—the massive axe hit the ground with enough force to have shattered her weapon. She lunged, catching the minotaur unbalanced, and pierced its chest. Withdrawing her blade, she danced aside as it fell.

Vayla spun to face another bull-creature, but Lorylla stole its attention when she descended onto its shoulders. The gray elf brought her red-hot sword to the monster's neck, and while it reached for her, she cut open its throat. She rode the beast to the ground as embers burned the hairs where the blade had passed.

A third minotaur approached, but it did not perform a single attack. It burst into flames and collapsed with a bull-like scream. A glance told Vayla it had been Wezlok's doing.

The air then grew deathly cold, shifting Vayla's attention skyward. The Death Lords were near, and their bone dragons wore armor. A log-missile struck one, but the steel plates allowed minimal damage and the dragon's path was only slightly altered. It discouraged Vayla that no other attacks came from the dwarfish archers, but they were likely occupied with the army to the rear. Hopefully they returned to task soon.

CHAPTER 44

THE COURTYARD

The Pavish began their march in the wake of the Dun Soldiers and next to Vecnor's force. Eraim's company had not painted their faces, but with all the commotion, no one seemed to notice. Neither did they notice when Eraim and her companions split from the barbarians. Surprisingly, Barrelda had joined them, and Desser and his wife both donned the war paint.

Eraim led the way along the base of the wall and out of sight of the citadel. Upon reaching the door she discovered the previous evening, she located the mechanism with ease and opened the panel enough to have a peek. The entrance was tucked away behind a large building, and she saw and heard nothing. She opened it further and slipped through.

To either side of the building were smaller structures, and beyond it was a road passing from the gate and to the citadel. A lane ran between the buildings and the compound wall to the left and right, twenty feet wide, and no creatures were present. Eraim motioned for the others to follow.

One by one, they filed through the secret door. Gruelenor came last and pulled the panel shut, but before he completed the task, a large metal hand seized it. The door opened and Vecnor entered.

"Vecnor!" gasped Magneer. "Thank the gods!"

Eraim could not help but smile. Vecnor did not reveal his plan to her, and she knew not whether he was to fight in the battle outside or within the citadel. She was grateful it was the latter.

An aura of ice invaded the courtyard, and Eraim looked skyward. A pair of undead dragons flew by. The chill faded as they disappeared beyond the wall, and the warmth returned.

Cavalor paled. "Cafior watch over Vayla."

"We're in the open," said Vecnor. "We need to move."

They crept to the nearby building and stood against the wall.

"The krahluks have been entering our world for the past couple of days," Vecnor said quietly. "They are tough, so don't underestimate them."

"What do you know of the zreekans?" asked Magneer.

"Only that their magic is deadly," Vecnor replied. "But they're not strong. If you can get in close, they are easy to kill. But beware of their tentacles."

Eraim eyed the nearby building. It had obviously been constructed in haste. There were so many handholds that she could probably climb it with her eyes closed.

"I will see what is going on," she said, and she immediately scaled to the flat roof.

Eraim remained low as she moved to the opposite side of the building. Below, the road split as it made its way around a few large trees, only to reunite before the bridge to Lormin Dmurr. There was no evidence the fissures had ever existed. Several buildings of various sizes lined both sides of the street, and hundreds of krahluks walked about on unknown tasks while Dun Lancers readied their horses. Meanwhile, the minotaurs carried logs and enormous stones from place to place, a task that might have been easier for the much larger krahluks.

There was no clear path to the citadel without alerting the entire compound. They needed a distraction. Eraim eyed a couple smaller structures to the left that were devoid of monsters. If she and Gruelenor fired arrows from that location, they might gain the enemy's attention. They could then race back to the secret door and escape while the others accessed Lormin Dmurr. Perhaps Eraim would find another way inside.

She returned to her companions. But before she uttered a word, Selanna spoke.

"I know," she said to Eraim. "But we cannot split up." Selanna pursed her lips, searching the dirt for an answer.

How did Selanna know what Eraim had seen? Unfortunately, that was the way of things lately. Selanna would not allow for Eraim's plan, so how were they to proceed?

CHAPTER 45

THE DEAD ARISE

The Death Lords swept low over the field, and the undead dragons released their sickly breath. Vayla heard the short-lived screams that followed, as well as explosions from the black spheres launched by Radaam. Worse still, the dead began to stir, and Blackfoot goblins, minotaurs, trolls, hobgoblins, and one-time allies, all slain in battle, arose to fight for Uustaag.

The rising of the dead was not unexpected, and Macurak blew the horn to signal a retreat. The allied forces withdrew from areas inundated by corpses, so as not to become surrounded, but not all of them escaped. Hundreds were slaughtered, only to rise again.

"Where are the dwarves?" Vayla shouted in frustration.

Assessing the battle, she saw the undead gathering to the right while the living enemies concentrated their efforts to the left. In areas where they mingled, the zombies showed no loyalty to Uustaag's soldiers, as if eager to increase the size of their force.

A blunted missile sailed across the sky, and Vayla's spirit rose as it scored a direct hit to a dragon's skull. The monster's helmet failed to protect it, and it crashed, sweeping dozens of undead with it into one of the larger fissures. The Death Lord leaped from the saddle in time to avoid sharing the mount's fate, and Vayla knew it to be Anduiff by the axe and sword he carried.

"Brondor!" Deeyon called out, advancing upon the Death Lord with several Kalmirans and Sards in his wake—the latter appeared hesitant and lagged behind.

Vayla needed to reach Anduiff, but fifty undead separated them, the lead figure a zombie minotaur.

"Zhokard Feint!" she said to Macurak.

She gained the minotaur's attention and danced backwards to allow the monster to press. Macurak struck it from the right, cutting loose one of its horns, and as the creature turned, Vayla sliced through its leg just below the knee. The minotaur fell, but it continued to reach for them, impervious to the pain. Vayla and Macurak moved on, leaving others to finish the task.

Vayla was separated from her captain as they slew well over a dozen more zombies, and four undead goblins were all that stood between her and the duel between Anduiff and Deeyon. The priest put forth an impressive display, twirling his blades until the Death Lord shattered one with the black axe. Vayla then gasped as the dark king's sword sped toward Deeyon's neck, but a ball of flame interfered, cast by Melac. Though the blast of fire brought no visible harm to Anduiff, the explosion deflected the evil weapon from its path and threw Deeyon from the area.

Macurak rejoined Vayla, bleeding from the scalp and left arm, and they defeated the goblins without delay. A massive claw then struck Vayla's shoulder—a living troll had flanked her. Her armor protected her from serious harm, but the force of the blow made her lurch. The monster pressed until fire engulfed it, and Vayla felt the intense heat as the troll screamed and was reduced to ashes in seconds. She nodded at Wezlok, who stood among battling allies with his hands extended toward the swamp creature. How had the elf managed to keep an eye on her with the chaos surrounding him?

Vayla shut out all pain and faced the Death Lord. Anduiff struck down the last of four Kalmirans opposing him, and the corpses rose as zombies to fight for the enemy. His eyes burned into Vayla as he approached on confident strides, and she took in a deep breath and readied her sword.

A dark presence appeared to Vayla's left. Radaam descended atop his bone dragon, releasing a pulse of black light, and from it Vayla sensed pure evil. Time slowed, and her eyes grew wide when Macurak jumped in front of her. But as the shadowy bolt arrived,

Wezlok was there. The Lorian wizard intercepted the spell, and the explosion launched Vayla several yards away.

Vayla lay on the ground, unable to breathe. Around her the battle continued, as if under water. Macurak and Wezlok were close by, both unmoving, and the elf's body was charred—that or a black substance covered him.

Somehow, Vayla was on her feet, and she turned to where her body was sprawled. How could she see her own body? Had she failed? It was the only explanation. Her grandmother had destroyed the master of all Death Lords single handedly, but Vayla could not find the strength to defeat even one. She would never be High Paladin. She would never be... anything.

"It is time," said a voice from behind Vayla.

She turned to see herself, as if looking in a mirror. But it was not her. The image was much older, dressed in a brown cloak with a golden mace strapped to her side.

It was Merssa.

"Am I...?" Vayla could not ask the question.

"No." Merssa walked over corpses and around soldiers that had slowed even further—they barely moved at all. "So keep your mind about you. You're no good if you're dead."

"But... what...?" Vayla stared at the late paladin.

"It is time to decide who you are!" Merssa's voice was firm.

What was this woman talking about? Vayla knew who she was.

"Your life lacks balance," Merssa said. "The final thread between you and Cafior is blocked. Your potential is chained."

"I know not of what you speak!" Vayla detested the accusation. "I *live* for Cafior!"

Merssa's expression moved to one of pity. "But the true path to Cafior is through love. You know love, but you resist. I once resisted too. But once I gave in, my bond with Cafior was stronger than ever."

"What?" Vayla furrowed her brow. "Macurak?"

"No," Merssa said plainly. "Your grandfather did not teach me to love *him*. He taught me to love life itself. *All* forms of life. But mostly, to love myself."

"I don't... dislike myself." Vayla mumbled.

"No." Merssa now stood before her. "But that is not love. You feel pressure. Pressure to live up to something that is not you. Pressure to be... me."

"You have haunted me my whole life!" Vayla hissed. "No one has ever seen me. They see you!"

"Did High Paladin Montac see me when he promoted you?" Merssa raised a brow. "No. He saw a strong bond between paladin and deity. Did holy warriors accompany me into Beit? Did soldiers follow me into Helmland? Did Macurak and Wezlok throw their lives into Radaam's spell to save me? It was all for you."

Vayla shook her head. "Wezlok sees you when he looks at me."

"Wezlok saw a reflection of me at first, back in Maple Lore," said Merssa. "Since then, he has grown to love *you.*"

"I don't know what you want from me." Vayla's voice trembled as she kept herself from shouting.

Merssa smiled. "I want nothing but your happiness. I want you to let Cafior in; to accept everything good in your life; to let yourself *live.*"

Vayla searched the ground. Since her youth, people had compared her to Merssa. She could see how this might have led to several of her decisions. Had she truly completed all of her deeds in the name of Cafior? Or was she competing with the legend that was her grandmother?

"Now you understand." Merssa extended a hand.

Vayla accepted the gesture, allowing Merssa to pull her in for a tight embrace. Years of frustrations melted away, and she was suddenly weightless.

"I have been watching you for so long," Merssa said softly. "And I am very proud. You share a greater bond with Cafior than I ever could have."

Vayla stepped back to look at her grandmother. "But you accomplished so much."

"Yes." Merssa nodded. "But my connection was not so strong that I could summon a spirit of Cafior to my aid."

"I... summoned you?"

"You did, my child." Merssa's smile faded. "I have done what I can, and now I must go. You will know what to do."

Vayla's eyes snapped open. Every bone in her body ached, but she forced herself to her feet. In her hand was a mace, golden in color, and from it she sensed the power of... Merssa? No. It was Cafior. She raised the weapon overhead, and a golden glow surrounded her.

CHAPTER 46

FOG OF SHADOW

Eraim led the others from building to building through the courtyard, avoiding enemy detection. The citadel bridge was not far, but there was no way to cross the last field without being seen. The best plan they came up with was for Selanna to destroy the bridge after gaining access into the stronghold. It was not a solid plan, and Selanna was not even sure it could be done. Why else had the bridge survived the first war against Uustaag?

Eraim took in a deep breath, ready to run, but a flash of golden light caused her to balk. It was more than a flash, for it continued to radiate from the battlefield beyond the wall. Eraim gazed in awe, reminded of Merssa, and she was suddenly inspired.

The rumbling horn of Lormin Dmurr vibrated the ground again, and the compound's enormous gate opened. All at once, the Dun Lancers rode forth, and the krahluks and minotaurs dropped whatever it was they were doing to follow. Eraim looked at Selanna, who shrugged and shook her head. As the last of the monsters passed beneath the portcullis, Eraim bolted across the field.

The bridge spanned fifty yards over the gap to Lormin Dmurr. At the opposite end, the opening to the citadel was uninviting. Eraim stepped onto the stones, and though the construction lacked the cold that penetrated her boots the last time, a chill ran down her spine. She and her companions moved swiftly across to the stronghold's entry chamber, where hallways stretched left and right and large doors ended the short passage ahead. As the last of them entered, a fog of shadow rolled along the corridors and seeped from the bottom of the nearby doors, engulfing the room. Visibility reduced to thirty feet, reminding Eraim of her time in Sistama.

"Trannum!" Selanna spat. "He knows we are here!"

"Of course he knows," mumbled Magneer. "He *always* knows."

"He does not know all," Selanna said with confidence. "And soon he will learn that truth."

Eraim detected rushing feet from both corridors, and they were closing fast. "Mees! Mees!"

Everyone readied their weapons.

Dark figures emerged from either side. Dun Soldiers. The large doors then opened and two shapes appeared. By the waving tentacles, they were zreekans.

While Eraim's companions met the charge of the enemy warriors, she sheathed Mithkahr and pulled her bow. The zreekans then moved closer, and her stomach soured when their grotesque bodies came into focus. Their skin was lumpy, and it looked as if it was crawling; as if thousands of black worms covered them. Four tentacles protruded from beneath the monsters but did not touch the floor, and the six-foot appendages writhed about, seemingly on their own accord. Eraim expected the tentacles' undersides to resemble that of an octopus's, but it was not so. Instead, slime reminiscent of ghoul blood coated them, complete with the rancid odor. The zreekans bore a single eye, comprising black irises upon yellow orbs with violet pupils, and their large mouths were filled with pointed black teeth and purple tongues.

The fiends seemed to gaze beyond Eraim, and their pupils pulsated. She loosed an arrow, piercing the eye of one, and the creature dissolved into a puddle of goop. The other zreekan fired a dark bolt from its eye and into the chamber, and an explosion followed.

Eraim readied another arrow, but a tentacle lashed out and snatched her bow from her. A second tentacle grabbed her wrist, inflicting searing pain. Vecnor then arrived, thrusting one of his swords into the monster, and the zreekan collapsed without liquifying. Eraim's arm was released.

Her eyes adjusted to the shadows and she could see twice as far. Dun Soldiers littered the corridors to either side, and the citadel entryway was larger than before. Though Selanna claimed the building to be indestructible, the zreekan's spell had demolished a portion of the wall, and Eraim was sure the portcullis would never close again. Magneer looked to have taken damage from flying debris, and he lifted himself from the floor.

The Dun Soldiers began chanting, and Eraim pulled Mithkahr, hoping for its protection against the evil drone. Her companions slowed, but as Mithkahr's glow intensified, she was immune to the effect. The runes on Baylun's axe lit up, and the krukari moved freely as well. Vecnor was surprisingly unaffected as he charged into the hallway on the right with both swords drawn.

Eraim joined Baylun to the left side. The young krukari swung the axe with speed and grace, killing four Dun Soldiers, and Mithkahr added two to the tally. Baylun received wounds to the leg and forearm, but the injuries closed quickly; and even as the dark veins inflicted by the evil weapons attempted to infect him, the webs vanished—obviously the work of the Nidor-jewel. Together, Eraim and Baylun cleared the hallway, and Vecnor did the same behind them. The Chant ended and their companions moved freely.

CHAPTER 47

DEATH LORDS

The golden mace in Vayla's hand was unexpected. Even more surprising was the glow surrounding her. It spread no less than fifty yards, reducing every zombie it touched to crumbling dust, and smoke emitted from the seams of Anduiff's armor. Only seconds ago, Vayla's entire body ached, but her wounds were gone. Not far away, Macurak and Wezlok stirred.

Vayla shifted her focus to Anduiff. The Death Lord charged with sword and axe, swinging them with lethal efficiency, and Vayla dodged and knocked aside every blow. Grimmen and the zhokards then arrived to give aid, but she waved them off.

"Secure the area!" Vayla commanded. "Anduiff is mine!"

She defended Anduiff's next barrage before countering, and her mace cracked the black sword. The weapons connected again, and the evil blade snapped with a flash of gold and black. Anduiff cast the broken sword aside and regarded Vayla, waving his axe back and forth.

"Zhokard Sweep!" Macurak shouted.

Vayla reacted without thought, and Anduiff raised the axe as she rushed in high. She dropped with a tumble, crashing the mace into the Death Lord's leg, and the golden weapon caved in the greave — she swore she heard the bone snap. She quickly rolled away, knowing her action to be risky, but the axe penetrated her left vambrace before she was clear.

Vayla regained her feet and took a defensive stance, but Anduiff did not press. The Death Lord leaned heavily on his good leg. Though Vayla doubted the undead king felt any pain, she was confident he could not walk on the broken bone.

There was an explosion nearby, and Radaam flew overhead. A glance told Vayla the golden aura affected the mounted Death Lord the same way it did Anduiff, and the dragon suffered a worse fate. The skeletal mount deteriorated rapidly, and it crashed to the east and beyond the holy light.

Around Vayla, Pavish barbarians assisted Macurak and the zhokards in keeping away minotaurs, trolls, and Dun Soldiers, and all allies within her aura battled with strength renewed. Once a terrifying presence, Anduiff stood alone, appearing smaller in her eyes. Blood trickled down her arm, but the wound from the dark axe failed in its attempt to spread its freezing pain. Vayla advanced.

The undead king took a defensive position, nearly falling every time he placed weight on the broken leg. The smoke issuing from his armor then became billowing steam as Vayla swung her mace from side to side and the golden light deepened. Anduiff raised his axe, and she knocked the weapon from his hand. She followed the attack with another, crushing the dark helmet. There was a final expulsion of smoke as Anduiff's knees buckled, and the Death Lord fell.

Vayla surveyed the field. Explosions launched allied forces into the air from Radaam's crash site. Hobgoblins and krukari continued applying pressure to the right, and minotaurs replaced the trolls to the left. To the rear, Nirans joined the dwarves from Morimont and Rornibur while they battled the flanking army of krahluks and dunarchins. Vayla was surrounded, and the otherworldly creatures drew nearer, tearing through her soldiers with strength no hands should possess.

She ordered the gray elves to concentrate their bows on the krahluks, but the Orlenfel warriors were busy with the minotaurs. The human archers were few and scattered after Radaam's dragon devastated them before it crashed. It seemed nothing existed to slow the gorillas' pace, but then a shower of arrows descended onto the giant apes. The monsters' silent mouths bared their hideous black teeth as they searched for the source of their pain.

To the west were greater than two thousand Lorian archers. Vayla grinned, and she turned to Macurak and Grimmen and raised her mace.

"To Radaam!" she commanded.

The zhokards cleared a path toward the last explosion, and Macurak remained at Vayla's flank, intercepting all attempts to hamper her progress. Upon nearing the crash site, Vayla saw Radaam wielding a pair of swords against Greyor and Deeyon. One sword bore hooks surrounding the guard, and the other was a smaller, curved blade. A group of Kalmirans confronted Sendor and Harbanian zombies nearby while a squadron of krukari and hobgoblins charged. But more pressing were the Dun Lancers approaching from the citadel with krahluks and minotaurs in their wake. Vayla needed to deal with the evil king quickly.

Macurak and the zhokards spread out to hold the perimeter against the krukari and hobgoblins, and Vayla moved forward, studying Radaam. She sensed his strength to be greater than Anduiff's had been, and she would not underestimate him. The golden aura reduced the zombies to ashes and smoke issued from Radaam's armor, but the Death Lord did not seem to notice as it released a dark bolt. Clanghorr's runes flared as Greyor lifted his axe, and the weapon appeared to absorb the spell, but the impact sent the dwarf tumbling.

Vayla charged while Deeyon put forth an exhibition, flailing his sword with great skill. Radaam was equal to the task, fending off every swing and trapping the priest's weapon within the hooks of the larger blade. Deeyon's sword was wrenched loose and thrown several feet away, and the momentum caused the Brondor priest to lurch. Before Vayla could arrive, Radaam's smaller blade pierced Deeyon's stomach to the hilt. The Death Lord yanked the weapon free, allowing the body to fall, and the cold eyes turned on Vayla.

She pulled up, taking a defensive stance to protect her wounded arm. But then Greyor returned, swinging Clanghorr's deadly edge and driving Radaam back. The dwarf pressed, placing too much strength behind every swing and becoming unbalanced, and Radaam hooked Clanghorr and pulled him in close.

Vayla would not allow the Death Lord to execute the same maneuver that saw Deeyon fall. Her mace struck Radaam's arm, creating a spark and knocking Clanghorr to the ground. A whispering chant then issued from beneath the black helmet, and Vayla collapsed, as if a boulder had landed on her. She could not rise.

Radaam kicked Greyor away and thrust the smaller blade at Vayla. A pair of arrows struck the undead king, one piercing the helmet and the other deflecting from his shoulder, and the pressure atop Vayla faded. She rolled, avoiding the dark sword, and scrambled to her feet.

To her left, Lorylla and Eimell fitted arrows to their bowstrings. Radaam cast a dark bolt at the elves, and Eimell jumped aside while Lorylla leaped into the air, reaching an unimaginable height. The spell struck the ground, issuing an explosion that Eimell could not completely avoid, and the elf's dive became an uncontrolled tumble for thirty yards.

Vayla advanced, but Radaam's body transformed into a wavering shadow, and he sped across the battlefield like a shimmering blur until passing beyond the golden aura. His true form then returned.

Charging past the Death Lord was the squadron of mounted Dun Lancers sent by Lormin Dmurr.

CHAPTER 48

DINING HALL

Eraim's wrist burned where the zreekan tentacle had grabbed her, and the wound was blackening.

"That looks like ghoul rot," Gruelenor said while Baylun worked his way around the hall with the Nidor-jewel. "Strange. You best have Baylun take care of it."

Eraim thought it odd as well. Did a relationship exist between zreekans and ghouls? Perhaps it was Trannum's connection with the zreekans that made it possible to fill an entire swamp with the horrid undead.

"That looks... bad," said Baylun upon reaching Eraim, and he handed her the fire opal.

Nidor's fiery healing challenged the burning injury, and the jewel won out. The wound vanished. Eraim nodded her thanks as Baylun tucked the gem into his pouch.

She attempted to retrieve the arrow she had fired into the zreekan's eye, but the missile had almost entirely dissolved within the creature's goop. Fine. It could keep the arrow. Luckily, her bow had dropped clear of the mess, and after wiping slime from the wood, she strapped it over her shoulder.

"What's that?" asked Magneer, staring at the ooze covering half the width of the corridor before the large doors.

"That is what happens when you shoot a zreekan in the eye with an arrow." Eraim wrinkled her nose. "I recommend avoiding the stuff."

She stepped around the puddle and over the tentacles of the zreekan Vecnor had killed, making her way to the doors.

"Brem?" Selanna's voice held alarm. "Are you okay?"

The priest was shivering and scratching. His spots were much darker again, and they oozed pus and traces of blood.

"I shall be well enough." Brem put forth his strongest expression while he continued to shake. "I'll not stay behind this time."

Selanna sighed and nodded. Kiryanna appeared she might argue the point, but her shoulders slumped and her mouth closed.

Eraim led the way through the doors and into the long dining hall. Fine furniture had replaced the broken table and chairs, and six krahluks occupied the room while the balcony held a dozen shadowy forms that were undoubtedly zreekans. The massive gorilla creatures made the chamber smaller, and they exhibited no regard for the new chairs as they advanced, crashing through everything in their paths.

One krahluk charged Eraim, mouthing its silent growls and closing the gap in little time as she darted to the right. Its enormous fist came across, and she ducked, leaving the attack to smash into the wall. She jumped aside, and its other fist created a recess of cracked stone as it punched the floor. Before the monster drew back, Eraim lunged, thrusting Mithkahr into its eye socket. The creature opened its mouth in a silent roar as the purple light went dark.

Cavalor struck the hulking beast twice with his sword, leaving a pair of fine violet lines on the perfectly black skin. The attack failed to hinder the krahluk in the slightest, and it snarled as it corralled Eraim into the corner. Cavalor then appeared atop its back — the king must have jumped as high as he could to scale the giant ape. One of his arms was wrapped around the krahluk's neck while his free hand clutched the black dagger Selanna had given him. The small blade cut easily into the smooth flesh, drawing thick purple blood.

The krahluk did not shift its focus from Eraim, and it thrust its fists to either side to prevent escape while bearing down with its long, pointed teeth. Eraim leaped at the last second, piercing its other eye socket with Mithkahr and extinguishing the light. Cavalor rode the ape to the floor as Eraim jumped onto its back to avoid being crushed.

Several explosions had occurred while Eraim battled the

towering foe. Nearly the entire table and all the chairs were destroyed, and nine zreekans released their evil magic from above. There had been a few more zreekans not long ago, and after seeing slime drip from above and Gruelenor release an arrow, it was obvious what had happened to the others. At the near side of the table, Barrelda helped Desser to his feet, but it otherwise appeared the zreekans' spells had surprisingly missed their marks.

A butchered krahluk lay in Baylun's wake, and he cleaved his mysterious axe into the flesh of a second, cutting deeper than Mithkahr would have. Kiryanna was nearby, assisting when possible while remaining out of the monster's reach.

On the other side of the table, Vecnor swung his large blades as if they bore no weight, and a krahluk fell to join another already at his feet. Magneer kept the attention of a third giant ape to Vecnor's flank, and Romik writhed on the floor, holding his arm.

A dark bolt raced toward Eraim, too swiftly for her to evade, and she braced for impact. There was a vibration at her waist, and the evil spell deflected into the chamber wall, fracturing the stone—the citadel was strong indeed! Smoke issued from the dagger Selanna had given her. It had protected her from the blast, and it now emitted warmth that penetrated her armor.

"We must stop the zreekans!" Cavalor ran for the stairs.

A single krahluk stood, and Baylun and Vecnor hardly needed Eraim's help. Pulling her bow, she sought the eyes of the enemies above. She hated to lose more of the precious gifts Tux had bestowed upon her, but she let loose a couple of arrows, each of them dissolving one of the creatures. Gruelenor destroyed another zreekan, and Selanna sent green balls of magic to drop two more. Only four remained.

Cavalor and Magneer reached the top of the stairs and split in either direction, and Desser and Barrelda were close behind. Eraim did not dare shoot any more zreekans—she did not wish to see what their slimy demise did to her companions.

"Use no more arrows!" she called out to Gruelenor, and she put away her bow and unsheathed Mithkahr.

Within the chamber, the final krahluk lashed out like a feral beast. But it was no match for Vecnor and Baylun and it soon fell. Baylun then raced up the stairs with Kiryanna, where the others had struck down two more zreekans. Vecnor did not follow. The large human released the sword from his right gauntlet, and Eraim noticed blood seeping from teeth-holes in the pauldron covering his shoulder.

She rushed to his side. "Are you all right?"

Vecnor grimaced, but he nodded.

Romik joined them and dropped to a knee, wincing while keeping his forearm close. "I think my bone is shattered!"

The sounds of battle ceased. The zreekans were defeated. Upstairs, Kiryanna pulled Cavalor to his feet; the king appeared to be fine. The balcony was destroyed in several places, and the upper-level walls revealed darkened cracks where zreekan spells had exploded. Baylun knelt in one of those areas, holding the fire opal over someone, and after a few seconds Magneer stood. Baylun then noticed the states of Romik and Vecnor and he rushed down the steps.

Vecnor nodded toward Romik at Baylun's approach, and the young krukari held the jewel against his brother's arm.

Nothing changed.

Baylun gazed at the gem. The flame still wavered inside. He touched it to Vecnor's shoulder.

Nothing.

Baylun shook his head. "I don't understand. It's warmer than usual... But—"

"Even when he lived," Gruelenor stared at the opal, "Nidor only had so much energy to give." He looked at Baylun. "And I saw you struck twice while you fought the krahluks. You're lucky to be alive."

"Yes." Kiryanna glared at Baylun. "You are a great warrior. But you need to take more care to defend."

Baylun gave a small nod. "I promise."

It surprised Eraim to hear Baylun speak so. Just as his father, he was not one to show emotions, but the sincerity in his expression while making his vow was genuine. And Kiryanna's fleeting smile-turned-stern-nod in response was unmistakable. Perhaps the marteese was good for the krukari.

Eraim prepared healing herbs at once. There was nothing she could do for Romik if his arm had truly been broken except make a sling, and she doubted she could treat the black marks on Cavalor's neck that had surely come from a zreekan's tentacle—she did not have the skill to cure ghoul rot, if that was what it was. When Brem applied a salve to Cavalor, Eraim was relieved to see instant lightening of the affected skin.

"Hold still," she instructed Vecnor as she packed the healing concoction into the teeth-holes in his armor. It was a horrible way to treat the injury, and she felt guilty whenever he cringed. But there was no time to remove the pauldron and care for the wound properly.

"You must hurry," Selanna said with urgency. "The enemy continues to prepare for us."

"Is there anything you can do for Romik?" Eraim asked Brem.

"I'm sorry." The marteese shivered. "His arm is beyond my ability at the moment."

Eraim sighed, and she tied a sling around Romik's shoulder.

Magneer led the way upstairs, with Baylun and Kiryanna close behind. Cavalor and Gruelenor went next, followed by Desser and Barrelda, and Vecnor and Romik trailed after with Eraim and Selanna ascending last.

"Why did you not tell anyone about the daggers?" Eraim whispered to Selanna.

"I said they might be effective against Thard'Dun creatures," Selanna replied.

"But you did not say they would turn away zreekan magic," Eraim pointed out.

Selanna furrowed her brow. An expression of understanding then lit up her eyes and she nodded. "Yes. I am sorry I left that out. But do not tell the others. I do not want anyone taking unnecessary risks."

Eraim was not sure, but it seemed Selanna was hiding something. Unfortunately, there was no time to pry.

Magneer opened the large door they had used months ago, when they first made their way to the upper levels. But the guardroom beyond was not empty. Two krahluks and an enormous minotaur stood waiting, and in the minotaur's hands was an axe three times the size of Baylun's.

Chapter 49

Reinforcements

L ancers!" Vayla was not the only one to shout the warning.

The Dun Lancers sped across the plain of fissures outside Lormin Dmurr, uncaring even as they lost several riders to the fiery cracks. Behind them, the krahluks trailed and the minotaurs split to the left.

Vayla looked around. Macurak and the zhokards were with her. Wezlok appeared haggard, while Melac stood tall with hands raised. Lorylla was at the lead of a couple hundred gray elves, likely all that remained of the Orlenfel warriors, and their grim faces awaited the next command. Greyor had retrieved Clanghorr, and he now led a squadron of Varlimor dwarves against trolls to the right while the Pavish rushed to challenge the approaching minotaurs to the left. Scattered were Sards, Sendors, Harbanians, Kalmirans, Marcs, Mocs, Nejans, Dales, and Philanders. More than half were locked in combat with hobgoblins, krukari, Radaam and the undead, or against the flanking dunarchins and krahluks, while the rest bore looks of defeat or fear—or both—as they stared at Vayla. The discipline of the Palidurians had kept the holy soldiers together, and what was left of them stood at attention. Vayla's forces outnumbered the enemy, but her confidence was shaken. The evil army was too strong.

Reaching deep, she found her courage and nodded to Lorylla. The Orlenfel commander shouted in her own language and the elves drew back their bowstrings.

"Shield wall!" Vayla called out.

Every abled foot soldier gathered to lift their shields. Some had retained their pikes, and others lifted those discarded or lost on the battlefield. They planted the handles of the long weapons into the ground and held them steady.

Vayla puffed out her cheeks as she exhaled, watching the enemy reinforcements. Though she had seen the monsters up close, she had never fought krahluks before. Eraim warned her about the difficulties of facing the nightmarish creatures, and now they attacked from both sides.

"Archers! Aim for the eyes of the krahluks!" she commanded. "Zhokards! Focus on the lancers!"

Three hundred Dun Lancers survived the myriad of fissures, and they lowered their long black weapons as they made their approach. Their horses pounded the hard soil, picking up speed, and like a dark wave they washed over the shield wall. Several mounts spilled their riders as pikes impaled the animals, but just as many pole weapons were turned away or splintered by the horses' armor.

Vayla thrust her hand forward, and the zhokards advanced. They joined the deteriorating wall of shields, fearlessly accepting lances into their bodies and throwing themselves into horses—anything to dislodge the evil riders from their saddles. Grimmen and his men suffered horrible deaths, but always they returned to the fray to continue their work—times like this made Vayla wish New Palidur had zhokards of their own!

Vayla and Macurak charged with the Palidurians, and Wezlok again produced duplicate images to confound the enemy. The unhorsed lancers were then swiftly defeated, and mounted warriors speared and trampled soldiers that were not there. In minutes, the cavalry's muster was cut in half.

The world trembled, and Vayla spied the approaching krahluks. Though the gray elves had slain over fifty of the rampaging gorillas, two hundred remained and they were closing fast.

Among the flanking army behind Vayla, the dunarchins were few, but the krahluks were breaking through the line—she wondered if any Stone Eagle dwarves still lived. Even with Varlimor dwarves charging to aid the Nirans opposing the advance, Vayla held little hope for success after zreekans appeared. The oddly shaped creatures unleashed dark magic reminiscent of Radaam's evil spells, killing allied soldiers within horrible explosions. Lorians continued to give support, but the number of descending missiles had decreased significantly—how much longer would their help last?

Vayla returned her focus to the surrounding melee. A pair of grounded Dun Lancers rushed Wezlok, forcing him to dismiss his illusions and defend himself with lightning, and the krahluks from Lormin Dmurr arrived. The apes smoked upon entering the golden aura, and Vayla thanked Cafior, hoping the divine touch made the krahluks easier to topple.

"Vayla! Your left!" warned Macurak.

She turned to see Radaam bearing down on her. The evil permeating the battlefield had been so thick that she did not sense his approach, and she barely had time to react as his larger sword struck her injured arm. The pain was excruciating. She fell, unable to defend herself, but a second blow did not land. A spell from Wezlok sent Radaam stumbling to the side and out of reach.

Vayla's arm dangled as she climbed to her feet, and she lifted the golden mace and faced the Death Lord. The arrow still protruded from Radaam's helmet, but he did not seem to notice and he readied his swords. To the dark lord's right flank, Dun Lancers on horseback charged to assist the undead king, but Lindow and a team of Nejans intervened. The mounted soldiers failed to reach their destination, and Radaam remained alone, his armor smoking.

The whispering chant returned, and the Death Lord's eyes grew bright. Every bone in Vayla's body felt as if they were being ripped from their sockets. She dropped to her knees with a scream, but the pain diminished when an explosion erupted at Radaam's feet, releasing her from the torturous magic. It surprised her to see it was Melac that had come to her aid.

The Kalmiran mage was casting another spell when Radaam thrust his fist forward. The Death Lord pulled back, and Melac flew across the field and onto the curved sword.

Vayla had rushed to prevent the wizard's ill fate, but she arrived too late. She struck Radaam's arm, and there was a spark as the evil king's bone snapped. Radaam lost hold of the smaller blade, and Melac fell to the ground, still impaled upon the weapon.

Vayla danced back, and the larger sword whistled just short of her nose. She advanced again, feigning a strike to the head, and as Radaam lifted his blade to parry, she dropped in an attempt to cripple her opponent. But Zhokard Sweep did not achieve the result she desired, and Radaam bore down while she attempted to roll to her feet.

Macurak shouldered the undead king before the sword struck, driving Radaam several paces. The pain of contacting the dark armor was obvious on Macurak's face, and his body stiffened as he collapsed. His situation worsened when Radaam's eyes turned his way and brightened.

Vayla charged as her captain's screams rose above the battle, realizing too late that she played into Radaam's hands. Her desperation had unbalanced her, and the Death Lord came around with his sword. Though the golden glow provided Vayla strength, kept her wounds in check, and weakened Radaam with every passing second, it could not stop the blade arcing toward her neck. Radaam's maneuver was disrupted again, however, and this time by Clanghorr.

Greyor severed one of the Death Lord's legs, and the evil sword narrowly missed Vayla's head. Radaam fell, and Vayla dropped to her knees, crashing her mace onto the dark helmet and extinguishing Radaam's left eye. She swung again and again, and the other eye winked out.

CHAPTER 50

BONES OF DUST

aylun stared at the giant minotaur from behind Uncle
Magneer. The beast was every bit as large as the krahluks
flanking it, but unlike the krahluks, it carried the largest axe
Baylun had ever seen. Its hair was greasy and its eyes red, and its
horns stretched at least eight feet across.

"Take the krahluks!" said Vecnor, pushing his way forward in
spite of his injuries.

While Magneer moved to the right with Desser and Barrelda,
Baylun went left. He knew Kiryanna followed.

The krahluk leaped, and Baylun jumped aside, barely dodging as
its fists smashed into the floor. The force of the blow cracked the
stone for several feet, and it surprised Baylun he and the ape did not
plummet to the lower level. He came across with his axe, slicing into
one of the krahluk's massive arms, and the beast opened its mouth in
a silent cry of pain. Kiryanna's weapon struck twice, but did not
pierce its hide — Baylun wished she would withdraw. The krahluk
swung its other arm, attempting to slam Baylun into the wall, and he
ducked before swinging upward. He sliced deep into the gorilla's
armpit and through half its shoulder, and he brought the axe back
around, cutting into its head. The monster was defeated.

Baylun turned to face the room. An arrow protruded from the
right eye of the other krahluk, and from the shaft he knew it to have
been fired by his father. The beast slapped Uncle Magneer's sword
from his hand, and Cavalor and Desser charged while Barrelda
moved to the monster's flank.

In the center of the chamber, the minotaur bled from its cheek and stomach, and Vecnor dropped his swords to grab its horns as it rushed him. Blood ran from his scalp and shoulder while he fought against the creature, and it drove him several feet and twisted its head, throwing him into the near wall.

Baylun charged, cutting deep into the back of the giant minotaur while Eraim added wounds to its thigh and stomach with Mithkahr. The beast roared as it brought its axe in a wide arc, and the attack passed over Eraim and toward Baylun. He dropped to the floor, narrowly avoiding the axe head, and the weapon decapitated the final krahluk and shattered Cavalor's sword—the Marcove king was nearly struck as well. Mithkahr inflicted a couple more gashes to the minotaur's leg, making it buckle, and Kiryanna thrust her blade into the monster's side.

Vecnor roared, shouldering the beast and driving it across the room. As he passed over his swords, he lifted one and plunged it into the minotaur's snout, and when the monster hit the far wall, the weapon was buried to the hilt.

The guardroom quieted. Vecnor withdrew his blade, allowing the body to fall, and retrieved his other sword.

"Do your best," he said without humor, handing one of his weapons to King Cavalor.

Cavalor eyed the sword with doubt, using both hands to keep it steady.

Brem moved to each of the company, praying over prepared herbs and applying them to injuries. Guilt gnawed at Baylun that he could not use the opal to mend their wounds. He wondered if Nidor had ever experienced such pangs of failure.

"Much better," Kiryanna said to Baylun with a firm nod.

He knew she referred to him dodging the attacks of the krahluk. Had he taken the fire opal for granted? Did his reckless fighting use up Nidor's strength? The guilt on his shoulders grew heavier.

"Perhaps you shouldn't engage with enemies you cannot hurt," he suggested to Kiryanna as gently as he could, knowing his voice to make everything sound harsh.

Kiryanna lifted a brow. "Do you not realize my distractions open the enemy up to you?" She gave a nod. "We are a good team."

She was distracting them? On purpose? Baylun could not fathom entering a fight with such intentions.

Brem finished tending to Vecnor, and the large warrior seemed better off than when Eraim treated him earlier. The priest's shoulders lowered, however, and his pale skin glowed within the shadowy citadel. As well, his oozing spots had nearly coated his face and hands and dark circles underlined his eyes.

Baylun approached Brem. "Here." He offered the fire opal. "The healing doesn't work, but it gives me strength. Perhaps it can help you."

Brem held up a hand to deny the gift. "Thank you, my son. But a strong Baylun will serve us much better than an ailing priest. I shall do what I can."

The marteese made no sense. The citadel would be the death of him.

"Thank you." Kiryanna touched Baylun's arm. "Master Brem accepts his fate, whatever that may be. But your offer of kindness shows strength of heart."

Baylun had a strong heart? It was nice to know Kiryanna thought so.

They exited the room, entering a grand hallway that arced to the right. Baylun eyed the high ceiling, but nothing moved. As they followed the curving corridor, a chill touched his soul, and he wondered if the others felt it as well. It was unnatural.

"Wait!" Selanna had halted. She fished a small bag from her pack and pulled loose the leather strap holding it shut. She stared into the sack for a couple of seconds, and it seemed a shiver traversed her body from head to toe. "Hold your weapons forth."

Vecnor was first to present his blade, and Selanna withdrew what appeared to be powder from the pouch. A handful of powder. She rubbed it onto Vecnor's sword, unflinching even as her hand passed over traces of blood from Vecnor's slain foes. She nodded upon completion, and he stepped away.

"What in Cafior's name?" Uncle Magneer frowned, offering his blade.

"Bone dust." Selanna wiped some on the ranger's weapon. "Trannum's bones," she added, turning to coat Baylun's axe. "It is believed that fighting him with his mortal remains will afford us an advantage. Perhaps make your weapons more effective."

"Perhaps?" Magneer shook his head. "I know I have not faced Trannum before, but trusting our lives to *perhaps* and *maybe* seems extreme."

"The dust is not the only plan," Selanna said. "Now ready your mind for Trannum. He is near."

She nodded to Eraim and Cavalor, who returned the gesture. Baylun was not sure what significance the motions held, and he probably did not need to know.

Once the weapons were prepared, Cavalor and Eraim took positions toward the rear of the company and on either side of Selanna. Romik lagged behind, his face pale and his eyes showing defeat. Baylun wished Nidor's healing would work just one more time.

"Let us move on," Selanna said.

Vecnor and Magneer continued along the wide corridor, and Baylun and Kiryanna walked to their left flank while Desser and Barrelda were to their right. Next were Brem and Gruelenor, and Baylun's father held an arrow to his bowstring. When the end of the hallway came into view, a large door barred the way.

Chapter 51

Healing Water

Vayla had little time to act. Most of the Dun Lancers were defeated, but the krahluks tore through the allied ranks and zreekans devastated her numbers. It was not fair. The creatures did not even belong in Vaeldor! Half of the zhokards had been ripped apart, and their black hearts lay scattered. Gray elves continued raining arrows with deadly precision, but most of the archers were forced to pull swords, and they now attacked with remarkable grace. The Pavish remained strong, and they were the chief reason Vayla found a moment to think.

Her arm dangled as she rushed to Macurak. Her captain struggled, unable to lift himself from the ground—his body shook after his confrontation with Radaam. Behind Vayla, dirt and scratches covered Wezlok and his hair was a mess, but his eyes were ever alert, scanning the battlefield and always returning to her. Greyor drew near, and he turned to face the enemy, as if to protect Vayla while she knelt next to Macurak. Lindow and Larman then barked orders for the Nejans to form a wall. Lorylla arrived, assisting Eimell to a position behind the line of soldiers and steadying him while he held his bow—it was surprising the Vermallon elf still lived after Radaam's spell.

The golden aura retreated as Vayla set her mace aside and retrieved the vial of Healing Water from her pouch. It would have done her well to mend her arm, but that would have to wait. She pulled the stopper with her teeth and poured the contents down Macurak's throat.

Macurak's body calmed in seconds; every wound he had taken

vanished. His expression was grateful, and he nodded his thanks.

Vayla stared into his eyes, knowing this might be the end, and gave him a brief kiss. "When this is over, we have much to discuss."

Macurak revealed his first smile in days. It warmed Vayla, fleeting as it was.

She helped her captain to his feet and lifted her mace, and the golden aura returned. Macurak raised a brow, gazing at the weapon, but there was no time for explanations as the enemy drew to within twenty yards. Would anyone believe the story anyway?

Vayla looked at Wezlok. The elf gave a firm nod. Turning to face the enemy, she took in a deep breath.

"Keep it tight!" Vayla stepped past the wall to lead the charge.

They advanced, and multiple images of Vayla and her warriors fanned out in every direction. This time, there were no less than a dozen illusions of herself, and she knew Wezlok to be expending every bit of energy he possessed.

CHAPTER 52

ROOM OF SHADOW

Selanna's heart raced. The final encounter with Trannum was at hand. It had to be the final encounter. Centuries of planning and the support of the vilest deity allowed the necromancer to mislead her for too long. But his ruse was known. And now it was *his* turn to be surprised. It had to be, or Vaeldor was lost.

Magneer threw open the door at the end of the hall. Though Lormin Dmurr had carried a shadowy atmosphere since they set foot within the citadel, the chamber beyond appeared to be the source of the fog. To the left, the wide staircase led upward to the gates of Thard'Dun; the *Portals of Ultimate Malevolence*.

A pair of glowing blue eyes materialized, hovering in the center of the room.

"Selanna..." came Trannum's voice from everywhere. "I knew you would come."

Vecnor and Magneer entered, their attention held by the eyes, and Baylun, Desser, Kiryanna, and Barrelda followed. Gruelenor remained in the doorway with bow ready—Selanna had prepped each arrow with the bone dust. But how were they supposed to combat the necromancer when he possessed no form? Selanna's shoulders suddenly felt heavy, but she needed to remain strong.

"This will be the last time we meet!" she said.

"How true those words are." The voice moved around the room, each word approaching from a different direction. "I have no more need of you, other than to procure that which you carry."

Selanna held her breath. How could Trannum possibly know? Elgarroth assured her the necromancer could not detect the crystal's

521

presence.

"Tell me," Trannum said. "What form have you and Elgarroth chosen this time?"

She exhaled. The black stick. Not the crystal. Trannum was *not* aware. Still, he reminded her they possessed the only item standing between Uustaag and Vaeldor. Long ago, Welmirth was in a similar situation, scaling Lormin Dmurr while Vennimor battled Uustaag's minions. Welmirth had been the most powerful wizard alive, something Selanna was not—not yet. But she had that which Welmirth did not: Uustaag's tool, and knowledge of its power. Of course, Trannum had not assisted Uustaag last time, but that was an issue Selanna was prepared to address. Uustaag would have to wait. The necromancer needed to be destroyed once and for all.

"No matter," Trannum said. "It shall be mine soon enough. Please, enter my chamber."

"Stop!" Selanna shouted as her companions crept deeper into the room, unsure of what trap the Shadow held ready for them.

"Oh, it is too late for that." Trannum chuckled. "You lost the moment you entered Lormin Dmurr. You see, I am here; in the corridor; in every chamber. I am everywhere. Including inside your very bodies!"

Selanna held an instant understanding of his words. The shadowy air *was* Trannum! He truly was everywhere, and he invaded them with each breath they took. He caught her by surprise—again! And this was confirmed when her body became rigid.

"We must act quickly!" she said to Eraim and Cavalor through clenched teeth.

Forcing her muscles to move, Selanna pulled the magic pouch Elgarroth had given her. It was small, but capable of carrying much more than one would think possible. She dropped to her knees and upended it, spilling the large blue crystal onto the hallway floor. It pulsated, glowing brighter than any of Trannum's orbs from the past.

Selanna forced her body away from the crystal. "Destroy it now!"

They could not. Try as they might, Eraim and Cavalor were unable to swing their weapons with any strength.

Trannum's mocking laughter resounded. "You have been to my old home." He sounded pleasantly surprised. "I forgot that little item existed. Thank you, Selanna. I shall keep it somewhere *very* safe."

Selanna stared in shock. She had failed again.

Nidor raced from the chamber, his body wreathed in flame. The Dale wielded Baylun's axe, and he said nothing as he brought it down in haste. With a single strike, the crystal shattered—the source of Trannum's immortality, gone!

"What?" hissed the necromancer.

The fog throughout the tower retreated into the room to form the Shadow, and everyone moved freely again. Selanna saw she had been mistaken about Nidor—Baylun stood above the glass shards with axe in hand. The young krukari was no longer on fire, but flames engulfed the head of his weapon and his eyes burned, just like Nidor's had in dire times. Without a word, Baylun returned to the chamber, followed by Eraim and Cavalor.

Selanna hurried to the doorway with Brem and Romik close behind. She had conserved most of her strength to this point, and now was the time to act. Trannum fell upon his dark magic, casting black darts, bolts of lightning, and red beams Selanna recognized to hold paralytic properties; and when anyone drew too near, he released waves of force to push them away. Just as she had with the zreekans' attacks in the dining hall, Selanna countered him, redirecting or dissipating his spells before they brought her companions harm. But Trannum was strong, and she could not stop them all. Vecnor and Baylun were launched into a wall, and lightning dropped Magneer to the floor, where his body convulsed. The others approached cautiously, doing their best to dodge the attacks. A dart reached Eraim, and the evil pulse caromed to the ceiling when her black dagger emitted a brief violet glow—Eraim had spoken the truth about the blade protecting her earlier. Unfortunately, the reflected spell rained stones onto Desser and Barrelda, and the two took injuries.

Baylun and Vecnor charged together, and though the krukari was again pushed into the far wall by an invisible force, Vecnor slashed through the necromancer's figure. The path of his sword left a violet line in the shadow that did not fade, and Trannum shrieked, reminiscent of an undead dragon's roar. Gruelenor pierced Trannum with an arrow, leaving a purple dot that expanded, tripling in size.

"Master!" Trannum's voice came from the shadowy form this time, louder than Selanna was accustomed to.

The necromancer attempted to flee up the stairs, and Selanna curled her fingers, as if she held an invisible ball between her hands. Trannum could not move. He continued unleashing spells, but the attacks became desperate and poorly aimed. Still, a red beam struck Barrelda, and the Bomahni warrior fell very near to where Magneer lay.

Vecnor cut into the Shadow again, and Kiryanna thrust her sword while Desser slashed with his, inciting more screams. Another arrow from Gruelenor's bow then passed through the necromancer as Baylun arrived with the flaming axe.

"Master?" The necromancer's voice grew weak.

Baylun's fiery weapon sliced through the Shadow, leaving a violet gap that expanded larger than any of the previous strikes. The darkness was consumed, and the purple haze faded into nothingness.

Everyone stood with weapons ready, searching the chamber. The room remained silent. It seemed to Selanna Uustaag was a cruel master, and perhaps Trannum had served his purpose.

"You may enter," a rumbling voice said from upstairs, shaking the entire citadel. "And bring me the Starrifix."

Was there no end to the Enemy's arrogance? Did he refer to the black stick? Selanna took in a deep breath.

Brem tended to Barrelda. The barbarian's leg was bleeding, but she appeared ready to continue. Kiryanna reported Magneer to be alive, though the ranger did not move, and Desser stood above his father with blood seeping from several small wounds. In fact, Selanna noticed that all of her companions possessed injuries.

"The easy part is over," she mumbled to herself, receiving a look of horror from Eraim. Selanna turned to Brem. "Please, do everything you can. And hurry."

CHAPTER 53

KRAHLUKS

Well over a hundred illusions rushed around the battlefield, frustrating krahluks that swung their enormous fists through opponents that were not there. The gorillas could not express their anger vocally, and they often pounded the ground while hopping—the resulting holes needed to be avoided by allies, lest they lose their footing. The enemy then became hesitant, and Vayla used this to her advantage to get in close. Her mace left violet welts upon their pure black flesh, inflicting visible pain, and she dropped three of the towering foes.

Not all of her soldiers shared in her victories, however. Many of those outside her golden aura failed to penetrate the dark skin, and purple lines were the only evidence their weapons had made contact. This resulted in a slow and costly process for defeating even a single krahluk. Greyor had the most success, as Clanghorr cut through the enemy with ease, and he severed limbs while killing eight that Vayla knew of. But the dwarf charged recklessly into his foes without utilizing his decoys, and she feared for him.

Macurak remained close, working with Vayla. They executed Zhokard Standard most often, splitting the attention of krahluks recognizing them to be actual combatants, and Zhokard Feint drew an unsuspecting monster into their trap. But they dared not perform Zhokard Sweep, for fear of being pulverized by the enormous fists. The giant apes then closed ranks, gathering into small groups to discern real opponents from phantoms, and this made fighting them one at a time impossible.

Vayla lost track of Greyor, but Lindow and Larman joined her and Macurak. Together, they battled three krahluks. Two of the gorillas were felled before a mighty fist struck Lindow, and the general sailed from Vayla's sight. But his false images continued to add to the third krahluk's distractions, and it was defeated shortly after.

Four apes then drove Vayla and her companions back. Lorylla bounded onto the shoulders of one, extinguishing its eyes with her sword and dagger and dropping it. Another krahluk grabbed the gray elf by the leg and tossed her no less than a hundred feet through the air. Eimell pierced the offending monster's eye sockets with arrows from twenty yards away, killing it, but a black bolt struck the Vermallon elf and his body exploded. The sight turned Vayla's stomach, and she gasped at the approaching zreekans.

"The rear guard has failed!" came warnings, too late to help Eimell. But Vayla's spirit rose when hundreds of Pavish intercepted the tentacled creatures.

Vayla, Macurak, and Larman retreated into a cluster of phantom warriors as the other two krahluks pressed, and the monsters were slain. The enemy persisted, however, and before Vayla realized it, six more gorillas advanced toward her small group.

Arrows descended in support, one at a time, and the shafts were long and black. To Vayla's surprise, a single missile was all that was necessary to drop each of the three krahluks that were hit. Turning, she saw Tux. She knew not where he had come from, nor did she care. He released four more arrows, slaying the other three krahluks plus another one nearby. Her hopes rose, if only slightly.

The false images disappeared. Wezlok lay face down, and beyond him hovered a pair of zreekans with their tentacles lashing about.

CHAPTER 54

THE TEMPLE

With the exception of Romik, the company was ready to proceed, even if their wounds were not fully healed. Selanna had watched Baylun and Kiryanna hold a conversation while Brem treated those in need, but their words did not register. It was the fire opal that piqued her interest. She did not know exactly what the jewel was, but it obviously contained a part of Nidor. And now Baylun emitted the same heat the paladin had. Unfortunately, it was not a topic she could pursue. The time to face the Enemy was upon them.

Vecnor led the way with Baylun close behind, and the group crept up the stairs and entered the large temple. The lights of the portals illuminated the chamber, and the air was uncomfortably warm. Amid the six pillars in the center, the altar was whole and covered in fresh blood, and beyond it was a single zreekan. Unlike the zreekans Selanna had seen thus far, its eye was red instead of yellow and it was visibly larger. To either side of the columns were four krahluks, and standing among the three gates was Uustaag. His Hezeb-Ragab helmet was beneath one arm, revealing his hideous face and eyes of red and violet, and planted on the long spikes on each of his shoulders was a human head—likely priests that had gladly parted with them, judging by the frozen expressions of euphoria. Uustaag's enormous sword hung at his waist and his hammer remained strapped to his back.

"You will surrender the Starrifix," the warlord said plainly, continuing to rumble the stone with every word, "and I'll allow you to leave this place alive."

"You will return to your world." Selanna maintained as steady a voice as she could. "You are no longer meant for ours."

"I see." Uustaag drummed his fingers on the pommel of his sword. "How many of you must I kill to change your mind?"

"You can try!" Baylun stepped forward with his axe, surprising Selanna.

"Where did you come by that weapon?" demanded Uustaag. "Torrac was lost long ago."

"I care not for your words," Baylun said.

"No matter." Uustaag's calm demeanor returned. "Though the fire is new, I killed its owner once. I shall do so again."

Uustaag donned his helmet and drew his sword. The blade was twice the size of one of Vecnor's, and wisps of violet smoke rose from its edge.

"This is your final warning." Uustaag's voice sounded more demonic when spoken through the Hezeb mouth. "And there will be no retreat."

The zreekan flailed its tentacles, and Selanna sensed the power the creature drew into itself. It was casting a spell. There was a distant explosion, and she was sure the bridge to the citadel was no more.

"You will not find us easy foes." Selanna hoped she sounded confident.

"Welmirth is long gone," Uustaag said. "Vennimor is dead. And now it's your turn." He stepped around the zreekan and through the pillars. "Dispose of these mortals!"

The krahluks advanced.

"Baylun left!" commanded Vecnor. "Cavalor right! Eraim and Gruelenor, your bows!"

They carried out Vecnor's orders. Magneer went with Cavalor, and Desser and Barrelda followed. Kiryanna joined Baylun. Brem readied his staff, his itching having faded with Trannum's demise, but he remained at Selanna's side.

Before the melee began, Gruelenor dropped a krahluk to the left, needing four attempts to pierce each of its eye sockets. Eraim killed a couple to the right, requiring a single arrow for each.

The runes on Baylun's axe burned brighter within the flames, and he squared off with two of the three krahluks on the left side. He severed the arm of one while easily dodging fists from both—it was as if he had been forewarned of their attacks. He then cut the second monster nearly in half. Next to Baylun, Kiryanna was as nimble as ever, dancing about while issuing small wounds to the third gorilla—her combative skills were reminiscent of Eraim's.

On the other side of the room, Cavalor swung Vecnor's sword with both hands. It surprised Selanna how well the Marcove king balanced the oversized blade, but Magneer had to keep a wide berth, for the arc of each swing reached out to Cavalor's sides. Cavalor issued a couple of wounds, but only managed to slow the monster's advance as he gave ground to avoid being struck. Magneer slashed the other krahluk, barely penetrating the ape's skin, and Desser and Barrelda offered aid, their weapons proving just as ineffective.

Selanna turned her focus to the center of the room—her companions needed to handle the krahluks without her. Uustaag stood, measuring Vecnor.

"You're the people's champion?" The warlord sniffed. "This won't take long."

Uustaag lunged, and Vecnor steered the large blade aside. He countered, and Uustaag was equal to the task. The two repeated the exchange a few more times, like a pair of savvy veterans feeling each other out.

Selanna cast three exploding green spheres, but they never reached the Enemy. The zreekan canceled her magic with its own. She took another approach, attempting to crash a pillar onto Uustaag. Again, the zreekan interfered, casting the column at her and Brem. She swiped her hand to the left, redirecting the projectile to a corner of the temple and nearly striking Romik. When did the young Lord of the Keep enter the room?

It surprised Baylun how easily he adjusted to the strange orange-tinted sight. It was as if each of his eyes saw the enemy, but in a different way—or perhaps in a different time. He knew exactly where the krahluks were, but he also saw what they were about to do just before they did it. And he had no difficulties telling the visions apart.

One gorilla lay dead, and the other was missing an arm. Baylun did not need to rely on any advanced warnings—the next move was obvious. He ducked well before the monster swung, and then rose, slicing his axe through the krahluk's remaining forearm and causing the ape to hop in either anger or pain—he did not care which. He followed the attack by cutting deep into its chest, and it fell.

Kiryanna occupied the other krahluk. Several purple lines decorated the gorilla's body where her golden blade had struck, and trails of its violet ooze seeped from a few. Kiryanna exhibited no wounds. Baylun roared at the monster, gaining its attention, and the marteese backed away.

The enormous foe came down with both fists, but Baylun perceived the maneuver and leaped back. Kiryanna then returned, holding the black dagger Selanna had given her, and she impaled it into the monster's flank. The krahluk spun with its terrible fist aimed at her head, but Romik was there, and he tackled her in time to avoid the strike. Baylun had not anticipated this attack—perhaps his prognosticative vision revealed only actions involving himself. He hacked into the ape's neck, and it stumbled sideways, placing a large hand over the wound as it sprayed the wall with purple blood. He issued another blow, killing it.

Kiryanna and Romik lifted themselves from the floor, and Kiryanna gave Baylun a nod of approval. Baylun did not know why Romik had joined the fight, but he was grateful for his brother's intervention—Kiryanna would have been pulverized.

In the center of the room, Vecnor and Uustaag did a dance of swords, attacking, parrying, countering, and deflecting. Neither had scored a hit.

"Hold back!" Baylun said to Kiryanna.

"I do *not* hold back!" she retorted.

"I didn't say not to fight," Baylun added hastily. "Just wait for your opening!"

Romik gave Baylun a nod.

Eraim stood next to Gruelenor while they trained their bows on the krahluks. The arrows Tux had given her continued to amaze her, as a single shot to the eye was all she needed to drop the massive beasts. To the left, only one gorilla remained, and Baylun issued a terrible wound to its neck, so she and Gruelenor concentrated on the enemies to the right. Unfortunately, the monsters turned their heads so often that clean shots were hard to find — they were surely aware that their weakness was known.

Eraim held her bow steady, waiting for an opening while a krahluk towered over Cavalor. She noticed Gruelenor doing the same with the ape attacking Magneer. Cavalor was driven to within ten feet of the temple wall, and he thrust Vecnor's sword into the krahluk's stomach. The blade did not penetrate far, but the creature certainly felt the sting, and it mouthed what Eraim assumed to be a silent curse as it smacked Cavalor with a backhand. The king crashed into the wall. Eraim released her bowstring, piercing the side of the krahluk's head to steal its attention, and the monster fell. She stared in shock, wishing she had known her arrows did not need to enter the eye!

Gruelenor still had no success with the other krahluk, and his arrows were nearly depleted. Magneer lay on the floor, and Desser and Barrelda fought the gorilla while Brem rushed to help. What was Brem doing? Eraim nocked another arrow.

"Eraim!" Selanna's voice was desperate. "The zreekan!"

Leaving the final krahluk in Gruelenor's hands, Eraim shifted her aim to the monster behind the altar. Its tentacles writhed while its red pupil remained fixed on Selanna. Selanna summoned a bolt of lightning, and as the zreekan's eye pulsated, the spell vanished. Before the pillars, Baylun raced to join Vecnor against Uustaag, with Kiryanna and Romik trailing after him. What was Romik doing?

Eraim shook her head, returning her concentration to the zreekan, and she released her bowstring. The black arrow sped toward its target, but a tentacle seized it at the last moment. The zreekan's eye then locked onto Eraim and fired a dark bolt.

"Down!" Eraim shoved Gruelenor to the floor, landing on top of him.

The evil magic struck very near—perhaps the dagger had protected them—and stones pelted Eraim from where it gouged the wall. But the pain was bearable, and she stood and drew Mithkahr.

Selanna sensed the explosion to her right. She feared for Eraim, but she had to trust that the dagger continued offering its unexpected protection.

While the zreekan focused on Eraim, Selanna launched three more exploding spheres. They struck Uustaag, but dissipated upon the krukari's armor. She felt foolish. Her fear of the spell not reaching the warlord led her to hesitate in using her full power. She immediately regretted that decision as the zreekan's eye returned to her.

"Now it is time to feel my strength!" Uustaag hissed as Baylun joined the melee in the center of the room.

The Enemy moved with impressive speed, beating Vecnor back several paces and not allowing for a counter. Baylun advanced from the side, swinging the flaming axe overhead, but Uustaag lowered his shoulder and thrust it into the young krukari before the weapon struck. Thankfully, Baylun avoided the armor spike, but he was knocked prone. Uustaag followed the attack with his sword, and Selanna reached out to steer the blade aside as it came down with the precision to slice Baylun lengthwise. Again, the zreekan opposed her.

She was powerless to help.

Kiryanna screamed.

The sword did not strike. A rush of fire surrounded Baylun, acting as a shield, and he was untouched. Vecnor used the opportunity to charge, but the warlord spun, forcing him to deflect the giant blade and return to a defensive stance.

Selanna's mind raced. She needed to find a way to help.

Eraim skirted the battle versus the final krahluk as she approached the zreekan. She stepped past the spot where Brem managed to drag Magneer, relieved to see the ranger still breathed. An arrow pierced one of the krahluk's eyes, and the ape thrashed about, forcing Eraim to jump away. Desser and Barrelda pressed as Gruelenor's next arrow penetrated the other eye, and the krahluk fell.

The zreekan's tentacles lashed out from inside the pillars, wrapping around Barrelda's waist and Desser's leg. The two cried out, and the barbarian woman rose ten feet up while Desser was dragged beyond the columns.

Eraim charged, and Cavalor was beside her with the oversized sword—he bled from both nostrils and his mouth, and he was in obvious pain. Having lost his blade, Desser pried at the tentacle wrapped around his leg with both hands. Barrelda slashed desperately at the appendage holding her while she was lowered toward the creature's gaping maw. The zreekan's other tentacles swung to intercept Eraim and Cavalor, its eye never veering from Selanna.

Baylun's vision of Uustaag was different, and he received less warning before the warlord struck. He saw enough to avoid the spike on Uustaag's pauldron—it possessed a bleeding head already—but being shouldered by the Enemy was like being rammed by a charging minotaur, and he crashed to the floor. He then thought his life to be spent when the enormous blade bore down, but flames arose to block the attack.

Baylun regained his feet after Uustaag pressed Vecnor, and the fire continued to surround him. The warlord drove Vecnor several paces before turning back to Baylun, but the eyes peering through the gaping, tooth-filled maw of the helmet focused farther on. Baylun saw briefly the Enemy lunging beyond him, and as Uustaag executed the attack, Baylun was given an opening to strike.

He did not. He could think of only one reason for Uustaag to charge past him, and he fell back, pushing aside a thrust meant for Kiryanna. Unfortunately, Baylun had not planned on his brother rushing to Kiryanna's defense again, and Uustaag's blade sliced through Romik's good arm. Baylun's momentum drove him into Kiryanna, and he knocked her to the floor.

The warlord laughed. It was as if he had performed the maneuver intentionally; as if he had known how Baylun would react.

Uustaag spun, raising his sword to defend against Vecnor's next strike. But the attack came in low. Vecnor cut into the Enemy's leg, and he was left vulnerable for his effort. Baylun roared to gain the warlord's attention. He brought his axe down with all the strength he could muster, knowing Uustaag would parry the blow, but he did not expect the flash of light that resulted. The evil sword was broken.

Uustaag bellowed, shaking the foundations and staggering Baylun again. The Enemy pulled the massive hammer with a sweeping motion, and the head glanced off Vecnor and crashed into Baylun.

Eraim thought of retreating to use her bow. Two of the zreekan's tentacles were occupied and it might not snatch her arrow this time. But she worried what the exploding goop would do to her companions. One tentacle reached for her, and she ducked beneath and slashed with Mithkahr, cutting the appendage loose. She then jumped aside as the severed tentacle continued to writhe.

The other tentacle wrapped around Cavalor's waist, and the king released Vecnor's sword and pulled his black dagger. The weapon sliced easily through the zreekan's skin, and the creature surrendered its hold.

Barrelda cried out as the pointed teeth sank into her shoulder, and Desser called to her, now upside down to await his turn. Eraim charged and thrust Mithkahr into the zreekan's bloated, potato-like body, and it quivered as it swung Desser like a club. She ducked to the side and spun, ready to strike again, but Uustaag emitted a cry that rattled the citadel. The violent shaking made it hard to move, and Eraim was sent tumbling when Desser smashed into her.

She halted upon hitting the wall, and her attention moved to the gates. The lights had become brighter shades of gray, red, and purple. From the red arch flew human-sized creatures on bat-like wings, emitting eerie wails from their toothless mouths. Their eye sockets were hollow, they had no noses, and gray hair streaked back from their skull-like heads. In place of their legs were scorpion-like tails with stingers at the ends, and four arms extended from their torsos, two from the shoulders and two from their midsections. All four hands held swords or daggers.

Chapter 55
No End in Sight

Vayla ran to Wezlok. He was alive, and there were no obvious wounds. Macurak and Larman joined her while Greyor, Grimmen, and six zhokards made a protective circle.

Wezlok stirred. "Ah, my dear Vayla." His voice was barely audible above the din.

"Where are you hurt?" Vayla dug into her pouch for the final healing vial.

"I am spent," Wezlok replied. "I have overextended myself." He took in a shaky breath. "Do not waste your Palidurian waters on me. Use it on your arm. You will be in need of it."

"He speaks the truth." Tux suddenly stood next to Vayla. "*Your* health is more important."

The gray elf put an arrow to his bowstring with amazing speed and released it; then another. He was effortless in his actions, and Vayla was sure two krahluks or zreekans had just expired. She looked at Wezlok, and his eyes began to close.

"I need you!" Tears issued as she pulled the stopper with her teeth.

"Please, no," Wezlok said weakly. "There is no time to argue. Your grandmother bought my life. And now I have paid her in full. With no regrets."

"No!" Vayla thrust the vial into his mouth, forcing every last drop down his throat.

Without waiting to see the results, she grabbed her mace and rose. Tux was no longer beside her—he stood fifty yards away, shooting his bow. The krahluks were very near, and she raised her weapon, stepping to Macurak's side. The golden glow intensified, lessening her pain as Cafior soared through her body.

An eruption resonated across the sky, but it did not originate from the melee. Half the citadel had crumbled. Many of the krahluk's hesitated, looking back as if plagued by indecision. From Lormin Dmurr, a cloud approached. But it was not a cloud. It was a swarm of flying creatures. Vayla did not know if the explosion was a good thing or bad, but the battle was not over.

She charged into the krahluks while they remained stunned, crashing her mace into the leg of one and knocking it to the ground. Macurak pierced his sword into one of its eyes, and Grimmen stabbed the other.

A roar sounded from the east, and a squadron of dwarves advanced on the zreekans, hacking and smashing into their ranks even as they were felled by deadly magic or thrown by tentacles. The Lorian elves followed the attack, filling the sky with arrows—there were at least a thousand! An arrow sailed just past Vayla, sinking deep into the head of a krahluk that had flanked her. It was from Tux, and he slew the monster with the single shot.

"To me!" Vayla commanded, realizing her men to be spreading too thin. She needed to keep them together.

Her order echoed several times, and soldiers able to heed the call retreated her way. Tux continued dropping krahluks, his focus seemingly bent around Vayla, and Greyor advanced, recklessly hacking into all enemies—it seemed the monsters regarded the dwarf with fear. The remaining host of the Pavish stormed the krahluks, and it amazed Vayla to see at least five hundred barbarians still fought.

The flying creatures arrived, appearing as demonic undead beings with four arms. They descended onto the battlefield, slashing viciously with swords and daggers and striking with twin scorpion-like tails. Victims of the stingers emitted gurgling screams as their mouths issued foam, and they collapsed—a process needing only a few seconds.

CHAPTER 56

STARRIFIX

The force of the enormous hammer inflicted pain unlike any Baylun could imagine. It was as if his bones had been crushed in a single moment. The flames surrounding his body winked out as he flew across the chamber, bounced off a pillar, and landed near the portals. It surprised him he could still see. He was amazed he still breathed.

Baylun sat up, even more shocked that he felt no pain and bore no injuries. He should be dead. He should be worse than dead. It had to be the work of the fire opal, and he thanked Silcor; he thanked Nidor.

The glowing of the arches intensified, and from the red portal issued hideous flying creatures. The heat of the opal then grew stronger than ever, though it did not harm Baylun, and he pulled it from his pouch. It was cracked. He was not sure why, but he knew what he had to do. He rose and cast the jewel onto the floor, shattering it and releasing the entrapped flame. It surged into a bonfire, and Nidor stood within.

Nidor gave Baylun a nod before racing into the midst of the three portals. The paladin swung his flaming sword faster than Eraim could release arrows from her bow, and each strike reduced an emerging enemy to searing ash. Even as krahluks charged from the gray mist and zreekans from the violet, Nidor allowed nothing to pass.

The scene was mesmerizing, but Baylun tore his attention away. Tears streaked Kiryanna's cheeks, and she held her golden blade ready while Vecnor continued the fight against Uustaag. Romik lay on the floor, and the arm struck by the evil sword had turned to ash with purple cinders.

Uustaag glared at Nidor from beneath the demon helmet, and Baylun sensed ire within the warlord's ensuing roar. The giant krukari went into a rage, swinging the hammer at Vecnor again and again. Vecnor steered the strikes aside as only he had the strength to do, but he would not last much longer.

Baylun charged.

Eraim did not know how, but Nidor was suddenly between the gates. Though several beasts had already escaped through the opening in the ceiling, the Silcor paladin fought like ten men to disallow any more. Eraim's spirit rose, and she returned her attention to the zreekan behind the altar.

Blood adorned Cavalor, both red and violet, and he had freed Desser and Barrelda using only the black dagger. Desser now pulled Barrelda's limp body away, struggling with only one working leg — the one the zreekan had constricted dragged behind him. The creature flailed its remaining tentacles at Cavalor, and the king dodged as he looked for an opening.

Eraim advanced, and the monster shot another evil bolt her way. She did not veer from her path this time, and as expected, the dagger gave off a vibration and the spell caromed into the wall. Eraim jumped over a tentacle as it lashed out, landing in a roll and rising with a thrust into the creature's body. While she executed the maneuver, Cavalor stabbed his black dagger into the zreekan's back and ripped the blade downward. The creature shook as its mouth opened wide, but it made no noise. A few seconds later, it slumped and ceased to move.

Turning to the center of the chamber, Eraim gasped when Uustaag's hammer sent Vecnor flying across the room. Baylun was no longer engulfed by fire, and he and Kiryanna rushed to attack the Enemy.

Eraim sprung from the pillars and charged.

Selanna continued searching for ways to aid her companions. How did the zreekan keep its eye on her while fighting Eraim and Cavalor? She then understood the reason for the positioning of the creature. The bloody altar intensified its power. That was how it nullified her magic.

A bright flame arose to the back of the chamber, and Selanna could not believe her eyes. Nidor had returned! All at once, the fire opal made sense. Nidor could not journey with them to Lormin Dmurr while he lived. Had he been with them, his presence would have been known when they approached from the south; when they hid among the Pavish; when they sneaked into the courtyard. Had any paladins accompanied them, the enemy might have overwhelmed them before they ever entered the citadel, and the black stick would have been lost. It was not a chance they had been willing to risk. Whether consciously or subconsciously, Nidor sacrificed himself in Darum Carumbor, and Silcor preserved his spirit within the gem. It was as if he had been born for this very purpose; a paladin out of Holindale, a realm often overlooked. Selanna doubted even Nidor was aware of his destiny until his demise.

And so, a part of Uustaag's plan had been foiled. Selanna had no doubt the warlord held back some of his troops, waiting for the right moment to devastate his enemies and break their wills. But with Nidor disallowing the evil reinforcements, that time would not arrive.

Amid the pillars, the zreekan slumped over the altar. Eraim and Cavalor stood on either side of the creature, splattered in its horrible blood. There would be no more interference!

Selanna's focus shifted to the battle against Uustaag. She stared in horror as the giant hammer crashed into Vecnor and he tumbled across the floor—never in her lifetime did she expect to witness such an occurrence. It then amazed her to see Baylun return to the fray. She thought the young krukari to be dead, but it was not so; and though he lacked the aura of fire and his weapon and eyes no longer burned, his expression showed no fear as he and Kiryanna advanced.

Uustaag readied his hammer for Baylun's approach, but then he spun away. Brem had joined the melee unnoticed, and the priest stabbed the warlord with a black dagger—Selanna did not know where the marteese procured the blade, since she had not issued him one. Uustaag brought the hammer overhead and straight down, and the citadel shook as Brem was crushed—Selanna averted her gaze at the moment of impact.

Uustaag turned, knocking Baylun's axe aside—the giant krukari was seemingly unconcerned with Kiryanna, allowing his armor to turn away her golden blade. Baylun then held a more defensive posture than usual, and he displayed surprising strength when he deflected the hammerhead again and again. But he found no room to counter.

Selanna needed to act. From the way her exploding globes failed to harm Uustaag earlier, she did not trust using fire or lightning, so she issued waves of force. It was magic similar to the bridge she created for her and Eraim to cross the Stony River, but utilized differently. Though the spells would not topple the massive warrior, she hoped to upset his balance; perhaps create an opening for her companions.

Eraim and Cavalor arrived, and Mithkahr cut into Uustaag's thick plates while Cavalor's dagger snapped upon its first strike. Uustaag spun with the hammer, nearly taking off Kiryanna's head, and Selanna released a burst of energy to lift the enormous weapon up and over Cavalor and Eraim as well. The hammerhead crashed through a pillar, spraying stones across the chamber.

"The time is now," a voice whispered, and Selanna was sure it spoke only to her. Was it Elgarroth? It might have been Nidor. No. It was a female voice from years ago. Merssa had uttered the words, and Selanna understood what she needed to do.

She pooled magical energy as her focus shifted to Eraim, the one companion Selanna knew to be the most difficult to trap. To capture.

To kill. She trusted no other to carry the reformed stick. Though the others possessed the black crowns remade into small weapons, Eraim's dagger was different.

"Eraim!" Selanna called out. "Your dagger!"

Eraim rolled safely away from Uustaag and rose to one knee. She frowned at Selanna without comprehension.

"Throw it to me!" Selanna said.

She was confident her friend knew better than to remain confused or ask questions, and in a flash, Eraim pulled the dagger and cast it at Selanna. Selanna released a bit of energy to catch the blade as it came to within reach, and she plucked it from the air. It transformed into the black stick, and then into something completely different.

Selanna held a dark jewel that burned with an inner violet light. It emitted a power so mighty that her own strength grew. But also it contained an element of nauseating waves that soured her stomach and made her insides rot. She felt more powerful than she could have ever imagined as energy rushed to her from distances she thought impossible; energy from another world. Selanna could destroy Uustaag if she wished; there was nothing he could do to stop her. To use such magic, however, would increase the decay that spread inside her.

She looked at her companions. They were different. They aged and withered before her eyes. She, on the other hand, was immortal, and her sight passed beyond Lormin Dmurr and across Vaeldor, watching all things birth, wither, and die. Except for her. She was the constant. She survived all. She *was* all.

Selanna shook her head. She sensed invisible tendrils rising from the jewel to pierce her skin, trying to take root, and they were pure evil. But the images were not from the item Uustaag referred to as the Starrifix. They were from Thard'Dun, sent to tempt her. She dared not use the power, not even against Uustaag, for it would give Thard'Dun a hold over her. Trannum must have succumbed to a similar temptation. And now Uustaag headed straight for her. He knew what she possessed.

Baylun swung the mysterious axe into the warlord's leg and cut deep. Uustaag barely noticed, and he knocked Cavalor aside with his gauntlet as the king attempted to impede him. Vecnor then slammed into the warlord.

Vecnor? He had not moved for several seconds, but he hit Uustaag harder than any of Selanna's spells. The two of them crashed to the floor, and it appeared as though the teeth of the Enemy's helmet were biting Vecnor while they grappled. Baylun dropped the axe, likely fearing to strike his companion, and joined the brawl. Uustaag released the hammer and attacked with his spiked gauntlets while the Hezeb jaws continued to gnash.

Thoughts, memories, and impulses flooded Selanna as Thard'Dun probed her mind. She resisted, trying to discern how to close the portals where Nidor fought to deny entry. Elgarroth did not have the answer. He said it would come to her, but she could think of nothing.

"Star affixed..."

The line from the prophecy escaped Selanna's lips; she knew not why. Starrifix! She had misunderstood it.

"Holy hand..." she whispered, watching Nidor. "Gates are, the key. Starrifix in holy hand. Flame not flame."

The gates are. They exist. The key, she held in her fingers. Holy hand... Flame not flame... the Silcor paladin.

"Nidor!" Selanna called out.

The burning Dale turned to face her, and she cast the Starrifix at him. He caught the jewel while krahluks, zreekans, and flying creatures slipped past, and its violet pulse weakened within his flames. Selanna sensed the power of Silcor wash over the room, and though Brem lay crushed and motionless, a green aura surrounded him and the strength of Frayorna was present as well.

Vecnor now bled from several locations, but he refused to yield, and he and Baylun kept Uustaag from regaining his feet—Baylun was also covered in his own blood. Cavalor, having gained possession of Kiryanna's blade, struck the warlord's helmet in a failed attempt to knock it free. Kiryanna joined the scrum, wrapping her body around one of the Enemy's arms to restrain it, and Gruelenor carefully thrust his sword into the armor plates. Eraim, meanwhile, used her bow to assist Nidor until her final arrow was spent.

The flying monsters continued to disappear through the opening in the ceiling while krahluks and zreekans swarmed Nidor. But even without Eraim's aid, the holy fire surrounding the paladin denied their attacks. Nidor then lifted the Starrifix and moved it about each gate, as if tracing runes in the air. His hand was surely guided by divine intervention, and one by one the glowing mists dulled.

"No!" Uustaag roared, likely feeling his connection to Thard'Dun's world dissipating.

Nidor continued in his task while the creatures desperately tried to stop him. Selanna cast spells to aid the Dale, not wanting to risk the enemy gaining possession of the jewel, and a surge of power encompassed the temple when the paladin lifted the Starrifix high.

There was a flash of golden light from the opening to the roof, and Selanna sensed the presence of Arronaus, Soleran, and Cafior. Amid the gates was then a puzzling sight. Standing next to Nidor was Nilborg, and Brem and Hubrid joined them. And then Merssa. They all clutched the jewel within their single fist. Another figure appeared, one Selanna recognized from her many trips across Palidur Bridge. It was Vennimor. The ancient paladin added his hand to those already holding the Starrifix. The jewel shattered.

A surge of violent energy filled the room. Selanna put forth all of her power in defense, but she sensed it was not her strength alone. Half of the chamber exploded, destroying the krahluks, zreekans, and arches while her magic protected the other side and all of her companions. The openings to Thard'Dun's world were gone, but unlike closing a gate, none of the invaders having entered Vaeldor were pulled back through.

Selanna's protection shielded Uustaag as well, and he rose in a fury, throwing Vecnor, Baylun, and Kiryanna from his body. Selanna turned on the Enemy, holding nothing back—there was nothing to hold back for. She wrapped energy around the large krukari to restrain him and toppled a pillar onto his head. She then released green bolts of magic to rip the flesh from his bones—an incantation she would never use on any living being under any other circumstances.

Even without the portals, Uustaag was pure strength, and he broke loose from the restricting spell while the column rolled from his evil helmet with little visible damage. The bolts, however, caused him to bellow as they tore open his skin in several locations.

More of the failing citadel crumbled, and Selanna rerouted her magic to hold it together. Kiryanna returned Baylun's axe to his hands, and he struck Uustaag in the side while Cavalor pierced the armor with the golden blade and Eraim drove Mithkahr into the warlord's stomach. Uustaag dropped his head back, roaring louder than before and shaking the foundations beyond what Selanna believed she could control. But then Vecnor plunged his sword into the open Hezeb-mouth, and the Enemy's cry abruptly ended.

Uustaag fell.

CHAPTER 57

LAST BREATH

Vayla prayed her father had survived the explosion within the citadel. She also prayed she had the strength to battle yet another foe she knew nothing about.

Hundreds of the flying demons had emerged from Lormin Dmurr, and Vayla braced herself as a score of the monsters headed her way. But as they came to within fifty yards, a loud *clap* resonated and they crashed into each other. It was as if opposing walls had collided, and their bodies plummeted, crushed and oozing black fluids. Behind Vayla, a very pale Wezlok was on one knee with his hands extended, as if he had just slapped them together.

Vayla could not help but smile. She wished the elf had the power to drop all the flying creatures from the sky.

She charged a nearby krahluk with Macurak at her side. But something had changed. The gorilla was like a feral beast. It fought with desperation, flailing its fists wildly as if cornered and fending for its life. Vayla was lucky to dodge the blows, but it was not so for Macurak, and he was knocked several yards away.

Vayla gave ground, taking a defensive stance. But the ape ceased its attack and grasped at its throat. All the krahluks did the same—it was as if the creatures could not breathe. They began collapsing, and so did the zreekans and flying demons, until all of them were motionless.

The combatants of the battlefield stared in disbelief. It was not a dream; Vayla's pain was too real. Though few, the Dun Lancers then resumed the battle, fighting until the last of them perished, while the minotaurs and hobgoblins fled into the south.

Vayla would have preferred to chase down the evil minions for their crimes against Vaeldor, but her warriors were exhausted. She was exhausted. Most of her men allowed their weapons to drop as smiles or tears invaded their filthy, blood-streaked faces. Several fell to their knees.

Vayla rushed to Macurak. He was alive, but badly broken.

"Healing!" she cried. "I need a priest!"

Her mind raced, desperate for a solution. She had not used her final elixir on herself—she counted on Cafior's protection to see her through. But neither did she save it. She wasted it on Wezlok! No. It had not been a waste. Wezlok needed it.

"I love you," Macurak managed through blood-covered, quivering lips.

A shadow fell over them as Wezlok moved unsteadily behind Vayla. He extended a shaky hand, and in it was the vial she discarded after healing him.

"Not a drop was lost," the wizard said.

Confusion threatened to overwhelm Vayla, but she could not afford such a reaction. She took the bottle and removed the stopper with her teeth. It was full. Pouring the contents into Macurak's mouth, she followed it with a firm kiss, in case it was too late. But his arms moved, and they drew her in tight.

Vayla pulled back, laughing and sobbing at the same time. She could not remember the last occasion she had cried as much. She looked at Wezlok, and tears filled his eyes as well.

"I told you it would do me no good." The wizard shrugged. "I did not allow a single drop to escape."

"Thank you." Vayla gently laid Macurak's head on the ground before rising to embrace the elf.

Wezlok did not flinch in the slightest, and he returned the hug.

After releasing the elf, Vayla noticed Greyor watching with a quizzical expression.

"Now I've seen everything!" The dwarf gave a hearty chuckle.

"Hail! Lady Vayla!" Grimmen dropped to a knee, and the

surviving zhokards did the same.

Vayla looked around. Most of the troops had drawn near, and they followed Grimmen's lead and kneeled upon the blood-soaked, body-riddled, broken field. Greyor took a knee. Lorylla arrived with a severe limp, and she kneeled. Vayla saw High Paladin Zeratar of the Arronaus Sector, and he was kneeling—she had not even known he was with them. Wezlok remained standing.

"Now what?" asked Macurak, appearing stronger as he pushed himself into a seated position.

Vayla faced the citadel. "We storm Lormin Dmurr! Leave no stone unturned! Destroy all evil hiding within!" She turned to her army. "And find our heroes!"

A roar resounded as everyone stood with a fist in the air, and they marched upon the walled fortress.

CHAPTER 58

AFTERMATH

Selanna held Lormin Dmurr together. She could feel the stones breaking apart, and it took nearly all of her strength to prevent it. One last gift from Nidor before he and the other holy spirits disappeared was a final blast of Silcor's Healing Flame, and everyone moved without assistance, including Romik and Barrelda. As for Brem, there was no way to carry his mangled body, so Selanna employed what power she could spare to lift his remains and bring him along.

They fled down the citadel to its entrance, where the bridge was no more. There, Selanna slowly released her support of the stronghold as she extended a magical force. She hurried the company across the invisible platform, even before the spell's completion, and the farther she stretched the bridge, the more Lormin Dmurr crumbled into the river.

Selanna was the last to step onto the far side, and she and the citadel collapsed in unison. Not a trace of the dark structure remained. She closed her eyes, wanting to sleep for a year, but Eraim shook her and asked repeatedly if she was all right. Selanna nodded and climbed to her feet.

It was not long before Vayla arrived with the army, and there was great relief and many hugs—none greater than that between Vayla and Cavalor. The grounds of Lormin Dmurr were then purged of evil, and a search for survivors on the battlefield began. The corpses of Uustaag's minions exuded fear even in death, making the process take longer than it should have, but hundreds of wounded soldiers were found. Lindow was among them, battered but alive, and the Nejans rejoiced—none more than Larman. Vayla was extremely pleased as well.

She and the paladins and priests administered every healing herb and spell they possessed, taking care of the worst cases first. Even after the herbal supply was depleted and divine magic exhausted, thousands were yet in need. Splints were then applied, and makeshift stretchers transported those unable to walk. As for the fallen soldiers, Vayla vowed to send wagons and remove the corpses to friendlier lands once time permitted.

Many thanks and farewells were given to Pargahnu and the Pavish, who departed into the west. Desser and Barrelda remained with the allied army, but Desser promised Pargahnu to return to Pavan soon.

The journey across Helmland took several days. Upon reaching Darum Carumbor, Vayla saw that Wezlok's spell of destruction had left the walls charred, but he failed to topple the structure. The army continued toward Beit, giving the tower a wide berth. Baylun refused to look at it.

Benzon lay half in ruin. The flanking legion of Helmland had stormed its walls with dunarchins, krahluks and zreekans, but in their haste to pursue the allied force, they moved on before the city was completely defeated. Nyer survived the assault, though barely, and he gave praises to Burnod, who led the defenses after he was unable to do so.

Onzac had not been so lucky, and the survivors were few. Palidurians were filled with sorrow upon learning of Grand Paladin Montac's demise, and his body was taken to New Palidur for a proper funeral.

Of the soldiers that fought against the forces of Uustaag and Trannum, they returned to their homelands to mend, and most refused to relive the horrors they witnessed at the Battle of the

Broken Land. But this did not stop the many celebrations that ensued, and it seemed even the evil creatures of the forests and mountains ceased with their raids for several months in recognition.

In Neja, Lindow and Larman returned with less than a quarter of what had marched into the war, and they were all regarded as heroes. Lindow was forced into retirement, for his right arm and leg were beyond repair and he was no longer fit for battle, but the people of Eastgate were happy to see him elevated to baron by the king of Neja.

Baron Lindow took the throne in Eastgate to govern the eastern border, ending the reign of the Karlsum line that lasted more than seventy years. Lindow promoted Captain Larman to general, and he converted several buildings into barracks to show a stronger military presence. The city then veered away from the lawless settlement it was infamous for.

The Nejan soldiers spoke often about Vayla, the fearless paladin, and how Cafior had influenced the war, and the religion spread throughout the region. To the surprise and pleasure of Lindow and Larman, Vayla visited whenever she was in the area. Unfortunately, those occasions seldomly came to pass.

The surviving gray elves were uncomfortable in the company of other races, and they returned to Orlenfel Forest shortly after the war. Lorylla, however, was at complete ease, and she celebrated months longer than those of her kin.

She traveled first to New Palidur, where she was honored, and then to the Varlimor Mountains to revel with the dwarves. She was a giant among the mountain folk, and many were hesitant in her presence, but Greyor included her in all festivities, making the days worthwhile.

Lorylla then passed into Kalmaar, where she spent a month in Darmhorng Castle. Queen Elloria and King Sullis welcomed her even more than did the Palidurians and dwarves, and she enjoyed time with her old friends before finally returning home.

After a couple of months in Philen, Romik resumed his duties as Lord of Ironside Keep in the Varlimor Mountains. He viewed the loss of his arm as a great disappointment, but his Granduncle Arkor found it amusing.

Arkor commissioned the dwarves to create an attachment for Romik's missing limb. It bore a hook at the end, but also it converted into a small crossbow. Romik's uncle spent months teaching him how to use the apparatus, and before long, Romik felt himself again — at least at heart.

He searched for the dwarf that had sold him Baylun's axe, hoping to learn more about the crafting of the weapon. But none of the local dwarves seemed to know of whom he spoke. He described the smith, mentioning how the dwarf's arms were larger than those of the Stone Eagle dwarves', to which the Varlimor dwarves appeared offended. But they insisted no such smith lived within Morimont. Romik thought it peculiar, but he gave up the search, not knowing where else to look.

His desire to spend more time with his family became unbearable, and since their lives were busy and they seldom found their way to Ironside Keep, he journeyed to Philen at least twice a year. He and Baylun grew even closer after the war, but he missed the days of being the protective older brother — Baylun radiated confidence and needed no protection.

Romik married two years later, after impressing a young lady in Denvale. Though she was a Marc, it was obvious from her dark skin that her family originated in Holindale. They were happy within Ironside Keep, and Romik was especially glad for her companionship when Granduncle Arkor passed away from old age.

During their second year of marriage, they were blessed with a child — the only one to result from their union. And though it was a girl, Romik trained her nonetheless to one day become Lady of the Keep.

Baylun and Desser returned to Philen with their fathers, Gruelenor and Magneer. Accompanying them were Kiryanna and Barrelda. The king of Philen spared no expense, providing grand celebrations for the heroes, and the festivities lasted half the year.

During that time, Magneer was named Duke of West Palidur, for the reigning lord did not survive the war. Magneer held mixed feelings with the honor bestowed upon him, for it would greatly reduce his ventures into the mountains to hunt, but his wife, Kalette, was very pleased.

Magneer informed Della of Daymyn's death, mentioning only that her son had been killed in battle. No one spoke otherwise, sparing her the heartbreak. Della moved in with Magneer and Kalette, where she lived until eventually finding happiness with a local farmer.

Desser broke the news that he was to live in Pavan with the survivors of Barrelda's tribe, much to the dismay of his relatives, and after three months, he made good on his word. But he visited Philen once a year. Barrelda became more fluent with the common tongue, though she never used it while among her people, and she enjoyed the annual visits to West Palidur, when she would dress as a princess and "feel pretty" for the entire stay. Her mannerisms remained barbaric, but no one dared to mention such things in her presence.

The Bomahni lost nearly three quarters of their population during the war. But their tribe was held high in Pavan, and all others stood in respect when they passed, foregoing the normal disputes over territories. Desser's skills in hunting continued to impress them, and he taught them everything he knew. Though he was never completely accepted as one of the tribe, life was good, and he especially enjoyed the large game Pavan provided. He even killed a golden bear, and he made a special journey to show the prize pelt to Baylun and Romik.

Barrelda bore six children, the eldest of which was eventually regarded as the greatest hunter of all Bomahni, and he rose to become chief.

Baylun was never the same after his time in Helmland. He became more outgoing, unaffected by the stares or teasing others held for him—there existed few that exhibited such behavior anymore. Most knew him to be a hero, and he was respected, and those that did not know him hesitated to gain his attention, for he was formidable to look at.

He enjoyed life, in large part due to Kiryanna's companionship, and they were married in West Palidur a year after the war's end. Kiryanna was the most beautiful bride in her golden dress. Baylun's mother could not believe his good fortune, and Lorin and Kiryanna spent lots of time together. Kiryanna bore three kids, two boys and a girl, and though none of them shared in her beauty, Baylun was happy that his daughter came close. Kiryanna and Lorin failed to notice flaws with any of them.

Duke Magneer made Baylun and Kiryanna captains among his army, and they often led forays into the wilderness to defeat raiding goblins or hobgoblins. They eagerly accepted every chance to fight side by side, exhibiting skills unmatched by any other duo within the realm, and Baylun especially enjoyed the opportunity to continue using his axe. After learning the weapon's name from Uustaag, Baylun tried and failed to discover what it meant. But he called it Torrac nonetheless, and it was not long before all of Philen knew of its might.

Gruelenor retired from fighting and hunting, settling down with

Lorin for good and caring for his grandchildren when Baylun and Kiryanna were away. He continued his worship of Silcor, and in taverns he shared stories of Nidor's amazing accomplishments, as well as the sacrifices the Dale made for all of Vaeldor. Together, Gruelenor and Magneer commissioned a grand church to be built in the fire god's name, and a statue of Nidor was erected in its courtyard.

Cavalor stayed in New Palidur for a couple of months after the war. But his realm had been without their king for too long, and he returned to Marcove and Castle Lambrak. With him were only five zhokards, as Grimmen requested to remain with Vayla as a personal guard, and Cavalor granted the application with his blessing.

The first order of business within Marcove was to visit the hill where Cavalor's mother defeated Cadorn, and he knelt before the statue of Merssa to give a full account. As he finished the tale, a warm breeze brushed over him, and he basked in his parents' love.

He also spent time in the western region of the realm to regale the Marc-Dale citizens with the heroics of Nidor. The people were proud, and Cavalor commissioned a church of Silcor to be built in every major city, so they could worship their deity and their hero properly.

Cavalor's daughter visited Castle Lambrak when she could, but Vayla became extremely busy as the years passed. It was her passion, however, and Cavalor loved that about her. She lived the life that was intended for him when he was young, though it was not meant to be. And she was better suited for it than he ever was.

Greyor arrived in Morimont a celebrated warrior again. They showered more praises upon him than after the last time he battled Trannum, and the occasion was more enjoyable, for he spoke of how Radaam was defeated, instead of how the Death Lord escaped. He also captivated his kin with the successes of Clanghorr, Destroyer of Evil!

Once the celebrations ended, Greyor returned to the work that kept him busy for the past twenty years. He still desired to return to Lornibur, the birthplace of the dwarfish race, and he sensed that time to be drawing near.

Vayla's life was forever changed. Though the comparisons between her and Merssa eased, she felt a strong kinship with the late High Paladin and found she missed them. She never passed through the Cafior Sector without stopping to pay respect to her grandmother's statue. "Thank you, Grandmother," she always whispered, no matter what kind of day she was having. She was raised to Paladin because of her connection to Cafior, but she discovered what it was to *be* a paladin during the war. And Merssa played a large part in that. Being a paladin was more than a title and battling evil in the name of Cafior. It was loving the world that He provided, and maintaining balance within all facets of her life.

Through Burnod, Vayla realized folks were not evil simply because of where they were born. She and the ex-general became somewhat friends, bearing much respect for each other, and she was glad to hear he had taken the throne in Benzon to begin Beit's reconstruction. Though the realm's citizens were thought to have been decimated, it was discovered that thousands of guards had used their Blood River potions for reasons other than why they were supplied. They kept their families alive and hidden among the wild. As well, those held prisoner in Maple Lore Forest were granted amnesty and released.

The Beitians worked to mend their cities, and Palidurian laborers assisted in the matter. Though there was friction in the beginning, they eventually learned to work together.

"You really must change the color of your buildings," Vayla said to Burnod. She and the ex-general were walking the streets of

Benzon during a visit to check on the city's progress.

Burnod frowned. "What? *White*?"

"What a wonderful idea!" Vayla held a mocking smile. "It is much more pleasant than that dark stone you people use."

"No." Burnod stopped. "Do you realize how much it snows up here? *Everything* would be white!"

"No." Vayla looked about the street. "Your black doors will stand out better, and people won't be so glum all year."

"No!" Burnod growled. "Do you know how hard it is to keep your eyes open in your ridiculous city when the sun glares off absolutely everything?"

Vayla resumed walking. "I think you should go with your first suggestion. White sounds marvelous!"

King Burnod painted the buildings light brown.

Upon returning to New Palidur, Vayla was shocked when Lord Rholmar informed her she was to ascend to Grand Paladin. It had been a unanimous decision of what remained of the High Order.

"I cannot take that title!" Vayla said. "Surely Nyer is better suited to—"

"My dear." Nyer almost smiled. "The position is not for the eldest, nor the wisest. That is why we have the High Order: to advise."

"Besides," added Lord Rholmar, "when Nilborg and I rebuilt this city, it was with the intention that the title be bestowed upon one that is respected, and not only within the city's walls. All peoples of Vaeldor hold your name in the highest regard. Even the great wizard, Elgarroth, is aware of your potential. He cautioned Montac that to proceed without you at the head of the army would bear disastrous results. He seemed to believe only *you* could lead Vaeldor to victory."

Vayla thought about his words. They made sense. And she could do the citizens a lot of good. There were a few minor issues about the Holy City she found irritating.

"Very well." She lifted her chin. "My first act will be to alter my surname. I shall now be addressed as Grand Paladin Vayla

Goldmace." She eyed Nyer. "And... High Paladin Nyer?"

"Yes?"

"It is Grand Paladin Vayla, or Grand Paladin." She gave the Soleran paladin a playful glare. "Not *my dear*."

"My apologies, Grand Paladin." Nyer grinned as he tilted his head.

Vayla returned to the Cafior Sector, still unsure about the change. But also she had an extra hop in her step as she hastened to tell Merssa's statue.

"Grandmother," she said with half a grin. "I have attained a position you never did. Ha!" And she stuck out her tongue. She knew Merssa was proud and would not mind the playful teasing.

"Grand Paladin?" Macurak whispered in amazement after Vayla shared the news. "That is great. But..."

"You needn't worry," she said. "I'll still need someone to keep me in line."

Macurak barely contained his smirk as he shook his head. "But how can I speak to the Grand Paladin the way I speak to you?" He maintained a low voice. "It is not an advisor's place."

"But it is within the rights of the Grand Paladin's husband." She gave him a sidelong stare. "So we best take care of that sooner than later."

Macurak blushed. He was not one normally given to acts of modesty, but Vayla could have said this in private, and not while sitting on the front pew in the Cafior church during a sermon. Grimmen sat next to Macurak, and the zhokard issued a playful elbow to the captain's ribs.

Vayla enjoyed Wezlok's company for several months after the war, as the wizard stayed in New Palidur longer than any believed he could stand to. She treated him as an old friend; perhaps an uncle. No one could recall seeing the elf smile as much—or at all, for that matter—though the occasions remained rare. Vayla offered to house Wezlok as a permanent resident and advisor after learning of her impending ascension to Grand Paladin. He assured her there were limitations to his tolerance of those outside Maple Lore Forest, and he eventually returned to his woodland home.

Though Wezlok would visit at least once a year afterwards, he gave to Vayla a ruby before he left the first time.

"If ever you have need of me," he said, "just shatter this gem, and I will come."

Vayla frowned. "I thought your debt to Merssa was paid?"

Wezlok held a wry smile.

"You know I'm marrying Macurak, right?"

Wezlok maintained the expression.

"What happens if I *accidentally* break it, and there's no emergency?"

The smile degenerated into a grave stare.

Vayla smirked and kissed his cheek. "If you're not here for my wedding, I shall smash it for sure!"

From what Vayla heard, Wezlok became a hermit within his forest. He made himself available to Lorians in need of counsel, but he preferred to live alone. Another rumor held him to have taken a wife, but Vayla could not get him to admit to it, and she never met such a person.

A week before her inauguration, Vayla spoke to the High Order, relaying her encounter with Merssa upon the battlefield but not mentioning everything that was said—the complete version was shared only with her father. Unfortunately, Merssa had already received every honor the city had to offer. Vayla then came up with an idea, and the Order backed her plan to have Varlimor dwarves erect a grand monument of the paladin hero at the northern end of Palidur Bridge. The task was completed without delay, and it stood both as a bastion to residents of Tedonis, and as a welcome home to Palidurians.

Though it took much more convincing, a statue of Nidor was eventually added to the silver street surrounding the Grand Cathedral. But Vayla did not accomplish this feat alone—Silcor was not a deity of worship within the Holy City. Approval was only granted after Selanna shared her story of the paladin's sacrifice in Darum Carumbor, and his integral part in defeating the Enemy once and for all.

Vayla's wedding was a grand affair, and people flocked from near and far, hoping to join the festivities. Every hero Vayla knew from the Battle of the Broken Land made the trip to New Palidur, and she hugged each one, saying "Thank you" in their ear.

Over the next eight years, she gave birth to three children, and she thanked Cafior none of them looked like her and her grandmother.

"If one did," she kidded Macurak, "I would fear another war was ahead!"

Macurak found no humor with the statement.

Vayla did not sit idle as Grand Paladin. Being young yet, she ventured from New Palidur often, defeating evil and giving counsel to lords and kings when necessary. These trips also served as excuses to enter Marcove on occasion, where she would spend at least two weeks in Castle Lambrak with her father, King Cavalor.

Vayla adored her husband, her children, her city, and her deity. She loved life.

"I cannot believe you gave me the black stick!" Eraim scolded Selanna once they were finally alone, several days after the war ended. "And without telling me!"

Selanna offered no excuses. There was nothing she could say to appease her friend in this matter, so there was no use in trying.

For many weeks, Selanna doubted what she saw at the time of the Starrifix's destruction. But Eraim witnessed the collection of past heroes, and she assured Selanna it had been real—that is, once Eraim was willing to speak to her. It warmed Selanna to know Merssa watched over them, and it made the world seem a safer place.

Selanna was pleasantly surprised by the changes in Vayla from the beginning of the war to the end. The young paladin no longer reminded her of Merssa, but Selanna no longer needed reminders of the late Cafior paladin. She wondered if Vayla had ever been like Merssa at all, or if it had been Selanna's own need that made her seem so.

Six months after the war's conclusion, Selanna journeyed to the House of Elgarroth with Eraim — it was the timeframe the elfish Seer allotted to enjoy their victory before Selanna took her new place in Vaeldor. She did not know why she was told to bring Eraim, but she was happy to do so. She still had not figured out how to explain the impending changes, and she hoped her mentor would be able to help.

The closer they came to the clearing, the more exhausted Selanna felt. The war was over, but her life was about to begin, and it would never be the same. It was both an exciting and a sad thought. Upon arrival, she was puzzled. Elgarroth sat on one of the four logs surrounding the fire, puffing on his long pipe as he often did. But why was Vecnor chopping wood?

Eraim smirked.

"Welcome." Elgarroth stood and smiled. "Please, have a seat."

They sat across from the wizard while Vecnor carried a pile of firewood into the house. Selanna was about to pry when Elgarroth spoke.

"Are you ready for your new life?"

"New life?" Eraim looked both curious and concerned.

"Now?" Selanna glanced at Eraim. Had Elgarroth forgotten they were not alone?

Vecnor returned, bearing a tray with five goblets. He served Elgarroth, then Selanna and Eraim, and he placed one on a vacant log and sat opposite from it with the last cup in his hand. They contained wine.

Eraim stared at Vecnor with a knowing smile, and she narrowed her eyes. "I knew you were the wood chopper."

Vecnor chuckled and drank from his goblet.

Selanna felt pity for Eraim. For years, Selanna watched the spark between her friend and the giant human sputter because they did not nurture it. Vecnor was often absent for long periods of time, and also there was the way Salenti elves were raised, frowning upon the mingling of elfish blood. But Selanna and Eraim had seen too much and met too many people from all walks of life to hold such archaic viewpoints any more. Besides that, it was no secret that Vecnor did not age normally—he was no mere human, of that there was no doubt. The worst part came after the war, when Eraim told Selanna she had expressed her love for Vecnor, and that the large warrior explained he could not return the sentiment. He further admitted he cared a great deal for her, but that his life was not his to give. He offered no more information on the matter, and Eraim was heartbroken. It was nice to see her smiling in Vecnor's presence, even if only due to the confirmation that she had figured out his little ruse.

Tux joined the gathering and took the unclaimed goblet from the log before sitting. Elgarroth and Vecnor did not acknowledge his arrival, but Selanna was sure they were aware of his attendance.

"You will want to live here," Elgarroth said to Selanna, again bringing confusion to Eraim.

"So soon?" Selanna still did not understand his candor.

"It is a job that has no holidays." Elgarroth's expression held no room for humor. "And it is time that you got to it."

"What about you?" Selanna asked.

He leaned back and smiled. "My days in this world are not yet spent. I shall remain, retired as it is. But I will be available for counsel, if you find need."

"What is going on?" Eraim rose to stand as high as those sitting around her.

"Selanna is the new Seer," Tux replied.

Selanna could not believe the words were uttered aloud. Elgarroth said no one else knew. Did Vecnor know as well? She regretted not preparing Eraim for this.

Eraim frowned. "But the Seer—"

"Is in Tikken City?" Vecnor raised a brow. "That's the human seer."

Vecnor *did* know!

"It is true." Selanna hoped to end her friend's anxiety. "Elves have a seer as well. That is what Elgarroth is. That is what he has been training me to be."

"How long have you known?" Eraim shot an accusatory glare at Selanna.

"Not long," Selanna said. "Just after our first meeting in The Jeweled Scabbard."

"But..." Eraim looked around. "What about Tux and Vecnor? Are they seers too?"

"They are my companions," Elgarroth said. "They are with me. Here to serve me."

"Companions?" Selanna was confused.

Elgarroth lowered his brow. "Did I not tell you? As seers, our lives extend beyond those of normal elves. I am just over a thousand years old, if I remember correctly. And it is essential we have companions. But we cannot be bothered with training new ones every time they pass on, so these two journeyed with me into Arman Forest to make their oaths. Their fates are tied to mine." He paused, as if musing. "I believe human seers can bond companions as well. All seers have the ability to enter Arman Forest, after all. Of course, the humans do not realize any of this, and it is not my place to tell them so."

"Companions!" Selanna smirked. "That is how you learn so much. Tux is your spy!"

"And Vecnor is my strength," Elgarroth added.

"Do I get a companion?" Selanna anxiously awaited the answer.

Elgarroth spread his hands before him. "You may have two. But no more." He looked at Eraim. "But it appears to me you have both spy and strength combined into one."

Eraim sat, her cheeks flushed.

"I do." Selanna could not conceal her joy. Eraim at her side for a thousand years? "I choose Eraim, without a doubt." She turned to Elgarroth. "But I shall still take a second, whether or not I am in need."

He lifted his brow. "Is that so?"

"Vecnor." Selanna gave a nod.

Vecnor choked on his wine. Eraim sat up straight.

"Is that possible?" Vecnor directed his question at Elgarroth. The wizard nodded.

Eraim darted from her seat, rushing into Vecnor and knocking him from the log. Selanna heard many kisses being planted, and she felt happier than she could ever recall. A thousand years with Eraim *and* Eraim's human sounded even better.

"What will you do?" Selanna posed to Tux, who had been staring into the fire.

Tux shrugged. "I still have time left. Perhaps I shall add to my legend. Maybe relax for a while." He looked at Eraim, now rising to her feet with the largest smile she had ever displayed. "And I will be around, in case advice is desired. Or, perhaps, to teach the secret of arrow crafting."

Eraim walked with Vecnor after the fireside conversation, just south of Elgarroth's house. Or was it Selanna's house? Maybe the House of Selanna and Eraim?

She had learned so much over the past hour. Before then, she felt alone. She thought she had been losing her dearest friend, and Vecnor had rebuked her without sufficient reason.

"Are you human?" she asked, her hand feeling secure within his enormous paw.

Vecnor chuckled. "Yes. I was born in Kalmaar. It was not such a nice place then. I was extremely pleased to see Karrak's line take the throne." He fell silent.

After a few seconds, Eraim changed the subject. "So you have lived a thousand years?"

"No." His forehead wrinkled in thought. "Tux was with Elgarroth from the beginning, well before they found me. Maybe eight hundred."

"And you are sure you can stand to live another eight hundred?" she asked.

He lifted her up. "Surely you jest. The next thousand will be fantastic!"

Eraim grinned. "This is going to be fun!"

Life would never be the same. It was going to be better.

This Concludes

EYES OPEN

in

SHADOWY HALL

and

THE FATE OF VAELDOR

TRILOGY

But the journeys continue…

Look for more adventures in Vaeldor in the future.

ACKNOWLEDGEMENTS

My first thank you belongs to my wife, Justiina. Her continuing support and patience go beyond expectation. To Ronnie, my son, I offer my deepest gratitude. I have enjoyed watching him bring Eraim's maps to life. When it comes to literary support, there is no one better than Mary J. Nichols. She has been with me every step of the way. To Bob, Scott, and Dale, thank you for your inspiration. And to Peggy Kattelus, I cannot thank you enough for your encouragement.

About the Author

Ronald G. Bellar was born in Ohio and raised in Michigan, one of the middle children in a family of ten. He has an associate's degree in electrical engineering and a bachelor's in automated manufacturing, but his love for numbers led him to a life in taxes and bookkeeping. His passion for medieval fantasy began at age 11, when he was introduced to *Dungeons & Dragons*, and it was cemented after reading *The Lord of the Rings* by J.R.R. Tolkien. He began writing when he was 15, but did not take it seriously until he was encouraged to do so later in life. After coaching football for 31 years, he retired his whistle to pursue his writing career, but his love for sports endures. He currently lives in Michigan with his wife and son.

Ronald G. Bellar has also written Books 1 and 2 of the Fate of Vaeldor Trilogy: *Alas! The One that Evil Brings*, and *Might and Strength of Evil Bone*. Beyond that, the adventures in Vaeldor will continue…

Visit Ronald G. Bellar's Facebook page at:
https://www.facebook.com/vaeldorhouse

Prophecy of Trannum

As told by Seac the Seer

Power of five, united by one,
Forth on journey, defy the sun.
Summer tastes winter, darkness draws near,
Sleeping do wake 'neath shadow of fear.

From edge of old, bond does break,
At last revealed, One all did forsake.
Evil long subdued, the One long sought.
Centuries pass, power hard bought.

Alas! the One that Evil brings,
Takes the lands, takes the kings.
Forces gather, dark secrets unknown.
Death march begins from One's throne.
Under sunless sky, o'er blanket of cold,
Fall of strength by treacheries unfold.
Dark power grows, living join through death.
By might of Lords, Hallowed Land is wrest.

Many a hero, born to die.

Trial of time, the battles cry.
Companies four, to take the test,
Set forth on perilous quest.
Seek to end at dark throne,
Might and strength of Evil Bone.
Power shatters, dust does fall.
Eyes open in shadowy hall.

Glossary of Names

Andria (an-DREE-uh): Barbarian realm north of Harbnum.

Andrian (an-DREE-uhn): Barbarian native to Andria.

Anduiff (AN-doo-if): Death Lord. First Lord of Benasti Forest. Disappeared after his undead dragon was blasted from the sky by Wezlok.

Arbiss (AR-bis): Lord over southern Sendorum.

Arbornum (AR-bor-nuhm): Militant city off Shield River. Guards the only bridge connecting Harbnum to Beit. Opposes the city of Onzac.

Arkor (AR-kor): Granduncle to Romik. Has only one arm. Governs Ironside Keep while Romik is away.

Arman (AR-muhn): Forest in northern Tenvale. Mysterious woodland known to possess magical properties.

Arrikan (AIR-ick-in): Deceased mountain ranger. Was married to Pallit. Mother of Magneer. Died of old age after the Necromancer War.

Arronaus (AIR-uhn-us): Deity of the sky.

Balgorn (BAHL-gorn) River in Helmland. Also called Blood River.

Ballrik (BAHL-rick): Son of Vikur and nephew to Arkor. Father of Romik. Saved realm of Nira from a demonic invasion by jumping through a gate to close it.

Barrelda (buh-RELL-duh): Pavish barbarian. Daughter of Pargahnu, chief of the Bomahni.

Batorn (buh-TORN): Gulf north of Kalmaar. Also a breed of horse from the region of the gulf, known for their beauty and great endurance.

Battle of the Dead Fields: Final battle fought outside of Burmagaard in Kalmaar. Area was never rebuilt afterward.

Bayn (BAYN): A marteese battlemage. Killed by the demon Ragab in Trannum's crypt over fifty years ago.

Baylun (Bay-luhn): Krukari son of Gruelenor and Lorin. Half-brother to Romik and cousin to Desser and Daymyn.

Beit (BAY-it): Realm of northern Vaeldor. Ruled by evil.

Beitian (BAY-shun): Citizen of Beit.

Beldara (bel-DAR-uh): Lake located in western Beit.

Benasti (be-NAS-tee): Forest in northern Kalmaar. Largely inhabited by evil tribes of hobgoblins and krukari.

Benzon (BEN-zin): Capital city of Beit.

Blackfoot Goblin: Tribe of goblins unseen since the days of the Ancient Enemy of the North. Served as the vanguard to the evil army.

Bomahni (boh-MAH-nee): Tribe of barbarians that live in Pavan.

Bormungdaher (BOR-muhng-DAR): Ancient dwarf king of Varlimor. Commissioned the construction of Palidur Bridge.

Borse (BORS): Priest of Cafior. Was married to Merssa. Father of Cavalor and grandfather of Vayla.

Brakkeet (brah-KEET): Expletive in the dwarfish language.

Brem (BREM): A marteese from Neja. Priest of Frayorna. Was present when Trannum was destroyed in the Necromancer War. Suffered permanent black spots on his skin from undead insect bites.

Brondor (BRAHN-dor): Deity of battle.

Burnod (ber-NAHD): General of Zurzak in Beit.

Cadorn (kuh-DORN): Death Lord destroyed by Merssa during the Necromancer War.

Cafior (CAF-ee-or): Deity of the land.

Cavalor (CAV-uh-lor): King of Marcove and father of Vayla. Adopted son of Merssa and Borse. Given to Selanna by Tarm when he was a baby and delivered to Merssa.

Clanghorr (KLANG-or): Ancient dwarfish battleaxe. Wielded by Greyor.

Council of Wizards: Group of eleven wizards, including the Seer, that rule over the free city, Tikken City. Responsible for keeping peace between nations, establishing a common language, and providing wisdom to kings and lords across Vaeldor.

Cramber (KRAYM-ber): Large village in northern Beit.

Dakreal (DAY-kree-uhl): Forest in Philen. Home to Dakreal elves.

Dandi (DAN-dee): Salenti horse belonging to Selanna.

Darmhorng (DARM-horng): Castle in Kalmaar housing Queen Elloria and King Sullis. Located outside capital city of Burmagaard.

Darmoor (DAR-moo-er): Militant city off Shield River. Guards the only bridge connecting Virch to Beit.

Darum Carumbor (DAIR-uhm cuh-RUM-bor): Ancient watchtower of Helmland during the reign of Uustaag.

Daymyn (DAY-min): Son of Solinin and Della.

Death Hunter: Hunter of the undead.

Deeyon (DEE-on): Priest of Brondor from Kalmaar. Sent by Queen Elloria to fight in the war.

Della (DELL-uh): Youngest sister to Lorin and Kalette. Was married to Solinin when he was killed by Gruzim in the Necromancer War. Mother of Daymyn.

Dellen (DEL-in): Former Captain of the Guard in Tikken City. Killed by the demon Hezeb in Trannum's cabin in Sistama.

Demoligius (dem-uh-LI-gee-us): Evil deity of fire.

Denvale (DEN-vayl): City in Marcove on the eastern edge of Varlimor Pass.

Desser (DES-sir): Son of Magneer and Kalette. Mountain ranger, skilled in tracking and hunting.

Dimarr (di-MAR): Former barbarian chief in Andria. Possessed one of Trannum's orbs. Killed when Merssa and her companions arrived to retrieve the orb.

Dominelli (DAHM-in-EL-ee): Largest village of elves in Salenti Forest. Home to Selanna and Eraim.

Dresnian (DREZ-nee-uhn): Lorian elf soldier.

Dun (DOON): Title given to most things associated with the evil deity Thard'Dun, including Dun weapons, Dun Priests, and Dun Soldiers.

Dunarchin (DOON-er-kin): Undead created from a firstborn. Elite warrior, able to walk beneath the sun.

Dunuthar (DUHN-uh-thar): Death Lord rumored to have been destroyed by Vecnor during the Necromancer War.

Eastgate: City on the eastern border of Neja. Keeps watch over the only bridge crossing the Stony River. Ruled by Baron Karlsum.

Elgarroth Sandanari (EL-guh-roth SAN-di-NAR-ee): Mysterious elfish wizard. Resides in the House of Elgarroth in Vermallon Forest. Mentor to Selanna.

Ellaville (EL-uh-vil): Village in northwestern Virch.

Elloria (el-LOR-ee-uh): Queen of Kalmaar. Former Brondor priestess. Led the army of allies in the Battle of the Dead Fields. Married to King Sullis.

Eraim (ee-RAYM): Salenti elf. Master of many talents and friend to Selanna. Wielder of Mithkahr.

Eslimil Tuxendora (EZ-li-mil TUX-en-DOR-uh): Legendary thief. Leaves the word "TUX" behind to take credit for his mischief.

Fellna (FEL-nuh): Deceased. Was married to Larman in Eastgate, Neja. Her son, Malen, now runs the inn.

Fendora (fen-DOR-uh): Kingdom in southwestern Vaeldor.

Fenreil (FEN-ree-uhl): The new Seer in the Council of Wizards of Tikken City.

Forban (FOR-buhn): Soldier in Darum Carumbor.

Frayorna (fray-OR-nuh): Deity of the forest. Mother of Nature.

Galenfial (guh-LEN-fee-uhl): Deity of the elves.

Gortran (GOR-tran): Skeletal wizard living in a forgotten village deep underground in the Stone Eagle Mountains.

Greyor (GRAY-or): Dwarf from Morimont in the Varlimor Mountains. Wields the legendary battleaxe, Clanghorr.

Grimmen (GRIM-min): A zhokard. Captain of the surviving zhokards under King Cavalor.

Gruelenor (GREW-len-or): Krukari. Married to Lorin. Father of Baylun and step-father to Romik.

Gruzim (groo- ZEEM): Death Lord destroyed by Vecnor with Gruelenor's help in the Battle of the Dead Fields.

Gulthar (GOOL-thar): Death Lord destroyed by Cavalor during the Necromancer War.

Harbanian (har-BAY-neeuhn): Citizen of Harbnum.

Harbnum (HARB-nuhm): Kingdom north of Sendorum. Protector of one of only two bridges crossing the Shield River.

Helmland (HELM-land): Wasteland north of the Stone Eagle Mountains where the Ancient Enemy of the North resided.

Hezeb (HEZ-ib): Demon possessing hundreds of teeth.

Holindale (HOE-lin-dayl): Barbarian territory south of Tenvale. Home to the dark-skins.

Hubrid (HYOO-brid): Former High Paladin of Arronaus in Palidur. Died protecting the retreat of the city's last survivors before it fell.

Ironside (EYE-ern-side): Keep on Varlimor Pass. Surname to Arkor and Romik.

Jurak (joo-RAK): Death Lord destroyed by Arkor during the Necromancer War.

Kalette (KAY-let): Middle sister between Lorin and Della. Married to Magneer. Mother of Desser.

Kalmaar (KAL-mar): Kingdom in eastern Vaeldor. Ruled by Queen Elloria. Known for its strong military and dedication to the worship of Brondor.

Kalmiran (kal-MAIR-in): Citizen of Kalmaar.

Karlsum (KARL-suhm): Baron of Eastmarch in Neja.

Karrak (KAIR-ick): Former King of Kalmaar. Died in battle in Darmhorng Dungeon after he was freed by Selanna.

Keelord (KEE-lord): Dwarfish general from Rornibur in the Stone Eagle Mountains.

Kembald (KEM-bahld): Capital city of Marcove.

Kiryanna (keer-YAHN-uh): Marteese warrior in Neja. Bodyguard of Brem.

King Arman (AR-muhn): The largest lake in Vaeldor. Located north of Arman Forest.

Kolermane (KOHL-er-mayn): King of the dwarves from Morimont in the Varlimor Mountains.

Korban (KOR-bin): Bridge spanning the Squire River. Built by dwarves of Rornibur and named after their king of old. Made of rorbak.

Krahluk (KRAH-luhk): Gorilla-like monster from another world. Hairless with jet-black skin.

Krukari (kroo-KAR-ee): One possessing both human and hobgoblin blood. Outcasts.

Ladonia (luh-DOHN-yah): Lady in New Palidur. Married to Rholmar, former Grand Paladin of New Palidur. Mother of Montac, the current Grand Paladin.

Lambrak (LAM-brack): Castle for King Cavalor in Marcove. Located next to Kembald.

Larkorn (LAR-korn): Capital city of Virch.

Larman (LAR-min): Captain in the Nejan army. Named after his grandfather, who owned Larman's Haven in Eastgate. Son of Malen and nephew of Lindow.

Lilli (LIL-lee): Salenti horse belonging to Eraim.

Lindow (LIN-dow): Son of the original Larman and Fellna. General in the Nejan army. Brother of Malen and uncle of Larman.

Lorian (LOR-ee-uhn): An elf from Maple Lore Forest.

Lorin (LOR-in): Eldest sister of Della and Kalette. Wife of Gruelenor. Mother to Romik and Baylun.

Lormin Dmurr (LOR-min duh-MER): Ancient citadel of Uustaag the Dark, Ancient Enemy of the North, in Helmland.

Lornibur (LOR-ni-ber): Ancient home to the dwarves. Original birthplace of the dwarfish race.

Lorylla (LOR-i-luh): Gray elf of Orlenfel. Daughter of Xorlunder. Fought in the Necromancer War.

Lothen (LOH-then): Forest on the border of Beit and Helmland. Home to the Guardians that keep watch over Helmland for any signs of the Ancient Enemy.

Macurak (muh-KYER-uhk): Captain in New Palidur serving under Vayla, Paladin of Cafior.

Magneer (MAG-neer): Mountain ranger. Son of Pallit and Arrikan. Married to Kalette. Father of Desser.

Malen (MAY-lin): Son of the original Larman and Fellna. Current owner of Larman's Haven in Eastgate.

Maple Lore: Forest along the Shield River. Home to the Lorian elves, a territorial race known to hold disdain for all other races.

Marc (MARK): Citizen of Marcove.

Marcove (MAR-kohv): Kingdom south of Kalmaar. Ruled by King Cavalor.

Marteese (mar-TEES): One possessing both human and elf blood.

Mayry (MAY-ree): Former queen of Kalmaar. Widow of Tarm. Married Gruzim after he killed her husband and became queen of Marcove. Biological mother of Cavalor and Solinin.

Mees (MEES): Elfish word for alarm.

Melac (MEL-ack): Wizard from Kalmaar. Sent to fight in the war by Queen Elloria.

Meldar (MEL-dar): Deity of the dwarves.

Merssa Goldmace (MER-suh): Late Cafior paladin hero of Palidur. Led in the Necromancer War. Died after destroying Cadorn, general of the Death Lords. Was married to Borse. Mother of Cavalor and grandmother of Vayla.

Millord (MILL-ord): Stone Eagle dwarf from Rornibur. Cousin to Poluran. Died in Lornibur during the Necromancer War.

Mithkahr (MITH-kar): Ancient elfish blade possessed by Eraim.

Moc (MAHK): Citizen of Moclen.

Moclen (MAHK-lin): Kingdom west of King Arman Lake. Home to Tikken City and the Council of Wizards.

Montac (MAHN-tack): Son of Rholmar and Ladonia. Grand Paladin of New Palidur.

Mordan (MOR-duhn) Steward to the Council of Wizards.

Morimont (MOR-i-mahnt): Largest city of dwarves in the Varlimor Mountains and home to the dwarf king.

Necromancer War: Battle against Trannum and his minions.

Neja (NAY-shjuh): Kingdom south of the Stone Eagle Mountains. The Bandit Kingdom.

Nejan (NAY-shjuhn): Citizen of Neja.

New Palidur (PAL-i-der): Name given to Palidur after the city was rebuilt, a task led by Nilborg and Rholmar after the conclusion of the Necromancer War.

Nidor (NYE-dor): Paladin of Silcor, the Fire God. One of the dark-skinned barbarians from Holindale. Possesses special abilities involving fire.

Nilborg (NIL-borg): Priest of Soleran. Fought in the Necromancer War. Worked with Rholmar to lead in the reconstruction of Palidur and renamed the city New Palidur.

Nira (NYE-ruh): Kingdom north of Kalmaar and south of Selt.

Niran (NAIR-in): Citizen of Nira.

Nomedd (NOH-med): Barbarian territory devastated by Trannum. Uninhabited.

Nyer (NEYE-er): High Paladin of Soleran. Member of the High Order of New Palidur.

Olinin (OH-li-nin): Marteese wizard from Neja. Killed by Trannum while investigating the Silent Marsh.

Onzac (AHN-zak): Militant city of Beit that guards the only bridge over the Shield River connecting Harbnum and Beit. Opposes the city of Arbornum.

Orbo (OR-boh): Berries that grow in Salenti Forest. Favorite treat of Salenti horses.

Orlenfel (OR-len-fell): Forest in northeastern Kalmaar. Home to the gray elves.

Palidur (PAL-i-der): Former Holy City in Sardina. Destroyed by Trannum's minions. Rebuilt as New Palidur by Nilborg and Rholmar.

Palidurian (PAL-i-DOO-ree-uhn): Citizen of Palidur.

Pallit (PAL-lit): Deceased mountain ranger. Was married to Arrikan. Father of Magneer. Killed by dunarchins in Trannum's stronghold during the Necromancer War.

Pargahnu (PAR-guh-noo): Chief of the Bomahni, a barbarian tribe in Pavan.

Pavan (puh-VAHN): Barbarian realm of the northwest.

Pavish (PAY-vish): Barbarian native to Pavan.

Philen (FYE-len): Kingdom in southwestern Vaeldor.

Philander (FYE-land-er): Citizen of Philen.

Poluran (POH-ler-uhn): Stone Eagle dwarf from Rornibur. Former owner of Clanghorr. Killed by Radaam in Ironside Keep.

Radaam (ruh-DAHM): Death Lord possessing both skills in both combat and sorcery. Disappeared through a gate at the end of the battle against Trannum in Nomedd.

Ragab (RAH-guhb): Demon with many horns and bone spurs protruding from its skin.

Rholmar (ROHL-mar): Paladin of Arronaus. Retired Grand Paladin of New Palidur. Married to Ladonia. Father of Montac. Worked with Nilborg to lead in the reconstruction of Palidur and renamed the city New Palidur.

Rivercross: Large city in Virch near the Korban Bridge. Famous for its markets.

Romik (ROH-mick): Lord of Ironside Keep. Son of Ballrik and Lorin. Older brother of Baylun.

Rorbak (ROR-back): Rare white stone native to the Stone Eagle Mountains. Used in the construction of Korban Bridge. Defies time.

Rornibur (ROR-ni-ber): City of dwarves in the Stone Eagle Mountains.

Rozall (ro-ZAHL): Captain of Darum Carumbor.

Ruson (ROO-sahn): Soldier in Darum Carumbor.

Salenti (suh-LEN-tee): Forest west of Moclen. Home to Salenti elves. Also a breed of horse that grows shorter and possesses long life and heightened intelligence.

Sard (SARD): Citizen of Sardina.

Sardina (sar-DEE-nuh): Kingdom east of King Arman Lake. Houses the free city of New Palidur.

Seac (SAY-ahk): The Seer. Member of the Council of Wizards of Tikken City.

Selanna (suh-LAHN-nuh): Salenti elf wizard. Friend to Eraim. Pupil to Elgarroth.

Sendor (SEN-dor): Citizen of Sendorum.

Sendorum (sen-DOR-uhm): Kingdom north of Sardina.

Shadia (SHAH-dee-yuh): Evil goddess of the darkness.

Shield River: River separating the evil realm of Beit from the rest of Vaeldor.

Silcor (SIL-kor): Deity of fire.

Sistama (SIS-tuh-muh): Elfish name for the Silent Marsh.

Slythe (SL-EYE-TH): Lieutenant in Darum Carumbor.

Soleran (SOH-ler-uhn): Deity of mercy and light. Defender of the Defenseless.

Solett (soh-LET): Former wizard from Tenvale. Possessed one of Trannum's orbs.

Solinin (SOH-li-nin): Son of Tarm and Mayry. Killed by Gruzim in Nira before the Necromancer War.

Soren (SOR-in): Paladin of Soleran. Killed by Radaam during the Necromancer War.

Star: Batorn horse owned by Vayla.

Starrifix (STAR-i-fix): Powerful magical item once possessed by Uustaag the Dark, Ancient Enemy of the North.

Stone Eagle: Mountains north of Neja. Home to Stone Eagle dwarves.

Stony River: Border between Virch and Neja. Flows from Stone Eagle Mountains to the Silent Marsh.

Sullis (SULL-is): King of Kalmaar. Paladin of Brondor. Lost his sword arm in the Battle of the Dead Fields.

Sylnor (SIL-nor): Small village in Beit. Home of Burnod.

Tarm (TARM): Former duke that conquered Kalmaar and became king. Was married to Mayry. Killed by Gruzim. Biological father of Cavalor and Solinin.

Tedonis (teh-DAHN-is): Former compound of Merssa's make before the Necromancer War. Evolved into a city and was named after the original surname of Merssa.

Tenvale (TEN-vayl): Realm south of Arman Forest. Kingdom of Wizards, known for its strange laws.

Thard'Dun (thar-DOON): Darkest of all evil deities. The Dark One.

Tikken City (TEE-kin): Free city located in Moclen. Governed by the Council of Wizards.

Torrac (TOR-ak): Mysterious axe wielded by Baylun. A birthday present from his brother, Romik. Purchased from a dwarfish smith in the Varlimor Mountains.

Trannum (TRAN-nuhm): Ancient necromancer, corrupted after researching Uustaag the Dark. Destroyed at the conclusion of the Necromancer War.

Tribenor (TRY-ben-or): Capital city of Sendorum.

Tux: Nickname of Eslimil Tuxendora.

Umbarc (UHM-bark): Andrian horse belonging to Vecnor.

Urell Coast (YOO-rell): Kingdom on the western shore of Vaeldor.

Uustaag (OO-stahg): Warlord of Helmland of old. Ancient Enemy of the North. The Enemy.

Vaeldor (VAY-uhl-dor): The continent of all known kingdoms.

Varlimor (VAR-li-mor): Mountains separating Kalmaar from Sardina. Home to Ironside Keep and Varlimor dwarves.

Vayla (VAY-luh): Paladin of Cafior. Daughter of Cavalor and granddaughter of Merssa and Borse.

Vecnor (VECK-ner): Mysterious human warrior. Also known as Black Rogue and Black Death.

Velgaad (VEL-gahd): Dwarfish Death Lord. Destroyed by Greyor during the Necromancer War.

Vennimor (VEN-i-mor): Paladin of Soleran. Founder of the original Palidur. Led the war against Uustaag in the distant past.

Vermallon (VER-muh-lahn): Forest separating Harbnum from Nira. Largest forest of Vaeldor and home to Vermallon elves.

Vikur (VIE-koor): Former Lord of Ironside Keep. Brother to Arkor. Father to Ballrik. Grandfather to Romik. Killed by Radaam in Ironside Keep.

Vircan (VERK-uhn): Citizen of Virch.

Virch (VERCH): Kingdom north of King Arman Lake. Known for its strong military. Protector of one of only two bridges crossing the Shield River.

Vol Maren (vahl MAIR-uhn): Capital of Neja.

Vronik (VRAHN-ik): King of Beit. Krukari.

Vou (VOO): Deity of magic. Provider of magical energy. It is said his mortal remains are buried in the center of Arman Forest.

Welmirth (WEL-merth) Ancient wizard that defeated Uustaag at the Battle of Balgorn.

Weslin (WEZ-lin): Baron of Arbornum.

West Palidur (PAL-i-der): City renamed by Rholmar when he was Duke of Philen.

Wezlok (WEZ-lahk): Lorian elf wizard from Maple Lore Forest.

Xorlunder (ZOR-luhn-der): Gray elf of Orlenfel. Killed by Gruzim in the Battle of the Dead Fields.

Zeratar (ZAIR-uh-tar): High Paladin of Arronaus in New Palidur.

Zhokard (ZOH-kard): Black warrior in the Andrian tongue. Creations of Trannum possessing black hearts. Neither living nor undead. Only known survivors after the Necromancer War work as bodyguards to King Cavalor of Marcove.

www.ingramcontent.com/pod-product-compliance
Lightning Source LLC
Chambersburg PA
CBHW051305190726
48290CB00001B/17